DEATH TUNNEL

Robert Curtis

DEATH TUNNEL   AN ORIGINAL NOVEL BY ROBERT CURTIS

THIS IS A WORK OF FICTION AND ANY RESEMBLANCE TO
CHARACTERS LIVING OR DEAD IS UNINTENTIONAL AND
PURELY COINCIDENTAL

ISBN: **1493524496**
ISBN 13: **9781493524495**
Library of Congress Control Number: 2013919325
CreateSpace Independent Publishing Platform
North Charleston, South Carolina

DEATH TUNNEL

Author's Note

Thuis is a work of fiction. There may be resemblances
to some real individuals but, if so, this occurs not
out of any intention to portray particular people, but
rather out of exploiting contemporary society's love of
the twin staples of book and film; murder and conspiracy. Quite why people these days are so fascinated with
murder escapes me. Obsession with conspiracy theories is quite another thing. Even those governments
bathing in the lustre of so called democracy are ultra-
secretive. The default mode of politicians and civil servants seems to be an imperative to keep the people they
are supposed to serve ignorant of everything they do.
The truth is that secrecy is not an essential element to
modern democratic government; it is rather an avoid-
able cancer that only succeeds in undermining the
fabric of a truly free and open society. Yet secrecy not
only persists, it grows. The general public knows nothing of the murky transactions that take place, for example, between government and big business; between
civil servants and the police; between the police and

the media; between the police and the judiciary. Is it therefore surprising that an increasingly sophisticated and informed public sees conspiracies everywhere and draws conclusions about events that support sometimes the most bizarre of explanations? At every turn one can be aware of the spin doctors' phantom hands seeking to manipulate occurrences that, in reality, need nothing more than to be disclosed to the general public as unvarnished truth. Only thus can true democracy be achieved for a well informed electorate.

However, those individuals who seek to perpetuate a culture of secrecy, politicians, organs of government, businessmen with financial and personal government connections, provide, for the novelist, the building blocks of their art. Such individuals, who conjecture as to the identity of fictional persona, ought to be the last to complain about tales woven around their imagined activities.

PROLOGUE

Kyoto - Autumn 1958

"The martial arts may be
An unfloatable
stone boat
But I am unable to discard
My weakness for this way"
Yagyu Muneyoshi Sekishusai 1529-1606
(Premier Japanese swordsman)

The garden had been artfully constructed to give it an appearance of raw undisturbed nature. The harmonious blending of the rich green, soft looking moss with, what looked like naturally fallen rocks shaded by ancient, gnarled trees, allowed only expert scrutiny to reveal how skillfully the scene had been created. Its architect and creator was the old kendo master Hanbei, who now stood silently on the carefully tended walk-way that skirted the whole of the garden side of the large old house he inhabited with his grandson. The front of his black silk kimono displayed an ancient family crest embroidered just below each shoulder, with a larger version decorating the centre back of the kimono. He stood completely motionless. A casual observer might not even have noticed his presence, so completely did he blend in with his surroundings. His careful gaze, directed at his grandson, seemed simultaneously to be deeply concentrated but also, to lack the intensity that might have caused the object of his attention to feel his presence. The twelve year old boy was standing on the worn, wooden bridge spanning the stream that ran through the centre of the garden into a carp pond, subtly designed to look as if it had been naturally formed by the slow passage of time. Although only twelve the boy could already execute perfectly the sixty four techniques and twenty two secret movements of the school of Heavenly Sword that the old man had created after a lifetime's study of fencing and other martial art techniques.

The old man had felt disappointment and shame when his daughter had first told him that she was intending to marry the Gaijin Major who was attached to the American occupying forces, after Japan's defeat in World War II. But the part of him that had never been prepared blindly to accept the teachings and morals of those who had instructed him in his youth, allowed him to understand how his daughter could turn against the traditions that had brought such disaster on their country and he had accepted her decision.

His first sight of his grandson had, miraculously, mollified his disappointment. The baby had the thick black hair of its Japanese ancestry and oriental features seemingly untainted by any hint of the occidental. As the boy grew older his oriental facial characteristics were somewhat softened by his European genes, but the boy could almost pass as Japanese. Even though he so resembled his mother, in certain lights it became apparent to a careful observer that the boy was contaminated with American blood. But, by then, the old man had come to love and, more importantly, accept, the boy whose spirit, if not his features, was pure samurai.

The boy had barely started walking when his mother and father were killed in a car accident near Hakone on a weekend visit to the sacred volcano, Fujiyama. There was never any question that the ascetic old man, who was the boy's grandfather, would immediately attempt to fill the void left by the death of the boy's parents. Hanbei was a man whose natural implacable will had only been fortified by years of disciplined practice of the martial life he had chosen. His determined resistance to the efforts of the father's family to have the boy repatriated to their home in California annihilated their every endeavor, until the American relatives graciously accepted an uneasy truce that allowed them to visit the boy in Japan whenever they wanted. This turned out to be no more than the insignificant irritant of a once, perhaps twice a year exercise, dedicated to the modest goal simply of maintaining a link between the two families.

From the inception of his guardianship Hanbei developed a fierce love for the boy. Perhaps the origins of that love were that the child represented the last living remnant of an adored daughter, perhaps they lay in Hanbei's vision of the boy as the ideal person to carry on the tradition and teachings of his school of swordsmanship. In truth, after his school had been decimated, with his best pupils failing to return from that terrible, pointless war and, then the death of his daughter, the boy became all he had left.

Hanbei had started teaching his grandson swordsmanship and martial arts when the boy was little more than a toddler. Taro, as he had been named, was a more than willing pupil. He had a natural ability and powers of concentration that made him more than happy to spend hours practicing the various movements. Although there was little overt display of affection between grandfather and grandson, Taro reciprocated his grandfather's love with the same ferocity he devoted to his practice. By the age of seven he was strong, skillful and more powerfully built than children several years his senior. Now at the age of twelve he could easily have passed for sixteen or seventeen. He was significantly more than a head taller than his Japanese contemporaries, well-built and extremely quick and powerful.

The old man scrutinized the boy's movement dispassionately as the almost imperceptibly swift flashing of the sword caught the dying rays of the sun. He watched as the dismembered body of the dragon fly floated gently down towards the rapacious mouths of the carp, frothing up the water in their anxiety to catch the insect that the boy had just sliced into several pieces as it had flown low over the water, reflecting that the technique he had just witnessed had been perfect in both timing and execution. No one looking at the old man's calm, impassive face at that moment would have imagined what an overwhelming sense of pride he felt for his grandson. Barely twelve months later, the old man was dead and the boy was on his way to California to live with the family of the father he had never known.

CHAPTER ONE

"To reach the way is not difficult
Only avoid picking and choosing
The conflict between right and wrong
This makes the mind sick" - *Shinjinmei*

Having advanced through many years and many experiences, I have concluded that Americans are brainwashed from birth into a deluded fantasy of existence that becomes problematic when colliding with reality. Take by way of example the famous and historic American detective agency, Pinkertons. Anyone who, like me, enjoys watching Westerns will have heard of them. I do not think that it is an exaggeration to say that they have become a part of American frontier mythology. A mythology that tells us, with some truth, that Pinkerton agents relentlessly chased desperate outlaws, then, more often than not, gunned them down and put them on public display in open coffins as a deterrent to other would be gunslingers who fancied their chances against the famous Pinkertons. Even dead bodies displayed in open coffins on Dodge City Main Street have a certain nostalgic romance about them. But how many of us know what has happened to that great nineteenth century legend. Well, in the twenty first century,

Pinkertons still exist. They have even prospered, with large, glitzy, glass and chrome offices strategically located throughout America. Although Pinkerton's founder, Allan Pinkerton, was originally based in Chicago, even hard headed realist that I am, I still like to think that the positioning of Pinkertons' current headquarters in Springfield Virginia is an acknowledgment of their connection to their roots in the romantic era of the Civil War, rather than a desire to be near our seat of government. Of course, Americans, who are so fond of their legendary frontier history and so proud of their traditions, for the most part remain blissfully unaware that Pinkertons are no longer an American company. They are owned by some distant, faceless Swedish company called Securitas. Of course they still draw their employees from the large pool of well-trained intelligence and law enforcement personnel churned out by the numerous agencies America maintains for internal and external security; the Department of Homeland Security, the police, the FBI, the DEA, the secret service and so on. For all I know they may even employ some former CIA operatives. But for me something got lost when they became Swedish. Perhaps I am over influenced by my weakness for the movies of the nineteen thirties and nineteen forties, but for me Swedes are the guys portrayed in those movies either as men who call their wives "momma" or as dimwit lumberjacks who can scarcely speak English. I may not be a pure bred hundred per cent American, but I am still entitled to have some pride in my American heritage and, having our most famous detective agency owned by Swedes and our largest car companies contaminated with German and Japanese components has never sat very well with me.

Now the company I work for is pure American. Of course they have not got the same history or pedigree as Pinkertons, but then they operate in a different sector and the chances of their being bought by some Swedish security conglomerate are absolutely nil. The company is called DNB Operational Services Inc. In my more poetic moments I think of the name as like some sexy, underdressed flirtatious babe who is constantly sticking her tits in your face but who flits away the minute you try and put your sweaty hands all over her. Why the analogy? Because most people have little chance of knowing exactly why we are called "DNB" nor of knowing precisely what we do. As of now however that changes, because I have never enjoyed being teased by flirtatious women who try to make themselves inaccessible. DNB stands for "Deniable", the operational bit, I think rather speaks for itself. I suppose that anyone who looked us up in the Yellow Pages might think that we service and repair vacuum cleaners or oil rigs or something like that. Actually, even though we are a private corporation, very private, for all practical purposes we also operate, unofficially of course, as an arm of the CIA, NSA and even, post 9-11, the military. Naturally, being a private corporation and not having any employees or shareholders who are on the official CIA payroll we are subject neither to any congressional nor any other oversight. A fortunate arrangement, because, overseeing us might give one or two congressmen a few sleepless nights.

Not, come to think of it, that I have ever encountered a politician who has sleepless nights about anything other than their popularity ratings, raising money or their sexual performance.

Anyway, as seems to be usual these days in so many businesses, not even our well known top ranking firm of auditors knows the business we are in. Of course, unlike such organisations as Pinkertons and Kroll associates, we do not employ ex cops. Until the Iraq and Afghanistan adventures expanded the company's business beyond its original frontiers, everyone who worked for DNB was ex CIA, ex NSA or former Special Forces. By the latter I mean Delta, Navy Seals or members of what used to be called the Intelligence Support Activity and which these days seems to change its name almost as frequently as I change my socks. Todays' DNB though, has a separate department that deploys former marines and rangers for specialist protective details in Iraq, Afghanistan, Pakistan and other hotspots.

Although varying in details, my background is not dissimilar to that of other DNB secret operatives. I lost my youth and a brief period of youthful innocence whilst serving in the French Foreign Legion Paratroops. My path to corporate America then led me through a Marine Reconnaissance Unit as a Sniper, the Studies and Observation Group in Viet Nam, Delta Force and finally the CIA. Up to now my seven years in the French Foreign Legion have been a matter known only to fellow legionnaires, as natural caution and, perhaps, unnatural youthful good sense, restrained me from disclosing this information either to DNB or any of my previous American military employers.

It is my belief that Special Operations personnel, in which broad category I include snipers, are born, not made. I knew from my Foreign Legion experience, fortified by training, that I was the type of soldier who preferred being on special missions, operating in small units. In transitioning from the Legion to the American military I also knew that a combat posting as a sniper would give me greater autonomy than being just another grunt. Therefore when I was offered the chance to go to the Marines' sniper school I jumped at it. The end result was that I obtained a fairly quick deployment to a very hot zone in Vietnam. Many people, many soldiers, would regard this as a distinctively unattractive outcome. I was of the opposite view because I had been suffering the effects of combat withdrawal. The Foreign Legion unit in which I had served was a front line special operations unit and I had missed the intoxicating feeling of adrenalin fuelled, heightened, highly tuned, sensual perception, which combat tends to foster and was what I had been seeking when I enlisted in the marines in the first place.

Without digressing too much, I was brought up principally by my Japanese grandfather. When he died I was left alone on the cusp of adolescence, apart, that is, from the housekeeper/cook and her husband, who had looked after the two of us ever since I could remember. I was perfectly happy to continue the life I had led with my grandfather until my American relatives turned up to remove me to the land of excess, where the disciplined daily routine my grandfather had imposed on me, which had become a part of my nature, had little place. These relatives were my father's brother and his wife. They were a sort of diplomatic delegation for the rest of the family, who comprised my paternal grandparents, another brother of my father and my father's still unmarried sister. Apparently the family had made a decision that the annual visits they made to see me when my grandfather was still alive were insufficient to secure my continued moral and intellectual development. They decided that, notwithstanding my tainted (half Japanese) origins and upbringing, they would save my soul and alternate me between the California mansion of my paternal grandparents and the Beverley Hills extravaganza that my father's brother, called home.

The Beverley Hills brother who turned up so suddenly in Kyoto was some sort of big shot lawyer whose client list included some of Hollywood's biggest names. I have to confess that their diplomacy was highly effective. Up to then the furthest I had ever been outside my grandfather's house was Mount Hiei just outside Kyoto. My uncle succeeded in making my future life in America sound exciting and attractive. The version I got was that I was going to spend my days playing in the swimming pools of the rich, famous, beautiful individuals that I saw from time to time on one of my very rare, privileged visits to the cinema. Do I have to say that, flawed individual that I was, I became a more than willing participant in their plans for my future. They were not bad people and the truth is that 99.9 per cent of children would have been more than happy to be in my place. The snag was that I belong to the odd 0.1 per cent who are never happy unless they are trying to decapitate someone with a single swift stroke of a Katana.

I have always had a facility for languages. I learned English in about three months and settled into my school fairly well, even though I may have acted with a minimal amount of arrogance because the rest of the children in my class and age group needed a few years to catch up with the severe academic standards my grandfather had imposed on me. Perhaps that was my real problem, rather than any incipient, irrepressible homicidal tendencies. Maybe it was the boredom of sitting in classes, where I knew not only most of what they were teaching, but knew it sufficiently well to recognise that it was culturally biased and frequently, simply wrong. Unsurprisingly, no one, from the teachers down to my fellow pupils, found my intellectual arrogance particularly endearing. Accordingly I was not enthusiastically discouraged from simply sitting quietly at the back of the class reading romantic stories about such things as the French Foreign legion. I am not much given to introspection but I suppose romantic adventure fantasy coupled with little significant social interaction could have actively nurtured my sociopathic traits.

My new family was not immune from the general consensus that I was startlingly eccentric. Their perception focused upon my insistence on maintaining a small Shinto shrine to my grandfather in my bedroom and continuing martial arts practice.

Every morning I rose at 5 o'clock to hone my techniques for three hours before trotting off to school. Americans have many virtues, but they seem incapable of understanding something else that my grandfather had deeply inculcated into me, a sense of duty. My duty to grandfather continued after he died and that duty was to continue with his teachings and, in due course, to pass on those teachings. Of course the latter goal has proved far more difficult and elusive than I would ever have dreamed at the tender age of thirteen.

Having endured some three years of dissatisfaction and boredom and, with my head full of Beau Geste and other such romantic nonsense, I ran away from home at the age of sixteen. I had decided to join the French Foreign Legion. In spite of my romantic notions I was sufficiently practical to have discovered that there is no recruiting office for the Legion in the greater Los Angeles area. I mistakenly believed that the nearest location for enlistment was Marseilles in France, being ignorant of the fact that there was also an office in Paris. Unlike the majority of my High School peers I knew not only the location of France but also Marseilles. My father's family had conveniently obtained an American passport for me before they brought me to America and were sufficiently organized to keep it with all their other important papers locked in my uncle's study. I marvel now that I had managed to reach sixteen without once being arrested, let alone having a lengthy criminal record. I was certainly sufficiently larcenous to be able to obtain my passport, traveling money and a credit card with a minimum of effort and a reprehensible lack of conscience.

A travel agent picked at random, showed more boredom than interest when I used the credit card to purchase a ticket from Los Angeles to Marseilles via Paris, where I had a brief stopover between flights. If I had known about the Legion's recruiting office in the French capital I might have saved myself two or three day's expense and a considerable amount of shoe leather. But I did not. My single minded destination was Marseilles and not even the hormones coursing through the body of a young, full blooded, sixteen year old alone in Paris were able to divert me from the noble purpose I had formulated in a Los Angeles suburb. I have always been single minded and not easily distracted from the particular current task that occupies my attention. My goal then was to join the Legion in Marseilles. I was not to be sidetracked by the bright lights of Paris. In any event, for the most part I did not at the time understand anything anyone said to me, although in truth and, lest you feel I am setting myself up as too much of a paragon, I did have more than a passing thought that some of the women who treated a young teenager travelling alone so sympathetically in his brief Parisian transit, sounded and looked most alluring.

Thinking about it now, I find it scarcely credible that the biggest problem to be encountered by a sixteen year old from Los Angeles trying to join the French Foreign Legion, would not have been getting to France, but finding the actual recruiting office in

Marseilles. It took me two days of searching and wandering the streets of Marseilles before I was face to face with a suntanned, ramrod straight sergeant in a khaki uniform whose creases looked like knife edges. He sported some medal ribbons and a large paratroopers badge above his breast pocket. That was when my heart actually started to beat faster for the first and perhaps the last time in my life.

Although I was big for my age, I had inherited the Japanese gene that stimulates hair growth on the head but not on the face. Not to put too fine a point on it, when the recruiting sergeant looked at me, he saw a fresh faced oriental looking kid who had not yet started to shave. As fate would have it there was a bit of trouble at the time in the Legion over split loyalties, arising out of the war in Algeria and they were looking for fresh blood or cannon fodder or whatever they were then calling it. With the peculiar sort of contradiction that I later discovered seems to run freely in the French intellect, I found out that, whilst the Legion were generally not too particular about where they got their new recruits, each potential recruit is also quite closely vetted by a French Internal security outfit called the Deuxieme Bureau. I am not quite sure what we were actually vetted for. Although one or two of my fellow recruits were booted out for failing the vetting, most were not and, if they were to be believed, their ranks contained as many thieves, murderers and assorted criminals as one could expect to find in a high security penitentiary. The supposedly anonymous ranks of recruits and legionnaires contained a lot of Germans, who I automatically assumed were ex Nazis. There were also numerous Italians and Spaniards as well as a smattering of Russians, Croatians and Yugoslavs. It soon became obvious to me that not one of my fellow recruits shared my romantic attitude towards the Legion (nor for that matter did the non- commissioned officers responsible for our initial induction and training, who told me constantly how tough my next five years were going to be).

It was a small step for me to assume that my fellow recruits were on the lam for one reason or another. Actually, in person, when you got past the bullying and the odd one or two who had to be dissuaded from their belief that my anus should have been a resting place for their sexual organs rather than for ejecting my bodily waste, they were not a bad bunch of guys. When the training had rubbed off all their rough edges you had a group of men who, for the most part, would stick with you without complaint when the going got rough, as it did quite a lot in those days.

After providing the minimum personal details, continually being asked why I wanted to join the Legion and undergoing a lengthy security grilling, I just scraped in as a recruit. I learned later that the French knew a lot more about me than they had let on, courtesy of the US Embassy in Paris and Interpol, but had decided that if I was foolhardy enough to want to join the Legion they could be foolhardy enough to accept me.

I had gleaned enough from the Beau Geste novels to know that prospective Legionnaires always use false names. My choice of fake name, Richard Pernod, was inspired by a large advertisement opposite the recruiting office for what I later found was a popular drink in the South of France. At the time I thought I was quite smart choosing this name. With hindsight I feel rather ashamed at the total lack of imagination I showed. Others who join the Legion, for the most part, put me totally to shame in terms of imagination; in all my time in the Legion I only came across two other Pernod relatives who, sad to say were singularly undistinguished in all respects. In a way I was lucky to join the Legion when I did at the very tail end of the Algerian war, when French President, General Charles De Gaulle had already announced that he was giving Algeria its independence and the diehard French colonists had formed the OAS to try and subvert the whole idea. With Algerian independence an established principle and France on the brink of civil war, I still got into the Legion in time to kill and torture a few Arabs without being too greatly exposed to the widespread terrorism that preceded Algerian independence.

I am giving these autobiographical details by way of brief introductory background to a later phase in my life when I became a fully-fledged, professionally employed, deniable black ops asset of the non-official arm of the intelligence community of our great country that I have previously named. I have no intention of making this a definitive autobiography so I will not describe all the aspects of my training or how, when the Legion says march or die, they mean it. Suffice it to say that I learned to march; I learned to speak French, Arabic and a smattering of other languages picked up from my fellow legionnaires and various deployments. I also learned the meaning of real physical fitness.

In addition I discovered that my grandfather had omitted several valuable lessons from my curriculum. One of these was how little food it takes to keep one alive. In the Legion our first food in the morning was a small piece of bread taken with coffee. We were always kept hungry in training and even had to fight to obtain sufficient to eat at mealtimes. That was how they taught us that all we needed to carry on is water and ammunition. I learned a multitude of useful things in the Legion, all of which stood me in good stead throughout my later career. I learned parachuting, about explosives and how to use and strip every conceivable weapon. I became an expert skier, scuba diver and driver. I was trained as a sniper and was sent for rigorous jungle training in French Guyana, in the Amazon basin. In the course of this training we were sent out into the jungle for 2, 3 or even 4 weeks and allowed only to carry food and ammunition for 48 hours. For the rest of the time we had to live off the land. It always amuses me when I read about, or see on television, these brave explorer types who walk to the North Pole or across the Gobi Desert, accompanied by a camera team and abundant supplies, constantly being replenished by air drops and everyone thinks they are so wonderful. What I think about these sort of exploits does not really bear writing, but, I would say, that I know, or have known, at least a thousand guys for whom that sort of jaunt would be a walk in the park and I am not talking about guys who would leave their wife and kids at home for a year or more just to get themselves on television for a few days.

I was just starting to enjoy my life as a soldier when Algeria had wound down and the rumours started flying about there being no further need for the Foreign Legion. By now I was fit and hardened and was not about to give up the fun life, so I volunteered for the elite 2nd Regiment of Paratroopers or 2eREP. This was formerly the 1st regiment which was disbanded after having been involved in the attempted assassination of General de Gaulle in the early 1960's for what they regarded as a betrayal, in granting Algeria independence. I was accepted, shipped off to the base in Corsica and underwent further training. This was where I really started to live the dream of an adventurous 18 year old. We were a small, elite unit, of some 1100 legionnaires and 60 officers. We spent our time, jumping out of aircraft, shooting, travelling, blowing up things and driving fast cars for all of which we actually got paid.

I served not only my contractual five years but, as I had become a sergeant a short time before my five years ran out, I signed on for an additional stint. I was proud of myself for making sergeant. It was no mean feat, particularly for someone as young as me. Only the best make non-commissioned officers in the Legion, after having gone through a special four month course. This course, like everything else in the Legion, is designed to crush those who are less than excellent. Non-coms in the 2eREP have to be able to do everything the grunts can do, but better. Still it had its compensations and allowed me to prance around wearing a black, as opposed to a white kepi, looking just like the guy who had recruited me so long before.

I never thought it would happen, but after seven years, I started to get bored. We were doing more training than fighting and, although it was still fun, the occasional operational forays into hot spots in different parts of Africa were not enough to maintain my adrenalin needs. I decided to leave and return to my adopted country America, which was becoming increasingly embroiled in South East Asia and Vietnam in particular, where they were filling the vacuum left by the departure of the French from that region. I thought that in Vietnam I might get some of the continuous action I had come to enjoy. By the time I enlisted in the marines, the war in Indo China had become fully Americanised with no further pretence of our being mere advisers to the Vietnamese. The extraordinary generosity of the French towards those who fight for them, allowed me to leave the Legion with everything I had learned about warfare, including looting, stealing and any number of amazing scams; a French passport in my adopted name, a telephone number I can always call wherever I am in the world, for assistance from fellow legionnaires and a small group of comrades who I know I can trust with my life. The Legion has a saying "Legio Patria Nostra", the Legion is our country. And so it is and always remains to ex legionnaires. As far as I was concerned I left the Legion with a lot more than when I had entered it.

I left my discharge papers, French passport and what money and other valuables I had managed to earn or steal, in a safe deposit box in one of the major French banks in Paris, before trotting off to the US Embassy who, obligingly renewed my old US passport. The Legion is not the best paying job one can find but, as a sergeant, I had been able to save enough to pay for my ticket back to the States and have a little pocket money. My father's family, who had long since decided that I was either dead or in prison, were guardedly welcoming, enabling me to make a peace of sorts with them, which I reinforced by almost immediately enlisting in the Marine Corps. Most of the men in my father's family had been in some sort of military service, although their career path usually took them through West Point. Still, they were reasonably mollified by my announcement that I had joined the marines with the intention of bolstering up our flagging military efforts in Viet Nam.

I suppose the point of my narrating a brief history of my time in the Legion is that when I got into the Marines in Nam in 1969 I was nothing like my fellow recruits. I was hard, tough and experienced, in jungle as well as desert warfare, with little in common with people who had been unwillingly conscripted into the American military. I had never been one of those bullying non-coms who like to shout at and torture the soldiers under their command but I made no secret of my contempt for individuals who lacked my experience, whether they were officers or enlisted men. I had been a tough sergeant in what, in my opinion, is the toughest unit in the world and I was still too young and too arrogant to have any patience for lesser mortals.

I saw too much slack discipline, drug taking and low levels of physical fitness compared to the Legion, all of which was totally alien to the ideas of soldiering that the French had instilled in me. My attitude, of course, did not endear me to anyone, except a hard core of similarly minded professional soldiers. Many junior officers in the field were a bit afraid of me and did not hide their resentment at what they thought was my insubordinate attitude until they needed me to get their patrols out of difficulties.

Whether or not the majority of the US army liked me, someone must have sung my praises, because I came to the attention of the CIA. I was one of the few eccentrics who actually enjoyed their Vietnam tours of duty and some perceptive CIA officer decided to put me with a group of like-minded individuals, shipping me off to MACV-SOG (Military Assistance Command, Vietnam - Studies and Observation Group). Contrary to what the title may imply, this was not a group of college professors carrying out an environmental study on the impact of military operations on Asian flora and fauna. It was a bunch of guys who were as sociopathic and had as little regard for authority as me, raising hell in places where, officially, there were no American forces.

After gaining a lot more experience and somehow or other surviving countless engagements, any of which could have seen me shipped back to America in a flag covered box, I was recruited by a tough, intelligent warrior called Colonel Beckwith. Our paths had crossed in my early days in Vietnam when he commanded an outfit called Detachment B52. A few years later, back in the States, he had been tasked with setting up an elite, Special Forces unit dedicated to counter terrorism operations. This unit, designated 1st Special Forces Operational Detachment Delta, is what is now generally known as Delta Force.

I do not need to go into my time as an operator with Delta, but when I was recruited by DNB I had been seconded to the CIA from Delta and become a contract operative for Langley on a more or less permanent basis carrying out the odd jobs that were off limits for career officers.

My recruitment to DNB took place shortly after I had returned from a particularly remunerative mission. A couple of colleagues and I had been sent to dissuade the Colombians from exceeding unofficial quotas that some bureaucrats had decided ought to be placed on importations of coca based narcotics. Apparently our combined powers of persuasion amounted to very little and we ended up with several bodies and a mountain of forensic evidence that even the Colombian police would have been unable to ignore. My colleagues and I were sufficiently realistic to know that politics frequently triumphs over command loyalty. As operators in the field we knew, however just our cause, the first rule was to leave no evidence. When I served in the Marines Corps the officers had always been at pains to impress upon us the importance of being able to improvise. This was quite ironic because the reality was that, in my whole time in the Corps, I do not recall officially ever being allowed to improvise about anything, including how to hold my dick when taking a leak. At all events, for my two colleagues and me, all alone in the depths of the Colombian jungle, improvisation was the order of the day. We stretched deep within our innermost resources and concluded that our best course would be to blow the bodies, the house we were in and all evidence, to kingdom come.

Whilst collecting together what we needed, we came across a very large, apparently walk in, safe, which looked as if it had been borrowed from Fort Knox. We all knew how to pick locks and open simple safes, but this monster was out of our league. Suitably intrigued we again improvised, deciding the explosives could be put to better use in gaining entry to the safe. Intellectual giants that we were, we had reasoned that nobody brings a safe like that into a house in the middle of the jungle as an interior decorating accessory. We were unanimous in agreeing that it was our duty to use our every resource to investigate the contents. We all had a highly inflated opinion of our expertise with explosives. It turned out that our self- confidence was seriously misplaced. In my colleagues' defence I would point out that their previous experience with explosives had either been blowing doors to gain quick entry into terrorist held areas, or blowing up vehicles and bridges. I have no such defence. I allowed my colleagues' eagerness to obtain swift access to the safe's contents temporarily to erase everything I had been so painstakingly taught by the explosives genius who trained us in the Legion. The force of the explosion very quickly restored my memory and common sense and my buddies discovered that opening safes requires a totally different technique from their usual mode of operation. The silence that followed the opening of the safe was broken by the string of obscenities with which I berated myself for having allowed my companions' enthusiasm to overcome my judgment. Instead of opening the door gently and walking away with the $100 million or so we estimated the safe must have contained, we managed comprehensively to destroy all but about $10 million. All of us were untemperamental, fairly philosophical individuals and little given to extended self-recrimination. We were soon reconciled to accepting that we had little to complain about. Before the mission we had speculated about the possibility of picking up a gold Rolex or two, but the $10 million was considerably more than any of our imaginations had been capable of envisaging. Mature consideration left us feeling elated. The only cloud on our horizon turned out to be the pilot who had been sent to exfiltrate us. He was some sort of religious patriot who had volunteered for the Agency because of a fanatic devotion to God and his country to the exclusion of all other human shortcomings. He arrived in time to see us packing up the money and patriotically insisted that it was our duty to turn it all in to be used for the benefit of our country. It soon became obvious to the three of us that it was futile to appeal to the man's non-existent cupidity. Fortunately one of our team was a crack pilot from the Special Operations Aviation Regiment and was able to replace the patriot at very short notice. The Patriot, regrettably, died a hero as a result of heavy hostile fire in the course of the extraction.

A refueling stop in Panama with a quick visit to the Panamanian office of the Union Bank of Switzerland allowed the three of us to arrive back in Washington feeling virtuous about a job well done and suitably sad about the fate of the poor pilot, without whose dedication and skill we would never have been brought to safety. In short we got the money and the pilot got a posthumous medal and a star on the wall of the Langley entrance hall.

Everyone was happy until I was summoned to the office of the CIA's Deputy Director Operations a couple of weeks later. I stood in front of him uneasily, whilst he fiddled with a pen and the papers on his desk. The man was a classic bureaucrat who preferred shuffling papers to operational activities. He would definitely have disapproved of my most recent adventure. I started to run through a quick mental check list of everything we had done since finding the money and wondering where and how we might have been spotted or who might have ratted us out. Eventually the DDO put me out of my misery.

"Ah yes, Traynor" followed by his burying his head in the thick file on the desk in front of him.

My immediate thought was that this was a classic interrogation technique, letting someone's feelings of guilt do the work for the interrogator. A skilled interrogator has many tricks and facets. He has the ability to make himself sympathetic and also to convince the person he is interrogating that he knows far more than he actually does. The person being interrogated becomes uncertain, confused, assailed by feelings of wanting to confess and ultimately, usually starts to let slip pieces of information. The interrogator then proceeds to use that information to extract even more. Talking at all is a slippery slope best avoided entirely. I was already at the uncertain stage, knowing I had something to hide. The question was, should I fall on my knees in prayer and start confessing or just kiss the guy's ring and offer him a share.

As I considered my options I allowed my gaze to wander over the DDO's desk. It was an impressive piece of furniture; a solid, antique, dark oak partner's desk with green leather covering the top apart from a small border the maker had left to show off the oak. The desk was clear, save for a couple of neatly arranged files, the DDO's elbows and two elegantly framed photographs. Both photographs showed the same people at different stages in their lives, a woman and two children. The first when the children were no more than babies and the second when both woman and children had aged considerably. I assumed that these were the DDO's wife and children and that he kept their photographs on his desk so that he would be able to recognize them when he returned home at night and thus know that he had arrived at the correct address.

This reminded me that the DDO was a bureaucrat not an interrogator and I therefore decided that my best course would be to adopt the neutral option of sitting rather heavily into what looked like the most comfortable chair in the room. This just happened to be a plush leather sofa whose colour matched that of the leather on the desk. The sofa was positioned to one side of the DDO's desk and my choice caused the DDO to twist his head uncomfortably when he next turned to look at me. I was reassured about my recent adventure when I saw him struggling to overcome his annoyance at my temerity in sitting down before he had invited me to do so. His skills at personal interaction ultimately triumphed, as he turned back to his papers without further comment.

After a few more moments of scratching away at the file in front of him with a rather old fashioned fountain pen, the DDO replaced the cap on the pen and rose gracefully, stretching out the trouser legs of an elegant $2000 suit as he joined me on the settee. I was assailed almost immediately by a most unpleasant stale, acrid smell, exuding from the DDO's mouth which made me stifle the breathe of relief that had started to escape me as he sat down. I suppose he thought that the heavy after shave in which he seemed to have bathed before my visit thoroughly masked every other body odour he exuded. Ever the diplomat, I took a tin of Peppermints from my pocket and offered him one before taking one myself. He took the sweet but I do not think that he got the point. For me at least, sitting next to him, now became marginally bearable.

He cleared his throat noisily before embarking on the purpose of his summons,

"I see you've been with us now a number of years on a contract basis as a very successful operator."

He meant that over the past twenty years or so I had killed a lot of people and never fucked up an operation. I was good but I was certainly not perfect. He did not have, nor did any of the official records contain, an entirely reliable account of my operations. One of the beauties of official files is that everyone who reads them thinks they are accurate. Those poor naïve individuals who make applications under the Freedom of Information Act think that what they uncover is the unblemished truth, just because it comes from an official file. What all those gullible simpletons forget or, more likely, never knew, is that, whilst the contents of the files come from a variety of sources, ultimately the results of live operations come from debriefing the operatives. Who are those operatives? I would broadly divide the Company into two categories, Bureaucrats and Bandits. The Bandits do the dirty work and the Bureaucrats get to make PowerPoint presentations to politicians with suitably enhanced satellite photographs. The Bureaucrats are, almost without exception, tight arsed, straight down the line never do anything that will get you a bad mark with your superiors, individuals. In other words, typical Washington grease balls, who will do and say anything to get ahead. Lest one forget, the CIA is based in Washington, a place which, in my experience, is unparalleled for its ability to produce bureaucrats. The Bandits are, for the most part, a bunch of villainous, double dealing liars. The one characteristic Bureaucrats and Bandits share is that they are trained, professional liars. To the former lying is a career path. To the latter it is often a lifesaver. All a Bandit's training and experience is based on lying. From counter interrogation to recruiting and running agents, bandits are taught and learn, to lie about everything, in every situation. We then spend years honing and developing these skills. We are trained to lie under torture, drugs. You name it. We get so accustomed to lying that sometimes we do not even know what the truth is. So why the hell would anyone think that we were going to change our deeply engrained habits just for the sake of a debriefing.

As for the debriefers. If everything turned out in the end as the agency wanted, they do not want extraneous details such as that the operation was a total cluster fuck until some lucky chance miraculously enabled you to achieve your objective. Neither do they want to hear that, of the $50,000 you were supposed to have spent bribing a top level official in a target government, $5,000 went on high class call girls, $25,000 went into your secret bank account and the rest went on sundry expenses like staying in a luxury hotel, buying clothes or alcohol. Or that the unnamed (sometimes even named) high level official was a figment of someone's unofficial imagination. A secret I learned early on from my Company mentor, the guy who recruited me, was that the Agency, like every other government department has a budget. If they spend, or better still overspend, their budget, they get more money the following year. And all government departments want more money. The more money they get the more prestigious they are. No one ever actually tells you this, but the truth is that everyone working for a government department is encouraged to spend money. Nowhere more so than in the intelligence community. CIA agents commonly carry thousands of dollars in cash, so that they are always equipped to handle most contingencies. I knew, therefore, that my file would be very popular with the DDO. I not only spent enough, all properly justified and carefully recorded of course, but also ensured that my debriefs read like paper-back novelettes. They provided a good yarn with a happy ending.

The DDO cleared his throat again, "You've actually got enough service you know to retire and get a pretty good pension."

A pretty good pension. The guy had to be kidding. Did he seriously think that people like me worked for the measly $70,000 a year less tax, a pension and medical plan? Well, maybe there were some, like that dick of a pilot who could have had a share of the money but whose misguided principles killed him. Maybe there were others who might have worked for the kicks. I am not saying that agents in the CIA are not patriots. Of course they are. But patriotism cannot stand alone against all the politics and bull shit. Most of the experienced people I know put up with the crap and stayed in, for the scams. Field operatives had it best. A posting in some Asian or Middle Eastern country where it was so difficult to get reliable intel that they found it did not make much difference if you sent back stuff that was invented. They got to invent their sources and, of course, their expenses. Before you knew it some of those guys were operating huge fictitious networks that were costing Mr. Middle American tax payer millions of dollars. And when someone like me flew in to do a job based on the Intel we had been getting, those local controllers had better be damn generous with the expenses or we would blow them out of the water.

Of course it was not all like that, but just let us say that, the more secret and delicate the mission, the more opportunity there is for skimming some dough. I have often thought it is much the same in private corporations where I am sure everyone has his hand in the cookie jar at the expense of the poor old shareholder. It is just that in my business you get to fly into places like Afghanistan with millions of dollars in cash to bribe locals to fight on your side. A prime example is the way the Agency dealt with Afghanistan after 911. The President decided he was going to make a big move against the Taliban. He asked the CIA, the Army Chiefs of Staff and various other members of the intelligence community to come up with a plan. I have always been in Special Operations and we special ops people do not share the same perspective as the regular army spit and polish brigade. In my experience nearly every senior officer I have come across in the army can be described in two words – "risk averse". When President George W Bush decided he wanted to take out Afghanistan the Generals were still traumatized by all the soldiers who had been killed in Mogadishu, Somalia, when a simple snatch operation had turned into an almighty gun battle with two Black Hawk helicopters brought down by rocket propelled grenades. So their idea of a plan was to try and take over Afghanistan without any American soldiers being involved. Luckily for them the Brits came to their aid.

The Brits have been involved in that part of the world for around two hundred years and had a pretty good understanding of what works. Their idea, which was shined up before being presented to President Bush, was to have a few operators in place to push things along, but mainly to pay the tribal chiefs, who made up what was called the Northern Alliance, to do the dirty work for them. So it was that a mixture of British and CIA spooks, Delta operators, Seal teams and British Special Forces landed in Afghanistan with millions of dollars in cash. Although I can pretty well guarantee that not all that money went into the pockets of the various intended tribal chiefs, the whole plan worked pretty well. But that is how the real world operates, in spite of the occasional self-righteous blitzes Congress or the FBI launch on practices that are deemed corrupt. Like the way the Justice Department and Army and Navy criminal investigation services descended on various Special Forces in the 1980's (which I avoided through being picked to work with the CIA) and for which a few hapless individuals spent time in Fort Leavenworth. By and large though, people get away with things. The biggest scams I have ever seen took place in Iraq. After the invasion, when Paul Bremer and his cronies were running things, money used to arrive in pallets of saran wrap packages of $500,000. Literally billions of dollars in cash, disappeared in Iraq, totally unaccounted for. Unfortunately I was not serving there when all that happened, although I did see, but was forbidden to touch, some of the mountains of neatly wrapped cash when I went to Iraq briefly for DNB.

The DDO was still speaking to me. "You're a contract agent so strictly speaking we'd be entitled just to terminate your contract, but we'd errm... we'd like to be fair... and we'd really prefer to retire you. Or rather we'd prefer it if you'd resign with immediate effect. We could then confirm all your pension rights etcetera etcetera."

Fuck. Now he was getting through to me. This was a blow from the blue. Thank god for that recent score. Up to then I had not been able to put that much money aside that I could afford to take early retirement.

He hurrrmed again before continuing, "the thing is Traynor, the agency is changing. We are considerably increasing our intake of electronic intel through the use of satellites, drones and so on... but I don't need to tell you that. Anyway with all the budget cuts, the... er... the sort of work you do, is no longer regarded as a suitable way to apply agency resources".

I could not help wondering where he was coming from. I might have been low down on the feeding chain, but even I knew that, for all the scams, the only really good intelligence came from guys on the ground and that, sometimes the only effective way to disrupt an opposing operation was to get your hands dirty.

He was now handing me something, a neatly printed card. It read "DNB Operational Services Inc" with an address in New York City printed in the bottom right hand corner and, neatly placed in the centre, in raised print, the name "Carl Standish - Admiral (USN retd).

Meanwhile the DDO was telling me that this company, DNB, was actively recruiting experienced operators like me for contractual work all over the world. That he was strongly advising me to call Admiral Standish as he was sure that they would be interested in hiring a person of my experience and qualifications and, obviously, salaries and fringe benefits in the private sector were often more generous than in government. That was all he knew. I could not imagine having pulled off a score like our last one in the private sector. I had initially been stunned at this bolt out of the blue. The idea that the government I had been working for so loyally and for so long, could just call me in one day and tell me that I was out on the street was something I had never considered. But as I listened to the DDO I began to realize that there was a little more to all this than I had thought. It turned out I was right. I knew all about Executive Order 12333 issued by President Reagan a few years before, forbidding the CIA to conduct assassinations, but I, probably like the majority of operational people always thought that was no more than a PR stunt. It seemed that, finally, the Executive Order was being taken seriously. In an effort to avoid any investigations by Senate Committees or the Justice Department, the CIA had decided that unpleasant tasks should be contracted out to the private sector, in particular this DNB outfit, set up by a former head of the NSA after he had retired. The same sort of principle had been adopted before with Air America and other entities. Apparently the idea had now been dusted off and refined to cover the sort of work I do.

The DDO stood up and that was it. Interview at an end. Time for the DDO to get on with some serious business, like planning a weekend in the country with his secretary. As I, too, rose to my feet, I found myself guided gently by my elbow to the door of his office.

Outside the DDO's office two people were waiting for me. The DDO's secretary, her admirable chest drawing my attention away from the pen thrust towards me, which I was supposed to take with minimum force and use to sign the various documents sitting on her desk dealing with everything, from the secrets I had to keep, to my pension rights. The other person was from internal security. It was his job to take away my entry card to the building and escort me directly from the premises. I had seen it happen before and had always deplored how one minute someone could be an employee with access to top secret information and the next could not be trusted to clear their desks by themselves and leave the building in their own time. I bowed to the inevitable, signed the various documents and allowed myself to suffer the indignity of being seen to be escorted from the building.

I tend to be a cautious person, both by temperament and training. As I drove out of the exit from Langley for the last time, I was carefully looking around to see whether anyone was following me. I spent a good hour satisfying myself that I was not under surveillance before going into a hotel, chosen at random, to use a public telephone. I am not one to hang around and brood. I like to know where I stand, so my first order of business was to call this Admiral Standish. I was greatly heartened by the fact that not only did he know all about me and was obviously expecting my call, but that our brief conversation included an invitation to fly up to New York to meet him the following day for which he had already arranged a ticket.

CHAPTER TWO

'He who makes a beast of himself gets rid of the
pain of being a man" –Samuel Johnson

D NB was housed on the sixtieth floor of a sleek
contemporary mid-town sky scraper. I subsequently found out that they also owned a large old
mansion in Upstate New York, housed in extensive
grounds, with all the facilities its operatives need to be
able to maintain their operational skills.

In order to reach Standish's inner sanctum one
had to pass through an office housing his two stun-
ning secretaries. I had always been impressed by the
DDO's private secretary, but these two were in a class
of their own. The security throughout was unobtrusive,
but impressive, with cameras and movement detectors
everywhere. Standish's office turned out actually to be
a large suite, with outstanding views of the Manhattan
skyline from the floor to ceiling glass windows.

My first impression of my prospective new boss
was of another immaculately dressed bureaucrat, with
a major difference. There is something about Special
Forces operators that, in my experience, makes them
instantly recogniseable to each other. Perhaps they
exude an air of physical confidence and calm that

comes from having been pushed to the limits of physical endurance and knowing they are capable of handling any situation, because they probably have. Whatever it is, Standish had it. I later found out that, for part of his time in the Navy, he had served with Seal Team 6, the anti-terrorist unit subsequently renamed Devgru. Anyway, whether it was mutual recognition of a fellow operator or the thick file he had on me apparently extolling my activities for Delta and the Company's Special Activities Division, I must have had one of the quickest job interviews on record before being put on the payroll. The job started off very positively. Once my new employment was confirmed I was told to take a couple of weeks off before reporting for duty.

I used my holiday time to visit some old legion pals in Europe whilst ensuring that no one was following me. At great personal cost to my liver I made the rounds of several of my less than salubrious friends, continually checking that I was not being shadowed. I had been lucky enough to have been removed from a special operations unit to work for the Agency just before several of my fellow operators were investigated for what might be called financial irregularities. The investigators offered the operators one of two choices. Either get prosecuted and be sent to Leavenworth or rat on your friends. Watching the process from the sidelines had taught me to be extra careful about concealing the existence of secret bank accounts. So before checking on my finances I wanted to be sure that I was not the target of some CIA internal investigation. When I was as certain as I could possibly be that I was clean, I very carefully made my way to the Principality of Liechtenstein to check on my finances and to arrange for the transfer of the funds sitting in Panama into what was for me a far more comfortable and secure zone.

Liechtenstein is a small area of land nestling between Austria and Switzerland and bounded by mountains on one side and the river Rhine on the other. I guess that it has closer ties to Switzerland than to Austria because it uses Swiss money and there are no border controls with the Swiss, whereas there are with the Austrians. Anyway it is a small, fairly agreeable little place, whose main industries seem to be selling postage stamps and money laundering. I arranged my affairs to my satisfaction and before I knew it was back in New York at the chrome and glass headquarters of DNB. Yes, just like Pinkertons, we were housed in a fancy chrome and glass building with a marble lobby. To my surprise I was given a special housing allowance to enable me to find suitable accommodation in the Big Apple before getting back to a demanding schedule of work.

CHAPTER THREE

Sicily – time the present

"It is blood that gives movement to the sounding wheel of history" – War memorial inscription - Piazza Armerina, Sicily

The cemetery descended from the sun baked hills in a series of irregularly spaced terraces. Whilst slightly reminiscent of some defunct vineyard, the descending rows of tombs bore no resemblance to the straight rows of neatly tended grape vines that occasionally dotted the Sicilian landscape. The graveyard was attached to and protected by a centuries old monastery that loomed high over it. The monastery was as sun dried as the rest of Sicily and seemed to have been infected by the lifeless tombs in its charge, for nothing seemed to stir behind its ancient, thick walls. Nevertheless, a deserted, thatched roofed, market stand with faded hand written price lists, provided evidence that the monks were still eking out their meager existence by selling a variety of herb based alcoholic drinks to the odd few tourists who were brave enough to undertake the drive up the narrow, winding, badly maintained access road. The road up to the monastery ended abruptly with a space that doubled as a turning area and car park. The market stall was built into the cliff to the left of the main monastic structure facing the parking area. The wooden signs, listing the products for sale and hanging limply from each of the two supporting pillars for the thatched roof, were the only hint of some living presence in the whole place. Now empty, the parking area was large enough for perhaps six or seven cars at any one time without the danger of one of them being displaced over the precipitous cliff edge that doubled as roadside and boundary to the extraordinarily elaborate cemetery.

Although it was only an hour or so away from the tourist resort of Taormina, the cemetery might as well have been on another planet. The beauty of the resort's bay, curving around the clear deep blue and green sea, was here replaced by rugged, unremitting red-brown earth, rock, wizened sun dried brush and the occasional olive tree dotting the otherwise arid landscape. Although it was not yet June, the hills were already assuming the parched appearance they adopted each summer until being temporarily revived by late autumn rains. Up here, at the base of the monastery, the harsh brightness of the sun seemed to be intensified by the strong radiation emanating from the ubiquitous white marble of the vast tombs.

I was working independently. Although DNB continued to pay me they had been underutilizing me for about three years and, with considerable time on my hands, I had been taking on some free-lance work. My target had visited the cemetery every day for the past three days. Always leaving the hotel in Taormina between 11.30 am and midday and always arriving at the cemetery at around 1pm when, according to the weathered sign nailed to its ancient, heavy, timbered door, the monastery was closed for an extended lunch hour. The tiled roofs and narrow streets of the village lying about a mile and a half below the monastery shared a conspiratorial like deadness both with the cemetery and its parent abbey, forming one enormous desolate, seemingly uninhabited, cloister. For the first two days that I had followed the target's car I had remained parked below the monastery, sitting quietly, unobserved in the apparently lifeless town, watching the man's movements through my high powered Leica Geovid binoculars. I can be stupidly mean about little things, but I never believe in stinting on equipment. I am a firm believer in quality. For me the high price of the binoculars was a minor irrelevance compared to the superb optics and built in laser range finder that allowed me precisely to measure distance and watch the target's every movement from so far away. But, even with lenses giving such perfect clarity that I could easily read the number plate on the man's car, I was unable to ascertain the precise reason for his daily visits to this isolated graveyard. Not that it was of any importance to me. I was there for one reason and one reason only and the motivation of the person I was being paid to eliminate, in carrying out this daily pilgrimage, was irrelevant to my purpose. Still, I suppose when it comes down to it, I am as curious as the next person and, in spite of myself, I was intrigued.

This third morning I had left the hotel early, before my quarry. In anticipation of my target following his pattern of the previous two days, I had positioned myself in the village, parking in a small side street just off a piazza containing in its center an elaborately decorated, but apparently no longer functioning, fountain. It had become second nature to me to choose good observation positions after all my years and experience as a former military sniper and Special Forces' operator. I was invisible to anyone driving through the village whilst maintaining a clear view of the monastery and cemetery. As my target's car arrived with the regularity I had come to expect, I was suddenly and uncharacteristically, overcome by immense curiosity as to what he was actually doing. It looked to me like a pre-arranged meet where failure by one party to turn up meant trying again the following day at the same time and place, but three days in a row was pretty poor tradecraft and perhaps it was something else. But what? Of course I had often been on jobs and been curious about particular people behaving as they had. Nevertheless I had long ago learned that curiosity got you into trouble and I had taught myself to repress feelings such as inquisitiveness, in favour of a natural caution and carefully acquired surveillance skills. I had spent countless hours, as a sniper in various parts of the world and in all sorts of different locations, immobile, observing, noting and waiting. In my time in the terminal years of the Vietnam war, in spite of being so much younger, I had been as patient as a hawk wheeling silently, high in the sky waiting to drop out of nowhere on prey unwise enough to expose themselves.

I think I have read somewhere that people become more patient with age, but the opposite seemed to be happening to me. In a mere two days my curiosity had developed from a slight tingle into an insistent itch demanding to be scratched. Today, as I watched my target commence what seemed to have become a ritual cemetery visitation, a sudden uncharacteristic impatience with the job made me decide to indulge my curiosity. The trained and experienced part of me made me wonder what the hell I was doing, but it was too late. I had already started the car and pulled out of the shadows to drive slowly up the hill towards the monastery.

As I reached the car parking area my target's chauffeur, who had been watching my progress up the hill, stared at me from where he was leaning against the side of his car, his arms folded across his chest. The target's car was a late model Alfa Romeo sedan, a well-designed, fast car. As I turned my car so that it faced back down the road slightly to the side of and behind the Alfa, I glanced at the chauffeur. He was wearing similar sun glasses to mine, the type favored by the United States secret service which seem to reflect everything around them without being overtly mirrored. I could not see his eyes but he was making no secret of the fact that he was staring at me unremittingly. As I got out of the car I glanced at him again, taking in his stance, posture and generally assessing his capabilities. I leaned back into the car to retrieve my camera like a dutiful tourist and covered the binoculars with my jacket, before locking the car and setting off down the steps into the cemetery.

The chauffeur was obviously doing double duty as Chauffeur/bodyguard. This could either be down to an imprudent piece of parsimony, or the target regarding himself as being relatively safe. Experience had taught me that it was very difficult effectively to combine the roles of chauffeur and bodyguard. You either had to be one or the other. In some exceptional cases the dual function might be necessary, but such splitting of roles always provides an assassin with an extra window of opportunity. Still the guy was obviously alert, looked fit and well balanced and had that quiet air of confidence that denotes someone who should not be underestimated. With that thought in mind, I descended the white marble staircase leading down into the cemetery, whilst at the same time scanning the tombs for some sign of my target. I could feel the chauffeur still watching me, but did not look back and was soon out of his field of vision.

The cemetery was much larger than it had seemed from the town below and the tombs bore not the slightest resemblance to the sort of graves to which I was accustomed. Many of the tombs were, in reality, massive, heavily sculpted monuments. A number of them were decorated with meticulous, almost photographic quality, engravings of the faces of their occupants as they must have looked in the prime of their lives. Above the main cemetery, built into the cliff that formed part of the monastery wall, were some mausoleums in caves carved out of the rock face. Those natural crypts contained sarcophagi and various religious statues. Wandering through the burial ground, trying both to observe my target and act the innocent tourist, I began to feel a strange fascination for this extraordinary cult of death that had produced such extravagant monuments to the defunct. My attention was momentarily drawn by the marble carvings and constructions surrounding me and I started to examine some of the pictures and sculptures more closely.

The sound of the Alfa starting made me realize that I had missed the departure of the man I had been watching. I looked up as I heard the Alfa's engine and was just in time to see the car begin a slow snaking descent back towards the village. I sighed to myself and shook my head at my loss of concentration. Uncharacteristically I was becoming careless and losing focus. I could not understand why. I had never before dropped my guard on a job, even on the many previous occasions I had been in hot places, where you have to fight off the natural tendency to torpor, because everything was so quiet and sleepy down to the occasional lazy buzz of a languid insect. I shook my head as I slung the camera over my shoulder and started to run back towards the marble staircase.

A tall, well built, heavily tanned man with black hair, albeit streaked liberally with grey, stepped silently out of the shelter of one of the tombs and blocked my way. I felt an immediate surge of adrenalin which I instantly controlled through a well-practiced breathing technique. I stood there, outwardly relaxed looking at my target. He was dressed in the light yellowish beige suit so favored by Italians in the summer months. The suit was well cut but the open jacket revealed the stomach of someone who was losing the middle-aged fight against excess weight. Sprigs of thick black chest hair sprouted through the open neck of his elegant blue shirt.

"Cosa voi?"

I knew that he could not see my eyes through my unfathomably dark sunglasses, that he was faced with an impassive gaze that merely reflected his own features and that those reflective lenses conveyed their own particular brand of menace. I wanted him to relax a little, so I casually dropped my hands to my sides and allowed the camera strap to slip through the fingers of my left hand, holding it so that the camera dangled innocently inches above the ground.

"Excuse me?"

"Oh, you are American." The English was good, but even in those few words there were traces of the man's native Italian accent.

"Why are you following me?"

"I'm sorry, I don't understand." My tone was intended to convey the uncomprehending puzzlement of an innocent tourist, mystified by the odd behavior of a local native, but it had no effect on the man confronting me.

"I want to know why you are following me. Is that so difficult to understand?" His voice was calm and patient; the voice of a teacher, patiently explaining something to a particularly obtuse pupil. I did not like the way this was heading. He was well balanced and confident, but not overconfident. There was nothing of the bullying braggadocio about him. I could see he was experienced and knew what he was doing.

"I'm sorry. I'm afraid you're mistaken. I'm not following you. I just came up to see the monastery and the graveyard."

Ever since the man had stepped out of the shadows and throughout the brief conversation, I had been mentally assessing my target and his likely responses, furiously working out whether I should try to bluff my way out of this situation or whether to do the job there and then. The man facing me was confident and reasonably relaxed. I was equally confident. I knew my abilities and that I was exceptionally skilled. I had no doubt about my ability swiftly to dispatch the man facing me. But whether or not I should was another question. From one point of view it would be convenient and quick. But I am very risk averse and hate acting on the spur of the moment without a detailed reconnaissance of the target area. For all I knew there could be dozens of eyes even now, peering curiously at this seemingly minor confrontation. There was also the consideration that I had been given very specific instructions for it to look like an accident. It had been emphasized to me, to the point of tedium, that there was to be no suspicion of anything other than accidental death. In the course of the three journeys I had made to the monastery I had almost decided upon a car accident. The steep, narrow, winding roads favoured such a solution. Regrettably, now my idiotic curiosity had jeopardized everything.

I felt my eyes narrow slightly beneath the shade of my sunglasses. The man's self-confidence was not misplaced and his speed belied his size. He was quick, very quick. He had produced the gun with the dexterity and speed of a skilled conjuror. All the same, it was not what I would have regarded as a professional's weapon. From where I was standing it looked like a .25 Calibre Beretta, carried with more regard for an easily concealed, lightweight weapon, rather than any heavy duty work. Still, it never did to underestimate an opponent. A good shot can do a lot of damage with a small caliber weapon and, if it was the Beretta it seemed to be, it had an eight round magazine and direct chamber loading. With the right ammunition and in skilled hands it was not a terrible choice for a close quarters' weapon.

"I asked you a question and I want an answer." The voice had developed a slightly exasperated pitch. "This is Sicily you know. Here it's easy to disappear with no questions asked."

I did not respond, but I thought to myself that that was very good to know. So, if it was so easy to make someone disappear here, why the hell had I been hired at great expense to fix some complex accident? Maybe my employer was not as familiar with Sicily as the man in front of me seemed to be.

The man's voice had betrayed the impatience he was starting to feel due to my failure to respond to him. He was clearly becoming disconcerted by my remaining so calm when a gun was pointing at me. Any lingering suspicion he might have had that I was some casual tourist would have been dispelled when I had failed to react to the gun by grovelling on the ground and begging not to be killed. I would have to act soon or things were going to get out of hand.

Fortunately he apparently liked to talk.

"I'm not some stupid amateur you know. I've noticed you following me the last two days. I've seen you in the hotel. So don't start giving me some idiot innocent act." The Italian accent was now much more pronounced as the man's agitation started to show.

In the distance I could hear the sound of a car, presumably the Alfa, starting to climb back up the hill. I had been set up and my situation was not going to improve. It was decision time. I slowly started to raise my hands as I said

"Look, just take it easy... "

The careful, measured, slightly submissive way in which I raised my left hand caused him to relax almost imperceptibly. It was then I suddenly snapped the camera whip-like towards his head whilst simultaneously moving my body to my left, away from where the gun was pointing. As my adversary moved instinctively to avoid the camera, I caught his gun arm at the wrist with my right hand whilst continuing the swing of the camera towards his head. He was already off balance and I prevented him from regaining his balance him by pulling on the gun arm, straightening it and pressing in on the wrist nerves where I was gripping him. At the same time, using the momentum of the camera swing, I wrapped the camera cord around the man's neck. The gun clattered to the ground as I swiftly changed my stance and pulled him backwards, ramming my knee into his back and half strangling him at the same time. I released his wrist and slipped my right hand under his right arm using it to grip the other side of the camera strap, whilst at the same time pushing his head down. He was now struggling violently, trying to lash out at me with his left hand whilst scrabbling to grab my right arm with his now free right hand.

The sound of the car grew louder and I turned to my right as I allowed him to break free from the strangling effect of the camera strap in my left hand. As I intended, the sudden release of his neck, coupled with his attempted twisting out of the strangle, made my adversary stumble forward, enabling me to strike the left side of his head in the temple area with the palm of my left hand, making him stagger and gasp. The blow knocked his head sideways, momentarily exposing and stretching out the side of his neck. In one continuous movement I swung my right arm across my chest and snapped down hard across my victim's carotid artery with the side of my hand. He collapsed immediately. At that point I did not care whether or not I had killed him. I was furious with myself for having been so stupid as to have allowed my curiosity to overcome my tradecraft.

As I stood over my supine victim I thought to myself that I was over age, overconfident and probably over the hill. I wondered, not for the first time, what deeply engrained machismo made me continue with this line of work. Everyone I knew, or had known, at the sharp end of the business was much younger than me. Those who had managed to survive their thirties and forties had either retired or had the good sense to become instructors or desktop security consultants, where, as independent investigations and intelligence advisors, they probably earned more than I did for doing nothing more arduous than giving security advice to overpaid, overly paranoid executives.

In the meantime I had to improvise a way to botch up this cluster fuck. Of the several serious problems I was facing the first and, most pressing, was what to do about the mark's bodyguard. Even now I could hear the car manoeuvering in the car park above. I looked down again at the figure slumped at my feet and the small gun lying in the thin layer of dust on the ground and made a quick decision. I could forget any elaborate car accidents. There was no way of staging anything like that here. In a very few moments I would have to deal with the chauffeur and that could be messy. Even if I could deal with the chauffeur discreetly and get the two of them into their car to drive them to a suitable spot for the "accident", I would then have the problem of returning to retrieve my parked car and driving it away, all without anyone noticing anything untoward. It was impossible; far too risky, with too many imponderables. I would just have to be a little creative and worry later about explaining myself out of any problems with a disgruntled client.

Decision made, I picked up the gun and with some difficulty, dragged the supine, formerly elegantly dressed, but still, thank goodness, breathing target, behind one of the tombstones. Then, crouching in the shadow of a vast black headstone surmounted on each side by a large angel whose spread wings sheltered the stone like a canopy, I called out loudly but indistinctly, "Eh! Eh!"

As I crouched there, waiting, I hoped that the inarticulate noises I was making would confuse the bodyguard and be enough to draw him within range of the small calibre Beretta. I had neither the luxury of being able to test fire the weapon and zero it nor the opportunity to check the magazine or the ammunition, so I had to take the chance that the weapon was fully loaded and in good working order. Certainly, from the weight, it felt like there was a full magazine.

I heard the soft crunch of slow, cautious footsteps before the guard came into view. The bodyguard had obviously been moving carefully from tombstone to tombstone, not wanting to expose himself prematurely. When he finally appeared, he was much closer than I had anticipated, but, as far as I was concerned, that was all for the best. He was holding much heavier duty artillery than the little Beretta in my hands, but that was of no concern. There are very few people like me, who have trained in elite military units for countless hours, using hundreds of thousands of rounds of ammunition, to obtain total mastery over hand and other guns. I could have done this in the dark, blindfold with exactly the same result.

I put the first shot into the bodyguard's throat and the second one through his abdomen, painful wounds, but the man would not have to suffer for very long. The bodyguard was wearing an open necked shirt so there was no chance of a concealed protective vest. I did not want it to look as if the man had died instantly. The scene had to look like a mutually destructive shoot out. Others would have to wonder why it was that a bodyguard should have decided to shoot the body he was guarding. It was the best solution I could think of on the spur of the moment. The bodyguard had scarcely dropped to his knees before I was dragging my target's bulk out of its temporary hiding place. He was not only still breathing, but seemed to be on the point of recovering consciousness. I was suddenly conscious of how extremely hot it was in that midday sun and realized I was sweating profusely. I propped the boss man up awkwardly against one of the angels, before retrieving the bodyguard's handgun. He was a game one and no mistake. In spite of his wounds, he had still been trying to reach the handgun lying in the dust, where he had dropped it. It was another Beretta, but a 9mm. A good weapon, the handgun of choice for more than one of the special forces I knew so well, but even so I could not help wondering whether Berettas were given away with packets of cereal in Sicilian supermarkets or whether Italians were just patriotic in their choice of firearms.

I straddled the bodyguard, easily pushing aside his feeble attempts to grab me and dropped into a very low crouch from which I fired at my target, hitting him in the stomach. The body jerked back against the angel before the legs slipped forward towards me. I took my second shot from an even lower angle, almost squatting on the bodyguard, whose throat wound was causing a sibilant gurgling, as blood mingled with air. This shot hit my target in the head, the exit wound leaving a nasty mess all over the bottom of the angel's wings as the body slipped all the way to the ground. I pulled my shirt out of my trousers and ripped off a piece from the end, which I used to wipe clean the 9mm before forcing it back into the dying bodyguard's hand. I have to say that he was game to the end. He still tried to resist me in spite of his wounds, but the effort was futile and failed to prevent me using his hand and fingers to fire two further shots in the direction of the mark. One of the shots hit the edge of the unfortunate angel's bloodstained wing and chipped away a large chunk of the marble. The other flew off in the direction of another tomb and I could hear it ricocheting around briefly.

I moved over to the mark's now still body and using the same piece of shirt wiped the little .25 before placing it in the appropriate hand. Trying to get the angle right, I saw that the bodyguard was still fighting, trying to sit up and aim the 9mm at me. I used my mark's lifeless hand to fire two further shots from the small Beretta. The first, a headshot finally put the bodyguard out of his misery whilst, with the other, I nicked the bodyguard's shoulder. I was breathing heavily as I stood up to survey my handiwork.

Nothing was going to elevate this into anything but crude but it would have to do. It was a real blood bath. There was blood everywhere, spattered over the tombs and seeping into and mingling with the dust. Now the main problem was to expunge any trace of a third person having been present at this little party. I also had to take the greatest care to avoid leaving any bloody footprints or other indication of my departure. I removed my shirt completely and used it lightly to brush the dust in the vicinity of the two bodies, whilst taking the greatest care not to go anywhere near the blood or disturb the ejected cartridge cases. I then stood back checking the area carefully to examine the scene. I desperately wanted to get out of there but it was no good rushing these things. I tried to survey the little tableau I had created with a dispassionate eye. I decided it was not too bad. With luck, the crime scene investigators would take things at face value and not carry out too rigorous an examination of the site.

Swarms of flies suddenly appeared from nowhere, eager to feast on the carnage. My next concern was witnesses. I brushed a few errant flies away as I looked around, carefully scrutinizing the monastery windows for some sign of life. I wondered how many people had to have been disturbed by all the shooting. I could see no-one and, amazingly, the graveyard had resumed its habitual quiet with only the frenzied buzzing of the flies to disturb the heavy silence. I continued carefully scanning the surrounding area, finding it scarcely credible that no one had flung open a window or come out to see what all the shooting was about, but there was not a sign of life. The whole area gave as much indication of human life as the surface of the moon. I had liked Sicily from the beginning, but now I was starting to develop a genuinely warm affection for a country where you could loose off several shots without even one curious curtain twitching. Where else in the world would that happen? Perhaps some of the Central or South American countries where I had served in the eighties, but nowhere else I could think of, not even Afghanistan. I glanced at my watch. It was only 1.35pm. I took another quick look around, checking the scene again, before gingerly picking up my camera and stepping carefully away from the bodies, to make my way swiftly back up the stairs to my car, the whole time using my shirt to brush out any traces I might have left in the dust of my progress.

Once I was sitting in the car I looked around again for any indication of someone watching, scarcely believing the degree of indifference I was experiencing. I saw absolutely nothing to concern me. I took the binoculars and carried out a quick 360 degree scan. Nothing. It was difficult to believe but it was what it was and even if there was some well concealed witness there was nothing I could do about it anyway. I switched on the ignition without starting the engine and quietly slipped the manual gear change into neutral before releasing the handbrake and allowing the car to start slowly rolling down the hill. Within a few seconds the steepness of the hill caused the velocity of the vehicle to increase. With the engine off, the power steering would not function and I had to struggle with the heaviness of the steering to manoeuvre the car around the sharp bends. The servo assistance for the brakes also, only worked with the engine running and I almost had to jam my foot through the floorboards to reduce the car's increasing speed. Perhaps a hundred yards before reaching the village I decided that controlling the car was becoming too difficult. I shifted the gear lever into the third gear and lifted my foot off the clutch. The engine caught immediately, allowing me to drive away smoothly and with a minimum of noise.

As I drove through the village, where, fortunately, there was still no one on the streets, I pondered my options. I was ostensibly in Sicily as a tourist, so it would be suspicious for me to return early to the hotel. I ought to do some sight-seeing and take some photographs to bolster my cover in preparation for a worst case scenario where I might be questioned by the police. But where should I go. I could take a tour of the volcano, Mount Etna, but that was perhaps a little too near the cemetery. What I really needed was some evidence that I had been far from the scene. By now I was well clear of the village, so I pulled off the road to look at my map. I did not want to get on the Autostrada where cameras at the tollbooths would give any police investigation a timed and dated picture of me sitting in my car without a shirt. My map only showed major roads. Not purchasing a detailed, large scale map of Sicily was another piece of sloppiness on my part. I could still see though, that if I avoided the Autostrada, I would be able to drive across country towards Enna and thence to the valley of the temples at Agricento. The temples were a major tourist attraction and would allow me to run off several pictures to bolster my cover. I checked the route again before setting off. The roads were almost completely empty and I was able to drive fast.

I stopped twice on the way. Once to put on a fresh shirt from the spare set of clothes I always tried to carry with me on a job. I had been driving for some thirty minutes on a long stretch of road, through barren hills, without seeing another car and decided not to push my luck by continuing to drive around without a shirt and thus attract extra attention to myself. I had pulled off the road and, in order to try and remove any possible gun-shot residue that might have contaminated my body, I washed myself down as best I could from two of the half dozen 1½ litre bottles of mineral water I kept in the car. I then put on a clean shirt, fresh trousers and clean shoes. A swift examination of the shoes I had been wearing had failed to reveal any blood spatter, but you could never tell these days when a spray of luminol could show up bloodstains invisible to the naked eye. I had then dipped the shirt and trousers I had previously been wearing into the car's petrol tank, before removing them and setting them alight, burning them together with the shoes and the piece of shirt I had torn off and used to wipe the guns. I looked at the shoes with a genuine feeling of regret that seemed to be reflected in the apparent reluctance of the flames to consume them. They were expensive Ferragamo loafers and I had been fond of them. Not only had they looked elegant but they had been extremely comfortable. The shirt and trousers burned well enough, but the shoes turned into an ugly, sooty, cracked apology for footwear with half melted soles. However, they were still recogniseable as footwear, even as I kicked over the dying traces of the fire and watched the last of the blue yellow flames flicker and die. Still mourning the loss of the Ferragamos, I reluctantly picked up their remains and threw them away in large curving arcs over two ploughed fields.

The second time I stopped was just outside Enna, when I filled up the car with petrol and oil. As I emptied the oil container into the engine I deliberately poured some oil over my hands, to give me an excuse to ask for some of the industrial strength dirt remover that garage mechanics use to clean their hands. The obliging mechanic not only gave me the special cleaning gel but helpfully offered me a carefully guarded key to the toilet, where, I was told, I could effect the necessary ablutions. The toilet turned out to be a dirty, foul smelling cubicle, with a large hole in the ground protected by a cracked, soiled porcelain surround that had been white in a previous incarnation. The washbasin was no better. It had apparently been used by several generations of mechanics for draining engine oil. I rubbed the gelatinous oil remover all over my hands and forearms before turning on the water tap to wash it off. As water jerked spasmodically out of the tap I washed my hands thoroughly before shaking off the excess water and wiping my damp hands on a miraculously present roll of toilet paper. As I returned to my car I was not sure if the relief I felt was at having escaped the toilet intact or having, with luck, destroyed any trace on my body and clothes of gunshot residue.

By the time I reached Agricento it was nearly 4pm. I parked and made a quick tour to take some photographs of the ancient Roman temples. Fortunately my camera was still working despite my having dropped it in the course of my brief struggle with the mark.

I was on the road again within twenty minutes and reached Enna fairly quickly. Having decided to try and bolster my tourist credentials by visiting the mosaics of the Villa Romana Casale, I turned towards the town of Piazza Armerina. Again I was lucky in not encountering any traffic and was able to reach the Villa by just after 5pm. My luck seemed to be holding because the site was still open for visiting for another couple of hours and I was able to take dozens of further pictures. Having dutifully taken photographs, I was able to relax a little and take the time to appreciate the amazingly preserved and varied mosaics. In fact I became so engrossed by the brilliant colours and variety of the mosaic pictures that I lost track of time. I have already mentioned that I inherited some of my Japanese grandfather's artistic skills and I was intrigued by the great diversity of subject matter of the mosaics. There were portraits; vivid hunting scenes, with humans and wild animals realistically depicted in all their natural ferocity; mildly erotic representations of bikini clad roman girls and many other skillfully conserved mosaics. In the end I remained at the villa until it closed. The sun was already starting to set by the time I ambled back to my car.

Driving back through the town of Piazza Armerina, trying to find the road to Taormina, I had to smile to myself as I passed the main square and saw inscribed on the war memorial the words "It is blood that gives movement to the sounding wheel of history." I started to feel more confident as I decided to take the words as a good omen for a successfully accomplished mission.

It was late by the time I returned to the hotel in Taormina. As I drove slowly up towards the hotel gates

I looked around anxiously for police cars, hoping that my nearly full, four gigabyte SD card of photographs would provide me with a strong enough cover and alibi to enable me to avoid any suspicion of having been involved in the shooting. On the drive home I had had plenty of time mentally to run through the scene I had left, checking and rechecking in my mind's eye whether or not I had eradicated all traces of my presence or whether I could recall anyone who might have seen me. It has become a habit with me to indulge in this type of mental debriefing after a job. I find it a useful way of checking myself, enabling me to be prepared to deal with any details I might have overlooked in the heat of the action. By the time I reached the Hotel I was fairly certain that there was nothing to link me to the carnage I had left.

At the hotel entrance, as I left the car for the concierge to valet park, everything looked normal. Still, even though there was no sign of any police cars, I braced myself to encounter the detectives I was sure would be waiting inside.

To my relief there were no police in evidence anywhere. I received no lingeringly quizzical looks from any of the reception staff. The receptionist listened to me politely when, in response to her question as to whether I had had a good day, I launched into a fulsome and genuinely enthusiastic description of the Temples at Agricento and the mosaics I had seen. My only moment of surprise was when the receptionist asked me whether I would be leaving the following day. As far as the hotel knew I was booked for a week and

I had been thinking up various excuses I might give for suddenly curtailing my stay. Then she produced the fax that had led her to ask the question. The terse document was from "Yellow Star Oil Exploration Inc, Equipment Supply Division". This was actually a genuine company partially financed by DNB. One thing that DNB Operational Services Inc knew about was discretion. They also knew that whatever I was doing would look a lot less suspicious to any relevant authorities if I was employed by an oil company rather than DNB who were known as a military personnel supply entity. Admiral Standish for all his years in the Navy and having run organizations like the NSA was no unimaginative bureaucrat. He was a tireless and innovative entrepreneur. He had expanded DNB's business base from merely carrying out unsanctioned operations and assassinations on behalf of the intelligence community, into providing general security services for multi-national corporations, including such things as negotiating with kidnappers and providing former military personnel to carry out many of the duties that the US armed forces sub contracted in places like Iraq and Afghanistan. He had then followed business necessity and logic by dividing the company into different sections and incorporating a number of innocent offshoots in different fields to provide cover for Black Ops personnel. The Diplomatic Studies Division to which I belonged carried out all black ops but we were usually accredited to other functioning organizations such as news agencies, computer software companies or, as in the present case, an oil exploration company.

Throughout the time I had been at DNB and, particularly since Standish had taken the helm several years before, DNB had become a successful private corporation with its CIA/NSA ancestry becoming more and more distant and obscure. I had been working for DNB for some fifteen years now. The work had not been very different from what I had been doing when I was with Delta and working with the Company, although there were no purely military operations. During the past three years or so my work had diminished considerably and extremely noticeably. It had seemed to me that I was being kept more on standby than carrying out any active functions. Nobody told me that I was being canned. I was just left to assume the worst. I suppose it was my age. It made sense really. No-one was supposed to be doing this sort of work in their late fifties even though I still considered myself at the peak of my powers. When I was not on an operation I trained hard on a daily basis and considered myself as tough and skillful, with or without weapons, as I had ever been. At least that had been what I had thought until my little fuck-up today. Today's episode had made me realize that I might still retain enough physical fitness for the work, but my mental sharpness was diminishing with age. I did not know whether DNB knew about my freelancing over the past years since they had started to underutilize me, but I did know that things like that were unlikely to have gone unnoticed and no one seemed to object as long as I kept them informed of my location. Certainly no one complained to me and my salary was still paid into my bank account at the end of each month, although those welcome bonuses after successful completion of an operation had become fewer and further between. Still, my freelancing was a lucrative alternative and I was not dissatisfied with my current status.

The fax was not addressed to me by name but merely stated that it was for my room number. I remembered that the message I had left giving my location and contact co-ordinates had given no more than telephone, fax and room numbers. DNB were being typically discrete not knowing what name I might be using. The fax was terse and to the point, typical of the director's secretary's feminist, Ivy League haughty disdain for mere operators like me. "Your presence required urgently in Rome to meet director. Telephone office a.s.a.p. for further details."

I read the fax three times and was probably frowning as I wondered what this was all about. The director referred to was, of course, Admiral Standish who, in the scheme of things, was no less a person than God. What, I wondered, could be that urgent that they were requiring a meeting with Standish in Rome. After a naval career that had taken him all over the world, Standish was notorious for his reluctance to travel any further from New York than the Hamptons, or at a stretch, Washington. Any misgivings I felt though, were more than offset by relief at having been given a solid reason for curtailing my stay. The fax, which had clearly been read by the reception staff, was a godsend. It gave me a legitimate excuse to leave abruptly, although Rome seemed a little too coincidentally convenient.

My client, for whom the current job had been carried out, was supposed to meet me in Rome in order to pay the balance of my fee. Although I was moonlighting, I wondered whether Standish might just be keeping a closer eye on me than I had imagined. I glanced at the row of clocks behind the reception desk that gave the time in eight different time zones. 3.30pm in New York. I was hungry and I decided that God's secretary could wait until after I had eaten for my confirmation that I would be in Rome the following day.

CHAPTER FOUR

Rome – Time Present

" And until you have possessed
dying and rebirth
you are but a sullen guest
on the gloomy earth " (Goethe)

Surprisingly Rome was even hotter than Sicily. At least in Taormina the heat had been mitigated by an almost perpetual breeze, but Rome was stifling and humid. I had left Sicily early, catching one of the first morning ferries to the mainland. Apart from wanting to leave before any over-zealous policeman decided to question fellow guests of the victim of the monastery shoot out, I had hoped to avoid any heavy traffic on the drive to Rome. A forlorn hope apparently. It seemed that however early one took to the road there were inevitable encounters with the surfeit of suicidal motorists who seem to be indigenous to Southern Italian roads. The journey had taken me about 5 hours. I was now sitting patiently waiting for the gridlocked traffic to move along the road beside the Tiber. I glanced around looking at my fellow motorists who, contrary to the popular conception of excitable Italians, were all sitting patiently waiting for the traffic to inch its way gradually along the road. Just above me was positioned one of the electronic signboards that were placed at intervals above the roadway. This one proudly informed me that the air quality today was tolerable. I looked at the thick black diesel fumes belching out of various trucks around me and wondered precisely what had to happen before the signboard would be able to announce that pollution had reached dangerous levels. Perhaps the arrival of a missile with a chemical or biological warhead. I decided that rather than open my window and take in hearty breaths of the tolerable air, I would continue to suffer the stale re-circulated air-conditioned coolness that I so used to shun in earlier days, when I had been more concerned with my macho image.

I glanced at the black face of the Tag Heuer look alike on my wrist. That watch had cost me ten minutes of bargaining and ten dollars in Bangkok three years before and was worth every penny. It kept perfect time, never complained when I knocked it, which I did frequently, and was always available to be given over freely to any muggers who might happen to accost me when I was in a generous mood. Unlike many of my acquaintances, especially the Russians, I did not like to wear heavy gold wrist or neck chains, but I did like watches. On three occasions in the previous ten years, after finishing particularly lucrative jobs and having been in transit for a day or so in Switzerland, a browse through the watch and jewellery shop lined streets of Zurich had resulted in my impetuously treating myself to extravagantly priced time pieces. I was now the proud possessor of Patek Phillipe and Frank Mueller wrist watches with complications and, a considerably cheaper, but still pricy, Breguet chronometer. Even though, for the most part, those expensive watches resided in a safe deposit box, I had never regretted the purchases. The pleasure I felt on the rare occasions when I wore one of my prized watches more than compensated for their cost. Indeed, despite my ignorance of the finer points of watch collecting, chance or perhaps inherent good taste, had guided my choice into rare examples, with limited production, whose value only seemed to have increased each year. On one occasion when I had chosen to wear one of my watches, even Standish, who made a fetish of looking elegant, commented with admiration about my choice of time piece. In the meantime, though, I had been working and my wrist was presently graced by a far from limited production example of Thailand's prolific craftsmen, which, even now, was reminding me that I was meeting Admiral Standish in just under two hours.

I saw a gap in the traffic and accelerated hard, narrowly missing another car that had spotted the same gap a couple of seconds later than me. I turned right into a narrow cobbled street constricted into barely one car's width by the mix of parked cars and a variety of motorcycles lining its two sides. I drove as far as I could down the street before being forced to make a right turn when the road turned into a one way system going in the opposite direction. By my reckoning I was now parallel to the Tiber and within walking distance of Piazza Navona. This is the large rectangular piazza which had, in the time of the Emperor Domitian, been flooded in order to provide Roman citizens with the spectacle of staged sea battles that had originally and less successfully, been staged in the Colosseum. Nowadays the gloriously profligate spectacles of ancient Rome were difficult to imagine in a Piazza Navona that had become a popular tourist destination, lined with open air restaurants and bars and whose central open space was filled to capacity with nothing more exciting than female tourists in skimpy tank tops, vendors of pictures and reproduction soccer shirts of popular teams, tee shirts and other shoddy, overpriced, tourist memorabilia.

I spotted a car manoeuvering out of a parking space fifty metres ahead of me and immediately accelerated into the vacant spot before anyone else could do so. I felt more pleasure in finding this spot than anyone has a right to expect. But I am no stranger to Rome and I knew that I could easily have driven around for an hour without finding anywhere to park. For the mission I was on, I had ruled out parking in a car park, to avoid any possibility of being logged by the ubiquitous closed circuit cameras with which all the car parks now seemed to be equipped. I estimated that I was about fifteen to twenty minutes' walk away from Standish's hotel and a few minutes' walk from the rendezvous point I had decided upon to complete the financial side of the business I had so recently concluded. I got out of the car, making sure that nothing inviting was visible to passers-by, before reaching inside for my camera and the cell phone I had stolen from a careless tourist at a restaurant in Sicily. I switched on the telephone, relieved to see that it was still connected, before punching in the local number I had memorized.

It had hardly rung once before being answered.

"Pronto"

"Hello." The guy did not know that I spoke quite good Italian and there was certainly no reason to enlighten him.

"Oh it's you!" the voice sounded aggravated. Not promising.

"What happened, it's been all over the news. Television, Newspapers... "

I could scarcely believe that the guy appeared to want to discuss our business on the telephone and wondered whether I had made a huge mistake taking on the job. Money is no good to you if you are sitting in a prison cell. I cut him short.

"Look, you don't want to talk about this on the air. I've got two hours before leaving the country. I need to see you now to conclude our business." There was a long pause followed by "Where are you?"

I did not like that pause. "I'm quite near Piazza Navona. Can we meet somewhere there?"

Another long pause. A bad sign. "Hello? Are you still there?"

"Yes." Further pause. Eventually he managed to squeeze out "I have an apartment in Via di Ripetta, by the Tiber, near Augustus' mausoleum. Can you meet me there?"

I wondered who the guy thought he was dealing with. Go into his place cold. Even if he was on the level, what idiot would want an assassin who has just completed a hit for him to come into his apartment? To do what? Sit down and have a cup of tea and wait for the Carabinieri to put two and two together?

I obviously needed to take the initiative, "Look, we have a very short transaction to conclude. I'm not going to your apartment. We'll meet in ten minutes by the Bernini fountain in Piazza Navona. Just bring what I need in a plastic shopping bag."

There was another, again far too long, pause.

"I'm not sure. Ten minutes... it's very short notice. I don't know if I can get there in that time."

"It's near enough to Via Ripetta" I snapped, irritably betraying my knowledge of Rome. "You can make it. Take a taxi if you have a problem. Just don't try and fuck me around."

I rang off without giving the man an opportunity to argue. I did not like the way this was starting to sound. Fucking Italians, you could never have a clean deal with them. They always tried to introduce some little twist or turn to try and screw you. Then they would turn around and try to charm you out of resenting them. Perhaps it has something to do with their relationship with their mothers. I remember reading somewhere that most Italian men remain living with their parents until well into their thirties. Be that as it may, I knew from past experience that, for all their undoubted charm, Italians are very difficult to deal with and in fact, when the job was first put to me and I had realized that I was going to be working for an Italian, I had wanted to pass on it. But then I am a greedy sonofabitch and the three hundred thousand dollars on offer was far too much to walk away from. Besides, I had already received half the money in advance. Even if the client welched on the balance it was still a good sum for a few days' work and no crew with whom to split the pay. But I did not want to start thinking like that. That would be just what the client would have in mind.

As I started walking towards Piazza Navona I took two Kleenex from my pocket. I held the phone with one and used the other carefully to wipe off any fingerprints or DNA residue I might have left. I was satisfied that the phone had been sufficiently sterilized by the time I passed one of the many trash cans that were thoughtfully placed all over the city by the municipality. This one was not too full. I glanced around to see whether anyone was watching before I dropped the telephone and the Kleenex into the middle of all the rubbish, making sure that it was not visible to any casual passer-by.

Piazza Navona was packed with people; the usual mix of traders and tourists. Apart from one or two attractive, skimpily dressed girls, the tourists were an unprepossessing lot. They all looked the same. Ugly, badly dressed and many carrying large backpacks on their backs. The sharp faced purveyors of art to the masses were operating their usual portable art galleries, selling photographic like paintings to ignorant foreigners who, for all I knew, probably thought they were buying some contemporary masterpiece to decorate their sitting room wall next to the flying china ducks. I passed a bench on which three English girls were sitting, apparently deciding which design henna tattoo they were going to have embroidered on their bodies. I was suddenly reminded of the biblical story of the Tower of Babel as I listened to snatches of German, Swedish, Russian, Japanese and three types of English; British, Australian and American, all accompanied by Italian continuo.

Just by the fountain where I had arranged the meet, four Chinese sat on stools, behind small trestle tables, offering tourists the opportunity of having their names inscribed in Chinese on a piece of paper, with an additional decorative hand painted image thrown in for the same price. I watched them for a few minutes as they worked. They were not bad at all. I mused that they probably offered as good a deal in art as anything else in the square.

It was time for me discreetly to blend in with the surroundings. I took my camera out of its case and stood by the fountain taking pictures, in imitation of everyone around me. Just another Japanese tourist. Then, still using the camera, I carried out swift sweeps of the square, seeking out my contact. I spotted him immediately. The man just had no idea. In his immaculate tan suit and elegant shoes he stood out from all the tourists as if he had been painted with a laser bomb sight. The only good part was that he was carrying a plastic shopping bag as he had been directed. I strolled over to him as if asking directions.

"Just point to the end of the square as if you're telling me where to go."

"What... oh... ". The man obeyed dutifully.

"I'm afraid you didn't give me enough time, I haven't got everything."

"You'd better walk with me. Continue pointing and waving your hand as if you're explaining something to me. What the fuck do you mean you haven't got everything? You know the rules. You knew I was coming back after the job to pick it up."

"I know, I know. But I didn't know what had happened. On the news it said there'd been a shoot-out with his bodyguard and that he'd been killed by the guard so I thought... ".

"You thought what? You told me you didn't want it to look like a straight hit. What the fuck do you think happened? That he and his fucking bodyguard decided to drive for an hour up to a fucking cemetery in order to blow each other's fucking heads off."

"Yes, but I said an accident... I never thought... "

"Well it was a fucking accident, wasn't it? An accident between him and his bodyguard. And I want my money now or you're going to be the next fucking accident."

I, who am normally cool and unemotional, was snarling uncharacteristically. Well, perhaps I was putting on a little bit of an act, knowing how Italians enjoy drama. But I was in no mood for any bull shit and I was not about to go into a post mortem on my hit in the middle of a public square, surrounded by a thousand curious tourists.

"There's no need to be unpleasant. I'll get the rest of the money. It'll just take a couple of days."

"I don't think you understand. Maybe I didn't make myself clear. I'm not going to be here in a couple of days. The deal was half in advance and the rest when the job was over. The job's over, you have to pay. One way or the other. If you don't pay cash now you're going to pay by joining your friend."

I had switched from psychotic, barely repressed fury, to ice cold matter of fact-ness. The effect was gratifying. The man's composure totally crumbled. He faltered, came to a halt and fumbled in his pocket for a silk handkerchief with which he wiped the sudden perspiration that appeared on his face. Although he was tanned I could actually see the blood drain from his face. His hands were trembling so much that he momentarily dropped his handkerchief as he groped awkwardly into his inside jacket pocket. I tensed briefly, reacting to the possibility that he was being stupid enough to reach for a weapon, but when I saw him starting to remove a thick envelope from his jacket, I covered the defensive movement I had started to make, by bending down and picking up his handkerchief for him. He had the grace to smile and say a nervous thank you, as he threw the envelope into the shopping bag, before offering the bag to me. I ignored the proffered bag and took my new found best friend's arm reassuringly in mine, as I steered him back to the end of the square from where we had both entered and well away from the group of Carabinieri standing casually surveying the crowd from beside their dark blue painted Land Rover.

In my experience there are always Carabinieri on duty in the piazza, armed with sub machine guns, on guard, no doubt, against some imagined terrorist attack feared by the Ministry of the Interior. In any event, I did not want my companion to get any cute ideas about shouting accusations to the Carabinieri that he was being robbed, with the possibility of my ending up on the receiving end of a good hosing down from a couple of Beretta SMGs on automatic. Fortunately, the client seemed unaware of my line of thought and accompanied me without demur. There was no more argument left in him. He had the good sense to know when he was defeated.

"I'm afraid it's not in dollars. I couldn't get dollars, I only had Euros. But it's better, much better. Less bulky with five hundred Euro notes."

"So how much've you given me?"

"One hundred and ten thousand Euros. The Euro is worth more than the dollar."

I knew exactly what the Euro was worth and made a rapid calculation.

"It should be a hundred and fifteen thousand minimum. You'll have to give me the extra five thousand."

The man stopped and turned to look at me, assessing me in silence for several seconds, before delving into another pocket and producing another thin envelope which he added to the contents of the shopping bag.

"I think I've underestimated you." A forced smile accompanied this admission. "If I need you again how do I contact you?"

"I don't think you'll need me again. I don't deal like this. This isn't a market place and you've turned what should've been a quick handover into a drawn out drama. This isn't some fucking child's game. We don't stand here and bargain about what you're going to pay me while ten thousand tourists include us in their holiday pictures and video films so that there's a record available of us meeting if anyone takes the trouble to investigate. You don't seem to have the sense to realize that it's as dangerous for you as it is for me. I don't like that and I don't like you. Take your fucking business elsewhere in future."

With that I took the shopping bag from his grasp leaving him standing in astonishment at my outburst. As far as I was concerned he could remain there all day with his mouth hanging open, but I had an appointment with God and within seconds I had disappeared into a large group of passing tourists.

I glanced at my watch as I slipped from one group of tourists to another. I still had forty five minutes before my meeting with Standish. I needed all of that time to ensure that I was free of ticks and there was no way I was going to head straight for my rendezvous. I also desperately wanted to delve into the carrier bag and open the envelopes to check the contents, but curbed my desire to do so. My first priority was to ensure no one was following me. I had no idea what my client's contacts or connections were with the dead man. I had carried out a careful check of the people around before approaching the client, but that would never be definitive. I had no way of knowing whether or not he had been tagged to the meeting place. If I had to say, one way or the other, I would not have thought so, but these days surveillance has become so sophisticated that you just never know, especially in cities when some invisible video camera could be following your every movement without any one coming anywhere near you.

Anyway I was going to spend at least 30 minutes checking for human tags and do my best to avoid appearing on camera before making the meeting with Standish. I promised myself that, if I had the time, I would check the money before my meeting. In the meantime I walked quickly, carving out a complex route through a series of narrow streets. Even on this bright sunlit day the streets were almost completely in shadow, although I had to be careful not only of tags but the veritable obstacle course composed of crap from the innumerable dogs who had been allowed to relieve themselves with total abandon and a complete lack of regard for the convenience of individuals who used the street as a means of walking from one location to another.

When I was as sure as I could be that I was not being followed I dived into a small bar next door to a restaurant where most of the outdoor tables seemed to be occupied by Americans. As I sipped a coffee and carried out a final check of the street I could not help hearing snatches of conversation from the neighbouring restaurant. An American with gray, well cut hair was regaling his companions with the tale of how he had almost bought Ferrari for sixteen million dollars "I'd even agreed the price with the Commendatore but then Fiat... ".

Maybe his companions were buying it. I suppose he thought the clincher was referring to Enzo Ferrari as "the Commendatore". They probably had no idea that anyone could have pulled that piece of familiarity out of any old newspaper.

I made one final sweep of the street to satisfy myself that I was free of ticks, before getting up to tear myself away from the world of high finance and big business. Even as I got up I could not resist a quick peek into the shopping bag. I was impressed. The client had been sufficiently switched on to put the bulk of the money into two large envelopes which in turn had been placed into separate plastic bags each bearing the logo of a different shop. The two envelopes, which I hoped contained the balance that I had forced the client to disgorge, sat on the top of the plastic bags. It looked like someone's innocent shopping. I checked out the street once more before leaving the bar. If I was being followed it would have to be by a full complement of professionals. Not at all likely, either from the client or the Italian police who, if they had been brought in, would surely have swooped by now to catch me holding the money.

Standish was staying at the Eden Hotel in via Ludovisi. I knew the hotel, having treated myself a couple of times when in Rome on Company business. I wished that I, too, was staying there. There are a lot of new, smart hotels in Rome these days, but cognoscenti still regard the Eden as one of the best hotels in Rome. Who was I to argue with them? My stays there had certainly been extremely comfortable.

Via Ludovisi runs between the famous via Veneto and via Capo la Casa. I hailed a passing taxi but, as I always prefer to be overcautious, except apparently on the job in Sicily, I had the taxi drop me off at the Excelsior Hotel. This is another large, luxury hotel situated on a corner of Via Veneto, directly opposite the street leading to the Eden.

I paid off the cab and ran up the entrance stairs into the palatial lobby which, with its magnificent high ceilings and massive crystal chandeliers, looked more like a vast ballroom than a hotel lobby, although it was broken up into different areas for sitting and drinking. I walked quickly along the decorative marble floor, pausing only briefly at a display cabinet showing off some choice jewellery on sale at a shop, whose address was shown prominently at the bottom of the cabinet. Using my peripheral vision I scanned as much of the entrance hall as I could for anything or anybody that seemed out of place to me. You pick up certain instincts after years of this work and it is surprising how well those instincts work and how attuned one can become to the minutest irregularity. There was nothing of that kind here today. I was almost satisfied as I looked carefully around the hall with what for me passed as a studied, relaxed casualness. Nothing; just the ebb and flow of groups of tourists and businessmen, meeting, entering, chatting. I looked at my watch. I still had some time before the meeting with Standish. I walked over to a wooden stand containing various newspapers in different languages, each attached to a wooden frame with a hook at the top to enable them to hang easily from the stand. I unhooked a copy of the International Herald Tribune and sauntered over to the sitting area that doubled as a lobby, lounge bar. It was a very large area, furnished with armchairs and settees placed around coffee tables of different sizes. I sat down on a sofa that was near enough to a group of business men to allow me to blend in with them and far enough from them not to draw me to their attention. I opened the newspaper, holding it up to glance at its contents whilst simultaneously surveilling the room. The ceiling of the hotel was extremely high and the walls were inset with large areas of pink marble that alternated with long, fairly wide, ormolu mirrors. Although the whole place was impressive and clean there was something about it that gave an impression of faded grandeur and past glory. The only person who seemed to be taking any notice of me was a waiter who slowly strolled over to ask me what I wanted to drink. He clearly was not concerned one way or the other when I politely declined his offer and he sauntered nonchalantly back to the bar.

When I was as satisfied as I could be that I was not under observation, I got up and returned the newspaper to its stand before turning and walking through to the back of the lobby, down a small flight of stairs. I knew from previous visits to Rome that there was an exit from the back of the hotel. The only thing that had changed was that on this occasion the exit had a large bilingual sign saying "Porta Allarmata - Door Alarmed". I continued down the stairs to where a corridor led to cloakrooms and went into the toilet while I considered whether or not I should risk setting off the alarm, if there really was one. I decided I would risk it and returned back up the stairs to the rear door which

I pushed open without any further hesitation. To my relief, no alarm sounded. Thank God for minor Italian inefficiencies.

Back on the street, I picked up another cab from the taxi rank at the side of the hotel. The Eden was not more than 300- 400 metres away, but I was still cautious enough not to walk directly to the rendezvous. Perhaps it was a reaction to my carelessness in Sicily, but I wanted to be certain that I was not being followed. I had the taxi drop me at a multi-storey car park opposite the Eden. I paid off the driver and entered the car park at the same time as a woman carrying a large shopping bag and an elegantly dressed man gently swinging a leather briefcase. I threaded my way through the parked cars as if searching for my own, but actually making my way diagonally across the garage to a position from where I was able to survey the street and the hotel across the road. Again I saw nothing whatsoever to arouse my suspicions. Finally satisfied, I left the car park and entered the hotel.

By now I was already five minutes late for the meeting but I thought to hell with that. I was no longer able to contain my desire to check the money I had been given. I walked straight through the small entrance lobby and up a few stairs into a sitting area which was comfortably furnished with a variety of armchairs and sofas. I sat down and casually glanced around. If the Excelsior was more like Grand Central station, the Eden resembled a private men's club with a few select members. The lobby was almost empty apart from the staff. An American couple who, from their conversation, appeared to be waiting for a guide, were occupying two chairs just below me. The only other person present was an attractive, tall brunette, carrying a Louis Vuitton attaché case and a pressed leather Chanel handbag. After a few minutes of looking too intensely at the brunette, I got up and walked up a further flight of stairs, through a secondary sitting area and into a small foyer containing a couple of exercise machines and a few dumbbells. Doors to separate men's and women's toilets formed part of the foyer. The men's toilet was small without the usual array of urinals and contained just two cubicles. I locked myself into one of the cubicles and was relieved to see that the toilet and cubicle were spotlessly clean and still retained a fresh pine odour from whatever cleaning agents had been used. So much of my life has been spent crawling through mud and earth; sitting motionless in some of the most inhospitable terrain in the world, trying to ignore the variety of wild life crawling over me, sometimes even attempting to nest in the warmest parts of my body, to say nothing about the days I have spent having to defecate into plastic bags and bury my excrement to avoid giving any indication of my presence, that when I am in civilized surroundings I have developed a tendency towards obsessive cleanliness. I cannot quite recall when it happened but suddenly, somehow, I acquired a compulsive repugnance, whilst in civilized surroundings, against touching anything where bacteria might repose or thrive. Even though the toilet was so obviously spotless, nothing was going to induce me to touch it. I pushed the seat and its cover with my foot, causing it to close with a loud thump. Having no other choice, I then sat down gingerly, without touching anything around me and balanced the shopping bag on my lap to enable me to examine its contents. I opened the envelopes carefully so that I would be able to reseal them. They contained bundles of 500 Euro notes as they were supposed to. I did not bother to count the money. It looked about right to my practiced eye. I was relieved that I had not been double-crossed. I took out ten of the 500 Euro notes and put them into my inside jacket pocket before resealing the envelopes carefully and replacing them in the shopping bag. I then covered the envelopes with the spare plastic bags before opening the cubicle. I was still alone in the toilet. Being unwilling to contaminate the carrier bag with whatever microbes infested the toilet floor, I held it between my legs whilst I carefully washed my hands. I always say that you can tell the quality of a hotel or restaurant by the quality of its toilets. In my opinion The Eden deserved the highest rating. Not only was the toilet apparently pristine, but guests were provided with a stack of neatly folded, freshly laundered, linen hand towels. Carrier bag still gripped by my knees, I shuffled awkwardly over to the stack of towels and removed one to wipe my hands. I then used the same towel to turn off the tap and open the door. As I held the door open with my foot I accurately threw the towel into the conveniently located wastebasket.

I was feeling quite pleased with myself as I left the toilet. Not only had I succeeded in remaining uncontaminated by toilet germs, but I had three hundred grand and no-one to share with. Not bad for less than a week's work. I decided that doing one of these a month would not be so terrible. I walked back down the two flights of stairs and approached the concierge. He was the usual slick, rather superior individual who thinks he is as good as the hotel's best guests. Notwithstanding his elevated status, he was only too pleased to accept the 20 Euro note I offered him for the privilege of looking after my shopping bag. Having successfully concluded that transaction I turned to the reception desk on the other side of the lobby and asked them to call up to Standish's room.

I retreated back to the sitting area and made myself comfortable. If I knew Standish he would keep me waiting anything from fifteen minutes to half an hour. I was quite surprised therefore when, after only ten minutes, Standish's traveling assistant came down in the elevator to escort me into the admiral's presence. Standish had officially retired from the Navy as a three star admiral. He had, for many years prior to his apparent retirement, been a senior figure in the US intelligence community. When he had been asked to head up DNB, as it had become known, Standish enthusiastically embarked upon his new career which, in the best traditions of CIA offshoots such as DynCorp and Aviation Development Corp, juggled clandestine operations with semi-official and purely commercial activities. Even though President Bush junior's policies had enabled the official intelligence agencies to regain responsibility for a considerable portion of the clandestine activities that had been forbidden to them for many years, the collateral culture of contracting out a proportion of military activities to private contractors like Blackwater, had enabled Standish's DNB to prosper beyond its founders' wildest dreams. It was sufficiently efficient, mature, well connected and represented by the top lobbyists to have grown into a billion dollar business. There was no question that the admiral relished the increased power that less oversight and commercial success bestowed on him as CEO of DNB. In his years in the intelligence community Standish had come to love all the trappings of power that accompanied jobs such as being Director of the NSA. He was not a person to whom it had ever occurred to try to slip away from his bodyguards. If he had some very private, delicate needs to attend to, his bodyguards just had to wait outside until he had finished indulging whatever personal necessity was currently demanding his attention. As CEO of DNB and master of his own budget, he had not been about to surrender his human status symbols. Now, wherever he went, even if it was 100 yards down the road, he travelled with an entourage of two secretary/traveling assistants and two body guards. In trips to dangerous parts of the world like Iraq he was better protected than the President.

I collided with part of Standish's ego in the ante room to the admiral's luxurious suite, when I was subjected to the indignity of a pat down by a bodyguard whose severely pockmarked face and dark complexion made me wonder as to his origins. Mentally I congratulated myself for having left the carrier bag full of money with the hotel concierge, thus avoiding any ugly confrontations that would inevitably have followed my refusal to allow the bodyguard access to the bag.

We eventually finished all the formalities attached to visiting a self- appointed head of state and I was shown into the presence of the man who DNB operatives like me privately referred to as the "capo dei tutti capi". The sitting room of the suite was suitably luxurious, with a large panoramic picture window at one end giving a magnificent view of Rome, with St. Peter's figuring prominently on the sky line. Standish was alone. He was a good three to four inches over six feet, very trim and distinguished looking, with commanding grey eyes. Impeccably dressed as always, he looked as if he had just stepped out of the display window of the Armani shop in Via Condotti. I looked at him sitting perfectly at ease in the lavish luxury of the hotel suite and thought that he looked more like an advertisement for luxury living than the head of a clandestine/military enterprise.

Years of practice have honed my self-control. I am so adept at beating the polygraph that I hardly have to think about it anymore. However, I do not know what it is, whenever I am in the admiral's presence I seem to become enveloped by a feeling of inferiority that I just cannot control. Perhaps I had inherited some particular servant gene that had developed over the centuries in a family that had served several generations of daimyo. Whatever it was I, who was always so cool and controlled, was unable to prevent it happening again and I silently berated myself for my weakness. There was just something about the admiral that always made me feel badly dressed, untidy, sweaty and out of place. The room was comfortably cooled by the air conditioning but, inevitably, I began to feel hot and uncomfortable. I could feel myself starting to perspire. I managed to restrain myself from smoothing down my trousers and wiping my palms as the admiral got up to shake hands with me in greeting.

The view and the old world luxurious surroundings seemed to have mellowed the admiral somewhat, because after cordially inviting me to sit on a comfortable sofa, he sat down next to me and offered me a drink of lemonade from the cooler standing on a coffee table close to the sofa. He then actually apologized for my having been searched, explaining that routines have to be observed or the guards get careless.

I accepted the drink cautiously. I was wondering what I was being set up for. Standish's reputation for hospitality vied with that of Lucretia Borgia, with the sixteenth century poisoness probably just being edged into second place. I knew that many a Washington power broker had over the years been treated to a sumptuous dinner only to be presented with a dessert of the poisoned chalice of being cajoled, or more probably blackmailed, into carrying out Standish's wishes.

"So how was Sicily? Beautiful at this time of year, isn't it? I gather that was your work that I read about in the paper this morning." The words were thrown out as nonchalantly as the arm movement that gestured towards the newspaper lying on a side table opened at a picture that seemed to have been carefully arranged so as to be visible from where I was sitting.

By now I was seriously concerned. Although I could see the newspaper easily enough from where I was sitting I needed a second or two to cover my reaction to the admiral's words. I casually leaned across to where the paper was lying and picked it up. The picture showed the two bodies lying in the cemetery in Sicily with a headline about treachery in a graveyard. I started to read the byline which speculated that this was a Mafia execution and described how the presumed Mafia boss had, in his dying moments, shot the bodyguard who had murdered him.

Before I had even begun to formulate a comment the admiral continued, with his inimitable ability always to maintain the initiative.

"Please, don't think there's any implied criticism. Of course it's a variation of a very old theme but I must congratulate you on an ingenious innovation. In a cemetery no less. My word, but you seem to be developing a macabre sense of humour as you get older."

His grey eyes focused steadily on me, that deadly alligator smile of his playing at the sides of his mouth. By a supreme effort of will I met his gaze without flinching, as he continued, saving me the embarrassment of attempting an unconvincing denial.

"As things are I'm not complaining about you carrying out the odd private job... provided of course, that there's never any conflict of interest." He smiled again in the face of my resolute silence. After my initial surprise, I had decided not to be drawn into any apologies or explanations. I wanted to know just how much Standish knew and how much he was guessing.

The admiral sipped delicately at his lemonade before continuing, adjusting his cuff slightly as he replaced his glass on the table.

"Well, it's easy to understand your interest in a little free lancing."

He picked up a file that had been lying face down on the table in front of him so that I had been unable to see what it was. As he opened it, making a play of flicking through some of its contents, I could see that it was my personnel file and I thought to myself that that was it. I was finally going to be terminated, although for the life of me I could not understand why he should have come all the way to Rome just to fire me unless there was going to be a considerable amount of prejudice in this particular termination. He continued talking as if he had not heard a thing I had been thinking,

"Yes. Apart from your retainer you haven't been getting much from us recently have you? Hmmm the last time you were operational was." Again, a quick flick through the file.

"Good gracious... two and a half years ago. I had no idea it was so long."

I had had enough. Fine if they were going to get rid of me. But I did not have to suffer all the extra crap that went with it. I decided to interrupt him. I may be a little old but I think that I am justified in still regarding myself as being one of the world's top assassins. Whether or not my ratings were dropping or I was developing a macabre sense of humour, one thing I did know, I was not some prize fish to be played at the end of an angler's line.

"Look Admiral, I know you've got better things to do than bother going through my file which, we both know, you know by heart anyway. Correct, I've been doing some, shall we say, non-contentious private consulting, but I sortta thought that you, or others"

I shrugged my shoulders carelessly as if to indicate the lack of importance of the whole matter,

" had kinda decided to put me out to pasture. I know that plenty of people around think I'm too old for field work. And I know that a lot of the work we used to do has gone back to the Company. I understand all that. And I'm happy. I've got no gripes. You guys've been real good to me. I get my full army pension. I'm still on retainer. Sure I like to keep my hand in. I like to go down to the range and practice. But you know all that, I'm sure. Surely you didn't come all the way to Rome just to can me. But if you did, that's fine. You don't have to dress it up. Though, if it's possible I'd still like access to the facility to be able to come down and get in time on the range. Keep myself up to scratch, you know. For personal satisfaction I mean. I guess you can understand that. I know you like to look after yourself."

The admiral smiled at me, opening his arms palms up in a subconscious gesture of honesty

"My dear John. I'm afraid you're way ahead of me and heading in a direction entirely opposite from mine. I have absolutely no reason and no desire whatsoever to "can" you, as you put it. And I certainly wouldn't fly all the way over here, however good it is to be back in Rome, just to tell you we're letting you go. I could do that by email. No. You've got it all wrong. On the contrary, I know your performance is as good as ever. After all you've managed to keep yourself out of trouble with your extracurricular activities. And look at your latest exploit. A masterpiece of black humour."

I frowned. I enjoy a good joke as much as anyone. However, even after all the years I had spent in this line of work, or perhaps because of those years, I believed in showing my victims a little more respect than simply referring to them as 'masterpieces of black humour'.

Standish continued, apparently not noticing my irritation,

"To be quite frank, your activities have been so discreet and well managed I have absolutely no complaints and no reservations whatsoever about keeping you active... whatever your age. These things are dealt with on a case by case basis and as far as I'm concerned you're still one of our best operatives. Of course, it's true, you've been somewhat underutilized recently, but as you ought to know that's due more to changes in the administration than anything personal to you." He sighed,

"Bush changed everything post 911. I can understand that he wanted everyone to understand American power but personally I thought he made several big mistakes. I and many people in the intelligence community never understood the man's obsession with Iraq. Attacking Iraq instead of the much more dangerous Iran; reverting openly to a policy of countenancing the use of lethal force against people we don't like. Virtually jettisoning the Geneva Conventions; the more or less open use of extra territorial rendition. Everyone knows we've got the organization, the ability... why emphasise it and shout it from the rooftops. It sometimes seems to me we're going backwards. The people who know to be afraid of us always knew anyway. But Bush, Rumsfeld, Cheyne, all seemed to think we needed to tell the whole world what we're doing. And what's the result? We're now on most of the world's shit list and that dithering wimp Obama has only made things worse."

He sighed, shaking his head in disgust, "And now, after an administration that started out frightening everyone with the invasion of Iraq and ended up being a poster boy for incompetence, we've got another administration earning the world's contempt for being irresolute."

Abruptly Standish stood up and turned to face the window, gesturing to me to join him, which I did.

"Magnificent view isn't it. This hotel has some of the best views in the whole of Rome. You know everyone talks about the Villa Medici. But I much prefer it here." I was not going to argue with him about that one. The view was very good and so was the comfort level of his suite. He turned to face me. The poet disappeared as abruptly as the bountiful host and he became all business.

"Anyway I've got something for you. It's more than delicate. It's classified above top secret. I had to meet you personally to tell you because, apart from the pleasure of being back in Rome, there is absolutely and, I mean absolutely, no documentation at all on this one. It's all being done through personal meetings; no video links, nothing exists of it except in the heads of a very, very small number of individuals. Before I left home I was summoned separately by the directors of CIA and NSA who each told me, in the nicest possible way, that my facility's resources were being activated at the personal request of the head of the British security service, MI6 and that the only person who was to know the precise mission was the operative to be utilized. I was told that this must be a totally compartmentalized, totally deniable operation. I don't know whether or not all this is mere hyperbole, because I know nothing about it. I was just told to activate my best man and to put him on call for a briefing by the Brits. I know nothing about the mission other than what I've just told you and what I'm about to say and I don't want to know. It's an all Brit thing and they seem to be in quite a flap. Anyway it's got them calling in all their markers and, for once, they don't seem to be worried about owing a few favours. I'm told it's something that the Brits've got to be totally dissociated from, which is why I've been asked to provide the personnel. Or rather" he corrected himself, "the person who will be running the job. Anyone else and you'll have to recruit them yourself. No Brits and no Yanks." He added firmly.

"This has got to be a false flag operation and everyone you use has to be expendable, so you might want to use Arabs or Yugoslavs, or whatever they call them nowadays, Serbs, Bosnians, Croats." He looked me directly in the eye, "Of course it'll be up to you, but you might think the more Muslim the better. Anyone you use might as well be led to think it's an Al Qaeda operation. They get blamed for everything these days as it is."

Standish paused and again beckoned to me to join him as he walked back towards the sofa. The admiral picked up his drink and took a sip. He seemed to be weighing carefully his next words, but I knew him well enough to be fairly certain that he had already rehearsed the entire scenario carefully in his mind, if not in front of the mirror.

"I have to be frank with you John. You and I have known each other a long time now. Maybe I shouldn't be saying this but you probably know my reputation for safeguarding my men."

I was puzzled for a moment until I recalled that Standish had at one time had overall command of the navy seal teams and it was reputed that he was responsible for the standing order that no man, whether wounded or dead, was ever to be left behind on an operation.

"I've said you'll use expendables. That means you'll be the only one to be left in the know. The only one who could turn around and blab. You know the Brits; they don't like to leave loose ends that aren't part of their precious little club. You're going to have to watch them John. Watch your back. They're also offering a lot of money here and you know how tight they are with their money. As I said, I don't know what this is about, but for sure it's murky as hell and, if I read this right, one way or another you'll be disappearing off the radar afterwards. You're going to have to make damn sure that you're in control of the disappearing rather than someone else. But... " He paused to take another sip of his drink,

"... I've got a lot of faith in you. I know you're capable of playing this hand so you'll end up with enough money to disappear in style." He laughed humourlessly.

My instinct for self-preservation that had been on the alert ever since I had heard that the admiral had come to Rome specially to brief me, immediately went up to the highest level of alarm. A queasy feeling hit me in the pit of my stomach such as I had not experienced for a long time. No, I was not being canned. I was just being offered up for a suicide mission which, if I was clever enough, I might survive with some money, as long as I buried myself somewhere no-one could find me. I thought of Monsieur Pernod and his French passport. That might do. Particularly as M. Pernod had had the foresight, over the years, to acquire for himself, two fairly isolated, but comfortable, farmhouses, one in France and one in Umbria, near Assisi, in Italy.

The admiral was continuing apparently oblivious to the effect his words were having on me,

"I suppose it's no secret I don't like the Brits very much and if it were up to me I'd let them stew in whatever it is they've got themselves into. But it's not up to me. Anyway, once I give them the OK. Your OK, that is, someone will come over and brief you. As I expect whoever comes, will be here in the next twenty-four hours, I've agreed to make this suite available for the meeting. Obviously I've had the room fumigated and put in our own babblers (counter bugging devices). I've also taken a room for you in this hotel and it would be preferable if you went out as little as possible to avoid any surveillance and any visual linking of you with our British visitor. You're not booked into any other hotel in Rome are you?"

Listening to this whole presentation, I hoped that outwardly I was impassive and neither giving anything away, nor showing the slightest interest. Inwardly, was a different story. I thought that I had trained myself not to react to things, but here I was, in spite of myself, feeling a little sick. My guts were churning over. I could not remember the last time I had felt so nervous. All I could think of was, when at the age of 16, I had stolen credit cards and shipped myself out to Marseilles to volunteer for service in the French Foreign Legion. I had felt the same stomach stirring sickness when my romantic ideas had first come face to face with the reality of the brutish drill sergeant who told the line of new recruits that the Legion's motto of "March or Die" was no empty phrase and that in the training to follow it would be keep up to the mark or die; that now we were in the Legion we had, to all intents and purposes, disappeared as individuals and either we would make good legionnaires or corpses lying in unmarked graves.

There could not have been a greater contrast than between the voice of the hoarse screaming drill sergeant and the soft spoken urbane admiral, but the message I was receiving sounded the same. I was wondering just what this job was all about. Standish's fairly overt warning, that I needed to take care, was completely out of character for the admiral. I knew from personal experience that he usually briefed operatives for the most dangerous missions with casual offhanded understatement. I knew that Standish had a thing about the Brits and had had a couple of nasty run ins with them, but what he was telling me did not have the ring of embittered malice. I did not know what Standish knew or did not know about the mission but I was prepared to bet that it was a lot more than he was letting on. And if Standish was not warning me that the Brits did not intend me to survive I had definitely ceased to understand English. I wondered if Standish was warning me because he disliked the Brits so much or whether he just felt some sort of obligation to me, as a veteran operative he had used so many times. I had heard on the grapevine that, before Standish had taken over DNB, he had missed out on the newly created job of Intelligence Supremo over all the intelligence agencies. That had been because of some political problem with the Brits over liaison with GCHQ (Government Communication Headquarters, the British sister organization and junior intelligence partner of the NSA). I also knew that it was said that when Standish was still in the Navy he had been denied his fourth star because of some problems with his British counterparts that had led to a complaint directly from the British Prime Minister to the President. If the rumour mill was correct it would explain Standish's resentment of the British.

As for the job itself, apart from the apparent difficulty I was going to have surviving, it must be something so unpleasant that even I would want to turn it down. I knew the British well. Years before when I had first been brought in to Delta Force I had been seconded to the

British Special Air Service for just over two years. I had not actually learned as much as I had been expected to learn, because I turned out to be far more experienced in certain areas than my hosts, who had been able to make more than good use of my own skills. But I had enjoyed my stint of being based at Bradbury Lines in Hereford. Although I had heard that since my time with the SAS things had changed quite a lot, not just the name of the base, which was now called Stirling Lines, after David Stirling who had founded the SAS during the Second World War. For one thing, a lot more American Special Service personnel were serving with the regiment. When I had been seconded to them only Captain Macwilliams had been sent with me, and we yanks were a rarity. However, something that I had learned from my time with the SAS was that the Brits were perfectly capable and more than well enough equipped, to carry out their own dirty work. If this really was the Brits and not some false flag operation I was being sold and the Brits did not want to have anything to do with the job, it had to be something really nasty.

"John?"

I was brought out of my silent analysis of the situation and reminded that I had not yet answered the admiral.

"No. I left Sicily early this morning and drove straight up here. I've got a rental car. I parked up some distance away before coming here. My things are still in the car."

"Fine. That's perfect then." Standish rubbed his hands together, "Why don't you get your car and bring your things up. I take it the car isn't rented in your own name. Perhaps you ought just to turn it in. Let the Brits supply you with any transportation." He added smoothly.

I looked at him, nodding my agreement as I wondered whether I ought to turn down the job now and thinking that, even if I took it, after what the admiral had just said, I was going to make damn sure that whatever the Brits provided by way of transportation would be parked a long way from where I intended to be.

"I haven't said I'll take the job yet. You haven't told me much to give me enough of an incentive."

"Oh, I'm sorry" said the admiral apologetically, "I haven't given you the clincher. They're paying $10 million."

I stared at the admiral trying to mask my confusion and wondering whether I had just heard right. Ten million dollars. Even allowing for the most extravagant expenses and a full crew I ought to be able to clear at least eight million. With the money I already had and my secret little farm houses in Umbria and France that no-one knew anything about, I would have more than enough for me permanently to disappear and enjoy a well-deserved retirement. I also still owned my grandfather's old house in Kyoto which I had inherited but which had been closed up for years. I had for some time nurtured a secret desire to go back there and perhaps re-open the old Kendo school. Frankly, however I considered it, the temptation was just too much for me. Whatever the risks it was going to be worth it.

I looked up at Standish, who now had the slightly smug self-satisfied expression of someone who had known all along that he was going to trap his victim.

"Pass me that bag will you." Standish gestured towards a brown leather case that was parked on an elaborate gilt dresser against the door furthest away from where I was sitting.

Without saying anything and without commenting on this exercise of control by the admiral, I got up, picked up the case and handed it to him before resuming my seat. Standish opened the case and probed in its depths for a few seconds before producing a medium sized brown manilla envelope. He handed the envelope to me unopened.

I made a big play of pulling out my Swiss army knife and slicing through the top of the envelope before emptying its contents onto the table in front of me. It contained a maroon coloured French European Community passport, a French identity card and driving licence as well as Visa and Mastercards issued by a French and Swiss Bank respectively. The documents were all in the name of Hassan Ben Kamal. The passport, identity card and driving licence photographs were sufficiently anonymous to have been me or any one of a hundred other people. I looked up from my examination of the papers. Notwithstanding the money on offer, my feeling of uneasiness had increased.

"Why the French Arab identity?"

"On what I've been told, this is an operation that should never come to light. However, one never knows in this day and age. It was my idea, without, as I have said, knowing anything about the operation, that, should, by some remote chance, an investigation be initiated directed towards identifying the individual or group responsible, that it would not hurt for that investigation to be directed towards individuals or cells linked to Al Qaeda. This documentation is simply laying the groundwork for that. You speak fluent French and, I believe, some Arabic. Your reservation here is in the name of Kamal. You know as well as I do that you have to give hotels in Italy an identity card and that the police take a record of all hotel visitors. We couldn't register you in your own name. Could we?"

"So, to all intents and purposes, for the duration of this operation I'm an Al Qaeda operative."

The admiral simply smiled, without saying anything.

I turned back to the envelope's contents and flicked through the passport looking at the various stamps on the pages. I wondered if this Kamal character was real or not. If he was real I wondered if he was locked up in Gitmo or somewhere else where these people are kept hidden. I also wondered if he was on any watch list that might endanger my own personal security.

I was extremely suspicious. One does not last long in this line of work unless you drive yourself mad suspecting everyone and everything.

"You wouldn't be setting me up here for something would you? Is this a real guy or is it part of a convincing legend?" I asked suspiciously, "While I understand what you're saying about the way the thing should be set up... these days... travelling around on an Arab ID particularly someone with North African origins. It makes me uneasy. A North African traveling around Europe on his own... it's like putting up a flag for the European agencies, and after what you've just told me... " I allowed my voice to trail off. I did not want to be too rude to the admiral. He could sometimes be a bit touchy about having his integrity challenged, but I also wanted to make the point that I did not want to use any identity that was on any watch lists.

Standish got it and was quick to reassure me. "Don't worry John. It's in no one's interest to jeopardize the integrity of your operation. Just look on it as providing an extra layer of security. A back up, if you will, if everything goes belly up. Once the operation's over you just dump the documents." He paused momentarily, "You only need use them selectively anyway."

Something else occurred to me "How come you're happy to have this Kamal, who may or may not be followed up later, registered at the same hotel as you?"

I did not know why I bothered.

"You needn't worry about that. That's all taken care of."

I did not want to be fobbed off. I always like to know what I am getting into, "But I do worry about little things like that. It's these little inconsistencies that always bother me." I looked up expectantly at the admiral. I might as well have looked at the wall. Standish just looked back at me expressionlessly.

OK, I thought, I give up. I looked down again at the various documents, "Are the credit cards good?"

"They're good for a couple of months. They've each got a limit of $20,000."

"Suppose I need them for more than a couple of months."

"Very unlikely. It's not anticipated the operation will last that long. My understanding, limited though it is, is that it's got to be over by the end of August at the very latest. After you've been properly briefed you'll know much more than me. If there's any change, or you need to extend, just call up Sophia and tell her to renew your cards. She'll arrange it."

Sophia was the cool, stylish, ivy leaguer who secretaried Standish and who, I assumed, with the cynical view I have of the world, did anything else he asked.

I thumbed through the documents again, before asking, without looking up,

"So when's this operation supposed to take place? You've just said we're looking at a short time frame here, so there must be some intel that you're not giving out. And... " I waved vaguely at the documents in front of me.

"And where is it? How many people will I need? " I looked up at the admiral before adding as an afterthought, "and why the warning about the Brits? That's a bit out of character for you, if you don't mind my saying so."

For the first time in all the years I had known the admiral I thought I saw the man's façade crack slightly. I could have sworn that a definite awkwardness crept into his demeanour and that a curious expression crossed his face fleetingly. I am not just a simple thug. One of the things I have had to do for years is observe people and gauge their reactions, probably before they even know how they are going to react. To my practiced eye, Standish actually looked conflicted.

"You don't really need to know this. I thought it was fairly common knowledge that I'm no great fan of the Brits. Had several run-ins with them when I was in the Navy. They ended up costing me my fourth star." I detected the slightest intonation of bitterness that had crept into his voice. "That's all you need to know and that's the reason for the warning. If they don't want you to come out of this and they're discomfited because you do, with a chunk of their money, it won't displease me. Also don't take the $10 million as gospel. There may be some room for negotiation, from both sides." He paused as I looked at him curiously.

He continued staring unblinkingly at me as if I was not really there,

"The team. I don't know how many and I don't know what sort of back up you'll need. You'll have to decide all that after they brief you. I would suggest you hit them for the money then, because you're going to have to pay your people yourself. A further word of advice. Take all the money you want up front."

This was another of the admiral's not so veiled warnings and I noted it carefully.

"As for the time scale," Standish continued, "it's going to be very soon. As I've already said, I don't know anything about the operation, but it's obviously urgent and I was told there are considerable time restraints."

"Just a couple more questions."

"Yes. What?"

"Why do you want me to do this job? Why me? You've got plenty of younger people. And," I paused, "have I got the choice of turning it down if I don't like it when I hear about it?"

Standish looked me straight in the eye, a thin smile spread across his face. His expression indicated that he thought I was some sort of mental defective

"Turn it down. You'd better tell me here and now if you're going to turn it down. The money that's on offer'll have people queuing around the corner to take your place. There's plenty of smart ex KGB operatives who'd kill each other for the chance of this one. Otherwise, assuming the money's satisfactory... " he smiled again, "... you're perfect. I know your work. I know you're reliable and thorough. In all the time we've worked together you've never put a foot wrong. You've never left any loose ends and you've never left any evidence of our involvement. Then again, we're deniable ops, a total shadow organization and you haven't done anything for us for over two years. You're even more deniable than us. And let's not forget the freelancing you've been doing. I know that you've been getting your jobs through two or three different third parties. So even if this thing, whatever it is, is traced back to you, there's quite a bit of distance between you and us and anything even remotely official. And, in the unlikely event that it is traced back to you, we can quite easily set up and deal with one of your other recent intermediaries."

I appreciated the admiral's frankness. I was not used to it. I trusted the two or three people he had mentioned as having given me jobs over the past two or three years, otherwise I would never have taken on anything from them. So, I did not particularly like the idea that one or other of them might be set up and eliminated without even knowing what they were facing or why. The admiral was continuing while I was thinking, I had never before known him to be so loquacious.

"You've established your own track record as an independent. Whatever I think about the Brits, I'm not in a position to fuck around on this. You're good, dependable. I know that you can set this up right. Also, you don't look American or British. With those oriental looks of yours you could be mistaken for Vietnamese, Chinese, Arab, anything. When I was first asked about this, I couldn't think of anyone better than you. And let's face it. I'm doing you a favour offering you this. You've been facing danger all your life, so the risks involved shouldn't bother you at all."

He stopped for a moment and gave me one of those steely eyed looks he was famous for, "You don't like being bull shitted, so the truth is I don't think from a technical point of view this is going to be a difficult operation for you to pull off. I've always liked you. Thought you were a hell of a good operator. You've done a lot for your country one way or another. But any way you look at it you're at the tail end of your career. How much longer can you go on doing this type of work, however fit you keep yourself. You can't go on forever and you're not the type to move into management. I'm giving you the chance to get out with a great chunk of money in your pocket. You'll have enough to keep you comfortably for the rest of your life. How many people do you know in this line of work who get a chance like that?"

I looked at him without saying anything. From one point of view he was right. I was getting too old to continue in this work. I was living on borrowed time and I would not be happy sitting behind a desk. I was also wondering though, whether he really had no idea of the different scams that operators like me got up to. That, even when I served with Delta, a few operations had enabled us operators to skim off sufficient money to endow quite a substantial special fund for unit operators who might fall on hard times or need special help. That fund had grown quite large and I and other former unit members received generous distributions on leaving the unit. Still, although I already had quite a decent nest egg, particularly with the properties I already owned, the money from this job would put me in the comfort zone for the rest of my life, even in the unlikely event that I lived to over 100. No, he was right. I was not going to turn this down, but I was not going to appear too eager either.

"Sure the money's great. Fantastic. But money's no good if you don't get to spend it. I get the feeling there's something you're not telling me. That feeling's making me wonder if I shouldn't just get up and walk away. I've lived this long by always listening to my feelings."

Standish looked at me again. He did not realize I was just bull shitting so as not to appear the complete pushover he obviously thought I was,

"Why do you say that?"

"I dunno' just a feeling."

"Well I'm going to answer you by asking you a question?"

"Sure."

"If you walk away from this with say $7million clear, will you do it? Whatever it is."

Now he was putting me to the wall and I knew the bullshit had to stop. I had played the lottery expecting less. Perhaps Bill Gates would have had the luxury of turning this down, but I was not Bill Gates. The payload on offer would enable me quietly to disappear and finally disentangle myself from all the people who seemed to have been controlling me for most of my life. Who knows, maybe I really would be able to return to Japan and set up the Kendo school as I knew my grandfather would have wanted.

"I guess. It's a lot of money."

"That's what I thought. So having said that... no, you can't turn around and change your mind. Once you've been briefed there'll be no going back. You understand fully my meaning here."

"Oh yeah. I read you four by four."

"There might, however, be one little snag I'd see as far as you're concerned." He was a bit of an actor and had a habit of introducing dramatic pauses into his speech which he combined with his steely look.

"You've always made it clear that you won't do women or children. It's funny. You've actually shown you've got some principles. Principles are not something that one normally associates with people in this game. I'll be frank with you John. I've always respected you for your principles and the fact that you've never ever compromised on that particular issue. You know, plenty of other operatives say the same thing, but when it comes down to it they end up justifying what they've done. But somehow I... er... how can I put this? As I'm being frank with you, well... I always rather suspected you because of your principles. Throughout your whole career; everything you did in Nam and later; everything you've done for us. You have a perfect record, but I always had this uneasy feeling that behind those oriental eyes of yours you weren't really on board, that somehow, somewhere you'd turn on us."

He paused again, pursing his lips before continuing, "you never did turn. You've always been the perfect soldier. And now, its become sort of a private challenge for me because I've got you on this one. If you want the money the probability is that your principles... your guiding light... whatever you call it, is going to have to go out of the window. Although the primary target is a man, he's apparently frequently in the company of a woman and I'm told that, however the operation proceeds, it is not to be pulled just because the woman might be damaged collaterally." He looked satisfied, almost triumphant as he finished speaking.

So he did know more about the operation than he was letting on. It was a hit on a man and a woman. In spite of myself, I frowned. I genuinely hated the thought of hurting a woman. The sinking feeling in my stomach suddenly became worse. My head started to throb as I remembered why I had always been so adamant about not killing women.

Only half listening to Standish, my mind wandered back to my second tour in Vietnam. It was the end of 1971. Everyone knew by then that the war was lost, even if they would not admit it, but the body count was still mounting. Although nominally I was still a marine sniper, I had been carrying out an increasing number of special operations, mostly for the CIA. Unlike other snipers who kept a close tally of their kills I had ceased to bother counting after my first tour. The number of kills meant nothing to me. I had become entirely caught up in the thrill of the hunt. I suppose I was obsessed. I had thought only of perfecting my skill at tracking; at moving silently through the jungle without leaving any sign of my presence. I was devoted to the single goal of completing my kill and then evaporating back into the undergrowth without leaving any sign that I had ever been in the kill zone. At the time I had felt in a strange way that I had been given a unique opportunity of learning to become completely at one with nature. Although some missions involved my working with a spotter I preferred working alone. I always tried to arrange solo operations. When I was out on a mission, alone, I somehow felt that I was an invincible predator, my prey the VC or NVA. Where most of the soldiers I knew would have done anything to avoid a patrol in enemy territory, I had always been eager to set out again on a feral expedition to hunt down and extinguish my current quarry. It came to the point where I needed the pursuit as much as normal beings needed food. In a way I was hunting for my food and my life- blood. Perhaps that was why I had become so good. I cannot say.

Something had changed for me though, when I was sent out to hunt the woman. More than 30 years had passed but I remembered her perfectly as I had first seen her through my scope. Her long, silky black hair, mostly tied in a tight bun; her black pyjamas; those black eyes; her small rounded breasts with the dark aureoles surrounding her nipples. She had been responsible for the deaths of many American soldiers, some of whom she had tortured hideously within earshot of American army encampments. She had been designated a serious danger to the morale and well-being of the army and I was the third of three snipers who had been sent out after her. The bodies of the two snipers and their spotters who had preceded me had been found nailed to trees on a patrol route, horribly mutilated. Instead of frightening me this had only motivated me more. Much to the relief of everyone who might have been chosen to spot for me, I elected to go out alone. I tracked her for ten days. Ten days of slipping silently through the jungle, often within feet of an unsuspecting enemy. I had lived on minimum rations supplemented by whatever nutrition I found in the jungle. I excreted into plastic bags that I buried deeply, where they would never be located to give away my presence.

When I eventually found her hideout I had watched her both through my range finder and my telescopic sight. I watched her bathe in the river flowing just by her encampment. I caressed her firm breasts and the curve of her hips with my eyes. I could have killed her several times, but always stopped short of squeezing the trigger. Something about her had evoked a strong sexual desire in me and, with the power either to nurture or destroy that feeling I had been numbed into inactivity even at the increasing risk to my personal safety. I had watched her and become seriously hard fantasizing about going down to the river and just taking her as she bathed naked. But, of course, I did nothing more than continue watching. There were, perhaps, two or three times I could have sworn that she knew I was there and was looking directly at me. Now, looking back, it seems ridiculous, but at the time I had come to feel a strong connection developing between the two of us until, finally, I had squeezed the trigger and blown her head to pieces. After that I felt different. The fervent congratulations showered on me back at base left me cold. I knew what I had done was wrong. For the first time ever I felt shame and regret for my actions. It was the end of the war. America had already lost, although there were still some who could not admit this. Killing the woman had been nothing more than a final act of spiteful revenge by an American military machine, whose might had been destroyed by the nationalist fervour of a peasant army. I knew in my heart that the woman had been a true patriot fighting for a cause in which she believed passionately. She had not tortured Americans out of sadistic pleasure as so many Americans had done to the Vietnamese. She had tortured them as an instrument of war; to strike fear into the hearts of her enemy, to sap their morale and destroy their will to fight. In the end she and others like her had succeeded. Compared to that I had been nothing more than a mercenary, at best a samurai whose only wish was to improve his skill.

I had no real friends in the army at that time. There was not the same camaraderie I had shared with my fellow legionnaires when I had served in the French Foreign Legion. I had never admitted to or told anyone how I had come to admire that woman and how much desire I had felt for her as I had watched her silently. In the end I came to believe that in killing her I had killed my desire for love. It seems stupid. But that was what I thought. I continued with my work but I swore to myself then that never again would I kill a woman. Years later, after a job in Hong Kong, I had gone back to Vietnam to try to find the place where I had killed that woman. I had found the grave of a woman resistance fighter who had been a heroine of the Vietnamese liberation army. Perhaps it was her, probably it was not. But the visit only re-awakened the sadness I had felt all those years before. Or perhaps I had not really been sad. Perhaps I was just a bit off my head from having spent too much time on my own in the jungle

Now I was being asked to kill another woman. Sure it was dressed up to make it seem as if the woman would not have to die. It was a collateral issue. But I was too old, too experienced and too realistic to believe lies like that. And I had changed. I no longer cared who I killed as long as the money was right. I no longer believed the lies I had told myself over the years, that I was a warrior with principles, a fine sword constantly being tempered in fire, seeking the perfection my grandfather, the great kendo master, had sought to instill in me.

Listening to Standish dangling all that money in front of me and acquiescing in the contract I had been offered, I faced the reality of what I had become or maybe what I always was, an unprincipled gun for hire, not caring who I killed or what I did in my search for that little extra financial cushion to take me into a comfortable and anonymous retirement – if I survived.

CHAPTER FIVE

London some 10 days earlier

"He had dared to commit terrible crimes and contemplated even worse ones; such as murdering the most distinguished of the senators and knights." Suetonius

The headquarters of the British Secret Intelligence Service, popularly known as MI6, is located in what some regard as a masterpiece of modern architectural design situated in South West London overlooking the river Thames at a place called Vauxhall Cross. The windows of the glitzy exterior are eavesdropping proof and the building conceals a host of measures aimed at preventing any interception of the personal and electronic information the building's occupant collects, analyses, houses and disseminates. To some observers the building looks like an elaborate wedding cake surmounted by two matching towers that could represent a bride and groom. In what would, in any other similar building, be the penthouse, was a suite of offices belonging to MI6's director, deputy director and other senior staff. The head of SIS was Sir Ralph (pronounced Rafe) ffitch- Stewart. No one quite knew why the first part of his hyphenated name was not written with a capital letter but apparently enough people had been sufficiently impressed by his double barrelled credentials to have appointed him to one of the most important intelligence positions in the Western world.

It is common knowledge that the British are very rooted in their traditions and the SIS was no exception. Acceding to a tradition that dated back to just before the first World War, Sir Ralph was known as "C", as had been all his predecessors since the first "C", Captain Mansfield George Smith-Cumming.

In truth Sir Ralph, or C, was not a man to be underestimated. As befitted one of the senior members of the British establishment, he was tall, aristocratic and good-looking. But his silver grey hair and aristocratic, slightly effete manner concealed a sharp mind and a tenacious personality. Many people had, to their cost, been deceived by his donnish, slightly absent-minded, self- deprecating facade. Beneath this veneer was a ruthless patriot, fanatically dedicated to the welfare first, of his Queen, then his country and finally significantly lower on the list and considerably less enthusiastically, to the government of the day. Being a servant of the Queen was no empty phrase to this C. Indeed, by a curious quirk of historical tradition, civil servants such as Sir Ralph and military personnel in Great Britain, still swear allegiance to the monarch of the day, serving first Queen and then Country.

Today as he sat behind an enormous and splendid antique desk that, surprisingly did not look at all out of place in the modern office, C was frowning at the documents that had been taken out of the file marked in large letters with the words "Umbra" "Zarf" and "VRK", code-words indicating that the contents of the file were of the very highest security, obtained from electronic surveillance and were of very restricted knowledge. The file contained numerous documents, including transcripts of recently intercepted communications. Spread amongst the papers, were some enlarged, colour, satellite surveillance photographs.

Sitting facing C was MI6's deputy director. Even taller than C's 6'2", with a full head of thick brown hair and a dark olive complexion which hinted at some perhaps Italian ancestry, Mark Everett Featherstonehaugh (pronounced Fanshaw by a similar esoteric quirk of the English language that had his boss's name pronounced 'Rafe') silently eyed his boss whilst C absorbed the contents of the file Mark had brought in ten minutes earlier.

He broke the silence as C looked up at him quizzically, "It looks pretty bad I'm afraid, sir" he said glumly. "I can't believe it would ever have got to this. That stupid, bloody woman! She's been warned umpteen times that whatever her personal differences are with her former husband, she is the mother of the heirs to the throne and needs to behave in a way commensurate with her position. So what does she do, she takes up with some bloody wog whose father is a known contributor to certain radical arab factions and is on better than nodding terms with Ayman al Zawahiri (Osama bin Laden's Egyptian born deputy)."

C raised his eyebrows as he interrupted his deputy, "Mark, you know as well as I do that these sort of expressions and racial epithets are politically incorrect, especially under our present political masters who, we both know, receive substantial funding from those 'wogs' as you call them." He spat out the final words with considerable distaste,

"and we both know, if we continue using these sorts of pejorative expressions within the privacy of these walls, one day the words are going to come out involuntarily and inevitably at a most embarrassing moment."

C's deputy smiled, "Sorry C. I got a bit carried away. I'm so furious about the whole bloody mess. It's so unnecessary and it's making us look stupid. As for the Royal family, I don't know whether you've seen the latest polls but they indicate that over 60 per cent of the population now thinks that the Royal family is outdated, out of touch and ought to be abolished. It's unbelievable what this country is coming too. It no longer seems to be the same place where I was brought up." He added unhappily.

C sighed in response, "Even more reason Mark why we have to handle this matter deftly and decisively. We are, it seems, the last line of defence for our most precious and important institution. By God!" he said suddenly banging a clenched fist on his desk, "do you realize, if we allow this pantomime to continue, the whole fabric of our society could collapse. Those half-wit politicians and journalists who blithely talk of doing away with the monarchy don't seem to realize that our whole society, our whole way of life, could collapse. And what would they put in its place. Bloody anarchy! We'd be like the yanks and every other bloody country with a politico as president. Which I suppose is what they really want. These days being Prime Minister isn't good enough for them. They want to be Presidents. Fucking idiots! Prime Minister or President, they'll be forgotten in twenty years. Who, except a few political historians, remembers Lloyd-George, Stanley Baldwin, Alec Douglas-Home, John Major? God, they barely remember Margaret Thatcher. No-one's got any sense of history or continuity today. All our great leaders seem to think of is how good they look on television and how to make themselves popular. They spend hours in front of the mirror, preening themselves, practicing their smiles and a look of sincerity, instead of spending their time dealing with the real issues facing us. I'll tell you Mark, within these four walls and I know you and I are at one on this, sometimes it really turns my stomach."

Featherstonehaugh was a little taken aback by the vehemence of C's outburst. He had only ever seen C as someone who was totally in control at all times; as a man who coolly weighed all his actions and carefully chose his words before expressing an opinion about anything. Secretly C's deputy felt honoured and not a little awed by the evident confidence his boss had shown in him by allowing him this brief insight into his true feelings.

C was staring moodily at the photograph of the Queen on the wall, a picture that seemed totally incongruous and slightly tawdry amongst the fine paintings that surrounded it.

"Well, we're seeing HRH at 1600. I have to report all this to him." He gestured towards the papers spread across his desk, "He's the only one who's got the gumption to say and do what he thinks." He sighed again. "What about the arab and his father?" C was unable to bring himself to call Mohammed Al Khalifa and his son Walid by their names."

"They've also had more than one warning that they were embarking on a very dangerous course by trying to cultivate a close relationship with her. They employ several ex SAS and Special Branch amongst their security personnel, who were approached unofficially and told to pass on our concerns. The father has just had another application for British citizenship turned down, as he was told would happen if he didn't stop trying to nurture his son's relationship with her. As for the son, he's as unscrupulous as his father but not half as smart. He's got huge debts in the States that he incurred trading on his father's name; he's also, God save us, got some outstanding breach of promise suit going on against him from some actress he promised to marry and a host of other things. It's been made perfectly clear both to father and son that they're swimming in dangerous waters. But the feedback I got was that the father blew up. Just talked about us being a load of pansies and boasting that his security people could look after anything we could throw their way. Robbins, our staff psychiatrist, thinks the man is out of touch with reality and doesn't think that there's any way, short of some really drastic action, to get through to him."

C sighed again, "I'm afraid I'd already reached the same conclusion. I just wish there was some other way. I hate to do this and I hate to use our resources for this sort of thing. Instead of going after terrorists we have to clean up what at bottom is no more than some silly little domestic dispute. To do this we're all going to have to put our heads on the chopping block. If it wasn't so serious it'd be amusing. "

He shook his head, "It's ridiculous. And to cap it all we're going to need all sorts of help from the cousins and probably also from Paris and we're going to end up owing too many obligations all round. I'm going to try to deal with everything on as personal a basis as possible. I'll probably have to end up retiring so that the service isn't burdened by having to reciprocate all the favours I'm going to have to beg."

"Do we really need to bring anyone else in on this, sir? Surely we've got all the resources we need. Why don't we go solo on this?"

"Don't think I haven't given it a lot of thought. But if, God forbid, anything went wrong, can you imagine the repercussions. It's going to need a team of at least six. That's too many for us to be sure about. You know as well as I do, nowadays it doesn't matter a damn how much you vet people, there's always some treacherous bugger ready to blow the whistle for the right incentive. No. No. In this particular case it's simply not possible to take the risk. We've got to bring in outsiders. It's unthinkable for anything to be linked to us in any way. It's got to be a hermetically sealed, false flag operation. Even bringing in the cousins, the only ones who will know anything are their two top men and probably that Standish person who runs their deniables these days. Although he makes me uneasy. He hates us you know, ever since that business with Cheltenham. Still I can't believe there'll ever be a leak from any of them. Then there's Jean-Michel in Paris. He's a good man. He understands what's at stake for us. One thing I'll say for the French, they're the tightest lipped, cover up bastards around and we can absolutely rely on them. Otherwise it's just you, me, HRH and possibly the aggrieved husband, if HRH decides to tell him."

"Ah, the Boy Wonder." Featherstonehaugh was referring to the way in which the heir to the throne was frequently referred to by his estranged wife in conversations with her friends, all of which C was having intercepted.

C looked at his deputy slightly reprovingly. He did not approve of disparaging members of the royal family. Still it was true that the heir to the throne was a little bizarre. Perhaps confused would be a better way of describing it. It was hardly surprising. Here was a middle aged man, brought up in ultimate privilege and yet apparently stuck permanently in the limbo between being monarch and a king in waiting. Some individuals might not have cared and just enjoyed their privileged existence, but the Prince was not like that. By all accounts he had a fearsome temper, frequently throwing at the current object of his displeasure whatever might come to hand. He combined a willful insistence on indulging himself without regard for the feelings of others, with a naïve, almost innocent obsession with the environment and love of the simplicity of nature that blended well with his undoubted skill as an artist. Yet his environmental credentials did not prevent him being an enthusiastic hunter and aficionado of fast cars.

"I rather think he's got a streak of ruthlessness running through him. There was that particularly convenient, somewhat suspicious accident that killed off the bodyguard of his wife's with whom she was having a rather indiscreet affair a few years back."

"Who knows what went on there? Everything was kept very in house with the Royal Protection Service. That Superintendent Chalmers who runs the Prince's protection is a canny, tightlipped bastard, totally loyal to his boss. He's perfectly capable of fixing up something like that and we'd probably never know. But accident or not you'd think that the wife would've learned something from that incident. She's very into conspiracy theories about everything, so she ought to have been the first to think it was all arranged. It doesn't make sense that she's now off flaunting this new relationship. Perhaps she's got a death wish, what with that bulimia thing and all."

C sat there, disconsolately looking down at the papers on his desk. In an attempt to break the melancholia that seemed to have descended on the old man, his deputy brought up the topic that had been the reason for the present meeting.

"What about this Major Cartwright?" C's deputy was referring to the SAS officer that they had agreed would be needed to liaise with whoever was employed at the sharp end and who would ultimately be charged with ensuring that no-one involved in their plan, however embryonic it was, would be left to disclose what they had done.

C looked up, once again his former crisp, analytic self, "Yes, Cartwright. I haven't decided about him yet. But I think he's going to be our man. He's got a first class record in these matters. Let's decide after we've talked to him."

"He's waiting downstairs now."

"Alright. If there's nothing else we need to talk about at this stage, wheel him in."

C's desk contained several telephones. One was for secure internal calls; another was a secure encrypted phone for secret external calls; others provided for secure communications to the British Prime Minister, the Foreign Minister, who was ostensibly C's boss and to the Chiefs of the armed forces. Featherstonehaugh picked up the internal phone, dialed a number and asked for Major Cartwright to be brought up to C's office.

Although Major Cartwright stood just over six feet tall he had to look up to address MI6's two senior executives. The army officer looked older than his thirty nine years. It was probably a combination of his rapidly receding, sandy coloured hair and a complexion that had seen too many extreme climates. There was nothing particularly remarkable about him other than his erect bearing which immediately betrayed his military background and his extremely strong handshake.

As they shook hands C said to the soldier, "Nice to meet you. I don't think we've ever met before. Do you know my deputy, Mark Fanshaw? No. Well take a pew, make yourself comfortable."

He looked at his watch, "Just time for a pre-prandial drink. What can I get you? I've got a rather unique old malt that I'd recommend."

Cartwright hesitated, "I normally wait till the sun goes over the yard arm, but perhaps a small one."

Whilst C walked over to a well-stocked drinks cabinet, Featherstonehaugh motioned Cartwright to sit on a three seater settee arranged with two matching armchairs by a large picture window that looked out across the river Thames.

"Great view you've got here Sir Ralph." Cartwright said as C brought over a small silver tray on which were placed three beautiful, hand cut, crystal whisky glasses, each half filled. C winced slightly at the mispronunciation of his name and, as he handed one of the glasses to the Major, said,

"Why don't you call me "C" like everyone else?"

Cartwright nodded his assent as he brought the whisky tumbler to his nose, "Hmm, terrific aroma."

"Yes, it's from a very small distillery that produces a special single malt that's aged for thirty years. They've been supplying my predecessors and me for the past hundred years or so. One of the perks of the job, along with the excellent wine cellar developed over the last century or so. Thank God that when they moved us into this monstrosity," he gestured with his arm, indicating the building they were in, "we were allowed to bring our wine cellar with us."

Having handed another of the glasses to his deputy, C placed the tray on a coffee table that separated the armchairs from the settee and sat down in one of the armchairs. He raised the glass slightly to the two other men saying "Cheers" before taking a small sip of the whisky. He swirled the liquid around his mouth before swallowing.

"Excellent." Putting his glass down on the table he looked at the Major,

"I suppose you're wondering why I asked you down here and what it is you've done that makes you deserving of us giving you lunch?"

Cartwright nodded his assent taking a further sip of his drink.

"Well, first of all we are extremely grateful for that little job you did for us in Latvia last month." He paused, "But that's not the main reason. However, before we come to that tell me a little about yourself?"

"Well C, can I be blunt? I'd like to say straight off that if this is a recruiting exercise then I'm not your man. I'm very happy in the Regiment. I'm a soldier. I like the army and I hope one day that I'll be made CO (Commanding Officer) of the Regiment. At heart I'm not really a cloak and dagger man, whatever little jobs I've done for you in the past."

"CO of the Regiment, eh" C mused, "well that day may be in the not too distant future Frank. You don't mind me calling you Frank do you?" C smiled charmingly.

Cartwright shook his head. "I don't quite understand. I'm not that close in line. Or am I? Is there something I don't know?"

"I would say that you're a lot closer than you might imagine." C took another sip of his drink. .

"I had no idea that you had anything to do with the selection process."

"I'm not saying that I have." He paused and looked directly at Cartwright. "Let's not talk about that for the time being. As I said, I'd like you to tell me something about yourself, your life, your hopes, your aspirations, your beliefs. What you think of the politics of this country for example, the Royal family, that sort of thing?"

Cartwright laughed nervously and shifted uneasily in his chair. "This sounds like some sort of positive vetting. I thought you had special people for that."

C said nothing in response, but merely waved his hand encouraging the Major to speak.

The soldier started to talk, briefly describing his career; his acceptance into the Special Air Service; various operations in which he had participated; the breakdown of his first marriage; his remarrying the divorced wife of a former colleague; his regret at not having children. C listened patiently and without interruption until Cartwright paused to swallow the last of his whisky, when C got up and, without asking, took the whisky decanter and poured another generous measure into Cartwright's glass. His next question came as he sat down again.

"What about politics Frank? What do you think of our present government?"

"Well C, I'm a soldier. It's not for me to think about politics. I do what I'm told."

"But suppose you're told to do something with which you disagree?"

"That's never arisen."

"But suppose it did?"

"I don't know. I'd have to deal with that when it arose. You can't talk about these things hypothetically."

"No." C drawled, leaning forward slightly. Featherstonehaugh was reminded of a snake about to strike its victim,

"Well, let me put a hypothetical situation to you. Suppose you had to choose between the interests of the Queen and the orders of the Prime Minister of the day."

Cartwright laughed, "Ha, that old chestnut. My oath of loyalty is to the Crown, not to the Prime Minister."

"Well I know that. That's all very well in theory, we all say that. But in fact we always get our orders from the government, mostly the Prime Minister of the day. No. Suppose you were really faced with the dilemma. Suppose the government of the day decided that the monarchy was losing its popularity and the Prime Minister, who relied for his support on republican minded MPs (members of Parliament) was pushed into deciding to abolish the monarchy. In fact perhaps he wouldn't need too much pushing. Perhaps he'd like the idea of replacing the monarchy with his own presidency. Take even our recently retired Prime Minister. His wife's an avowed republican; a smart woman. Suppose, like Lady Macbeth, she had persuaded her husband to mount a coup against the monarchy; well let's not say a coup, let's say he was persuaded to use his parliamentary majority to force through the abolition of the monarchy. It's not that improbable is it? And, according to the polls one reads, such a move might be supported by the majority of the country. And let's just suppose the monarch of the time, the present Queen, or whoever inherited the throne, decided that they weren't going to take this lying down and called on the armed forces for support. Where would you stand? How would you react?"

Cartwright again shifted uncomfortably in his chair, "Where are we going with all this?" He laughed a little nervously, "You're not plotting a coup d'état are you?"

C continued, ignoring the interruption. "Let's continue supposing shall we. Suppose that the monarch of the day thought that with sufficiently strong leadership and the arrest and possible assassination of three or four of the most prominent politicians they could resolve the issue. You and your SAS chappies would be on the front line. Who would you support? The monarchy or the politicians?"

"Well the politicians are the elected representatives of the people. What you're talking about is a coup d'état or perhaps civil war. The prospects of that are very remote. At least I'd think they were. In my lifetime anyway."

"Major you're prevaricating. Is that how you'd like to answer? By equivocating?"

Cartwright pursed his lips and took a deep breath. "If there were the sort of civil strife that you predicate, first I would have to consider that the Colonel in Chief of my regiment is the heir to the throne. Then I suppose that I'd have to consider that my oath of loyalty was to the Crown and that my own personal sympathies would be in favour of supporting the monarch." He paused and took a quick swallow of whisky, before muttering, "even if it meant one or two targeted assassinations."

He looked up at C and said with a bitter laugh, "Well, there you are. Is that the end of my career for expressing too radically a right wing opinion?"

"Not at all, Frank. Not at all." Responded C soothingly. "I am considerably heartened and relieved to know that, for all the so called democratization of our social and military institutions, there are still to be found officers with some sense of historical continuity and values. And that's all I wanted to know."

C looked at his watch, "Why don't we go into lunch now and talk about this some more. I'm afraid it's not going to be anything very elaborate, but I hope it will be adequate."

He got up and led the way through a door that Cartwright had not previously noticed and that brought them into a large conference room where a table long enough to accommodate at least thirty people was set at one end for a meal for the three of them. A large sideboard against one wall of the room was covered with a white linen tablecloth on which had been placed an array of different salads, cold fish and meat dishes as well as two bottles of white wine in individual coolers, which had been set slightly to one side of a large selection of other bottles.

After they had helped themselves to food, Mark poured a generous measure of the white wine into each of the large crystal glasses resting by the table settings. They sat down and C took an appreciative sip of the wine.

"This is a rather good Batard Montrachet. Very difficult to find these days and horrendously pricy, but again, one of the perks of the job."

Cartwright who could not tell a Batard Montrachet from a South African Chardonnay smiled in feigned appreciation.

They ate for a few moments in silence before C resumed questioning Cartwright. Notwithstanding that C was an expert interrogator it took nearly an hour before he felt sufficiently comfortable to explain to Cartwright the job for which he had been chosen.

The soldier was stunned. "You don't mean it. You can't really mean it. It's another of those tricky questions isn't it?" He looked expectantly at the two MI6 bureaucrats who merely returned his gaze without saying a word.

"My God. You're serious." He continued looking at C and his deputy who still said nothing.

"As you know I've been on some pretty dicey jobs... but getting involved in killing her. God I don't know. I don't know if I can do that. I really don't." He shook his head in confusion.

"Well I'm delighted to hear you say that," lied C.

"We're not interested in working with psychopathic killers. We're all men of conviction and integrity here. How do you think we feel about this? Do you think that we haven't spent sleepless nights, worrying, wondering, trying to think of some other way out of the situation? I can tell you we've tried everything. There've been warnings galore. The bloody woman's either got a death wish or thinks she's totally untouchable because she's the mother of heirs to the throne. The final straw, of course, is that she is definitely considering marriage to this Walid character. I am sure that a considerable part of it is just the desire to cock a snook at her former husband and the Queen, because we know from our intercepts that she's got plenty of reservations about this Walid. Thinks he's too addicted to cocaine; got quite a history with prostitutes. Things like that. But it seems her desire to inflict some sort of harm on her former husband and the monarchy is stronger than any reservations she might have. What it really comes down to is that we are being forced into action because she is being stupid, stubborn and arrogant."

He sipped from his third glass of wine, looking into the middle distance and almost seeming to be talking to himself.

"Not much of a reason really for such drastic action is it? If it were we'd be having mass institutionalized executions of politicians at the opening of Parliament. The irony is, that a woman living out some sort of fantasy has now managed to drag us into her Alice in Wonderland world and I've been cast as the Queen of Hearts saying 'off with her head'. I can still scarcely believe that we are being placed in the absurd situation of taking totally disproportionate action merely because of a unique set of circumstances and dysfunctional individuals who seem to be too stupid to know when they ought to back off."

He paused to take another sip from his glass,

"So we are now in this terrible position that no-one wants."

In the brief hiatus that followed these words C leaned across the table to cut himself another piece of cold salmon.

"Excellent salmon, this." Lifting his wine glass, he took another sip of the Batard Montrachet, holding it briefly in his mouth to savour the flavour.

"How do you like the wine? A 1996, an outstanding year for white Burgundy."

"It's delicious" responded Cartwright dutifully, wishing he had the courage to ask for a glass of beer instead and wondering at C's ability to switch from a discussion of committing a horrendous crime to the triviality of food and wine.

C continued as if he had made no comments about the food or wine,

"But anyway, you're not to be involved in any of the unpleasantness."

He looked up at Cartwright,

"In truth I think you must realize that I didn't have to tell you any of this. We could have had it all done and then sent you after the participants on a routine mop up operation and you'd probably have been none the wiser. But I want you fully on board and I want your whole hearted participation even though, initially, your role will be restricted to attending the briefing of the operative. With Mark here, acting as your liaison you'll

be keeping close tabs on the operatives and finally... "
He allowed his words briefly to hang in the air,

"... finally, when it's all over, you're to see that our little secret remains a secret. You can use a small team of your own people for that purpose. Members of your Special Projects team would be suitable. It would fit in with their counter terrorism role. But obviously, I hardly need to stress that no one on your team is to have any idea what's really going on. You'll have to sell them on something like they're being on an anti Al Qaeda mission. We'll settle the details later. We're still not yet sure how this is all going to play out, but, if all other options are exhausted and we are forced to proceed, it'll be down to your team to clear up afterwards and tie up all the loose ends without their knowing exactly what it is they are cleaning up. Are you reading me?"

"Oh yes. Loud and clear, sir. And let me say, I've taken the decision and you will have my one hundred per cent loyalty and participation." Despite his brave words Cartwright was making an enormous effort to control the fear gripping him at what he was committing himself to.

"Good man, Cartwright. I knew we'd be able to rely on you."

C leaned across the table and warmly patted Cartwright's arm.

Noticing a slightly puzzled frown that appeared on Cartwright's face, C asked

"Something troubling you, Frank?"

"Only... well... it's just that... well my men aren't fools. In fact they're quite bright and knowledgeable.

That's one of the reasons they've been badged (made permanent members of the SAS).I think the major difficulty is going to be pulling the wool over their eyes."

C nodded, "A good point. We'll have to give that some more thought, but I don't see we've got much option other than for it to be sold as a counter terrorism operation. We're doing them all the time. It's going to be of the utmost importance though to keep the principal operation and the clean up afterwards entirely compartmentalized from each other. After all, the principal operation is, to all intents and purposes, going to be seen as an accident, whereas you will be conducting an entirely unconnected anti-terrorist operation. It is all going to be a matter of perception and with the appropriate groundwork your team ought not to have the slightest suspicion of any connection between the two."

Cartwright sat back in his chair listening to C and drawing on the large cigar that C's deputy had offered and lit for him moments before. He was even able to put aside for a few brief moments the profound fear that had been gripping him since committing himself to become a co-conspirator to what by any standards was a heinous and cold-blooded assassination plot, allowing himself a brief moment of reverie. Being privy to a secret like this was tantamount to being offered an entry into the highest levels of British society. For a moment he imagined himself as Commander of the Special Air Service, with perhaps a knighthood or even a baronetcy. Who knew where this could lead. Of one thing he was certain; he had advanced a long way for the son of an undistinguished mid-level civil servant. He restrained his brief mental indulgence, realizing that he was allowing the alcohol to blunt his senses.

"How close am I to get to the actual operatives?" he asked

"As close as you can. Apart from running your team at the end, as I've said, you're going to be our liaison man with the people doing the job. We need to be able to know exactly where they are at all times. We'll fix you up with any electronic gizmos you'll need. Can we count on you?"

"I've already said you can, sir."

"I can't say how delighted I am to have you on board." C stood up and patted the Major on the back, before walking over to the array of bottles spread out on the sideboard.

"Can I offer you some port? This is a very excellent, rare 1893 bottle. It's quite an experience."

"Well... " Cartwright responded a little nervously, "I'm not really used to drinking so much at this time of the day. I've already probably had more than I should."

"Oh come on man. I know what goes on in the officer's mess and this Port is quite unique."

Cartwright sighed, "Oh well, in for a penny. Thank you very much, sir."

They drank the port with Cartwright dutifully making what he considered appropriately impressed noises of appreciation, though in truth he cared no more for port than he did for wine. The job he had been given both frightened and excited him. He realized that he had become privy to what was destined to become one of the greatest secrets of modern times. He also knew that the responsibility he was being given was a once in a lifetime opportunity that was certain to lead him to the promotion that he craved and who could tell what other honours.

"One thing I haven't yet told you."

C's words interrupted Cartwright's speculation about his future prospects. "HRH himself wants to meet everyone on the team. So we've got an appointment with him in about an hour. He's coming over here. The woman and her boyfriend are on holiday at the moment cruising around the Med. We've got a satellite visual due over them and HRH is coming to have a look. He'll probably give the final OK, or not, then."

CHAPTER SIX

"There are very few things impossible in themselves; and
we do not want means to conquer difficulties so much as
application and resolution in the use of means."
Francois Duc de La Rochefoucauld

MI6's operations room is, effectively, a large control and communications centre housed in a sub-basement deep below the headquarters building. It actually comprises several rooms; a main conference room for senior staff, with six flat screen televisions for video conferencing and all the requisite technology for linking the screens to a variety of international locations (including the CIA and NSA) through encrypted networks, as well as for downloading satellite images in real time; five additional video conferencing rooms, all similarly equipped to the main conference room, but with only two flat screens each; finally a large situations room with watch officers and analysts located in two large semi-circular tiers of individual computer terminals. On the wall facing the tiers of technicians who man their computer terminals 24 hours a day, seven days a week, are a series of clocks, each labelled with the particular location in the world whose time it displays. Underneath the clocks is a very large flat panel television screen equipped to receive video conferencing, data and satellite transmissions, flanked by two slightly smaller flat panel displays with similar technology.

The walls of the whole of the sub-basement, including the walls of the individual conference and video conferencing rooms, are all made of fabric wrapped, special acoustic wall panels, designed to absorb all external noise and to protect the rooms against any unauthorized eavesdropping. Additionally each room contains sensors to detect the presence of all prohibited devices, such as cell phones. Every ceiling is equipped with high resolution digital cameras capable of recording and broadcasting documents or objects in the rooms or on tables in the rooms. Access to the centre is closely restricted to those with top security clearance, who include the technicians operating the vast complex of electronic equipment it houses.

For the present, apart from some of the computer monitors, all the screens were dark and the normally crowded room was relatively empty. A skeleton staff of technicians busied themselves at their work stations as Cartwright and Featherstonehaugh waited for C to re-join them. C in his turn was waiting at the small, inconspicuous secret underground entrance for the arrival of HRH. It was Cartwright's first visit to the operations room and Featherstonehaugh gave him a brief explanation of how the centre operated and the capability to monitor in real time, operations as far afield as Afghanistan, from that subterranean nerve center in central London. Cartwright was not unintelligent but he had always found electronic equipment difficult to comprehend and had minimal computer skills, so he found the control centre rather overawing and his frequent nods and grunts in response to Featherstonehaugh's summary, expressed only perfunctory comprehension of the explanation he was being given. Fortunately he was saved from the embarrassment of responding to Featherstonehaugh's query as to whether he had understood the previous ten minutes of technical explanation by the entrance of HRH and C.

The two protagonists were followed closely by a tall, thin, good looking, immaculately dressed, middle-aged man, before the large blast proof doors slid silently shut.

Even the technicians stood as HRH entered and Cartwright, too, found himself straightening to attention without thinking, as C introduced him to the Royal personage. At 80 plus years of age the man C had referred to as HRH still retained some of the debonair good looks that had made him so handsome in his youth. He had probably shrunk a little from his original height of fractionally over 6 foot but he walked with a vigorous upright stance and only his heavily wrinkled neck gave an indication of his advanced age. He retained the piercing blue eyes that must have cast fear into many a junior officer's heart throughout his career in the navy and still preserved a naval officer's bluff, forthright way of talking that had, over the years, cost him so much popularity. He was not a man to court popularity for its own sake; he despised politicians and, whilst his honesty and bluntness had earned him many enemies, it had also endeared him to the likeminded people he cared about. As he shook hands with Cartwright and looked piercingly into the soldier's eyes his voice was surprisingly mellow.

"Glad to have you on board Cartwright. I expect when this is all over we'll be having you over to the palace to give you a little something in recognition of the inestimable service you're rendering us, eh Colonel?"

"Er... it's Major your highness," stuttered the soldier.

HRH's eyes twinkled and he smiled warmly, "No Cartwright. You're mistaken. It's Colonel. And that's only a minor acknowledgment of the service you're performing for us."

Cartwright had difficulty restraining a smile of pleasure from crossing his face as he bowed to HRH muttering his thanks. HRH smiled again before turning to the man who had been following just behind him ever since he had entered the room.

"Let me introduce my special senior equerry, Brigadier Sir Peter Joynson-Murray."

The Brigadier shook hands with Cartwright as for the second time within a few seconds he was addressed as 'Colonel'.

At this point all eyes in the room turned towards the large screen as it lit up and one of the technicians addressing himself to C, said, "We're just coming on target now sir."

The real time images starting to appear on the screen were being received from the joint UK and

US spy satellite operations, mostly by courtesy of the United States National Reconnaissance Office which, from its headquarters in Chantilly, Virginia manages the American spy satellite system whose mainstay is the KH-12, Keyhole spy satellite. The exceptionally clear images now being provided showed a large yacht cruising all alone in the deep blue of a perfect Mediterranean afternoon. Three or four faint specks were visible on various parts of the yacht as a disembodied voice echoed from somewhere amongst the bank of computers in the room, "Zooming in now sir".

Almost immediately the deck of the luxury yacht appeared in close up, showing a man and woman sitting at a well laid table in the middle of the sun deck. The man was dark skinned with thinning, wiry black hair surmounting his round, heavily tanned face. His stocky frame was covered in black hair matching the hair on his head. His apparently formerly muscular body was well past its best, showing definite indications of rapid degradation, with soft rolls of fat developing around his middle and sides and his pectorals losing their definition in incipient flabbiness.

The angle of view from the satellite did not allow the woman's face to be shown until she was shaken by a clearly raucous laugh that caused her to throw her head back, briefly showing the room the face of one of the world's best known women. The dark skinned man got up and walked around the table to the woman, lifted her face, kissed her and in one swift, simultaneous and obviously well practiced movement, removed her bikini top.

HRH's voice broke the silence, "Nice pair of jugs, what." He paused momentarily before adding with a laugh, "Can we get a close up of those."

Before anyone could say anything a disembodied voice emanating from the general direction of the technicians responded with a "certainly sir" followed by a choked laugh emitted from the same source.

Almost before the sound of the voice had died down the camera had zoomed in on the woman's breasts, to the accompaniment of an admiring murmur from HRH

"Always admired her, never realized how well racked she was. Makes you wonder even more about the boy doesn't it?"

The embarrassed silence that followed his comments was accentuated when, in clear view of those watching in the operations room, the camera zoomed out again to show the man pushing his swimming trunks against the woman's breasts and then her face. She laughed as she playfully pushed him away before pulling him back towards her by the elastic of his trunks.

A throat-clearing cough followed by C's voice broke the silence in the room. "I think we've seen enough"

The images in front of them continued playing for a few more brief moments to the accompaniment of one or two more uncomfortable coughs and throat clearings, before the screen blanked out and the lights came on.

The return of the lighting failed to extinguish the almost tangible sense of embarrassment that pervaded the room. Cartwright, who had risked a quick, side long glance at C, saw the MI6 director avoid looking at HRH, apparently being engrossed in operating the keys of the computer nearest to him, although Cartwright also noticed that he actually seemed to be tapping the keys at random. The SAS man stole a quick glance at HRH who was standing stock still, a slight smile playing around the corners of his mouth as he remained, momentarily, gazing at the blank screen as if it was continuing to display the images they had been watching moments before. Featherstonehaugh broke the silence,

"Might I suggest that we adjourn upstairs C?"

C nodded gruffly and without meeting HRH's eyes motioned to the door with his hand as he said, "This way sir."

Cartwright followed the others to the elevator that whisked them all to the top floor in silence.

No one spoke until they were in Sir Ralph's office. HRH was the first to break the silence as he wandered over to the window and took in the view.

"Damn good view Rafe. My first time up here y' know. You chaps do yourselves proud." He turned towards the others but fastened his gaze on C.

"Well, what do you think?"

"To be brutally frank, sir, I don't really like to say what I think."

"Well we know she's a stupid little chit. Great body though. I s'pose not too much harm in her having a bit of a fling, eh? Be a bit of waste if she didn't. 'Course the big problem is her choice of partners." He ran his hand over the top of his thinning hair and down to the back of his wrinkled neck, which he rubbed briefly before asking

"S'pose that all gets recorded?"

"Absolutely sir," Featherstonehaugh replied. "Even if it's not on screen it's all recorded digitally, if not by us then by... "

HRH finished the sentence, "the Yanks, I s'pose?"

"Yes sir."

"Hmmm. Think there's any point in making a few choice prints and showing them to her. Sort of pointing out the bloody folly of her behaviour." He added after pausing briefly, "In fact I wouldn't mind a couple for me own collection."

His laugh was as spontaneous as it was infectious and Cartwright found himself smiling. HRH's admiration and pursuit of members of the opposite sex was a more or less open secret in the corridors of power of his wife's kingdom.

C ignored HRH's personal request and instead slowly answered the principal question, "with the greatest respect, sir, that's probably a question you're more able to answer than us. After all no-one here knows her better than you do."

HRH who was as well known for his sense of humour and lack of tact as he was for his amorous adventures, quipped back without hesitation,

"Well, obviously... and regrettably... not well enough."

Featherstonehaugh, in an attempt to bring the conversation back to a more serious level, coughed drawing everyone's attention as he addressed himself partly to C,

"If you'll recall sir, she has been approached several times and had pointed out to her, her continuing responsibilities as the mother of the heirs to the throne and the folly of pursuing relationships with errm... undesirables."

Before C could say anything HRH interjected,

"I remember. In fact we've been through all this a few times before haven't we? If I remember rightly, there was that thing with that Indian doctor wasn't there? A couple of years ago. What was his name?"

"Ravindra Singh," Featherstonehaugh provided the name before adding, "a distinguished cardiac surgeon."

"Yes, he appeared to have operated very successfully on her heart, if I recall." The seriousness of the meeting was apparently not resulting in any dampening of HRH's humour, "but he broke it off when he was told to, like a good boy, didn't he?"

"He did indeed, your highness" C answered this time. "We gave him the stick and then the carrot of a knighthood. He took very little persuading, even though she seemed to think he was the love of her life. The Al Khalifas', though, are a completely different kettle of fish."

"So? What? Now it finally comes down to making a bloody decision. Is that it?" HRH paused and started to pace the room slowly with his hands folded behind his back as C, Featherstonehaugh and the other two stood silently watching him. Finally he turned to them, folded his hands across his chest and sighed,

"It's damned difficult. Always liked the girl. And the boy" it seemed to Featherstonehaugh that HRH always referred to his middle aged son and almost certainly the next English King in this deprecatory way, "treated her bloody badly. Never made any allowances for the fact that she was just a young inexperienced gal. Preferred an old nag to a young filly. Could never understand him m'self, perhaps he couldn't take the pace. Even more difficult to understand having seen that just now. Hmmm, I don't bloody like it, but I s'pose the good of the country's got to come first and those bloody wogs really seem to have their hooks into her, damn their eyes."

He paused and looked C directly in the eye before saying slowly, "Here's what we'll do. We'll make one last effort. We'll send someone who she might listen to, to talk to her. I'll call her m'self, to tell her someone's coming. If she's really determined to marry the man and this final approach doesn't work, we'll have no option but to go with your plan and hope to God we can avoid anything happening to her. We're also going to have to be sure that absolutely nothing'll be left to chance."

"Well sir," C answered, "I've spoken to my counterparts at the NSA and CIA as well as the DGSE in France. They all understand our predicament and have promised me every assistance in whatever action we choose to take. The cousins have even offered us the services of one of the clandestine organizations they use."

HRH held up his hand to stop C saying anything more.

"I don't want to know the details. I just want to know the thing's going to be dealt with discreetly and with no comebacks. Also it's got to be clearly understood that every effort has got to be made to prevent anything untoward happening to her. If at all possible any action's to be restricted to the man."

He appeared about to say something else but then just shrugged, shook his head and said "Damn difficult, damn difficult."

He turned to Cartwright whose presence seemed to have been forgotten up to that point.

"Colonel, if the worst comes to the worst and, God only knows how I hope that it's not going to come to that, it's going to be on your shoulders to ensure the absolute discretion and maintenance of secrecy of any operation. Is that clearly understood?"

"Yes sir. I understand sir." Cartwright had seen combat in various parts of the world. He had been wounded in secret operations, both during the first Gulf War and in Afghanistan. He was a brave man, but not a stupid one. He had never set out on any operation without being frightened, but he could not remember ever before feeling so strongly the icy grip of near panic in his chest. HRH's words had sent sharp spikes of dread shooting through him at the reality of the responsibility he was being given. He felt faint and wondered if his legs were going to give way. His one wish was to sit down. Somehow however, he not only managed to stay on his feet but was able to retain the power of speech.

HRH was still addressing him, "I know you will m' boy, I know you will. And I can promise you, after a suitable time they'll be a 'K' in it for you." He took Cartwright's hand and shook it warmly.

"Thank you, sir." Cartwright managed to avoid stuttering. His thoughts had been fixed on commanding his beloved SAS regiment but now, presumably in addition, he was also actually being promised a Knighthood. Even the exultation he felt at the prospect of sudden advancement in the ranks of English society was unable, though, to still the beating of his heart and the fear that had almost so overwhelmed him. He wondered for the first time whether, for all the apparent routine that the job would probably entail for him, he might not be destined to survive or, worse still, that it might turn into the most almighty mess and he would end up disgraced, a sacrificial lamb to the goddess of failure. He had no illusions about how power operated at the stratosphere into which he had just been admitted and how, as the most junior member of the elite group, he would be the first to be regarded as expendable.

As HRH took his leave, C turned to Cartwright and said,

"Frank, I'd be grateful if you'd stay behind a little while. They're a few details we need to go over,"

Without waiting for a reply he followed HRH out of the room, leaving Cartwright alone with Featherstonehaugh. The latter indicated to the soldier that he should be seated before himself sitting down in an adjacent seat.

"From now on all the operational details will be dealt with purely between the two of us. That is, assuming that this actually becomes an operation. Although HRH has basically signed off on this, we're obviously still going to make every effort to try and disengage the woman without having to resort to the sort of drastic action we've touched on here. So I'd say that, basically, over the next few weeks or so, your job is just going to be to make sure you're available at very short notice and to train up an anti-terrorist team for the possibility that they'll be required in the aftermath of this operation."

Cartwright nodded and an awkward silence ensued which Featherstonehaugh broke by picking a file off C's desk and rifling through it, as if looking for something in particular when, in reality, both men were actually just waiting for C to return and give Cartwright any final instructions before dismissing him.

It was approximately ten minutes before C breezed back into the room. Without speaking to either of the two men waiting for him, he walked over to an antique sideboard on which stood an impressive looking chrome and black espresso machine with a number of white faced dials. After several loud gurgles and other assorted noises, whilst the machine was apparently clearing its throat prior to making some sort of speech, a thick dark liquid dripped out of a nozzle into the espresso cup C had previously put into position.

"Coffee anyone? " C turned as he addressed the question to the two men. As both men gave a nod accompanied by a "thank you sir." C turned back to the machine and made it work its magic twice more before the three men sat down for a few minutes further discussion.

C sipped his coffee slowly, appearing to savour each drop as he simultaneously addressed himself to Cartwright.

"Mark will have told you that for the time being you'll just be on standby and holding a suitable team ready in the event that we have to proceed. Unfortunately, it's my reading of the situation that there's at least an eighty per cent probability that we're going to have to take action, but we all have to pray that the woman sees reason and, even if she doesn't, perhaps we can get her out of the way and this can be dealt with without any ancillary damage to her."

He paused, "If we can get her out of the equation perhaps she'll have learned her lesson."

A gloomy expression crossed his face before he sighed and put down his coffee cup,

"By the way Frank, your promotion to Colonel, full Colonel that is, we're letting you skip a rank, is being gazetted tomorrow. Congratulations." He lifted his cup again, took one last sip and stood up, as did Cartwright and Featherstonehaugh. Walking round to his desk he picked up a large manilla envelope marked "Ultra" and leaned across, offering it to Cartwright.

"You're to study everything in there. Memorise the information. The papers have to stay in this building. There's a room next door." He pointed to another cleverly concealed doorway, which Cartwright had also not previously noticed,

"Make yourself comfortable. Take your time. Anything you want that's not in the room, call Mark. Just lift up the green phone it's a direct line to him."

C shook Cartwright's hand as he said, "We probably won't be meeting again for the foreseeable future.

You'll be dealing with Mark from here on in and he'll keep you up to speed. Best of luck Colonel."

Almost before he realized it Cartwright had been gently ushered into the neighbouring room where he settled down to go through the papers he had been given. The envelope was large and contained probably several hundred sheets of paper. There were surveillance photographs of Mohammed Al Khalifa; his son Walid and the woman whose face was so well known. In addition, the file contained abridged transcripts of monitored telephone conversations that had taken place over the course of the previous three months between the two Al Khalifa's and the Al Khalifa's and the woman, as well as calls from the woman to various friends and, apparently, a lawyer. There were photographs and detailed plans of the layout of the "Cleopatra", Mohammed Al Khalifa's luxury yacht, together with photographs and biographies of all crew members.

The papers also contained photographs and biographies of all Mohammed Al Khalifa's personal staff and security personnel. Cartwright was particularly intrigued to see that Al Khalifa employed five ex members of the SAS, three of whom he knew personally, as well as a former officer of the French internal security service, the DST, as chief of his extensive security unit.

Some two hours passed, in the course of which Cartwright had not only studied the papers he had been given, but had also browsed through the cupboards in the room. He had helped himself to a packet of chocolate biscuits he had found, as well as having made himself some tea with the tea bags and electric kettle that, thoughtfully, had been placed in full view on one of the cupboards. There was a knock on the door and Featherstonehaugh entered.

"How're you getting on?" He looked at the tea cup and the empty biscuit packet, "I see you've made yourself at home."

Cartwright flushed slightly, but said nothing.

Featherstonehaugh was holding two files, the thinner of which he handed to the soldier with his left hand before sitting down next to the Colonel.

Cartwright opened the file. It contained a full face photograph of an oriental looking man with close cropped salt and pepper hair as well as single sheet of typed paper containing a brief and uninformative biography of the man in the photograph. It was difficult to tell the man's age from the photograph. He could have been anything from late 30's to 60 but there was something about the man's eyes that indicated he was probably much nearer the higher number.

Cartwright read the biography and turned to Featherstonehaugh. "Not very enlightening. Who is he?"

"He's the person we're being given to set up and run the operation. We're told he's a certain Hassan Ben Kamal who's a free-lance operative who has carried out clandestine operations for our American cousins. Supposedly North African extraction. In fact we believe he's actually a man we know as John Traynor."

"Well he doesn't look very arab. Looks more Chinese."

"We think he's half Japanese, half American. We don't have too much information about his antecedents and, for all their assistance, the cousins are not telling us that much about him. If he is this Traynor fellow, he's someone who's cropped up on our radar screens from time to time as a top assassin and, he's someone of interest on whom we've developed our own file. I don't know why, someone in records must've slipped up, but Traynor's never, until now, been cross checked through the computer with other records. Anyway we've done it now and what do you think?"

Cartwright did not know what to think, so he looked suitably nonplussed without saying anything.

Featherstonehaugh handed over the second file, "It seems he was attached to your mob from Delta Force shortly after Charlie Beckwith set up Delta and started up a programme of cross training between our special forces. He was with your lot for around two years."

"He was attached to the Regiment?" Cartwright was surprised. He opened the second file which contained several photographs and much more information. The photographs showed a much younger man who was, however, still easily recogniseable as the older man in the later photograph.

"Hahumm." Cartwright nodded as he flicked quickly through the various photographs and other papers the file contained, which all looked as if they had been copied from a microfiche.

"You probably know this already, but Colonel Beckwith was one of the first Americans to serve with the SAS. He wanted to run Delta along the lines of what he had seen at Hereford and he started sending over both officers and non-comms to learn how we did things. Since then of course, I hardly need tell you, it's developed into a substantial exchange programme, also involving joint exercises and inter service competitions. Anyway this Traynor was one of the first Delta people to be sent over here and apparently everyone was very impressed with him."

"I can see." Cartwright was studying two sheets of paper that he held side by side. "He must have been one of the first of the cross training people we took on active ops. Of course, nowadays we're so short on good personnel that the people seconded to us go on active operations as a matter of course, but I didn't know they did it with these earlier guys, particularly not in a sensitive place like Ireland. He seems to have a pretty impressive record, but what a risk sending him out to Northern Ireland at that time."

"Funny" he mused. "I wonder why I never came across him." He continued to scrutinize the file and the old pictures.

"You know what, perhaps I did come across him." He scrunched up his eyes thoughtfully,

"Yes, that's it. I think I remember now. If I recall correctly, the man was a superb sniper. Got hits at incredible distances."

"Hmm." Featherstonehaugh was non-committal. "Why don't you just familiarize yourself with him? If it's the same man and not some Algerian lookalike, he wasn't just operational in Ireland. There's bits of hearsay in there as well. The sort of stuff picked up in conversation and reported back. Reading between the lines he seems to have had quite a record in Vietnam. Of course he must have been pretty young then. We don't really know his real age or what he's like now. If it's the same chap, he's at least got to be in his late 50's, which strikes me as a hell of an age for someone in this line of work. But then you can never tell. I've known of a few good operatives who were still at the top of their game when you'd have thought they ought to be drawing their pensions."

"Well what would you say are the implications of their offering us a chap like this?"

"I don't know. But the way I'd read it, they reckon it's pretty routine stuff, however important it is to us and they've given us someone who's either fully or semi out of the game, so there are no strong links with any particular organization. They probably also regard him as totally expendable at his age. However you look at it, he's got to be at the end of his operational life. They know we won't want too many people around writing this into their memoirs, so they offer us someone they won't miss. Anyway I'll leave you with those," he pointed to the files. "I suggest you take another hour, two hours whatever, then when you've got a better handle on everything, we can talk through any questions you might have."

Left alone again, Cartwright looked curiously at Traynor's file. The man had served in Ireland at a time when the war against the Irish Republicans had been quite hot. He was an expert marksman with both rifle and handgun and had chalked up more kills than any other of the personnel who had served in the Province, notwithstanding that, because of his oriental looks he had not been suitable for most undercover work. As Cartwright had remembered, he was an accomplished sniper. Cartwright had a healthy respect for expert snipers who were able patiently to stalk their targets and lie in wait for as long as was necessary before making their killing. According to the information in the file, this Traynor had carried out kills at distances of well over 1500 yards which, by Cartwright's book, put him into a very rare, elite group of extra special operatives.

His operational reports also rated his unarmed combat skills as exceptional, to such an extent that his tour with the Regiment had been extended at the request of the then Commanding Officer to enable him to run a course teaching various special, but unspecified techniques, to selected troopers and officers. The only question mark that anyone had noted against Traynor was that he was labelled a complete loner and not a team player. Cartwright wondered whether it had ever occurred to whoever had carried out the psychological evaluation he had just read to question whether a team player would be capable of lying absolutely still in hedgerows for hours, possibly days on end in order to gather information or make a kill from a mile away.

It was clear to Cartwright from the information he had in front of him that this Traynor had been an exceptional soldier in every sense and at the top of his game. He wondered what he was like nowadays. It was approaching thirty odd years since Traynor had served with the SAS and Cartwright knew how quickly even highly trained people could lose some of their skills, but the fact that Traynor was apparently still operating made him a man to be wary of.

He turned back to the file that he assumed had been provided to C by the CIA. As he looked beyond the brief biography at the few other sheets the folder contained, he smiled to himself. The sheets contained mostly blanked out spaces interspersed with a few, very few, type written sentences. All that Cartwright was able to glean was that Traynor had served two consecutive tours with the Marines in Vietnam. Then after a gap of a few years, during which he had apparently been a prisoner of war, he surfaced in Delta Force. The prisoner of war thing looked a little curious because it was noted that there had never been any official Vietnamese confirmation of his even having been captured. On the other hand, the Vietnamese had a record of concealing the capture and location of some of their prisoners. The years following his induction into Delta were a total blank save for his having been honourably discharged in 1990.

The only other information the file contained was that Traynor had been awarded various decorations. The decorations were listed but not the circumstances in which they had been won. The British military, with an assumed supercilious superiority, were sure that they were the best in the world. Members of the SAS regarded themselves as the best of the best. Part of

British military ethos had always been to hand out decorations with grudging reluctance and the British view, never expressed to their American colleagues, was that Americans handed out medals to their military personnel like Christmas decorations. There was no British equivalent to the Purple Heart. The most a wounded British soldier could expect from his high command was medical treatment. Even so, Cartwright was impressed by the number of decorations that Traynor had been awarded for gallantry, including the Navy Cross, the Distinguished Service Cross and the Silver Star, all with one or more oak leaf clusters, indicating that the medals had been awarded on multiple occasions.

After approximately another hour and a half, Featherstonehaugh returned and asked Cartwright whether he had finished and whether he had any questions. Cartwright stood up, stretched and looked at his watch. He felt confident that he was fully conversant with the information contained in the files.

"I don't think so" he said as he pushed all the documents back into their folders and offered the files back to C's deputy.

Featherstonehaugh nodded as he took them and then walked swiftly over to one of the cupboards which he opened to reveal a large safe. Cartwright had never seen a safe like this one. There was no lock and no combination dial. Instead the massive metal door contained a hand sized screen and a retinal scanner. Then Featherstonehaugh did something that Cartwright had not been expecting. He spoke to the safe giving his name and a code number before having his retina and palm scanned. After a slight pause, the safe responded, saying in a hollow sounding disembodied voice, "Opening for Mark Everett Featherstonehaugh Thursday at 1846 hours."

Cartwright was suitably impressed.

"God, I've never seen a safe like that before. We've got these great big blast proof things that'll open up if you give them a well-placed kick," he laughed to show he was joking.

The MI6 man finished placing the files in the safe and closed the door, holding it shut for a brief instant with the palm of his hand over the screen.

"Mark Everett Featherstonehaugh closing safe, Thursday 1847 hours".

"Is that safe as foolproof as it seems, because if it is we could do with one of those down in Hereford?"

"Absolutely fool proof. Works on all sorts of obscure algorithms mixed up with the identification procedures. It carries out instant voice, handprint and retinal scan recognition and then matches them up, as well as digitally photographing the user, all in fractions of a second. It then logs everything into our mainframe and double checks the digital photograph with the other recognition features and also checks the known location of the person who's identified, to make sure that that person is not logged into some other part of the building, or out. If there is any mismatch the security alarm is immediately activated and the building locked down."

"Bloody incredible. Who makes these things? I thought I was up to date with all the latest security equipment, but I've never seen anything like that."

"All done in house. Our tech people produced it. I think it's something they developed in their spare time, just for the fun of it. Anyway, as far as I know it's unique. I don't think even the cousins have such a comprehensive system."

Featherstonehaugh took one last look around the room before ushering Cartwright into the corridor towards the elevator. When they reached the elevators, Cartwright looked for a button to press. Featherstonehaugh laughed and swiped a card through a card reader placed on the wall.

"The cousins and probably most everyone else still think that the Brits are a load of bumbling amateurs who only think of hunting and shooting. They all get the surprise of their lives when they come into this building and see all the sophisticated electronics we use. Funny how they all have the idea that we're a bunch of amateurs, when we probably have one of the oldest traditions of this sort of service in the world. And one of the most effective." He laughed again.

As they waited for the elevator's arrival Featherstonehaugh handed Cartwright a card printed with two telephone numbers.

"Check in with me every couple of days, whatever's happening, whatever you're doing. I know where to get hold of you. You're being kept down in Hereford at least for the next month, so use whatever time we've got to put a team together and keep them up to the mark."

Cartwright nodded his acceptance as he stepped into the elevator accompanied by C's deputy.

"I'll see you down. If there's anything you think of in the meantime give me a call and we'll meet up."

The two men shook hands in the lobby and Featherstonehaugh watched the soldier as he negotiated the security barriers and disappeared through the front entrance.

CHAPTER SEVEN

*"We must beat them every time because British vol-
unteers are superior individuals than Anatolians,
Syrians or Arabs." General Sir Ian Hamilton
at the time of the assault on Gallipoli.*

Featherstonehaugh was back in C's room within
minutes. C was sitting facing Brigadier Sir Peter
Joynson-Murray, who had returned to the building unknown to C's deputy. They were sitting by the large picture window sipping cups of coffee.

He greeted the guest before addressing himself to
C.

"Oh, good evening Brigadier. Sorry to disturb you
C, but I thought you were alone."

C waved his hand airily at his deputy, "No, no, come
on in. This also concerns you. Get yourself a coffee."

The deputy director walked over to the coffee
machine and made himself a cup before joining C and
Joynson-Murray.

"We've just been going over all the options again.
HRH is apparently very reluctant to do anything that
might or could result in any harm to the woman"
explained C.

"Yes" added the Brigadier, "he's quite fond of her really and thinks she's just a little misguided and been getting influenced by malicious friends of hers. He's worried that if she's constantly in the company of this Al Khalifa chappie she might inadvertently get caught in the cross fire so to speak."

"Well that's a problem we've all been grappling with" Featherstonehaugh responded, a worried wrinkle forming across his forehead.

C looked at him keenly, "What's bothering you Mark? Is it that you don't think our soldier is up to the job?"

"Good God no! I think he'll be perfect. No it's not that." He paused, stood up and walked right up to the window and looked out, before turning back towards C and the Brigadier.

"It's just that I've got exactly the same concerns the Brigadier has just expressed. And the other thing is that I don't want us going off half-cocked here. We may be falling into the trap of entering into this woman's stupid little game. She may be doing nothing more than having a bit of a fling spiced up by the knowledge that she's actually getting to us. She knows if she wasn't striking a few nerves we wouldn't be bothering ourselves sending out these little warnings and generally making it clear she ought to behave herself a bit better. She's immature, irresponsible and pretty malicious. It's my reading, that at the moment she lives for nothing more than really to stick it to her ex-husband and the rest of us, who she thinks have been ganging up on her. In a way I can understand her. God knows the man deserves everything she's been throwing at him. He hasn't exactly been the soul of discretion over his relationship with that other woman.

What I'm trying to say is, whatever it looks like, is it really that serious? And are we embarking on a cure that might turn out to be worse than the disease? Then the other thing that bothers me is that we're going to be entirely dependent on an unknown team. This Traynor who's being put up to us was obviously a top operative. But what's he like now? Is he really up to this? Can we rely on the cousins' choice of personnel? There are so many imponderables and so many aspects that we just cannot control."

C stood up, walked over to his drinks cabinet and poured out three large whiskies before responding.

"I know exactly what you mean Mark. And I fully share the concerns that you and the Brigadier have expressed. Lord knows, I've had the same thoughts myself. But I think you're misjudging the Al Khalifas. They're the real problem here. I think they've got their grubby little hooks into her and I don't think she has the wit or the will to get out of their clutches. The father's manipulated some of the richest, most influential people in the world. What chance does she stand? As for the son, yes, he's a bit of a playboy - but a dangerous toy for her. Then, from some of the intercepts we have, it sounds like her brother, who ought to know, thinks she's gone a bit off the page." He turned to a small folder that had been tucked into the larger file sitting on his desk and pulled out a couple of sheets before saying

"I quote... 'your mental problems... your fickle friendship...

I know that manipulation and deceit are symptoms of the illness that afflicts you and I pray to God that you are getting the appropriate and sympathetic treatment you need'."

He looked up from the sheet of paper from which he had been reading aloud and raised his eyebrows.

"I know that the brother is not exactly whiter than white, but he ought to know his sister and, apparently, his analysis is sufficiently strong for him to have thought it necessary to express to her, what on any showing are pretty strong views."

Featherstonehaugh shrugged and murmured "Hmmmn" before adding "Well that's one view but the other would be that those comments might have been applicable a year or so ago but, apart from her frolics with the Al Khalifas, I would say that over the past few months it looks pretty much as if civilities have been restored between her and our much beloved heir to the throne."

C shook his head sadly before saying slowly, "If I thought we were going off half-cocked I'd stop everything right now. But I don't. My every instinct tells me that if we don't do something quickly, this thing is going to spin totally out of control. And don't think for one minute that I'm a novice at this type of operation. I will only go ahead when I'm certain that everything will be dealt with with the utmost discretion."

Featherstonehaugh still looked doubtful, "Well you say that, but you never know how these things can turn out. Apart from my concerns about this Traynor character, we're involving the cousins and you know as well as I do that somehow or other everything they do seems to get out, either by way of rumour or congressional enquiry. Things aren't like they used to be. We can't do what we like anymore. You know how the cousins like to document everything and the next thing you know some fucking jew boy journalist starts applying for documents under their Freedom of Information Act and we're all fucked."

The Brigadier grunted something that sounded very much like a murmur of agreement with the sentiments that Mark had just expressed.

"Oh come on Mark, Brigadier. I can't do this job acting like some bloody old woman frightened of the shadows she sees at twilight. You know it's not going to be like that at all. I've already had informal, totally undocumented chats with my counterparts at CIA and NSA. They've not only promised me their unqualified support, but say they are offering me this Traynor because he is a top deniable operative. I am assured that he is as solid and reliable as they come. And you know as well as I do that any problems of leakage have generally only ever come from official sources. Think about it. When has anything ever come out about their deniable operations when they are carried out by an independent, commercial entity?"

"Like Air America, sir?" Mark gently chided his chief.

"No, not like Air America." C responded sharply, "The outfit run by Standish is a first rate organization.

And, whatever I think of Standish personally, there has never been the slightest hint of a leak of their nefarious activities. None of the Directors of the CIA, NSA or Standish are going to put their heads on the block to allow them to be chopped off by some senatorial or congressional enquiry. They're all too experienced and wily for all that. They are the only people in the know. There's no one else to leak information."

"Yes. But what are they going to want in return. We're going to end up being bought and paid for."

"Well that's a point" added the Brigadier.

"Oh come on." Replied C, "face the bloody facts. As far as the cousins are concerned, we're all bought and paid for now. Have been for years. Just look at how our PM goes crawling on his hands and knees for a brief glimpse of the President's arsehole."

The Brigadier made another indecipherable noise and gave C a quick look of disapproval, which C ignored as he continued,

"Our most important intelligence gathering operation, GCHQ, is run by the fucking cousins. We're entirely dependent on their elint (electronic intelligence) and their satellites. For Christ's sake half the SAS is made up of yanks these days. Look at Iraq. Bush and his cronies get some bee in their bonnet about Saddam Hussein; they think they can just walk in and grab the world's second largest oil reserves when we're all saying leave Hussein alone. The country's stable, it's not a threat to anyone, we've got them completely boxed in and the downside is exactly what's happening now; and we're soon going to have another fundamentalist regime there that'll be a real danger to the world."

He glared at the Brigadier, "Do you want to see the original report we prepared for the Prime Minister when they first started talking about attacking Iraq? For once we and the Joint Chiefs (the heads of the armed forces) saw completely eye to eye. We gave a report that stated explicitly Saddam Hussein had no operational weapons of mass destruction; that it was going to require at least half a million troops to maintain control over the country post war and that we could not see that sort of man power being available for any or any extended period; that the alternative was a descent into the sort of tribal anarchy that actually followed and is still continuing, even if these days it's kept out of the news for the most part. That report went to the Prime Minister and to Washington. What came back from the Americans? We don't want to know any of that. It's just timid speculation. We're doing this with or without you. If you want a share of the spoils you'll join us. So either rewrite your fucking report or fuck off back to your silly little island.

The Prime Minister couldn't bear that could he? As the Americans say, he was already a legend in his own mind. He had to be seen as an important player in the world. So, I got an urgent summons to Downing Street where I was told, in terms, that we didn't know what we were talking about. That the Prime Minister was embarrassed by the total failure of our intelligence services to have provided him with a reliable up to date briefing. I was handed a copy of a confidential report for the

President's eyes only. I've still got a copy if you want to see it. It was some load of crap that God knows who had cobbled up and I damn well knew it hadn't come from the CIA because I spoke to their Director about it. But what the hell, the Americans had already decided to take over Iraq and nobody cared what the intelligence agencies said? So off we go following Bush, Cheney and Rumsfeld, the three stooges, into exactly the mess we had all predicted.

No. The reality is they whistle and we come running. That's the truth and the whole bloody world knows it. We became their colony a long time ago. If I can use another Americanism, get real."

The Brigadier's face flushed with annoyance. "I don't think it's like that at all. We're equal partners in a mutually beneficial alliance."

C looked at the equerry in disbelief. "And when did you last do something the cousins disagreed with? When did you last adopt an independent line? We're so independent that when the CIA started calling itself the Company, we suddenly became the Firm."

The Brigadier stuttered before muttering unintelligibly into his glass.

"Anyway" C continued as if he had never been interrupted, "We're getting off the point, which is how to take out the arab without involving her and that's something we're all going to have to work on."

He stood up with an air of finality that clearly indicated both to Featherstonehaugh and the Brigadier that the discussion was over.

CHAPTER EIGHT

*"There are bad people who would be less dangerous if
they were quite devoid of goodness."*
Duc de La Rochefoucauld

Sakurako Yoshida,   Kyoto, 1995

Jun? Jun? Oh, you mean young Taro. Of course
I remember him. Do you think that just because I'm
old, I'm senile? I looked after him from when he was
a baby and before that my husband and I were looking after his grandfather since I can't even remember when. His grandfather, the old Master, I can tell
you there were times when I really wondered about
him. The way he made young Taro work. Hours and
hours, every day. Practising with the sword, then fighting with wooden swords. But I can't deny Taro San
seemed to love it. He was always a very serious boy,
very obedient to his grandfather, maybe old before his
time. The old master was really more like a father to
him from when he was a baby, because his real father,
the American Colonel, was always away travelling
around Japan and goodness knows where. Taro wasn't
allowed out of the house much then, there was a lot
of ill feeling against the American occupying forces
even though the war had ended quite a time before.

Still what with the Colonel's work, it was some sort of secret stuff you know and, Taro being the child of a Japanese American marriage, well you know what people are like…..anyway it was always thought safer to keep Taro in the house unless he went out with the old Master.

I have to say though, all that practicing in the old Master's dojo didn't seem to do young Taro any harm. He wasn't one of those young hooligans you get nowadays, who go out beating up poor folk just for the fun of it. Oh no. He was a good boy. Very obedient. Whatever his grandfather asked, he would do. The old man sometimes used to make nasty comments about Taro being polluted with American blood, but anyone could see that the old man was proud as anything of the boy and with good reason. You should have seen the way he came to handle a sword and at such a young age. That wasn't all. Bright as a button he was and you should have seen him draw and paint. Sometimes I thought he was better than his grandfather. Sad, I never heard anything more about him after those American relatives came to get him when he was about twelve. I wonder what became of him. My husband and I went on looking after the house for years until my husband died and then it all got too much for me. We used to get money four times a year, sent from America to pay our wages and for expenses for the house, but no-one ever came to visit, certainly not young Taro. I would imagine that by now the house has gone to rack and ruin even though I closed it up ever so carefully when I retired.

Richard Traynor, attorney at law retired, 1998, Los Angeles

I've had a very successful and interesting life. As a lawyer I was retained by some of the most successful names in show business. As a matter of fact I became a bit of a celebrity myself. No doubt you've read about me or seen me on television from time to time. A successful advocate learns to concentrate on the positive aspects of his client's case and of course to minimise any negative elements. I suppose it was much the same when we went to collect John from Japan. He had led a very sheltered life. When my brother was still alive it was a time of great social upheaval in Japan so John was usually kept in the house and grounds in Kyoto. Actually it was a very spacious house with, unusually for Japan, quite large grounds. After my brother died, that sort of seclusion became something of a lifestyle and I think the only time John left the house was to go for walks or to the movies. So, of course, quite naturally he was very interested in hearing about my clients and that when he came back to LA with us he would probably often be rubbing shoulders with some of the stars he saw on the silver screen. Once he'd made up his mind to come with us he could hardly wait to leave.

Naturally nothing's ever as easy as you imagine and John never quite fit in with the family. He was always a very odd, rather introspective boy. I suppose it had to do with his upbringing by that crazy old man. I mean when you met the old man he was always very courteous and polite, but I know he used to have young John working out at those martial arts for hours on end. It's not surprising that John turned out to be so strange. We should really have brought him back to LA when his father and mother first died, but the old man was very resistant to our overtures and made such a fuss that in the end we gave in. Of course, by the time the old man died and we managed to get through all the red tape necessary to bring John back I suppose it was already too late, he'd already been moulded into what he was, which I can tell you wasn't like any teenager I've ever come across. It's not as if he was involved in drugs or crime or anything like that. Absolutely not. From that point of view he was a very good kid. It was just that he didn't seem to be interested in the same sort of things as other kids of his age. Not that he was any trouble, I mean until the day he ran away, just shy of his sixteenth birthday, we never really had any complaints about him. He was clean, tidy, kept himself to himself. He was generally good at school. Learned English in record time and then we found out one day he'd picked up pretty good Spanish from the help. Quite a talent for languages that boy had. Could probably have made a good career for himself in the Foreign Service. He was also a pretty good artist. We've still got some of the pictures he painted of the family. I suppose he inherited that from his grandfather, who I understand was also quite a well-known artist. He certainly didn't get it from his father. It was just that strange insistence on those pagan practices of worshipping ancestors. It was quite disturbing really. Bizarre and a bit unsettling. He kept a little shrine in his room to his grandfather and God knows who else. Never called his grandfather by his name, always used to call him "Shihan". That's apparently some sort of Japanese honorific for a very senior martial arts instructor. We tried to discourage the ancestor worship and he did use to come to Church with us, but he would never let us remove that shrine. Whenever we even suggested it he'd give us this cold look... quite disconcerting it was. Then of course, every day he was up at around five in the morning practicing those martial arts of his for two or three hours. I can't say I actually disapproved of that. The family has something of a military tradition and one thing you have to credit the boy, he certainly had incredible self-discipline. You don't often see that sort of discipline in youngsters not then, not now.

It was quite a surprise to us when he ran away. It wasn't as if we left money and credit cards lying around. He did quite a professional job of breaking in and stealing what he needed. That was the last we heard of him for years. After all we'd done for him. Then suddenly, one day, completely out of the blue, we got a call from the US Embassy in Paris. They were checking up, trying to verify that John was who he said he was. Anyway, within a few days he was back in LA. I don't think I'd ever have recognized him, except there were times when I could see his father in him. He'd grown what, maybe 7" – 8". I have to say he'd become a fine figure of a man. He was lean, muscular, very fit looking. One of my clients saw him in my office one day and wanted to cast him in a movie. John wasn't interested. He'd hardly been home when he enlisted in the marines. We didn't see too much of him after that. He came to visit a few times over the years. We went to a couple of ceremonies when he got decorated. I'd say he turned out well enough; became a credit to the family. Those are some of his citations on that wall over there. Impressive aren't they.

Martha Traynor, Los Angeles, 2006

Richard didn't know squat about John. He was never home, always at his office or socializing with his clients. I was the one that had to deal with the boy. All Richard knew or cared about was those citations for bravery on the battlefield and how they reflected on what he called the family's tradition. The only time I could drag Richard away from his office was when we were invited to see John being decorated. I had to deal with the problems at school. It wasn't as if John was intrinsically bad or difficult. First of all, when Richard and I went to Japan to collect John, after his mother's father died, I suppose Richard did lay it on a bit thick about mixing with movie stars and so on. The boy was very impressionable. After all, the grandfather had taught him at home for years and he wasn't used to being with people and wasn't worldly at all. So when he got here he was soon disappointed that he wasn't meeting movie stars and had to knuckle under and go to school. Then, I don't know what his grandfather had been teaching him, but he thought he knew everything. He used to argue with the teachers telling them what they were teaching was nonsense or culturally biased. Can you imagine that? A young teenage boy trying to lecture his teachers. Well, I seemed to be up at the school all the time. If he'd been at public school he would have spent most of his time being suspended. Then he went to the opposite extreme. Stopped taking part in the class and would just sit at the back reading all those silly romantic novels like Beau Geste and the Scarlet Pimpernel. Filling his head with all sorts of stupid ideas about the French Foreign Legion, saving aristocrats during the French Revolution, that sort of nonsense. And at home, when he wasn't practicing his martial arts he'd be off to the cinema to see the same sort of nonsense he was reading about. Errol Flynn films that sort of thing. Don't get me wrong. I don't think there's anything wrong about enjoying a good action film, but in John's case it seemed to be all he was interested in apart from worshipping his grandfather and early morning practices. Then one day he was gone. Just like that. He left a short note. Funny sort of note. Thanked us for looking after him, apologized for stealing our money, he called it "borrowing" I recall and said he hoped to be able to pay us back one day. Well, of course we were disappointed in him, but in a way it was a bit of a relief for me really that he was gone. All he took with him apart from our money and his passport was his grandfather's sword and the shrine he kept in his room. The sword was very old, worth a lot of money I believe. It should have been in a museum, not carried around by some young boy, but then Richard just used to take the path of least resistance and let the boy keep it in his room.

I was sure that sword would be lost or stolen but when John came back years later he still had it. I remember the day he returned. Richard refused to go and pick him up at the airport but I sent Manuel in the car. Even after all he'd done, John was still a Traynor and he was still my nephew. Anyway I heard the car pull into the driveway and a few minutes later John walked through that door there. I didn't recognize him. He'd become so tall and strong looking. He was quite handsome even with his oriental features. You know how some Eurasians can be very good looking, well he was. He didn't give me a hug or anything. The first thing he said after "hello" was, "I've brought your money back".

He'd been brash and arrogant before but now there was a confidence and strength about him that made me feel very secure when I went out with him. I can't remember how long he stayed. A couple of months maybe. Maybe not even that, maybe it was just a couple of weeks before he disappeared off again. The next thing we heard was he'd joined the marines. Sure enough he turned up again one day in Marine uniform. I remember being surprised he'd been made a sergeant so quickly. After that we hardly saw him. He shipped out to Vietnam where he did a couple of tours before the knock on the door telling us that he was missing in action. The marines sent his things back. There wasn't much. Quite a few medals, which Richard displayed in the library. They're still there. I can show you, if you like. Funny thing was his sword wasn't among the personal effects, but I understand he always carried it with him everywhere and we assumed it was lost with him. The family held a bit of a wake for him. It was surprising, it got quite emotional really; his picture and all those medals for bravery, he even had some from

France. With all that on display no wonder the family was proud of him then, even those who hardly knew him. On top of everything else he was given a posthumous Navy Cross. I think it was the second time he was awarded the Navy Cross, it's the Navy's second highest decoration you know, after the Medal of Honor.

Then after all that John suddenly turned out to be alive, after, what was it? Five years, six years I can't remember. All I remember is that when we thought he'd been dead for years he suddenly turned up again like the proverbial bad penny. Over the years he's come back to see me from time to time but I haven't seen him for quite a time now. I wonder if he'll come to my funeral.

Jacques Renardier, Florence, Italy June 2010

How well do I know John Traynor? As well as anyone you've known for forty plus years; someone you served with in the Foreign Legion for seven, eight, nine years, whatever it was. I can tell you, that when you serve in the Legion with someone, you soon come to learn everything you need to know about them, particularly when you're stuck in some nasty situations for days on end and people are trying to kill you the minute you relax or get careless. And this is going on twenty four hours a day. I've used the word people because I have to watch my language these days. You call them by some other more specific pejorative term which we all actually used to use the whole time and someone is going to start abusing you, calling you a racist and the next thing you know is you're in a fight with someone twenty or thirty years younger than you, probably with his friends too, when all you wanted was to go out and have a quiet dinner with your wife. So anyway I watch what I say these days unless I'm with friends like Traynor when I can relax and be myself.

John isn't the sort of person who talks about himself very much. Of course, over the years little bits and pieces came out. From what I pieced together, he was brought up for many years by his grandfather, who was some sort of super martial arts expert of the old school, not the sort you have today. I suppose it was from him that John learned that martial arts are for fighting and not for things like the Olympic Games. Apparently even when John could hardly walk his grandfather had him practicing swordsmanship and martial arts eight hours a day. And of course it had an effect; John was good, very good. I'll tell you a little story later about the first time I saw how good he really was. Anyway, for sure all that training also taught John coolness under pressure and self-discipline. I never saw him panic or lose his head whatever the circumstances.

I had already been in the Legion for a couple of years when I first met him. I didn't actually find out until years later that his name was John Traynor. Like so many others in the Legion in those days he had adopted a false name, Richard Pernod, of all things. We used to kid him about his name, nicknamed him "Pastis" which is another similar drink to Pernod. Actually we first started off giving him the nickname "Anaise" which was a sort of play on words. Pernod and Pastis are "anise" drinks. They taste of aniseed. "Anaise" is a girl's name and he was a fresh faced young kid and we'd joke around saying he was like a girl, that sort of thing. Sure he was tall and well-built but you know how Orientals don't seem to be able to grow much facial hair, well John was like that. I don't think he even started to shave properly until he'd been in the Legion for about three years. Of course he pretended to shave, along with all the other guys in the morning, but we all knew it was just pretence. It was a bit of a joke for a while. Not for too long though. He soon showed us how easy it is to underestimate someone when you don't know them. Of course you can understand us. I mean how would any group of tough, hardened guys have reacted to some youngster, who we saw at the time as a gook kid who hadn't even begun to shave, which of course he was, even though he'd had an American father? We were a pretty tough lot in those days, not used to mixing with innocent looking kids. I wasn't untypical. I'd joined up because I had to. It was either that or prison for me. If I'd known then what things were like in the Legion I might have chosen prison, but when the Judge offered me life in prison or the Legion it was a no brainer. Still, even though the Legion was no picnic in those days, it did allow me to get my life back. Overnight the miraculous happened. The police, who had me on their list of most wanted, suddenly lost all interest in me. That's France for you; practical and down to earth. I don't think there are too many other countries prepared to give you a completely new start just for putting on a uniform and doing some of what you used to do before but this time in the French

National interest. I can tell you that I wasn't the worst there either, not by a long shot. There were criminals from all over Europe; quite a lot of Germans too. No one much liked them but, if the Legion was prepared to accept them, they had to be tolerated.

Anyway Traynor was a real oddity. He tried to fit in and keep himself to himself, but in a way that made him stand out even more. He was the youngest recruit I ever came across. I never understood how they let him join in the first place, although, as I've said he was big and surprisingly strong for a youngster like that. Of course being a bit of a pretty boy he soon attracted the attention of elements who didn't care who they had sex with, just as long as they had somewhere to rest their dicks. I remember this one guy, he was a big bastard, a German, older, but very fit. A bit of a keep fit fanatic in fact. I think he had been in the SS at the tail end of the Second World War. He never bothered me, but there were a lot of guys who were frightened of him. Well, when he saw Traynor I think it was love at first sight or whatever else got him going. I can't remember all the little details now, it was a long time ago, but I think Traynor had just started basic training, or perhaps he had just finished and we had decided that he was alright and no one much was bothering him anymore. Anyway this German made a bee line for him. What happened afterwards is something I'll never forget. It was like David and Goliath and no one gave Traynor much of a chance. Well, although Traynor kept backing away from the German, I could see that he wasn't scared and his eyes were darting around the room the whole time, even though he was watching the German very carefully. I was sort of half thinking I ought to intervene and stop it all except that the way Traynor was made me interested to see what he was going to do. I think the others felt the same way, including our sergeant who just happened to have slipped into the barracks unnoticed. Well, the German was advancing on Traynor, getting more and more confident with every step when suddenly Traynor just darted forward and did these lightning fast kicks to the German's knee, chin and between his legs. I can tell you that everyone in that room, including the German, was totally shocked. I've already said the German was big and fit, so although he was momentarily stunned and was rocking on his feet a bit, he wasn't stopped by a long way. But I have to say Traynor was really fast. I don't think I've ever seen anyone move as fast as he could when he was fighting. He wasn't just fast, he moved so easily and smoothly, it was like someone dancing. Having kicked the German, he then dashed into the corner where there was a broom and other stuff for cleaning out the barracks. Traynor grabbed the broom and, in one movement, had kicked off the brush part. By this time the German had recovered and was again rushing towards Traynor but, as I recall, I think his lust had at least partly been replaced by rage and he was shouting as he ran towards the kid. Traynor met him head on, side stepped and before you could blink had hit the German two or three times with the broom handle in his solar plexus, his wrists and head and had followed up with more kicks to the German's knee and head. Anyone normal would've been down and out, certainly've had enough, but not that big Boche. He did falter and drop to one knee but he wasn't anything like finished. Well, Traynor then moved straight in again, no hesitation at all. I don't know how many times Traynor hit him, but that broom handle was moving so fast and from so many angles you couldn't keep count. At first the German had his hands up trying to defend himself and grab the stick but Traynor just kicked his arms away and within seconds the German was on his hands and knees, covered in blood. In fact there was blood spurting everywhere. I, along with everyone else, was stunned. We all knew how to fight but I don't think anyone had ever seen a big fucker like that German taken apart so quickly and efficiently. I'm pretty certain that if the sergeant hadn't then stepped in, Traynor would have killed that German.

But it wasn't as if Traynor had just gone berserk, oh no, he was cool as ice and the sergeant merely had to touch his arm for him immediately to stop his attack. The German immediately collapsed on the floor into a pool of his own blood. He was at least three weeks in the hospital afterwards and I can tell you that the Legion doesn't just let you stay in hospital to have a rest. After that everyone looked at Traynor in a completely new light and no one ever messed around with him again. One of the other funny things was that after the sergeant had got a couple of the men to carry the German off to hospital, he turned round to Traynor, nodding at the blood everywhere saying "you made this mess, now you clean it up". Traynor, still cool as a cucumber, just saluted smartly and said "Yes, sergeant" before getting to work scrubbing up the barracks.

That's Traynor for you in a nutshell. A cold, efficient, unemotional, killing machine. That's what he was and for sure he still is. Will be till the day he dies. He's just one of those guys who seem to have a particular talent for fighting and killing. Give him any weapon and I guarantee that, within a short time, he'll be better than any expert. It was the same with rifles and handguns. Almost from the word go he was shooting better than the instructors. I think he's the only person to have won the French military shooting competition for both rifle and hand gun for, what? Five years in a row, I think it was. One thing about Traynor though, if he's on your side he's the best friend a man could ever have. As long as you remain loyal to him, he'll go through fire for you. There aren't too many people around like that, although I'd never want to cross him, if you understand what I mean.

Pierre LaCroix civil servant retired, formerly of the Deuxieme Bureau - Spring 2007

It so happens that I remember the Traynor case very well. Very young man; made his way here from America to join the Foreign Legion. At the time it was my job to vet Legion recruits. The general perception is that the Legion accepts everyone whatever they've done. There is an element of truth in that of course but, as with every truth, there is also another side that shows us that truth is not the absolute some philosophers make it out to be. To an extent it's true that the Legion has all sorts of riff raff in its ranks, but once someone is accepted they might carry out all sorts of classified missions so, obviously, we need to vet them before they're accepted. We also used to weed out anyone who might have been a potential source of embarrassment or difficulty for our government or high command. So for example, whereas we might have taken in some low level Nazi's after the Second World War, any prominent senior official who was likely to attract the attention of the Israelis, for example, was a complete no no.

I remember Traynor because he was a potential problem of a different sort. He came to the Legion calling himself Richard Pernod. That's indicative of how innocent and lacking in imagination the boy was. Pernod, hmmph! And he didn't speak a word of French. Not a word. He claimed to be 18 but it didn't take much digging for me to find out that he was actually 16, although he was pretty big for a 16 year old, particularly amongst the French who, I must say, even though I am French, are a pretty scrawny lot before they fill out on wine and foie gras. Ha, ha. So, Traynor. As I recall, the FBI had sent out a circular about him which had gone through Interpol. In fact, to this day I have no idea how he even managed to get into France through immigration control. I suppose it's because the police at immigration and the gendarmerie, who have such a high opinion of themselves, can't tell the difference between one oriental and another. Whatever the reason, he was in France and, at the time I became involved, a potential Foreign Legion recruit. Initially I was minded to reject him. Not only was he too young to join the Legion, but also there was that little problem of him being on FBI and Interpol notices. In the end what swayed me though and made me approve him was a visit I made to the American

Embassy in Paris. They had a resident FBI agent there who had no conception of my seniority and the important position I was in and who tried to strong arm me into putting out a full police alert for Traynor. His family obviously had some political pull that had the FBI guy all hot and bothered. Anyway this FBI agent had been posted as liaison to Paris without being able to speak a word of French. Then, without even asking me, he just assumed I understood English. Personally, I may be a bit old school, but I don't think you're entitled to come into someone's country, supposedly to liaise with the local police and not speak the language and automatically assume that everyone is going to speak English. And they call the French arrogant.

Well, not only did this functionary from Washington try to lay the law down to me, but he treated me like some third rate provincial, when anyone could see he was the unsophisticated provincial. I don't think he realized for a moment that I knew exactly where Traynor was and, should I have felt inclined to do so, could have had Traynor brought to the Embassy in a matter of hours. In France we believe in Liberté Egalité and Fraternité. Not everything is about power and money here. We respect freedom of choice and individual liberty. I decided there and then, if Traynor wanted to join the Legion, I wasn't going to stop him.

Retired General Phillipe St.Clair Comte de Roche Lafont, Paris, June 2010

The Foreign Legion. Oh yes, that was in my youth when I was young and couldn't get enough action. A long, long time ago. Almost a lifetime, in fact. I come from a military family you know. My father, grandfather, great grandfather and so on - all cavalry officers. We trace our roots back to the Middle Ages. My ancestors were aides to several Kings; one was a general under Napoleon; so we're a pretty distinguished military family in this country. If you look at the battle flags decorating the wall over there, you have displayed pretty much the whole history of France. Well you can imagine, with my family background, what the family thought when, after, what even though I say so myself, was a pretty sterling performance at the St. Cyr military academy, I ended up an officer in the Foreign Legion, commanding the dregs of humanity But let's be fair, the detritus of society they may have been, but they were good soldiers and in the end my time in the Legion didn't hurt my career at all. In fact I think it rather helped it. I served as a junior officer in Algeria during the war there and transferred to the Legion in, I suppose it was the late fifties. Anyway the Legion and the paratroops had made a bit of a name for themselves in Indo China at Dien Bien Phu. Even though that was an enormous defeat for France, in a way it was also a symbol of our country's glorious military tradition. Do you know that the final message the officers sent out as they were being overrun, facing certain death, was "Vive La France"? That's the true spirit of the French army. And, if truth be told, it wasn't so much the troops who were defeated; it was the imbeciles who were in command at the time. At all events the Legion had not only been heavily involved in Indo China, that's what it was called then, before being split up into Laos, Cambodia and Vietnam, but were seeing a lot of action in North Africa where our other colonies decided to seek the same independence the Vietnamese had obtained.

Being a young career officer I realized you don't get decorated sitting in an office shuffling papers, so, when the opportunity came up I had myself transferred to the Legion and then to the 1st regiment of Foreign Legion paratroops. This actually led me into a bit of difficulty because the first regiment became very politicized, very anti de Gaulle and very much against granting independence to Algeria. I'm sure you remember that the commanding general at the time and some of his senior officers considered President de Gaulle a traitor for granting independence to Algeria and ended up trying to assassinate him. In fact they very nearly succeeded. I was very lucky, I could've got myself into all sorts of trouble, but I was sensible enough to keep out of all that and was able to distinguish myself for my patriotism by passing on what I had heard of the plot through back channels, via my family connections. Even patriotism aside, I couldn't have taken a more intelligent step because most of the first regiment's officers ended up in prison, murdered or fugitives and the regiment itself was disbanded and reformed as the elite 2nd Regiment of Paratroopers or 2eREP.

I came out of it all with a promotion and, although not formally commanding officer at the time, was, by virtue of my position, in almost de facto command of the regiment. We were based in Corsica. The way things had turned out in Indo China had made us realize that warfare was changing in the twentieth century and my eleven hundred odd men were being trained as Special Forces operatives. We trained in all the usual things special forces do; parachuting; scuba diving; skiing; jungle training and so on. All of my men were experts in the use of every type of weapon, explosives and the like. We also trained in the techniques used by the intelligence and counter intelligence services, fast driving, car handling, communications, surveillance and so on and so forth. Of course these days the Special Forces units have proliferated, everyone wants a share of the anti-terrorism pie.

It's been so many years since I left the 2e REP and I served mostly as a staff officer afterwards, so it's all part of a distant memory and I am not current with what they do today, even though of course I'm still in touch with the High Command. But today when they seek my opinion it's usually about general strategy not particular regiments.

There are still regimental reunions of the 2e REP of course and I sometimes go, just to put in an appearance. It's expected you know. I think that it was at one of those that I may have come across Sergeant Pernod again. I remember him well. He was unusual in the Legion because, if I recall correctly, he was of Japanese extraction although he was a big man for a Japanese, maybe 1 metre 87 centimetres, a good 6 foot plus in your imperial measurements.

As I recall he had applied for a posting to the 2eREP quite a short time after it was created. His acceptance was what I think what you Americans call a "no brainer".

He was exceptional at all forms of personal combat. In fact I think I can say in all honesty that in my whole career I never came across anyone who could approach the level of skill he had. Remember too, that he was very young. Much younger than the average member of the regiment. He was also an exceptional marksman. Before he joined us he was the sniper of choice in his previous unit and had several long range kills to his credit. If I remember rightly he also cleaned up all the prizes at shooting competitions for a good few years.

I have no idea what became of him. He's probably dead. In my experience people like him don't get to live very long. They're always on the edge, pushing their luck and one day their luck runs out. But he was a credit to the Legion and a credit to France. He was offered a commission in the regiment, you know. Have you any idea what an honour and how rare it is for an enlisted Legionnaire to be offered the chance to become an officer. He was not even French but he had been noticed. He was a damn good non-commissioned officer, I'll give him that, but what do you think he said when he was offered a commission. He laughed. He actually laughed. To my face. Then he told me that he was intending to leave the Legion because he was beginning to get bored and thought he might get himself involved with the Americans in Vietnam. Anyway I was pretty disappointed by his attitude. I thought he was damned ungrateful. Here he was being offered an honourable career and he thought it was funny. Shortly after, I signed his discharge papers. I don't know anything further about him. I may have seen him at some regimental reunions afterwards, or it may be I didn't, I can't really be sure.

Former Gunnery Sergeant Lloyd USMC retired, Florida October 2003

Vietnam... that was long time ago. I trained a lot of men who fought in Nam. I remember a few of them of course but it's difficult to recall the names. Have you any idea how many marines I trained? Traynor though, oh, yes, I certainly remember him. He was not the type of person you forget. In my entire career I never came across anyone really like him. He was in a platoon I was training at the Island. He became a topic of speculation in the sergeant's mess within a few days of arriving. The first thing you learn when you start to train men is that you have to break them down before turning them into marines. Well that Traynor, actually we called him "Yoshi" because he was a Jap, some of us thought he was a bit of a show off. I'd work the men all day until they were ready to drop but Yoshi, he didn't drop, he'd then go off for a couple of hours run, even sometimes missing mess call. It doesn't take much of that to get you noticed in the Corps. Also his marksmanship was outstanding and he could strip a weapon down faster than anyone I've ever seen, even blindfold. It was pretty obvious he was no ordinary recruit and that he had been in the military before, except that he wasn't that old so it was a bit of a mystery that he acted in every way as if he'd been in for at least ten years.

Well, after a couple of weeks of basic training even the officers started to notice him and I was asked to make some discrete enquiries. I don't know what they meant by discrete. I had him report to my office, where I put it to him straight that he had obviously previously been in the military. I asked him where and with whom he had served. The question clearly rattled him and he looked a bit shifty for a couple of minutes. Actually correct that, a lot of orientals look shifty to me, I think it's just an oriental thing, so he probably looked pretty normal. He didn't answer me at first. For sure he was thinking what lie to tell me. He then came out with a real whopper. I'll give it to him, the guy had imagination. He said he had served five years as a British paratroop before being honourably discharged as a non-commissioned officer, adding that he had not previously disclosed this because his last two years had been spent in a special unit whose activities he was obliged to keep secret. I confess I didn't know what to think. He clearly knew all about soldiering, as much as me, probably even more and I'd been a marine for nearly fifteen years by then. To give myself a little time to think I asked him how many parachute jumps he had made. He hesitated for a few seconds before replying that he couldn't remember the exact number but it was something of the order of 1000, most of which were operational. He certainly got my attention with that statement. No one makes up that sort of shit. I thought to myself that, wherever he came from, he was just the sort of experienced soldier we needed out in Nam. From what he had said it seemed obvious he had considerable combat experience, no doubt a lot more than me. I started to wonder how I could fast track him to a recon unit and asked him if he was interested in being sent to sniper school if I could arrange it.

Well to cut a long story short, it took a while but with the CO's help we cut through the red tape and got him into sniper school from which I heard he managed the quickest graduation on record before being deployed to Nam where he covered himself in glory and medals. I am proud to think that I did my little bit in training him to become the marine he did.

Former Gunnery Sergeant Michael ("Fat") Platt USMC retired, West Virginia, 2003

I don't remember how I got the nickname "Fat". I was never fat when I was in the Corps. I suppose some unimaginative, wannabe fucking comedian worked out that "fat" rhymes with "Platt". Anyway the name stuck. Of course I remember Traynor. He's not someone you forget easily. No one ever called him "brainer" or said there was no one "saner". No one would've dared. He was "Yoshi" for a short time before people wised up to the fact that it was better not to say anything even slightly derogatory about him, at least not to his face. Then they started calling him "ice man" and with very good reason. I was paired with him as his spotter at sniper school and we were deployed to Nam together. He was called "Iceman" because that is what he was. It didn't matter if all hell was breaking out around him, he'd calmly and carefully take his shot or decide on a course of action. I never saw him panic or lose control, not once. No, I can't remember him ever being anything but totally cool and calm. The way he was actually had a beneficial effect on anyone who was with him, on patrol for example. You know how people can lose their heads under fire; well one look or a touch on the shoulder from him would make most people calm down. I supposed that he was what you might call a natural leader. Although funnily enough he preferred to be out fighting on his own, definitely not leading men. That was never his thing.

Well I suppose the truth is he despised most of the men he had to lead from time to time, because he felt they slowed him down and just got him into unnecessary trouble. I've been with him in the jungle and I was always a pretty good hunter because my father used to take me hunting from when I was very young. I had nothing on Iceman though. He could be a couple of feet away from you and you wouldn't even know it. So you can imagine what he thought about a platoon of grunts trampling through the undergrowth and even smoking as they went, so that you could smell them miles away. You'd be surprised how smell carries in the jungle. Anyone who knew what they were doing would try and eat Gook food so that they would start to smell like the Gooks. Most of what I learned about jungle fighting was from Traynor. He could spot a booby trap ten feet away and he was the one who taught me that if I wanted to stay alive it was better to make one's way through the thickets rather than taking an easy trail which, all too often ended in an ambush.

Actually, because of his skill in jungle fighting Traynor was quite in demand for patrols, which was a bit paradoxical because the same officers and men who felt comfortable with him along, were the ones who called us snipers "Murder Incorporated" and other such pejorative names. We got called "assassins", "killers", you name it. They didn't like snipers very much in those days. Not like today. The majority of ordinary military regarded snipers, almost without exception, as nothing more than murderers and avoided us like the plague. Of course we were murderers and, I have to say, pretty damn good at it. But that was what we were all supposed to be there for, wasn't it? The irony was that, whilst the whole American military machine seemed to be obsessed with "body count", if you could kill a hundred or more of the enemy using no more than one shot each, you were a goddamned assassin. I never could understand it. If every soldier in Vietnam had killed as many, or half as many, of the enemy as we snipers did, we would never have lost that war. I often wondered how those guys who used to call us such things as "Murder Incorporated" thought of themselves. Some of those same guys had massacred civilians at places like My Lai. In all the time I served in the US military I never came across a sniper who knowingly or wantonly killed any non-combatant.

Anyway, I'm getting off the point. If I had to sum up Traynor in a couple of words I'd say "stone cold killer". The real McCoy. Though talking about it like this reminds me that he wasn't just some mindless assassin. He seemed to quite like the Gooks, I s'pose because he was a Gook himself. Jap, Gook, they're all the same. He wasn't one of those you dropped in some VC village and let them loose on the local population.

He wasn't like that at all. I saw him upset a few people when he stopped them killing some of those villagers. In fact don't say you heard it from me... if anyone asks I'll deny it even though it was a long time ago, but you know the military, you don't want to start stirring things up. Well there was one patrol I remember. Traynor and I were making our way back from one of those special ops he always seemed to be chosen for. We knew there was a village a couple of Klicks ahead, we'd skirted it on our way out. Anyway we heard some shooting from around where the village was. I wanted to go on and ignore it, but Traynor insisted on taking a look. I suppose we both knew it was our guys doing the shooting, we could hear from the sound of the firing it wasn't AKs. Well we approached cautiously and when we got to the edge of the village we could see what looked like a rifle squad of our men laughing and generally horsing around. Well one thing I learned early on was it doesn't matter how friendly you think people are, you don't just walk into a position without taking a good look and making sure no trigger happy, doped up grunt is going to take a pot shot at you. So we lay there at the edge of the village and took a look through our scopes. What we saw wasn't very pretty. There were quite a few bodies lying around, women, old men, a few kids even. I heard Traynor cursing under his breath and looked around at him. It looked like he was aiming his rifle at one of the huts to our left. I shifted my view to take a look and could see that six or seven of our men seemed to be raping a couple of girls. As I looked I could hear the girls screaming and then I saw the head of one of the soldiers who was on top of a girl disintegrate and that familiar pink spray erupting into the air. Then another one went down and a third. I wasn't even aware of hearing the shots. By the time those soldiers realized what was happening every single one of them was dead. By now the rest of the squad was firing wildly into the jungle. I don't think it took Traynor more than five minutes to kill them all.

I'm not your average nervous type of guy, but I can tell you I was shit scared. In fact I don't think I've ever been so scared in my life. What I was thinking was either Traynor was going to waste me next or, even if I managed to get away, I'd be facing the gas chamber or life in Leavenworth. I looked at Traynor, looked back at the village, it was like a dream to me, I've never experienced anything like it. I suppose I was in a bit of shock. It wasn't like when we were out on a mission or we were under fire. Traynor had just taken out a whole squad of our own men. I saw the two girls who'd been raped, getting up and looking around like they couldn't believe what had happened. Well I was finding it pretty difficult to digest too. I heard Traynor say "Let's go, c'mon, the rest of the platoon maybe around somewhere." and I got up and just followed him back into the jungle.

I didn't know what to do. I thought I ought to report it but the truth is if I'd found Traynor intimidating before, now I more or less pissed myself every time he looked at me sideways. I don't know what came over me a couple of days later but it was like everything suddenly bubbled up and I couldn't control myself. I told him I wanted to talk to him. He just looked at me coldly and said, "They weren't real soldiers. They were just shit." Then he turned and walked away from me.

The whole thing worried me for a long time; I thought for sure the army was going to have a big investigation. I mean Traynor had killed ten or twelve of our own men, one shot each. Anyone finding them had to be able to put two and two together. We never heard anything about it though. I suppose it was all those dead women and children, the top brass probably didn't want to stir up a shit storm. And the NVA did, of course, have their own snipers, who weren't half bad even if they might not've been up to our standards. So, thinking about it now, it probably never even occurred to anyone that that squad had been taken out by our own side. Even so I had flashbacks for a quite a few years, until the more I thought about it the more I knew Traynor was right. If those men had been real soldiers, not only wouldn't they have murdered a lot of innocent people but they would have set up a proper perimeter around the village. They didn't know if there were VC around or not. They were in the middle of a really hot zone and were acting like they were at some extreme frat party. Real soldiers would still have been alive today. So I don't worry about it anymore. Traynor probably gave those guys a quick merciful death when they could easily have been captured and tortured by the VC or NVA.

I haven't seen Traynor since I shipped back Stateside and got my discharge and quite frankly I wouldn't be sorry never to see him again.

John Traynor, Umbria, Italy, 2010.

I think of myself as a soldier, but let's face it, I'm really a killer. I used to have these romantic notions about soldiering and I suppose I could have made a conventional career in the military and ended up as one of those respected, grizzled nco's or perhaps even an officer, but things never seemed to go like that for me. I was always being drawn in a different direction. In retrospect, my life seemed to develop with a sort of elegant inevitability. The one thing that amazes me now is how the thin thread of fate weaving through my existence allowed me to develop numerous, high level military skills whilst keeping me clear of any serious harm. Sometimes I think that I have just been extraordinarily lucky. Over the years I have been in combat far too often to count. I have stood or lain next to people who have been riddled with bullets or blown to pieces and have always walked away with nothing more serious than minor flesh wounds. I have been in helicopters that have crashed; had teams of assassins target me; my enemies have even rigged cars I have been using with explosives, all with negligible adverse personal consequences. In my experience most combat soldiers come to believe in luck or talismans, but I always remember my grandfather telling me that, whilst something unexpected can always happen, it will be my training and ability to react to unanticipated events that will save me. So, as I trusted in and believed my grandfather, my creed was training, skill and tradecraft. I never lost my faith and was never betrayed by it.

My parents died when I was a baby and I was brought up by maternal Japanese grandfather until he died when

I was entering my adolescence. My grandfather was an exceptional man. He was not just a pre-eminent practitioner of martial arts, but was also famous in Japan for his calligraphy, poetry and painting. In fact he was regarded as a National Treasure after the Second World War. He tried to teach me calligraphy, but I'm afraid I wasn't very good at it. I don't paint badly though. I like to paint and it's been quite a useful cover for me from time to time because everyone always seems to think that artists are harmless eccentrics. Anyway, my grandfather certainly wasn't harmless. He was a tough taskmaster I can tell you. In all the years he was bringing me up I never called him anything but Grandfather or Shihan, which translates to something like "Master Instructor". Not only did he make me practice martial arts eight hours a day, he would then spend another few hours teaching me writing, history and all the conventional educative curricula that are supposed to provide a basis for success in the modern world. I never minded the hours of physical practice. In fact the better I became, the more I came to enjoy carrying out the different techniques.

I've only ever met one other person who was anything like my grandfather. That was an old Chinese doctor up in the mountains of Southern China, close to the border with Vietnam. I had been working with the CIA and had also been attached to MACV-SOG (Military Assistance Command, Vietnam - Studies and Observation Group). Operating mostly in Laos and Cambodia, we were quite a successful team, obtaining intelligence, disrupting enemy supply lines and, most of all, killing a lot of the enemy.

It was the very tail end of the Vietnam war, shortly before the evacuation of Saigon. I was sent out on one of those missions dreamed up by the top brass that have no real military objective but were intended to be more of a warning that, although we were being defeated, America still had teeth and was not shy about biting. I was tasked with carrying out an assassination mission targeting some Russian officers who were directing some of the Vietnamese war effort from just over the Chinese border. Everything went fine. Better than fine in fact, because not only did I nail the two generals who were my primary target, but I also managed to knock out half their staff. I succeeded in extracting myself from the immediate vicinity of the operation with little or no difficulty and made my way to the exfiltration point. That was where the wheels came off. The chopper home turned up on time and had lowered the Stabo rig that was supposed to lift me out of hostile territory. Luckily for me, before I could reach the harness, half the NV army started to open up on the helicopter. The poor bastards didn't have a chance. I watched as my recovery aircraft was blown up in mid-air with no chance that anyone who had been in the chopper had survived. The guys who flew and manned those helicopters were pretty good guys, they saved a lot of lives. It was bad luck for them that day, but good luck for me. Another few minutes and I would have been dangling in the air when the NVA opened up. Well, that's war for you. Nothing ever makes any sense.

However I was left with the serious logistical problem of being in the middle of nowhere, surrounded by half the NVA and several million hostile Vietnamese and Chinese and no one from my side knowing what had become of me. Even now I'm not one to give myself up easily, but in those days I was young, gung-ho and fancied myself the Superhero. Somehow or other I managed to evade the teams sent out to find me, thanks, probably in no small measure, to the pepper spray we Special Forces used to carry to thwart tracking dogs used by the NVA.

After several weeks living off the land, a greatly slimmed down version of the superhero managed to drag himself into a small hill tribe village high in the mountains of Southern China. I think my luck must have been working overtime. The villagers' principal occupation was growing and selling opium and its derivatives, so they were as concerned as me to avoid alerting the People's army and state security about my sudden appearance. Best of all though, as far as I was concerned, the village was cared for by an old traditional Chinese doctor who turned out to be an outstanding exponent of Chinese martial arts and in particular Dim Mak, or the specialized art of fighting using "touches" or strikes on various acupuncture points on the body. I've said that the old doctor was like my grandfather and, in a way, being with him was like being a young kid again. I spent four years living in that village learning from the old doctor. He taught me things about martial arts that I don't think even my grandfather knew. Also, I actually learned as much about healing as killing. I think if the old doctor were still alive he would probably be very disappointed that

I had become a professional assassin rather than setting myself up as a practitioner of Traditional Chinese Medicine. On the other hand maybe he wouldn't be disappointed. I think he knew me pretty well, maybe better than I know myself, so he probably always knew I would never become a healer, even though I do get a kick out of sometimes doing my healing bit and I always keep different Chinese medicinal herbs and acupuncture needles in my travelling bag.

When the old guy died I left the village and the disappointed villagers, who had thought I was going to be curing their arthritis for the next 50 years. In the following few weeks I walked towards where I thought Thailand ought to be. It was not easy and I had a few close calls, but finally I managed to present myself at the US Embassy in Bangkok. I had a bit of a time getting in because I looked and smelled worse than the dirtiest vagrant you could ever imagine. Neither should it be forgotten that I look far more oriental than western. I didn't resent the way I was treated. I realized that to the trimmed, starched marines on guard duty I looked like some gook bum off the street trying to get to America. Again, though, my luck held and finally one of the marines on duty was credulous enough to listen to my "semper fi's" and how I was MIA and had managed to escape from a Vietnamese POW camp before walking to Thailand. After they cleaned me up I became quite the celebrity. Nearly everyone at the embassy at one time or another hosted me to a variety of entertainments in order to hear first-hand about my fictitious captivity and the true account of my walk to freedom. I had honed the fiction throughout my weeks of working my way through the jungle, so you can imagine how unassailably pat it all came out. My credibility was bolstered by the chief CIA spook in Bangkok who turned out to be one of my former buddies from the Studies and Observation Group. He testified to my being an unimaginative simpleton without the capacity for telling a tale of even a fraction of such complexity if it were not completely true.

By the time I was repatriated to America I was extremely sorry to leave that hot, dusty Shangri-La. My regrets multiplied daily as, once back in the USA, I had to undergo debriefings and countless hours of interviews and form filling in order to regularize my status and obtain several years of back pay. There were several occasions when I yearned to return to Bangkok and the beautiful, willing, constantly smiling women I had left behind. Finally the bureaucracy became bored with torturing me and went on to focus on some other poor bastard. I was given a furlough before being told to report for duty at Quantico.

After subjecting me to the full intensity of their bureaucracy, the High Command, in their wisdom, apparently decided to bestow a little kindness on me. They gave me a job training snipers. This may have been good for the trainee snipers, but I found the tedium of it life sapping, until one day Charlie Beckwith turned up to save me by offering me the opportunity of selection for Delta. Our paths had already crossed in my early days in Vietnam when he commanded an outfit called Detachment B52. When, a few years later, back in the States, he was tasked with setting up an elite, special forces unit dedicated to counter terrorism operations, 1st Special Forces Operational Detachment Delta, he got out his address book of sociopaths and looked me up along with others like me.

CHAPTER NINE

Hereford 10 days after Cartwright's lunch at Vauxhall Cross

"Secret Intelligence has never been for the fainthearted"
– Richard Helms – A Look Over my Shoulder

Cartwright stirred uneasily as he dreamed of being cornered by the fierce looking Adou tribesmen. His whole troop lay dead around him and the tribesmen were coming in to finish him off. He could see their dark eyes and ragged beards as they levelled their automatic Russian weapons at him and opened fire. But, when he looked down at his chest to see how many hits he had taken he saw only the red tie and flannel shorts that made up the Sunday best in which his parents had dutifully dressed him when he was a little boy being taken to the Church in Essex, every Sunday morning. The Church bell was ringing so loudly and insistently that he could not hear the vicar's sermon. As he strained to try to catch some of the words he woke up.

The insistent ringing of the church bells had turned into the sound of his mobile phone. He glanced at the luminous dial of the Rolex wristwatch that he almost never took off, a gift from his parents when he had graduated from the military academy at Sandhurst. The dial read 4.35. It was still dark outside.

He leaned across to the bedside table where he had left his telephone, trying to stop the incessant ringing before it woke his wife and still struggling to clear the vivid images of his dream from his mind.

"Hello, Colonel. Colonel? It's Mark Fanshaw. Sorry to disturb you at this hour but things are moving rather faster than we anticipated."

Cartwright's head cleared immediately, "What do you want me to do?"

"There's a chopper on its way to collect you and bring you up to meet me at Northolt. I'll brief you as we're flying. You'll need kit for a couple of days, maybe a little bit more, hot weather, European hot. See you in a couple of hours."

By the time the helicopter arrived half an hour later, Cartwright's dutiful wife (who had become even more dutiful since she had learned that her husband was involved in a secret operation that, at the very least, was going to elevate her to becoming Lady Cartwright) had made him coffee and a scrambled egg whilst her husband washed, dressed, shaved and packed. Actually he had cheated on the packing, because experience had taught him always to keep ready a packed bag so that he could travel within minutes of being required to do so, which had often been the case. In point of fact he kept four bags constantly packed, the contents of which he changed seasonally. One was for Europe and Northern Europe, a second for the Middle East and desert, a third for the tropics and finally one that was really two bags containing uniforms and his black kit, the Nomex suits and assault kit used for special operations, along with a variety of weapons.

He also decided, on the basis that he was flying from the military airfield at RAF Northolt, rather than on a commercial airline, that he would bring a weapon with him. Although he doubted that he would have any need of a gun, he felt more comfortable knowing he was armed. Many of his troopers were wedded to the Sig Sauer as a side arm. His personal preference was for Heckler & Koch products and he decided to take a sub-compact Heckler & Koch P2000SK 9mm pistol. It was a light, easily concealable, handgun. He threw three spare 10 capacity magazines into his bag together with a box of cartridges.

Featherstonehaugh was already seated on the aircraft by the time Cartwright's helicopter landed. The transport was a BAE 146 VIP transport plane used by the Royal Air Force for the transport of senior officers and other VIP's. Its use was not restricted to the air force and it was frequently used, not only by the security services, but also by members of the Royal family. In addition to its crew of 6, the aircraft was equipped to take up to 19 passengers. Today, however, Featherstonehaugh and Cartwright were alone. Their flight plan provided for them to land at Ciampino military airport near Rome. The BAE 146 had a maximum speed of 400 mph and the flight was expected to take between 2 ½ to 3 hours depending upon the prevailing headwinds. Cartwright had been in air force transports more times than he cared to remember, but this was the first time that he had been offered coffee and breakfast by a pretty young air force warrant officer who was the day's flight attendant.

"Very nice" commented Cartwright settling into the comfort of his seat as they were taxiing for take-off. "Surely though, with the nature of what we are doing, we ought to be a bit more anonymous."

"There's a European Union agricultural meeting in Rome over the next two days. There's already a full complement from the Ministry of Agriculture and we're just two more senior civil servants from the ministry hitching a free ride. No detailed records, nothing to connect you or me. In fact I've got a diary full of meetings in London over the next two days and I believe you're off training on your own in the mountains of Wales. Just remember the drill, no names at any time over the next day or so, apart from…"

Featherstonehaugh added, as an afterthought, "Marcello di Stefano of the SISDE, Italian secret service. He's meeting us at Ciampino. He'll get us through everything anonymously."

After the plane had taken off and the warrant officer flight attendant had disappeared to join the rest of the crew, Cartwright sipped his coffee before taking a bite out of the croissant he had selected from the range of breads and pastries that had been placed in front of them.

"What's happened that's making this suddenly so urgent?"

Featherstonehaugh finished putting some jam on a piece of bread he had previously buttered and took a bite, which he chewed briefly before replying.

"Well there's quite a lot been going on. The first thing is that HRH's attempts to reason with the lady in question came to nothing. Rather, I should say, they elicited a totally unexpected fact that rather threw everyone. She told the person who was sent to see her that, not only did she love Al Khalifa and was going to marry him, but she was going to have his baby."

"What." Cartwright was startled. He stared at Featherstonehaugh in astonishment, "that can't be true".

"That was our initial reaction; that she was just trying to stir the pot even more. But then we picked up some more intercepts that led us to a doctor she had been seeing. We had someone go and take a look at her medical records and you can probably guess the rest."

"She's pregnant."

"Indeed she is. She's in the first trimester, so we can expect it to start showing in the not too distant future."

"Good grief! I can hardly believe it. Surely she understands the implications of all this. She can't seriously be intending to have it."

Featherstonehaugh shrugged, "I don't know about that, but I can tell you that

Al-Khalifa went out to a very well-known and exclusive jeweler and bought her an extremely large and expensive diamond ring."

"I see." Cartwright rubbed his chin thoughtfully, "So this means what... that we are not only go, but the whole timetable is moving into high gear?"

"Well we can't exactly have her walking around showing off her pregnancy. Everyone has now signed off on this. The pregnancy has changed the whole dimension. Unfortunately it's made her a primary objective in herself because no-one can work out a scenario for leaving her untouched whilst provoking a spontaneous miscarriage. I don't need to elaborate for you what it would mean for the mother of the heirs to the throne to give our future King a muslim half-brother."

"God, what an almighty mess. Jesus, how can she be that stupid?"

"I don't know if she is. I think she's fully aware of the risks she's running. She's told various people that the Royal family is going to try and get rid of her. She's apparently pretty chummy with her butler and one of our intercepts picked him up speaking to a pal of his, saying that she wrote a letter to him nearly a year ago, in which she said she was certain she was going to be killed in a car accident her ex-husband was planning in order to make the path clear for him to marry his mistress. We're attempting to get hold of that letter. It wouldn't do to have something like that floating around. I don't know where she got it all from, but if that's what she believes, then I can't understand what she's thinking, continuing to flaunt this present relationship in everyone's face. Maybe she thinks the Al Khalifas can protect her. Who the hell knows? Anyway the short point is that we're on our way to a meeting with Standish and his operative, this Traynor chappie. The message we are carrying is that the operation is an immediate go. I've got a briefing prepared for them. Your active participation shouldn't be necessary. You're there to listen, meet Traynor and arrange liaison procedures with him."

The rest of the trip was spent in almost complete silence with Cartwright trying to adjust his thinking to the reality of the situation that was now confronting him. Since he had joined the army he had never at any time, not even for one moment, considered that he might one day be involved in the officially sanctioned assassination of a member of the Royal family. He remembered the Princess well. She was deeply concerned with some charitable NGO (Non-Governmental Organisation) involved with mine clearance throughout the world. She had become something of an official spokesman for the lobby who were trying to have mines totally banned under international law. Three or four years previously Cartwright had been on a jungle training exercise in Papua, New Guinea when he had received orders for him and four of his troop to break off training and accompany the woman on a visit to Cambodia where mine clearance was still being carried on. Some bright spark, who had been asked to organize her protection, had apparently glanced at a map and thought that Papua was just a few minutes away from Cambodia. It was a close run thing but he and his team had just managed to arrive in Cambodia in time to meet her off her plane.

They had then spent four days in close company with her, carrying out close protection duties. He recalled that she was not only beautiful, but had been absolutely charming to them all. In addition she had a natural ability to make everyone around her feel that she was as concerned for their well-being and comfort as they were for her safety. After she had left Cambodia to return to England, even Cartwright and his hardened team were more than a little in love with her.

And now he was an integral part of a small group of individuals who were planning to kill her. If they were successful and there was not much chance that they would not be, in a very few days that lively, charming and beautiful woman was going to have her life snuffed out. Not for the first time Cartwright wondered whether he was doing the right thing and what he had got himself into.

CHAPTER TEN

Rome

"Take what you can from the situation and pave the way for your influence, though you have but little strength your influence will be great" – Ancient Chinese military strategy

After being dismissed by Standish I returned to the lobby of the hotel, collected my carrier bag full of money and then used the passport Standish had given to me to check in for a room. Everything went like clockwork, as it usually did when Standish made the arrangements. My room even exceeded my expectations. I had half expected to have been put into the sort of semi cupboard that some of the smarter Italian hotels reserve for what they regard as their less salubrious guests. But no, there I was with my carrier bag in a large deluxe room with a well-stocked mini bar. I had several things to do, like getting rid of my car and starting the preparations for putting together a team. I knew just who to go to for that. My old pal from the Legion, Jacques Renardier. Jacques was quite a bit older than me. He had already been in the Legion for two or three years when I had joined and had taken me under his wing immediately. He had joined up after getting involved in a few very nasty incidents and chose the Legion as a preferable alternative to a long prison stretch. I did not care what he had done, any more than he cared what I did. We had served in the paras and been on the sergeants' course together. We had been in situations where you find out what people are really made of. He had always proved himself a solid and reliable pal who would stick with you through anything. I had not seen him for several few years, although we had maintained long distance communication. Although he was considerably longer in the tooth than me, he was not the kind of man to accept a peaceful retirement living on his reminiscences. He was someone who jealously guarded his position in the social substratum that I and people like me inhabited. I knew that he owned some sort of antique shop in Florence where, I assumed, amongst his other activities, he fenced a variety of stolen objects.

I thought of trying to cram the carrier bag full of money into the electronic room safe, along with the new documentation I had been given and the other two different passports and matching documentation I was carrying, but I distrusted hotel room safes. They are far too easy to open. I have done it enough times myself. All it needs is a small electronic device that plugs into most hotel safes and opens them in about 20 seconds flat. There is in fact no really secure place in a hotel room, unless you are adept at dismantling parts of the room to make a secure hiding place. Even then, in my business the greatest enemy is a professional like me, who will stand in a room for a few minutes deciding where he would hide things. I have found that when you think you have a good idea it is normally not unique to you, so I decided long ago not to keep things in hotel rooms. If you are really stuck it is better to take a room in another hotel in a different name and hide things there, even though this has its own problems.

In any event I decided not to leave all that cash in the hotel room, which, having been chosen by Standish, I regarded as a hostile environment. There was not much danger in my carrying everything with me. I always carried a couple of money belts with me and it is surprising how much one can stuff into those without looking much more than the paunchy middle aged guy that your grey hair declares you to be. Anyway no-one was likely to try and mug me between the hotel and my car.

The hotel television, as in many hotels these days, was set up to provide internet access. Normally I would not even think about using the internet in a hotel, certainly not in my room, but what I was interested in was fairly innocuous; finding the nearest location for the car hire company I had used. Still I did not want to be too obvious. I checked the websites of every car hire company whose name appeared in the telephone yellow pages that conveniently had been placed just by the telephone. For good measure, I also looked up some hotel sites in places where I had no intention of ever going and checked a few dates, two and three weeks ahead, just to provide anyone who might check on me with a few false leads to keep them occupied.

As luck would have it, the car hire company had an office in the car park across the street from the Eden. Having weighed the pros and cons I decided that there was no necessity to return the car to some more distant location. My only other problem now was to contact Jacques to get him to put in hand the obtaining of everything I needed and to start putting together a team. I decided to buy an anonymous telephone card and call him from a public telephone chosen at random, on my way to pick up my rental car. I was intending to take my time over all this in spite of the fact that it was already late afternoon. Going to the meeting with Standish had not been too much of a problem because there was unlikely to have been any surveillance on me. That had all changed in the hour or so I had spent with Standish. I knew the Brits. They had a meeting fixed with Standish and me the following day, which probably meant that they had already established surveillance on the hotel.

Cars were parked all over the street outside the hotel and there were buildings all around, any of which would have provided an ideal location for observing the hotel. I would just have to be extra careful to get rid of any watchers. I thought that it was unlikely anyone except the Italians would be able, in the short time they had had, to mount a full scale surveillance operation, which would require a lot of people as well as vehicles. I estimated that, if there was already surveillance on the hotel, there would probably be no more than two, possibly three watchers involved and it ought not to be too much of a problem to flush out and evade that number.

My first action on leaving the hotel was to go into the garage across the road to try and find the rental car office. In fact two car rental companies had offices in the garage and the company from whom I had rented had their office conveniently located, so that even in the gloom of the car park I could speak to their agent at the same time as keeping an eye on who entered and left the car park. It turned out that I had until 8pm to return my car because the agent had some work to catch up on and was going to be in the office until that time. Whilst I was in the office talking to the agent the only person who had entered the garage was a young, attractive, well-dressed woman. The problem, as far as I was concerned, was that although she had entered the garage shortly after me she had not driven a car out; even though I spent about ten minutes in the car hire office.

Having arranged the return of the rental car with the agent for approximately 7.30pm, I slipped out of his office and walked as rapidly as I could in the direction of the Spanish steps. It was about 70 metres from the garage entrance to the steep, narrow street that led down towards the main shopping area of Via del Corso. The road itself was undergoing some repair and there were various, rickety, lopsided wooden barriers at the top of the road impeding, but not making impossible, both pedestrian and vehicular access.

The watchers were not very good. One had positioned himself at the corner of via Ludovisi. He was of medium height, rather thin build, probably in his thirties. He was putting on far too much of the impatiently waiting for someone act, by looking around and looking at his watch every few seconds. As I walked past him on the opposite side of the road I saw, out of the corner of my eye, the woman I had noticed going into the garage. She was now walking quickly towards Mr.Impatient.

I ran through different options in my mind. A lot of central Rome is restricted to cars that have a special permit. There are other areas that are almost exclusively pedestrian. I had to assume that the watchers would have vehicular support and that their vehicle would have the necessary permit to drive around the historic centre. Even if the watchers were easy to spot it did not mean that it was going to be equally easy to lose them. I did not want them seeing my car or seeing me return it and I did not want them to see me using the telephone. I wondered if I should just take them down a quiet street somewhere and put them out of action for a while, without hurting them too much. That might be a worthwhile tactic. They did not look Italian, lacking that very distinctive, scruffy sort of elegance that seems to come naturally to Italians. So, if I decided to put them to sleep for a short time, it would be unlikely immediately to provoke ten thousand Carabinieri into launching themselves at me. I decided to walk around a little, to see if I could lose them before taking more physical action.

I scrapped my original idea of trying to lose them amongst the tourists at the Spanish Steps and, instead, strolled down to the via del Corso. I had already formulated a plan. I took my time, looking in shops and sometimes going in and generally acting in a way that caused the watchers to become even more conspicuous. There were in fact three of them. One, a younger looking guy dressed in a leather bomber jacket and blue jeans, had walked past me and was staying in front of me, boxing me between himself and the man and woman following behind. I turned left into via del Corso and started walking towards Piazza Colonna where the square is divided into two by a richly carved Roman triumphal column. Across the road opposite the square is a department store called Rinascente. An indoor shopping centre takes up the whole of the next block over in the direction of Piazza Venezia, where the enormous memorial to King Victor Emmanuel acts as a gateway to the Imperial Roman Forum. What I liked about Rinascente and the shopping centre was that they were on square blocks and each had four separate entrances leading into four different streets. The buildings are also very close to the metro entrance. In other words it is a bit of a watcher's nightmare because there is so much to cover.

The block immediately before Rinascente is occupied by a large fast food restaurant called Autogrill. Although it is a busy restaurant with a fairly heavy flow of people, as far as I recalled, it only had one main entrance so I doubted that I would be able to shake my shadows there without finding a hidden corner in which to conceal myself for an hour or so, until I could be certain that the watchers would have given up and decided they had lost me. But I did not have an hour to waste. There was too much for me to arrange before dropping my car off and getting back to the Eden. I wondered how well my little threesome knew Rome and whether they realized that I was intending to use Rinascente to lose them. From the way they were acting I doubted it. They had obviously not yet realized that I had made them and they were giving me plenty of space, but there were too few of them to cover the parallel streets. For what I wanted to do I needed to get the threesome to close in on me.

Autogrill has three floors accessible to the public, including a basement with toilets. I went in, bought myself a cup of coffee and carried it to one of the standing tables provided for short term customers. Two of the watchers followed me in. The girl bought a coffee and positioned herself quite close to me. A bit risky for an attractive girl like her, not many men would fail to notice her standing 10 feet away from them. To me, it just emphasized that this must be an inexperienced team put together in a bit of a rush. Before I finished my coffee I saw the third watcher loitering by the door. That was my cue to move. I took a slow sip from my already empty cup and casually replaced the cup on its saucer. The girl was nonchalantly sipping from her cup, probably also empty by now. Her partner was behind her further into the store, standing in the interior supermarket studying a shelf of pasta. The guy at the door was still hanging around. Time for action. I started to walk in the direction of the basement where the toilets were located. The watcher at the door thought he was anticipating my move and entered the shop to be able to intercept me as I went towards the toilets. His only problem was that I changed my direction mid-stream and walked extremely quickly out of the Autogrill and, without looking back ran across the road in front of a turning car, straight into Rinascente.

I glanced into the store windows as the Rinascente door swung open for me. I had caught them completely unawares and I could see the three of them reflected in the glass door, still over the other side of the road. I was through to the other side of the store and out again in a few seconds and then straight into the shopping centre. I had lost sight of them and for sure they had lost sight of me. Having made the mistake of all entering the Autogrill I doubted that they would repeat their error and all enter Rinascente after me together. I expected one would have followed me and the others would have run around to the sides to try and cover the other exits. Except they were too slow and had missed my run into my present location. Having lost sight of me, I calculated that they would have to verify that I had not remained in Rinascente, which had about five or six floors of shopping area plus a basement. I decided that rather than conceal myself in the shopping centre for a little while, I would take a chance and use a different exit and then try to get out of the area as quickly as possible without being spotted. I had to rely on speed as I had nothing with me to change my appearance.

I managed to cross over into a narrow street leading off the Via del Corso without them spotting me. The street was empty and almost entirely in shadow as the late afternoon sun started its inevitable decline. I kept close to the buildings for maximum conceal-ment as I moved down the street. The entire area in front of me was completely empty of pedestrians and I kept looking behind me to see whether my flight had been picked up. After what I had just done there was no point in being surreptitious about checking behind me. I was definitely not being followed. I ran to the end of the street and into a cross street and then ran on again until I was able to enter another small street that led in the approximate direction of Piazza Navona, near where I had parked the car. I con-tinued walking through different streets. I was by now certain that I had lost my pursuers, so I stopped at a small shop to buy a telephone card before continuing on my way.

I entered Piazza Navona from a side street about half way down the square and went directly to a pay phone located by the junction of that street and the Piazza. Whilst looking around, I replaced the Sim card and battery in my smart phone. I use several different Sim cards and, even so, those and the battery spend more time out of my phone than in it. If I could man-age without a mobile phone I would, but these days they are far too useful to be without. I looked up Jacques Renardier's telephone number before putting the calling card I had purchased into the appropriate slot in the public telephone and dialling. I continually scanned the area around me whilst listening to the ring-ing tone. The Piazza was becoming crowded with tour-ists who were starting to fill up the various restaurants lining the two sides of the Piazza. It was a beautiful evening, with the fading light giving the buildings of the Piazza a warm reddish tint that highlighted their elegant proportions.

"Pronto"

"Jacques?" I talked quietly not wanting any curious passerby to hear me.

"Qui parla?"

"C'est moi Jacques. John Traynor".

"John, ce n'est pas possible."

He actually sounded pleased to hear me. I decided to switch to English.

"Jacques I'm in a bit of a rush and just wanted to touch base with you. Have you got another number I can call?"

Good old Jacques, no unnecessary questions or ifs and buts. He just rattled off a number which he said was his telefonino, his cell phone, which I immediately tapped into my phone.

"Give me ten minutes then call me and I'll give you another number."

I replaced the receiver and crossed the road to a bar where I stood at the counter and ordered a coffee.

After ten minutes I went to the payphone on the wall at the back of the bar and dialed the number Jacques had given me.

He answered immediately and gave me another number which I again recorded on my phone. I replaced the receiver and immediately dialed the second number.

"What's going on? Are you in trouble?"

"No. Nothing like that. Are you up for working with me?" Jacques knew perfectly well what I did.

"Of course." Good old Jacques. There was not even any momentary hesitation. What do you need that's not going to aggravate my rheumatism?"

"A couple of sets of papers, transport, plus a team of say, five, preferably from the area where we first worked together, if not from there then from East of here."

"You're near."

"A little south. I'll be with you in a couple of days, tops."

"How long do you need them for and what's the rate?"

"A week, ten days perhaps. 50 large Euro in advance, plus terminal bonus of same at the end."

He whistled, "Pretty generous."

I paused for a second or two, I did not like to say this over an open line but I thought I owed it to Jacques to give him a heads up. If anything went wrong he needed to be able to protect himself, both from the people he was using and those using me. "The bonus part is likely to be problematic. The contractors are running a very tight operation and won't want any loose ends." Before he could respond I added, "That might include us."

There was a slightly too long silence at the other end of the line.

"So what's new? I get it. Call me on the cell number when you need to speak again."

"One more thing. Have someone stand by to deliver the transport. I'll probably need to make a very quick exchange of cars within the next two or three days. I'll explain more when we meet."

"No problem. But this line should be pretty secure, let's fix a spot now."

I thought for a minute.

"It's got to be near you, but somewhere where no-one will know which way I might have gone."

"How about a rest stop on the Autostrada? There is one after Arezzo at Incisa. From there you can go off in about four different directions."

"Sounds perfect. I think I know it. Next time I call I'll give you a time and other details but I won't mention where."

"Good. I'm looking forward to seeing you again."

"See you soon."

I replaced the receiver and looked at my Tag clone. 6.30pm. Time to return the car and have a decent dinner.

On my way back to the car I passed a luggage shop and bought a large brief case with two combination locks. Before driving off I removed my money belts and put the money and passports into the case, setting each of the locks with a different combination.

I got the car back to the rental company and returned to the hotel carrying my luggage without incident and without seeing the three watchers. Whilst one of the porters took my suitcase I asked the concierge to look after my new briefcase with its valuable contents. When he suggested that I leave it in the hotel safe I gave him a 50 Euro note and told him that I would prefer that it was immediately available to me if he would be so kind as to ensure that he and his colleagues kept an eye on it for me. He was more than anxious to oblige. By then the other porters on duty had caught a whiff of money and were starting to hover within earshot of our conversation. I doled out some more 20 Euro notes to each of the circling staff members and considered it money well spent.

As I went up to my room I wondered first how the Brits had known who it was they ought to follow. It did not need a genius to work out that they already had at least some information on me, as well as my picture. I wondered if Standish had given them a picture of me. Somehow I did not think so. This meant they must have their own file on me, which in turn probably meant they had dug up a file the SAS must have kept on me from my time with the Regiment so long ago. In those days I had not yet become so paranoid about my security and from the SAS records the Brits would be able to run up a pretty good profile of me, something I did not like at all.

I went on to consider why the Brits had put people on me so quickly. All I could think was that they wanted as much information as possible about my contacts and movements, better to enable them to keep tabs on me. Before entering my room I looked for the imperceptible tell I had left at the top of the door. It was gone. Someone had been in my room whilst I was out. I opened the door cautiously to its fullest extent and looked into the room. There was no one there but the bed had been turned down and a chocolate left on my pillow. So much for leaving indicators to tell me when someone had been in the room. Of course if I had thought about it I could have left a "do not disturb" notice on the door to exclude the housekeeping staff, but I actually like to have my bed turned down in hotel rooms. As I had not left anything in my room, I had not bothered to leave indicators inside. Nor had I bothered checking for bugs, I was not going to have any confidential conversations in the room and I did not talk in my sleep.

I had been in the room for about 30 seconds before the porter who had taken my suitcase delivered it to my room.

By now it was nearly 8pm and I decided to take a shower and get into some clean clothes. The phone rang whilst I was in the shower but I did not bother to answer. As I was drying myself off I noticed the message light flashing, indicating that whoever had called had left a message. It was Standish telling me there was a meeting in his suite at midday tomorrow and I was on my own until then. Normally, in this sort of situation, I would have had a meal in my room, in front of the television set, particularly as I was not paying. But too many of the luxury hotels in Italy these days think it is more up market to provide pseudo French cuisine and I preferred to go out to eat something simpler and more genuinely Italian.

As I walked out of the hotel entrance I saw leather bomber jacket loitering on the other side of the road. I ignored him. They could follow me now to their hearts' content. There were quite few Trattoria type restaurants in the vicinity of the hotel and whilst choosing one I saw the rest of the watching team. I assumed the woman would follow me into the restaurant with one of the men, which is exactly what happened. Bomber jacket was the unlucky one left standing outside.

They came in a few minutes after me and were given a table close to mine, by which time I was already looking at the menu. They must have been hungry because they had hardly been seated before they started to munch on a packet of bread sticks. In between crunches I saw the man talking into his sleeve. He was probably telling their third wheel to take the opportunity of filling up his own tank because, with the bottle of wine that had appeared so quickly on my table, they could see I was settled for some time.

The meal turned out to be very good and the wine was on the plus side of acceptable. I was glad I had decided to eat out of the hotel. Also I was beginning to feel very attracted to the girl watcher. She was not just good looking, but had an intelligent alert look to her that I liked. I overheard her talking to the waiter and she spoke perfect Italian. As the level of my bottle of wine dropped so did my usual caution and I started to wonder how I could detach the girl from her partners and see whether I might get anywhere with her. I thought to myself that she ought to be keen to get closer to me, because that way there would be less chance of them losing me again. I was not drunk, but I realized that I was getting there. I again thought to myself how I was allowing my professionalism to be compromised far too often. Lucky that this was going to be my last job.

I finished my meal and the bottle of wine and accepted a glass of grappa the restaurant owner apparently offered to all his clientele. In spite of my work I am basically not an unkind person and I knew how difficult it could be to try and maintain constant close surveillance on someone. All things considered I thought that the watchers deserved to finish their meal in peace, particularly after what I had done to them that afternoon. They certainly looked considerably more relaxed than when they had first come into the restaurant after me. I started to wonder if they realized I had lost them intentionally in the afternoon, or whether they were so inexperienced that they were not aware that I had identified them. Thinking about it from their point of view, I would have had no reason to believe that I would be followed from the Eden and I might just have been taking the normal counter surveillance measures anyone like me could be expected to use. They could have put losing me down to simple bad luck. Whatever they thought, I did not really care. They would stay with me only as long as I was prepared to tolerate their presence.

They finished their meal at around 10.30pm just as I was getting a little impatient to leave. I was not sleepy. It was a pleasant evening and I did not have to be up early, so I decided to take a stroll. I left the restaurant with my entourage in tow and wandered up to the Via Veneto towards the Porta Pinciana, before crossing the road just by Harry's Bar and then walking back down towards the Westin Excelsior. There is an outdoor café that is part of the Excelsior where there were two or three unoccupied tables. I decided to have a nightcap before returning to my hotel. The three English watchers had managed to stay with me this time, with two behind me and bomber jacket on the opposite side of the road. I sat down at a table facing the street, with my chair back against the hotel's exterior wall. The other tables were occupied by a mix of Arabs and Americans. Two hookers were sharing a table just across the pavement from me and were eyeing me up, assessing whether or not I was a suitable prospect for the evening. As I sipped the Irish coffee I had ordered I was tempted, but I found my gaze constantly turning to the English girl who had sat down with the other watcher at a table about 10 metres from me and lost interest in the hookers.

I got back to the hotel just before midnight, still accompanied by my faithful shadows. I assumed that they would wait around outside for at least another hour to make sure that I was safely tucked in for the night. That was their call. I was looking forward to spreading myself out in a comfortable king-size bed

CHAPTER ELEVEN
Rome – the following day

"Force the enemy to change his formation fre-
quently wait for him to lay the seeds of his
own self destruction then take advantage of
this'" – Ancient Chinese military strategy

Cartwright watched out of the window as the BAE 146 came into land. They had barely finished taxiing before he saw a dark blue Lancia sedan, flanked by two Carabinieri Land Rovers, racing across the apron towards where the aircraft was being parked. By the time the door had been opened and the steps from the aircraft put into place, four Carabinieri in their dark blue uniforms and gleaming white bandoliers, were in place around the aircraft, each one holding a Beretta sub machine gun. Featherstonehaugh was first out of the plane and as he reached the tarmac he was greeted by a smiling, ebullient Marcello di Stefano.

"Marcello. Come stae?"

"Bene, bene". The Italian took Featherstonehaugh's proffered hand firmly between his two hands and shook it warmly.

"You look very well my dear fellow. How long has it been since we were in Venice together? Nearly a year I think. Marvellous to see you again."

"It is good to see you too. We are going straight to your meeting at the Eden Hotel. I'll drop you there and you can call when you have finished, or if you need anything. Here... "

Di Stefano handed a card to Featherstonehaugh that contained nothing more than two telephone numbers.

"I don't know whether you'll be staying the night but I know you love our cuisine and just in case, I've arranged a very special restaurant for us tonight." He put his arm around the Englishman's shoulders smiling, "You ought to stay anyway."

"I'm not sure yet what we are doing. But it is possible we might have to stay and then I would be more than delighted to accept your hospitality. I certainly prefer not to miss one of your dinners."

"Bene. Bene. Perfetto. And this is" He turned towards Cartwright who had by then joined Featherstonehaugh on the tarmac and stood by a little awkwardly as the Italian greeted C's deputy.

"Oh, I'm so sorry. This is Mr. White." Featherstonehaugh offered no further explanation of who Cartwright was, or what he was doing accompanying him and Di Stefano seemed to take the lack of explanation as perfectly normal behaviour.

"Yes. I see. Most pleased to meet you Mr.White." Notwithstanding his apparent lack of curiosity about Cartwright, the Italian still looked the soldier over appraisingly as he moved to shake hands.

For his part, although Cartwright estimated that Di Stefano was probably in his fifties, the Italian looked fit and tanned, with only a slight trace of middle aged spread, that was almost totally disguised by his immaculately cut grey suit. Cartwright knew that a lot of English soldiers held the Italian armed forces in contempt, but Cartwright's experience was that, although Italians liked their food and clothes, possibly in that order, they not only had a very efficient security service, but also ran some of the best teams of special forces in the world including the Italian State Police counter-terrorism unit, the NOCS, or Special Operations Central Nucleus. Cartwright had trained and been on joint operations with some of those units and did not share the average Englishman's disdain for what they thought were foppish, decadent Italians.

The Englishmen handed their bags to Di Stefano's driver in response to his gesturing to take them. With their luggage safely stowed in the Italian's car, Cartwright and his companion got into the Lancia as the four Carabinieri smartly saluted them and Di Stefano before returning to their Land Rovers.

Cartwright sat in the front next to Di Stefano's driver, who turned out to be a frustrated racing driver. They were hardly seated before the driver took off accelerating hard. From then on the acceleration barely faltered until they became caught up in the traffic approaching the centre of Rome. Taking full advantage of the blue strobe light flashing away on the roof of the Lancia, the secret service driver got them into Rome in what seemed no time, at speeds that, at times, exceeded 100 mph. Cartwright was relieved when they finally drew up safely and smoothly outside the entrance to the Eden. There was a glass partition between the front and rear seats and it had been up throughout the whole journey, so Cartwright was unaware of the content of Di Stefano and Featherstonehaugh's discussion, but he had noticed that they were deep in conversation. He assumed they had other topics of mutual concern that had nothing to do with the reason he was in Rome.

When they arrived at the hotel the driver took care of their overnight bags whilst both Featherstonehaugh and Cartwright retained hold of the attaché cases they each carried which contained, in Cartwright's case, his gun and spare magazines.

A tall, well-built, fit looking man with a sallow complexion and severely pockmarked face was waiting for them at the entrance. After they had both shaken hands with the departing Di Stefano, this man took them up in the elevator to meet, as he said, "the admiral".

The first thing that struck Cartwright, as they were ushered into the "Admiral's" presence, was the incredible view the room gave of the whole city of Rome. Although the room was luxuriously furnished the large picture windows that extended to three sides of the room completely dominated first impressions.

Featherstonehaugh seemed unaffected by the view and walked over immediately to greet the man who had risen when they had entered the room. Cartwright assumed that this was "the Admiral". He was very tall, tanned and good looking with short cut, steel grey hair. Although Cartwright would have put him in his mid-sixties he looked very fit and moved with the easy, graceful elegance of an athlete. Although the "Admiral's" military bearing was unmistakable, Cartwright thought he looked more like a film star than a military man, an impression only strengthened by what were obviously, a very expensive suit, perfectly laundered white shirt and designer silk tie. Cartwright felt a little shabby standing there in his tweed jacket, cavalry twill trousers and desert boots. To cover his discomfort he turned towards the man who had been seated next to the Admiral and who now rose to shake hands with him.

Cartwright examined Traynor curiously. He was taller than Cartwright had imagined, probably about six feet. He was slim but had broad shoulders and a vice like grip. His oriental eyes were devoid of any expression and to Cartwright his face was that of the archetypical inscrutable oriental. If Cartwright had not known Traynor's approximate age, he would have found it difficult to say whether he was in his early forties or late fifties. The oriental's face was smooth and totally unlined. Cartwright had the passing thought that he might have undergone plastic surgery. As far as the SAS man was concerned the only clue to Traynor's age was his salt and pepper, grey and black hair.

They all sat down as they accepted the coffee the admiral offered them.

As they drank their coffee and the admiral and Featherstonehaugh made small talk about the view and Rome generally, Cartwright found himself under scrutiny from Traynor, who thus far had said nothing, other than to greet the Englishmen.

After an appropriate interval the Admiral stood up.

"I know you gentlemen have things to discuss that have nothing to do with me. My function, which I believe I have fulfilled, was simply to arrange this introduction and provide you with secure facilities where you can talk freely and openly. I'll therefore leave you. If you need anything at all, please feel free to call either myself or my secretary on the extension numbers I've left by the telephone... " he indicated the telephone on a table beside the sofa where Traynor was sitting, whilst simultaneously gesturing towards double doors that Cartwright had noticed when he entered the room before adding

"There's another room in there with some sandwiches and drinks, if any of you want anything. You'll probably want to open the doors anyway to verify that you are as alone, as I have told you you will be."

Featherstonehaugh stood up as well.

"Thank you admiral. I am very grateful for the way in which you've arranged everything. I think that I can take it from here. I will of course inform you when we have finished and if there is anything that we need, although I wouldn't anticipate there will be. Thank you again."

As soon as the admiral had left Featherstonehaugh delved into his briefcase and handed an electronic device to Cartwright,

"If you would just do the honours please, Frank."

Cartwright took the instrument and holding it out in front of him, very carefully started to go through both rooms checking everywhere for listening devices. It took him some ten minutes before he handed the device back.

"It's clean. Nothing here except babblers."

"Good." He turned to Traynor whilst, at the same time, taking a thick file out of his brief case,

"I understand that you have agreed to undertake a small contract for us. I need to brief you and I have to tell you that we have a very limited time scale which is critical... ".

Traynor leaned against the back support of the sofa where he was sitting and gazed steadily at Featherstonehaugh without expression, "You need to hold your horses just a little bit. Before you go on, there are certain preliminaries we have to sort out."

Traynor's voice was quiet, not at all what Cartwright had expected. As Traynor was speaking, Cartwright realized he had expected him to speak with a Chinese intonation, instead of which Traynor spoke with just the slightest trace of an American southern accent.

"First, there's the money. Second, method of payment. Third, I understand you want me to use my own team and I need to know how many people I'm likely to need. Fourth, is method and then time scale.

So, money. The price is 10 million Euros paid in advance. I'll want the funds in cash. Half in Euros – 500 Euro notes and half in Swiss francs – 1000 franc notes. That way I reckon you can get it all into a duffel bag... "

Featherstonehaugh interrupted him, "There must be a misunderstanding Mr. Traynor. I don't know where you get your figures from but we agreed to pay a total of 5 million pounds, that's about 7 million Euros, to include your whole team, half in advance and half on completion of the job."

Traynor stood up, "Well in that case we've got nothing more to talk about. I've told you the figure and, with a job like this, there's no question of paying half on completion. I'm not staying around to get dickered about on payment or worse. When the job's finished I'm gone."

"Well that's all very well" Featherstonehaugh spoke smoothly, completely unruffled by the other man's attitude, "but, although you come very highly recommended, I don't think, assuming we accept your figure, that you can seriously expect us just to hand over that sort of money to someone we don't know and then hope that you'll complete the job and not just disappear with the cash." He raised his eyebrows enquiringly at Traynor as he finished his sentence.

"Well, I can understand your dilemma. But you've got the admiral and DNB vouching for me and the people who recommended them. I'm afraid payment is not negotiable."

Featherstonehaugh sat back and looked appraisingly at the American. He had complete discretion as to amount and method of payment, but he had anticipated paying on his terms. The two tranche system was fairly standard for hired killers and he had not expected any argument over this. In fact he and C had discussed the payment and had thought that they might get away with a transfer to a Swiss or other bank account and that they would then deal with the team before or at the time of payment of the second half and, with a little luck they would not only be able to avoid paying the second amount but might be able to recover the first part. It was clear from Traynor's attitude that this was not something that was going to wash at all. Featherstonehaugh felt both frustrated and relieved at the same time. Traynor was at least sufficiently professional to minimize any risks he might face from MI6 and would probably be equally professional in his execution of the contract.

He made his decision.

"Just a minute. Please sit down. I am prepared to agree to your terms subject to one condition."

Traynor looked at him warily and raised an eyebrow in query.

"You are going to be in possession of a large amount of our cash. We'll pay you an immediate advance of, say three and a half million Euros. You'll prepare yourself and get your team together. You'll be paid the balance in cash, as you request, just before you get the go. Once we are sure the mission is a go, Mr. White here," he gestured towards Cartwright, "will accompany you throughout the performance of the job. This will be both to safeguard our money and to ensure that implementation is in accordance with the strict requirements that we are going to discuss now. I should perhaps add, that you would, in any event, require quite close liaison with Mr. White because the operation is intel driven and up to date intel will be critical to successful completion."

Traynor had sat down while Featherstonehaugh was talking. He looked steadily at the Englishman for a long time without saying anything. He then looked over at Cartwright. His gaze was so cold and so obviously calculating and assessing that Cartwright felt as if he was being measured for a coffin. The Englishman shuddered imperceptibly.

"Agreed in principle, but I'll want you to make the first payment four million euros. Can you get it to me today?"

"I'm not sure. But if not today, then, early tomorrow."

"Alright. So let's discuss the job. What've you got there?" He indicated the file Featherstonehaugh was holding.

CHAPTER TWELVE

Rome mid-day the same day

"Rather than trying to be too clever and acting indis-criminately it is better deliberately to look foolish and refrain from action" – Ancient Chinese military strategy

I was feeling quite pleased with myself. I was going to get paid 10 million Euros. Standish had told me that the job would pay 10 million dollars but I had changed it to Euros which, at present rates of exchange was about thirty per cent more or about 13 million dollars. I thought I had done very well swinging that one. The very tall, well dressed, smooth Englishman obviously suffered from the sense of superiority that seems to infect nearly all the English I have come across. He had started off talking down to me, but he had not put up much resistance when I had insisted both on 10 million Euros and payment in advance. I would have accepted half of that amount if he had dug in his heels, but I realized, when I made my play, that they would probably be stuck if I walked out on them, because I had little doubt that they had already planned their operation around me. Still, I had taken something of a risk, because I knew half a dozen good people from Eastern Europe who would have taken over the job from me for a lot less than I was demanding and with no questions asked.

I was not too happy about the other man baby-sitting me but, when I agreed to the terms for payment, I had already decided that they would probably want to impose their own man on me and that this "Mr. White" was probably their chosen representative. The man that had been introduced to me as "White" was clearly a British army officer. The way he dressed, the way he held himself, his weathered complexion, spoke louder than words. I assumed that he was an officer in the SAS and that he was capable of handling himself in most situations. In any event, I did not need to worry about him until the job had been completed. They were not going to mount and pay a huge amount for an operation and then go and abort it by getting rid of me too soon.

So I went along with the compromise that was offered to me. I was going to have to give White the slip at some stage so that I could either put the money in a safe deposit box somewhere or get it in to my bank in Liechtenstein. I would deal with that problem too, when the time came, there was no sense in worrying about it now, although I would give it some thought in the meantime. I noticed from the slight bulge under his jacket that Mr. White was armed. There was no need for him to come to this meeting heeled. The fact that he was, told me that he was probably one of those people who are so used to carrying weapons that they feel uncomfortable going about unarmed. This was a useful piece of information for me to file away for a future date. In my experience people who are weapon dependent often hesitate when disarmed, sufficiently to give their opponent a slight edge. When you are fighting for your life a slight edge can mean the difference between life and death.

Once I agreed to his terms the Englishman in charge was all business. He had a file that contained pictures of a number of people. There was the primary target, an arab called Al Khalifa, who was probably in his early forties. Nearly all the arabs I have come across of that sort of age are going to seed and well on their way to their third chin. This Al Khalifa was different. He looked reasonably trim and fit. Then there were some pictures of the woman. There were one or two with both her and Al Khalifa from which it looked like the two of them were at the extreme side of very friendly. The rest of the pictures were of Al Khalifa's father, who was a wealthy businessman and security personnel. Al Khalifa's head of security, Bernard Picard, was apparently a former officer in the DST, the French counter espionage service -Directorate for the Surveillance of the Territory, which operated under the Ministry of the Interior. I learned later that he had become an informant for the DGSE (the French sister spy agency to the CIA and British MI6)providing to them, on a regular basis, information about the Al Khalifas, including details of their movements and the movements of the woman, which DGSE obligingly, immediately passed on to their counterparts in the British security services. The Al Khalifas must have been anglophiles because, apart from a couple of French, all their other security people were British, either ex SAS or former paratroops.

Let me be honest here. A phalanx of bodyguards, or what is now called personal security detail, might be a great status symbol at a swanky restaurant or the Academy awards. They might even be effective at manhandling obnoxious paparazzi, but they are completely useless against someone like me. To be effective against an assassin, PSD's have to be part of an active intelligence organization which not only maintains a completely up to date threat assessment but which also actively seeks out potential threats in order to neutralise them before they can materialize too close to the principal. In other words they have to be part of, or strongly linked with, governmental or quasi-governmental intelligence organizations. Perhaps that was the thinking behind employing ex members of the SAS. But, whatever information such people obtained through their own grapevine, it was never going to be sufficiently good or current to protect against someone like me. So I was not particularly concerned by the bodyguards.

"This is the Al Khalifa's yacht, the Cleopatra. She was the beautiful mistress of Julius Caesar."

He was talking down to me again. I knew all about Cleopatra, I had seen the film with Elizabeth Taylor. While giving me the history lecture, he was showing me some pictures of what must have been the ultimate in personal maritime transport. As he described it, with its flat screen televisions, Jacuzzi, its own speed boats and helipad it sounded like the ultimate seagoing luxury hotel and probably for the first time in my life I began to wonder why I had not been born into a family of billionaires.

"It's approximately 80 metres long with a crew of 35 plus five personal security detail. At the moment they're anchored off Sardinia, although they do a bit of cruising around on odd days. They are scheduled to remain around Sardinia for the next week and then they are going to spend a few days in or off Corsica before heading into Monte Carlo, where they will probably dock for a week or so before she is due to fly back to the UK."

I interrupted him because all this talk about the boat had given me an idea for doing this job without having to share with a full team.

"Before we go any further. If you get me a full schematic of the boat and some plastic explosive we can make the whole thing disappear at sea. End of story, tragic accident, no survivors. There's some deep water out there. Where the Tyrrhenian Sea is, it's well over 3000 metres deep and in the Ligurian Sea, North of Corsica it's nearly 3000 metres deep." I knew that part of the Mediterranean well from when I had been based in Corsica with the 2e REP and I had done a lot of my dive training there. I continued.

"A properly shaped explosive can make a hole big enough so the thing sinks within a few minutes and won't leave any inconvenient debris. I could probably have it all set up to go by the time they set off for Corsica."

"But you'd be killing nearly fifty people. We can't do that." The Englishman looked horrified.

I was puzzled. Personally I do not see the difference between killing one or two innocent people and fifty. It's just a difference of scale.

"The fact that there are so many that die is a factor to make everyone believe it was an accident. Look at your reaction. Who's going to believe we've murdered fifty people in order to target one or two?"

I could see that I was freaking out the two Englishmen. I was surprised that the SAS guy, Mr. White should have reacted in that way. He was a soldier as I had been. He must have been in war zones, like for example Iraq or Afghanistan where hundreds, probably thousands, of innocent people, women, children and babies, were being killed all the time, sometimes for no better reason than that someone who had a minor grudge against someone else reported to the US military that that someone else was a terrorist with a cache of weapons.

The lead Englishman had recovered from his astonishment at my proposal and was talking again.

"Putting aside for a moment the unacceptable level of casualties, there are far too many improbables. How, for example, would you approach the ship undetected when it's at sea? How would you be able to set the explosive and detonate it so that the boat sinks in sufficiently deep water, so that it's never detected? How are you going to prevent some salvage team searching out the wreck, possibly locating it and then either through divers, a camera equipped deep sea submersible or an autonomous underwater vehicle, finding out that there is a bloody great hole in the hull caused by an explosion. How could you ensure that there were no survivors and no survivor was picked up by another vessel? The Med is crowded at this time of the year."

He paused shaking his head, "And then God knows what photographic satellite reconnaissance might pick up and record. It would be perfectly feasible for the whole explosion to be filmed and the next thing you know we'd have pictures of the whole thing circulating on the internet. No. No way. We've got to have this handled with the utmost care, so that the whole world can have no doubt that it was an accident."

He had been looking at me the whole time to see my reaction. It was true that there would be logistical difficulties in getting out to the yacht and laying the explosive charge, particularly if the yacht was equipped with an underwater surveillance system. But that could probably be resolved. I was not convinced about the satellite problem though. I had in the past arranged a few "accidents" with boats and they had all worked out very well. In fact boats had become something of a specialty of mine for arranging sudden disappearances of people who owned, or habitually went out on boats. Of course I had no experience of such a big boat. My previous efforts had involved boats of 40 to 60 feet, no more than a quarter the size of the Al Khalifa's yacht.

Mr. White decided that he had something to contribute.

"Even if, in theory, you could blow this boat up in such a way that it sank immediately, with the explosion restricted entirely to below the waterline, so that it would not be picked up by satellite, in order to get it right you'd have to practice on something of a similar size and construction. That could never be done in the time period we're talking about. Assuming we could even find a similar type of boat, I'd reckon you'd need a minimum of one month's preparation probably longer, to get it just right. There's quite simply not the time to do what you suggest properly."

I looked at him nodding. He had a point. The first time I had done a boat it had taken me nearly five weeks of full time effort to get it all worked out. Just getting hold of similar boats to practice on had taken nearly two weeks and then arranging the practice efforts, in a clandestine location, had been a logistics nightmare and, at that time, I had had the full co-operation both of Delta and the Seals.

The two of them were obviously firmly against my proposal so there was little point in pushing it, even if I thought I could resolve all the logistics. I reluctantly expressed my agreement, "Yeh. You're right. It's impractical within the time constraints. So how is it that you want this handled?"

"Simple, straightforward. A motor accident. We provoke their driver into travelling at high speed and then cause them to crash."

I was curious. They obviously had something very specific in mind. In my experience car crashes were all very well but were a bit of an unknown quantity. I had quite a lot of experience with cars and it was amazing how crashes very rarely turned out the way you expected. For example, if you are following a car you can make it spin around in a fairly predictable way at certain moderate speeds. But go beyond those speeds and things start to happen very quickly and with a lack of predictability that increases in direct ratio to the speed. It would not be that complicated to come up behind them on a mountain road and give them a nudge off at a sharp bend. But again I would have to make sure I knew the road and be certain that they would be in the right spot at the right time. Of course if they were thinking of a car with an electronic not a mechanical accelerator, it was possible to fit a device electronically to control the accelerator, so that the car could be made to accelerate at a dangerous location without the driver being able to control it. Not difficult to do if you had sufficient access to the vehicle but, again, the result could not always be certain.

"What are you thinking of? Fitting something to control the accelerator and make them accelerate when they would normally be braking?"

"No. Absolutely not." The emphatic response came from the senior Brit, "There's to be absolutely no tampering with the car. It's likely to be taken apart after the event by crash investigators over whom we have no control and we do not want them finding anything suspicious."

"Well, in that case, in my experience there's no such thing as a simple straightforward, high speed accident. I'm not saying it's impossible, but you have to ensure the target vehicle is on the road you have planned the incident and that there's no one else around to prevent your manoeuvre. It's doable. But it has also got its risks."

"We have a way to minimise the risks." White decided to give me the advantage of his expertise.

I looked at him, "OK. Go on. Tell me."

White looked at the other Englishman, who nodded almost imperceptibly.

"You were in the American special forces, so you must be cognisant with laser dazzling weapons."

I smiled. I did indeed know of those weapons. In Delta we had used them in various situations. One type, in the general category of such weapons is the flash bang grenade. First developed by the SAS, it combines a dazzling flash with loud noise to disorient the opposition in a restricted space. The flash bang is a basic operational weapon for taking down buildings or aircraft in a terrorist hostage situation. Different types of laser based Dazzler were used in general combat situations both as an anti-personnel weapon and as a means of disabling laser targeting systems. However, as I recalled there had been a number of attempts to ban their use because they could blind people. The various international rules about use of different types of weapons have always amused me. Under international law it is permissible to kill enemy forces in any number of ways, although certain weapons and munitions are banned. I've always found the rules completely incomprehensible. To me killing has always been killing and should be done in the quickest, most efficient way possible, with whatever weapon happens to be available. Whilst war might be a continuation of diplomacy by other means, in my experience it always involves killing and maiming as many of the opposing forces as you can. I could never understand the incongruity of trying to regulate methods of killing and maiming.

They were waiting for my response, "Yeh I know all about that and the use of green spectrum laser dazzling devices. If I remember rightly the Chinese produced a laser dazzling device that they attached to their main battle tank in the 1980s which had a range of up to about 10 klicks."

Mr. White nodded his agreement with me.

I continued, "As I recall there's some international convention that made those types of weapons illegal, isn't there."

"There is an international protocol on dazzler weapons" answered the taller Englishman, "but your country does not regard itself as bound by that and, I don't know if you know, but similar devices were used effectively both in Iraq and Afghanistan. Indeed, our navy used a dazzling laser against enemy pilots during the Falklands war, as far back as 1982."

"Yeh, I remember" I said " so I take it that you're going to provide me with one these dazzlers, so that when the target's car is driving along at 100 plus miles per hour I operate the dazzler from some convenient spot and the driver is instantly blinded, disoriented, and drives off the road."

Apart from equipment we had used in Delta, I had never in my civilian career used the sort of weapon they were talking about. I thought it was a good idea but I could see all sorts of drawbacks. If you operated the device from a static location you'd have to be very precise about where you used it and it would require a sniper's skill (which fortunately I possessed) to fire it at just the right time. But one would need to control the road, ensure that no one else was around to be affected by it. Finally you had to ensure that the target was travelling fast enough so that mere braking, if he happened to react in that way, would not help him, he'd go off the road whatever he did. I knew from experience that it would be difficult to control all the variables in order to be 100 per cent certain of the result.

I shared some of my thoughts with the Englishmen.

"It could be a good idea. But in order to work there are a lot of variables to control. First we have to ensure the target is travelling fast enough so that nothing he does is going to prevent him crashing. That also applies to the location. The attack will have to be timed to perfection on a stretch of road where the slightest error can be disastrous for a driver. That's quite a lot of different variables to get right. I'll have to look at using the device both from a static and moving location. My instinct tells me though we are probably going to have to act from a moving platform, car or motorbike."

The Englishman, whom I had come to think of as the boss in the short time since I had met the two, nodded his head vehemently.

"That's what we think too. A static location is probably not going to work."

I wondered how big and unwieldy the device they were going to give me was

"How big is this dazzler thing? Is it easy to carry around and operate? Is it going to work if it's raining or misty?"

Boss man could not hide his pride in his country's technological achievements, "We've developed a device rather like one produced in your country called the Glare Mout. The Glare Mout has an effective range up to 2 kilometres. The device we've developed is specifically for much closer operation, maximum 100 metres, but its been miniaturised. It's about the same size as a reflex camera, so it's easily transported and equally easily operated. It can be used in rain although, depending on the intensity, its light might become diffused. It's waterproof down to about 20 metres. It will cause temporary blindness in whoever it's directed towards, but will leave no trace on the retina. There's no burning or any other physical damage, even from close up."

I was curious to see this device of theirs.

"Have you got this device with you? Can I see it? I'll need to test it to make sure it works before I base the whole operation around it."

The boss man suddenly became more cagy. They were not giving me any of their little toys until they absolutely had to,

"Oh, you can take my word for it. It works alright. You won't need to test it other than to check that it's operating properly. It's rather heavy on batteries, so you'll have to carry a few spares. We haven't got it with us. Mr. White will be in charge of it and will lend it to you to enable you to familiarise yourself with it just before it's going to be used."

I could not restrain myself from commenting that their obvious lack of trust in me, both in respect of their money and their device, was touching. Surprisingly my comment elicited a laugh and seemed to make them both relax. I suppose it rather highlighted the cultural differences between Americans and Brits. If I had said the same thing to one of my superiors in the army or the CIA I would have been reprimanded for impertinence. The Englishman continued.

"I want to add this. We've considered our time scale, the movements of the target and the requirements of the operation. Based on all those, we consider that the optimum location is going to be Monte Carlo. We're not yet sure whether or not they will be staying on their boat when they get there or if they'll stay in a hotel. But it is almost certain that whilst based in Monte Carlo they will travel to Cannes or Antibes, where they both have friends. So you should be planning to do this between Monte Carlo and say, Cannes. Probably nearer Monte Carlo because the road is less crowded up there. There's a lot of traffic all the time around Cannes and Nice which would probably rule out anything there."

I had to agree with him. He did not know I owned a little bolt hole up above Cannes that had once been the secret hideaway of one my targets. The target had purchased the house in the name of a Panamanian Corporation. He had no idea that I had discovered the location of the house and he had felt secure enough to stay there alone without any bodyguards. After completing my business with him, I had taken the time to go through his house and had found all the property documentation that showed the house was unencumbered by any mortgages and that the title was registered in the name of the corporation. Conveniently, the corporate documentation was also there, including a book of bearer shares that bestowed ownership of the corporation on whoever possessed the shares. It was as easy as writing to the lawyers in Panama who administered the company, to tell them that I was now the owner. That house turned out to be one of the better bonuses I had picked up in the course of my work and all it cost me was the annual fees for maintaining the corporation.

Anyway the point is that, although I was not saying anything, I knew that part of the South of France very well. Boss Englishman was right. There was no practical way of carrying out the operation around Cannes or Nice. If the targets used the Autoroute, as they probably would, the ideal spot would be after Nice, heading up towards the Italian border and just before the exit for Monaco, or alternatively driving to or from Monaco. I recalled that there were some tunnels in and around Monte Carlo, including a long tunnel shortly after one came in off the highway. A tunnel would be ideal. There was little space for a target to manoeuvre and we could use people at either end to prevent or impede access to any civilians.

In my business it never does to reveal too much to those who contract your services, so I simply said, "I'll get up there as soon as I can; drive around, survey all the routes to and from Monte Carlo and see where might be the best place."

Both Englishmen nodded their agreement.

"There are some things I'm going to need that it'll be better if you provide."

"We can provide most things within reason. What is it that you will require?" The answer came out smoothly without any hesitation.

"First I'll need, regular, reliable intel about the targets' movements. How big a group they travel in? How many cars? If they travel in convoy, where in any convoy the targets will be located? How many bodyguards they have in the car with them? The woman is a media magnet. I'll need to know whether they are going to be constantly under the eye of the media and whether or not they get followed around all the time by paparazzi. In other words all the variables that are going to affect how I need to approach the target and execute the operation."

"We understand all your requirements for precise intel. Up to date intel will be provided on an on-going basis. Mr. White will liaise with you over that." He picked up his briefcase and once again delved into its inner recesses to produce another buff coloured envelope.

"In there you'll find a lot of the additional general details you've mentioned. Travelling habits etcetera etcetera."

I nodded. These guys were as professional as I would have expected from my experience with the SAS so many years ago.

"I'll also need, immediately, a couple of decent handguns and plenty of ammunition. One of the guns should be able to be fitted with a noise suppressor. My preference would be for a Heckler & Koch USP Tactical, not the 9mm, the .45 with silencer please. I'll also need a car. Something fast, but not overly conspicuous. A top of the line Audi A6 or S6 would do, preferably without any of the go faster badges. Oh and a secure, untraceable mobile phone, for communicating with you."

For all their obvious professionalism they could not prevent themselves from exchanging a quick glance. I could almost read their thoughts. They were first wondering why I was asking for handguns for a job that was unlikely to require the use of firearms. They were also wondering why I was being so obliging as to give them the means to know my location at all times. I could see that they were a little puzzled that I was being so accommodating and I wondered whether I had over played my hand a little and was trying to act too much the naïve simpleton. I was not going to explain that, in relation to the firearms, I liked to have a weapon available in case of some unforeseen necessity and thought, in any event I would take advantage of my position in order to acquire a couple of decent handguns that might otherwise cost me an arm and a leg on the black market. With regard to the telephone I thought I had perhaps better kill their doubts. I gave them my most innocent face,

"Do you think you'll be able to arrange that at short notice? Normally I wouldn't want one of your phones, for obvious reasons, but as you're foisting Mr. White on me I'll need to be able to talk to him because, however close he would like to stay to me, I've no intention of sleeping and showering with him."

I avoided any explanations about the car, it was a fairly standard request and I could see that my other comment had allayed any doubts I might have caused. The boss simply said

"I should be able to get what you want. Because we've got such a tight timetable I'll try to arrange it all for tomorrow evening."

That suited me fine. It would give them time to fix up the car with GPS tracking devices and possibly microphones but I hoped that they would not have time to do anything too elaborate, like installing a live video feed.

The taller man, who had still not introduced himself, stood up, followed by Mr. White.

"I don't think there's anything more we need to discuss right now. I suggest we meet again here, tomorrow at... what do you think Mr. White, 1700?"

White nodded his acquiescence and his companion turned to me with a quizzical look,

I also stood up. "Fine. See you tomorrow. Oh, one other thing."

"Yes."

"I believe you had some people on my tail last night." I held up my hand to stop the protest of innocence that I could see forming on his lips.

"I need you to remove them. I have things to arrange. Confidential things. I don't want to have to waste time losing your watchers, or even perhaps", I looked him full in the face with the hard threatening expression I had developed over the years,

"taking them out of circulation."

I could see that my point had gone home. He nodded.

"I'll look into it."

I did not trust him to remove the watchers, but he might. At worst he would ensure that they were more discrete, which meant that they would have to keep their distance and would therefore be easier to lose. In the last resort he would not be able to complain if I decided to leave the three of them lying asleep in a doorway.

I walked out of the suite with them. The admiral was not around, but the pockmarked bodyguard was sitting just outside the door. He told me that the admiral was out and would not be returning until an indefinite later. Now that it looked as if the job was a go I needed to speak to Jacques to organise everything required for the job. Whilst talking to the Englishmen I had formulated in my mind an outline strategy and started to consider what was required. I knew the approximate location of the hit and I had already half decided to use one of the tunnels in Monte Carlo. Of course this was all subject to the targets behaving as the Englishmen were predicting. There were a considerable number of unknown factors, but I knew enough to be able to carry out some provisional planning. I would probably need two men to follow the targets from their point of departure and possibly to run interference on any additional cars in a convoy or any following media. If I completed the job in a tunnel I would need, in addition, at least two men at each end of the tunnel to slow down or block any traffic for the time I needed to carry out my task. That would be six bodies and at least three, possibly five cars. I might need the people at the ends of the tunnel to masquerade as police. If so we would need uniforms and the strobe lights the police use. Possibly even painted up cars.

One very positive advantage in carrying this out in the first tunnel into Monaco was that, in an area where both French and Monegasque police might operate, we could take advantage of potential confusion between the different police forces. I needed to spend some time by myself to study the contents of the envelopes I had been given and to try and prepare my strategy and decide exactly what resources I would need. I also had to formulate some preliminary ideas about how I was going to evade Mr. White, particularly after the job was concluded.

CHAPTER THIRTEEN

Rome 1400

"Ask not what you can do for your country.
Ask what's for lunch." (Orson Welles)

Featherstonehaugh and Cartwright left the meeting with Traynor and walked out of the hotel. The first thing Featherstonehaugh did as they started to walk towards the Via Veneto, was to take out his encrypted mobile telephone and dial the number of the MI6 head of station in Rome.

He did not waste time on preliminaries.

"David,Fanshaw here."

"Yes sir. Welcome to Rome."

Featherstonehaugh ignored the greeting.

"First thing. The person you put the watchers on for me yesterday, turns out he's not the European end of the drug cartel we thought he was. He's someone quite different, so you can take the watchers off tout de suite, although I'd still like to see a copy of their report before I leave Rome.

Then I'm going to need a couple of rooms at a decent hotel overnight tonight if you could please fix that up asap. Our bags are with the concierge at the Eden Hotel, so perhaps you could get one of your people to pick them up and drop them off wherever we are going to stay.

Next, I'm going to need a car tomorrow. We'll probably need it for a week or ten days. Something reasonably anonymous looking preferably not registered to us or the embassy." He paused,

"Probably something in the Audi A6 category. You know, something that'll move but not draw too much attention."

"We've got an Alfa V6 that'll fit the bill. It's fast and blends pretty well here and it's off the books."

"An Alfa? Bit flash isn't it? I think we need something a bit more low key."

"No, no. The Alfa will blend in fine. There are a lot of them on the road here it won't stand out at all."

"Hmmm." Featherstonehaugh was not convinced. "Still, I do think that something like an Audi A6 would be more suitable. Don't you have anything like that on your books?"

"Well, we've got an S6 without any badges, but I'm not sure it's available." the head of station made little effort to conceal his reluctance to part with the car.

"That'll do fine. Make sure it's available for tomorrow afternoon. Also I need you to ensure it's equipped with a GPS locator, so we know where it is at all times. If you've got the time I'd also like you to fix it up with a microphone and concealed video feed."

"I'm not sure we can do all that if you need it by tomorrow afternoon." The resident officer was still unable to keep out of his voice the resentment he felt over having to give up what was apparently a vehicle over which he had some proprietary feelings.

"Well, just do the best you can. The GPS though is essential." Featherstonehaugh's brusque, authoritative tone curtailed all further inclinations to rebellion from the MI6 resident.

"Then finally, I'll need an anonymous cell phone and a couple of hand guns. If you've got a .45 HK USP Expert fitted with a suppressor that'll be perfect and perhaps you'd better make the other one an HK compact, if you've got one, or a SIG or Glock."

The MI6 Rome resident had heard enough to feel that he was justified in interrupting the Deputy Director of his agency.

"With all due respect, sir, it sounds as if you're running some sort of operation. I'm sure you're aware, sir, that the SOP is for all operations in my domain to go through me. I'd like to point out that I've heard nothing at all from London asking me to mount an operation here. You must realise we've got to be extremely careful not to step on any toes. We co-operate very closely with the locals here and they are not going to take too kindly to some off the books operation taking place."

Featherstonehaugh was starting to become impatient with the local officer. Neither he nor C were used to subordinates arguing with them.

"I'm afraid you're forgetting yourself David. This is a matter that's above your pay grade. You needn't worry about the locals. I'm in direct liaison with Marcello Di Stefano over this and he's personally handling the local side of things. All you are required to do is provide me with any logistical back up I need. Is that clear?"

The voice at the other end of the telephone sounded suitably chastened, "Yes sir. Absolutely. I'll get on to your requirements immediately."

"Thank you David, I'm very much obliged. I'll call you in fifteen minutes for the details of the hotel. I'd also be grateful if you'd call Di Stefano for me – do you have his private number? You do, fine – would you tell him, please, that we are staying the night. Tell him where we are staying and that we'd be delighted to accept his invitation and I'll call him later."

Featherstonehaugh turned to Cartwright, "Let's have a spot of lunch shall we Frank? One of my favourite restaurants is just around the corner and I'm absolutely famished. You must be too, neither of us has had anything since that snack on the plane over."

The restaurant turned out to be Harry's Bar, at the end of the Via Veneto. Featherstonehaugh was immediately recognised and greeted effusively by the staff, with an excess of enthusiastic hand shaking. When they were finally seated at a quiet corner table and had ordered, Featherstonehaugh turned to Cartwright.

"Well we've got quite a few things to sort out. Before we discuss those and hand over all that money I'd like to have your opinion of this Traynor fellow."

Cartwright leaned forward in his chair, placed his elbows on the table with his hands together before resting his chin on his fingertips.

"Well, from the way in which he immediately wanted to blow up their boat, irrespective of how many died, we can certainly say he seems to be lacking in any humanitarian instincts."

Featherstonehaugh smiled as Cartwright continued,

"From the file I read, he's clearly very competent and, meeting him, has given me no cause to change that opinion. He seems to be on top of the technical side of things. I must say, though, he certainly doesn't look as if he's been in the business for over thirty years. He's got that really fit look about him but I don't think I would ever have put him at over forty. Neither do I think he's someone to be under estimated. He seems to know exactly what he's talking about and I'm sure he's already had enough from us to know what he needs by way of a team and other logistics. I'm a little puzzled about his taking a car and a cell phone from us. In his place I'd want to make my own arrangements. If he trusted us, he wouldn't have insisted on being paid everything up front, would he? So there must be some reason that he's allowing us to give him the means to keep tabs on him."

Featherstonehaugh was nodding his agreement, "Yes. I don't quite get the request for a car and phone. My guess would be that he's intending to use them to decoy us. I hope we can get the video feed installed, then we'll be able to know. In the last resort it doesn't really matter, because we don't have to know where he is at all times before the job is done, we need to have him tracked afterwards and at that point you'll be with him, so it'll just be a matter of keeping the coms open between us."

They both fell silent as the waiter approached and laid a pasta course in front of them. Cartwright had ordered a standard penne arrabiata whilst Featherstonehaugh, who was more adventurous, had chosen tagliolini with truffles and porcini mushrooms, although neither of those delicacies was really in season. As Featherstonehaugh commenced expertly to wind his pasta around his fork and Cartwright impaled the penne with his, the MI6 man continued voicing his thoughts aloud.

"If we give Traynor his four million Euros tomorrow, it will enable him to set up his team and get together all the equipment he needs. He's obviously going to need to acquire another couple of vehicles. He's going to have a lot to do. As things stand at the moment, we've actually got a window of nearly three weeks to do this job, but we'll get this Traynor ramped up to be ready next week. The sooner we give him the rest of the money, the sooner you become part of his team. So we'll arrange to pay him on a timetable that'll enable you to have at least a week to look him and his people over and decide the best way to handle them after they've finished the job. You'll also, in that time, be able to get yourself embedded in the job, so that you can ensure that everything goes smoothly and there is no suggestion of the thing being anything but an accident."

"That sounds alright." Cartwright had finished his pasta and was scooping up the remains of the sauce with his fork.

"This is really delicious."

Featherstonehaugh looked pleased that Cartwright seemed to appreciate his choice of restaurant,

"Yes, it is rather good isn't it?" He looked at his watch, "I'd better phone the resident back and find out where we're staying. Then I'll have to speak to C and get him to arrange to have the money with us by tomorrow, when we hand over the car and other things." As he was speaking he pulled out his phone and pressed the redial key.

They were booked into the Excelsior Hotel, a short distance across the road from where they were eating. Cartwright had no idea what any of the hotels in Rome were like, but the choice seemed to please Featherstonehaugh.

They continued discussing the operation for a little longer before Featherstonehaugh changed the subject and started to give a short lecture about Rome. The deputy head of MI6 had at one time taught classics at Balliol College Oxford and he lapsed easily and fluently into a short history of the Roman Empire that Cartwright, rather to his surprise, found extremely interesting and informative.

After finishing lunch and a very good bottle of red wine from the small Tuscan specialist producer of Castello dei Rampolla, Featherstonehaugh led his companion across the Via Veneto to the Excelsior Hotel, which Cartwright found rather grand and slightly intimidating. Unlike many British army officers he was not independently wealthy and survived on his army pay, which did not allow him to indulge in frequent stays in luxury hotels. In fact, the only occasions when he had enjoyed the best of accommodation available to travellers was when his expenses were being met by his government, a government noted more for stinting than for cosseting its armed forces.

They had hardly arrived at the Excelsior before Featherstonehaugh received a telephone call from Di Stefano. The Italian security chief was intent on firming up his dinner invitation. He arranged to collect them at 9.15pm, which Cartwright thought was rather late, but was a time Featherstonehaugh accepted without demur. Before they went to their respective rooms Featherstonehaugh explained to the soldier that Italians were in the habit of dining late and that the time given by Di Stefano probably represented a slight concession to English sensibilities. He also suggested to Cartwright they could meet for a pre-dinner drink at 8pm, which would give the SAS man three or four hours to wander around Rome on his own, a suggestion Cartwright was pleased to adopt.

CHAPTER FOURTEEN
ROME Same day 1700 hours

"Pacifying the tiger and leading it from the mountain means enticing your enemy by scattering bait he is liable to take and thus showing him the opening where you wish him to strike." (Ancient Chinese military strategy)

After my meeting with the Brits I went back to my room, in order carefully to go through the contents of the envelopes they had given me. There was a lot of information to assimilate but after nearly two hours or so I was able to formulate an outline action plan. I spent approximately another hour working out different permutations for completing the job and what I might need. When I was satisfied with my provisional plan, I set the room safe and locked my notes into it. My current reading of the situation was that Standish, rather than wanting to know what I was doing, would positively prefer complete ignorance, so I had no further concern that my room might become a target of surreptitious enquiry. I still had no intention of calling Jacques from the room, nor of doing anything else from there that might at some future date provide a link between me and the activity for which I was being engaged, but I felt considerably more relaxed about any sort of surveillance on me.

I was stiff after sitting working at the desk for the past two hours and I started to do a few stretches. I then decided that I did not need to rush out and would exercise for a while. I started with push ups and sit ups and continued on from there. I then finished off with a couple of sets of ninjutsu katas that I adapted to include some Dim Mak techniques. Even with the air conditioning blasting away, after over an hour of practice I was sweating profusely by the time I finished and I decided to shower before going out to call Jacques. Coming out of the shower and towelling myself off, I looked at myself in the mirror. Some people might regard me as being a little narcissistic but I did not think I looked bad for someone of my age. My body had not really changed for the past thirty years. I still had the same musculature, without any trace of fat, although if I was honest with myself constant exercise was becoming increasingly burdensome and difficult for me. I had noticed that even that Brit, Mr. White or whatever his real name was, had the slightest beginnings of a spare tyre around his middle. Still I felt good and charged with energy as I dressed.

Before leaving the room I called Standish's suite on the internal phone. His secretary told me that he was not available and that, unless there was something particular, it would be unlikely that we would need to meet again before my departure. I was also told that the suite had been made available at 5pm the following after-noon, for a further meeting with the two gentlemen I had met that day. I was not bothered. I did not need to see Standish again. Once I had collected all that lovely money from the Brits, I would get the job done and disappear. No more having to be polite to people like the admiral. I was quite looking forward to that.

I went down to the lobby, exchanged a couple of words with the concierge and told him that I would like him to hold my bag for another day or so, before put-ting myself back on the streets of Rome.

The Brits seemed to have indulged me. There was no sign of the previous night's trio, nor of anyone else taking too much interest in me. Still, there was no point in being careless and I spent nearly an hour walking, apparently aimlessly, but in fact taking evasive action, in case I was being followed. Finally I went into a pleas-ant looking Trattoria and sat down at a table. They had just opened and I was their first customer. I ordered a bottle of red wine and a large bottle of mineral water and asked if I could use their payphone before order-ing my meal. The phone was in the basement near the toilets and as there was no one around I had complete privacy.

Jacques answered almost immediately. I gave him the number of the telephone and he said he would call me back in about ten minutes. In fact I only had to wait about six minutes. I did not have to ask him if we were secure.

"Lucky I was out across the other side of town, so I didn't have to travel far to find an anonymous phone."

I grunted. I took it for granted that he would not have called me back until he was certain we could talk freely. That is the way it is with the very few guys you know you can trust.

"I'm going to need someone reliable to meet me tomorrow night, at the place we discussed. He'll need to be around my height and build and wearing... " I thought for a second deciding what I would wear tomorrow, "pale beige slacks and a short sleeved blue Polo shirt. I'll need to change cars with him and he'll have to take mine on a trip. He should reckon on being away about a week. I'll tell him what to do and give him enough money when we meet. We'll need to meet inside – I think there's a restaurant there isn't there?"

"Yes. Is it going to be safe? I'm thinking of sending my son. He's a good boy. Very reliable. Not stupid. He's a bit taller than you and doesn't look Chinese, but he'll pass in the dark. But if it's... ".

"Your boy'll be fine. I just need to spend some quiet time on my own, preparing. I need a little misdirection and he can learn what it's like to have an expense account."

Jacques chuckled. "Don't give him too free a rein."

"We'll discuss the other stuff when we meet, but I'm thinking we'll need another half a dozen guys or so depending whether you're too old to give me a hand."

A snort came down the line. "If I'm too old, then so are you."

"Don't think that thought hasn't crossed my mind."

"Anyway I've got six possibles who are all available."

"Good. I'll see you after I've sent the kid on his way. What car is he going to be driving? I'll meet him inside the restaurant but I'll need to transfer my bags into his car immediately I get there, so no one following me will see me carrying out the change-over."

The answer came back immediately, "He'll be in a silver Alfa 159 Sportwagon, with Florence plates including the numbers 7 and 3."

"Fine, tell him to leave it unlocked and to leave the key on the left front tyre."

"OK. See you tomorrow. The car's got a navigation system. I'll set it for my address so you don't get lost and I'll change the language to English for you. I know your Italian is horrible."

"I can't speak to you for two minutes without you insulting me, can I?"

A chuckle came down the telephone line.

I put down the phone thoughtfully. It looked like phase one was coming together. As long as the Brits came up with the money tomorrow.

I went back upstairs. The restaurant was still almost empty, apart from a couple, probably in their thirties and obviously American, who were already well into a plate of mixed ante pasta.

I had hardly sat down before the waiter came over to take my order. He was short, very slightly plump, probably in his mid-forties with a permanently worried expression on his face.

He made some suggestions, but I decided to have a simple plate of spaghetti with oil, garlic and chilli peppers, with a rucola and tomato salad followed by some roast lamb Roman style.

It turned out that chance had brought me to an excellent restaurant where everything, including the wine was delicious. Around 8.30 pm the restaurant started to fill up mostly with Italians and the quiet gave way to a boisterous buzz of conversation. There was still no sign of last night's shadows, nor anyone else looking like their replacements. It really did seem as if the Brit had been as good as his word, at least for the time being.

It was around 9.30pm by the time I left the restaurant. The walk back to the hotel took me nearly half an hour, which was quite welcome, because it gave me time to digest my meal and enabled me again to check whether I was free of ticks. Again I saw no sign of anyone following me.

A message was waiting for me at the hotel. Standish must have given the Brits the name under which I was registered. I did not much care. There were two uses to which I was going to put the identity documents Standish had given me. I would hide the passport and driving licence in the car the Brits were going to give me, in case I needed them in the course of the operation. For the time being though I had no intention of using them. The credit cards were going to Jacques' son, with instructions to enjoy himself for a week. I knew that Standish was smart, very smart, but I wondered why he had gone to the trouble of preparing a false identity for me. Did he seriously think that I was going to use it to allow him to track me on an unsanctioned operation?

But I suppose that is the difference between operatives who work in the field and bureaucrats. No one experienced in field work would have gone to the trouble of providing me with the means to operate a little disinformation by my giving the credit cards to someone who was not going to be anywhere near me. It was the same with the car the Brits were going to provide; just another convenience to allow me to throw them off my track while I made my preparations.

The message simply confirmed our meeting for the following day at 1600 rather than 1700 and that all the documentation I had requested would be available by then for my inspection.

I went to bed partially satisfied with the knowledge that, within a couple of weeks, if everything went as planned, I would be able to enjoy a comfortable retirement, although a slight nagging uneasiness made me unable to sleep. I lay there physically relaxed, concentrating on trying to focus on what was worrying me. After a few moments a mental picture formed of the two Englishmen. The very tall, thin one, assumed the shape of a snake in my imagination, whilst the other one, Mr. White, remained as he was when I had left them, broad shouldered, upright, strong and with a cold look in his eye. I wondered then whether I was going to have to kill him too. As that thought crossed my mind I pictured him facing me, his right hand moving to draw the pistol that I had been sure he was carrying and, as he moved, I drew my own gun and fired twice, seeing the two round holes appear just above his suddenly sightless eyes. Throughout my whole career, the one thing I had never lacked was confidence that I was going to prevail in any form of combat. The half dream that I now experienced on the cusp of sleep, dented my usual assurance, tainting it with a slight uncertainty.

CHAPTER FIFTEEN
Rome the following day

"One of the very nicest things about life is the way we must regularly stop whatever it is we are doing and devote our attention to eating". Luciano Pavarotti and William Wright, Pavarotti, My Own Story

Featherstonehaugh was up early notwithstanding the late night he and Frank Cartwright had had with Di Stefano. The Italian had taken them for a superb meal of several courses, at which they had consumed a number of different bottles of wine. Di Stefano made it clear when he collected them from their hotel that work was taboo that evening. The evening was dedicated to a leisurely, relaxed meal between friends. Even Cartwright, who was initially stiff and formal, relaxed as the evening wore on and imbibed his fair share of the free flowing wine.

Featherstonehaugh had spent the afternoon before that memorable meal in his room, speaking to C on the encrypted telephone he carried. They had discussed the initial payment to be made to Traynor the following day. C was initially aghast that his deputy had agreed to pay Traynor so much. He was certain that Traynor would have accepted a lot less, but Featherstonehaugh made a strong case for not wanting to scare off the assassin. They had no time to rewrite the operation and the whole plan now revolved around Traynor. C reluctantly accepted the opinion of Featherstonehaugh, who was, after all, the man on the spot. Once this hurdle had been passed C had made another suggestion.

"We can of course pay the man in funny money. We can get our hands on some very good stuff that'll deceive almost anyone. Then it won't actually cost us a penny."

"With the utmost respect sir, I don't think that would be very wise at this stage. Perhaps we'll think about it again for the second stage payment, but for now he's going to be getting together a team who he's obviously going to have to pay something. The payments are undoubtedly going to come out of what we give him and it's a certainty that he's not just going to walk around with the rest of it. He'll be getting it into some bank. The best we could hope for is that he'll put it into a safe deposit box. But we've got to anticipate that the other people he's going to pay and people at one or more banks are going to be examining the money. It only needs one of them to raise the alarm of forged money and that'll be the end of our operation and probably a hit on an unsuspecting Cartwright when he meets Traynor in a week or so. We can't possibly risk that sort of disaster at this stage. If we aren't prepared to pay the money, we ought to call off the whole thing now. It's not as if we can't keep tabs on him. He's going to be using a vehicle we provide and can track and where's he going to go with a couple of million in cash? Either it goes into a safe deposit or a bank. He can't put it into a bank in Italy and, unless he's got some long established banking relationship in Switzerland, no Swiss bank will take in that sort of money in cash. In the time he's got that only leaves Liechtenstein. I'd be prepared to bet that, at some time before the next payment, he's going to be heading for Liechtenstein."

"Yes. Yes. No. You're absolutely right. I'm just being too much of the tight fisted civil servant I suppose. We'll just have to see what we can find out about where he puts it and what we can do about getting the money back, after the whole thing's over."

"I think that's the wisest course sir."

"When have you got to pay him?"

"Well, I told him we'll make the initial payment some time tomorrow, latish afternoon."

C sighed, "Alright. I'll send a courier over with the cash tomorrow. It should be with you by early afternoon. If you're going to keep an eye on him from now on you'll need a fair sized team. I'll send a few good chaps over with the courier, to boost your team over there."

"That's another thing, sir. The people over here can only be used in support."

"Why's that?"

"Well, you know we put them on him when we knew he was going to be meeting with Standish."

"Yes. So?"

"Well I'm afraid, sir that he made them immediately; gave them the slip and then told me to keep them off him or he might decide to put them out of action."

"Really." C sounded reflective, "he must be a lot better than I thought he'd be. He doesn't sound like the common or garden thug that I'd imagined."

"Oh no. I don't think he's that at all sir. Very far from it. He's older, as you know, but he looks very, very fit and I would say that he's definitely not to be underestimated. The speed with which he flushed and slipped our team here is, I would say, indicative of the level of his tradecraft. From the point of view of the operation I'm very satisfied with what I've seen of him. Post operation though, I think we're going to have to be very careful. I'd be surprised if he didn't prove more difficult to remove than we might be anticipating."

"Hmmph." C did not sound convinced, "we'll worry about that then. I think we've got sufficient resources for most eventualities."

Featherstonehaugh did not respond. He knew that his organisation was extremely efficient, thoroughly ruthless and more than capable of holding its own with the best in the murky world of international intrigue, but this Traynor fellow made him feel slightly uneasy. He was simultaneously both typical of the operatives Featherstonehaugh frequently came into contact with and completely atypical. First he was completely calm. One of the initial thoughts that had flashed through Featherstonehaugh's mind at their preliminary meeting had been "immobile as a statue". Traynor had betrayed nothing; had no little nervous characteristics; did not fidget and did not seem to display any of the micro-expressions that Featherstonehaugh had been taught to recognise; and when he moved he exuded a sort of quiet, deadly confidence that Featherstonehaugh had rarely seen before. All in all, he made the MI6 number two very uneasy.

The following morning, Featherstonehaugh was enjoying a leisurely breakfast by himself, when the rather attractive dark haired waitress with a seductive smile walked over to his table, holding a portable telephone.

"You are Signor Funcho." She made him sound Chinese, but he found it rather charming. He smiled at her winningly as he acknowledged his name.

"A call for you sir."

The voice of the Rome Head of Station grated on his nerves. The man was still unable to conceal the resentment in his voice at having his routine and resources totally usurped by the interlopers from London.

"Just to tell you, I've received a flash. A courier's due to arrive around midday. I'll arrange a car to collect him."

Featherstonehaugh gave his response in the same clipped tones used by the caller.

"You'll need at least two cars, possibly three, or a minibus, if you've got one. There'll be a few people to collect. And we'll probably need some more accommodation. Needn't be anything fancy."

The silence at the other end of the phone spoke louder than any words. Featherstonehaugh was beginning to wonder whether he had been cut off when the telephone crackled into life again.

"Very well. Is that all sir?"

"I don't want anyone taken to the embassy. Bring them directly here please."

"Very good sir."

He had just returned the telephone to the waitress and engaged in some suggestive banter with her, which managed to eradicate his annoyance at the clear hostility manifested by the resident officer, when Cartwright appeared in the breakfast room. He was dressed in shorts and running shoes. His white tee-shirt was soaked with sweat, with dark patches forming under his arms and around his abdomen.

The SAS man bounced jauntily towards his superior's table, picking up a piece of cake as he passed the breakfast buffet and then sitting down next to his superior as he simultaneously bit into the cake.

"Morning sir. Beautiful morning isn't it. Quite a change from the cold, grey drizzle of Hereford."

Featherstonehaugh ignored the greeting as he looked his companion up and down, barely disguising his distaste

"You're dressed in a rather unsavoury manner for breakfast Frank."

Cartwright was untroubled by the almost overt criticism. Having finished the cake he had taken a roll from the bread basket on the table and was busily applying a thick layer of butter,

"Just been for a run round the Borghese gardens and then spent an hour in the gym," he said happily as he bit into the roll,

"You saw that Traynor fellow. Got to keep myself in trim if I'm going to keep up with the likes of him. How's the grub?"

Featherstonehaugh sighed and waved his hand airily towards the buffet table by way of reply.

"Hmm. I'll take a look. I'm starved." Cartwright got up brushing crumbs from his tee-shirt onto the floor.

To Featherstonehaugh's horror he returned to the table with two plates laden with scrambled eggs, ham, sausages and cheese and, with barely a pause, commenced to demolish the pile of food with an efficiency that even overawed the MI6 man. In between mouthfuls, he described to a silent Featherstonehaugh the various pleasures and pitfalls of running in the Villa Borghese.

When Cartwright's plates were empty and the buffet table seemed severely depleted, Featherstonehaugh leaned back, sipping at the cappuccino the waitress had just replenished for him.

"If you've finished Frank I'll tell you the programme for today."

CHAPTER SIXTEEN

Rome to Florence

"The good fortune of the foolish youth, he fol-
lows orders and thus is docile" (I Ching)

I was up early. A good night's sleep in a comfortable bed had banished all my concerns and doubts. I decided to have a work out. I had already seen what passed for a gym at the time of my first meeting with Standish at the hotel. I hoped that they had somewhere better equipped, but my enquiry about this merely led to a disappointing negative answer. Apparently the guests at this hotel were more concerned with their comfort than their physical condition. What passed for a gym was a small atrium close to the lobby toilets, with a bicycle, a couple of treadmills and a few weights lying about. I spent an hour on the treadmill and then went through various exercises both with and without the weights.

I had nothing really to do until my meeting with the Brits later in the day to collect my money and their car. Now that I knew the Brits would be coming at around 1600 I calculated that I should be able to leave Rome by 5.00 pm to 5.30pm. Apart from the morning rush hour, this was the worst time to get on the road. However, even allowing for heavy traffic out of Rome I still thought I ought to be able to make the rendezvous with Jacques' son by 7.30pm to 8.00pm. That would be perfect. Either it would be dark, or the light would at least be poor enough to allow me to effect a seamless change with the boy, with little chance of being spotted.

There were a few things I needed to buy and I decided to go out and also call Jacques to ensure that his son was at the rendezvous by no later than 7pm. Before leaving the hotel I packed, ensuring that I had left nothing lying around in the room.

I walked from the hotel down to the principal shopping area around Via del Corso. It was, as usual, so crowded that I was frequently forced to walk in the road to avoid the throng. As far as I could tell, I was still not being followed. I made some purchases and then used a public telephone chosen at random to arrange the rendezvous with Jacques' son, which took all of fifteen seconds. I had a couple of coffees and then wandered down to the Via Flaminia to pick up a slice of Pizza from what I consider to be one of the best pizzerias in Rome, where they sell, by weight, slices carved from large rectangular pies. The choice was even wider than I remembered and I ended up by eating three generous slices with different toppings, comforting myself with the thought that I would probably not have another chance to eat before driving up to Florence.

Before I knew it, it was time to return for the meeting with the two Englishmen.

They had arrived a little early and apparently with a full complement of backup. My instincts clicked into gear immediately I saw the two cars. One was parked unobtrusively nose into the kerb on the same side of the road as the hotel and alongside a number of other cars similarly parked. The other was parked on the other side of the road. The only difference between them and other parked cars was that they were the only cars that were not empty. It looked as if they were four people in each car but I was walking quite fast and had no time to take more than a cursory look. A gleamingly clean, silver Audi S6 was parked directly outside the front entrance, being guarded by a man who was remarkable for being so ordinary looking that, even for me, it was difficult to remember what he looked like once I was in the hotel. As I walked swiftly through the lobby I wondered if that was my designated drive.

The tall, urbane Englishman and his military companion were waiting for me in Standish's suite. My attention was immediately drawn to the large holdall occupying the centre of the coffee table that divided the two sofas in the sitting area.

I greeted the two Brits with my customary charm by nodding my head slightly in their general direction.

"Is that it?" a second nod took in the holdall.

They obviously preferred my initial form of communication as the man in charge delivered his own nod. Never one to stand on ceremony, I walked directly over to the holdall and opened it. A very gratifying sight met my eyes. Bundle upon bundle of 500 Euro notes. I pulled out a bundle at random from the centre of the bag.

"You're not going to count it are you?" the Englishman seemed horrified at such a preposterous notion.

I turned to him, the bundle of money still in my hand.

"Why? Can I trust you?"

"Of course." He sounded quite indignant.

My response was to peel off the rubber band that held the notes and to fan them open like a hand of cards, before counting how much was in the bundle. Fifty thousand Euros. I replaced the elastic band and looked into the holdall to make a quick estimate of the number of bundles. It looked about right to me, around eighty bundles. I threw the bundle I was holding back in the bag and took out another. As I peeled off the elastic band I heard an exasperated snort from the Englishman. I took out two or three notes at random and subjected them to the ultra violet false note detector I had purchased earlier in the afternoon. According to the instructions that I had read over a coffee, the notes seemed to be genuine. I glanced over to the two Englishmen. The soldier had obviously never seen so much money before in his life. He was leaning forward, his eyes trying to bore into the depths of the holdall. The expression on his face managed simultaneously to convey curiosity, amazement and greed. I mentally filed away the thought that this might be a man who could be bought. The other Brit was leaning back on the sofa with a bored supercilious expression that was obviously intended to and succeeded in, aggravating me. He was right. I was not going to spend the next, however long it was going to take, counting the money. My cursory inspection would have to do. If there was anything wrong or it was short, I would not do the job and I might even decide to take out that greedy soldier boy into the bargain.

I casually threw the bundle I had been checking back into the bag along with the ultra violet light.

"Looks OK. I'll check it more carefully later. What about the other things I asked for?"

By way of response the supercilious one reached down for an attaché case that had been placed on the floor, at the side of the sofa where he was sitting. Without saying anything, he placed the case on the table, twirled the combination locks decorating the side of the case and opened it with a loud click. The back was up facing me, so that I was unable to see the contents, but he reached in and placed on the table a Heckler & Koch P2000SK sub compact pistol. A lovely piece of work, with a pre cocked hammer system for easier and more reliable combat use. I picked it up, pulled back the slide and checked the magazine. It was fully loaded and ready to go. As I was doing this, the Englishman placed another pistol on the table. Another H&K, a USP tactical 9mm with silencer already attached. They certainly were not stinting on the firearms. Heckler & Koch weapons are, quite rightly in my opinion, generally regarded by those in the know as amongst the best.

I put down the compact and picked up the USP which I also checked and which was also fully loaded. The USP comes in three principal versions including the 9mm with a 15 cartridge magazine and a .45 with a 12 cartridge magazine. The one in front of me was the 9mm which I preferred for its larger magazine. The sub-compact too, was a 9mm with a 10 round magazine.

"Very nice. How about spare cartridges?"

He answered by delving into the attaché case again and producing two spare magazines and two boxes of cartridges. Well at least they were dealing with this properly.

He had apparently now decided to talk to me.

"There's a silver Audi S6 outside the hotel. Here are the keys." He pushed a key ring across the table, with one of those black, a little bulky, computerised keys attached. I did not say anything about his only having given me one key. I assumed they had retained the other one or two keys the manufacturer supplied, in order to be able to get into the car at will. They were dreaming if they thought I was likely to leave anything in the car for them to find. I had even bought myself a packet of thick surgical gloves, so as not leave any prints in the car. And I intended to give Jacques' son a couple of pairs so that he, too, would leave the car clean.

"I need a number to call you when I'm set up, so that your Mr. White here can come and deliver the rest of the money and start to baby sit me."

The Englishman delved into his attaché case one more time and handed me the mobile phone that he had retrieved.

"The number is programmed in. Once you're ready, you call us. Or, if there's anything you need in the meantime. How are we going to get hold of you if we need to give you some up to date intel?"

The question was posed casually, as if they were not going to be attempting to track me at all times. That bloody mobile phone was a bit of a killer for me. It probably had a GPS tracking system built in entirely independent of the GSM chip and probably worked both off the telephone battery and some other battery they probably had buried somewhere in the telephone electronics. Well I was not going to need to contact them for at least a week, so I would give the phone to Jacques' son and tell him to take good care of it and not to use it for any calls to his father. In fact, I was going to have to give him a quick course in field security before I sent him off on his holiday to Monte Carlo.

"You won't need to contact me. In fact it's better if you don't. The less contact we have the better. I'll call in about a week. I'll only need your intel when the operation is set up and ready to go."

"Well... ", I got the impression that there was more than a little play acting in the reluctance he was showing, "if that's the way you want to play it. But we need to have a way of contacting you in case of emergency."

"Just call the phone you've given me."

"Of course." He laughed, "I must be suffering jet lag or something. I hadn't thought of that. I rather thought you might have kept it switched off when you weren't using it, so we wouldn't be able to track you."

Very clever. He thought he was throwing me off the track by bringing the subtext of our discussions into the open.

"Yeh, well you're right. But I'll tell you what I'll do. I'll switch it on at odd times in the day. If you want me you'll either just have to keep trying until you get me. Or leave a message. I assume there's a number programmed into the phone to call for messages."

He nodded.

"If there's nothing else, I'll be on my way." I threw the guns, ammunition and cell phone into the hold-all, zipped it shut and looked up at the supercilious Englishman enquiringly. He nodded his acquiescence to my leaving. As I picked up the holdall I glanced across at Mr. White. His eyes went from the bag to me and back to the bag, before finally settling on me. The way he was looking at me, I could see that he had already measured me for a coffin. With my free hand I picked up the car keys which still lay on the table and left the room.

I went straight to my room where I emptied the safe and called for the porter to take my bags down. I did not have to wait very long and I let him carry both my suitcase and the holdall with the money. We walked together to the elevator and then through the lobby, where I saw the two Englishmen in conversation. They barely glanced at me as I asked the porter who was carrying my bags, also to collect the bag I had left at the concierge's desk. As we walked outside I operated the remote control on the car key and the silver Audi outside the front entrance gave me a big hello, flashing all four indicators at me at the same time. The remote control had a button to operate the trunk. I activated it and the trunk swung open just as the porter reached the car. He put my three bags in, closed the trunk and smiled his thanks as I tipped him an overgenerous fifty Euros. The money was apparently sufficient to cover his opening the car door, which he closed after me with a soft clunk and wishes for a good trip home.

The car started immediately with a soft purr, which turned into a low and rather satisfying growl as I put the automatic box into drive and moved off up towards the Via Veneto. I was not supposed to turn left at the top of the road but I did anyway and drove straight up to Porta Pinciana and then headed right, going towards the Corso Francia and thence onto the via Cassia, from where I intended to pick up the Autostrada towards Florence. The traffic was not as bad as I had anticipated until I got to the Cassia. There it was stop go for about fifteen minutes before I was able to accelerate into a gap and outdistance the cars around me. The Audi responded eagerly to the accelerator and as I made the turn off towards the Autostrada into faster travelling traffic I enjoyed the surge of power that rapidly brought my speed up to 150 kilometres an hour. I pulled into the far left lane and continued to accelerate. There was a lot of traffic but I managed to keep the speed between 150 and 180 kilometres an hour as the cars in front of me rapidly pulled out of my path when they saw the fast moving Audi looming up in their rearview mirrors.

Of the two cars I had seen parked near the hotel and, which I had assumed were sent to follow me, one, as far as I could tell, had followed me to the Corso Francia, but I had lost him in the traffic before I reached the Autostrada. I assumed that they had a location device planted somewhere in the Audi and that they would be able to track me, whether or not I was visible to them. I preferred though, to put a decent distance between us so that, if possible, I would be able to effect the change-over with Jacques' son without being observed.

I had to slow down as I approached the toll barrier for the highway going to Florence, in order to take a ticket. What I had not noticed was that the car was equipped with a telepass that automatically registered the car and lifted the barrier. I only realised this as the barrier lifted for me without my having to take a ticket. Well another good mark for the Brits, they were saving me the hefty toll that I would otherwise have had to pay.

The road after the toll was much clearer of traffic and I realised that I ought to be able to make good time. I decided to pull into the side of the road just after the toll in order quickly to check out the car for listening devices or cameras. Whatever they had put in I could not find in the few minutes I gave myself. A microphone transmitter could have been installed in any one of a number of places and I was not going to knock myself out trying to find it. A camera was different; it would have had to be positioned to give a view of the whole interior and there were only a few suitable locations. I could see nothing and felt fairly confident that they did not have a visual on me, which was my principal concern as a possible factor in spoiling my plan to divert everyone's attention from where I was actually going to be.

As I pulled back onto the Autostrada the car that had followed me from Rome came through the barrier. Well we would soon see what sort of a driver they had. There was no traffic in the outside lane ahead of me and I accelerated hard. The Audi was a joy to drive. It was sharp, responsive and the power seemed endless. I was soon travelling at 240 kilometres an hour. The following car disappeared somewhere, far behind me. I had to slow from time to time, as I bore up on cars that were a little leisurely about getting out of my way, but I was able to maintain an average speed that worked out well over 110 miles per hour. I passed two or three speed cameras, only one of which seemed to be working as I caught the brief flash in my rear view mirror. I was not concerned; let the Brits sort that one out. I was wearing the same short sleeve blue Polo and beige slacks that I had told Jacques his son should wear. In addition I was wearing a red baseball cap and large Ray Ban sunglasses, both of which I had bought in Rome. I had in fact bought two identical sunglasses as I intended to give one pair to Jacques' son. If Jacques and his son had followed my instructions, it was going to be almost impossible to tell us apart, even from quite close up. Someone, of course, might notice we were wearing different shoes, but the car following me was full of men and, whilst it is not an immutable rule, it tends to be women, rather than men, who notice things like shoes.

I made good time to the service area and arrived just after 7.30pm. The light was fading and the sky was settling into a deep night blue, although it was still tinted rose by the glowing embers of the setting sun as I pulled slowly into the parking area. There were a dozen or so cars parked outside the red-signed Autogrill and perhaps an equal number of heavy trucks, sitting in the separate area provided for larger vehicles. No one was in any of the parked cars. I saw the Alfa Sportwagon immediately. It was parked away from the restaurant area, near the trucks. He had obviously deliberately placed it where other cars were unlikely to park next to it and sure enough it had a free parking space on either side. I pulled in next to it and switched off the Audi's engine. My rear view mirror and a quick look around, confirmed that no other cars had followed me into the rest area. I quickly got out and, continuing to look around for anyone watching, casually walked between the two cars and bent down by their front wheels to retrieve the Alfa keys. I then opened the back hatch of the Alfa, before also opening the Audi's trunk. I put the case that was resting in the Alfa into the Audi, before transferring my suitcase and the holdall with the guns and money into the Alfa and then locked both cars with their respective remote controls. I kept with me the case with the money I had earned in Sicily as I swiftly walked into the restaurant. The whole operation had taken me no more than thirty seconds and no one seemed to have noticed.

In order to get to the restaurant area I had to go through a small barrier, into a shopping area stuffed with a large variety of Italian comestibles, olive oil, salamis, cheese, pasta in a dozen different shapes and colours, and wine. On the other side of this demonstration of the Italian love affair with food was an area containing toys, magazines, music, films, in fact anything that a lone or family traveller might want or need to make a journey that much more bearable.

As I walked into the restaurant area I looked around for someone dressed like me. A young man sitting at a table facing the entrance raised his hand slightly and I walked over to him, feeling rising irritation because he was wearing a faded beige suede jacket zipped up to just below his neck rather than the blue polo shirt I had stipulated. He must have seen my annoyance because as I sat down he immediately said in French,

"I've got a blue polo shirt underneath my jacket. I thought we might draw too much attention if people saw us dressed exactly the same way."

I checked my irritation. The boy was smart.

"That's good." I nodded my approval, took off my baseball cap and put it on the table next to the boy. I put the keys to the Audi on the hat. It's a silver Audi S6, parked next to your car. I'll give you some other stuff in a minute and some money. I want you to drive to Monte Carlo. I've got a room booked at the Monte Carlo Beach Hotel- it's the only hotel in Monte Carlo with a proper beach and I thought you might prefer that. The room's booked in the name of Hassan Ben Kamal. I've written the name and the hotel down on a piece of paper you'll find in an envelope in the glove compartment in the car. From now on you are Kamal.

I've programmed the hotel into the navigation system. Also in the envelope I've put 10,000 Euro,"

I paused as the boy's face lit up with pleasure. I imagined he had never seen so much money, let alone been given it to spend. I had even better news for him.

"There are also two credit cards in the envelope in the name of Kamal. You'll need a credit card when you check into the hotel and you can spend up to 5000 Euro on each card." The boy looked as if he had died and gone to heaven.

"Now listen very carefully. You've got a lot of money to play with for the next week, but don't go spending it in the Casino. No gambling please. Not at all. Not even slot machines. It's very important you don't draw any attention to yourself and don't get into trouble." He was looking at me intently furiously nodding his agreement.

"Otherwise, sun yourself on the beach, go out, go to discos or whatever you young people like to do these days. The money's yours to spend as you like. I'll be in Monte Carlo in about eight days. I'll come to the hotel and we can change cars again and you can return home. Whatever you do don't talk on the phone in the car. In fact don't talk in the car at all, there are probably going to be people listening. There are also going to be people following you to the hotel and probably in Monte Carlo. They might decide to stake out your room, so, when you go out, try to keep the baseball hat and these glasses on," I pushed a case with the Ray Bans across the table to him.

"If no one follows you from the room then you can lose the hat. I want them to think you're me for as long as possible, so they don't start trying to find me. When you leave here take the Autostrada towards Pisa and then turn off to La Spezia and Genova. You just keep going and you'll see the signs to Monte Carlo after you cross the border into France. As I've said, I've set the navigation system in the car for the hotel you're booked in, so you shouldn't have any problems. I'm going to the toilets now. Wait five minutes, pay for whatever you've had and come there. We'll do the change in there. One more thing. You'll see I've left a cell phone in the glove compartment. Whatever you do, don't use it. Just leave it there. Don't use the hotel telephone to make calls. Try not to make any calls, but if you have to, then buy a phone card and use a public phone well away from the hotel. Use a different phone each time you call. Any questions?"

"No sir. Well perhaps one thing. Do you want receipts for the money I spend so you will have a proper account of what I give you back?"

I smiled at him and thought bless his innocent little heart.

"I don't need any receipts. The money's yours to do with what you like, as long as you don't throw it away gambling. A bit of advice – use the credit cards to pay for things and save the cash." I paused again looking him in the eye,

"If you do a good job for me I'll give you another 10,000 Euro when I see you in a week."

303

"Really" he could not prevent a huge grin spreading across his face.

"Yes really. I think you're father's right. You're a good boy. But I can't stress enough how careful you need to be. I don't want anyone to find out who you really are. It could be very dangerous for you later."

He did not look concerned, but he was young, thought he was bullet proof and did not know what he could be letting himself in for.

"Don't worry. I'll be careful."

As I got up I said

"Oh, when you leave here you'll need to fill up the car. You can pay with the credit card."

I left the baseball cap on the table for him to pick up and walked towards the toilets. I did not see anyone I thought might have been watching me, but did not expect to. At the speed I had been driving I thought that I had to be a minimum of five minutes ahead of the English watchers and I had only been in the rest stop for that length of time.

As usual I was lucky. No one was in the toilets and the first person to come in was the boy.

"Right. Now take off your jacket and give it to me. Put on the baseball hat and glasses and one more thing." I produced surgical gloves like the ones I had worn in the car.

"Put these on and keep them on whenever you're in the car or touching the car. They're not very comfortable, particularly in the heat, but it's a lot better than leaving your fingerprints anywhere on the car. If you get hot just keep the air conditioning on. Any questions?"

He was starting to look a bit scared. That was good. The sooner he realised this was not a schoolboy game the better. He shook his head.

"Ok. Off you go. Remember, there is no such thing as being too careful. Good luck."

He pulled on the baseball cap, glasses and gloves and hesitantly offered his hand to me, which I shook, slightly surprised at the gesture. I had the feeling he actually wanted a hug of re-assurance. When he left he no longer seemed the self-confident young man who had been sitting at a table waiting for me.

After the boy had gone I locked myself in a cubicle, put the seat cover down with my foot and sat down to wait. While I was sitting there several people came in and out. I waited twenty minutes before getting up, putting on the boy's jacket and doing it up. It fitted me well because we were the same size and build although the boy was probably two or three inches taller than me. I put on a pair of slightly tinted glasses with clear lenses and a woollen hat, both of which I had purchased in Rome. The glasses hid my eyes sufficiently for people not to notice that I looked oriental. I opened the door cautiously and shuffled out with my head down. There was one other person in the washroom who looked like a lorry driver. I put my case down, washed my hands and dried them under the hand dryer. I then picked my case up and with my head slightly bent forward shuffled out in what I hoped was a fair imitation of an elderly man.

I went back to the restaurant and sat down where Jacques' son had been sitting, facing the entrance. A waitress came over and I ordered a plate of pasta and a salad. The whole time I was looking around for some indication that the English watchers had failed to fall for my ruse. By the time the waitress brought my food I was satisfied that everything looked normal and that there was no indication of anyone paying any attention to me at all. I hoped that, if the Audi had the tracking device I expected, the people following would not have arrived before Jacques' son was at the petrol filling area and that the stop would have been short enough for them to think that it was no more than a quick pit stop.

I finished my food, paid and shuffled out. There were very few cars now in the parking area. I paused for a moment, pretending to rub the small of my back as I carefully scrutinized the car park and neighbouring gas station. Nothing either attracted my attention or alerted my senses. I shuffled over to the Alfa, unlocking it with the remote before I reached it. I got in and was pleased to note that the interior light had been set so that it did not come on when the door opened.

I started the car and switched on the navigation system, which, as promised, spoke to me in English. Within no more than ten minutes I was off the Autostrada and driving through the centre of Florence, satisfied that I had lost my pursuers. There was definitely no one following me. I heard a telephone ring and looked down quickly. I had not noticed that a cell phone had been left on the front passenger seat. It was not easily visible because it had slid back against the seat squab. I picked it up and answered it cautiously in Italian.

"Is that you John?"

It was Jacques' voice.

"Is everything alright? I expected you to be with me by now."

"Everything's fine. I just took my time making sure that everything worked out ok. I sent your son on his way about an hour ago. He's probably well on his way to Genoa by now."

I paused to listen to the calm woman's voice talking to me from the Navigation system as I looked at my position on the screen.

"I'm very near your place now. I'll see you, I think, in a few minutes."

I had just crossed the Arno along a bridge a short distance downstream from the Ponte Vecchio and was now driving slowly along a narrow, dark street that ran parallel to the river. I did not know Florence very well, having only been there three or four times before, and following driving instructions from a pleasant, but robotic, female voice emanating from a computerised navigator is not calculated to help one orientate oneself. As far as I was able to ascertain I was somewhere near the Medici Palace. I had just made a right turn, followed by a left turn into another dark street, when I saw the tall, rangy figure of Jacques. He was standing in the middle of the street waving me down. I had last seen him several years before and, apart from a rather grizzled look, resulting from a few days of unshaven, grey facial growth, he looked much as he had when we had last been together.

Even though we did not communicate on a regular basis, he was a good friend and obviously genuinely pleased to see me. He almost pulled me out of the car to give me a crushing bear hug. He stepped back as I gasped,

"Look at you, you Jap bastard. You haven't changed at all. You still look like the youngest sergeant in the Legion. How do you manage it?"

"You look the same too. Still that filthy, unshaven look you think makes the women love you."

He laughed, shaking his head ruefully "That's all over for me. Carolina barely lets me out of her sight. She's been having a go at me all day for sending her beloved Paolo out for you. Get the car out of the street and then we can catch up. You'll see the garage three doors down."

I looked up and noticed, for the first time, a large archway flanked by two huge, open wooden doors, on the right side of the street ahead of me. I got back into the car and drove through the archway into a long garage that seemed to stretch the whole width of the street into the parallel street behind. Two other cars were already parked there and I pulled up directly behind them.

"Have you got somewhere secure where I can dump my stuff?" I asked, as I removed my bags from the rear hatch of the car.

"Of course. You're staying with us," Jacques responded, as he picked up my suitcase and the holdall with the money and started walking towards an open door cut into the wall of the garage.

"What've you got in here? Its heavy." he said slightly raising the holdall.

"All in good time Jacques. All in good time."

He laughed as he led me into an ancient stone, vaulted kitchen.

"This house is over four hundred years old, in fact parts of it, like this kitchen, are even older, they date from the Middle Ages."

"You'd never know it." I said, looking around at the shining steel work tops and beautifully polished wood cabinets that seemed completely out of place in the mediaeval room.

"I've knocked three buildings together. You can't tell from the outside. I was lucky to be able to pick them up over the years we've lived here. This used to be a Trattoria, but the old couple who ran it had no children and decided to give it up and go and live in the country. They loved Paolo and offered me the place when they decided to sell. It was a real steal."

I grunted appreciatively as he led me up a narrow winding staircase and through another arched doorway on which I almost hit my head. The door opened into a large, well lit bedroom, luxuriously furnished and dominated by an immense, wooden four poster bed. The bed was obviously very old. It was made of dark oak, carved with all sorts of intricate twining plants, interspersed with a variety of animal heads.

Jacques was obviously very proud of the bed and started to extol its virtues and history, without neglecting to tell me that the springing and mattress were modern and would provide me with a comfortable night's rest. He put my bag down before showing me the spacious marble bathroom that led directly off the bedroom.

"It's all self-contained. No one will bother you here."

I wondered whether Jacques and his wife had given up their own bedroom for me and voiced the question.

"No, no. This is a guest room. The family bedrooms are on the other side of the building."

"Well," I said admiringly, "you certainly seem to have done well for yourself."

He looked me directly in the eye, "I don't do badly and most of it is legit."

Jacques had been an expert gunsmith almost as long as I could remember. In the Legion he had always been modifying his weapons to make them more accurate or smoother to use. So, having seen the lavish way in which his house had been constructed and furnished, it did not surprise me too much when he said,

"I've got a workshop and quite a nice little shooting range in the basement."

I chuckled in response. Part of my amusement lay in the fact that in the old olive oil mill that I had purchased as a hideaway, several years ago, deep in the Umbrian countryside, some of the first work I had carried out had been the conversion of part of the huge cellars into a shooting range and armoury.

"I'll leave you to settle in. When you're ready, come on down. I'll be waiting for you in the kitchen."

I nodded. He turned and left the room, carefully closing the door behind him. The door had a key in the lock. Jacques, like me, was very keen on privacy. Even though I trusted Jacques completely, I went to the door, locked it and took a quick look around the room to see if there were any concealed video cameras. Carrying out checks like this had become second nature and, knowing Jacques as I did, it was not beyond the bounds of possibility for him to want to keep an eye on his guests. My check revealed nothing. I took a quick look around the bathroom. The walls and floor were entirely covered in marble. The mirrors over the hand basin and above the bath might have concealed video and recording devices, but I doubted it. One corner of the bathroom was taken up by a large shower with an opaque curved glass door. The shower was large enough to sit in and, indeed, a marble bench extended out of one of the inner walls.

I went back into the bedroom and retrieved the holdall that contained the money and the guns the Brits had given me. I carried the holdall into the bathroom and then into the shower, before closing the shower door and settling myself on the bench. I then opened the holdall, took out the guns and ammunition and emptied the money over the floor of the shower. I started to count, putting everything I had counted in piles of 50,000 Euro, each pile containing 100 of the 500 Euro notes. As I was counting, I examined the bank notes for markings and also, randomly checked them with the ultra violet light I had purchased for detecting forgeries.

Counting the money took me less time than I had anticipated. When I had finished I felt quite elated. Even with the expenses I was going to incur and even allowing for an immediate down payment to Jacques of 500,000 Euros, I would still be clearing at least 3 million Euros and this was just the first tranche.

Before replacing the money in the holdall I put aside ten piles that I intended to give Jacques and another five piles to use as an advance payment to each of the crew we were going to recruit. I transferred these latter piles into the bag I had bought in Rome.

It was now approaching 9.30 in the evening and, as I was preparing to go downstairs to see Jacques, there was a knock on my door. I unlocked the door and opened it. Jacques stood there looking at me for a moment before saying

"We're going out to eat. There's a very good Trattoria quite near here where we shouldn't have a problem getting a table."

I did not answer him directly, because I noticed that his gaze had extended beyond me to the bed, where I had placed the money I intended for him and the two guns.

"Come on in. Let's have a quick talk before we go out."

He followed me obediently into the room, closing the door behind him.

I pointed to the money and said,

"That'll be for you, if you want to partner me. I'll need good, reliable back up."

He did not say anything but simply walked over to the bed and picked up one of the piles of 50,000 Euros which he counted quickly and professionally. He whistled through his teeth as he finished counting and looked at the other nine piles.

"That's a lot of money. When did you suddenly get so generous? It must be a pretty nasty job."

"That's just a down payment. Half for you now and half later; a total of one million Euros."

He looked at me steadily, riffling the bundle of notes in his hand.

"You know, I'm a married man now with a family. I've got the son you met, a daughter and another younger son. I make enough without getting myself into too many problems. I can't get into anything that might affect my family. Not even for a million Euros." He threw the notes he was holding back onto the bed.

"Jacques, I'll be straight with you. I'll tell you the whole thing, then you can decide. If the people who are running this op know you're involved the likelihood is they'll come after you. I don't think they want anyone around to be able to cause any problems for them later, real or imagined. So it's in my interest to keep you unknown to the other players, including the guys we recruit. You're an essential part of my exit strategy and that means keeping you completely under wraps."

Jacques nodded. As I had been talking he had picked up another bundle of cash which he was fingering and looking at as he spoke, "Fair enough. I think you know you're one of the only people I'd trust with the lives of my family. All I ask is you respect that trust, whatever the cost."

I nodded in turn, "Jacques, none of this needs to be said between us. We've both proved that to each other more than once."

He replaced the cash on the bed before picking up and examining each of the guns in turn, "Have you checked these out yet?"

"No time."

He threw them back on the bed and scooped up his money, cradling it in his arms, as he started to walk out of the room, "Bring the guns along. We'll try them out quickly before dinner. Follow me." Jacques had obviously become so integrated into the local culture that eating out around 10pm was obviously normal to him.

As I followed him I took the key out of the lock and locked the door from the outside, slipping the key into my pocket as I descended the stairs.

From the bottom of the stairs Jacques led me through the kitchen, along a narrow corridor into a comfortable looking sitting room, where one wall was lined with a wine-rack containing perhaps a hundred or so bottles. The wall that angled the wine rack faced a large settee and was taken up by a large wooden unit housing a flat screen television and a variety of other home entertainment devices. Jacques, still cradling the money he had taken from the bedroom against his chest with one hand, used his other hand to pick up what looked like a universal remote control. He pressed a button and the complete unit with the television, stereo and DVD player started to glide silently open. Jacques looked at me with a proud grin on his face.

"Not bad eh? Leads down to my secret hideaway. You know Florence is full of all sorts of secret passages and I happened to stumble on this after I had been in the house for a couple of years."

I followed him down another narrow staircase that seemed to have been carved out of solid rock. The walls were smooth stone, worn shiny over the centuries and they gleamed in the light of the fluorescent bulb that shone from the ceiling. At the bottom of the stairs there was a narrow passage that seemed just to end in a stone wall. With his empty hand Jacques fumbled for something on the wall that I could not see and then seemed to press the wall, which, in response, slid open with a high pitched buzz. Jacques turned and grinned at me again. The opening in the wall revealed a large, cavernous room that must have stretched a good hundred metres to another wall that I could barely see. Then, as Jacques flicked a switch, the whole area lit up. I am rarely surprised, but what I saw did the trick. One wall was racked from floor to ceiling with a huge variety of different weapons, from ancient flintlocks to modern light machine guns and LAWs (light anti-tank weapons). I could see now that the wall at the end of the room contained some targets. Just by the right hand wall were two shooting stands each containing a table and chair, the latter facing a small screen and some controls. I realised that Jacques had installed an electronic targeting system, which displayed on a screen at the side of the shooter the precise location of the hit on the target at the end of the gallery. It made the pulley system that I had installed in the basement of my Umbrian house look prehistoric. The room also contained a work bench, equipped with everything any gunsmith could want, including a lathe. Jacques threw the money onto his work bench and walked over to a large floor to ceiling combination safe which he opened. I was polite enough not to look inside without being invited. No invitation was forthcoming, apparently friendship stopped at the safe door, as it would have done had the safe been mine. Jacques scooped up the money again and disappeared with it into the safe, whilst I walked over to the shooting stands and placed my guns on the table by one of the television monitors. I took out the magazines of both guns and checked the loads before picking a pair of ear muffs from one of the hooks on the wall next to the shooting stand. I put on the ear muffs and picked up the gun with the silencer as Jacques walked over to me, having closed the safe.

"Before you do that I need a couple of pictures for the papers you asked for."

I nodded and removed the ear muffs and stood patiently whilst Jacques produced a digital camera and snapped off some pictures. He then disappeared up the stairs, returning five minutes later.

"My daughter's taking the pictures round to the paper guy now. Everything should be ready for you by the morning."

I trusted Jacques absolutely, but I was not happy to leave my picture with some unknown forger who might be arrested at any time. However, before I could say anything, Jacques, who had obviously been reading my mind, added,

"Don't worry she's not leaving the card with the pictures on it and I'll make sure when I collect the papers that he hasn't made any copies of your picture. He knows better than to fuck about with me" he added menacingly, before continuing,

"Put the ear muffs back on. I'll set the target for 30 metres, it's too far at the moment."

I replaced the ear muffs as Jacques pressed some buttons and the targets moved nearer. There was a bar code reader on each of the tables, with a sheet containing pictures of different targets, followed by a bar code for each type of target. Jacques ran the reader over the bar code for a target with the outline of a man and then nodded at me,

"It's ready. You can shoot."

I emptied the magazine in bursts of two shots fired in quick succession at each of the head and heart areas and without looking at the monitor.

When I had finished, I looked down at the monitor.

"Pretty good. I see you haven't lost your touch. The monitor shows hits to within 1 millimetre" Jacques was nodding approvingly at the monitor which showed that there was barely any distance between the shots at each area of the target.

"I'd be quite upset if I couldn't do that pretty well blindfold. It'd be time for me to stop working. Move the target back twenty metres." As I spoke I picked up the compact.

As the target moved back, I commenced firing alternately with right and left hands until I had emptied the magazine. The monitor again indicated a tight grouping around the head and heart areas that I had targeted.

As Jacques reset the target I picked up the shell casings that had been ejected from my guns and threw them into a plastic dustbin that sat meekly by the side of the table with the monitors.

"I could do with adjusting the trigger pressure."

Jaqcques nodded as he picked up each of the H & K pistols in turn and dry fired them,

"Leave it to me. I'll sort these out for you."

He was examining the gun with the silencer attached. I had ejected the magazine immediately after firing it and he was stripping down the rest of the gun. I was examining some of his extensive arsenal, when I heard him give a sharp exclamation, that caused me to turn around immediately. Jacques was grunting to himself as he delved into the butt of the gun with a long pair of tweezers.

"Well, what have we here?" He was holding something between the prongs of the tweezers. I walked over to look. It was a tiny, very flat miniature electronic microchip. I did not have to be an electronics expert to recognise state of the art equipment. I felt a sinking feeling. I had seen things like that before. It was a GSM tracking device powered by an ultra-miniature battery. It was the sort of thing that can be implanted under the skin and operated by a body's electrical current. Jacques, who had always been much more technically minded than me, was obviously familiar with these devices. After a few seconds of poking and pushing at it he grunted again.

"Hmmn. Well that's disabled. Let's see whether there are any more." He picked up and stripped the compact H & K and examined the parts carefully.

"This one's clean." He announced, "Clever fuckers" he muttered admiringly, "who'd of thought of bugging a gun?"

He turned to look at me, "Well my ice man friend, you've gone a bit pale. What's happened to that famous sang froid? You must be getting old."

"Why do you think I've decided this is going to be my last job? I can't keep up with all this electronic shit. Will they have been able to track me here?"

"It's possible, but what I think is this. This type of device can be switched on and off remotely, to preserve battery life and to reduce risk of detection. Unless they had some reason to think they'd lost you, they'd be unlikely to switch it on. They'd lose any signal in here anyway, what with these thick walls and the sound-proofing I've put in. And if they're following Paolo in your car and, for sure they'd have that set up to track it, there'd be no reason to check on this secondary device. But just to be sure we'd better be careful. The upside is that they can't carry out any sort of physical surveillance on this place without my knowing. I've got some miniature concealed cameras for keeping an eye on the streets around here. Come and look."

He led me over to a corner of the cellar that I had noticed previously as emitting a low glow. Several monitors were attached to the wall, showing images of the outside of the building and the streets to the back and front of the house. Even though it was dark outside, the cameras recorded extremely good definition. We watched for a few moments in silence. There did not seem to be any activity at all outside the house, not even anyone walking around. I turned to Jacques,

"It could be a big problem for you if they find out about you. That's what bothers me."

Jacques shrugged, "I understand. But what's done is done. We've just got to be extra careful from now on. The only people using devices like that," he nodded towards the work bench where he had left the miniature transmitter, "are governments. Governments who've got access to sophisticated satellite imagery." He added. "If they catch on that it's not you they're following and they can't get a fix on you with that," he nodded again at the transmitter, "they'll probably try and get satellite images of your drive from Rome and they'll be examining all the cars at any places where you stopped, to see if they can pick up the changeover. The upside is, that with all this electronic stuff, people get lazy and tend to rely on it too much, so as long as they're getting all the right signals they probably won't be questioning who they're following."

He picked up a telephone and dialled a number saying to me "Paolo" as he dialled.

The call was answered quickly. He spoke to his son in rapid Italian, telling him to be extra careful that no one following him realised it was not me and not to take any chances on being spotted as having taken my place. He told him only to use his cell phone in a serious emergency and if he had to call for some reason to try and use landlines. The call took all of thirty seconds.

Jacques looked at his watch, turned to me and grinned, "Time to eat. Let's not forget the important things in life."

I was not feeling very hungry. Frankly, I was more worried about the miniature tracker than Jacques seemed to be. As I followed him out of the cellar, I asked,

"Can we reactivate that tracker?"

"Sure. In a couple of days we can send your friends on a nice goose chase. Is that how you say it in English?"

"Wild goose chase."

"Oh yes. Wild goose chase. Yes, that is where we can send them. Don't worry I have a plan."

"I'm not worried Jacques. I also have a plan." Indeed I did. Within the next couple of days I needed to get all that cash into Liechtenstein, after approving the personnel Jacques was suggesting I recruited. Thousands of trucks went north from Florence up the autrostrada and then into Austria, Germany, Eastern Europe. You name it, they went there. I had decided that one of them would be taking a re-activated tracker with them.

CHAPTER SEVENTEEN
The Autostrada to Monte Carlo

"Concealing a dagger behind a smile means using a friendly manner to put your enemy at ease whilst making secret preparations to implement your strategy" (Ancient Chinese military strategy)

One of the two men in the back seat of the 5 litre Mercedes E Class leaned forward towards the man in the front passenger seat, who was looking at the computer screen of the laptop he was balancing on his knees.

"We need to step on it. He's getting too far ahead."

"I'm already doing about 130 miles per hour" complained the driver.

"Well, unless he stuck our locating devices on an aeroplane flying North, he's going quite a bit faster and he's moving away from us all the time."

The fourth man who had been sitting in the back seat with his eyes closed, chimed in "It doesn't matter how far ahead he gets. We can keep tracking him.

We've got the tracker in the car and in one of his guns if we lose him."

"Yeah, but we're too far away to pick up anything on the radio mike in the car" said the other back seat passenger, as the walkie-talkie on his lap crackled into life,

"Bob, you'd better slow down. There's a police car coming up behind you fast. We don't want any problems." The disembodied words came out of the walkie-talkie which was transmitting from a second car of watchers driving a couple of miles behind the Mercedes.

Bob, the driver, glanced in his rear view mirror as he lifted his foot off the gas pedal, just in time to see a flashing blue light in the distance, but moving closer all the time. By the time the blue and white Subaru Legacy station wagon drew level with them, he was travelling at the legal limit of 130 kilometres an hour. The police slowed as they drew level and looked curiously into the Mercedes containing four men. After driving alongside for what seemed several minutes, the police apparently decided that whatever suspicions the Mercedes had aroused, it would have been a waste of time questioning the occupants of a car with diplomatic number plates.

As the police sped off, disappearing into the distance, Bob slowly built up his speed again until they were again travelling at around 210 kilometres an hour.

"Those cops must really be banging on. They've totally disappeared." The words came from the back seat.

"Or they've turned off. Whatever, we've got to try and get closer to that bugger. He's further away than ever." As he spoke, the driver accelerated.

The man in the back seat, who was holding the walkie-talkie, spoke quietly into the device, updating the car behind and telling them to speed up.

Approximately an hour later, the two men who had been catnapping in the back seat were woken by the front seat passenger exclaiming, "He's stopped."

"Probably taking a piss, having coffee or filling up with petrol" yawned the man with the walkie-talkie, as he relayed the information to the car behind them.

"Well whatever, it'll give us a chance to catch him up. How far ahead is he?" the driver turned his head slightly towards the man beside him, as he asked the question.

"He's about" he was squinting at the computer screen and running his finger along the map that was displayed along with the flashing point that gave the location of Traynor's Audi, "he's stopped just before Florence. I think it's a service area. He compared the screen to a paper map he was holding. Looks like Incisa. If so, we're here" he was muttering almost to himself, "he must be around 40 or so klicks ahead of us. Shit, he must have been driving at around 150 miles an hour plus. A regular, fucking Michael Schumacher ain't 'e."

"Well we're doing 220 kilometres an hour now, so it should take us," the driver paused as he made the mental calculation, "it should be about 9 or ten minutes. Is that right?" he again half turned to the man beside him, who was by now using the computer's calculator.

"Yeah, we should do it in about ten minutes and change."

In fact they arrived at the service station just as Paolo had finished refuelling the Audi and was pulling away from the petrol pumps.

"There he is. There. Just pulling away." said the front seat passenger pointing at the Audi.

"We might as well take the opportunity to fill up." Commented the driver, as he pulled up to one of the petrol pumps. "You getting anything on the audio?"

"I could do with a decent coffee." The left back seat passenger spoke as he fiddled with the dials on what looked like a larger version of the walkie-talkie held by the man at his side. "Oh yeah. Loud and clear. I'm getting the car radio. Horrible fucking taste in music; Italian fucking rap. God, sounds like the same sort of crap my teenage son listens to translated into Italian. Huh."

As the Mercedes was being refuelled, a 3 litre Alfa Romeo saloon, also with diplomatic license plates drew up behind them. The front seat passenger got out of the Mercedes and walked over to the Alfa, speaking through the open window of the passenger side for a few minutes before returning to the Mercedes which was now refuelled and ready to leave.

As he got back into his car and closed the door, he said to the other occupants,

"I told them our target pulled out a few minutes ago, after filling up. They asked me whether we had switched on the locator that we were told was planted on the target himself."

"Not much point in doing that and wasting good battery time we might need later, when we've got visual on him," interjected one of the men from the back seat,

"That's what I told them," replied the man from the front seat as he turned to the driver, saying, "come on, we'd better get after him."

The driver nodded as he started to guide the car out of the petrol station and back on the Autostrada. As he accelerated back up to 200 kilometres an hour, the man beside him plugged the computer into a power socket in the fascia before resuming his study of the computer screen. After a few minutes he said in a puzzled voice, addressing himself to the driver,

"Heh. You'd better slow down. He's going a lot slower now and we're catching him fast. In fact we ought to be visual within a few minutes. Wonder why he's suddenly slowed down like that."

One of the back seat passengers was quick to offer an opinion, "First he was probably desperate for a piss, like I am now and secondly he's not a young guy. Now it's dark he probably doesn't see so well, so he's slowed down."

"If you need a piss I'm afraid you're going to have to use the bottle. Whoops, there he is if I'm not very much mistaken." He looked back down at the computer screen, "Yeah, we're right on him."

"I've got him" said the driver as he eased their speed back to the equivalent of about 100 miles per hour.

Thereafter they travelled within visual distance of the Audi, which slowed its average speed even more as they entered the narrow Autostrada that runs along the

Ligurian coast and winds its way curving through innumerable tunnels up to and beyond Genoa and then on to the French Riviera.

The rest of the drive was uneventful and, by the time they finally drove into the tiny principality of Monte Carlo just before midnight, only the two drivers of the cars of English watchers were awake.

The passengers stirred when the Mercedes stopped just across the road from the Monte Carlo Beach Hotel, where the Audi had drawn up. The occupant of the Audi had scuttled so swiftly into the hotel, that only the driver of the Mercedes had caught a quick glimpse of him, as he had left his car in the hands of a yawning concierge.

"I'd say that's him for the night. What are we going to do about setting ourselves up for surveillance?" asked the front seat passenger of the Mercedes, as he stretched out his arms and legs?"

One of the men in the backseat, who seemed to be in charge of the team, answered, opening the door as he did so, "I'll see if we can arrange a couple of rooms for us in the same hotel. We can't all roll up at the same time and take four rooms, it'll look too suspicious. B team'll have to find somewhere else to stay. But let's see first whether we can get rooms here. You two stay put for the time being."

As he had got out of the car he had paused and taken a deep breath of the sea sprayed air, before leaning back into the car to address some final instruction to the driver and front seat passenger.

By now the second car had pulled in behind them. Although the night was dark, the occupants of the cars were easily visible in the light coming from street lamps, shops and not least the moon, which was almost full and whose reflection off the smooth sea gave additional illumination.

Whilst his colleague entered the hotel across the road, the driver of the Mercedes used the Navigation system in his car to find the locations and telephone numbers of nearby hotels. There were not many. It seemed that the Monte Carlo Beach Hotel was located on its own, away from the main centre of the principality, where the other hotels were clustered. As he was using the navigation system, one of the occupants of the Alfa Romeo walked over and climbed into the back of the Mercedes. They all listened in silence as the driver telephoned one of the numbers he had obtained from the navigation system. As he made the reservation, one of them pulled out his wallet and produced a credit card which he handed to the driver, when he realised from the driver's responses that the hotel was asking for this.

As he terminated the call, the driver turned to the two men in the back seat handing back the credit card as he did so,

"I've booked two double rooms in a hotel down the road," he pointed in the direction that the navigation system's map had indicated as the location of the hotel.

"You'd better hang on until the boss comes back and says how we're going to divide up the shifts."

A few minutes later the man he had described as "the boss" came sauntering across the road. As he approached the Mercedes he leaned into the car through the driver's window, which the driver had previously opened.

"It's a bit of a fuck up. This hotel's full, except for a suite that's a fucking fortune a night. Anyway I've taken the suite for one night and we'll see if we can arrange something else for tomorrow. Two of us'll stay in this hotel. I'm afraid that you two, he indicated Bob the driver and the man sitting next to Bob, are going to have to stay in the car. It'll be one man on and one man off. The one who's off'll have to sleep in the back seat."

"Yeah, didn't I fucking know that," muttered Bob.

"Sorry mate" said the Boss, "I'll make it up to you tomorrow. And if our man stays here for the next few days, as we were told he probably will, you'll get plenty of r & r. We'll probably only need one team on him at a time when he goes out."

"Yeah, yeah" responded Bob, in the tone of someone who was resigned to his fate. "I've booked the other team into a hotel down the road. Can they go off or do you want them to hang around some more."

"No. No reason for them to hang around. But two of your team," he looked at the man in the back seat who had come from the Alfa, "are going to have to relieve Bob and Jock at say," he looked at his watch, "say 0700."

"Ok boss." The man in the back seat nodded, got out of the car and walked back to the Alfa, which almost immediately drove off in the direction of the other hotel.

The Boss walked around to the trunk of the Mercedes, where he was joined by the other back seat passenger. They opened the trunk and removed two large soft bags. The Boss, holding one of the bags, walked back to the driver's door and told the driver which room they would be in, before turning to join his companion who had crossed the road back to the hotel.

CHAPTER EIGHTEEN

"With order motion is eager; eagerness with order
moves, this is the way of heaven and earth then
will the subordinates operate and armies move"
– Commentary on Chinese military strategy

I woke up early the following day, notwithstanding that after dinner Jacques and I had spent a couple of hours going through his list of possibles for my team. I had been thinking about the operation throughout the whole drive to Florence. I had almost decided, based on my knowledge of the Cote d'Azur, that I would carry out the operation in the tunnel that connects Monte Carlo to the access road to the French Autoroute. Based on that premise, I worked out that the minimum manageable safe team would be five plus Jacques and myself. Jacques would keep well away from the rest of the team and act as my personal back up for the escape route that I had sketched out in my mind. I had been open with Jacques about the risks of the operation and the probability that all our operatives would be the subject of a further operation by the Brits to liquidate everyone who was involved, so as not to have anyone writing about the operation in their memoirs in years to come. Whether or not the individuals we were recruiting would be able to survive to reap the financial reward I was going to offer them, would be up to them and their own individual abilities. My criteria were to have reliable people who knew their way around and could handle themselves in a tight corner with a sub-category, that had been stressed to me by the Admiral, there should be no possible tie in with the Brits. I eventually decided on two Serbs, a Croat, a Russian and a Syrian. Three of them spoke French and all were experienced operatives. I had included the Syrian as something of an afterthought and with some reluctance. From the biographies Jacques had shown me I suspected the Syrian had ties to Pasdaran, the Iranian Revolutionary Guard. Jacques told me that he thought the man had a history with Hamas and some Hezbollah splinter group. Neither Jacques nor I liked the idea of using someone like him but, again, bearing in mind what the Admiral had told me, I thought it might be useful to use him as a little element of misdirection. Although the whole idea was to make the operation look like a road traffic accident, I did not think it would hurt to leave a shadowy dead Syrian around, who could be linked to Iranian and Arab terrorist groups. I had not worked out in my mind how something like that would play out, but thought it was something I could keep up my sleeve.

After we had decided upon the team, I asked Jacques who he had used to contact the individuals and how quickly we could bring them into the area of operation.

"I'll come with you and introduce you to the guy. He's German, but lives in Bologna. We can make a meet between here and Bologna and get him to get things moving."

"Uh, uh. I thought I made it clear. I don't want you openly involved in any way. Call him up and arrange for me to meet him. Tell him I won't tell you what the whole thing's about and that all you know is I'm recruiting 5 mercenaries for a job for around a couple of weeks, which pays 100,000 Euros for the job with 50% down and 50% when the job's finished and he'll get a finder's fee of 10,000 Euros."

"I've already told him all that" answered Jacques looking at me thoughtfully, "He's a solid guy. I don't think he'll be any problem, but I suppose you're right. Better to play it carefully. I'll set up the meet."

I continued.

"In the meantime I'll need you to rent us two suitable places in or around Monte Carlo. One'll be for the team and one for you and for me to work from and come back to afterwards. Maybe even hole up for a few days, after the job. I'll also need a car for a trip North and then to the South of France and that we can also use for ourselves later. For the operation we're going to need two motorbikes, the same colour and make the French Gendarmerie uses. Also, two other inconspicuous cars, at least one that could pass as a French police car. We'll also need police uniforms for the team. You and I will be the ones to carry out the hit. We'll use one of the bikes. Can you manage all that in a short time?"

Jacques grinned. "As long as you give me the money, I can manage anything. What about weapons?"

"I'm thinking about that. I haven't decided yet, but this isn't a go in shoot 'em up job. We're setting up an accident. It musn't look like anything else. We're going to have to do it and be out within a few minutes, without leaving any trace that we've been around. If we get it right there shouldn't be any problems on our escape route and no big police activity afterwards. I don't think we'll need anything other than the side arms to go with the police uniforms. Although" I added an afterthought as I formed a mental picture of the two Brits in Rome staring at me, "it won't hurt for you and me to have, just for us, say a couple of automatic shotguns and maybe a couple of MP5 SDs" I was referring to the Heckler & Koch submachine gun with a full time steel sound suppressor. I went on, as a further afterthought,

"I don't know whether you could also get hold of an MP7" I was referring to another sub machine also produced by Heckler & Koch but which was compact and lightweight, combining the portability of a hand gun with almost assault rifle performance. It used special 4.6mm ammunition designed to penetrate several types of body armour. It was a gun I had never used, but I knew was well thought of, like most of the H & K products and had been adopted by several special forces.

Jacques grinned at me as he said, "As a matter of fact I can. You remember Stefan," he was referring to a huge Serb who had served with us in the Legion and who was as smart as he was big,

"Well Stefan's become a big businessman. He's even got his own planes. He's been supplying bodyguards for various people in Iraq and Afghanistan and they've been using the MP7. I was speaking to him last week. He knows how I love guns and he's been down in my cellar and seen the set up. He was telling me about the MP7 and said he would get me a couple with a couple of thousand rounds of ammunition. I should be getting them within the next two or three days.

Just then Jacques' mobile phone started to beep. He lifted it up and looked carefully at the screen. After reading what was obviously a message, he turned to me handing me the phone, saying as he did so "It's an sms from Paolo"

I looked at the message which read "arrived safely at friend's do not 4get 2 feed cat. 8 kisses a mama".

I frowned "what's he saying here?"

Jacques laughed, "For a clever guy you're sometimes a bit of a dummy. He says he's in room 428 at the hotel. It's pretty obvious isn't it? After the warnings I gave him he wouldn't just send a message for the sake of it and we haven't got a cat."

I forced a smile, feeling stupid. It was the simplest imaginable code, that a child would have figured out in nanoseconds.

Jacques then called up the contact who was supplying the labour. In the briefest of conversations he arranged for me to meet the man that evening. The meet was fixed for a hotel in a service area just by the main highway at Modena, which was more or less halfway between Florence and Bologna.

We continued discussing the various requirements for a little while longer before Jacques went off to arrange a car for me. He promised to return within two hours. While he was away I went back up to my room and divided the money up into what I was going to bank, the individual amounts for the hired help and a bundle for expenses. This did not take me very long and I then went out for an hour, wandering around the neighbourhood, looking out for any sign of surveillance. I was still nervous about the locator that had been placed in the handgun the Brits had given me. By the time I returned to the house I was satisfied that the watchers who had followed me from Rome had probably not activated the transmitter in the gun and were, no doubt, this very moment, enjoying the delights of Monte Carlo.

I had been back at Jacques' place for about half an hour and was busy chatting up his wife. Initially she had been a little hostile to me. She had hardly spoken to me at dinner the night before, but now seemed to have warmed up considerably.

When Jacques returned we must have been looking a little too cozy, because the first thing he said as he walked into the kitchen where we were sitting was

"You just leave my wife alone, you fuck. She's off limits."

His wife laughed flirtatiously, as he walked over to her and put his arm around her protectively. Giving her a kiss, he released her, instructing me to follow him.

He walked into the sitting room, where the concealed entrance led down to the cellar and sat down.

I sat next to him as he opened the leather attaché case he was carrying. He pulled out a large brown envelope and emptied the contents onto the coffee table in front of us.

"There's three sets of papers. Italian ID card and driving licence for you to use in France if you want. French ID card and driving licence for you to use here if you need to and Japanese passport, license and credit cards The Japanese stuff is stolen and altered, so be careful with it. The credit cards are ok because they're just clones, so they should not have been cancelled. I don't reckon that someone looking like you is going to get checked too carefully when he produces a Japanese passport. As far as I know we don't have too many Jap villains wandering around Europe. The car's outside. It's a rental. Rented in the Jap name. No sense in risking driving around in a stolen car. I know the guy at the rental place and told him we'll pay the bill in cash when we return the car. So there's not going to be any trace on the credit card, but he had to take the number for the time being, just in case."

He paused, "I've also, to go with the Japanese image, put some camera gear in the trunk. When you're driving around you ought to keep it handy, just to keep in character."

I laughed. I had always appreciated the careful way in which Jacques liked to cover most of the angles. The two identity cards had my picture on them, but when I opened the Japanese passport and flicked through it I saw that the picture probably belonged to the original owner.

"I suppose, if no one looks too carefully I could pass as this guy." I said.

Jacques took the passport from me and scrutinised the picture. He shrugged, "It could be you. It could be anyone. It's well known all orientals look alike to us Europeans and we all look alike to them."

"I think that's an urban legend. But it'll do."

He produced a piece of paper with some numbers written on it.

"That's what everything cost."

He had listed out the cost of the papers, cameras, money to the car rental guy and two mobile phones. It was very reasonable. It came to just under 6000 Euro. The papers alone would have cost me twice that in America. I pulled out a bundle of notes from my pocket and gave him twelve 500 Euro notes. I then followed him through the house to his garage, where he had parked the rental car.

It was a BMW 535 Diesel Estate car. I walked around it slowly, looking at it before saying to Jacques, "What the fuck is this? A diesel estate car?"

Jacques laughed, "First, no-one in Europe is going to look twice at an estate car. It's totally inconspicuous. As for the diesel, that's what people are driving these days. It's not like the old diesels you know. This is a really fast car. It'll get up to a hundred kilometres an hour, that's sixty miles an hour plus, in under six seconds and it has a top speed of well over 250 kilometres an hour. Added to that the fuel consumption is really good, so you'll be saving money and won't be fuelling up all the time."

I shook my head ruefully. "If you say so. I must really be getting out of touch. I still think of diesel engines as smelly, noisy and slow."

"Just trust me, jeune homme. This car is perfect for your needs."

It was by now nearly 1pm and I wanted to get on the road, but Jacques was insistent that we went out for lunch before I left. Clearly, living in Italy so long had corrupted his sense of values so much that having a meal had become more important than getting on with work. Eventually he persuaded me, arguing that it would take me no more than two hours to get to the hotel in Modena and I was not due to meet his contact until 9.00pm.

In the event, I only managed to get on the road in time to hit the rush hour just before 5pm. After we had finished lunch we had returned to Jacques' house for him to adjust my two guns as he had promised. He also spent a little time showing me how to re-activate the locating device he had uncovered. I had told him that I wanted to attach the locator to a truck going some long distance, so he also gave me some superglue to enable me to do this. Jacques had made some preliminary enquiries, through a contact of his, about houses around Monte Carlo. Rental was going to be expensive, even though it was still not yet high season. He had been told that what we were looking for would cost between 10,000 and 20,000 Euros for two weeks plus security deposits. I left him with an additional 100,000 Euros to cover this and the cost of the vehicles I had asked him to arrange.

The rented BMW had a navigation system but I did not want to leave any record in the car of where I had been travelling and I had bought a portable navigation system when we went out to lunch. Jacques had told me to stay off the Autoroute going out of Florence as, particularly at that time of day, the highway was completely jammed up. Instead he programmed in a route through Florence, then out towards the Futa pass. He told me that, after the pass, a road joined the Autostrada shortly before the junction between the North South highway and the principal East West axis running between Milan and Bologna.

As usual Jacques had been right. There was hardly any traffic on the route I took and the car was fast, responsive and handled well. It seemed to take no time to reach the road leading to the Autostrada. However that final, short stretch was narrow, winding and quite heavily trafficked and took me almost as long as the drive from Florence. When I finally passed the toll onto the highway I found it packed with what seemed to be thousands of trucks. Although there were three lanes, because of the density of traffic, my speed varied between 90 - 100 kilometres an hour with occasional bursts up to 160. It was annoying and frustrating and I was irritable by the time I reached Modena.

The hotel that had been fixed for the meet was just off the Autostrada, separated from a rest stop by a low evergreen hedge. The rest stop was packed with parked trucks. I noticed on the road that led to the rest stop, three scantily dressed hookers displaying themselves sensuously. Two of them were large

African women, whose clothing exposed more of their enormous breasts than it concealed. The third girl was much younger than the other two, probably Eastern European. She was blonde, thin and much more attractive than one would have expected at the side of a busy road. In fact she strongly tempted me, but it was by now after 7.30pm and I was anxious to send the locating device that had been concealed in the gun, on its way.

There was no point in my going on anywhere after the meeting so I had decided to spend the night at the hotel. I checked in under the Japanese identity, talking to the receptionist in a mixture of Japanese and pidgin English. She did not raise any queries about the passport. Maybe all orientals did look the same to westerners after all. Obligingly, she put my large bag, containing money and one gun, in the hotel safe deposit for me. I kept the pistol with the silencer on me, just in case.

By the time I had checked in and taken my case to my room it was nearly eight. I was still digesting the remnants of lunch with Jacques and decided to get rid of the locating device and, if I was then hungry, eat dinner after my meeting. I wandered out to the rest stop and down the road to where the hookers had been standing. They were no longer there. With no one apparently around to see me, I walked through the ranks of parked trucks. Most of them were Italian, but there were several with French and Dutch plates. I was considering attaching the device to a truck registered in Holland, when I noticed two trucks parked side by side, with the same company name emblazoned on both of them. I knew enough to recognise Polish and, in particular, the name of the town printed just before a telephone number. I remembered that Gdansk was far in the North of Poland. I assumed the trucks would be heading back to their home base. That was perfect for what I wanted. I walked under a street light, took out the locating device; activated it as Jacques had shown me, before walking back to one of the Polish trucks and used the superglue to stick it underneath the trailer, where no one would ever find it. That ought to keep those Brits occupied and confused. I then walked back to the hotel and sat in the lobby to wait for my contact.

My man arrived dead on 9pm. He came barrelling through the entrance doors, stopped, looked around the lobby and then walked directly towards me. He was quite tall, although slightly shorter than me, but there any resemblance ended. He must have been in his late sixties and was a good thirty or forty pounds overweight, with his large stomach protruding out over the belt that hitched his trousers almost up to his navel. For all that and his almost bald head, his clothes were expensive and his dress sense gave him a certain elegance despite the best efforts of his body to ruin the impression.

He sat down heavily next to me and pulled out a handkerchief, which he used to mop away the sweat that had been gathering on his face and forehead.

"I think you're waiting for me." He spoke in English with a noticeable German accent. I recalled Jacques had said he was German.

I answered him, mimicking a Japanese accent, although not laying it on too heavily.

"Yes. I am most pleased to meet. We have some business to arrange."

He ignored what I had said and asked "Have you eaten yet?" and without giving me time to reply added, "Let's go into the restaurant. I'm hungry."

He got up without giving me a chance to object and led the way into the hotel restaurant. I had no option but to follow him. The restaurant was comparatively empty, with less than a quarter of the tables being occupied. In the circumstances, it was probably a better, less conspicuous place than the lobby to discuss our business.

The German did not seem particularly inclined to open a conversation about our business. He was too occupied calling the waiter over to take his order of ante pasta, pasta, a main course and a bottle of red wine. I was a little nonplussed by the time the waiter turned expectantly to me. I looked at him and then at my companion, who had already started making serious inroads into the basket of rolls that had been on the table when we sat down. I decided to be polite and ordered a plate of tagliatelle with wild mushrooms and a salad.

It would be impossible for me to describe the German as having impeccable manners or even as matching the politeness that I thought I had been showing. It was apparent that his social graces only extended as far as tasting and approving the wine. He had already emptied his glass and was gesticulating for the waiter to give him a refill, before the poor man had finished pouring me a glass. I did not mind. It suited me if he was going to be a big drinker. I like wine but try not to mix alcohol with work. It is bad enough mixing my work with my age, without alcohol added into the equation.

After downing a second and third glass of wine in quick succession and demolishing his plate of ante pasta with impressive speed, the German, who actually turned out to be an Austrian, deigned to address me.

"So, we are going to agree on these contractors you are employing." Our pasta had arrived and somehow, he managed simultaneously to speak intelligibly and attack his plate of pasta with the same efficient voracity he had displayed towards his first dish. Even though it was revolting to watch him, there was something fascinating about the way in which he was able to destroy a plate of food with the only trace of anything ever having been there, being one or two small tomato stains on the tablecloth. With some difficulty I stopped staring at him and delved into my shirt pocket.

"Yes. I've got the names of the people I want." I fished out the folded piece of paper on which I had written the names I had agreed with Jacques.

For a few brief seconds he seemed lost, with only an empty plate in front of him. Then his fat, stubby fingers flew over to the bread basket and ripped the packaging off some breadsticks, which swiftly followed everything else, into his mouth. Now that his mouth was again happily working, he took the paper I was offering, looked at it and nodded.

"You're paying half now and half at the end and it's for a maximum of two weeks?"

"Yes. They'll need to be available to start in about a week or so; maybe a little longer. But once I call them, they've got to be where I tell them within a day."

"Where will that be?" the question came out very smoothly as he munched on the last of the breadsticks.

"I'll tell them that directly, after you put us in touch."

He looked at me sharply, "OK you give me the money for them and I'll get them arranged."

"No. You put me in touch with them. When I've spoken to them and agreed everything and am happy we're a go, I pay you your introductory commission. Where are these guys now, anyway? Are they in Italy?"

"Three are in Italy, two in Croatia. Very close." I moved my head slightly to avoid the crumbs of breadstick flying towards me through the air.

"Can they meet me here tomorrow? I'll pay 1000 Euros each expense money to get them here. If you can get them here tomorrow there's an extra 5000 Euros in it for you."

His main course had now arrived, along with the second bottle of wine he had ordered, to replace the one he had finished.

"I'll get them here for tomorrow evening. But you'll give me 20,000 Euros for my fees and expenses, as well as the 5000 Euros for them."

I wondered if it was all that wine and food that was making him so smart, or whether he was just naturally quick. I hated to destroy the man's self- confidence but there is no point in allowing people to think you are a pushover.

"I've already said I'll give you 15,000. The expenses and everything else I deal direct with the contractors. If you don't like it fuck off." I still had some pasta left in my plate and turned my attention to that.

His only reaction was to drain another glass of wine. The second bottle was now three quarter's empty and my first glass still sat untouched.

He had now finished his main dish, nearly two bottles of wine and everything in the breadbasket but still did not reply to me. The waiter interrupted the silence between us, wheeling over a trolley full of desserts and, then, at the direction of the human food blender sitting next to me, filled a large plate with a portion of everything that was creamy and sugary. When he was satisfied that there was no room to cram anything else on to his plate, the waiter was dismissed with a quick nod and allowed to wander back to his station, shaking his head in wonderment.

"My usual fee is 10%. 20,000 is not unreasonable. It's not even 5% of the 500,000 you're going to be paying out. I can get everyone here by 6 o'clock tomorrow evening for you to approve them. But I can assure you you'll be happy with them. They're all good men. The best. Lots of experience. But I want half my money up front, now."

"I told you I'll pay 15,000. If you want anymore get it off the guys you're contracting. This is a great deal for them. No one pays this sort of money for a couple of weeks work. And you'll get your money when I see and agree the contractors. I don't know you, you don't know me and for all I know you could be just a rip off merchant."

He stopped in the middle of a mouthful.

"Look, I was in GSG 9 (*Grenzschutzgruppe 9* - a counter terrorism_and special operations unit of the German Federal Police, considered to be among the best of its kind in the world) for fifteen years. I think you know what that means. It means I'm not a cunt. I supply mostly Russian, Eastern European and South African ex-soldiers for hire all over the world. I supply some of the biggest companies; Blackwater, Spartan, Hart. You've heard of them?" He continued, without waiting for my confirmation that I knew the companies he had mentioned.

"They're all perfectly happy to pay me deposits for the work I do. It's time and money for me coming to meet you here and there's no reason for me to change my business practices just because you don't like it."

"OK. Let's understand each other. I don't give a fuck about GSG 9 or anyone you work with and, I'm not about to start taking up references for you. All I know about you is you like to eat and drink and you're out of shape and overweight. I'll be in the lobby at 6 tomorrow evening. If you're there with the contractors we've got a deal. If you're not I might even decide to come after you for wasting my time."

He looked at me hard for a few moments before cracking a smile and thrusting a podgy hand across the table at me.

You've got a deal. Just one thing I ask. Any commission I take off the guys I'm bringing, you deduct it and pay direct to me." I was not sure whether he was asking a question or making a statement, but if everyone agreed I certainly did not object.

I took his hand and shook it, "if we're all up front with each other and the men agree to that, I've got no objection."

"Just one more thing" he tapped the side of his nose with his right index finger, "the separate money you're paying me... just be between the two of us. Understood?"

"I've got no problem with that."

He actually started smiling, "Let's have a grappa before I go on my way."

"Do you think you should if you're going to be driving? You've already drunk nearly two bottles of wine"

"It's no problem, it's no problem" he answered expansively as he motioned to the waiter to come over.

It was another ten minutes before he was lumbering out of the door towards his car. Amazingly he walked perfectly straight and gave no indication of being drunk. He had made no effort even to offer to pay the bill and had simply got up and shaken my hand again, with a "see you tomorrow" before walking out. I was left at the table, amongst the ruins of his dinner, with the waiter bringing me the bill which I paid in cash.

CHAPTER NINETEEN

"Increase moves and then follow through"
—Chinese military strategy

I was woken by the rumble of early morning traffic, which intruded into my room even through the double glazed windows. It was still dark outside, although light from the sodium street lamps provided enough illumination in the room for me to see clearly. I looked around wondering for a moment where I was. My Thai reproduction Tag Heuer had long since lost any ability it might once have had to display its numbers in the dark. I looked towards the television, the base of which glowed 06.20 at me. I lay there not wanting to get up, wondering what I could do usefully to spend the day, whilst waiting for my Austrian companion of last night to arrive with his cohort of mercenaries.

After a few minutes I got out of bed on the side by the window and looked out. I had a magnificent view of the rest stop and truck parking area. The vehicles of the previous evening had all gone and there were only two cars and one or two trucks sitting there. The British locating device was apparently well on its way to Gdansk.

I switched on the television, climbed back into bed and lay there using the remote control to flick through the channels until I found CNN and the news. I watched for a while before getting bored with the parochial reports, pre-digested for an American audience suffering from attention deficit disorder and changed the channel to the BBC and the completely different British news. At least they provided a reasonably balanced view of what was going on in the world and spoke slowly enough for my brain to digest and think about what was being said. I was about to switch off when the announcer said something about the princess who was the current object of all my activities. My concentration returned as I watched. The woman was apparently going to Monte Carlo as the guest of Prince Albert for the Formula 1 Grand Prix being held the following week. She was then going to spend further time on the French Riviera, either staying in Monaco or on a friend's yacht. They showed a few long distance shots of what was, from my recollection of what the Brits had shown me, probably the Cleopatra.

I made a quick calculation based on the following assumptions. First, that Jacques would be able to set up the safe houses and get everything else I had requested; that the team being presented to me tonight was satisfactory and that I got the rest of my money. If those three uncertainties could be resolved, I ought to be able to do the job towards the end of the next week. It would be rushed, but in essence it was not a complicated operation. Everything depended on the target's movements. We just needed to ensure we were in the right place at the right time. One advantage of speeding up the timetable was that it would give the Brits less time to prepare to fuck me.

It was nearly 8.30am by the time I had showered, dressed and watched some more news. I went downstairs to see what sort of lavish breakfast the hotel was including in the room rate. I found a buffet with about ten different types of cake, some rolls, cheese, yoghourt and tinned fruit salad. I do not like yoghourt, rarely eat cake and never for breakfast, so I settled for a small bowl of fruit salad and a roll. The former tasted as if it had been sitting stewing for days and I pushed it aside. The roll was tasteless and I left that too, after one bite. Even the Foreign Legion gave us better food than this. At least the espresso was good. After three more espressos I thought I had better eat some more of the roll to avoid heartburn. Even after trying to get through that without breaking a tooth, I was unable to make the breakfast last longer than ten minutes. I went to the reception area to tell them that I would be staying another night.

I had watched television, had breakfast and it was not even 9am. How was I going to kill time until the Austrian brought the men for me to look over? I had to call my banker in Liechtenstein to arrange to deposit the cash. If the men passed muster I would be able to get there the following day. I intended to do some more work on the planning for the job, but all that, including finding a public phone well away from the hotel would not take me more than a couple of hours. I remembered that Modena was where the Ferrari factory is situated.

I wondered if I should go there. I had enough money not to notice the cost of ordering a new Ferrari and I had always had a secret hankering for one. Perhaps it would be a little premature, but then I remembered hearing that there was a waiting list of about a year for the cars, so why not order one now. Fate had placed me in Modena with nothing to do all day. I decided to make a decision after I had dealt with everything else. I went back to my room, took out a pen and paper and started working on my plan of operation. My first step was to draw a rough map of what I remembered of the road system around and between Monte Carlo and Cannes. I have a good memory for that sort of thing and I knew the area quite well. After about half an hour, I thought that I had produced quite a good representation of the roads in and around what was going to be our area of operations. I then spent another hour and a half working out different scenarios. It was nearly lunch time by the time I had finished. I left the hotel and drove towards the centre of Modena. I got lost in a one way system and ended up on the other side of the town. As I was trying to get back into the centre I passed a small Trattoria which looked quite welcoming. I went in to find the place almost full. They still found a small table for me and a waitress with a black moustache rattled off the different choices. I soon discovered why the place was so busy. Their three course set menu, including a choice of pasta, main dish, a litre of wine and a litre of mineral water was provided for 20 Euros. I thought ruefully of the meal the previous evening which had cost over 150 Euros.

I was not intending to drink the wine, but the food was very good and so was the wine. By the time they brought me 3 large pieces of cheese as dessert I found that I was almost down to the end of the bottle. I was not feeling in the least drunk but I was in a pleasant frame of mind.

I left the restaurant just after 2pm after having used their payphone to call Liechtenstein. I told the banker that I was not sure when I would arrive the following day but he said that he would wait for me.

Apparently, either the food or the wine had improved my sense of direction, as I found my way into the centre of Modena without difficulty. I walked around the town for an hour or so but there was little of interest to me. After a coffee, I drove back to the hotel. Just before I got to the hotel on one of the roads leading off the Autostrada I passed the hooker I had found attractive the evening before. These girls either have exceptional eyesight or psychic abilities. I would have sworn that I had barely glanced at her, but there she was, stepping out in front of my car giving me a smile that seemed to tell me we were alone in the world. I had plenty of time before my meeting. I stopped. Her Italian was almost non-existent, but she spoke good English. I let her get into the car. She came from Moldova which had been a satellite of the former Soviet Union and was astonished when I told her I had been there, as I had a few years before. We quickly came to an arrangement and I took her back to the hotel for what turned out to be a couple of very pleasant hours.

I got out of bed just before 5pm and took a shower. While I was in the shower an idea had started to auto-germinate in my brain. Within the next few days I had to cross at least two borders with guns and a very large amount of cash in my car. It was something that had been bothering me. Border controls between European countries had almost been done away with but checks were still made from time to time, particularly between Switzerland and the members of the European Union. Whilst I could conceal the guns and cash from a cursory inspection, any, even limited, search could easily uncover them and throw a wrench into my whole operation. I had already considered taking a train from Italy to Switzerland and then renting another car in Switzerland and taking a train back to France, because inspections on trains in Europe can be perfunctory, but, again, that is also not always the case. Neither did I really have the extra time that taking a train would entail. I now had a girl in my room and I was thinking that a man travelling with a woman is far less conspicuous and less likely to be stopped for inspection than a man travelling alone. The girl had already said that she wanted to stay with me for the evening and I had no objection. Indeed, once she had taken off her cheap clothes and cleaned herself up in the shower, she turned out to be a beautiful young woman with a perfect body. Also I liked her. A lot of people might consider me to be a cruel, heartless master of destruction and chaos. I suppose I am. But I also have a bit of a weakness for strays. Stray cats, stray dogs, stray children; I have looked after them all within the constraints imposed by my life.

There was something of a stray about this beautiful young girl that appealed to me as much as her physical attraction. I later realised that, although there was no physical resemblance, she reminded me of someone I had shacked up with when I was in El Salvador in the early eighties. Another young, attractive hooker, who had adopted me after one night together. We were together for more than three months, when one day she just disappeared. I was more disappointed than I cared to admit at the time, which was probably why I just shrugged my shoulders and got on with my work. Then, about ten days after she had disappeared, I was back in my apartment, having a few beers with one of my colleagues, when there was a bit of a commotion outside. We went down to see what was going on and there she was. What was left of her; a crumpled mutilated doll lying naked in the dusty street with the words, "puta" and "FMLN", carved both into her abdomen and forehead above the eye sockets, from which the eyes had been removed. My job at the time was assisting the Salvadorian government's fight against the Farabundo Marti National Liberation Front (FMLN). Thereafter, until I moved station, members of the FMLN I came across found very little compassion at my hands.

I finished showering and went back into the bedroom, drying myself off. She was lying naked on the bed, enjoying the comfort of the air conditioning, but looked up a little warily as I sat down beside her. I stroked her body and asked

"Do you have a passport?"

She sat bolt upright, "Why do you ask?"

"Because I was just thinking. I like you and was wondering if you'd like to come on a little trip with me for a few days. I'd make it worth your while of course."

I have known a lot prostitutes over the years. Some quite well. I know that many men who frequent prostitutes and lap dancers deceive themselves that any warmth and affection shown to them means that the women genuinely like them. I do not consider myself as susceptible to self-deceit. I know that, as a rule, the warmth and affection these women show are as simulated as subsequent orgasms and used only to extract increased payment. Of course working girls are as capable of genuine feelings as anyone else, but the principal feeling they derive from their "johns" is the pleasure of counting their takings after waving goodbye. Accordingly, I was astonished at the girl's reaction to my suggestion. She burst into tears. Instead of throwing some cash at her and telling her to fuck off out of there, I surprised myself by trying to comfort her. I held her, wiped her tears away and made stupid soothing noises. That was enough to stimulate her into pouring out her whole story.

It was nothing unusual. She was 23. In spite of a University education she had been in a dead end job, in a dead end town, in a dead end country. Hollywood films, which were about the only form of entertainment for her and her friends, had filled her with all sorts of romantic ideas about life in the West. The advertisement in her local newspaper for dancers in an exclusive club in Western Europe and the rates of pay quoted, had been irresistible to her. The reality had been the taking of all her documents, multiple rape and transport across Europe locked in a dirty truck with other girls, with more rape at each stop. Finally, only a few weeks previously, she had been sold to a gang of Albanians who put her out on the roads abutting the Autostrada. So no, she did not have a passport and if she tried to get away the Albanians would kill her. In the normal way, with a few days in hand I could easily have got her a set of false papers. But I did not have a few days. Thinking that at least I could give her a few hours of peace, I left her in the room full of false hope, telling her not to worry about the Albanians and I would see what I could work out.

I went down early to my meeting, having abandoned the idea of taking the girl with me. Then fate took a hand. Just as I got down to the lobby, it became flooded with people. A coach full of Czech tourists had stopped at the hotel for the night. They were milling around chaotically, with the two receptionists desperately trying to cope with the confusion and register each individual's passport. Three or four blonde women in their thirties or early forties were chatting together incessantly, as they removed their passports from their bags and placed them carelessly on the reception counter in front of the harassed receptionists. It was the work of a moment to brush past and slip the passports off the counter, into my pocket. No one noticed a thing. I strolled casually outside to the car park and got into my car. The street lights provided sufficient lighting for me to look at the passports. I chose one, of a woman who was quite fat in reality, but whose passport picture did not show her bulk. She was thirty five and the picture could have been any rather attractive but non-descript blonde. I locked the passport into the glove compartment and returned to the chaos in the lobby, pretending to pick up the two other passports from the floor and replace them on the counter. No one noticed this either.

Fifteen minutes later the lobby had cleared and everyone had disappeared into their rooms, leaving the reception staff with a large pile of passports and identity documents to enter in their computer. It was unlikely to be morning until the loss of the passport was discovered and I intended to be on the road very early.

My group arrived together, shortly after 6.20 pm. Clearly my companion of the previous evening had not been sufficiently intoxicated for it to affect either his driving or his business dealings. I did not need to spend very long with the proposed members of my team to know that they were going to be more than adequate for the operation. Apart from the Syrian, there was instant mutual recognition between us of what we were.

The Russian was a large, surly, ex Spetsnaz who had seen action in Afghanistan and Chechnya and thereafter worked as a "bodyguard" for various interests. It was obvious to me that "bodyguard" was a euphemism for doing the same sort of work I did. The three guys from the Balkans had all seen a lot of action there and had latterly been working on contracts in Iraq. The two Serbs seemed as hard and morose as the Russian, but the Croat, by contrast, was quite an engaging, jokey guy who feigned an American accent and idiom he had obviously adopted from the cinema.

The Syrian was entirely different. I did not like him at all. He made my hackles rise. His head was shaven down to a heavy black stubble, which failed to improve his sharp, pointed face. He had narrow eyes that never seemed to want to look at you directly and were always darting from side to side. Neither clean shaven, nor bearded, his face matched his head. Perhaps it was the way he dressed and his shifty look that reminded me of the Iranian president, Ahmadinejhad. In spite of those darting sideways looks, his eyes reflected the internal fire of a zealot. He made little effort to disguise his dislike of the other members of the group. The feelings were clearly mutual and I thought to myself that at the end of this job we were going to be fighting over who got to waste him. I wondered why he was taking the job and asked the question.

As he answered he half covered his mouth with his hand and looked down and to the left, saying the money was good and he needed it. It would have been obvious he was lying, even if his body language had not been so palpable. My reasons for including him no longer seemed so compelling. If he had his own agenda he could sabotage the whole operation. I had no choice though. I would just have to take a chance. If everything went down the next week it was too late to change personnel. All I could do would be to see if I could eliminate him from the job at the final planning stage or, at the very least, allot him one of the least important parts. I would also, when the opportunity presented itself, have a private word with the others and tell them to keep an eye on him.

I told them that I would need them the following week. I did not tell them where, but said that it would not be too far from where we were now and that they should allow a day for travel. I took cell phone contact numbers and promised to give them as much notice as possible and full details of where we were going to meet. I told them if they would come outside with me, away from the lobby I would give them 1000 Euro each for their expenses for coming and an additional 5000 as an advance on their fees with a further 45,000 when we met the following week. I had started to get up when my overweight friend of the previous evening threw in his oar.

"These men have to pay me 10% of what they are getting as a finder's fee. I need you to pay me that direct now, because my job is finished. That's 10,000 each. 50,000 Euros."

I looked at him and at the men who, said nothing but nodded and shrugged their shoulders.

"Suppose one or more of them don't turn up," I said.

"They will. They're all first rate, reliable men." He sounded like the madame in a brothel, describing her girls.

"We need to discuss this. Why don't you guys go to the bar and have a drink on me." I gave a 100 Euro note to the Croat and they all got up and left me with the Austrian.

After five minutes haggling I agreed to pay him 40,000 Euros all in, being the 15,000 I had promised him the evening before and 5,000 each for the men, to be deducted from what I paid them.

We got up and joined the men who were sitting at a table in the bar area away from anyone else.

"I've agreed to pay this man," I nodded towards the Austrian, "5,000 each out of what I'm going to pay you. I'll also give you the 1000 each I promised for today's expenses and a 5,000 Euro advance. That means that when you come to join me you'll be getting 40,000 Euro each advance payment and a further 50,000 at the end of the job. Is that all right? All agreed."

They all nodded their agreement and I said, "I'll just go and get the money and then you can all go and be on your way."

I got up and walked to the lavatory that serviced the restaurant and bar. Locking myself in one of the stalls, I performed my usual trick of shutting the toilet cover with my foot and sat down. Earlier that morning I had taken several large envelopes from the receptionist and had already put 6000 Euros into each of five envelopes, which I had left in the room safe and removed before coming downstairs. In addition I had been walking around most of the day with 50,000 Euros stuffed into the inside pockets of my jacket. I now took out 10,000 and put it back in my pocket and divided the balance between two other envelopes. I used one of the envelopes to unlock the stall door and returned to the bar holding all the envelopes in my hand. I sat down and handed them out, giving the Austrian his two envelopes. The others took the money and put it away without opening the envelopes and checking the contents. The fat man however, looked in both envelopes and quickly counted the notes without taking them out. Having finished the count he looked at me and nodded.

I stood up. "OK. I'll be contacting you guys at the numbers you've given me and we'll be meeting next week."

They all drained what was left of their drinks and stood up. The Croat delved in his pocket and pulled out some change and bank notes, offering it to me.

"That's the change from the drinks." I took the money, thanking him.

We then all shook hands and I accompanied them as they walked out of the hotel. They squeezed into a new model S Class Mercedes driven by the Austrian and off they sailed. I made a mental note of the registration number of the Mercedes. One never knows.

After they had left, I went into my car and wrote down the Mercedes registration number on piece of a paper I had in the glove compartment. I put the piece of paper in my pocket and retrieved the passport I had stolen. It was 7.30pm. Just about time for dinner. I wondered if the girl was still going to be in my room when I went up.

She was. She had dressed, made the bed neatly and put on the bed cover on which she was now reclining, watching television. She looked up as I came into the room. I fished the passport out of my pocket and threw it on the bed next to her, asking,

"Do you think you could make yourself look enough like that to pass a border?"

She picked up the passport, looking at the cover before opening it at the page containing the picture and personal details. She studied the picture and other information carefully with her face screwed up in concentration. I liked that. She was not yet the careless, drug addict she might have become. Eventually she answered me.

"Yes, I think so. I change my hair, the makeup... but where did you get this?" She was fingering the passport nervously.

"Never mind about that. I just need to know if you think you can pass through a customs inspection using that passport. I think you can. But I need to know that you believe you can."

She looked at me, still twisting the passport around in her fingers, "I... I... yes, I can make myself look like this woman, but... but"

"What?"

"I... I'll need some clothes. I have nothing. Nothing. No. This is not possible. They will kill me." She put the passport down on the bed and looked as if she was about to burst into tears again.

"Don't worry about them killing you and don't worry about clothes. Don't worry about anything. We can fix all that. We can fix everything" I said soothingly, although I was becoming a little irritated by her uncertainty. I hoped that it was nothing more than an act to try to get me to buy her a new wardrobe.

"Really." She said, "really. You really mean this. You really want to take me with you. Away from these Albanians."

It was apparent that her hesitation came more from the difficulty she was having in believing that I wanted to take her with me, than in any inherent lack of belief in her own acting ability.

"Look" I said, "I got you that didn't I?" pointing to the passport, "I got that very quickly. And I can assure you I can handle any Albanians."

She looked at me. She was more confident now. "I can make myself look like that woman. I will make a whole story about who I am, how we met in Prague, how you became my boyfriend and took me with you here."

This was more like it.

"We'll talk about the cover story while we're driving. I'll get you some clothes tomorrow and whatever makeup or other stuff you need. Let's go out and have some dinner now. We're going to have to leave early tomorrow."

She seemed really pleased. As we went downstairs she started firing questions at me, asking me where we were going, what it was like and a host of other inconsequential questions. I decided to take her to the hotel restaurant. The food had been quite good the evening before and I did not want her new found confidence destroyed by letting her see the road outside where I had picked her up, to remind her of what she was. Neither did I want to start getting involved in any problems with her Albanians. She had told me that they cruised around throughout the evening checking on their girls. I did not want any unexpected encounters that might lead to me having to waste someone.

I preferred to run the risk of her seeing the woman whose passport I had stolen. As it turned out I did not need to worry. The Czech coach was no longer in the car park and it had obviously taken its contingent of holiday makers out somewhere else. I noticed, as we passed the reception desk, that various passports were now all neatly filed in different pigeon holes where the keys for individual rooms were kept.

CHAPTER TWENTY

*"There are no good girls gone wrong - just bad girls
found out."*
Mae West

After dinner last night, Natalya, for that was the name of my new girl-friend, and I made love again. On this occasion she was considerably more affectionate, open and relaxed than in the afternoon. I enjoyed her but could not help reflecting how influenced a girl can be by the promise of a few clothes and a short trip.

I woke her up at 5am, expecting complaints and an extended stay in the bathroom. She surprised me. She was not only good humoured but it took her no longer than five minutes to shower and dress. We were on the road before 6am. Although we were passing Milan, I did not think we needed to go to the design capital of the world to outfit her with clothes. Milan, like every commercial centre these days, seems to become nothing more than one extended traffic jam between the hours of 8am and 7.00pm and I wanted to pass it before the morning rush hour started to build up. I thought there would be sufficient shops in

Como, just before the Swiss border, to enable me to buy Natalya whatever she needed.

She was chatty and did not seem to mind my fast driving. The traffic was still quite light and I was able to keep up a high average speed. We had passed Milan by 7.45 and half-an-hour later were driving into Como. The journey had been much quicker than I had anticipated and no shops were yet open. I found a parking space and took her into a hotel near the lake for some breakfast.

By the time we had finished breakfast, the streets had come alive with people ambling into work and the shops had started to open. Natalya scored more points with me when, at first, she was quite diffident about choosing clothes. On the demerit side, she had no idea of what was elegant and kept gravitating towards hooker-wear. She was better with the make-up. In the end, with my help, we managed to put together a reasonable wardrobe and a few pairs of shoes, most of which went into a cheap suitcase I also purchased. She needed little persuasion to wear one of the new outfits and to throw away the street-whore clothes supplied to her by the Albanians. I put everything into the trunk of the car alongside my bag of money which, with utter recklessness, I had left locked in the trunk, camouflaged under a covering of my clothes. In order to help encourage Natalya to spend my money, I had purchased a couple of shirts and two pairs of shoes which, I added to the clothing covering the cash.

Having relieved ourselves of our purchases, we went back to the hotel where we had had breakfast. Natalya went off to the ladies' room while I waited for her in the lobby. I was astonished when she came back. She had done an amazing job with the makeup, changed her hairstyle and with her new clothes looked completely different. I asked her for the passport which she had taken with her to guide her transformation. She handed it over. As I compared how she looked now to the passport picture, I realised this girl had quite a talent. I began to think I might have discovered a real treasure. No-one at any normal border inspection would be able to tell she was not the woman in the passport. When I said as much, Natalya looked really pleased.

There was one other thing to take care of when we returned to the car. The guns. Without tools and with little time to prepare, I had decided to use duct tape Jacques had given me, to tape the guns underneath the front driver's and passenger's seats. It was not a very good hiding place and would not withstand a determined search, but I had already checked and for a cursory examination, even if someone passed their hand under the seats, the guns would be undetectable. Natalya's eyes widened a little when I produced the two fire arms and started taping them in place, but she said nothing. Having finished and satisfied myself that the now concealed weapons would pass any brief inspection, we got back into the car. There were no questions from the girl as I started the engine and headed out of town, back towards the Autostrada and the Swiss Border. That was something else that pleased me about her. Most women would have been unable to restrain themselves from asking about the guns. Natalya, however, remained silent until we were in a queue of cars inching our way slowly towards the Border control.

"Can I ask something?"

"What?" I did not mind talking as we approached the customs post. Chatting to your girl-friend looked natural and innocent, it averted suspicions.

"Who are you exactly?"

She said it so seriously that for some reason it made me laugh.

I glanced across at her, "Does it really matter?"

"No. No. It doesn't. But you make me feel very safe." She snuggled across the seat and into my shoulder, just as we approached two Guardia di Finanza who were inspecting vehicles on the Italian side of the border. They barely glanced at us, casually waving me through. The Swiss Border guard however, looked at our car and directed me into an area where two other cars were already sitting, apparently being inspected. I relaxed, controlling my breathing and watched as a border guard approached my window. He greeted me in Italian but, in keeping with my Japanese persona, I pretended not to understand him and asked him haltingly if he spoke English. He did. He told me that I did not have a sticker to travel on the Swiss Highway and I would have to purchase one for 45 francs. Relieved, I asked how many Euro that was and in exchange for the money, I was handed a small sticker indicating the year. He stood there watching while I stuck it to the windshield and then smiled and waved me through welcomingly into Switzerland.

Natalya had been smiling at the guard and acting as if she did not have a care in the world. But as I drove away from the border she put her arm through mine and confessed,

"I was so frightened when he stopped us. I thought for sure we were going to have a big problem. I can't believe you could stay so calm."

I laughed, "You seemed to me to be pretty calm yourself."

"Yes, but inside I was shaking all over."

"Well, it's what's on the outside that counts."

I was pleased with the girl. So far she had not put a foot wrong.

It took us a little over four hours to reach Liechtenstein. Although Liechtenstein is an independent principality with its own police force and army, there is no border between Switzerland and the principality. We drove into Vaduz, which is the main town and into the grounds of the Park Hotel. I had stayed there before and found it pleasant. It also had the advantage of having a gym and spa facilities. Natalya, who had at first been excited to see the lake at Lugano and the mountains around the San Bernardino pass that we crossed, had fallen asleep about an hour before we arrived in Vaduz. She woke up as I stopped and I told her where we were, in response to her question.

The check in was quick, but it was nearly 3pm by the time we were installed in the room and I was impatient to get to the bank. Natalya started to ask me questions about what we were going to do and could we eat something. I told her I had to go out to a business meeting and that she could order whatever she liked and, if she wanted, go to the spa and charge everything to the room. I then left, taking my bag of money with me.

The bank was no more than a ten minute walk from the hotel. Entry was gained through an automatic door controlled by one of three concierges who also took me to a conference room whose windows were covered with thick drapes. I accepted the coffee that I was offered and which was brought to me within five minutes on a silver tray containing a cup of coffee, a small jug of cream, some paper wrapped sugar lumps and a few assorted biscuits.

I was left alone with my coffee for at least ten minutes and I spent the time munching on the biscuits until a knock at the door was followed by the entry of Herr Von Auer. The banker was a tall, balding, portly man who tended to peer at one myopically through his smart Cartier, gold framed glasses. He greeted me as effusively as decorum and the character of these bankers allowed, which meant he shook my hand, smiled and used my name. Or rather, the name in which I had opened the account, "Mr. Chau".

I have probably already mentioned that, throughout my operational years, I managed to build up an enviable collection of different passports and other identity documents. At the time I had opened my account with this bank, I had been on an operation during which I had had to adopt the identity of a Singaporean Chinese businessman, which had given me access to a Singaporean passport. I had used that passport when opening the account. As the balance increased, I had, on the advice of the bank, incorporated a Panamanian company in whose name the funds were now held. Various named individuals held a power of attorney from the company enabling them to utilise the funds in the account. These named individuals were all in fact one and the same, myself, but I was the only one to know this. The practical reason for all this subterfuge was that I used different names in different places and at different banks. No questions were raised when I instructed the Liechtenstein bank to transfer funds to banks where I held funds in other names, which were also signatories to the corporate account.

After we had finished the social pleasantries of talking about the weather and the world economic situation, I told Von Auer that I had some funds to deposit. He produced a folder with some printed deposit slips and asked me how much I was depositing. By way of reply I took my bag, placed it on the table and opened it for him to see,

"Good gracious," he was unable to contain his surprise. I do not think that even in Liechtenstein he was used to seeing so much money in cash.

"How much is there?" he asked unable to take his eyes away from the interior of the bag.

After I had paid out Jacques, the other members of the team and the intermediary and added in the money I had received from the job in Sicily, I had just under 3.5 million Euros on me.

I thought that I would keep back around 100,000 Euros for immediate expenses and therefore responded, "I want to deposit 3.4 million Euros. There's more than that here, but I'm going to keep back the approximately 100,000 extra."

"Very well. We'll have to check the amount of course. Do you wish to leave the money here for us to check and come back later or... " he stopped when he saw the look I was giving him,

"I'll get a money counting machine in here."

"Yes. I think that's a better idea."

He forced himself to take his eyes out of my bag, got up and went out of the room.

It was another ten minutes before he returned, accompanied by a younger man who was carrying a counting machine. Polite as ever, he introduced the young man to me, although I did not catch the name. The machine was placed on the table and the young man then started crawling around on the floor trying to find an electrical outlet to plug in the machine. I watched in silence as he tried to get the plug into various sockets which were all too far for the length of the cord. Eventually, just as I was about to say something, he moved the machine to the end of the table, nearer to a socket. He and von Auer then started to take out the bundles of 500 Euro notes and run them through the counter before placing piles of counted money on one side of the table. The machine was very fast. I was surprised at how quickly they accumulated 68 bundles of 100 notes each.

"3.4 million. Is that right? That is what you wish to deposit" Von Auer was looking into the bag trying to calculate how much I was holding back.

"Yes. That's right."

He started scribbling, filling in the deposit slip and then handed it to me to sign. I signed it using Kanji characters and pushed the slip back across the table to him.

He said something in German to the young man, who scuttled out of the room, bowing to me. The younger man returned a few minutes later with what looked like a large plastic crate. The two of them then shovelled the money into the crate with their hands, before each picked up an end and carried the money out of the room.

After they had left I was once again on my own. Having finished my coffee and biscuits I started to flick through an International Herald Tribune that was on a side table with some German language newspapers. Von Auer did not return for another fifteen minutes, by which time I had been able to glean a fair idea of what was happening in the world and in the world's financial markets.

When Von Auer re-appeared, he gave me a receipt for the cash and an updated copy of a bank statement for my account, which included the money I had just given him. He sat down again opposite me.

"So, Herr Chau, just what would you like us to do with this money. I have some investment suggestions I would like to make."

I listened to his suggestions and discussed them with him. He, like nearly all bankers, wanted to have a complete discretion as to how to handle my funds. In the innocence of my youth, I had once given such discretion to the bankers at a Swiss bank where I had opened my very first account. I had soon learned that I would have been better off entrusting my funds to an untrained chimpanzee with a pencil and a list of shares. I soon took over the management of my own funds and found that following companies was not much different than following horses; one examined the track record, the management and the product and did not get too excited by exceptionally good odds. At least my capital had increased every year, even if I had not made any fortunes. In the end, with Von Auer, I decided to invest half a million of what I had given him and leave the rest as cash, gaining interest for the time being. Before leaving him I made a request to warm his heart,

"Do you have a branch or correspondent in Monte Carlo?"

"Yes we do. It is not a branch exactly. It is a correspondent bank who maintain a small sub office for us."

"I'm expecting to pick up some more cash. Maybe a little more than what I've just deposited. I'll need either to deposit it in a safe deposit or else have some secure method of getting it delivered to you and credited to my account."

Instead of replying he started to write on the writing pad he had on the table by his side. When he had finished, he tore off the piece of paper he had been writing on and handed it to me. It contained a bank name, the name of an individual, an address and telephone number.

"This is who you will need. When do you expect to carry out this transaction?"

"Sometime within the next three, four, five days. I'm not quite sure."

He picked up the telephone and dialled. After a few moments he started to speak in German. My German is not very good but I got the gist of what he was saying, which was that a very good client would be making a delivery of a substantial amount of cash that was to be routed to them through some account whose details I did not understand.

He put down the phone,

"It's all arranged."

I needed to be convinced. It was a lot of money, "Are you sure it's going to be alright. It's a lot of money. I don't want to have any problems."

"You don't need to worry sir. We do this sort of thing all the time. He will count what you give him in your presence and will give you a deposit slip from this bank."

I thought for a couple of minutes before answering, "Maybe your other clients are more trusting than me. I need to be reassured. I want a letter signed by you and by someone in this bank who is authorised to sign cheques and pay out money, addressed to me and saying that that man" I gestured towards the paper he had handed to me,

"That man is authorised to receive deposits on behalf of the bank and the bank will honour any receipt signed by him for an unlimited amount. Can you do that?"

"I will have to ask." He got up, "if you'd be so kind as to wait a little longer."

He left the room again and I resumed my perusal of the Herald Tribune. A further twenty minutes passed before he returned. I was staring to become impatient and a little irritable. After all I was trying to arrange to deposit a large sum of money with the bank and I did not appreciate being made to hang around kicking my heels. I was just about to pick up the phone and ask for Von Auer when the door opened and he entered the room with another man, equally tall, silver haired, extremely well groomed and wearing a beautifully tailored suit.

"This is Herr Kessler. He is a senior director of this bank."

I got up and accepted the immaculately manicured hand Herr Kessler offered to me.

"Please sit down Herr Chau." There was a polite pause as we all made ourselves comfortable.

"Herr Von Auer has explained your requirements to me and I would like to assure you that the arrangements for the delivery you are anticipating are one hundred and ten per cent secure and you need have no worries. The money you hand over will be credited to your account within 24 hours."

"That is all very well Mr. Kessler and I appreciate your assurance. But you must understand, this is a lot of money for me. In fact I think it's a lot of money for anybody. It's not unknown for sums like this, or even greater, to go astray. I'd hate anything like that to happen - for all our sakes." I paused and gave him one of my long practised, very hard, blood chilling looks before continuing, "therefore, to avoid any difficulties or misunderstandings and so that I can rest peacefully at night, I made a simple request that ought not in any way to embarrass you."

Kessler looked at me without speaking. When he did reply he did so in a measured and relaxed way,

"Your request is very unusual. We do this sort of thing quite often. The problem would be, if we gave you the sort of letter you have requested... if somehow it left your hands and fell into the hands of others... it could, at the very least be embarrassing to the bank and at worst might have very bad consequences."

I leaned back in my chair, "I can understand what you are saying, but you still have to realise that I need some reassurance here. So what reassurance can you give me?"

"How will this be sir? You make the delivery. The money will be counted in your presence. We will then speak on the telephone. You can speak personally to me. After I have verified the amount with our agent, I will immediately fax to you a receipt for your money that I personally will sign."

I thought for a minute before agreeing, "OK. That'll be fine with me. I'll call your guy in Monte Carlo before I come in so that you'll know to be available."

"That will be satisfactory. I am glad that we were able to come to an amicable resolution. It was a great pleasure meeting you, perhaps on your next visit, if you give us some notice, we can invite you to lunch." Kessler got up, shook my hand and left the room. Von Auer was all smiles, fussing over me, as I too prepared to leave.

I had been away from the hotel for approximately two hours. Natalya was in the bedroom when I returned. She had discarded the persona of the Czech passport and transformed herself back into a rather more sophisticated version of the girl I had originally met. She had been too shy and diffident to go to the spa and was even apologetic about having ordered a plate of pasta from room service. I told her to relax and that, as I had now finished my business, we had a couple of days in which to take a lazy drive to the South of France. It was not yet time for dinner and I wanted to speak to Jacques privately. Against her half-hearted protests, I insisted on taking her down to the spa. She was unable to hide her pleasure as I arranged for her to have a massage, facial and pedicure.

I returned to the room to call Jacques, using a telephone he had given me for communicating with him. I brought him up to date and told him that I planned to be in Monte Carlo the day after tomorrow. He told me he had managed to rent a small house for the two of us in La Turbie, just above Monte Carlo, and another place in Beaulieu for the team. He gave me the addresses, which I wrote down. The rentals, with the cash deposit demanded, were a small fortune. I did not care, Jacques still had more than enough to cover the cost of the vehicles I had told him to acquire and any other expenses. In the overall scheme of things the house rentals were a small amount and both places were furnished and ready for immediate occupation. I told Jacques to get up to France at once and prepare everything for me and the team. I also said I was aiming for the team to get to their house in three days, the morning after I expected to arrive.

Jacques also told me that his son had spoken to him and reported that, for the past day he had not noticed any sign of surveillance. I listened. Jacques' son was not exactly experienced in these matters and the surveillance team was bound to be professional. Still it was possible they had lifted the surveillance. It no longer mattered very much. I had had the time to do what I needed and was intending to make contact with the English people the following day anyway. The principle problem to be avoided was for the English to be able to identify Jacques' son in order to make the connection with me. As they did not know the name under which Jacques' son was registered they were unlikely to be able to make the connection, even if they realised it was not me they had followed to Monte Carlo.

After speaking to Jacques I went out to buy a telephone card and then used a public telephone to call each of the men I had recruited. In turn, I told them to meet me in three days' time at the Cafe de Paris, next to the Casino in Monte Carlo. I gave them all the same meeting time. There was no point in telling them in advance where they were to be housed, particularly the Syrian. I then went to a bar and ordered a glass of wine while I once again mulled over my plans before going back to the hotel to join Natalya.

CHAPTER TWENTY ONE

Monte Carlo

*"As the innumerable shells creep around the great
rock so will I with the Imperial host encompass
the Prince of Tomi on every side that there may
be no outlet for him to escape." (The Kojiki)*

The two men sitting in the Mercedes outside the Monte Carlo Beach Hotel stretched as the sun rising over the distant sea hit their eyes. The one known as Bob groaned,

"I'm fucking exhausted. All the other buggers are tucked up nice and comfy in their hotel rooms and I think I've really buggered my back up, what with the drive up here and spending the night in the car."

His companion was watching a man use a water hose to wash down the pavement outside a cafe, approximately 100 yards from where they were parked,

"I think that cafe's open. I'll get us a couple of coffees."

Bob was anxious to get out of the car, "Why don't we both go. We can see the hotel from there just as well as from here and I need some air and a stretch."

As the other grunted his assent, they both got out and sauntered towards the cafe.

In the hotel, the one they had all addressed as "Boss" was in the shower. After he had checked in with his companion, they had unsuccessfully tried to discover in which room their target had registered. They were unfortunate in that they dealt with the night manager. Not only was he was not giving out information, but he took offence at the offer of payment for information and threatened to call security to eject them from the hotel. The Boss had eventually succeeded in calming down the irate manager and been accepted for one night only. After taking their bags up to the room, they had sat in the lobby and wandered around the public areas in an attempt to locate their target; all to no avail.

The Boss decided that today he would make another attempt to ascertain in which room this Traynor guy was located and also have the team sweep through the hotel to find him. He would also put a permanent watch on the Audi. He switched on the portable locating device that should have activated and picked up the transmitter hidden in the gun handed to Traynor by Featherstonehaugh, but could not get any signal. He cursed, "These damn things never work when you need them."

He turned to the other operative, with whom he had shared the room,

"You'd better go down and check on the two in the car. If the other two've relieved them, tell them to come up here to clean up and have a rest. Then get the rest of the other team over here. We'll have a conference in say," he looked at his watch, "one hour, when I'll assign the work load."

The other nodded and disappeared through the door.

After a day in which the teams thoroughly combed through the hotel and car park trying to locate Traynor and organise blanket surveillance, the Boss was becoming increasingly frustrated. He had a car with two of his team sitting permanently in the garage watching the Audi. The Audi had not moved all day. Neither had they been able to spot Traynor, although they all knew what he looked like, having watched him leave the hotel in Rome.

The head of the team had called Featherstonehaugh, who was already back in London, to report their lack of success. Featherstonehaugh had by then asked his technical division to try to activate the locating device in the gun, also without success.

"It very much looks as if he must have given you the slip at some time after he arrived in Monte Carlo," mused the MI6 deputy director.

"That's next to impossible sir. The car hasn't moved since it arrived and we've been covering all the exits and entrances, of which there aren't too many. The only way he might have got out would have been to swim away, early in the morning and I don't think that's very likely."

"Well, if no other explanation fits we've got to go with what's left, however improbable."

"He'd either have to be a very good swimmer or have had someone pick him up offshore. I suppose that's a possibility."

"Give it another day and see if we get anything. If not, there's no point in your continuing to stay there. You'll have to take the cars back to Rome before returning to London. But speak to me tomorrow morning and we'll make a final decision then."

Before terminating the call the watcher made another suggestion.

"We could give the car in the car park a bump and then tell reception and try to get the room number that way, or the car's owner down to speak to us to exchange insurance details."

"No. I don't want you to do that. That's the sort of thing hotel staff tend to remember and I don't want to draw you to their attention."

While this was going on, Paolo had a good night's sleep and, for most of the following day, enjoyed himself at the hotel pool, which looked out on to a private beach area. Never shy, and now particularly stimulated by being on what he regarded as an espionage mission, he had started talking to two attractive girls who were in Monte Carlo for the Grand Prix that weekend. The watchers had seen him walk through the lobby with the two girls but, in the microseconds in which their eyes passed over him, their brains instantly filtered him out as having no resemblance to the fifty something year old oriental who had glided past them in Rome. Neither was Paolo's position damaged by the intelligence numbing effect of the two girls who drew the watchers' glances and attention for far longer than any professional should have allowed. The result was that they did not even consider the young man with two girls as having anything to do with the person they had been seeking all day.

Paolo, on the other hand, not only noticed, but identified as suspicious, the men who spent their whole day in the hotel lobby, notwithstanding that immediately he looked away from them it seemed almost impossible to remember their nondescript faces. To satisfy his suspicions, Paolo had wandered into the basement car park where he had the good sense to observe from some distance away, that the Audi seemed to be under observation from a car parked close by. He covered his appearance in the garage by pretending to retrieve something from a convertible Porsche that was sitting on the other side of the car park, open and unattended.

After a completely fruitless day, the watchers held out no hope that the following day would be any different and were mentally preparing themselves for the trip back to Rome. It was with some surprise therefore that, when the following morning the Boss tried again to activate the locating device that had been concealed in Traynor's gun, the signal came through strongly. The electronics technician who was part of the team tried to obtain a precise location through his laptop. The results considerably dented their professional pride, because it was obvious they had either lost their target or he had discovered their device and sent it on a long trip. As the Boss reported to Featherstonehaugh immediately they had the location,

"He's apparently, someone in North Germany up near the Polish border."

Featherstonehaugh was nothing if not decisive, "OK. Pack up. Go back to Rome. I'll have a plane collect you at Ciampino tomorrow morning. You can liaise with our man at the embassy for details and transport arrangements."

Paolo, who started the day cautiously probing the public areas of the hotel, noticed the absence of the watchers quite quickly. He waited until the late afternoon before checking the garage, to see if the Audi was still under observation. As far as he could see it was not. But by now he regarded the car with considerable distaste and kept away from it for the rest of his stay.

CHAPTER TWENTY TWO

"When you think that your method of defence is infallible
your vigilance will inevitably slacken."
(Chinese military strategy).
London SIS Headquarters

Featherstonehaugh went directly to C's office after having instructed the team of watchers to return. C, polite and urbane as always, insisted on giving Featherstonehaugh a coffee from his machine before listening to his update.

"I fear that we may seriously have underestimated this fellow Traynor. He gave an experienced team the slip and we have no idea where he is. The tracking device we put in one of the guns we gave him was off the air for at least a day and, when it resurfaced, it was giving out a location somewhere in North Germany. Now, it's not impossible that he's putting a team together in Germany up near the Polish border. In fact, it's perfectly feasible that he's recruiting East Europeans. But somehow I don't think he's doing it where our tracker is placing him. I should add that, the last time I got our bods to check the location of the tracker it was over the Polish border moving North at about 50 miles per hour. I had always thought that, within a short time of getting the money from us, he would be making his way to somewhere he could deposit it and I surmised that Liechtenstein was probably a best guess, although he could have some existing arrangements in Monaco. I couldn't imagine him carrying it all around with him throughout the whole operation and, to the best of my knowledge Liechtenstein's the nearest place that'll still accept so much cash. So Germany would have almost squared with that hypothesis. But Poland, no. Anyway, the fact is that the car we gave him is in Monte Carlo and the tracker from the gun is in Poland somewhere. He can't be in both places at the same time, so what I deduce is that, somehow or other, he must have found our device and then dropped it into some other vehicle, at some point between Rome and Monte Carlo. It's always possible he did it in Monte Carlo but he'd have had to be very lucky to find a car or truck there that was travelling and en route to Poland.

I think what's more likely, bearing in mind the only time he was out of visual contact with our watchers on the drive up to Monte Carlo, is that he carried out a switch somewhere in Italy. The Italian Autostrada are teeming with long distance lorries and I am sure that there are plenty going to Eastern Europe."

C watched Featherstonehaugh as he talked, developing his hypothesis, unconsciously stroking his lips and chin with the forefinger of his left hand whilst he voiced his analysis of the various possibilities.

"I think that the logical probability is that he lost the watchers in Italy by switching cars and having someone else drive our well prepared vehicle up to Monte Carlo. To me that, in itself, indicates a considerable degree of organisation and planning."

"Are we sure that the only time visual contact was lost was in Italy?"

"That's what the watchers told me. Excluding the time following his entry into the hotel, visual contact was lost only between Rome and Florence. They said he was going too fast for them safely to keep up, but they weren't worried because they had him on their computer screen the whole time. Apparently he was moving the whole of the time they were out of visual contact apart from a brief stop to fill up with petrol just before Florence. And they were able to resume visual just as he was leaving the filling station. After that they had him in sight the whole time, up to the moment he checked in to the Monte Carlo Beach Hotel, when he then disappeared."

C grunted, interrupting his deputy's analysis,

"You're assuming the only place he could have given our people the slip is when he stopped at Florence, but he could have gone into the hotel in Monte Carlo and slipped straight out again without checking in. It was the middle of the night, dark, he could have laid up for a couple of hours, waited for our watchers to grow a little careless and then just slipped away. We've done similar things hundreds of times. You gave him the bugged gun in Rome didn't you?"

"Yes. He then left almost immediately, which is why I tend to treat Florence as the fulcrum. He couldn't drive and go through his things so carefully that he was able to spot the tracker in the gun. He couldn't have found it with any detector, because it wasn't switched on and wouldn't have given out any signal until it was. Even if he had stripped the gun down at once it's most unlikely he'd have found the device. No, I think he must have carried out the switch in or around Florence and then gone to ground somewhere where he had the leisure carefully to go through what we'd given him."

"Yes, that's all very well, but suppose he didn't go through his things. Suppose he just dumped the guns we gave him, didn't want to risk them being found on him. That would be the work of a couple of seconds and we could just be driving ourselves mad based on a perfectly sensible decision of not wanting to be found in possession of two illegal weapons. He may just have asked for them to see to what extent we would comply with his demands. He may never have intended to hang on to them. At the speeds he seems to have been driving it's perfectly feasible he might have decided that he had a fair chance of being stopped by the police somewhere and was risking all sorts of problems by keeping the weapons. At all events, I don't suppose it would do any harm to check on the Echelon records of telephone calls in the period during which he left Rome and stopped in Florence and carry out a comparison with calls from Monte Carlo after the Audi arrived there. We could see if there is any correspondence between numbers." C was referring to the European wide electronic surveillance system operated by the American National Security Agency in conjunction with British Government Communications Headquarters at Cheltenham, England.

"Actually, I've already done that, sir" replied Featherstonehaugh, "all it has thrown up is a series of local numbers and you'd be astonished at how many Italians are apparently calling Italy from Monte Carlo. There was, though, one SMS the computers flagged as possibly suspicious. It came from Monte Carlo, shortly after our teams arrived there and was sent to a mobile phone registered to someone in the North of Italy."

He handed a piece of paper to C containing a copy of Paolo's message to his father and the caller's and recipient's numbers and names and addresses.

"One of the reasons the computers picked out this message is that the call was made from and sent to numbers that were also in use in other parts of Italy at around the same time."

He handed another piece of paper to C, "those are the details of the other calls made around the same time in different locations, which makes me inclined to believe that the phones are cloned. Now there might be all sorts of other reasons totally unconnected with our operation for cloned phones to be in use but, just in case, I've arranged for all communications between those numbers to be flagged and reported to us."

"Those numbers on that message might be a simple code. Did you try getting through to that room number at the hotel?"

"We did, but the hotel wouldn't put the call through without us giving the name of the guest. I didn't want to push it so we just rang off. After all, it really isn't that critical that we track Traynor at this stage and, if it all goes belly up, we don't want hotel staff remembering a lot strange incidents involving the man in room whatever."

"Hmm. You seem to have covered just about everything. Good work." said C, thinking that, every day his deputy was becoming more suitable to be his replacement when the time came for him to retire, which, in all the circumstances, he thought might be very soon.

CHAPTER TWENTY THREE

"Gaudeamus igitur juvenes dum sumus" –*('Let us rejoice while we are young'-Student drinking song)*

Paolo, like most young men of his age, had manifold faults. He was inclined to be impetuous, impatient and brash. In one respect, however, he was exemplary. He adored and admired his father. Even when he chose to defy or argue with Jacques he always respected the calm, measured and thoughtful way in which his father approached the slightest problem or dispute. Not even his most outrageous exploits or blatant defiance had ever caused his father to explode with anger. Instead Jacques listened carefully, before quietly defusing any explosive situation. This was not to say that Paolo regarded Jacques as a soft touch. On the contrary, he would always remember how, when he was about twelve, the whole family had been out for Sunday lunch in a restaurant near the Piazza della Signoria in Florence. Towards the end of the meal, three very large young Germans, who had been sitting at a nearby table and staring unashamedly at Paolo's still very beautiful mother, started making offensive comments, fuelled by the grappa that had followed the several bottles of beer that littered their table. Although Paolo had become incensed at their increasingly rude behaviour, Jacques and his mother had ignored the Germans. However, when they had left the restaurant, the Germans had followed them outside and the situation had started to take a very ugly turn. Initially Jacques had spoken to the three foreigners quietly and politely. They had interpreted his calm remonstrations as weakness and grown bolder, even to the extent of trying to fondle Paolo's mother's breasts and attempting to kiss her. Jacques' response had been immediate and devastating. Within seconds the three Germans were lying on the ground, semi-conscious or unconscious and probably requiring hospital treatment. Jacques had left them lying there, like so much garbage, as he walked off without a backward glance, dragging Paolo and his younger brother and sister along with him as they sought to linger, to marvel at the stricken Germans.

From that day on, apart from minor displays of defiance, Paolo listened when his father told him something and obeyed any instructions given in the quiet and solemn monotone Jacques used when wishing to impart something important. When Paolo had met Traynor he was struck and awed, by the fact that the latter displayed the same calm quietude as his father. No, actually with Traynor, there was something more, an immovable almost tangible menace. So when Traynor told Paolo not to use a portable phone and his father reiterated the same instructions, Paolo was going to listen. He had slipped up by sending an SMS announcing his safe arrival in Monte Carlo to his father, because he thought it was important, but the message had hardly been sent before he was worrying whether he had perhaps done something wrong. Therefore, when he had satisfied himself that the watchers had truly gone, he did not even think of imparting this information to his father through the telephone he had used previously. He purchased a telephone calling card and found a public phone near the famous Casino and well away from his hotel, before making the call. The number he called was not the same number to which he had previously sent the SMS. His father had given him a list of four numbers which he had been instructed to use in sequence should the need arise. Instructions he now followed to the letter.

As a result, the information gathered through Echelon and passed to Featherstonehaugh over the following couple of days showed nothing of any interest to MI6 and no further correspondence between the numbers he had previously flagged and subsequent calls. Sighing, Featherstonehaugh pushed the list to one side, having decided that, without pinpointing specific numbers and recording all conversations from those numbers, he would be unable to obtain any further useful information. It was another dead end and as much of a waste of time as leaving the watchers in place would have been. Traynor had now been totally off the radar for three days. He wondered if they had been had and the 4 million Euros he had paid out to Traynor had just been thrown away and they would now be no nearer carrying out a necessary operation than they had been weeks before. He dispelled such black, depressing thoughts by reassuring himself that Traynor had come into this through Admiral Standish, who was thoroughly reliable and respectable, even if he did not like the English and that they had been steered to the admiral by the directors of the CIA and NSA themselves.

Featherstonehaugh, therefore, waited patiently for a call on the secure phone whose twin he had left with Traynor. He was not to be disappointed. Three days after he had called off the watchers the telephone rang. Featherstonehaugh waited before answering to enable his technical department who were, on his instructions, monitoring the numbers, to start a trace.

"Hello."

"Is that Mr. White's friend?"

"It is indeed. I've been waiting for your call. You've been a bit off the radar."

A dry chuckle came over the line, "Lost me did you? Well don't worry I'm ready to meet you or Mr. White and continue with our business."

"That would be acceptable."

"Is the rest of what you need to deliver available?"

"Of course." Responded Featherstonehaugh smoothly, "Where do you propose meeting."

"How about my hotel in Monte Carlo?"

"Which one would that be?"

Again that dry laugh, "I think you know that sir. Shall we say tomorrow? The afternoon, at 15.00 in the lobby."

"That'll be satisfactory."

"And will you be coming sir, or will it be Mr. White?"

"It'll just be Mr. White."

"Very well." Click. The call was disconnected.

Featherstonehaugh picked up the internal phone and dialled a number.

"Did you get a location?"

"Not a precise one sir. It's somewhere in the South of France near to Draguignan. I think he pulled out the battery and SIM card because we tried to switch the phone back on remotely, but couldn't get anything. Sorry sir."

"Don't worry. No more than I expected."

He replaced the receiver and leaned back in his chair thinking for a few moments, before using his outside line to dial through to Cartwright.

CHAPTER TWENTY FOUR

"Once a woman has given you her heart you can never get rid of the rest of her" – John Vanbrugh

Having finished my business in Liechtenstein and arranged for the team to meet me in Monte Carlo, I had had two days free to enjoy with the girl. She now seemed to have lowered all the barriers, to the extent that, sometimes she seemed to be like a little girl in the way she enjoyed simple pleasures. It appeared that she had jettisoned any reservations she might initially have had about me and no longer considered me as someone who could potentially pass her on to another gang of slave traders. She was correct. For all my defects I have always tried to adhere to my own particular code of conduct and I have always abhorred people who trade in women and turn them into prostitutes, drug addicts and the like. Those are a species who appear on my black list, next to paedophiles and politicians.

I had decided to head into the south of France, through Geneva and Lyons and then down along the Rhone valley through Provence. It was the long way around to Monte Carlo but, from my point of view, it was safer, because we only had to cross one border, at Geneva. I knew from experience that that particular border was not subject to very stringent controls, probably because of the large number of people who lived in France but worked in Geneva and travelled to and from that city every day.

We left Liechtenstein early in the morning and arrived in Geneva at lunchtime after an uneventful trip. We passed through the border without being checked, before stopping to eat something. Natalya had never in her life been on this sort of a trip. By mid-afternoon we were near the town of Taine on the river Rhone and, as I regarded myself as on a short holiday, took the time to stop off at this wine making centre. We went into the premises of two of the largest wine producers, Jaboulet and Chapoutier. After a session of wine tasting, I ended up buying a couple of cases of wine, although as I did so, I wondered what I was doing and what I would do with the wine over the next few days, when operational necessity was going to preclude any serious drinking. I finally sated my conscience with the thought that anything we did not drink I could give to Jacques' son to take back to Florence for me.

We spent the night in a luxurious hotel in Avignon, where I splashed out on a suite and an expensive dinner. I had decided that I might as well enjoy my time with Natalya, who was proving to be an interesting and intelligent companion. The worst possible thing was happening. I had picked her up on the spur of the moment, to use as a prop to enable me to travel around without drawing attention to myself and now I was actually enjoying her company. As for the attention side of things, with the clothes I had bought her and the care now being lavished upon her, she was positively glowing with beauty and drawing admiring looks from a whole cross section of the male population of Southern France, to say nothing of the people who stared disapprovingly at the two of us and so clearly wondered what a beautiful young girl was doing with that much older oriental man. I dispelled my doubts by convincing myself that she would fit in perfectly amongst the smart set in Monte Carlo and the Cote d'Azur and that, when I finally dumped her, she would no doubt be able to fix herself up with some aging billionaire with a 200 metre plus yacht.

On the drive from Avignon to the Cote d'Azur the following morning, I was working out in my mind how I ought to handle the changeover with Jacques' son and my move into the house that Jacques had rented for the two of us to separate us from the rest of the team. I was also undecided about what to do with Natalya. I did not trust her sufficiently to leave her in my house near Cannes, which was a secret hideaway even Jacques knew nothing about. That house was well provisioned for emergencies. I could stay there secluded for two or three months at a time, without even going down to the village shops, but I was nowhere near ready to disclose it to the girl. Neither did I want to take Natalya to the hotel where Paolo was installed. I did not want her anywhere near the team I had assembled. Although I did not know what sort of place Jacques had rented, there was an argument for installing Natalya with us.

A couple of friends staying in a house in the South of France, with their wives or girlfriends, would not attract much attention, even from the pathologically curious French. Jacques, of course, did not have his wife there, but that was something that could be resolved fairly easily. The practicalities depended upon my plan.

There were two separate contingencies for which I thought I needed to plan. The first was, if the whole operation went according to plan. If that happened, attention was going to be focused on an accident investigation, not a manhunt directed towards my team or me. So, in the normal course of events, we would all be able to carry on as if nothing had happened. The only element likely to impact on this was the Brits seeing my team and me as a loose end, quietly to be liquidated after the operation. Standish had given me a veiled warning about this, which was augmented by my own impressions, derived from the meetings I had had with the two Brits in Rome.

Like all operations, there are tiers of operatives who have different levels of knowledge and pose different degrees of risk. Here, the first tier was the few, however many, individuals, who decided upon and approved the operation in the first place. That would include Mr. White and his boss, who, presumably, were regarded as totally secure. The second tier was me, with a level of knowledge almost as great as the first tier. The third tier was my team. My team and I were simply operators. Operators were always regarded as expendable by the bureaucratic first tier. In such a sensitive, secretive operation as this, we would be considered a positive liability; the only possible source of an authoritative leak that the "accident" was not an accident at all.

In fact, as the prime operator and planner I had the same concerns as the tier one group. I wanted to finish the job with enough money to disappear into an obscure retirement. For me the security of the operation and my security were symbiotic elements. I did not want, any more than the Brits, one of my team being hauled in by the police on some totally unrelated matter and then trying to work out a deal for himself by giving away the details of this operation. My instinct was that the Russian was solid enough and that nothing was likely to make him talk. As an old hand, whose life had depended on making quick, accurate assessments of people, I pegged the Russian as a member of an elite group, skilled in carrying out sensitive assassinations on behalf of political leaders. These people knew the downside of having loose lips and could be relied upon. The others, apart from the Syrian, would probably also stand up. But there was never any certainty. Jacques was the only person I was sure about and it had taken me thirty or so years to acquire that sort of confidence in him. I had already decided that the Syrian was not going to be left around, so the fact that I did not trust him was not a concern. I decided that I was not going to make any plans to deal with the other members of the team. If the Brits wanted to take care of the members of my team that was a matter for them, as far as I was concerned they deserved a fighting chance.

So my concern was myself and my safe disappearance with Jacques after the operation, without leaving any trail to be followed. All my experience and my every instinct told me to operate on the basis that the Brits were planning a clean-up operation after we had done our work. I did not know what myth the Brits were going to sell to their clean up team to explain their actions, but it was a virtual certainty they would use a team from the SAS or the Increment (an SAS team seconded to MI6) who would be goal oriented and, to set their adrenalin going, would only need to be told we were a fanatical terrorist cell planning a large operation in England or mainland Europe. This sort of thing goes on all the time. For every terrorist you read about who is brought to trial, there are many more who have been targeted in drone attacks or otherwise quietly disposed of. Even though they would be operating in the same vicinity as our "accident", an SAS hit team would have no reason to associate the two events. For them it would just be one of life's little coincidences. I had already prepared the groundwork for ensuring the Brits would be unable to come after me by arranging to separate myself physically from my team. The rest would involve maintaining careful security.

The other possibility that required pre-planning was if anything went wrong for reasons beyond my control and we were unable to deal with whatever problem arose. If this involved a full scale police operation we would either have to get out of France immediately or, alternatively and, probably more realistically, go to ground until any initial manhunt had died down. I was fairly confident that this was no more than a remote possibility. The essence of the operation was a controlled fatal accident, not an overt hit. I was very experienced in planning and controlling operations and was confident that there were only two potential problems. Too many bodyguards around, disposing of whom could make the whole thing messy and blow the whole accident scenario, in which case I would abort the operation. The other possibility was a witness being in the wrong place at the wrong time. That was something to be dealt with on the spot.

Having considered the different scenarios, I decided against taking Natalya to the safe house Jacques was setting up for us. If there were unforeseen difficulties she would just be another burden. The best thing for both of us would be for me to put her in a hotel. She could stay there for a couple of weeks. If she was still there when I judged it was safe to move, well and good. If she fixed herself up with someone else in the meantime, well that would also be alright.

We were coming up to a service area and, as we had been driving for some time, Natalya asked if we could stop for a coffee. I pulled into the service area and sent her inside while I used the navigation system in the car to obtain the telephone numbers of three first class hotels in Monte Carlo, the Metropole, the Hermitage and the Hotel de Paris. When I called them, the latter two were fully booked. Before hearing about it on the BBC news on television at the Modena hotel, I had not realised a Formula 1 Grand Prix was taking place the coming weekend and that, consequently it would be difficult to find a hotel room; another black mark for me. The Metropole only had a junior suite available. I booked it for ten days in the name of the passport that Natalya was using. I felt relieved. That was one problem disposed of for the time being.

I got out of the car and joined Natalya in the restaurant. She was sitting in front of a plate piled high with food, which she was making impressive progress in consuming. One thing I had noticed about Natalya was that she loved her food, but still managed to maintain her perfect figure. I wondered if she was simply making up for the months when she had been kept on a subsistence diet by the Albanians, but did not say anything to her. I was not hungry, but picked briefly at her plate and drank a coffee whilst she finished eating.

When we were back in the car and had re-joined the highway, I told Natalya that we were going to Monte Carlo and that when we arrived there I would have to go away, alone, for some days on business. I glanced at her from time to time while I was talking and could not help noticing that, after an initially pleased reaction at the thought of time on the French Riviera, she reacquired that guarded, closed up look she had had when I first met her. I tried to reassure her. I did not want some sulky female on my hands when I had other things to concentrate on.

"I told you when we first met I had business to attend to. You'll be in a good hotel, a nice room. I'll leave you enough money to take care of yourself and when I've finished my business we'll take off together."

"Who're you trying to kid, sport. I've heard it before. This is the kiss off isn't it? ".

I had noticed that Natalya had a tendency to pepper her speech with a vocabulary that seemed to be derived mainly from American films of the 1940's and 1950's.

"I was starting to think I was more than just some bit of fluff to you. Well don't worry I'll manage, somehow." She reminded me a little of Lauren Bacall and, in spite of myself, I could not help laughing at the way she had expressed herself. When my final chuckles had subsided I glanced over to her and in response to the confused expression on her face said:

"Look. This is not the kiss off. If I wanted to do that I could have left you at the rest stop just now. Just driven off when you went inside and that would have been that. I've no intention of dropping you. I really like you. You just need to understand, when I say I've got business to attend to, I mean it. The money for staying in these luxury hotels and eating expensive meals doesn't drop out of the air, you know. If I could take you with me I would. But it would be too difficult. Just stop worrying. I'll try to stay in touch and, don't worry; I'll come back for you."

She sat there silently for a while, obviously thinking over what I had said. From time to time she glanced across at me and then after about ten minutes I could feel her starting to relax.

"OK. I believe you. I want to believe you. I need to believe. You know you're the best thing that's ever happened to me in my whole shitty life and I don't want to lose it."

She leaned across and brushed her lips softly against my cheek. I really was getting soft. In spite of myself I felt good. No, I felt affection. For this street whore. I tried to tell myself that, whatever misfortunes had befallen her, she was still a whore and just doing her job, but part of me wanted to believe her. I did not remember the last time I had had any sort of normal relationship with a woman. Perhaps, if the job went as planned, perhaps I might just give a real relationship a try, notwithstanding the age gap and who and what we each were; the killer and the hooker. Maybe we were not such a bad match after all. I smiled again, it even sounded a bit like a 1950's B movie.

It was late morning by the time we came onto the stretch of highway that skirted that section of France known as the Cote d'Azur, the blue coast. It could never have been bluer than that morning. The air, as yet unpolluted by the day's traffic, was sparklingly clear. The sea betrayed scarcely a ripple, shining a deep cobalt blue, that reflected the clear cloudless sky above it. The incredible depth of sea colour was accentuated by the lighter colours of a white and rust brown coast-line. It was a magnificent day and a magnificent view. Looking at it made even me feel good. Natalya was unable to restrain gasps of admiration that she emitted in her native Russian.

Between Cannes and Nice we hit traffic, with the French displaying their usual lack of consideration for other drivers. I just relaxed, saving my concentration for avoiding the not infrequent lunatic manoeuvres undertaken by drivers around me and otherwise allowing the current of traffic to push and pull us according to whatever whim dictated its movement at any particular time.

Notwithstanding the traffic it was just after 1pm when we pulled off the highway towards Monaco. It was almost gridlock as we moved slowly into the principality. It must have taken nearly ten minutes just to pass the toll booth at the exit to the highway. Edging forward into the long tunnel leading to that legendary playground of the rich and the royal, Monte Carlo, I was not displeased at our slow progress. This tunnel was to be at the centre of my operation. Driving through it at this pace was giving me an unexpected and unusual opportunity carefully to survey the killing ground without drawing attention to myself.

Another forty five minutes of slow progress brought us to the hotel. The whole centre of Monte Carlo had been transformed into a Grand Prix racing circuit, festooned with all the placards and hoardings that seem to accompany every Formula One race. It seemed as if every spare inch of space announced different products, or banks that all poured their money into the ravenous mouths of the Formula One organisation. I had a very cynical attitude to sponsorship of these so called sporting events. In my opinion, Companies that pour millions of shareholders' money into such events, do so for the benefit of a privileged few directors who, in return for all that money, are given a front row seat, with enough supporting space to keep them and their guests supplied with ample quantities of food and drink throughout the event.

I had been present at this type of event before. I had even participated in one or two, in a peripheral way, dressed as a waiter, circulating cocktails specially concocted for one particular personality. People in my business welcomed occasions like this, not for the social networking they fostered, but for providing an environment where even the most vigilant of targets felt able to relax and enjoy themselves, in what they mistakenly thought was a moment of complete security. The realisation that they were not as secure as they had believed, normally came in the few seconds before they were granted their wings to a better place. By that time I, the messenger, would also be on my way, although to somewhere more mundane.

As we approached the hotel, some of the road was entirely blocked off for the race. One could hear, from behind a high hoarding that hid the cars from view, the shrill, high pitched whine of racing engines being blasted around the circuit. Eventually, with the help of my portable navigation system which I had fixed to the windshield in the car, I managed to circumvent the roads that had been incorporated into the race track for the weekend and found myself outside the Metropole Hotel. The concierge took Natalya's single, rather pathetic looking suitcase out of the trunk of the car with barely disguised contempt. He aggravated his offence by leering openly at my companion. In the normal way I would barely have noticed this sort of conduct. I was used to porters who seemed to think that carrying suitcases for the wealthy in some way elevated their social status sufficiently for them to look down on lesser mortals. On this occasion, however, I felt an uncharacteristic surge of anger. I charged through the doors of the hotel across the lobby to the reception desk, by which time I again had my feelings under control.

Natalya trailed behind me, a little bewildered by my sudden rush to check in.

The porter who had annoyed me brought Natalya's case up to our room and then proceeded further to aggravate me with a detailed explanation of everything in the room, from the flush mechanism in the toilet to the minibar. After a while it finally dawned on him that I was ignoring his explanations and fiddling with the television because I had no intention of tipping him. With that realisation he curtailed his explanations and left us in peace.

Immediately we were alone Natalya slunk over to me, put her arms around me and said, smiling seductively,

"We should test this bed. It looks sooo comfortable."

I was strongly tempted but I had a lot to do. I gently disentangled her as I replied,

"I'd like nothing more, but I've got a lot to do. I've got to get going." She pouted, kicked off her shoes and threw herself back on the bed, allowing her skirt to ride up high on her thighs. I looked at her with considerable regret.

"You've got to listen to me. It's important. I told you I have to leave you here for a few days, while I do some work. I don't know if I'll be able to come back and see you at all in that time... " she sat bolt upright at that, looking at me in alarm, inducing me to lie to soften what I was saying, "I may be able to get back for a day or so here and there, but I've got some travelling to do and I'm going to be very busy."

Sometimes this woman was a little too sharp. "What do you mean get back for a day or so here and there? How long you will be gone? I don't believe it. This is the end, yes? I thought. I thought... so you just bring me to this nice hotel to airbrush me."

I frowned wondering what she was talking about, until I realised that, even with her excellent, Hollywood based English, she occasionally got her idioms confused.

"Brush off"

"What?" It was her turn to look puzzled, wondering why I was smiling,

"Brush off. The expression is brush off, not air brush. Air brush is something photographers do to pictures to make them look better."

"Oh." Now she looked crestfallen, like a little girl who had just had her school work criticised.

"I'm not giving you the brush off. I'm giving you a few days holiday, when you can just sit by the pool, go shopping, have your hair done. Do whatever you like, until I come back. I'll leave you with money. It's only a few days. The time'll pass quickly."

"But I don't want to do any of those things without you. I love you. I want to stay with you. Can't I go with you? Even for a few days. I won't be any trouble."

Fucking hell, I thought to myself. What have I got myself into here? Yet, in spite of myself and in spite of the fact that I did not believe her, I felt pleased. I had read about mid-life crises, but had never thought that sort of thing applied to me. Now I was beginning to wonder. Ever since I arrived in Sicily I had been making one bad judgment call after another. I looked at Natalya wondering whether I was ever going to see her again and felt a pang of genuine regret. I opened my attaché case and counted out 20 five hundred Euro notes.

"There's ten thousand Euros to keep you going for the time being. Put it in the safe and just carry around what you need. Anything in the hotel, charge to the room. I'll be back with you before you know it. I have to work. This money," I gestured towards the money, that I had placed next to the television, "doesn't grow on trees. I have to work for it. The work is hard and its... " I hesitated, wondering whether I should add what I was about to say. Finally I decided it was perhaps the best and most persuasive thing I could say,

"and it's dangerous. Very dangerous. I don't want to put you in a position where you're in danger."

She sat up abruptly and slid to the edge of the bed towards me, looking at me seriously,

"I know all about danger. Maybe I can help you."

"No. You can't. The best help you can give me is to stay here. I don't want to have to worry about looking after you."

"You are a spy! I knew it. I knew it from the way you so quickly got that passport. The way you look all the time to see if someone is following and you sleep so... " she was searching for a word, "you sleep so... so softly. And the way your body is so hard like you train all the time. I knew it."

"Look, don't worry about what I am or what I do. Just take it easy; enjoy yourself for the next few days. Oh, I almost forgot. I need to get you some proper papers. I'll need some photographs of you."

My final request succeeded in mollifying her more than all my other attempts at persuasion. She got up, went to her bag and took out the small digital camera I had bought her in Liechtenstein and handed it to me. After I had taken the pictures I removed the SD card and placed it in my shirt pocket. I then picked up my bags, kissed Natalya goodbye and left.

CHAPTER TWENTY FIVE

Cote d'Azur

*"In gardens, beauty is a by-product. The main
business is sex and death". (Sam Llewelyn)*

Once I was in the car I programmed the navigation system with the address Jacques had given me for the house I had instructed him to rent. It took me about an hour to negotiate my way out of Monte Carlo and to the village of La Turbie, where the house was located. It turned out to be a large rambling villa, hidden behind a pleasant garden that shrouded the house with trees and a variety of exotic looking shrubs. The garden itself was enclosed within a wall that was at least three metres high. The only way into the property was through large ornamental iron gates operated remotely from the house.

I stopped the car and leaned out of the window to press the entry phone system. Almost immediately the gates swung open. As I drove through the garden, around a long driveway ending in a large gravelled semi-circular turning area, I was enveloped in a sense of well-being that was in no small part fuelled by the fragrance wafting through the car window from the profusion of flowers and blossoms growing abundantly everywhere. A medium size van, three cars and two motor cycles were parked outside the house. Two of the cars were blue Renault Lagunas with French license plates that I noted could easily pass as police cars. The third car was an Audi S4 estate. The motorbikes were both powerful BMWs, painted in the blue favoured by the French mobile gendarmerie.

As I got out of the car, Jacques' rangy figure sauntered out of the house. At first I thought he was completely naked until I realised that he was wearing a skimpy pair of swimming shorts. I greeted him

"You look very sportive"

He laughed and spread out his arms in an expansive gesture,

"What do you think? Not bad, hein?"

I looked around, "we're not here on holiday you know." I nodded towards the cars and motorbikes. "You've done well. They're just what we need. How did you get them here?"

He gave a sardonic snort, What do you think? I drove them myself? I had some boys bring them up. There's quite a lot of gear, so I needed the van."

I raised my eyebrows,

"Don't worry. All they knew was they got paid to drive up here for some rich client and they'll come up to collect them when I tell them."

"So what about the rentals? Did you have any trouble with ID's for renting the places?"

"Cash covered all that. A month's rental paid in advance and two more months security deposit."

"Phew. How much did that cost."

"Enough. Don't worry. With everything, I've still got change from the hundred grand you gave me. And, if there are no problems, we get the deposits back."

I nodded. The job was paying a lot and I could not afford to skimp on small details.

"Come on in. Have a drink. You must be thirsty."

He was right. It was hot and I was.

The interior of the house was comfortably furnished and there was a constant, almost imperceptible cool breeze whispering through it.

"It's great. When you open the windows and the doors by the pool you get this cool air coming off the sea."

I nodded as Jacques handed me a tall glass of homemade lemonade that he had poured from a jug he took from the fridge in the kitchen.

"This is delicious." I was surprised, "Did you make this?"

"Sure. You think you know me, but I've got many talents you couldn't even guess at."

"Yeah right. Listen. The crew's arriving tomorrow. I want to be sure their place is ready and everything's set up for them. Then I've got to meet someone in Monte Carlo this afternoon and we've got to get your son out of the hotel and exchange cars without anyone picking us up. We ought to do that before my meet, so we'll need to get going soon. The traffic in Monaco is a bitch with the Grand Prix on."

Jacques nodded, "When are you going to tell me what the job is?"

I put my empty glass down on the kitchen table, "Is there any more of this?"

Jacques went over to the fridge, retrieved the jug of lemonade and poured me another glass before looking at me expectantly, "Well." He raised his eyebrows questioningly.

I did not want to go into a long explanation so I synthesised the brief operational facts, "It's a hit. We've got to make it look like an accident. I'm getting a special piece of kit to help us. I want to do it in the tunnel just before you get into Monte Carlo from the Nice Autoroute."

Jacques wrinkled his forehead, "How are we going to know where the target is going to be? Are we going to have to set up a whole surveillance operation? And how are we going to be able to make sure we can get into the right position?"

"I'm being fed, what I hope is up to date intel. What I'd really like is to try and get a link into the Autoroute and Monte Carlo traffic cams. I don't know if it's going to be possible, but I'm going to ask the people who are providing the intel."

Jacques looked thoughtful. "These people. Are they in a position to get you anything you want?"

"I'd say so. It's off the books but officially sanctioned."

"Government?"

I shrugged. "What's government? I'm dealing with what I'd say are high level spooks." I hesitated and Jacques looked at me expectantly. After a pause I continued. There was no reason to hide anything from him. From the other members of the team yes, but not from Jacques.

"As far as I know it's an all British, SIS operation. They've given me a liaison guy, who I reckon is an SAS Rupert."

When Jacques and I were in the Foreign Legion paras we had trained and worked with British SAS units. He knew, as I did, that the troopers called their officers "Ruperts".

Jacques whistled, "Why do they need outside contractors? Those guys can do anything themselves. What's the catch?"

"Well, when I tell you the target you'll understand that it's something where they can't risk any English operative ever being identified. For sure there's going to be a whole big stink afterwards, accident or not. If everything goes ok we needn't worry about any police operation, but we're going to have to watch the Brits."

"Who's the target then?"

I told him as I had been told and that the woman was not to be harmed if possible, but that we all knew she was not likely to survive, not with the sort of accident being planned.

Jacques looked thoughtful. "So for sure with this target, this type of operation, they're going to have a secondary team hanging around somewhere in there to mop us up afterwards."

Jacques rubbed his head as he was thinking, "They can't come after us immediately after the hit without compromising the whole operation. Unless they've got us identified before, they're going to have to try and identify us and come after us afterwards when we're well away from the scene. If they put a surveillance team on us to try and identify us before the op, security at their end might also be compromised and they'd have the same problem with their people that they must think they're going to have with us. Too many people in the know. Also, if they come after us immediately, someone on their side might start wondering and putting two and two together."

"I agree with you about the surveillance but I don't think we can rely on them waiting before going into action. They'll sell the whole thing to their team as a long planned anti-terrorist operation. That's why I think they've brought in the SAS guy and aren't doing this in house at MI6. The accident'll be just that; an unhappy coincidence. And if any of the operatives start wondering, they'll probably be shipped off to Afghanistan where they'll be dealt with blue on blue, by friendly fire."

Jacques nodded his agreement. "You're probably right. So however they handle this we're going to have to be very, very careful."

I had not yet told him one important element. "I ought to tell you. This liaison guy, the SAS Rupert, he's going to be in a position to ID the members of the team. It was something I had to agree to."

"Well that's easy. We'll just take him out before we go into action."

"If we can manage it. The timing'll be critical. We'll need him because he's going to be providing up to date intel on the movement of the targets. By the time we get into the final phase, things could be moving too quickly for us to have time to deal with him. It'll be tricky and we've got to plan for a situation where he's going to be around after the op to come after us. That's why I wanted this safe house, to keep you well away from him and other members of the team. As far as he's going to know, my team'll just be the others."

Jacques nodded thoughtfully before changing the subject, "you know with the webcams, Paolo's a bit of a computer genius. I'll bet he can hack into the whole system and get us a direct feed."

I thought about this for a couple of minutes before deciding this was just the sort of tempting idea that, if adopted, could make an operation vulnerable to exposure, "I don't want to get your son involved any more. It's too risky. If anything happened to your family, how do you think I'd feel?"

"I understand. But what's the risk? Paolo can stay here the whole time, well away from the action, do everything from here."

"Yeh, but then he's going to know what we're doing. He's young. Suppose he says something in an unguarded moment. And we all know how snafu's (situation normal all fucked up, military slang) happen. It's much too risky."

"Hmm."

I could see that Jacques was not convinced. I did not say anything, but thought to myself that his normal sound judgment was being outweighed by his pride in his son. However, Jacques immediately came up with another idea.

"I'll tell you what we can do. If we get him to set up the computer so we can get into the system whenever we want, then we can send him home and he'll be none the wiser."

I considered this possibility. As long as his son was safe back home when we went into action and had no idea about the operation we were carrying out, I could not see any objections.

"If he can do that. OK. Otherwise not."

Jacques nodded again and headed for the stairs. "I'll get some clothes to change into before we head off to Monte Carlo to go and pick up Paolo and switch you two back over. I'll only be a couple of minutes and then we can drive over to the other place I rented. The keys are over there," he pointed to a set of keys with a label attached to them that I had previously noticed sitting on a coffee table.

In a short time we were on the road, heading towards Beaulieu. Jacques was driving the van, which we used to transport one of the motorbikes, after man-handling it into the back of the van to leave it at the team's house. I followed him in one of the Renault's.

The house Jacques had rented for the team was as ideal as the villa we had just left, albeit a little distant from our area of operation. It had four bedrooms, so the team would have to do a little doubling up, but that was no problem. There was a large sitting room, dining area and well equipped kitchen. The secluded garden even contained a ten metre pool. I thought back over my long career and how I would have been in heaven with this sort of set up on some of my old ops. Comfortable housing was just the thing to put the team in the right frame of mind and get them well prepped.

We wheeled the motorbike out of the van and then spent about fifteen minutes inspecting the house before I turned to Jacques to ask a question that had been bothering me since arriving,

"If you wanted to carry out surveillance on this house where would you do it from?"

Jacques looked at me for a moment before responding,

"The house is hidden by the garden. So the only practical place would be from high up."

"Yeah, that's the way I figured it. Let's go into the garden and take a look."

Jacques followed me into the garden and we both looked up towards the hillside that overlooked the house. The only property which gave good visibility over where we were standing was an ultra-modern house on a slope about a kilometre above us. Jacques gestured towards it without saying anything. I raised the binoculars I was holding to examine the object of our attention. Although the house seemed to be made entirely of glass, it was impossible to see inside it even through the binoculars, because of the tinted windows and strong reflections from the sun and the surrounding trees.

As I scanned the house and surrounding area with the binoculars Jacques commented.

"That's the only possible place. It gives a good view of both the house and the garden. Everything else is shielded by the trees" he paused for an instant,

"Unless of course, whoever you're thinking of is going to be using thermal imaging equipment. Then it's not going to matter much where they are as long as they've got a direct line of sight to the house."

"Well, if it were me I'd want both direct visual and thermal for inside and parts where there's no visual. I can't believe they won't come prepared for that." I lowered the binoculars, "Let's go up the road and take a look at the place."

I glanced down at my watch, "I'd like to leave the Renault here and pick up the Audi from the other house. Do you think we're going to have time for that?"

Jacques, in turn, looked at his watch, "Should be able to. It's much closer to Monte Carlo. We'll stop off on the way. Just let me change quickly into my Monte Carlo outfit."

He picked up the large carrier bag he had brought with him into the house and disappeared into one of the bedrooms, re-appearing a few minutes later dressed in a well fitted blue blazer and immaculate white trousers.

I put the Renault keys on a table just by the front door before locking up the house, pocketing the key and climbing into the van next to Jacques.

The road that led up to the house overlooking the property Jacques had rented was narrow, winding and dusty and we left a cloud of swirling dust in our wake as we drove up the hill. Approaching the house we could see that it had been built on the crest of its own hill. It was surrounded by a large wooded garden and was only partially visible from the lower level of the road outside. The long driveway that led through the trees to the house was blocked by a large iron gate running the whole width of the drive, approximately ten feet in from the road. Two video cameras sat on poles above and on each side of the gate. The whole property seemed to be surrounded by a wall, probably four metres high, covered at the top with rusting barbed wire. Jacques had driven up to the gate and I got out of the van, walked around to the intercom and pressed the buzzer. There was no reply. I pressed again three or four times with the same negative result. I turned towards Jacques, shrugged my shoulders and indicated with my thumb that one of us ought to go over the gate to look inside the grounds.

He leaned out of the window of the van and said "You do it. I don't want to get myself dirty. And anyway I'm too old for that sort of shit."

I laughed as I nodded my head in assent and he started to manoeuvre the van so that it partially shielded me, before waving at me to proceed. It was easy enough to get over the gate but it was a deceptively steep climb up to the house. The house seemed to be unoccupied and locked up. I walked around it and could see that it gave a completely clear view of the whole property Jacques had rented. The Brits would be able to figure things out in much the same way as Jacques and I had. If the house was empty it would make an ideal observation post for the house below. There was an alarm box sitting prominently on the outside wall of the building, but an alarm would present no problems to a well prepared and properly equipped team. As I walked back down the driveway towards the gate I had climbed I noticed that there were at least two other video cameras providing surveillance of the grounds.

Having climbed back over the gate and brushed down the dirt I had acquired on my clothing, I got back into the van.

"That's the place they'll use. It's got a great view of the house below. There's an alarm but... " I shrugged and Jacques nodded. I did not need to tell him about things in which he was an expert.

He turned the van around and headed towards La Turbie where he exchanged the van for the other Renault and I climbed into the Audi. We then drove in convoy to Monte Carlo.

I had previously discussed with Jacques how we were going to effect the removal of Paolo from the hotel and my taking his place. We had decided to park the two cars away from the Monte Carlo Beach Hotel, perhaps in an underground car park. I would leave the Audi there so that I would have a clean vehicle to use when I needed it.

There was the usual traffic jam driving into the Principality. Amongst the equipment Jacques had brought to France were some walkie-talkies, which we used as we approached the hotel. As we drove around the hotel I spotted an underground car park a short distance from the hotel and told Jacques I was going to go in there. He followed me.

Having parked the cars, I walked towards the hotel, with Jacques following 150 to 200 metres behind me. He was wearing elegant white trousers, a blue blazer and sun glasses topped by a Panama hat. A silver topped cane completed his ensemble. He looked just like one of the many older, wealthy inhabitants of Monaco out for a late morning stroll. Jacques was something of a perfectionist about these types of things. One of the reasons I was always happy to work with him was his total professionalism.

I walked into the hotel lobby and looked around. There were a few people sitting in the variety of arm-chairs that decorated the lobby, mostly couples; certainly no one who looked either out of place or like a watcher. I relaxed as I surveyed the area, allowing my instincts to take over and invisibly feel every hidden corner of the lobby that my eyes might not consciously register. In the meantime Jacques had followed me into the hotel and marched unchallenged directly to the bank of elevators, as if he were a guest. As long as Paolo was in his room, we should be able to carry out a brush past handover to me of the room key and keys for the car Paolo had driven up there, and no one would be any the wiser about the part Paolo and Jacques had played.

Paolo was the first out of the elevators. He was dressed in beach shorts, with a short sleeved polo shirt hanging out over the shorts. The plastic strap of the back to front baseball cap he was wearing girded his forehead like a semi-circular crown. It was almost impossible to distinguish him from the other young men in the lobby, at least three of whom were also similarly wearing reversed baseball caps.

Out of the corner of my eye I saw Jacques leaving another elevator and slowly walking towards the reception desk. He was carrying a hold all in one hand, that I assumed was Paolo's and in the other a large Ferragamo carrier bag. I turned and also walked towards the reception desk, arriving there at the same time as Jacques, who put the holdall down on the floor next to him, but placed the carrier bag on the reception desk. There were two receptionists both dealing with other people. I leaned on the desk with both hands and slipped the envelope Jacques had placed partly under the carrier bag into my inside jacket pocket. I was confident that no one would have noticed the smoothly executed manoeuvre. One of the receptionists, having finished with her customer, came over to Jacques who asked her where she thought the best place would be to view the Grand Prix. Whilst she was going through a lengthy explanation of the merits of different locations and trying to sell him a place on the hotel boat, which was going to be moored in an excellent location for viewing the race from the harbour, the other receptionist came over to deal with me. I told him that I was not sure if I was going to need to check out or spend another few nights in the hotel. I extracted a concession that I could wait until 4pm before confirming either way. I walked away from the reception area and took the elevator up to the floor where the room, previously occupied by Jacques' son, was located. I was alone in the elevator and took out and opened the envelope Jacques had passed to me. It contained a plastic key card for the room and the keys of the British Audi.

I entered the room and looked around. Fortunately it had been cleaned and made up by the housekeeping staff, although the bathroom was in the sort of state that I know young men are prone to create, with wet towels everywhere and urine stains on the floor by the toilet bowl. I picked up the house telephone and dialled housekeeping who I asked to come to clean the bathroom.

I still had a couple of hours before I was due to meet Mr. White. I thought wistfully of Natalya. I could just imagine spending two pleasant, early afternoon hours with her in this bedroom. I went out on the balcony, which overlooked the swimming pool and beach beyond. I was going to give Jacques 20 minutes or so to get clear before picking up my bag from the back of the car that I had left in the car park and bringing it into the hotel room.

CHAPTER TWENTY SIX

The VIP lounge Heathrow

Aiport, London

*"The supreme art of war is to subdue the
enemy without fighting" (Sun Tzu)*

The six tanned, fit looking men sitting enjoying the
drinks and waitress service in the VIP lounge of
the European terminal at London's Heathrow Airport,
looked very unlike the normal visitors who passed
through that area and the head of protocol, whose job
it was to handle real VIPs, scowled at them, in spite of
his best attempts to conceal his displeasure at their
presence. These men were not supposed to be in the
VIP area which was usually reserved for royalty, heads
of government or celebrities. Equally out of place were
the men's black canvas holdalls, which were carelessly
strewn over the thick pile carpet that usually cocooned
Louis Vuitton luggage.

"I don't think he likes us very much" one of the men commented to the group, indicating the protocol chief with a movement of his head.

"Screw him. Fucking twat." responded another of the group as he took a swig of the 16 year old Glenfiddich whisky that the pretty waitress had given him in response to his request for a scotch.

"You think he remembers Andy and me from the last time we were through here B G 'ing (bodyguarding) that Saudi prince?" asked a third member of the group.

"Who the fuck cares" said the man who had first spoken. "I don't think this counts as prime time (slang for free time) so let's get another drink before the boss comes back to ream us out for drinking on the job."

They all laughed and drained their glasses as the one called Andy motioned to the waitress to come over.

While the SAS team were taking advantage of a rare moment of relaxation, Cartwright was sitting with Featherstonehaugh in a stationary limousine with darkened windows, parked just outside the VIP area.

"Your intel liaison in Nice is Phillipe Esclimont. He's got an informant on the Al Khalifa's security detail. Here's his number." As Featherstonehaugh handed Cartwright three sheets of paper with the names, pictures and contact details of particular individuals, he added, "the others are in case you need any logistic help. Jean-Michel Dumont is the DGSE Chief. He'll do anything he can to assist you. But try not to contact him. We don't want him more involved than absolutely necessary."

Cartwright nodded. He did not say anything to Featherstonehaugh, but he had already made his own arrangements for local help. Over the years since the 1970s, as international terrorism had grown, so had the various special forces of different countries to combat that terrorism. Throughout the second part of the twentieth century, military thinking and tactics had evolved to combat changing threats and strategic interests. This had resulted in different countries, including America, adopting the Special Forces model of the British SAS. Exchanges of information and techniques between different military units had always existed. Officer cadets from a variety of different countries attended the British Officer academy at Sandhurst. America also provided training for officers from different countries. It was inevitable with the military exchanges that take place, that Special Forces too, with their particular specialised requirements and training, should have developed their own private networks for exchanging techniques. Nowadays units like Delta, Navy Seals, the SAS, Germany's GSG 9 and KSK and the numerous units operating under the French COS (Commandement des Operations Speciales) not only frequently train together; they have exchange programmes for personnel and even assist each other in operations. On a non-operational level they compete against each other in international special forces' competitions that extend from such things as shooting and close combat to dealing with various terrorist scenarios. The result is that, whatever the political differences countries might have with each other, in this contemporary age, Special Forces have a network of back channel communication and assistance that is as unofficial as it is effective.

Cartwright and his men were travelling on a commercial flight to Nice Airport and he had arranged for them to be met and escorted by Hubert Ducrest, his counterpart at GIGN (Groupe D'Intervention Gendarmerie Nationale), a Special Forces unit that was a part of the French Police. Through the operation of the curious subculture that exists in Special Forces' circles, Hubert had agreed to provide vehicles and whatever other logistics Cartwright required. He was also attaching two GIGN operators to accompany the British team to deal with any local police who might inadvertently inhibit the British operation. This enormous degree of co-operation was taking place entirely unofficially and unknown even to the French Interior Ministry or the DGSE. The French and English Special Forces had a particularly close relationship and, as far as Hubert Ducrest was concerned, he was merely reciprocating the assistance the SAS had given his unit previously, including an operation two years before that had involved removing two dangerous Islamic terrorists of Algerian background from England to France. This sort of clandestine operation was now a frequent occurrence in a world where combating ruthless terrorism had forced democratic countries sometimes into adopting operational methods that were distinctly undemocratic and often illegal. It was a rare occurrence for any information ever to leak out about these activities, mainly because they took place, for the most part, under the radar of politicians, or even members of governments.

There was a rap on the window of the limousine and Cartwright opened the door in response. It was the seventh member of his team, Ken Collier, Regimental Sergeant Major, the backbone of the Regiment and one of Cartwright's most trusted men.

"All the gear's stowed in the baggage hold sir, where we can remove it whenever we want. They've finished loading passenger luggage and they're going to start boarding in ten minutes, so I suggest we get on board now."

"Very well Ken. I'll be with you in a couple of minutes. Get the men into the cars that are taking us to the plane."

Cartwright closed the door and turned to Featherstonehaugh.

"Well we're all ready to go. I just need the money to give to Traynor."

"It's in a large bag in the boot." The MI6 deputy chief looked slightly embarrassed as he added, "Well Frank. The very best of luck to you." He held out his hand to Cartwright who took it for a brief handshake before opening the car door again and getting out. Cartwright went to the rear of the limousine and opened the trunk. It was empty apart from a large black canvas holdall that was almost indistinguishable from those carried by his men. Cartwright, who had all too frequently been let down by MI6 or other government departments, unzipped the bag to check the contents. It was full of 500 Euro notes in what looked like 50,000 Euro packets still with their bank wrappers. He pulled out one bundle at random and flicked through the notes to make sure it was all money. Satisfied, he checked two more bundles, before again zipping up the bag and removing it from the trunk and walking into one of the waiting Land Rovers which, by now, contained his team.

They were the first to board the aircraft and had been given three rows right at the very back of the cabin to keep them away from the eyes of the majority of passengers. They tried, in the limited space available to stow their holdalls and themselves but the complaints started even before take-off. Andy was the first one to utter a complaint to Ken Collier,

"Hey sarge. I thought we were going business class not cattle class. There's no bleeding room here."

"Ross, you don't hear the Colonel complaining do you? What's good enough for him ought to be good enough for you. So shut it."

As he finished talking the RSM turned to glance quickly at Cartwright, who was sitting by him, separated only by the holdall full of money. Cartwright glanced back at him and made a face as he tried to move himself into a comfortable position. Then he turned towards the seats behind him,

"It's as difficult for me as it is for you lads. It's only a short trip. It'll soon be over and I won't be looking if you take advantage of any drinks they bring round."

One of the men responded on behalf of the others, "Thanks Boss." They all laughed.

The flight to Nice took an hour and twenty minutes and, if the other passengers had but known it, they were cleared to land immediately thanks to Hubert Ducrest, who had informed the flight controllers that a flight was coming in with VIPs that he was meeting.

As they descended from the plane, the arriving passengers glanced curiously at the group of gendarmes standing to one side of the aircraft, next to four large Citroen cars with tinted windows and assumed this was simply part of the heightened security that one saw at airports so often these days.

The SAS men only descended from the aircraft after all the other passengers were in the terminal and out of sight.

Cartwright was the first to descend the aircraft passenger stairs and be greeted by a smiling Hubert Ducrest.

"Welcome to France, Frank."

Hubert, a commandant of the GIGN was of medium height but was almost as broad as he was tall. He had the build of a weight lifter, with wide, muscular shoulders and barrel chest that looked as if they were about to burst the seams of the short sleeved shirt he was wearing. His grip as he took Cartwright's hand was like a vice and the simultaneous bear hug he gave the Englishman nearly took Cartwright's breath away.

"Hubert. You don't know your own strength" Cartwright laughed as he disentangled himself from the Frenchman's effusive greeting. He half turned towards the rest of his troop who had followed him down the stairs.

"You know RSM Collier, of course and I think you also know Ross, Peters and MacCallister."

The Frenchman nodded as he shook hands with the other members of the unit. After greeting Ducrest the group wandered over to shake hands with the rest of the GIGN reception party and it was apparent that some of them already knew each other.

Cartwright looked at his Rolex watch, "Hubert, I want to drop the men off at the hotel, but I've got to get up to a meeting in Monte Carlo. Can I get someone to drive me there?"

Ducrest laughed, "Don't be ridiculous Frank. I'll drive you myself and while we're driving you can tell me about this little operation you're on."

Cartwright nodded "Thanks, Hubert."

"Have you actually arranged a hotel? Or would you prefer to stay in our barracks? You know it would be much more private for you."

"We've arranged a hotel. I don't think it would be a good idea to stay in your barracks. Better to keep everything very, very unofficial. We're booked in at the Holiday Inn in Nice."

Hubert nodded, "Not a bad choice. The hotel's ok. Off the main beach road. It gets a lot of businessmen, so no one's going to notice you very much."

He turned to the GIGN operators who were helping the SAS unit remove some bags from the hold of the aircraft whilst the baggage handlers were kept at bay by another GIGN operator. Speaking rapidly in French he told his team to take the SAS men to the Holiday Inn and await further orders before he turned back to Cartwright.

"OK Frank. Let's go. Do you need any equipment?"

Cartwright motioned to the holdall that had been virtually glued to him since he had collected it from Featherstonehaugh.

"That's all I need."

"Do you need a weapon?"

Cartwright responded to the question by patting the left side of his chest where he had a pistol holstered underneath his jacket.

Collier approached him as he was following Ducrest to one of the parked Citroens. "Do you need me to go with you Boss?"

"No thanks, Ken. Get the chaps sorted at the hotel. Get yourselves some grub and we'll have a head-sheds meeting when I get back and I can give you all a sitrep."

Collier nodded and walked back to the men, who were now grouped around the other cars chatting with the GIGN operators.

Cartwright threw the holdall into the backseat of the car in which Ducrest had by now squeezed himself into the driver's seat. The Colonel opened the passenger door and sat down. Ducrest was so broad that when the two men were sitting side by side, Ducrest's shoulders kept brushing against the Englishman.

"Have you put on weight Hubert? You almost fill this car on your own."

Hubert laughed as he put the car into gear, revved the engine and drove off with a loud protesting squeal from the tyres.

They were barely out of the airport when they hit the traffic.

"It's that damn grand prix. The whole of the Cote d'Azur is full, from the Italian border to past Cannes. Thank God, it's over this weekend." He hit the siren and picked up the blue strobe light sitting on the fascia, leaning out of the driver's window to put it on the roof of the car. He then accelerated, weaving quickly and expertly through the traffic which parted in front of him, allowing him to pass.

They soon reached the Autoroute where the traffic was much lighter. As Hubert drove through the toll barrier without slackening speed, he switched off the siren and reached out of the car to retrieve the strobe from the roof.

Cartwright, who, in spite of having been on a number of high speed driving courses, had never quite managed to overcome an inherently cautious approach to motoring and always preferred to travel at a more sedate pace, gripped the side of his seat tightly as the Frenchman raced along the Autoroute at nearly 120 miles per hour with little regard for anyone in front of him.

It was no more than twenty minutes before they were exiting the Autoroute and entering the principality of Monaco. Cartwright had never before been to Monaco and he was anticipating with a certain amount of eagerness his first view of the famous millionaires' playground. As they followed the road from the highway into the principality, they entered a long, well lit and well maintained tunnel. Driving through the tunnel Cartwright's professional instincts took over and made him think that this would be a more than suitable location for the sort of car accident that had been conceived for the operation. He did not want to alert Hubert to his interest in the tunnel and contented himself with observations made directly ahead of him as they drove. Whilst hurtling along the Autoroute, Hubert had asked him about the reasons for his presence in the South of France. He had given the cover story about Al Qaeda using foreign mercenaries to prepare an attack that they thought was either going to be directed at the financial centre that Monte Carlo had become or by assaulting the yacht of a prominent member of the Saudi Royal family, which even now was moored in the principality's harbour. He had said that the information was imprecise but their objective was to capture these mercenaries and their handler and then try and obtain valuable intelligence from them. Hubert nodded, understandingly. These types of operations were all part of the on-going intelligence war against Islamic extremism. They were not infrequent and went on all over the world, often resulting in the turning of one or more of their targets into informants or even double agents.

Cartwright went on to explain that MI6 had managed to plant a mole in the terrorist team and that he was now due to meet that mole and obtain further information from him. He had indicated the holdall and, tongue in cheek, had told Hubert that he was handing over some equipment that the team had requested and that the mole had undertaken to obtain and that this was expected to bolster the mole's credentials.

"Quite a sophisticated operation" remarked Hubert at the end of the narrative, "why not keep it going rather than pull the cell in?"

"It'd be too dangerous" responded Cartwright, "our man in their team says that he can't control what they are doing and he thinks we'll get much more information from pulling them in. We're going to watch them for a few days, but, as you know, we're not normally sent in for long term surveillance."

"Two questions then; first why don't you have me and my boys help you out when you pull everyone in? Secondly, why are you personally running this operation when you ought to be back at Stirling Lines administering the Regiment?"

Cartwright answered cautiously, "Well, as for you helping us out, there's nothing I'd like better but, as I am sure you know, we have people in Saudi pretty much all the time doing training, so we have close contact with the Royal Family. We promised to keep this operation completely to ourselves. The ruling family are petrified that if there's the slightest hint that they might be at all vulnerable it could stir up all sorts of problems. There's already quite a lot of dissent and discontent with them that they are desperate to keep suppressed. As for me running this, if you don't mind Hubert, I'd rather not discuss that. There are some things I think it's better you don't know, but it has to do with my knowing the mole personally and his being in a position where he's afraid of traps being laid for him." He paused for a moment, thinking how unconvincing his explanation of his presence sounded and then added,

"Besides, I've been in the field my whole career. To tell you the truth I can't get used to sitting behind a desk doing administration. Things being what they are with this mole, I grabbed at any excuse to get in on the operation."

Hubert, who had just been nodding at Cartwright's narrative without saying anything, laughed.

"I know exactly how you feel. For everything we do, I have to fill in ten forms. Sometimes it drives me mad. I came out to meet you as well and to drive you to get out of the sacre bureau."

Cartwright heaved an inward sigh of relief. He did not like to lie to Hubert, but this was a mission that no one could know about. As they drove through the traffic in silence Cartwright thought that, even if he had told Hubert the truth, Hubert could probably be trusted with the secret. In their line of business everyone had dark secrets that they were adept at keeping buried. However, Cartwright recalled something that he thought Benjamin Franklin had once said, that three people can keep a secret if two of them are dead.

As they pulled up at the Monte Carlo Beach Hotel Hubert turned to Cartwright,

"Do you want me to wait for you? Or what would you like me to do?"

In truth Cartwright did not know. He had planned on trying to stick close to Traynor and wanted to be able to identify Traynor's team as soon as he could. His next move really depended on the American.

"I'm not sure how this is going to play out. Can you perhaps be somewhere where I can contact you in the next hour and let you know what I want to do?"

"Sure" The Frenchman pulled out a pen and wrote a number on a piece of paper, "that's my portable. Just call me. If I don't hear from you in an hour I'll head back. Will you be back in Nice tonight? If it's possible the boys and I would like to entertain you."

"I think I will. When I've had my meet I'll know more about how I need to assign the men, so I'll want to try to get back to Nice."

Hubert nodded and, having left Cartwright at the hotel entrance drove away. Before entering the hotel lobby Cartwright watched the Frenchman's car until it was out of sight. The GIGN commandant for his part watched Cartwright in his rear view mirror as he pulled away. He was curious about what Cartwright was really up to and he wanted to satisfy his curiosity. Personally he liked the Englishman, but the English were operating in his backyard and he needed to know what they were really up to. The truth was, for all their friendly relations and joint training, when it came down to it everyone operated in his own national interest. He might like the English, even admire their professionalism, but you could never trust them. He drove a short distance and then pulled into a turning, out of sight of the hotel, before parking his car in a zone where parking was prohibited. As he left the car he pushed the sun visor down to display his free parking police credentials.

He walked back to the hotel slowly, keeping a careful eye out in case Cartwright had had him drop him there to deceive him into thinking that the meet he had talked about was taking place there when, in reality, it was somewhere else. Having reached the entrance without encountering the Englishman, he peered through the glass entrance doors but was unable to see Cartwright. He entered the hotel, looking around carefully as he sidled close to a pillar that partially concealed him from anyone in the lobby. A tall, slim oriental man coming out of the elevator caught his eye. It was difficult to describe what attracted his attention about the man. There was something about the way he moved and seemed to exude a type of energy or power that put all of Hubert's police instincts on fine alert. He watched the oriental curiously as he made his way into the bar area. Then he saw Cartwright. The oriental was the person the Colonel was meeting. The two of them shook hands briefly and then walked together towards the elevators. They entered one just before the doors closed. Hubert walked over to the bank of elevators and watched as the lights for various floors lit up as they were reached and passed, until the light for the fourth floor stayed lit, indicating that Cartwright and the oriental had probably got off there. Hubert wandered over to the reception desk to see if he could obtain some information about the oriental man.

Cartwright was both relieved and uneasy when Traynor turned up at the time agreed with Featherstonehaugh. After the most perfunctory of greetings Traynor had suggested adjourning to his room. Cartwright did not like the idea of entering an unknown location with a known assassin and a holdall containing six million Euros. Surreptitiously he patted the gun under his coat for reassurance as Traynor led the way to the elevators. He was on full alert as he followed Traynor into the hotel room, although logic was telling him that he was there to hand over the money to Traynor so that there would be no reason for the American to take any offensive action against him.

He relaxed a little when Traynor sat down on one of two adjoining armchairs and indicated to him that he should do likewise. Traynor seemed to be reading his thoughts as the first thing he said was, "You don't need to worry. I'm not here to ambush you. If we're going to work together we need to establish a little bit of trust."

Cartwright shifted uneasily on his chair. He doubted that the man next to him would ever trust him. He probably suspected that it was part of Cartwright's job to ensure that he did not leave the South of France alive. Traynor was sitting back looking at him in a relaxed but extremely alert manner. He wondered if this man was going to be a little too difficult to deal with. So far he had acted like a supreme professional and not made any mistakes.

"Is that the money?" Traynor was pointing at the holdall which Cartwright had placed on the floor by his side.

"Yes."

"May I?" Traynor asked. When Cartwright nodded his assent, he reached across, pulled the bag towards him and unzipped it. He looked inside before standing up, carrying the bag over to the bed and emptying its contents over the bed cover. Cartwright stood up nervously as Traynor crossed the room and disappeared into the bathroom for a few seconds. He relaxed when Traynor reappeared carrying a portable ultraviolet light and started picking up various bundles of money at random, flicking through them and randomly checking notes. Cartwright hoped to God that MI6 had not filled the bag with forged notes. Traynor was now carefully examining every bundle. To conceal his anxiety Cartwright walked over to the sliding door and looked out towards the swimming pool and the sea beyond.

"Nice room. Pleasant view" he commented. Traynor did not respond. Cartwright returned to his chair, relegated to watching silently for the nearly ten further minutes Traynor took checking the money. Finally the American appeared satisfied and started to shovel the money from the bed into a large duffle bag that Cartwright had not before noticed and that had been sitting at the side of the bed, partly concealed by the bed cover.

"You can have that bag if you like" offered Cartwright, indicating the holdall in which he had carried the money from England.

Traynor gave him a look that managed simultaneously to convey contempt and incredulity that Cartwright would even have made such a stupid suggestion. "I don't think so." He picked up Cartwright's bag, closed the zip and handed it back to the soldier.

CHAPTER TWENTY SEVEN

"Let your plans be dark and impenetrable as night, and when you move, fall like a thunderbolt." (Sun Tzu)

I had collected my things from the car in the car park, taken them up to the hotel room before checking the Brits' Audi that Paolo had left in the hotel car park. Nothing seemed amiss and there did not seem to be any physical surveillance.

I made myself at home in the hotel room, spreading out my things and putting out my toothbrush and other wash things in the bathroom so that it would look as if I had been staying in the room to anyone who might decide to come in and look around. Just before the time came for me to meet Mr. White I took the elevator down to the lobby.

I paused as I exited the elevator and looked around carefully. The first thing I noticed was a short, squat guy built like a tank, trying to conceal himself behind one of the decorative pillars in the lobby. It was a hopeless task because the guy was about twice as wide as the pillar. There was something quite comical about it, but he looked more like a cop than the people the Brits had used to carry out surveillance in Rome. I wondered what was going on. Surely the Brits had not got the French police involved. It would not make any sense. I thought I might as well put the question to Mr. White because it made a big difference to the operation.

He was sitting in the bar area, looking around nervously, with a large black holdall on the ground between his legs. He got up as I approached and offered his hand to me. Fine. I shook hands.

"Why don't we go up to my room. It'll be more private." I suggested immediately. In response Mr. White nodded his assent, picked up his bag and started to follow me towards the elevators. When we were nearly at the elevators I jerked my head towards the pocket Hercules helping to prop up the lobby pillar and asked him, "Is that one of yours?"

He knew what I was talking about because, without looking, he replied, "Sort of. He was my ride down here but he wasn't supposed to have stuck around."

"What is he? Local fuzz." We were in the elevator by now, almost up to my floor. I looked at him and could see him hesitating, wondering whether or not to tell me the truth. He answered me as I led the way out of the elevator towards my room.

"He's a colleague from GIGN doing me a personal favour. He's got nothing to do with what we're doing. I rather suspect that he just got a little curious and decided to do some spying on his own." I noticed that he did not try and explain GIGN to me and took it for granted that I knew what he was talking about. So he probably also realised that I knew he was SAS.

I opened the room door. He followed me in and I motioned him to sit down. Before doing so he looked around carefully, taking in the whole room as well as the bathroom, whose door I had deliberately left open to enable him to see inside. I wanted the guy to feel relaxed. I sat down on one of two chairs I had earlier moved together. Eventually he seemed satisfied and sat down next to me.

"Do you want a drink or anything?" He shook his head. He was not yet at ease. That was OK, if he wanted to get straight down to business. I indicated the bag,

"Is that the money?". He nodded.

"May I?" He nodded again and I picked up the bag, put it on the bed and unzipped it before emptying the contents across the bed cover. It made me feel good looking at all those bundles of 500 Euro notes, but I did not trust the British and I still needed to check the money. I went into the bathroom to retrieve the ultra violet light I had bought in Rome, which was supposed to be able to help identify forged currency.

Mr. White was standing up, still looking nervous as I came out of the bathroom. I ignored him and started picking up bundles of notes and checking them under the UV light, while he tried to disguise his nervousness by walking over to the window and looking out.

It took me about fifteen minutes to check and count all the money. I could not afford any mistakes. I did not want to look a chump when I took the money to the bank guy for delivery to Liechtenstein.

When I was as satisfied as I could be that the money was genuine and all there, I pulled out a large waterproof duffle bag that I had put under the bed. As I was putting the money away, Mr. White told me that I could use his holdall if I wanted. I gave him a look intended to convey that if he thought I was that stupid he ought to take his money and go elsewhere.

I glanced at my watch. There might still be time for me to meet the bank guy and get rid of the money, otherwise I would have to put it in the hotel safe overnight. But I also wanted time to get to know my friend a little better. I zipped up the bag and threw it on the floor.

"So, I know you don't want to tell me your real name, but can I know your first name. If we're going to work together I can't keep calling you Mr.White."

He hesitated again, before answering, "It's Frank."

"OK Frank. You probably know my name's John.I suggest though, that if at any time we're in the presence of members of my team we stick to Mr. White for you and Ben for me. That's the name I'm registered under here" I added.

He took the opening I had given him, "When can I get together with your team?"

"Any time you like, from tomorrow. I've got a few things to sort out. But what I'd like to know first is how you're going to figure in all this. You're not thinking of coming on the op are you? I thought the whole purpose of using me and my contractors was to keep you people well away from the action. And if you're not coming on the op you shouldn't really be coming into contact with my people, it might spook them."

I do not know how he thought all this was going to play out, but what I said seemed to stop him short and make him start thinking. Before he could say anything in reply I went on,

"As I understood it, you were going to be providing me with up to date intel from a source close to the target and you were also going to be providing me with a piece of equipment. I'd like to go over the plan with you so we can both be happy that the equipment you're providing is going to be right for the job." He nodded his acquiescence as I continued, "Where are the targets now? When are they coming in?"

"They're here now. They're staying on the Al Khalifa's yacht. They came in for the Grand Prix and then they're staying on for the Cannes Film Festival next week. The woman might also be staying a few days at the palace, as a guest of Prince Albert and his wife. But we don't know yet. We do know that a security detail drove down from Paris in three cars including an S600 Mercedes they normally drive around in.

I listened carefully and I did not like what I was hearing. If they were going to the Cannes Film Festival there was no reason for them to stay in Monte Carlo. They had their own boat and they could moor it in the harbour in Cannes. Why should they bother driving backwards and forwards to Monte Carlo when they could simply walk down to the harbour and board their boat. I voiced my concerns to Frank.

"The intel we're getting so far is that they won't stay in Cannes. The harbour there is too crowded during the film festival and they'll be much more private moored in Monte Carlo. They've had problems with paparazzi and they're much too easy a target for the paparazzi in Cannes. I'm told that a decent intimate picture of the two of them, maybe kissing, can fetch a shitload of money, so you can imagine the sort of photographers' feeding frenzy they're causing."

Yes. It made sense. I would never forget the one or two times that I had seen the news media chasing down a celebrity on the street. They had been worse than starving wild animals fighting over a fresh kill. I felt reassured.

"What about the dazzler? Have you got it with you? I need to try it out."

"I suggest we meet tomorrow. I can give it to you then."

As a matter of fact I wanted to see where he was staying to carry out some observation myself, in order to see if I could get some idea of how many men he had brought with him and what they looked like. It always helps to be able to look over the opposition.

I was quite casual about it, "Fine. Why don't I pick you up tomorrow from wherever you're staying, collect the dazzler and take you over the route where I think we can carry out the op."

Again the hesitation. This man was not an experienced undercover operative. That was good. He was a soldier. After serving in the military for twenty five years I understand soldiers. They are conditioned by their training to think and act in a particular way. It makes them predictable.

"Why don't we meet here tomorrow?"

I shrugged, "If that's what you prefer. Why don't we say here, at 1600 then?" I had to give myself time to collect my team, drop them off in Beaulieu and get back.

He frowned."1600! That's a bit late in the day isn't it?"

I shrugged again. "I've got a lot to sort out. I've got to make sure my team's ready to go at short notice and it's not so easy to get around with all these grand prix people about. It's the last practice day tomorrow, you know, before the race on Sunday."

He grunted, "OK then. Tomorrow at 1600."

"Is your friend going to be chauffeuring you again tomorrow?"

"I don't know. Probably just a driver." He paused "Oh. One more thing." I could see that he had been restraining himself for some time before adding what he wanted me to believe was nothing more than a casual afterthought.

"Could you please make sure you keep the mobile phone my colleague gave you turned on, so that I can contact you at any time. Good communications between us are going to be vital." As he finished speaking he wrote a number down on a piece of paper and handed the paper to me,

"That's the mobile number I'm using. It'll be on night and day." The implication was that I, too, should keep my mobile on 24 hours a day. The Brits' major priority now would be to know where I was at all times. I did not say anything. I was wondering whether Jacques' son would be up to the task of hacking into the French mobile phone network to enable me to pinpoint the location of Frank here and, probably, his band of merry men, if they did not locate themselves where Jacques and I had anticipated they would choose.

I looked at my watch again. I needed to hurry if I was going to make the bank. I stood up,

"You'll have to forgive me. I've got something to do. Can you see yourself out?"

He stood up. Picked up his empty holdall and left the room after once more shaking hands with me.

No doubt he and his GIGN friend would be waiting for me in the lobby, or just outside, to try and follow me to see where I was going. If the way the GIGN man had tried to conceal himself earlier was any guide, I ought not to have too much trouble losing them, but, in any event, I already had an alternative plan. I had arranged for the hotel to rent a speed boat for me for the afternoon and even now as I looked out of my window, I could see it anchored, waiting for me in the deeper water adjacent to the beach area.

I had earlier used an outside telephone to call the banker. I had arranged that, unless he heard from me to the contrary, I would be making my delivery some time that afternoon before 18.00. I put on some swimming trunks and then double wrapped a couple of towels, a shirt, a pair of slacks and trainers in two plastic laundry bags that housekeeping had thoughtfully provided in the room cupboard. I picked up the duffle bag and checked it to make sure that it was properly closed and completely watertight. I had purchased it on my way back to the hotel from the garage after I had collected my bag from the car. I had passed a dive shop, just across the road from the hotel and having gone in and seen the large waterproof duffle bag, had instantly formulated my plan for getting out of the hotel without passing the front entrance.

Duffle and plastic bags in hand I made my way down the service stairs. The beach and pool were on the level below the lobby and where the stairs ended was an exit that led along a corridor straight through to the pool. I carefully avoided a couple of dead cockroaches that I preferred not to have plastered all over my bare feet and slowly pushed on the fire door that opened out onto the poolside. With the door half open, I peered out looking around. The pool area was quite crowded and there were the usual array of loungers, umbrellas and bare breasted women being ogled by men of all ages. I did not see Frank, or his heavily built colleague. Nor did I see anyone who looked even remotely like a watcher.

"Can I help you sir?" One of the pool staff had opened the door wide and was addressing me.

"I've rented a boat. I think it's that one." I indicated the sleek motor boat sitting out on the water. The pool boy followed my gesture and nodded.

"I'll get you the key sir. It's Monsieur... "

"Kamal."

"Very good monsieur. If you'll just wait a moment."

I watched him as he walked to a door just to the side of the toilet/changing rooms and disappeared inside. A few moments later he reappeared dangling a key attached to a red flotation device. He walked back to me and handed me the key,

"Would monsieur like to be taken out to the boat?"

"No. It's alright. I think I'll swim."

He looked doubtfully at the duffle and plastic bags, "Is Monsieur sure? It's no problem to take you."

"No I'm sure. I can do with the exercise." He still looked doubtful but shrugged and turned away to answer the summons of someone who was, no doubt, a much better prospect for a tip.

I walked down to the water's edge. The boat was moored about 50 metres from the beach. The bags and the key were a bit of a handful, but I managed to wade out into deeper water before slipping onto my back and kicking my way out to the boat. Although it was a hot day the water was colder than I had imagined, but my inelegant splashing soon dissipated the initial chill. Once I was on my back, with the things I was carrying clasped to my chest, they ceased to cause me any difficulty. I got to the boat quickly and, treading water, threw the boat key and bags with my clothes into the boat, before manhandling the duffle bag out of the water. This proved more difficult and eventually I submerged myself under the bag and pushed it into the boat with both hands. I managed all this, as well as hauling myself into the boat, without capsizing it, although I had it rocking fairly violently. It was still in the final throes of its rocking as the engine started with a deep, throaty roar.

The hotel was located in a small bay to one side and out of sight of the main harbour. I pulled up the anchor and turned the boat out to sea as I opened the throttle. I soon cleared the bay, at which point I could see the main harbour and the town centre rising above it. The harbour was thronged with boats and, as I eased back the throttle and cruised in to find a berth, I looked around for the Al Khalifa's yacht. If I had not remembered it from the pictures I had seen, I would have had no problem identifying it. It was one of the largest, if not the largest, of the boats in the harbour. The clean, smooth lines and the sharply swept back bow gave an impression of speed even though the boat was anchored peacefully, with the water lapping softly against its side. A helicopter sat on a landing area at the stern, with its main rotors tied together. I had always been content with my life, even throughout some of its vicissitudes, but as I looked at the boat and some of the almost equally impressive neighbouring yachts, I could not help feeling a slight pang of envy at the sort of immense wealth that some people enjoyed. I felt a rather malicious satisfaction that, for all their wealth and privilege, a couple of these people's lives were resting in my ruthless hands. I thought to myself, let them enjoy their wealth for the few remaining days left to them. In a few days they would own nothing more than a slab in the mortuary and that would only be a short term rental.

I passed close enough to be able to read the name "Cleopatra" on the stern and to see the faces of two of the crew who were immaculately dressed in white uniforms. Viewing the boat curiously, I wondered if I might catch a glimpse of my targets, but the two crew members were the only visible life forms.

Although the jetty was quite crowded with a wide variety of boats with little in common other than their synchronised splashing to the rhythm of the waves, I found a mooring space and eased my boat in before jumping out and tying it up loosely, leaving it free to join in the bobbing dance of its companion boats. I sat on the jetty where I had moored my boat and opened the laundry bags to remove a hotel towel in order to complete the drying process that had already been initiated by the sun and wind. Having dried myself, I dressed quickly and threw my wet trunks and the laundry bag back in the boat before hoisting the duffle bag onto my shoulder and walking to the road running alongside the harbour. Quite a few taxis were waiting, presumably hoping to pick up the only moderately wealthy visitors from the yachts in the harbour who did not have their own cars waiting for them. I jumped into one of the taxis and gave him the address of the bank.

Everything went like clockwork at the bank. I had not had the opportunity of carrying out a careful count of the money but the bank did it all for me. Of the six million Euros, I retained one million to cover the balance of the money I had agreed to pay Jacques and the rest of the team and to leave me enough cash to be able to keep me going in any emergency. That million went back into the duffle bag along with a faxed receipt from Herr Kessler.

The bank office was in a building that housed an arcade of shops and the principality's main post office. I had noticed a sign for the post office as I had entered the building. After I left the bank I followed the sign indicating the post office and saw that the post office was still open. Whilst looking for somewhere to purchase an envelope, I noticed a section with a rather bored looking woman sitting behind a counter reading a magazine. Her section specialised in sales of philatelic items and sold decorative envelopes that were used for sending out stamps on the first day of issue. I purchased an envelope and a set of stamps before writing on it my address in Umbria and placing the receipt for the five million Euros into the envelope. I was able to post the receipt just as the post office was closing.

CHAPTER TWENTY EIGHT

When Cartwright left Traynor he went directly down to the hotel lobby and looked around for Hubert. He could not see the Frenchman so he telephoned the number the GIGN man had given him.

"Hubert?"

"Oui."

"It's Frank. Can you collect me?"

"Sure. I'll be about ten minutes."

Cartwright seated himself on an easy chair from where he had a good view of the elevators. He wanted to know if Traynor was going to keep the money he had been given in the hotel, or whether he was going to take it somewhere else. If the latter, Cartwright had made up his mind that he would try and follow. He had not wanted to get Hubert more involved than necessary, but it was better to find all of Traynor's locations than to keep the Frenchman totally in the dark. Besides he could work any surveillance into the cover story he had already told Hubert. He hoped that the Frenchman arrived before Traynor appeared. Cartwright was almost completely ignorant of the intricacies of international banking and was unable to imagine that Traynor had arranged to deposit the money with a bank and that, by the following day, Traynor's account in Liechtenstein would be credited with the money he had handed over. He made the mistake of assuming that Traynor was as unsophisticated about finance as he was. Neither did he imagine that, even as he was sitting there, Traynor was making his way to the speed boat moored by the beach.

He started to think about the money, which led him to wonder whether, after the operation and after they had disposed of Traynor and his crew, he might be able to recover the money and manage to take it for himself. He might have to do a split with the members of his team, with a chunk for the sergeants' mess and another chunk for the troopers' mess. It would not be the first time. Yes, with a little luck he might come out of this operation not only with enhanced status but also the cash to maintain a better lifestyle. Throughout the whole of his military career he had felt inhibited by the lack of a private income enjoyed by so many officers in the British army. It had always been an uphill battle for him to manage purely on his army salary.

His reverie was interrupted by a tap on the shoulder. He jumped in surprise. He had not noticed Hubert creeping up on him. Hubert sat down next to him.

"Are we going? Or are we waiting?" He was staring unblinkingly at the Englishman.

"We're waiting a little while." He paused, then looked at the Frenchman with a smile,

"By the way Hubert. You know you're not the most inconspicuous of individuals. Did you think I wouldn't see you trying to hide behind something that's half your size?"

Hubert was unfazed, "Just a little curiosity my friend. This is my territory you know. I need to know what goes on here." He paused for effect, "whatever I am told."

"Listen Hubert. We've both got our orders and priorities and I think we understand each other, but please don't let's go falling over each other. My contact also took all of two seconds to make you. I like you Hubert and I know we're in your neck of the woods, but please don't do anything to fuck up my operation."

The Frenchman nodded, "Fair enough. Fair enough. I'll try not to let my personal curiosity interfere with my unofficial duties."

They sat for a few moments in silence before the Frenchman asked, "Are we staying here? Or are you ready to get going?"

"I wanted to wait a little while and see if my man came down. I thought we might follow him. I like to cover as many of the angles as I can."

Hubert nodded. After a further ten minutes had passed without any sign of Traynor, Cartwright stood up decisively.

With a brief "Wait here for me Hubert" he strode towards the elevators and entered the first one to arrive. Having pressed the button for the fourth floor, he was again outside Traynor's room within minutes and knocking on the door. There was no reply. He knocked again, louder. There was still no reply. He was examining the lock, wondering whether he would be able to open it, when he heard the clanking of a cleaner's cart. He looked up in time to see a maid pushing a cart along the corridor. He called to her and when she approached him asked her in French if she could open his door for him because he thought he had left the key in the room. She hesitated for a moment before deciding that he had an honest face and using her pass key to open the door. He thanked her politely and gave her a warm smile as he entered the room.

The room was empty. Not a sign of the assassin. He stood in the centre of the room for a moment, looking around carefully before opening the single cupboard in the room and peering inside. A jacket and two pairs of trousers hung from the rail. Two pairs of shoes, both with rubber soles were placed neatly side by side on the floor of the cupboard. He slid the door of the cupboard to open the other, previously closed, side. There was a room safe and below it three or four drawers. He tried the safe door. It was closed. He pushed one of the numbers and the word "closed" appeared in red letters. He wished he had thought to bring with him the pocket sized device that could open these electronic hotel safes in about fifteen seconds. Unfortunately he had left it with the rest of his equipment in Nice. He opened the drawers. Some underwear and four or five shirts. He closed the cupboard and walked over to the luggage stand where Traynor's bag was sitting. He opened the bag. It contained the UV light Traynor had used to check the money, a few more clothes, a couple of paper-back books and a drawing pad. He took out the drawing pad and opened it. The first four pages were filled with diagrams of what looked like roads with various crosses and arrows dotted around the page. Cartwright was fairly certain that this was a schematic for the operation. He sat down on one of the armchairs in the room and looked more carefully at the diagrams. He felt a sense of relief that at least Traynor seemed to be planning the operation and was apparently not just going to disappear with the money he had so meekly handed over a short time before. Some of the other pages were filled with sketches of people. He looked at them curiously. They were very good. He was no art critic but it seemed to him that, surprisingly, the assassin seemed to be quite a talented artist.

He closed the drawing pad, replaced it in the bag and then started to feel around the bag for concealed areas. If there was a concealed area he could not find it. He wondered where Traynor had put the guns and ammunition they had given him in Rome, to say nothing of the money. The room safe was too small. Surely Traynor was not walking around the streets carrying two concealed pistols and six million Euros in cash. Cartwright closed the bag trying to restore it to its original position, although he did not much care if Traynor realised that his room had been searched, he ought to be expecting things like that and Cartwright was not going to be embarrassed even if he was caught in the room. He stood again, looking around the room carefully, wondering where he would conceal something. His eye fell on the air conditioning duct. Pretty obvious, but you never knew. He dragged a chair underneath the duct and stood on it to give him access. Peering into the slats he could not see anything. It looked pretty dusty and dirty and certainly did not look as if it had been removed any time recently. Again, though, you never knew. He delved in his pocket for the knife that was his constant companion, a large model Swiss army knife with, amongst other blades, different screw driver heads. Opening the knife, Cartwright selected a screw driver to fit the screws holding the duct in place. It took no more than a couple of seconds to remove the duct, but his only reward was to have his hands covered in dirt. As he replaced the duct he smudged some of the dirt that now covered his hands on to the wall. Cursing quietly, he climbed down, put his knife on the chair and went into the bathroom to wash off the grime. Professional pride restrained him from being too obvious and instead of wiping his hands on one of the pristine towels hanging on the towel rail, he pulled off some toilet paper, dried his hands and flushed the paper down the toilet bowl.

Going back into the bedroom he looked around carefully, as he folded up the blades of his knife and replaced it in his pocket. Where could Traynor have hidden the money and the guns? He could not see any-where. Traynor had not come into the lobby whilst he was waiting, so could not have deposited the money in the hotel safe. That meant Traynor had some other loca-tion that he felt was safe enough to keep the money and weapons. Trying to imagine himself in Traynor's posi-tion Cartwright decided that the assassin was unlikely to keep all that cash in the same place where he would have established his base of operations and support team. That indicated that he had probably arranged a separate safe house, or maybe just another hotel room. Cartwright sat down on one of the chairs looking out at the balcony and the sea beyond. He was starting to get a very bad feeling about this operation. He had not anticipated Traynor using two different locations for himself and his crew and he did not have a large enough team to carry out surveillance on multiple locations. He thought back to what he had read in Traynor's files, mentally comparing it to the man he had met, his quiet confidence, his smooth gliding movements, the power he had felt through a mere handshake. Perhaps this Traynor was going to be too much for him. Then again, from everything he had read and seen, was Traynor really going to be any threat after he had concluded the operation. The man seemed to be a consummate professional. Certainly not the type to rush off and try to sell his memoirs, or even crack under interrogation. He shuddered and stood up. What was he thinking? He had a job to do and he had better do it to the best of his ability, as he had in the past done every job with which he had been tasked. Gazing out of the window a thought struck him. He slid back the sliding door to the balcony and stepped outside. Leaning over the edge of the balcony he looked out at the swimming pool area, the beach beyond and the small floating raft about 50 yards from the beach with two people sunning themselves on its surface. Two or three small motor boats were moored near the raft, floating gently on the calm water. How could he have been so stupid? Traynor must have left the hotel by boat. He would not have needed to go through the lobby to get to the beach.

Before leaving Traynor's room Cartwright gave the room a quick visual check to ensure that nothing was obviously out of place. As he returned to the lobby he was again wondering if Traynor, who up to now had been completely outthinking the British, was going to prove too much for him.

"He's gone. Slipped out of the back while we were sitting here." Cartwright announced to Hubert as he walked up to the Frenchman.

Hubert just shrugged in response and stood up, "Does that mean we're going back to Nice?"

Cartwright nodded.

CHAPTER TWENTY
NINE

Though you may be victorious
In the arts of war
They are but a stone boat
That will not cross
The melancholy sea of life
Yagyu Muneyoshi Sekishusai 1529-1606

As I left the post office from where I had posted my receipt I could not help noticing that it was just around the corner from the hotel in which I had placed Natalya. I imagined her waiting for me naked on her bed and immediately felt myself getting hard. I looked around carefully, wondering whether I dared risk a quick visit to her. The feeling in my groin became too insistent for me to ignore. I was as sure as I could be that no one was watching me. Perhaps I was thinking with my lower extremities. I remembered a line from an English film I had seen some years before, "When the balls are full the brain is empty." All too true. I was still debating with myself the wisdom of my actions by the time I was in the lobby of the Metropole dialling Natalya's room from the house phone. She answered almost immediately with that drawling pronunciation that I realised I had come fondly to associate with her.

"Daaarleeng," she squealed, "where are you? Can I see you. I meees you."

I will not pretend that I was not pleased at her reaction to my call. I had not gone directly to the room because I had half suspected she might already have found some other companionship.

"I'm in the lobby. I managed to get away for a short time." I restrained myself from adding that I had been thinking about her and wanted to see her.

"Come up at once." I need hardly say that I required no further encouragement before making my way to the room. When I got to the room the door was slightly ajar and the entrance and sitting room to the suite were dark. However, a thin sliver of light came from the bedroom beyond. I entered and shut the door silently. My senses were, as nearly always, alert for anything wrong as I put down my bag, slipped off my shoes and walked quietly towards the shaft of light. She was lying on the bed, naked except for a thoroughly revealing diaphanous black lace teddy that was a new addition to her wardrobe.

"I've been hoping you would come" were the last words she whispered in my ear before I sank into her arms.

The lovemaking was even more satisfying than it had been previously and as we lay on the bed afterwards, with her half asleep, snuggled closely against my chest,

I started to have thoughts that I had never previously allowed myself. There had never before been room for any woman, even semi-permanently, in my life. Sure I had known lots of women, but they were either prostitutes or female agents operating in the nether world I inhabited. Throughout my life I had used women as tools of my trade or for instant gratification. As I listened to Natalya's shallow breathing against my chest, felt the softness of her hair on my skin and smelled the mixture of perfume and sex wafting in the air around us, I tried to convince myself that this was just another street hooker on the make who had been lucky enough to find a temporary protector to latch on to, but I found it almost impossible to re-impose the icy objectivity with which I was usually able to keep relationships at a distance. I felt hungry and looked at my watch. I had been with Natalya for nearly three hours and had not eaten all day. I tried to shift my right arm which was trapped under Natalya's body. My movement merely caused her to move more closely against me and to run her lips against my neck and chest. I reasoned that there was nothing pressing to prevent me from spending another few hours with her. After all I was as entitled as anyone to have a few hours of leisure; I might never again have the opportunity.

We spent another hour in bed before ordering a meal from the room service menu. I eventually left around 1am. Uncharacteristically I was reluctant to go. I could not remember the last time I had felt so relaxed, at ease and unthreatened. Before dressing I had showered and looked at myself in the bathroom mirror, thinking that I still looked quite young in spite of the grey hairs. I had the well-muscled body of a much younger man. I imagined myself on a slab in a mortuary with a pathologist dictating notes over my body, "Asian male of indeterminate age could be anything between 35 and 50 from the physical condition of the body; well-developed musculation; good skin tone. Two old, probably gsw scars on the side; what seem to be other shrapnel scars on legs and torso. Three gunshot entry wounds to the rear of the head and back... "

I left the imaginary post mortem uncompleted and finished dressing. Natalya had asked me if she would be seeing me again soon and I had replied honestly, that I did not know.

I walked from the hotel to the Casino. Several taxis were waiting patiently for those late night gamblers who still retained sufficient funds to cover a taxi fare. The lucky driver who took me back to the harbour where I had left my boat, received a tip in addition to the fare.

It was a beautiful warm, moonlit night and even at this late hour there were quite a lot of people around with sufficient romance in their souls to be enjoying the way the moon was reflected in the dark stillness of the water of the bay and backlighting the looming hulls of the different boats darkly outlined against the horizon. I had had some doubts about navigating back to the Beach Hotel in the dark, but in fact the moon provided sufficient light to make it an easy, enjoyable trip across smooth water that was barely ruffled by a very slight, warm breeze.

Once again I passed close to the Cleopatra. In contrast to the quiet it had exuded when I had passed it earlier, it was now brightly lit, not just from the interior, but with lights strung over the helicopter pad and running the length of the ship from stern to bow. I could see several men and women, sitting on the rear deck, listening to music and obviously drinking. Easing back on the throttle, I allowed my boat to drift close to the side of the yacht whilst just maintaining slow forward progress. I looked carefully at the people on the deck but was unable to identify my targets with any certainty. The thought crossed my mind how easily I could probably get on board from underneath the bow without being detected. Once aboard I could identify and silently take the Al Khalifa man and drop into the water with him, letting him float free after I had drowned him. That would be it. Job over. Accidental death after falling over board, unnoticed during a party. No need for a complicated car accident. No collateral damage. The woman could get on with her life, without knowing how close she had been to dying. And I could be on my way out of the country before that SAS man would even be awake. I could leave Jacques to pay off the team I had engaged, they would not even know what they had been paid for.

As I slowly passed the length of the ship, mulling over the idea, it started to become a very attractive option. I just had to calculate the risks of being able to get onto the yacht and off it again, with my victim, without being seen.

I cut the engine further, reducing its sound to an almost unobtrusive putt, putt, putt, as I steered, starting to circle the yacht, looking both for entry points and a clear view of my primary target. Whilst the party seemed to be in full swing in the stern area I could discern no movement around the bow. I cut the engine completely, allowing my boat to drift under the yacht's bow and against the anchor chain. The slight scraping noise it made was followed almost instantly by a woman's voice floating out of the darkness.

"Hello? Is there someone down there?"

A man's voice came from the same dark area where the woman's voice had emanated, "There's no one there. Don't be silly."

"I know I heard something."

I made a quick decision and called out, "My engine cut out and I drifted into you. I'll restart it and be on my way."

The outline of a woman's head appeared above me as she leant over the rail to look down at me. Almost immediately a second outline appeared beside her,

"Hello there. Why don't you come on up and join the party?"

"Oh come on Cynthia, it's late the man's trying to get home."

The woman was apparently not so engrossed with her companion that she was prepared easily to give up her idea of getting me to join the party.

As I listened to this brief exchange and the further argument that ensued, I was rapidly considering my options. Responding affirmatively to Cynthia's invitation would be a simple and effective means of getting on to the yacht. I could mingle with the guests, find my way around the yacht and probably much more easily take Khalifa and deal with him. But once his body was found the police were bound to launch an investigation, even if it was regarded as an accident. That would inevitably lead to an enquiry about the guests who were present throughout the evening, amongst whom I would stand out like a beacon. A stranger, suddenly appearing in a boat, out of the night. Even the dimmest, laziest detective would want to follow up on that one.

"Perhaps another time. Your friend's right. It's late and I'm tired." With that I re-started the engine and sped away.

The tired, older Traynor, who had been making so many mistakes recently, regretted not having taken advantage of an opportunity to look around the yacht, observe the targets close up and perhaps deal with Al Khalifa that very night. Fortunately the cautious professional Traynor prevailed and, at least for the rest of that night, I remained a ghost disappearing into the dark of the night. I was going to stick with the plan and deal with any problems from Mr. White and whoever he had with him as best I could.

I got back to the hotel without difficulty. I had had my exercise for the day and had no desire to do any more swimming. I slowly brought the boat inshore until I felt it start to scrape against stone and sand. I threw out the anchor, making sure that it was firmly embedded before jumping into the water and wading the final few feet to shore. Not bothering to put on shoes, I left wet footprints all the way from the pool area to the lobby reception desk, where I returned the keys to the boat before going up to my room. I entered the room, threw my bag down by the bed and undressed. As I was walking into the bathroom my unconscious nudged to the surface something it had registered instants before. My case had been moved. When I stay anywhere I usually place various "tells" in and around the room to give me some indication as to whether someone has visited in my absence. It might be a thread apparently caught in a zip, or a hair stuck across a door. In this case I had arranged my suitcase at a slight angle to the case holder on which it was resting and had placed one of the internal straps so that it stuck very slightly out of the edge of the closed case. The case now rested squarely on the folding support where I had placed it. Before opening it I felt along the edge for the inside strap. It was no longer there. I opened the case. The strap that ought to have protruded sat coiled up beside my clothes. I switched on all the lights and looked carefully around the room. It could have been just the maid who had moved the case, but I wanted to make sure. I saw a dirty mark on the wall next to the air conditioning vent. That had definitely not been there before. I notice things like that. An intruder examining the vent would have had to stand on something. The chair at the desk was the obvious choice for climbing to a higher level. I pulled it out and looked at the cushion. There was the faintest trace of a rubber soled footmark. The Englishman had been wearing rubber soled desert boots. He must have come in after I had left and been through my room. I took the chair and used it to climb up to look at the air duct. The accumulated dirt and grease had been disturbed. He had not been very careful this Englishman. Either he was not very competent at carrying out clandestine searches or he had not cared or, better still, thought I would not notice anything. I hoped it was the latter which would mean that he was seriously underestimating me. I chuckled to myself. He must have thought that I had hidden the money and perhaps the weapons behind the air duct and then got himself dirty taking off and replacing the grill before messing up the wall.

By the time I was ready to fall into bed it was nearly 2.45am. I set the alarm clock for 8.00 am, just in case I did not wake on my own and, putting one of my pistols under the pillow and one just under the bed, I lay back and fell into a dreamless sleep.

CHAPTER THIRTY

*"Victorious warriors win first and then go
to war, while defeated warriors go to war
first and then seek to win" (Sun Tzu)*

I woke just before the alarm rang. I had had five hours of good sleep and felt refreshed. The idea that I was shortly going to be starting the action stimulated me. I washed, dressed and threw the guns into the bag with the money I had retained. On my usual principle that it is always best to eat when you can, I decided to have breakfast at the hotel restaurant downstairs. I carried with me the bag containing the money and guns.

After finishing breakfast, I went down to the garage to take another look over the Audi the Brits had loaned to me in Rome. It was a bit dusty, but it started immediately. I had decided to use that car to pick up my team and transport them to Beaulieu. No doubt the Brits would get all excited when their car re-appeared on their radar, moving again. They would have no idea that it was part of my plan to lead them to my team in order to distract them from coming after me and, that I wanted to give them sufficient time to set themselves up somewhere near the Beaulieu house, so that they would be well away from where I was locating myself. I hoped that I was not being a little too clever by making their task that much easier. I locked the car up and went back up to my room before switching on the mobile phone I was using to communicate with Jacques.

He answered my call immediately.

"John"

"Yeh. I'm getting ready to pick up the package and deliver it. It'll become live when I leave." I was telling Jacques that I was using the bugged car and did not need to add that he therefore had to stay well away from me until I again came back to the hotel and switched cars.

"Mother's going to put the kids in bed and do a little shopping before going home." I was not being especially abstruse and anyone connected with the operation would probably have been able to figure out what I was talking about within a few minutes, but I was talking for the benefit of the computers that analyse the millions of conversations monitored by Echelon, the Anglo-US eavesdropping system that listens in to all European communications. Words like "mother" "kids" and "going home" would be most unlikely to raise a sufficient flag on the computers to send the conversation for further analysis.

A lot of civil rights activists have been vocal in their objections to the huge increase in governmental information gathering but, as an operator who knows the system, my attitude is let them gather as much information as they can. I think that the megalomaniac bureaucrats and politicians who implement these systems are just shooting themselves in the foot and overloading themselves with huge amounts of information that no one will ever get around properly to analyse. I am not saying that the incredible amount of surveillance that goes on in our society today has never produced results, but I do not believe that it produces any greater results than carefully targeted observation. In the United Kingdom today and, to a somewhat lesser extent, in some of the American cities, one cannot walk for two minutes without being recorded on camera multiple times. This mass surveillance was sold to a gullible and unsuspecting public as a crime prevention tool. But, in the years since the cameras have proliferated all over London, far from decreasing, crime has increased, as has the wearing of hoods by street thugs to prevent their being identified on film. For the criminal a simple, low tech answer to a high tech problem. I also ask myself how it is, if high tech surveillance is so effective that, notwithstanding George W Bush's administration's introduction of so many new surveillance measures, the murder clear up rate in the US in the past twenty years has plunged from something like 90% to around 65%.

Having spoken to Jacques and let him know that I would be turning up later in the day, after having settled the team into their quarters, I opened the bag with the money and made up five bundles of 40,000 Euros each, which was the money I had agreed to pay the individual team members as an advance payment when they turned up in the South of France, with a further 50,000 each at the end of the job. I put the bundles totalling 200,000 Euros in a separate smaller case before taking the two bags containing money down to the garage. I put the duffle bag with 800,000 Euros in it into the trunk of the car and threw the other bag into the rear seat.

As I drove the car to the garage entrance I realised I had forgotten to obtain a ticket from reception that would enable me to leave and enter the garage at will. I delved in my jacket pocket and retrieved Kamal's credit card, which I then ran through the ticket machine that had been sitting patiently waiting for my payment, unlike the irritable Frenchman behind me who had started sounding his horn when I had failed to pay within ten seconds.

It had been an ill-considered idea to meet my team by the Casino on the final practice day before the Grand Prix. Sitting in traffic, listening to the angry buzzing of the high revving grand prix cars racing around the circuit behind the giant bill boards that hid them from sight, I soon gave up the idea of driving to the Casino. I turned away from the circuit at the first turning I could find and after a few minutes was fortunate to spot a parking space. I left the bag in the trunk untouched but took out the bag with the money for the team and locked the car before heading on foot towards the Casino.

I spotted them from more than 100 yards away. They stood out sharply from the crowd of beautifully dressed millionaires, celebrities and well-heeled motor racing fans who thronged the streets.

I must have been as conspicuous as I thought they were, because they started walking in my direction within seconds of my having spotted them. I turned and let them follow me, checking from time to time that they were actually following. When I reached the car I opened it and sat in the driver's seat. Within about a minute the other doors opened and my team squeezed themselves into the car. The Russian, who was at least a head taller than anyone else, had gone for the relative comfort of the front passenger seat. Somehow the four others managed to squeeze themselves into the rear passenger cabin. The furtive looking Syrian was almost completely obliterated by the men on either side of him. I handed the case I had been carrying to the Russian and said,

"The down payment I promised is in there. You can dole it out now if you like, or you can wait until we get to our safe house."

The Russian grunted and opened the case to look inside before taking one of the bundles in his massive hands and counting it as I drove off in the direction of Beaulieu. The others seemed more concerned with surviving the journey without being crushed to death and no one commented when the Russian, apparently satisfied with the count put the bundle back and closed the case.

The relief was almost audible when we finally arrived at the house in Beaulieu and the team vacated the confines of the Audi with an impressive display of alacrity and agility. I unlocked the house and let them in. I instructed them to make themselves at home and sort out their own sleeping arrangements and said I wanted to meet on the terrace in ten minutes to discuss the operation. They nodded their response and proceeded carefully to prowl through the villa, like a stray cat trying to decide whether or not premises were suitable for it to take up residence.

Jacques must have been back to the house before me, presumably with Paolo, because not only was the second Renault parked outside but, as I entered the kitchen, I noticed that two loaves of fresh bread had been placed on one of the counter tops. I opened the fridge and a quick glance indicated that Jacques had been as efficient in this department as in every other, as it was now stocked full of eggs, cheese, cold cuts and steaks. It looked as though there was enough food there to keep the team surviving for at least five days.

As I closed the fridge door I felt, rather than heard, someone enter the kitchen behind me. I turned to see the Syrian standing in the doorway, leaning slightly against the open door. He was looking at me contemplatively, with half open eyes. He was no more endearing to me now than when I had first met him. In fact I had to control my outward reaction to him to bland indifference, so that he would not be able to sense how he was making my hackles rise. I could see that he was also making an effort to be pleasant,

"Thanks for the money. I have to say you've been absolutely straight with us so far, I wasn't quite expecting that."

I was surprised. What did he expect? I am a professional and I have always been reasonably straight with other professionals I work with unless they have given me some reason to be otherwise.

"What did you expect? We're professionals here. I treat you the same way as I expect you to treat me. You do your job. You get paid. You go home. That's the way I do business."

Well perhaps not quite. And with a high degree of probability, not in your case my friend, but then I do not think that you are being entirely open and frank with me.

Before either of us could say any more, the rest of the team, led by the Russian came into the kitchen. The Russian just pushed his way past the Syrian without a word, in the process making the Arab stumble forward towards me. These were not men who would usually let such conduct pass, but the Syrian's only reaction was to shoot an angry glance at the Russian that spoke more than words. The glance bounced harmlessly off the Russian's hide, as I am sure would have a more physical reaction and he continued, without pause, towards the fridge. He opened the door, looked in and gave a satisfied grunt as he extended an enormous hand inside the fridge. He pulled out a couple of packets of cold cuts before turning towards the bread. Within seconds he had converted the bread and meat into several appetizing looking sandwiches. Everyone, apart from the Syrian, fell on the food like a pack of ravenous dogs.

The Russian turned to me, explaining through a mouth full of food,

"We haven't eaten since meeting last night and heading up here. We didn't even stop for coffee."

I took the hint and filled a kettle with water, before putting it on to boil. I had to look through a couple of cupboards before finding a packet of coffee, which I measured into a large size cafétiere to await the boiling water.

The group meanwhile spread themselves around the kitchen table as they consumed their sandwiches and waited for the coffee. It was the Croat who broke the ice. He had been making some jokey comments about this being a self- service hotel, when he turned to me,

"So when are you going to tell us about the job? I wanna say, all joking aside, I'm impressed at the way you've set us up and dealt with us so far. We can all recognise you're a hands-on guy who's seen plenty of action and you understand how to look after your men. You've got us. You've paid us. We're in the comfort zone. So now what's the job?"

As he spoke the others sat up, instantly alert, paying careful attention to my response. I did not answer directly. Instead I placed my drawing pad on the table along with a map of Monte Carlo and the surrounding area.

"Ok. So here's the general outline of the job. Your parts are not going to be that complicated. And it shouldn't be dangerous. I could tell when we first met that you're guys who can handle yourselves, but none of that should be necessary. I'm the one who's going to be doing all the heavy lifting here. Your task is going to be to run interference and keep me free to do what I've got to do for, probably – maximum five minutes."

They were looking puzzled and shifting awkwardly in their seats. I knew what they were thinking and the surlier of the two Serbs voiced it in his thick accent.

"What sort of interference? Really no gunplay? Shooters like us? Big pay for little work, so what's the catch?"

"No catch. But it's a big job. While it's not too complicated, what I do I like to do right. And I like to work with reliable people. If anything goes wrong and I'm sure we all know how the easiest of jobs can become a clusterfuck, I want to know my team can handle it and they'll be there for me."

They were all nodding along with me, except for the Syrian who just glared at me balefully from the sidelines, as I continued,

"So, there's going to be a target car I'm going to hit. There's very limited protection and I don't expect any support vehicles. The real problem is the celebrity nature of the target, which means they're likely to be followed by a whole group of press reporters. Your first job is going to be to slow down the reporters and then keep them away altogether."

I paused to point to a section of the map in the general area of the tunnel I had already selected,

"I've marked off a section of road here. It's a tunnel, so we can control it with probably one or two guys at each end. Whoever's going to be running interference with the reporters will be following the target and will then join the group waiting at the end from which the target enters the kill zone. We're going to have to be a little flexible about everyone's actual disposition. It'll depend on the up to date intel I'll be getting just before the op, the final deployment of the target vehicle and the following reporters. We may possibly need to put someone on higher ground to shoot out a couple of tyres to slow down the press."

One of the Serbs interrupted. "I can do that. I'm a pretty good sniper."

The other Serb sniggered. It was the first time I had seen anything even approaching a smile on either of their faces, "Yeah an' you had plenty o' practice."

I nodded, "Fine. But the position's flexible for the time being. We can't firm up till later on."

The Serb who had volunteered to act as a sniper interrupted again, "What sort of rifle will I have and what's the likely range? Will I have a chance to pick my spot?"

"Don't know yet. Don't know and probably. Do the tools matter to you?"

"Yes. Depending on the distance, I have my preferences."

"Well don't worry. If it takes place it's not going to be any spectacular distances, probably no more than 300 metres."

The Serb nodded, apparently satisfied.

I took out a diagram I had drawn in my sketch pad, showing where I had preliminarily envisaged everyone's position. After I had explained my various markings, I looked up at the Russian, "How's your driving?"

He looked at me and made a bit of a face.

"So you're not going to be running interference on the press. Who's comfortable enough behind a wheel at high speed to be able to stop people following without killing himself?" I looked around the table. After a brief pause both the Syrian and the Croat said almost simultaneously, "I can do that."

There was no way I was going to trust the Syrian on his own. I wanted someone to be able to keep an eye on him at all times. I pointed towards the Croat, "OK that's you" before looking at the Syrian and telling him, "I seem to remember you speak good French. I'm going to need you to team up with him," I indicated the Russian, "He doesn't speak any French and the people on the road will need to have at least one French speaker." I did not know whether or not he had bought it and the Russian was looking even more sour than usual, but they knew better than to argue. I made a mental note to have a private word with the Russian.

"Which of you can ride a motor bike?" The Syrian clearly thought this was his way out of his incipient partnership with the Russian and was the first to say that he was a pretty good rider. He straightened up proudly and gave a humourless smile,

"I know all bikes. Many times I've used them in operations."

"Good. So you'll be rider and Ivan over there will be pillion passenger." His face froze. That was not what he had intended at all, but it worked perfectly for me.

The Serb who had not volunteered for sniper duty now piped in,

"I also can handle a bike. The one outside – the BMW – no. I know this machine."

I looked around at the others, who simply shrugged. The Syrian had resumed sulking in his corner, "OK. If we need to use another bike, you'll have that. But we probably won't need more than one bike."

The Croat then asked, "This stopping the press following your target – this will be done with car or bike?"

The Russian, who had just finished the last of the sandwiches and was wiping his mouth against the back of his hand answered before I could,

"Must be with car. Too dangerous with bike and not sure."

The Croat signified his agreement with a quick nod of his head, "I agree it has to be with a car. I can do this. I'm a very experienced driver."

The Russian looked over to me, a sly expression on his face, "Cars, bikes. Same colour like French police. We have uniform, lights, siren?"

Apart from the Syrian, whose presence I was already regretting, I had picked these people for their experience, so I was not surprised that the Russian and, probably the others, had drawn a particular conclusion from the vehicles sitting outside. They had probably all carried out very similar operations in the past using the same basic format.

"We have the uniforms, the strobes, but not the sirens."

As we had been talking a further idea had come to me. The SAS officer was clearly working with the GIGN. If there were a gaggle of reporters hanging around the Film Festival, waiting for the targets to come out, why should the SAS guy not get the French police to hold up all the press for a while and prevent them following the couple as they were leaving? Something like that would neither be out of place nor, probably, very unexpected. It was not likely to be something, even in the aftermath of the accident, that was going to raise any questions. I made a mental note to speak to the Englishman about it when I met him later on.

I thought my crew had been sufficiently briefed. They knew the general outline of what they had to do. I could leave them to take it easy for the rest of the day and discuss amongst themselves any questions they might have.

"You've got the outline. We're going to have two or three days at least before we have to go into action. I don't want anyone leaving this place and drawing any attention to themselves. You can take it easy here, it's comfortable, it's got a pool. There's plenty of food and there's beer in that cupboard over there." I indicated a walk in larder, where I had noticed that Jacques had, thoughtfully, placed four large crates of beer. One of the Serbs, who was obviously not a particularly trusting type, got up, opened the larder door, looked in and then closed the door again, nodding his head as he did so.

"I've got things to do. So I'll leave you to make yourselves at home. Just take it easy for a couple of days. I'll be back some time on Monday and I'll probably have some more intel for you by then. I want to stress though, I don't want anyone going out and drawing attention to themselves. You're big boys. You've done this sort of thing before and there are worse places to be holed up. Is that clearly understood?"

I looked around the group as they nodded their agreement, even the Syrian, albeit he was a little slower than the others at giving me the confirmation I had asked. Satisfied I turned to the Russian and inclined my head towards the front garden, "Ivan, I need to have a word with you."

He stood up, growling at me, "The name not Ivan. Is Vladimir" and shambled out after me.

I walked well away from the house, out into the open where no one could hear us or approach without my seeing them. The Syrian had followed us out, but he stood in the doorway, looking at us without attempting to come any nearer. When he saw me looking towards him he disappeared back inside the house. I turned to Vladimir, speaking quietly,

"Look, I'm not very happy about that Syrian, which is why I teamed him with you. He gives me a bad feeling and I don't want him fucking up this operation."

The Russian, who was a good three or four inches taller than me and was leaning towards me in order to hear me, nodded slightly,

"Me too. And the others. We don't like this guy. Don't trust him. Draco... ", he was referring to one of the Serbs, "say he kill plenty like him in Bosnia. They come from all over to fight Serbs. I also see guys like him in Chechnya. Many times. Only one thing to do with these guys." He made a chopping motion with his hand, "You want me to do this?"

"Yeah I do. But not just yet. We still need him. You can do it when we're sure we don't need him anymore. But I don't want any mess and I don't want him left around where we've been operating. Also I want some-one to keep an eye on him at all times. Will you tell the others?"

"I tell them." He paused before asking," I kill him. I can take his money?"

"Of course. And the balance I'm going to pay. You can either have it or share with the others. It's up to you."

He nodded, satisfied, before turning and walking slowly back into the house. I watched his retreating fig-ure for a few moments before getting into the Audi and driving back towards Monte Carlo. As I drove I thought about the Russian and then about the other three from the Balkans. They were on the ball and did not seem bad types as far as these things go. A bit dour perhaps, apart from the Croat with his fake American accent, but they knew what they were doing and seemed thor-oughly professional. I wondered if I should perhaps give them a heads up about the Brits. Somehow it did not sit very well with me not to say anything. But then I reasoned that any good professional ought always to expect the unexpected. The Russian knew what I had in mind for the Syrian; it would not be much of a leap of imagination for him to think that perhaps I would be telling a similar story to each of them and that my real intention was just to have to deal with the last man standing. Fuck it. It seemed to me that as I got older I was getting softer and more stupid. Why should I warn these guys? They were experienced killers. Did they go around warning their victims? I did not think so. I was just being a fucking dick even thinking about this. My only concern should have been how Jacques and I were going to make it out alive, rather than worrying about a group of killers who I had only just met, knew nothing about and whose only concern would be to take the share of any dead fellow team member.

CHAPTER THIRTY ONE

Nice

"Regard your soldiers as your children, and they will follow you into the deepest valleys; look on them as your own beloved sons, and they will stand by you even unto death." (Sun Tzu)

In Cartwright's opinion Hubert and his GIGN colleagues had taken rather too seriously their obligations as hosts to the visiting SAS group. As Commander of the Regiment he had tried to maintain sufficient dignity and sobriety as were commensurate with his rank and status. It had been an uphill and ultimately losing battle, faced with the Frenchs' steadfast determination to prove that they led the world as hosts and bons viveurs. The men under Cartwright's command had shown none of his qualms. They were battle hardened veterans who knew only too well to accept whatever bounty they could whenever it was offered, because who knew what the following day would bring or even if there would be a following day. It had been a noisy, shambolic group that had returned to the Hotel in the early hours of the morning and had left a small smattering of urine stains in the Hotel hallway. Cartwright did not know how his men had fared but, apparently, he had been sufficiently compos mentis to undress before falling into bed, although he had no memory of doing so.

He looked around the room, bleary eyed, desperately trying to focus and saw, to his surprise, that his clothes of the previous night had been neatly folded on a chair and his jacket hung from the trouser press/hanger that sat in a corner of the room next to the clothes cupboard. His head hurt and he felt slightly sick as he gave in to weakness and fell back onto his pillow. He decided that he was getting too old to abuse himself in this way. It was not as if he particularly liked drinking, but the wine had been endless, then there was the cognac, that other thing, what was it, vieille prune and ultimately that other drink - absinthe. Just thinking about it made Cartwright feel like throwing up. He turned on his side deciding he would go back to sleep for a little while, but the insistent buzzing by his head prevented him from dropping off. He lifted his head and looked around again before finally realising that the buzzing was the telephone. Struggling to sit up he leaned across the bed and fumbled for the phone.

"Colonel Cartwright?" French accented English registered on the Colonel's half conscious brain,

"Yes" it came out as a gruff, throaty, half cough followed by a full blooded choking cough.

"Colonel Cartwright. Are you alright?" the voice sounded alarmed.

Cartwright fought to control the coughing spasm before answering and, when he did speak, his voice sounded almost normal,

"Yes. I'm sorry. I seem to have developed a bit of bad throat. Who is this by the way?"

"You don't know me sir. My name is Phillipe Esclimont. I work for Jean-Michel Dumont." There was a pause whilst Cartwright tried to forget the pounding in his head and concentrate on identifying who the hell Jean-Michel Dumont was. The voice, apparently realising he needed prompting, dropped to a whisper and added

"The Director General of DGSE. I am your liaison here. We need to meet face to face so I can update you."

"Christ!" he had been so tied up with GIGN and back channels that he had forgotten all about liaising with DGSE. Featherstonehaugh had told him that the Director of DGSE was providing a direct link for up to the moment intel from within the ranks of the Al Khalifa private security detail.

"Yes. Of course. Where and when can we meet?"

"Well, I am now downstairs parked outside your hotel... ".

Cartwright sat bolt upright. He looked around the room. It was in reasonably good order considering the state he had been in last night. He sniffed the air. God, the room stank like a brewery. He could not bring anyone up there until the room had been cleaned.

"If you give me a couple of minutes, I just have to finish off some work I'm doing and then I'll be down to see you."

"Good. Walk out of the main entrance and turn left into the street at the side of the hotel. I am parked about 50 metres up the street. It's a black Citroen."

The telephone went dead as the Englishman thought to himself cloak and dagger and black Citroens. He leapt out of bed, now fully awake and went into the bathroom, where he took a quick shower. His head still throbbed, but by the time he was dressed he was feeling a little better. He was downstairs, out of the hotel and looking for the Citroen inside ten minutes. It seemed to be the only black car in the street and was noticeable from yards away. Was this the inconspicuous spy? The driver's side window was open and the man inside glanced at him, before saying,

"Colonel Cartwright. Get in."

Esclimont was a well groomed, expensively dressed, thirty something year old. Cartwright noticed that his hands, which were resting casually on the steering wheel, had long tapering fingers ending in beautifully manicured nails. The Frenchman had a languid manner and way of speaking that made the Colonel think that he was probably some sort of French aristocrat.

Esclimont turned to look at the Colonel, scrutinising him at length before continuing his turn, to enable him to lean towards the back seat and retrieve a large manilla envelope. He handed the envelope to Cartwright,

"This contains the couple's programme for the next five days. You will see that they are attending the Grand Prix in Monaco tomorrow, followed by a Gala party at the Palace hosted by Prince Albert and his wife. The following day they are entertaining Prince Albert on the yacht Cleopatra for lunch; expected to last until early evening, when they will be attending another party given by Crown Prince Abdullah of Saudi Arabia on his yacht. He has the largest yacht moored in Cannes; you can't miss it when you look out at the harbour. They are not scheduled to attend events at the Film Festival until Wednesday. You will see the programme. The preliminary events pencilled in for them have been highlighted. As a rule my informant finds it convenient to meet me between 5pm and 6pm each day in the bar of the Metropole Hotel. Those hours, until around 8pm, are normally a quiet time for him. So I would usually be in a position to give you updated information by 21.00 each day. Do you have a cell phone I could call you on?"

Esclimont's slightly effete, foppish looks, were belied by his crisp, no nonsense approach to the task in hand.

Cartwright took out a pen and wrote his cell phone number on a piece of paper and handed it to the Frenchman without saying anything. He was starting to feel sick again and could hardly wait to return to his room, or at least to try and eat something that would soak up the alcohol that was, no doubt, still swishing around his system. The Frenchman took the proffered paper and folded it precisely into four, before slipping it into an inside pocket of his jacket. He then started the engine, turning slightly towards Cartwright as he did so, as if surprised that the Englishman was still sitting beside him. The Colonel took the hint and got out of the car, simultaneously saying,

"I'll wait to hear from you."

He barely had time to close the door before the Citroen was speeding off down the road, leaving him standing in its wake. Still standing in the road he opened the flap of the envelope and peered inside, pulling out the topmost of the small number of sheets of paper within. It was a neatly printed schedule of events, with their respective dates and times. He slipped the sheet back into the envelope, stepped back onto the pavement and wearily returned to the Hotel entrance.

"Morning boss." The Colonel looked up at the chorus of voices that greeted him as he entered the lobby. Four of his men were sitting there drinking coffee. They all looked clean, spruce and shaven. Cartwright realised, self- consciously, that, in his haste to meet Esclimont he had omitted to shave. He restrained an impulse to run the back of his hand against his cheek to test the stubble and returned the greeting. He sat down on a spare chair and dropped his voice to an undertone.

"If you haven't done so already, I want one of the GPS receivers set up in a car to see if we're picking up any signals from the transmitter." He was referring to the transmitter that had been installed in the embassy Audi Traynor was driving.

"Already done that, Boss. In fact while we were setting up we got a hit around 10, about twenty five minutes ago. It was moving towards the Casino in Monte Carlo, but then it stopped and was stationary when we last checked." The speaker paused, allowing his superior officer a short time to respond if he wanted to. When no response was forthcoming, he continued,

"Apart from stuff we're going to need up here that we can carry around with us, we've packed the other gear ready to stow in the vehicles we'll be using. Oh, Commandant Ducrest called. He said he wanted to know what, if any vehicles we need or whether there's anything else he can do. I think he was just checking though, to see whether we'd survived last night."

The others all laughed. It seemed to Cartwright that none of them were feeling any ill effects from the previous evening. He wondered if they were more resilient than him simply because they were ten or so years his junior or whether NCOs simply had better genes than officers for that sort of thing. He realised he was still being a little slow because, although they had been talking about the GPS tracking system in the car, he had momentarily forgotten about Traynor's cell phone.

"What about the cell phone I asked you to track?"

The slim, sandy haired soldier who answered to the nickname of 'Digger' chimed in, "I've been on that sir. We're patched into Cheltenham who are passing on real time intel. The last we got, the phone's switched on and a fix put it in the same location as the car. After the car stopped though, the phone started moving. Apparently always going in the direction of the Casino. Should I get an update now, boss?"

"No. Leave it until shortly before we're ready to leave." He stood up, "I've got to do one or two things. We'll meet down here again in say," he looked at his watch, "half an hour. Digger."

"Sir?"

"Is our GIGN liaison around?"

"I think he's having a spot of breakfast with the RSM, sir. Do you want me to get him?"

"No. Whilst I'm grateful for their help I don't want them muscling in too much. This is our op and it's nothing to do with the Frogs. I noticed there's a Hertz office in the hotel and I'd just like you quietly to go and rent us a couple of cars. Here... " he opened his wallet and took out a credit card that Featherstonehaugh had given him, in the imaginative name of 'Peter Jones'. He also took out one of the old style British Driving Licenses that had not yet been entirely supplanted by the new standard European Union model photographic license. The old style license, which was also in the name of Peter Jones, contained only licensee's name, address and birth date but no picture.

"Gotcha, Boss" responded Digger as he took the proffered licence and credit card from the officer. Then, addressing the rest of the seated group,

"Ross, you want to come with me. Two cars. Two drivers."

The two of them wandered off in the direction of the Hertz office whilst Cartwright made his way back to his room where he went into the bathroom. He looked at his face in the mirror as he prepared to shave. Thank God he did not look too untidy. He grunted to himself as he imagined the debonair Esclimont looking with disgust at his unshaven face and slightly dishevelled appearance, before covering the dark stubble that had formed overnight with a thick layer of shaving soap.

As he shaved, he started to plan out the day in his mind. He would get the GIGN driver to take him up to Monte Carlo for the meeting with Traynor to hand over the dazzler. He would also go through the couple's schedule with Traynor, so that they could try and make a preliminary decision as to the time and place of operation. He also wanted Traynor to take him over the killing ground, to enable Cartwright to satisfy himself as to its suitability. He would have to dump his driver for that. That should not be too difficult, he would send him to the bar for a drink and they could then slip away.

Before he met Traynor however, he wanted to get his men prepped to allow them to trace the location of Traynor's team and set up an observation post. He wiped his face on a towel and looked again in the mirror, from where a cleaner, tidier, more military looking individual stared back at him. Satisfied with his appearance, he straightened his tie, put on his jacket and went back to rejoin his men.

The whole group including RSM Collier were now sitting together with the GIGN liaison officer in their midst. Cartwright caught Collier's eye and signalled him to come over. The RSM sat on for a short time with the others before quietly detaching himself from the group and joining the Colonel.

"Is your room in a state for a headsheds meeting?" Strictly speaking the headshed nomenclature was an SAS colloquialism for people in authority, but Cartwright was using the expression loosely to include all members of his SP (special projects) team. He thought that the reaction of a slightly embarrassed look, flitting ever so briefly across the RSM's face, was an indication of the room being in disarray after the previous evening's frivolities. He was mistaken.

"Yes, sir. It is. In fact, sir, I've got a little extra space that makes it quite suitable for meetings."

"What do you mean, Ken?" The Colonel was puzzled.

"Well, sir, errm, it seems somehow errm, the room I was allocated, seems to be one of the larger ones. A sort of suite, if you will."

"You've got a suite!"

The RSM studied his shoes waiting for the inevitable storm to pass over him.

"Ken, did you say you've got a suite?"

"Err, yes sir. I don't know how it happened sir. It was obviously a mistake. And then before I could discuss it with you and arrange to change rooms with you sir, you dashed off for a meeting and by the time you got back we all went off with GIGN and things sort of got lost."

Cartwright was put out. He, like previous commanders of the Regiment encouraged self-reliance and initiative in his men and he knew that they were only too ready to take whatever advantage they could of any situation in which they found themselves, but this was bloody cheeky. He had left the arrangements for the trip to be organised by the RSM with a counterpart at GIGN that the RSM personally knew very well. He had no doubt that the better room had been arranged between the two of them. He decided, however, that there was little point now in making an issue of it. He would let it pass.

"Very well. Meeting in your... your suite in ten minutes. What's the room number of your suite?" He said gruffly, emphasising the word 'suite'.

Collier gave him the number and he stalked off leaving the RSM standing alone until the soldier called Andy walked up to him.

"Upset the CO have we Boss?"

Collier just scowled and snapped, "Meeting, my room ten minutes. Team members only." He was making it clear that this was not for the GIGN. He also then marched off in a fair, but unconscious imitation of the Colonel.

Andy sauntered back to the group smiling, "I think the CO's just found out the RSM's bagged himself the best room in the house."

As the others started laughing he added, "We've got a meeting in the Presidential Suite in ten minutes and when the CO actually sees the room I don't think it's going to be pretty."

The others laughed even more heartily, whilst the GIGN man looked puzzled, until Ross explained in French why they were laughing.

The RSM's suite comprised two bedrooms, one on either side of a large sitting/ dining room. The dining area was almost entirely taken up by a long rectangular table large enough to seat twelve. The sitting area was comfortably appointed with a four seater sofa and two armchairs arranged to face a large flat screen television fixed to the wall.

The six other members of the team had not delayed going up to the suite, they all wanted to be there to see their commanding officer's reaction when he walked into the room. They were to be disappointed as they noted no reaction apart from a slight scowl that crossed his face as he entered and looked around the room.

"We'll sit around the table. Who's got the GPS locator?"

"Me sir" followed by a slight thump as the device was placed on the table.

"Anything on it?"

"I'll have it for you in a minute sir"

No one said anything as MacCallister fiddled with the device and brought it on line.

"Looks like they're still parked in Monte Carlo. Hasn't moved from its last location."

"Ross, check with Cheltenham the present location of the cell phone number we've been tracking. I want to know movement and locations."

Cartwright paused, surveying the men around the table,

"Right. You've already been briefed on the op and the targets. First order of business today is to locate their safe house and then to set up an OP (observation post) so that we can start to monitor them and decide when we're going to take them out. I'm working with an inside contact, so I won't be able to participate in the surveillance. I suggest two teams of three. One team on static surveillance, one mobile. Ken Collier will be control. Change the formation any way you like as long as we have full cover of the targets. I'll leave you to sort out amongst yourselves communications etcetera. Weapons to be hot, but try and avoid any contact with the targets. For the time being this is strictly a surveillance and intel gathering operation. Any questions?"

"Do we know how many there are in the cell?"

Cartwright thought back to the diagrams he had seen in Traynor's sketch pad, trying visually to recall what had seemed to be positions of members of the assassination team, "Not sure at the moment. Present indications are that it is probably five or six. I hope to have more precise information later today."

He continued, "I'll take the GIGN chappie as my driver. That'll keep him out of your hair. Make sure you're not being followed. Hubert Ducrest is a little curious and proprietorial about what goes on his neck of the woods. I told him politely to mind his own business, but he might still decide to try and track us. Hence the hire cars. Leave the spare GIGN car here as a reserve."

They spent another hour and a half pouring over maps of Monte Carlo and the South of France, familiarising themselves with the road network, discussing the implementation of their operation and checking their equipment. They were still deep in discussion at lunchtime. Napoleon had once observed that an army marches on its stomach and this was as true today of the SAS as it had been of the armies of the Napoleonic era. It was Andy who first raised the subject,

"Perhaps we should break for lunch, Boss."

Cartwright looked at his watch, it was almost 1pm. He realised that he had not eaten since the previous evening.

"Good idea. Perhaps we should stay up here though and have them bring something up. Is there a room service menu anywhere?"

Collier stood up, "There's one on the sideboard." He walked over to fetch it and then read aloud what was available, translating from French for those members of the team who did not speak that language. After everyone had chosen what they wanted and the order been given, Ross noticed that the tracker was indicating movement from the car that was being monitored.

"Sir, looks like the car's on the move."

"Good. Keep an eye on it and when it stops locstat it (record and save the co-ordinates). Then give us the location on the map."

Ross nodded. There was nothing further to be done for the time being. Shortly thereafter the food came and the next half hour was spent eating and washing down the food with glasses of beer. By the time they had finished, the GPS monitor showed that the car had stopped in Beaulieu.

Cartwright stood up, "OK lads. It looks like it's off to Beaulieu for you. A couple of you load the equipment into the hire cars. Load as much as you can. I'd prefer not to leave anything much here. Ken, are the satcoms working?"

"All tested and running, sir." The British were using the American Milstar satellite communications system. It was the most advanced military communications system available. Operating from a satellite in Geosynchronous orbit twenty two thousand miles above the earth, it provided worldwide secure, jam proof communications. Collier turned and burrowed into a Bergen lying on the floor next to one of the armchairs and produced a handset which he handed to the Colonel,

"Yours sir."

Cartwright nodded his thanks as he briefly checked that the handset was operating and the battery fully charged.

"If there's nothing else sir, we'll be off."

"No. Off you go. Good hunting. If I don't hear from you in the meantime, I'll contact you sometime around 18.00."

The men all filed out, followed by the Colonel, who returned to his room to pick up the dazzler and schedules he had been given by the Frenchman Esclimont. He still did not trust Traynor and decided that, although he still had a couple of hours before they were due to meet, he would prefer to arrive at the rendezvous early, to give himself an opportunity to ensure he was not being set up. There was no reason why Traynor should be setting him up, but it was worth taking some extra time to reconnoitre, if only as an exercise to keep himself sharp.

Having collected everything he wanted and put them into a holdall, he opened the room safe and took out the compact 9mm USP Heckler & Koch pistol he had previously put there. He checked the magazine and engaged the safety before slipping it into a holster that fit neatly under his left arm. Extending his hand into the safe again he took out two spare clips of ammunition and put one in each of the pockets on either side of his jacket. As he locked the safe he took one last glance around the room to check that he had left everything looking normal. Then, picking up the holdall, the Colonel went downstairs to find his GIGN driver.

CHAPTER THIRTY TWO

Beaulieu

"Crushing the enemy's body and spirit means you degrade and humiliate him the instant before going in for the kill" Miyamoto Musashi - The Book of Five Rings

Ross sat in the front of the lead car, with the RSM driving. He held a computer on his lap into which he had plugged the GPS locator. The software automatically started up and within a couple of minutes he was staring at a detailed map showing the precise location of the car they had been tracing. Speaking over the Milstar link to the British Government Communication Headquarters in England he gave them the map coordinates, for them to cross check with the location of the cell phone that was also being tracked. Within minutes he had the information fed into the computer which showed the two locations corresponded.

He then fed the address into the GPS Navigation system with which the Renault car they had rented was fitted and within seconds the RSM was being given driving instructions by the soothing female voice emanating from the device.

When they could see that they were approaching their destination, the RSM slowed down and Ross informed the occupants of the other car what they were doing over the secure individual communications device they were using for team communication.

The two cars cruised slowly past the villa that Jacques had rented for Traynor's team, taking both still photographs and video footage as they passed. The villa occupied a plot of land in a quiet street planted with an abundance of trees. The houses, or villas, all seemed to have large gardens full of trees and bushes. Whilst it seemed there might be ample concealment to set up an observation post, at first sight the villa was scarcely visible from the road and seemed to be almost impossible to monitor externally with direct visual equipment.

Andy's voice came over the radio,

"This is going to be a fucking bitch unless we insert into the garden itself. What do you think Boss?" The question was addressed to the RSM who had been thinking exactly what Andy had voiced aloud.

"It's risky going into the garden. We could blow the whole surveillance. I'm not going to OK that until we've discussed it with the CO. For now let's go higher. It's quite hilly around here, we'll see if we can find somewhere that looks down onto the house."

He drove following the road and took a turning that presented itself, which seemed to lead above the road they were on. This secondary road wound round in a series of tight curves, constantly turning back on itself as it rose above the coastline. Eventually the RSM brought the car to a halt on a piece of wasteland that the map on the computer indicated was almost directly above the house they needed to watch. Ross looked around at the dry, dusty, scrubby wasteland, with its shrivelled but dense, bushy undergrowth,

"I don't suppose you could've found anywhere more uninviting for us to set up could you Boss?"

"Let's just see what we can from here and then take a general look around. I reckon that a lot of these houses are just holiday homes for people and they get rented out. We might get lucky and find an empty one we can break into."

Ross and MacCallister, who was also in the car with them, got out as the RSM switched off the engine. The rest of the squad had stopped behind them and had got out of their car and started to look around. The RSM joined them as they stood looking down at the houses below. He put the high powered binoculars he was holding up to his eyes and scanned the properties beneath them before passing the binoculars to the nearest man, who happened to be Andy.

"That's the house isn't it?" he pointed with his finger, "Actually, from up here you get a pretty good view of it, both front and back. I could see two or three guys sitting around the pool." As the RSM spoke, Andy lowered the binoculars and looked around at the houses neighbouring and above the land on which they were standing.

Indicating a modern structure that seemed to be nearly all glass, Andy suggested, "Up there. We ought to take a look see. If it's empty it'd be perfect for us and we wouldn't have to lie around on this desolate jebel."

There was a murmur of agreement from the others. Digger volunteered to take a look and was already moving across the road towards the house Andy had been talking about.

Whilst they were waiting, two or three of the men lit up cigarettes. The RSM continued carefully to scan the target house through his binoculars.

As the minutes passed and Digger failed to return, some of the men started to become anxious.

"It's been nearly fifteen minutes Boss. Perhaps someone else should go up and see what's happened to the Digger."

"Digger can take care of himself. Knowing him, he's probably got inside and having a quick kip while we hang around out here."

"We'll give him ten more minutes. Then Andy and Ross can go up take a look see." The RSM's decisive voice settled the issue

As it happened, that proved unnecessary, because Digger reappeared within minutes. He was sweating and breathing more heavily than normal.

"Jesus, Digger. You go on a short walk in the suburbs and come back huffing and puffing like a steam train. Next thing you'll be RTU'ed (returned to unit – the ultimate disgrace for those who had been badged) for not being fit enough.

"Fuck you MacCallister. It's fucking hot and that house is perched on top of a fucking mountain. You couldn't even get up there."

"OK, OK" the RSM interposed, "so is it empty or what?"

Digger smiled triumphantly, "It's empty. I disconnected the alarm and looked around. There's a pile of mail and it looks like no-one's been in there for months. Bad news is the water's turned off but as I came out I spotted an outside spigot that probably turns it on. Electric's on though. I managed to get the front gate open. You can't see it from here, but I suggest we get in there ricky ticky and close the gate again before making ourselves at home. There's a great view of the target house."

The RSM rubbed his chin thoughtfully and looked around at the uninviting scrubland where they were parked before making the decision, "Right. Let's get up there then. But someone's going to have to be on permanent watch to make sure we're not disturbed."

"Why don't we get GIGN to speak to the agents or the owners and say they're commandeering the house for a few days?"

"That'll be up to the CO. I'll speak to him about it. It's a better option than them having to bail us out if we get in any problems."

They piled back into the cars and drove into the house, hiding the cars out of sight before setting themselves up. As Digger had claimed, there was an extremely good view of the target house below them, even allowing them to look into part of the interior through some of the windows, once they had stabilised high powered binoculars onto a tripod.

Whilst his men were setting themselves up, Cartwright was sitting waiting for Traynor in the lobby of the Beach Hotel. He had arrived an hour early for the meeting and, after telling his driver to come and collect him two hours later, had spent half an hour walking around the hotel, checking all the exits, entrances and the underground garage. By the time Traynor arrived he felt confident that he knew his surroundings thoroughly and that Traynor was alone without anyone backing him up.

He had also had a call from Ken Collier to report that the men were set up in an empty house overlooking the target property. He did not say anything to discourage the RSM, but was slightly concerned that the men should have broken into a civilian's house. A whole variety of problems could arise from that. He wondered if perhaps he should get Hubert to clear it with the owners. For the time being however he shelved his concerns. First things first.

He neither saw nor heard Traynor arrive. The first he was aware of the assassin's presence was when he felt a tap on his shoulder. The surprise of it made him jump and he turned rapidly, trying to conceal his involuntary reaction. The oriental was regarding him without expression, but he was sure underneath that impassive exterior the man was silently laughing at him. He felt a chill, like a presentiment of death. Everything this man did, his conduct, his planning, the way he dumped the people who had been following him. Everything told Cartwright that this was a man to be feared. Yet again he could not help wondering if he would really be able to take him.

"So do you have it?" Cartwright had not noticed before but the American had a very pleasant voice and a certain calm that, if it were not menacing, would be quite soothing. The Colonel had heard of Ninja mind control and had always dismissed it as a fable, but it crossed his mind that this man was trained in all kinds of exotic martial arts, perhaps there was something after all in this mind control business. He forced himself to answer the question.

"Yes. Can we go up to your room? I'll show you how it works and how to keep the battery charged to full power."

"Lead on. I think you know the way." It could have been a perfectly innocent suggestion, but Cartwright had the feeling that Traynor was telling him he knew the Englishman had searched his room.

Once in the room, Cartwright removed the dazzler from his bag and unwrapped it. It was about the size of a small ultraportable computer, but bulkier. It came with a fitment that allowed it to be mounted on a motorbike or the window ledge of a motor car and swivelled through 360 degrees. Traynor examined it with interest, turning it around, weighing it in his hand and testing the mounting mechanism. Then, without warning and completely to Cartwright's surprise, he switched it quickly on and off, whilst directing it towards the soldier's face. For the instant that the device was on, Cartwright was blinded and disoriented. He staggered forward with arms flailing outwards and would have fallen but for the strong hands that gripped him vice like, whilst guiding and pushing him into a chair. The Colonel felt dizzy, nauseated and completely confused. He was blind and helpless. The effects lasted several minutes. He was not sure how long. It seemed endless. Gradually however, his vision started to recover and he started to feel better. It was a good thing the man had pushed him into a chair because, otherwise he would definitely have collapsed. Even ten minutes later Cartwright felt slightly sick and giddy, fearing that if he got out of the chair he might collapse.

Throughout the time that Cartwright was incapacitated Traynor said nothing. Presumably he was examining the device more carefully. Finally he broke the silence.

"I'm sorry about that Frank. I had to test it and better sooner than later. We have to be sure it works, don't we? In fact it's pretty impressive. I don't think it was on for more than a fraction of a second and look at the effect on you."

Cartwright felt an almost uncontrollable rage building up against this fucking, grinning American monkey. Who did he think he was, using him, a senior British officer, the commanding officer of the SAS, as a human guinea pig? He swallowed hard, struggling to master his feelings and not show how murderously he felt towards the American. Thinking how he would be able to repay this arrogant son of a bitch soon enough enabled him to calm himself sufficiently to say,

"I don't think that was really necessary. Do you?"

Traynor looked at him thoughtfully before answering. "Necessary. We probably have different concepts of necessity. What might be necessary for me may not be for you and the other way around."

Cartwright found the assassin's steady gaze disconcerting, but he could not help wondering what the American was talking about, did he now think he was a bloody philosopher or what?

"Do you have anything else for me?"

So that was it? No apology. Nothing. Just straight on to the next topic. Cartwright checked himself as he felt his anger building again. He swallowed hard and, very carefully, stood up. He felt it was important not to show any weakness in front of this hyena.

Walking stiffly towards his briefcase, which he had left on the floor when he had given Traynor the dazzler, he pulled out the envelope given to him by Esclimont and, without a word, handed it to the other man.

Traynor took it, also without saying anything, opened it and pulled out the papers inside. As he was looking at them he sat down. Cartwright watched as the assassin slowly read one sheet after another. Finally, the American looked up.

"Well, if this is accurate. I would say that Thursday looks best for carrying out the operation. They've got an early evening film performance followed by a reception. That would mean they'll probably be heading back to Monte Carlo," he looked down at the schedule of events, "around say... well let's say sometime between 23.00 and mid-night, one a.m." He paused, thinking.

"That'd be perfect. They'll all be tired. The bodyguard or guards'll be sleepy after a long day; the place I've decided upon is probably going to be empty. And

Thursday'll give me four clear days to get everyone prepped."

Thursday, Cartwright thought. I cannot wait. He would go over the killing ground with this jackanapes and then join his team to plan the removal of this bunch of killers and the one in front of him in particular.

"I'd like you to take me over your proposed location. As you might imagine, I've also had a bit of experience in these matters and might have some useful input for you."

Traynor shrugged, "It's your dime. We can go now if you like. I'll drive. I don't suppose you want your driver to come with us. We don't want to start him wondering, after everything's happened, why you and I were wandering around the exact site several days before the accident, do we?"

A note of caution again sounded in the colonel's head. The way he referred to the driver was not a guess. It meant Traynor must have seen him arrive and would therefore have been waiting and watching, even though Cartwright had been an hour early. He really had to be careful with this one. A couple of advanced micro transmitters had been stitched into the dazzler's carrying bag and Cartwright was heartened by the thought of their presence, which he thought the American most unlikely to discover.

Traynor had turned and was looking at him again and Cartwright had the totally illogical, but nonetheless uneasy feeling, that the American was reading his thoughts. He was therefore only partly startled by the man's next words.

"There's something I think we need to discuss. I've worked in the past with you Brits and I know you're not to be trusted."

Cartwright opened his mouth to protest but the American gestured to him to stay silent, "Just let me finish please, and then you can say anything you want... As I was saying, it's my experience you Brits are unreliable allies. You've always got your own agenda and you always think you know best."

That was more than enough for the Colonel, "I do not think that it is either profitable, constructive or, for that matter, helpful, for me to have to listen to you express your dislike of us."

"Please let me finish. I didn't say I disliked you. I said you can't be trusted. That's something completely different. Anyway, as you seem so impatient... "

Cartwright frowned and would again have interrupted if Traynor had not again forestalled him with another motion of his hand.

"I'll get straight to the point. You're not what I would regard as the usual type of liaison man. To me you look like army. I'd guess SAS. So I have to ask myself, now why would the Brits be sending an SAS officer, supposedly to deliver money and liaise with me. Not just an officer, but someone who must be fairly senior, because when we first met he was with someone who was obviously a pretty senior spook. So I ask myself, is this just liaison or is it something more? Then I think to myself... and I'm just thinking aloud here. So I think to myself. Normally the Brits are perfectly capable of doing this sort of operation themselves. So why have they brought someone like me in, at very, very great expense" Traynor emphasised the 'very' before pausing momentarily,

"Well, I answer myself, probably two reasons. One, this is much too sensitive for any Brits to be involved if anything should go wrong. And I'm sure we both know how easily and how often things do go wrong. Two, they've paid over all this money without very much argument, which, knowing how tight-fisted you Brits are, is most unusual. At first, I thought you'd pay me in funny money, so I checked it carefully and also had someone else check it. But it was ok. So then I thought, they've got to be thinking they've got some way of getting at least some of the money back. Well I think to myself, how would I do that. Of course there's only one way. I'd have to kill the guy I gave it to. In your position I'd probably want to kill him anyway – and his team, so there'd be no-one unreliable to brag about the operation afterwards."

Cartwright was now listening very carefully. He was wondering why Traynor was telling him all this. If this was the way he was thinking then the sensible thing would have been to keep it to himself and take counter measures. Having disclosed to the Colonel what he was thinking he was enabling the SAS man to plan on countering any counter measures the American was considering. He subconsciously made an infinitesimal hand movement towards the gun nestling in his shoulder holster before realising what he was doing and checking the movement. The only problem was that damned man in front of him seemed to notice everything. A compact Heckler & Koch pistol suddenly appeared in Traynor's hand. It was almost like magic, Cartwright had not even seen him move.

"Is this what you're feeling for?"

This time Cartwright could not control himself. His hand shot to his shoulder holster and felt... nothing. Just an empty holster! Before he could voice the question the other man gave him the answer.

"I felt it when I helped you into the chair a few minutes ago and thought I'd better perhaps remove it while we had a little chat."

Cartwright had not noticed a thing. The dazzler must have affected him much more strongly than he had realised. He felt even more frustrated with the man in front of him. This was a situation where Cartwright should have been in complete control, but he was not. All the initiative seemed to have been taken over by the other man. In fact, as Cartwright rapidly ran through in his mind the other meetings he had had with Traynor, he realised that either overtly or more subtly, it was the American who had, each time, taken control over the interaction. What the SAS man was really feeling and not quite able to formulate in word or thought was that the American had, from the moment they had first met, imperceptibly been establishing mental dominance over the Englishman, the whole time keeping the English soldier mentally off balance, both by his actions and his carefully chosen words. Cartwright had been trained to withstand torture and he had also been trained in techniques to establish physical and mental control over people, but somehow Traynor had taken the initiative and upended the whole process. In spite of himself Cartwright began to feel an aura of invincibility emanating from the man facing him, who even now was pressing his psychological advantage.

"I imagine you're wondering why I should be telling you all this and showing my hand. I'll tell you why. You might not want to hear this but, I'm sure, somewhere or other, at the back of your mind, you've realised I'm a lot better than you. If we have to go head to head, I'm going to kill you and I'll kill everyone working with you. I know you've got a team hanging around in the background, probably even now, taking a look at my people."

The Englishman was a little shocked at this blunt statement of the American's superiority. The problem was that he was beginning to believe it.

"I've been in this business a long time and, actually I've reached a stage in my life where I've realised that the best way is not always the easy way of just killing the opposition."

Killing the opposition was the easy way for this man, Cartwright thought in wonderment, as the American continued talking,

"I've found it's sometimes easier to do a deal with the opposition rather than everyone trying to kill each other. That's what I want to talk over with you. You must've realised by now I'm not the sort of guy to go around bragging about this job after it's over. I'd have to be out of my mind to do that. And I'm certainly not nuts." He chuckled as he added, "Crazy maybe. But not nuts." He laughed again, a broad smile breaking across his face,

"The truth is I want a quiet life. I realise it's time for me to get out of the game. I've had a good run. I want to be able to enjoy the money I've got and not be looking over my shoulder all the time. Anyway, however it all plays out between you and me, I'm going to disappear. You can be dead when I disappear or alive and, maybe," a sly expression crossed Traynor's face as he ended his sentence,

"maybe, just maybe, you can not only live through this, but you can also be a little better off." He paused allowing the thought to ferment for a short time in the Englishman's head.

"In the end it's got to be your choice. You can make a bad choice or you can be clever enough to make a good choice."

Cartwright felt a little numb. He wondered what it was precisely that this man was offering. A number of conflicting thoughts and emotions sought to crowd into his mind at the same time and he drew a deep breath as he tried to control himself.

"What exactly are you proposing?" he asked cautiously.

Traynor paused and looked at him appraisingly before replying.

CHAPTER THIRTY
THREE

"Pacifying the tiger and leading it from the mountain means enticing your enemy by scattering bait he is liable to take and thus showing him the opening where you wish him to strike." (Ancient Chinese military strategy)

There have been many great and famous swordsmen in Japan. Among the greatest was Miyamoto Musashi who is known to have had more than sixty duels in his life and never once lost. Musashi and other famous swordsmen, whatever their different styles or philosophies, were all agreed upon one thing. That in order to beat an opponent it was important to distort and warp his mind, by deception and any other means a swordsman could think of. What this meant was taking and holding the psychological advantage at all times.

I first learned this lesson from my grandfather. Then experience taught me how important a lesson it was. Psychology therefore became simply another weapon in my arsenal.

My assessment of the English officer was that while he displayed the typical arrogance I associated with the officer class in general, he also seemed to have some feelings of inferiority. It was obvious that he had the confidence in his physical abilities and skills that all special operations personnel share, but it was his weakness I wanted to exploit. I had thought long and hard about whether or not I should tell this English officer that I knew what his real function was and to attempt, basically, to bribe him into leaving me alone.

There had been a time in my life when I would simply have bulldozed over the Englishman and any support team he had with him and kill them all as quickly and efficiently as I could. But I had changed. I had come to realise that one can sometimes overcome the opposition without killing them. Such a course particularly appealed to me on this job because, quite frankly, I did not want the problem of disposing of a number of bodies without any possibility of their ever being found. It was essential for the "accident", never to be re categorised as anything else and several bodies of British soldiers lying around was only going to be grist to the mill of inevitable conspiracy theories that were bound to start up. I had gone over very carefully in my mind my appraisal of the English officer before deciding that he might be very susceptible to being suborned. If I had been dealing with the other man who had been with him in Rome, I would not have given the idea a moment's consideration. That man had been an archetypical, arrogant upper class Englishman, who would not have considered for a nanosecond the proposal that I believed might very well appeal to the army officer.

Having decided that I was going to proposition the Englishman, I made up my mind first to establish psychological domination over him. Once I had him mentally off balance I would put my proposition to him. Then and, only if he did not go along with me, was I going to have to kill him and his whole team.

I had arranged to meet him at the hotel at 16.00. I wanted to get there in good time so that I could see him arrive. I was in fact able to get away from my Russo-Balkan-Syrian group by just before 14.00 and was back at the hotel by 14.30. The Englishman had not yet arrived so I installed myself in a quiet, virtually inaccessible corner from which I could watch people arriving at the hotel entrance. He arrived just before 15.00. A good hour early. He turned up in a Citroen driven by a hatchet faced individual with close cropped hair, whose eyes never ceased looking around as he dropped his charge. I watched as the Englishman entered the hotel and the car and driver disappeared down the road away from the hotel.

Like the good and efficient operator that I was sure he was, the Englishman, thinking he had arrived a long time before me, reconnoitred the whole hotel before settling himself in a chair from which he, too, had a good view of the whole lobby and entrance. I had discreetly followed him throughout his walk through the hotel. He was not that good, because he had no idea at all that I was following him which, as we were in a fairly confined area, he ought, in my opinion, to have realised.

I let him sit for about ten minutes, content just to watch him. You can learn a lot about people watching them when they do not know they are being observed. Eventually I decided it was time to make contact. I was able to get up right behind him without his noticing my approach, or without drawing any attention to myself from other people in the lobby. I stood behind him for a minute, practising negative presence. This was an ancient ninja technique my grandfather had taught me, the purpose of which was to place yourself close up to a target without them sensing you are there. The technique was the converse of another technique for sensing an attacker's presence when you could not see them.

Eventually, I touched him gently on the shoulder. He jumped as if he had received an electric shock. I suggested we adjourn to my room and continued pressing the psychological advantage I had gained through my initial stealthy approach, by hinting to him that I knew he had been through my room. It was satisfying to see my barb strike home. I felt a little sorry for the man. He seemed so transparent and easy to read. I wondered how he had apparently survived so long in the secret world of special operations.

The next shock that was in store for him was when he took the dazzler out of his bag to show it to me. I looked at it carefully. I had never before seen a miniaturised version of this device. Operating it was obvious and easy, but I wanted to see how it worked and how effective it was. I also wanted to press home to my English friend the point that I was the one in control.

After I had examined the dazzler for a few minutes, I casually turned it towards the Englishman and flicked the on switch, for probably about half a second or even less, before flicking it off again. I have to admit to being quite impressed with the result. It was a most effective device. The Englishman staggered, put his hands up to his eyes and would have collapsed if I had not half lifted, half guided him into a chair. He sat there in a confused, semi-comatose state for six or seven minutes and for another four or five minutes was blinking rapidly, evidently trying to regain control of his sight and faculties.

As I guided him towards the chair I felt the weapon under his coat and, once he was in the chair removed it without difficulty or protest. In fact I was fairly certain he did not know what I was doing. More out of habit than design, I tucked the gun into the waistband of my trousers in the small of my back. I then sat down opposite the Englishman to await his recovery. Whilst sitting there with nothing much to do, I reached for my drawing pad, which was sitting on the side table where I had left it and started a pencil sketch of the English officer. I kept it flattering and portrayed him sitting with his eyes open. It turned out very well and was finished by the time he had pretty well recovered. At first he did not say anything, although I noticed he found it difficult to look at me. He stood up, rather unsteadily and walked towards his bag, from which he extracted a brown envelope he then handed to me. I opened it and examined the contents, which comprised a few sheets of paper with a schedule of engagements for the next few days and notes about the people who were going to be present at different events.

As I examined the sheets of paper and, in particular, the schedule of events, the day for the operation virtually chose itself. On the Thursday, the woman had a lunch engagement at the Royal Palace in Monte Carlo followed by a visit to sick children in a Monaco hospital accompanied by the wife of Prince Albert. She was then due to travel to Cannes with Al Khalifa, to attend an early evening premier of one of the show-cased films at the Cannes film festival. The screening was to be followed by a charity dinner, hosted by the Elizabeth Taylor Foundation to raise money for AIDS research. This event was scheduled to end around 11.30pm or mid-night. The couple were then returning to Al Khalifa's yacht in Monte Carlo to spend the night, with a morning and afternoon of leisure scheduled for the Friday. She was due to return to Cannes on Friday afternoon and would then be spending four days at the Carlton Hotel in Cannes, apparently by herself.

I looked up at Frank who was regarding me with an expression of what I can only describe as unadulterated loathing. I thought for a minute that perhaps I was not after all going to be able to corrupt this army officer and that the apparent hate I had been able to provoke in him might overcome the obvious advantages to him of the proposition I was proposing to make. Wondering whether I had perhaps gone a little too far in using the dazzler on him, I decided that I had better try to dispel some of the antagonistic feelings I had engendered, before putting some additional grease to the wheels of corruption I was about to set in motion.

I ignored his overt hostility and told him, holding up the schedule, that Thursday looked like the best day for carrying out the operation. That day also had the advantage of allowing me two or three days to prep my team and to carry out a couple of practise runs, which I also articulated. The Englishman immediately became more soldier like and less the sulky schoolboy. He agreed that the Thursday had also seemed to him suitable and asked me if we could take a run over to the area where I was considering carrying out the operation so that he could make his own assessment of its suitability. I had no objection and told him so, but first I wanted to initiate our little talk so that he would have something to think about whilst we were driving.

I put to him, quite bluntly, what I considered was the real reason for his presence, rather than as a supposed liaison officer. Without beating about the bush, I said that I had no doubt he was with a backup team whose purpose was to eradicate my group and myself. Once again his face and gestures gave him away. He looked almost shocked that I should be quietly sitting opposite him telling him this and made the slightest, involuntary movement towards his left armpit where he had holstered the gun that I had removed.

I produced the gun, asking him at the same time whether that was what he was feeling for. Now he looked panicked and made no effort to conceal a hand movement towards his holster. I handed the gun back to him. I had achieved dominance, now I wanted to establish a little trust and goodwill.

I told him that he had no chance of besting me and that, if I wanted to do so, I could kill him and his whole team, but that I preferred to come to an arrangement with him that would enable me just to slip quietly into the shadows.

The poor guy. I suppose that he was not used to dealing with complicated situations. He was used to being in control and probably in all his previous experiences everything had always been a simple black and white for him. He had, no doubt, anticipated that this job was going to be more of the same. But here I was, some awkward motherfucker who, up to about ten seconds ago, he had been thinking of killing, making things difficult and intricate for him. He looked very confused and when he finally spoke it was slowly and cautiously.

"What exactly are you proposing?"

"Before I put my proposal to you I think I need to tell you one more thing." I paused. Once, way back in my distant, barely remembered Californian school days, I had had a drama teacher whose words had somehow stuck with me through the years, that, in drama, one can never overestimate the effect of a well-timed pause. I had found that applied in life just as much and so I introduced what I thought to myself to be a well-timed pause.

"If you have any thoughts at all about recovering the money I've received from you Brits, you can forget it. Even if you and your team somehow, miraculously, managed to kill me and my men, you'd never get the money. It's gone. Well hidden from you and your masters and nowhere you'd even know where it is. That's why what I'm about to suggest is such a good deal."

He looked surprised. I had been right. The man had no idea of the way the international financial system worked. I continued,

"I'm not interested in what happens to my men. So you can have them. If I can walk away quietly from all this, with no hassles from you and no bodies around for me to clear up, I'll give you 500,000 Euros."

I repeated the figure "Half a million Euros. That's somewhere around 400,000 British pounds. Pretty near half a million. The sort of money not many people ever get the opportunity to amass."

There it was the look of greed. I do not care who it is. Everybody is greedy. Rich, super rich, poor. They are all the same. Everyone is greedy for something. For most it is money. For some it is sex and for a very few others something else. Money though, I have found, usually works on 99.9% of people. In any event I could see the Englishman was interested. I had originally thought of offering him 250,000 Euros but had decided to increase the amount after seeing the way he had looked at me following my having tried out the dazzler on him. Being a bit too clever with the dazzler was costing me and somehow I thought that perhaps I ought to try and clinch the deal by sweetening the pot just a little. After another short pause I continued.

"I'll tell you what. You're English, you operate in pounds; I'll make it up to half a million pounds. What do you think?"

He did not reply and I started to wonder whether I had explained myself sufficiently. Anyway I decided that there are times when it is better to repeat oneself, rather than to risk leaving a situation unclear.

"I want this to be crystal clear, so I'll run over my proposal again. What I'm proposing is this. After the operation, I allow you and your gang to take out my men. That gives you a body count to report back to your bosses. As for me, one of my men is an arab, Syrian in fact. I have some French arab identity documents with my picture on them. When the time comes for you to clean up, I'll give you all those documents, so that you can, so to speak, recover them from the body of the Syrian. I'm sure I don't need to tell you how to make him instantly unrecogniseable to your men. Then, as far as your bosses are concerned, you'll be able to report you've successfully taken all of us out. I'll disappear and no-one will ever hear from me again. You'll be made a general and, with half a million pounds cash, tax free, you'll have a nice little nest egg to help ease yourself into retirement when your time comes to retire."

I looked at him expectantly. I did not think I could have made myself any clearer. He looked back at me, this time straight into my eyes. Then he rubbed his chin and looked slightly away from me to his right. After a few moments of silence he nodded his head slowly.

"Alright. You've been open and frank with me; I'll do you the courtesy of reciprocating. Basically we're both nothing more than simple soldiers doing our job. Just supposing, talking hypothetically, I were to be interested in your proposition. How do you say everything would work, so that I could be one hundred per cent sure I could trust you to live up to your end of the bargain, pay me and that there wouldn't be any comebacks for me. You say the money's gone, irrecoverable for us. If I were interested, how would you pay me then? How could I be comfortable that, after I've let you disappear, I'm not just going to be left holding nothing but my dick?"

"Well, talking hypothetically, just supposing you were interested, how would you want to be paid?"

He looked a little perplexed, "I don't know", he replied thoughtfully,

"In cash I suppose." He paused again, "And before the operation, so you don't just disappear without paying me."

I sat back in my chair without speaking. It had taken me years to learn the ins and outs of international banking and, even then, the banks were constantly changing the rules because they had thought up some little dodge to enable them to chisel a little more money out of their customers. Did I really want to educate this soldier boy, who was still barely managing to mask his greed? Eventually I supposed I was just going to have to bite the bullet.

"Look, just think about it for a minute. Would you really have to worry about me gypping you? Isn't the other way around more likely? Isn't it more for me to worry whether you'll keep your end of the bargain? If I try to fuck you over there's nothing to stop you coming after me. And once the job's over I won't have any of my team to help me out. So, if we come to a deal, it's to my advantage to pay you. I'd have absolutely no reason to do anything but play it straight. Surely you realise that if I were thinking that way there wouldn't be any point in our having this conversation and my tipping my whole hand to you. On the other hand... " I paused again to give him time to think,

"If I pay you first there's at least a 50 per cent chance you're going to decide to try and take me out anyway. What a result that would be for you! You'll've done your job, have a sack full of cash and no-one around to know anything about it. Great for you; not so good for me."

As he looked at me a smile crossed his face. It was the first time I had seen him smile. "You really like to try and think of everything don't you?"

"I try, but one thing I've learned in this game, you can never figure out all the angles. Experience has taught me that it doesn't matter how much you plan or think, there's always a curved ball going to come at you from somewhere out of left field."

He grunted noncommittally. I did not know whether or not he was agreeing with me. "Well, let's say I do go for your little scheme. You seem to have some experience in these matters. Tell me clearly how you are saying it would all work?"

That was it, time for the Traynor crash course on the clandestine handling of illegal funds. I thought for a moment before replying, "Monte Carlo's a tax haven. There are plenty of banks here from different countries. I think you should go to one of them, a branch of maybe a Luxembourg, Swiss or perhaps Austrian Bank. Somewhere where there's still some element of secrecy left, however little and your government can't automatically access accounts. You go to the bank, ask to speak to a director and then tell them you want to open an account, either to operate from here or from whatever country you choose. I'll give you a 100,000 Euros, no, say pounds, on account, to pay into them for opening the account. You then give me the bank details and account number. I'll then send you another 150 to make up a quarter of a million, which you should get within a day or two. I'll send the rest of the money a couple of weeks after the job, when I'm out of the danger zone and sure you're keeping to our deal."

He sat there silently, for a few minutes considering what I had said. He really had nothing to lose. Whatever he decided he was going to be at least 100,000 British pounds better off. He obviously realised this and eventually nodded again.

"OK, I'd say we're going to have a deal. You show me you're genuine and help me out with the details and it'll be a go. I've got no experience with the banking side, so I'm going to need your help with that." He looked at his watch,

"I don't suppose we're going to be able to do any of that over the weekend, so can we arrange that for Monday? Would you be ok with that?"

I shrugged and nodded my acceptance. I had decided I did not mind helping him. It was in my interest to make things as easy as I could for him. He immediately offered me his hand to shake, as a gesture of agreement. I took it. His handshake was firm, with none of that extra strong competitive squeeze that some people like to try. Our bargain was sealed and I had every hope that he was going to keep to the agreement.

"Before we go and check over the terrain I'd like to give you something." He looked puzzled and questioning. I did not want him to worry that I was intending to try out the dazzler again so, with barely a pause, I turned to the table where I had my sketch pad, carefully pulled out the drawing I had made of him, turned and handed it to him. He looked at it as he took it from me.

"When did you do that?"

"A short time ago. When you were, er, resting."

He actually looked embarrassed as he looked at the drawing "That's really good. Very good." He continued to examine it carefully before looking up,

"Thank you."

He seemed genuinely pleased and his hostility towards me seemed finally totally to have evaporated. If that was the case, the drawing had worked its magic. Giving someone a drawing has helped me on more than one occasion. It makes you more human to the person you've drawn. I suppose that it is fairly obvious that in any painting, sculpture or drawing there has to be some level of intimate connection between artist and subject. The level of intimacy varies with the work and the length of time spent on it, but it is something always present. I had deliberately drawn a portrait of Frank, not to establish any feelings of intimacy from my side. I was immune to being influenced by whether or not I had sketched someone, but it was clear to me that Frank was not the sociopath that I was. Having established dominance over him, I wanted to establish in him feelings of goodwill, trust and intimacy that would make it that much more difficult for him to betray me. My idea was that the quickest route to this objective was through the making of and giving him, a drawing.

As we drove towards the location I had chosen for the operation, I tried to cement whatever feelings of goodwill I might have established with Frank, by chatting to him and telling him some of my more whimsical and less contentious experiences. I glanced over to him from time to time and it was clear that he was becoming very much more relaxed in my company. He even laughed out loud at some of the stories. As we approached the tunnel I had chosen as the site of the operation, I explained briefly to Frank my plan to block either end of the tunnel with my people in police uniforms whilst I initiated the crash well into the tunnel and well away from the potential witnesses, who, if there were any, would be held back at either end.

Entering the tunnel, I drove through slowly, giving Frank ample opportunity to look around. Having exited at the end, near the entrance to France and the Autoroute, I turned around at the first opportunity and cruised slowly back, giving Frank plenty of time to continue his inspection and make his own assessment. In truth I was not averse to any comments or suggestions that he might make about something I could have missed. We had reached somewhere around the middle of the tunnel when Frank asked me to stop the car. I dutifully pulled up, activated the car's hazard warning lights and pulled the hood release handle. We both got out of the car and, as I raised the hood to give anyone who passed the impression we had stopped for some mechanical problem, Frank looked around and walked up and down a short distance away from the car in each direction.

"If you want to spend any time here, I'd better put up the warning triangle. It's obligatory in Europe you know."

"No, that's ok. I've seen enough." Before getting back into the car and as I closed the hood, Frank delved into his pocket and pulled out a piece of chalk. He walked across to the other side of the road and made a chalk mark that no one would ever have paid any attention to. He then returned to where the stationary car stood and made another chalk mark in a similar location on our side of the road before saying "Let's get going" as he got back into the car.

I started the car, and then waited for another car coming through the tunnel to pass me before moving off.

"You can do it where I've marked the spot. It's a good location. On a straight, in the centre of the tunnel. If you can keep people out of the tunnel for two or three minutes you'll be able to carry out the whole operation and no one'll even know they were kept out of the tunnel before the accident, they'll think they were blocked because of the accident. Also, at that spot the target should probably be travelling at a good speed, accelerating again if they had previously slowed at the entrance to the tunnel."

I have always found it is better to say nothing rather than to allow yourself to say something that you might regret later. I therefore refrained from telling Frank that I had already mentally designated as the killing zone, the approximate place he had marked, without the necessity for making physical chalk marks that some curious and particularly observant policeman might notice and wonder about. I confined myself to a brief

"I agree. I'd already planned to do it around the middle of the tunnel."

"I understand. But we need to have everything planned to precision. Not leave anything to chance."

I did not have to be too astute a psychologist to comprehend that Frank was trying to overturn the dominance I had established in our relationship and to regain his confidence in his supposed position as the man in charge. The fact that he did so in this way told me that he was probably a little inflexible in the way he went about things; the sort of person who liked to make a detailed plan and then follow it through meticulously. I also liked to make plans and thoroughly prepare my operations, but I never allowed myself to become fixated on the details. One of my grandfather's golden rules, perhaps the golden rule, was never to allow your mind to rest on one movement, one goal or one opponent. Always keep your mind in motion, allowing your body to flow unceasingly from one action to another.

In the metaphysical and apparently irrationally perverse world of Zen, this was called the inflexible mind.

However, my function was to kill people, not to educate a potential opponent into the finer aspects of martial arts and I therefore maintained my silence as we drove back towards the hotel.

The Englishman broke the silence first,

"Is it going to be practical for you to take me to a bank and give me the first hundred thousand on Monday morning?"

I did not answer immediately because I had already been thinking about the difficulties these days of walking into a bank in most countries with a bag full of cash. I had managed to do so in Liechtenstein only because Liechtenstein banks were still flexible about dealing in cash and I already had a well- established relationship with the bank that enabled me to arrange my deposit. Frank though, was going to be turning up out of the blue with a bag of cash. Banks were so nervous these days about being accused of involvement in money laundering, that even on opening an account in a tax haven or country purporting to maintain secrecy, such as Switzerland, one would be questioned about oneself, one's assets and the source of the funds.

"I've been thinking about that, because it's not as easy as it used to be to deposit large sums of cash in a bank. They can quite easily report these things, if they are the slightest bit suspicious."

"What about a Swiss Bank? There shouldn't be any trouble with that should there? They have strict secrecy, don't they?"

"Not anymore. Not in my experience. It depends on the Canton where the bank is situated. But generally all Swiss banks will eventually give out information. The most you can hope for is to delay the process, which, as I've said, depends on the Canton. Zurich for example is absolutely hopeless. You can't delay the process there for more than three or four months. Other places are much better. It can take a couple of years or more. The other problem with Swiss banks is that generally, unless they know you well, they won't take a deposit of more than around 50,000 francs in cash."

Frank was frowning. He was obviously rethinking his position. He was realising that taking a large cash bribe was not as easy as it used to be.

"But I've got a suggestion as to how we can do this. If I remember correctly you need about 500,000 Euros in cash deposits in the bank if you want to establish residency in Monaco. I think you should go into whatever bank you choose or feel comfortable with... with... say 20,000 Euros or pounds, in cash and tell them you want to open an account, because you're thinking of establishing residency. You'll need to show them a passport or identity document. If you've got a false ID, that'd be best. I don't suppose you came here under your own name."

He did not respond. He simply stared straight ahead out of the windscreen, so I continued,

"Then, when the account is open, I'll immediately send through to you, instead of the first 100,000 pounds I was going to give you, say a quarter of a million, less the cash I give you to open the account. How would that be? If you get the account open on Monday. I should be able to get the money through to you by Tuesday or Wednesday at the latest. You'd have it before the op and know that I wasn't bullshitting you. Then we'll both be clear and know exactly where we are. I'll be as sure as I can be that you're not going to try and fuck me because, otherwise, you'll never get the rest of the money. It'll be a lot for you to give up. Then, as we discussed before, when I'm satisfied I'm free and clear, after a couple of weeks say, I'll send you the rest. Another quarter of a million British pounds."

As I spoke I wondered if I were making a mistake in upping the initial payment from 100,000 pounds. I was really gambling on Frank's cupidity. Nearly everyone I have ever come across wants to receive more money than they have been paid or earned. But just suppose I totally miscalculated and Frank was content with just a quarter of a million pounds and prepared to forgo receiving another quarter of a million for the sake of tidying up all loose ends. Well I had said it now and would have to live with any adverse consequences. I was effectively gambling that, when Frank saw that he had a quarter of a million pounds, sitting in cash, in a bank account, he would be greedy enough for the other quarter of a million to keep to the bargain with me. If I knew anything about human nature, once the Englishman held a bank statement in his hand showing a 250,000 pound credit, he would hardly be able to contain his impatience before receiving another quarter of a million. I sighed to myself. My human nature was making me wonder whether I was not being a little too free at dispensing money. The expenses were starting to dent my little nest egg.

We had reached the hotel and I drove the car down into the underground garage. As I cut the engine Frank turned to me,

"What you've suggested sounds good to me. One thing I would appreciate. I don't know very much about banks or banking. You seem to know a lot. I'd be grateful for your help in choosing a bank where I'm going to have maximum secrecy and minimum difficulty."

I nodded, "Sure I'll help you. It's in my interest to see you're happy. Let's meet here Monday morning at 10 am and we'll get you sorted by noon."

He seemed quite affable now. Not a single trace of the hostility he had shown after I had used the dazzler. You never know though. Maybe he was a quick learner and becoming better at concealing his feelings. In any event, he nodded his approval and, once again, offered me his hand to shake, before getting out of the car with a brief,

"Monday morning, then. Your room".

Within seconds he had disappeared in the direction of the entrance to the lobby.

I sat in the car for a few moments, wondering whether I had read the Englishman correctly and played this right. Perhaps I should still plan on taking out him and whoever he had with him. There were unlikely to be more than ten of them and with my team, the element of surprise and perhaps Jacques participating, they might not be too much problem. I thought about my team. I was pretty sure the Russian was former Spetsnaz, Russian Special Forces. They were good, so he would be a reliable operator to take out two or three of the Brits. Jacques and I could probably account for another five between us. That might leave two, three, perhaps four to the Jugoslavs and the arab. They were an unknown quantity. I had no idea how they would perform against SAS troopers, who were amongst the best in the world. All things considered, perhaps the odds were not really that good. In any event, what the hell would we do with the bodies. And what if some of my people got hurt and I was left short-handed. I might not be able to carry out the operation without messing it up. Of course I could try to hit the British team and fly the coop without carrying out the operation. That would not be any good either. I have never, in my whole career, reneged on an operation I have been paid for. I was not intending to start now. Strange as it may seem I do have some professional pride in what I do and, however bizarre it might seem, I regard myself as having some integrity. Besides, I had to look at the practicalities. If I walked away with the money without doing the job, the probability was that Admiral Standish would send people after me because, ultimately, it was his head on the block. He had chosen me. Neither was it beyond the realms of possibility that I would be labelled as having gone rogue and the CIA and whoever was presently doing their dirty work, would be brought in to deal with me. No. There was no question of not carrying out the operation and antagonising people who would otherwise be prepared to ignore me. Nor was it going to be practical to take out the Brits. I would have to live with the bargain I had made with Frank and hope that he kept to his end of it.

I got out of the car, locked it and entered the hotel lobby. I looked around carefully, but it seemed that Frank had already gone. Before going back to my room I made a circuit of the hotel, going to the pool area and the beach. I went up to the room only after I was satisfied that neither Frank nor any of his French friends were carrying out surveillance on me. I only stayed in the room long enough to collect everything I needed, before taking the elevator downstairs and leaving through the hotel's front entrance. I stood in the entrance for a moment, allowing my eyes to adjust to the bright sunlight. As I became accustomed to the light, I scanned the street around the hotel. Seeing nothing suspicious and no sign of the Englishman or the car he had arrived in, I started to walk down the street towards the garage where the spare Audi was parked. I took my time, casually glancing in shop windows as I passed, to see whether I was being followed. If there was anyone keeping tabs on me I did not want them to think that I was operational.

The light was beginning to fade and the lengthening shadows made it difficult to distinguish between what was real and what was imagined. I passed a shop selling expensive women's lingerie and thought of Natalya. The thought was involuntary and all the less welcome for disturbing my concentration when I should have been devoting my attention to uncovering ticks. I decided that going into the shop could serve two purposes; helping me flush out anyone following and buying a present for the girl. I chose a couple of very erotic items that would probably have been cheaper if they had been manufactured in gold. As she was wrapping them up, I asked the shop assistant to allow me to use her telephone. As I dialled Natalya's hotel I carefully scanned the street through the shop window. When the hotel operator answered I asked for the girl's room. Once again she immediately picked up the telephone, so, unless she had someone in the room with her, she must have been waiting for me to call. She sounded as pleased to hear me as the last time I had called, but seemed disappointed when I told her that I was some distance away and would be unable to see her today. Against my better judgment I promised to try and come to her hotel the following afternoon and spend the evening with her. I felt that I was being reckless rather than careless. The distinction being, that I knew what I was doing and did not really care about any consequences. At the same time part of me was asking the other part what the hell he thought he was doing. The fact that I could not see anything in the street to concern me assisted my attempts to silence the thoughts that were seeking to impose some element of sense on my recklessness. I put down the telephone having promised to see Natalya around 7pm the following evening, after the Grand Prix, when I could lose myself in the crowds I expected would be thronging the hotel, with members of the various teams no doubt celebrating success or failure with equal fervour.

I left the shop with beautiful underwear, beautifully packaged. No one followed me as I entered the garage.

I made two or three circuits of the interior before making my way to the car. Driving out of the garage I was alert for any indication that I was under mobile surveillance. Nothing triggered my internal warning systems, but I still took a circuitous route towards the safe house established by Jacques in La Turbie, which took me nearly an hour. When I was as certain as I could be that I was unaccompanied, I drove into the house.

I arrived to find Jacques in the kitchen preparing dinner. His son Paolo was in the sitting room, typing away feverishly at a laptop computer. Paolo looked up at me as I walked in and gave me a lopsided, slightly guilty looking grin as if I had caught him in the midst of some illicit activity. As I followed the delightful smell emanating from the kitchen I realised that I was hungry. Jacques was very busy. He was someone who had always taken his cooking very seriously. He had covered his outdoor clothes with a striped apron that ran down from his neck before being double tied around his waist. He looked up as I entered the kitchen and nodded a greeting before turning back to whatever he was focussing on.

"I'm just preparing dinner. I hope you're hungry."

"I am. What are you making? It smells great."

"You'll see. Paolo's been working on getting into the traffic surveillance system. Why don't you go in and get him to explain it to you while I finish up here."

Jacques was simultaneously tasting something, stirring one of the pots in front of him and talking to me. I left him to it and went to talk to Paolo.

"You working on getting into the traffic system?"

"It's done. Come. I'll show you."

I sat down beside him and, within a couple of minutes, was watching the traffic flow on the Autoroute between Cannes and Monte Carlo. He explained to me how he had been able to hack into the system but, although I use computers frequently, Paolo had totally lost me within minutes in describing the technicalities of what he had done. I had thought the boy was smart when I first met him but Jacques was right, he was a computer genius. He was not only a technician, but was also able to explain to me, so that I understood clearly, how to access the system for myself. He made sure that I understood how to switch between different cameras on different stretches of road, identify the particular sections of road and how to split the screen in order to show several sections at once. He made me practise for about twenty minutes under his watchful eye; until he was satisfied I was adept at doing exactly what I needed.

By the time we had finished Jacques was calling us in to eat. The table was neatly set and there were several steaming dishes sitting between the place settings. As we sat down Jacques turned to me and said,

"So what do you think of my boy?"

"He's very smart. You were right."

Jacques beamed with pleasure as I praised his son. The proud father was a side of him I had never really seen before and it made me even more aware of the necessity to remove Paolo from the danger zone. Jacque's son was a distraction. If he was around, then because of my relationship with Jacques, I would be worrying about his son and not devoting myself wholly to the things I should be concentrating on. As I helped myself from the different dishes I murmured quietly to Jacques,

"You need to get your boy out of here. Now wouldn't be too soon. He's done a great job but I wouldn't forgive myself if anything happened to him."

Jacques nodded, "If you're happy you can work the computer I'll have him out of here tomorrow, even though he wants to stay to watch the Grand Prix."

"Forget the Grand Prix. Get him away from here. He's explained everything I need to know to access the camera system for the Autoroute."

"Are you two talking about me?" Paolo asked the question in Italian. I had been speaking to Jacques in French. I turned to the boy, answering him in the language in which he had spoken.

"Yes. We're talking about you leaving here. Tomorrow."

Paolo frowned, "While I was here I wanted to watch the Grand Prix. I met a couple of great girls and promised them I'd go with them to the race."

"Sorry. No way." I got up from the table whilst I was talking and walked over to where I had left my bag. I unzipped the bag and stuck my hands in to count out ten 500 Euro notes which I then took out. I walked back to the table and pushed the money towards Paolo as I sat down,

"That's to help you forget the girls and not to contact them again. I don't want anyone around here knowing you or that you've been here."

Paolo looked at the money doubtfully as Jacques sat back in his chair looking at the two of us. Eventually Jacques' son reached for the small pile of notes,

"Well. Alright. Thank you."

I stretched out my hand and caught Paolo's as he was drawing the money back towards himself. He looked up at me and I gave him one of my killer looks,

"I'm serious. This isn't a game. If you don't leave you're going to be as much of a danger to me as to yourself. So don't play around."

The boy looked a little shaken. He was not used to someone like me staring at him in that way and gripping his arm hard enough to stop the flow of blood. As I released his arm he looked around to his father, perhaps expecting some paternal intervention. But Jacques knew better and had resumed eating, pointedly concentrating on the plate in front of him.

After we had finished dinner, Paolo disappeared into one of the spare bedrooms and I was left to discuss with Jacques the outcome of my meeting with the Englishman.

As we sat down Jacques turned to me, saying reprovingly,

"You were a little tough on my son back there."

I looked up at my friend, "You think. Better a two second reality check than a bullet in his head."

Jacques nodded thoughtfully, "You're right. Kids these days think they're bullet proof. They take drugs till they're coming out of their ears. Smoke three packs of cigarettes a day and never think they're going to be the ones to get sick and die. Things were different when we were younger. We were tough and disciplined."

"That was after we joined the Legion. How were we before that?"

Jacques laughed, "Doesn't bear thinking about. Anyway what happened with that English guy?"

By way of answer I dragged my bag over to where we were sitting and pulled out the case containing the dazzler, which I opened before handing the device to Jacques.

"Take a look at that. What a piece of kit that is... don't point it at me please. I already gave the Englishman a quick dose and he was out of it for about ten minutes. Come up alongside a car and stick that in the driver's face as we're accelerating past... pooof... watch the fireworks."

"Hmmm, really. I'd like to try it before the op." He was examining the device carefully, without switching it on.

"Take my word for it. It works. It works very well." I paused before adding, "Anyway you'll see it in action soon enough. It looks like we're going to be on for Thursday."

"Thursday, eh." He was still examining the dazzler," you remember the gun John? The one the Brits gave you?"

"Yes."

"Are you sure they haven't done the same with this?" He looked up at me, "and maybe also the bag it came in?"

So much had happened that, in truth, this was something that I had overlooked. My discomfort must have shown on my face. Most people were unable to read me, but Jacques had known me for so long that I think he was often able to sense my thoughts.

"Let's look at the bag. As for this" he lifted the dazzler, waving it slightly in the air, "I've got another way we can deal with it without my having to dismantle it and perhaps fuck it up." He put the dazzler on the table and got up, throwing the bag it came in at me, as he walked out of the room, "Take a careful look at that. I'll be back in a minute."

I started to examine the bag, inch by inch. Feeling every slight indentation and using my knife to cut out anything suspect that I felt. By the time Jacques returned, the bag was in shreds and I had four very small suspicious pieces of metal on the table. Jacques put down on a chair what looked like a large blue apron which, from the way he handled it seemed to be quite heavy. He also put down on the table a bottle he had also been carrying, with what looked like about half litre of clear liquid. He picked up the pieces on the table and immediately discarded two of them. As he examined the other two he grunted, before opening the bottle of clear liquid, carefully unscrewing the top and gently dropping the two pieces inside the bottle. The liquid in the bottle immediately started bubbling. Jacques screwed the top back on the bottle, picked it up and took it outside into the garden, returning without it. He looked at me as he sat down again,

"Acid. Left it in the garden in case the chemical reaction makes it explode. You never know with that stuff. Anyway those two bugs are finished. Shame I couldn't take the time to examine them more carefully. I don't often get a chance to look at stuff that advanced. I'm surprised you even found them."

I glanced towards the bag, "Well I did rip that thing to pieces didn't I? What's that?" I indicated the blue apron.

"It's a lead apron. Same as they use in hospitals to shield people from xrays. I thought I'd bring it along, just in case. We'll wrap this in it... " He picked up the dazzler, "if your people've planted anything in this it'll almost certainly shield the signal. We'll just keep it wrapped up until we use it, then wrap it up again."

I nodded, "I knew I was doing the right thing bringing you in on this. You're just the steadying hand I need."

Jacques laughed as he finished wrapping the dazzler in the lead apron.

"So tell me. Do the others know when the job's on for?"

"I'm intending to brief them tomorrow. Going there might be a little bit of a problem though." I thought for a minute before continuing,

"I had a little chat with the Englishman. He didn't say so, but I'm pretty sure he's already got a team watching the house. Probably from that place we looked at."

"We expected that. Though I thought you wanted them to keep tabs on the house, so they'd be comfortable with knowing that the people they were watching had a base to return to."

"Yeh. It's just that... "

I sat back and told Jacques the proposition I had put to the English officer.

Jacques furrowed his eyebrows in concentration, "And he went for it?"

"Seemed to."

"Hmmm." He sat silently for a while thinking.

"You know it doesn't sound like any English Ruperts I know. I think they call them Ruperts because they're too fucking stupid to go for the money. Just making the offer probably hurts their pride. The fact that you should even think they might go for something like that'd be an insult to them."

"Maybe. But they're human like anyone else. There's an old saying that you catch more flies with honey than with vinegar and if you can't catch a fish with one bait you use another. I happen to think that this particular one is hungry for money. Of course it doesn't mean he's not thinking of fucking me over. He might be thinking he'll take the money I'm going to give him before the op, then forget the rest and take my head instead. If that's what he thinks I'm going to have to kill the fucker aren't I?"

"If you're going to kill him, why give him money in the first place?"

"Because the way I reckon it, if it all goes bad and he decides to try and kill me along with the others, at least I'll have bought us some time."

Jacques shrugged, "I don't see why we couldn't just take him out when he comes to give you a final briefing and the up to date intel."

"I could, but then we've got to get rid of him. It's the same problem with the rest of his team. We might be able to remove them all without much of a problem. But what do we do with them afterwards. The actual operation's got to be perfect, so that no one goes crying afterwards to my boss about what a fuck up I've made. If we mess up, I'm going to have my boss, probably the CIA and who knows, every clandestine agency that doesn't exist, all after me. If the job goes well, there's nothing to complain about and my people are going to be happy quietly to forget about me and that they had any sort of involvement in the operation. They know it'll cause more problems to come after me than to leave me alone. If they've got no reason to come after me they won't. I've seen it before."

Jacques looked sceptical, "I hope you're right. But if it were me I'd cap the lot of them, otherwise you're going to be looking over your shoulder all the time. If they're sitting in that house we looked at, we could go in and take them all out. Tomorrow, or the day after. There's plenty of places to get rid of bodies in the hills. Fuck, how many of them can there be? A small special ops group. Eight? Ten? Twelve max. I could go out, buy a truck load of acid. We could dissolve their bodies in a few hours. There are plenty of empty houses around waiting to be rented out. We could empty a small swimming pool, fill it with acid and... pouf" He accompanied the sound with an expansive spread of his arms and hands.

I sat there looking at Jacques, thinking about what he had just said. I could not be sure whether or not he was serious about filling a swimming pool with acid. Although he might have been right in principle, he was losing sight of the overall picture. If we got lucky and were able to get rid of all the Brits without the team being compromised, they would then probably decide seriously to come after us. Intelligence services and secretive units have long institutional memories. They do not like taking losses and this would be a big hit for them. If we got them really worked up by killing a whole team, to say nothing of the senior officer in charge, they would certainly be pushing buttons everywhere and pressuring my side to help them. I did not want any of that. I was a bit surprised that Jacques, who was usually so careful, was sounding a bit reckless and making it all seem too easy. I preferred to stick with my plan. If the English officer kept to his agreement with me there would be no comebacks. Everyone who mattered would think I was dead. I preferred to take a risk on being right about the Englishman, than risking a much bigger mess with who knows what consequences. If I was wrong and everything went bad, I would just have to try to handle it. It would still be easier than having a bounty on my head and every assassin in the world trying to collect. In the end just leaving the Brits alone would result in a lower level of risk and if I could not handle things... well that was always a risk in this business. As the saying goes, 'if you can't do the time don't do the crime'. If I was not ready to die at any time I should be in a different line of work.

"I'm sticking with what I've decided," I said finally, "there's too much possible downside to doing what you're suggesting. If this were a private job, that'd be something else. But we're dealing with official people here. I just don't want to fuck around with MI6 and the SAS if I don't need to. These people have long institutional memories and I don't want to be on everyone's watch list for the next fifty years."

Jacques shrugged again and nodded without saying anything, then stood up and walked out of the room. I looked at his disappearing back and the empty doorway, thinking about our conversation, until he re-emerged a few minutes later. In each of his hands he held a Heckler and Koch MP5 SD sub-machine gun, one of which he held out to me. The gun was familiar to me. It is used by many special operations forces. It is extremely reliable, with full time sound suppression. The version that Jacques handed to me was the SD6, with a retractable butt stock and three firing modes, single shot, automatic or three shot burst.

"Just in case," Jacques said, as I checked the weapon, "and I've got plenty of ammunition." He added grimly.

I handed the gun back to him, "Let's hope we don't need them."

CHAPTER THIRTY
FOUR

"The world says: "You have needs – satisfy them.
You have as much right as the rich and the mighty.
Don't hesitate to satisfy your needs; indeed, expand
your needs and demand more." (Dostoyevsky)

W hen Cartwright left Traynor he had a lot to
think about. He was both excited and nervous
and, strangely, felt a sense of liberation. He did not
quite understand the complex cocktail of emotions he
was feeling. First he wondered just how far he could
trust the American. The money on offer was more
than tempting. It would be something of a godsend. As
Commander of the Regiment he had certain demands
on his finances that were difficult to meet just on his
salary. Since the 17th and 18th centuries when wealthy
gentleman had raised and uniformed their own regiments, the British army had maintained something of
a tradition of having an officer corps drawn from the
sons of prosperous landowners, for whom their army
pay was nothing more than a small supplement to their
own private income. With the first and second world
wars and conscription that had followed, the elite club

of rich officers had been infiltrated by middle class individuals without any family resources to finance themselves. Even with the breaking down of class barriers that occurred in the twentieth century, it was still almost impossible for anyone but the rich to become an officer in the fashionable Guards or Cavalry regiments. It was simply too difficult socially, to maintain the requisite standard of living in those regiments on a government salary.

Cartwright had dreamed of being a soldier ever since he could remember. As a boy he had imagined himself as an officer in the Coldstream or Grenadier Guards, dressed in the elaborate uniforms of those regiments. He was not particularly academic and, with a father who was a medium grade civil servant, he had been lucky to gain admission to a minor undistinguished university. He had started to fulfil his military ambitions by enlisting with a Territorial Army unit and undertaking part time training in parallel with his academic studies. It was in this period he had realised that he had no chance of acceptance as an officer into one of the elite regiments he had dreamed of. Having graduated from University, his reality had been an acceptance by a rather different elite, the Parachute Regiment. Having served with the Parachutists for a number of years, he had applied for and passed, selection into the SAS. The Special Air Service was not only a military elite, it was also probably the most egalitarian unit in the British army. Professionalism, not wealth was the watchword; non-commissioned officers and even troopers had as much input into operational activities as the officers themselves. Even so finances could be a strain for an officer, particularly of the upper echelon. Because of its many clandestine activities and generous budget the SAS did provide opportunities for individuals to supplement their incomes from time to time and both the sergeants' and officers' messes had managed to accumulate capital to fund their activities.

Notwithstanding the supplements, which were not so easily accessible to the senior officer that Cartwright had recently become, the financial strains remained. Half a million pounds, with no comebacks, seemed very attractive to the British officer as he was being driven back to the hotel in Nice. He thought ruefully of his bank overdraft, which had now crept up to around thirty thousand pounds and had been causing him sleepless nights, wondering how he was ever going to pay it off. Now, suddenly, with the prospect of the money promised by Traynor, his overdraft seemed insignificant. If everything went as the American promised, he was not going to have any more financial worries.

His thoughts turned to Traynor. Strangely enough, in spite of his initial anger at being the subject of Traynor's experiment with the dazzler, Cartwright had found himself warming to the American. When they were not discussing business Traynor was an engaging conversationalist, an amusing companion and a talented artist. Part of Traynor's skill as a conversationalist was his ability to listen, although the greater part of the time he had been talking, not listening. He also had a real understanding of pace and timing and knew exactly when and how to bring his narratives to a close.

Cartwright took out the drawing Traynor had made of him. It was not simply a good likeness, very professionally executed, but seemed to capture, in a few deceptively simple strokes, some of the inner conflict that so often seemed to afflict the Englishman.

As he continued to look at the drawing, Cartwright's feeling that he could trust Traynor solidified. Suppose he complied with what Traynor wanted, who would know? What were the chances of anyone finding out? There was no reason for the assassin not to disappear into the shadows as he had promised. Why would he not? He had every reason quietly to retire. He had a sum of money that to Cartwright seemed huge. More than enough for someone to live on for the rest of their days. In fact probably enough for several people to live on. He had almost certainly set up one or more alternative identities that would make him virtually impossible to trace or identify. If everything went as planned on this operation and it was designated the accident it was supposed to be, no one who mattered would have any interest in digging into deeply buried secrets. Of all the secrets that Cartwright had interred in his years of special operations, this secret was going to be the most deeply buried and least likely to be exhumed. What it amounted to was, that he could probably take Traynor's money in complete safety. It would be that much better though, if he could take the assassin's money and also dispose of the assassin. As Cartwright was mulling over that idea and how it might be accomplished, they arrived at the hotel.

Cartwright dismissed the driver and went up to his room, from where he immediately called his RSM on the secure communications network. He arranged for the RSM to send one of the men to collect him and bring him up to the observation post they had set up.

Whilst waiting, he made a secure call to Featherstonehaugh, whose office was also connected to the Milstar system. With his natural caution honed by years of experience in clandestine operations, Cartwright refrained from being too specific, notwithstanding the secure line.

"I've met with your chappie and it seems that he'll be active Thursday. In the meantime, we're in a good position to look into his staff and should be able to monitor their performance fairly closely."

"That's good news."

"There's one thing I wanted to ask you."

"The rather bulky delivery made to the chap. The second tranche of the two lots of equipment... "

"Yes. I'm with you."

"Well, I took a look after the office closed to see whether he had set it up but there was no trace of it. He later told me that he had removed it to another location that was not accessible to us. That rather concerned me, because you had indicated that we should do our best to recover that equipment afterwards. I don't think that's going to be possible, unless you have any suggestions as to how we might go about that."

There was a long pause from Featherstonehaugh. Cartwright waited for his eventual response,

"Hmmm. That's a tricky one. There are ways of tracking shipments like that because there is an international system for transferring that type of material. But it is very problematic for two reasons. First you would be most unlikely to have a shipment that was just those goods. They would probably be mixed in with other shipments. Secondly, the goods might not be shipped at all, they might just be kept by the recipient and used in situ. I think, without any further information we're probably going to have to write this one off unless you pick up some useful lead that might help pinpoint the shipment."

What Featherstonehaugh was seeking to communicate to Cartwright was information about the way sums of money were transferred internationally. Most banks have either branches or correspondent banks in different countries. Transfers of money between banks are carried out by interbank transfers. In Traynor's case, the logistics would have been effected in one of the following ways. Traynor could have delivered the cash to a correspondent of his Liechtenstein Bank. The cash would then have been paid into the Liechtenstein Bank's account with its correspondent without any reference to Traynor. If the cash were actually transferred to Liechtenstein it would not be identifiable as a separate amount because, in all probability, it would be included with other cash transfers, of which there are many every day and, been sent through the interbank system. On the other hand it was most likely that the money would not even have been transferred. It would probably simply have remained in Monaco in the account of the Liechtenstein Bank at its correspondent's premises.

Whatever the position, Cartwright understood that the money he had handed over to Traynor had almost certainly become untraceable. Set against that scenario the American's offer seemed even more attractive to the Englishman.

Cartwright's ride to the observation post arrived in Nice over an hour after he had finished speaking to Featherstonehaugh. It was Ross who was driving and as he drove he reported to his superior what the team had done and how they had set themselves up, as well as the results of the surveillance so far. Cartwright listened but scarcely spoke; making Ross wonder what was up with the boss.

Ross pointed out the house where Traynor's men were set up as they drove past, before climbing the hill to the contemporary structure that had become the SAS men's observation post. The team had been busy. They had disarmed the alarm without activating the signal to the central station, but had managed to connect up the video surveillance system for the property, as well as the electrically operated entrance gate.

Cartwright walked around the house, carefully checking everything his men had done and the way they had set themselves up. The house had seven bedrooms and the men had not hesitated to make themselves at home in the comfort it provided. At first Cartwright thought of reproving his men for the liberties they had taken with someone else's property but, when he thought about it further, he decided as long as they left no fingerprints and nothing was taken, the worst that the owner or the owner's agents would think was that some homeless people had taken up residence briefly. Anyway, he thought to himself, he would have the men clean up properly before they all cleared out. After all, they were only going to be in the house for four or five days.

The surveillance equipment they had brought with them had been carefully set up in the room that overlooked the house under observation. It included long range high quality laser and parabolic microphones designed to reflect low frequency sound and reject unwanted background noise, as well as other highly sensitive omnidirectional microphones with extremely high gain amplification. They also had an array of equipment for monitoring cellphone conversations and photographing and video recording their subjects. For night time and monitoring their targets inside the walls of the house, they were using long range thermal FLIR (forward looking infra-red) imaging systems. They had even assembled, but not yet put into operation, a small unmanned aerial vehicle also equipped with infra-red imaging. The observation room, as the men had named it, was itself in total darkness save for the glow from the screens displaying the images of the people in the house below them.

As Cartwright finished his inspection he was approached by the RSM accompanied by one of the other men,

"Cuppa tea, Boss?" Ah, the ubiquitous cup of tea that was the English soldier's mainstay wherever he might find himself,

"Thank you Andy, that would be very nice" answered Cartwright graciously, as he accepted the steaming mug that was being offered to him. He turned to the RSM,

"Ken, why don't we go and sit in the kitchen and you can give me a sitrep."

The kitchen blinds, like the curtains throughout the rest of the house, were firmly closed and the men had, in addition, covered the windows underneath the blinds with brown paper, to prevent any light showing outside. Even so, the only light in the kitchen came from a torch that had been placed on a countertop to the side of an electric ceramic hob unit. The torch had been so positioned as to shine on the ceiling casting an eerie, shadowy muted glow over the room that was, nonetheless, adequate to light the room without totally destroying everyone's night vision.

They made themselves comfortable, Cartwright enjoying the pleasure of slowly sipping the steaming tea,

"Well, sir, as you can see we're all set up and operational. We've identified five tangos. We've labelled them simply T1 to T5. Haven't picked up anything much in the way of information from their conversation. Two of them, Ts 3 and 4 seem to be Serbs. At least they're speaking Serbian. As you know Macallister and Ross speak some Serbian from their time in the Balkans. One of them, T1, is definitely Arab. He went off into the garden by himself at one point and we picked him up speaking on his cell phone." He put a clipboard on the table with a large number of writing pages attached to it and quickly went through the pages stopping at a particular point and showing it to his superior,

"That's his cell number and the one next to it is the one he called. We asked Cheltenham to locate it for us and whoever is using it is in Marseilles. Anyway we recorded the conversation and Ross and I've done an approximate translation. It's quite interesting. Sounds like they're arranging for the guy here to pick up what they described as a "package", so that he can complete his mission. So I'd say we're definitely onto something. The question is should we bring in GIGN and if so when, or do we run solo on this?"

Cartwright listened silently. He was intrigued. What was going on? Traynor was supposed to be running the operation. From what he had seen of him and the way he operated and the fact that he had offered up the men he was using to Cartwright after the operation, he was unlikely to be entrusting any significant aspect of the operation to one of these men. He made a mental note to speak to Traynor about it.

"Any idea where T1 is from?"

"I can't be certain. My Arabic's a little rusty. Ross though says T1 sounds Syrian and he thinks the guy in Marseilles is Palestinian."

Cartwright furrowed his brow. Was it possible that by some strange chance Traynor had recruited an active terrorist?

"Have you been able to get a picture of T1?"

"Nothing clear. We've got the thermal images, but of course they're no good for identification."

Cartwright was tempted not to wait until his next meeting with Traynor before speaking to the American about T1 and, to try to get Traynor on the cell phone they were supposed to be using for communications. Perhaps he would try later on. He was curious to obtain whatever information he could before he saw Traynor on Monday morning, but did not want any of his crew to know what he was doing. He had still not decided whether he was going to go through with the arrangement Traynor had proposed to him. However, if something was going on with T1, it might provide a sufficient distraction for him to be able to implement the arrangement with Traynor.

"Nothing much else to report sir. They cooked themselves a meal about half an hour ago and they're either watching television or playing cards or something. It doesn't look like any of them are going out at all."

Everything seemed to be under control. Cartwright really had nothing to do. It looked like being a few days of standard monotonous surveillance for the men, with nothing much to alleviate boredom. At least he had the excuse to go out and meet up with Esclimont and Traynor. The men had already arranged between themselves who was going to be on watch and who was going to be resting and when. He turned to the RSM,

"I haven't eaten. Did anyone by any chance buy anything?"

"Well no, I'm afraid not, boss. What with setting ourselves up and getting stuck in, it got rather late to send anyone out to buy food. We do have a few MRE's (meals ready to eat) though, boss."

Cartwright frowned looking at his RSM incredulously, "You've got to be kidding me. We're in France. The world's culinary centre. We've got a fairly generous expense allowance and you're offering me an MRE. There's probably some starred Michelin restaurant just around the corner. What's the time?"

He looked at his watch. Just after 21.00, 9pm. There had to be a restaurant open nearby.

"So I take it that you and the men haven't eaten yet."

"Actually, no sir. As a matter of fact some of the chaps were thinking... " his voice faltered and tailed off,

"Yes." Cartwright snapped impatiently.

"Well, when we did a recce of the area, we did actually spot a rather nice looking little place about a mile down the road. We thought maybe you'd ok our going there, but we didn't want to go off without your say so. It just didn't seem that it might be any problem if a couple of the lads stayed on watch and the rest of us went out for a bite."

Cartwright looked at his sergeant major. He could not see any objection to the suggestion being made. The people they were watching seemed to be settled in for the night and were unlikely to cross their path. Even if they did they would have no reason to suspect that the British team were watching them. He did fancy a decent meal, even after or perhaps because of, the excesses of the previous evening, which, in any event, seemed to have been such a long time ago.

"I don't see any objection. Yes. Let's go. I take it you've arranged who'll go and who'll stay. Have you?"

"Yes Boss." Collier jumped up and was out of the kitchen with an alacrity and eagerness Cartwright had rarely seen him display. He heard the RSM's voice bellowing to the men,

"Right lads. Those going out, on your bikes and into the cars chop, chop. Don't worry lads, we'll bring you something back." The last comment was shouted from the front door at the two soldiers left on surveillance duty in the house.

By the time Cartwright was outside everyone was already in the two rental cars waiting for him to join them.

CHAPTER THIRTY FIVE

Sunday

"I once spent a year in Philadelphia,
I think it was on a Sunday."
(W. C. Fields)

I could not remember the last time I had actually rested on a Sunday. The fact that I was staying in a house in a village above the Mediterranean, where warm sea air wafted into my nostrils in the early morning and I had nothing very much to attend to, did not prevent me from waking up early. I found the sea air sufficiently invigorating to be motivated to go into the garden and perform some formal martial arts exercises for an hour or so. I was about half way through when I became aware that I was being watched by Jacques' son. I continued, ignoring the boy's presence. Jacques had seen me doing these sort of exercises many times and lacked the interest shown by his son, who walked over to me as I finished.

"That was fantastic," he said admiringly, "I've done some kickboxing and karate back home but I've never seen anyone move the way you do.

It's like... " he struggled for a minute to describe his impressions, "like your movements come from your breathing, like... I don't know... like everything is so smooth and flowing. I don't suppose you could teach me some of that stuff."

Even though he was taller than me he had an eager little boy look to him. I patted him on the shoulders,

"Sure, let's see you do something."

I watched as he moved into a Karate stance and directly into a kata sequence of formal techniques. He performed tolerably well and had obviously been practising for a number of years. As he was performing, Jacques came out and stood watching until Paolo finished the kata, when he walked over to us.

"Did he tell you he was Italian kick boxing champion for the last two years?" he asked proudly.

"No, he didn't."

Paolo looked embarrassed.

"Why don't you have a go with him, see what he's like? An old guy like you might just find him a bit of a handful". It was the proud father speaking, not the Jacques who had been with me when I had, within a few minutes, dispatched seven opponents armed with knives and machetes in a back street in Rio during a week's leave from jungle exercises. True, that had been more than thirty years ago and he probably thought I had lost it. All the same he was laying down a challenge and his son had asked me for a lesson. I turned to

Paolo and told him to attack me whenever and however he wanted. He hesitated for a moment before slipping into a forward side stance and feinting with a punch at my head followed up with a side thrust kick to my head before twisting smoothly into a roundhouse kick with his other leg, also to my head. The boy was fast and moved well, but I had no difficulty in avoiding his first kick and catching his foot at the apex of the round-house kick with the side of my right hand, as I moved in closely and hit him with the palm of my left hand just below his buttocks. In the real world I would have dealt him a crippling blow to his testicles, but we were just playing. The simultaneous movements, coupled with his momentum, sent him sprawling sideways and it required nothing more than my grasping his trouser leg and shoulder with a quick twist of my hands to land him heavily on the ground on his back.

I glanced quickly at Jacques as I moved towards Paolo to give him my hand to help him get off the ground. Jacques' disappointment that his son had failed to kick my butt was palpable. As for Paolo, he had fallen so heavily and unexpectedly that he was winded. I squatted beside him, sat him up and administered a technique that enabled him to recover instantly.

As Paolo and I stood up I said, "Your movements are good, fast, but you were telegraphing your intentions beforehand. I could tell what you were going to do before you did it. I know that some Taekwando and Muay Thai experts can be very effective with high kicks, but to me, I think they look good and, if they come off are very spectacular, but even if you're very fast, they take that much longer to connect than a short powerful blow and if you miss you're wide open. Let me show you something." I looked around until I saw some long sticks lying near the house. I walked over and picked up two that seemed to be pretty solid. I handed one to Jacques and one to Paolo.

"Now both of you, attack me, as hard as you can."

They had barely started to lift their sticks before I moved in close to the side of Paolo. I caught his arms whilst they were still bringing the stick down to where I had been. He was completely off balance and I easily twisted him around to where Jacques was wielding his stick. Using my grip on Paolo's arms, I pushed the stick, which he was still holding, up to block Jacques' downward blow. Even as the two sticks hit with a loud thwack I continued my movement but twisted to reverse the direction in which I was moving Paolo, simultaneously throwing the son against his father. As Paolo's body cartwheeled to the ground Jacques was caught a glancing blow which unbalanced him backwards and made it easy for me to turn my body, sweeping him with my right arm, followed by a light blow to his throat with my left hand the combined effect of which was to send him down hard on the ground with his legs flying up into the air. In his case, I grasped him by the shirt and his trouser belt as he was falling, so that he did not land with any force, I had no desire to see him injured.

The two of them lay on the ground looking up at me, wondering what had happened. Jacques's shirt had been torn where I had held him and he looked at the ruined shirt ruefully,

"Thanks very much. One of my favourite shirts."

"I'm sorry. I didn't want your old bones to crack as you hit the ground." I turned to Paolo, "Anticipation of your opponent's actions, flowing explosive movement in response. There are only so many ways of attacking. Once you realise what your opponent is doing it's important not to focus on that but to move into your response and then, without hesitation, flow into the response to the next attacker. Paolo, I could have avoided your blow and done a high kick to your head or a side thrust kick and then tried to do the same to your father, but what I did was faster to execute and more effective. Your father could have been dead. I touched his throat, but could easily have shattered it, before turning to finish you off."

They both started to stand as I was speaking, "There's a big difference between sport kick boxing or taekwondo for example and real combat. Personally I don't believe in turning martial arts into a sport. The aim of martial arts is to destroy your opponent, mentally and then physically. Focusing your attention and power on crushing one or more opponents has nothing to do with trying to score points."

Father and son were, by now, standing looking at me, Paolo seemed awestruck whilst his father looked chastened. Lest I be misunderstood, I am not trying to suggest that either Jacques or Paolo for that matter knew nothing about combat. On the contrary, I knew Jacques as a fierce and formidable fighter, I had seen him in action. What I had briefly seen of Paolo indicated to me that he, too, was very good. But I have been studying and practising martial arts since I could barely walk and have had the advantage of learning from incredibly skilled and knowledgeable individuals who analysed and thought deeply about their art and whose skill had transcended the mere physical into the realm of the metaphysical. I was, quite simply, in a different category. Jacques broke the silence first.

"Let's go inside and have some breakfast. Then we'll have to get Paolo on his way." He turned and started to walk towards the house. I followed and Paolo fell in beside me,

"That was great." he said, "The way you put me down. I've never felt anything like that. It felt as if... as if I was being pushed through the air by some huge, unstoppable force. I didn't really know what was happening." He paused as we entered the kitchen, "I really wish, if you ever have the time, you could start to teach me."

"We'll see. Maybe it'll be possible." I meant what I said. I liked the boy, perhaps a little of Jacques' paternal affection had rubbed off on me. I had my place in Umbria which was not that far from Florence. Perhaps when things settled down, I might take some time to try and teach Paolo. Maybe he could be my first pupil.

Another thing I liked about Paolo was that he cleared away the breakfast things without anyone asking him. In the meantime I spoke to Jacques,

"Where are we going to take Paolo so that he can get back?"

"Probably easiest to cross the border back into Italy and take him to a station in one of the towns there, from where he can get a train to Florence."

I agreed, "Can you manage that by yourself? I've got some things to do and it's best we're not recorded together crossing the border or getting onto the Autostrada."

"You're right. I'll take him. It's no problem. Maybe I'll even drive him home; it won't take more than three or four hours from here."

"It's up to you. There's nothing to be done here today. Nor probably tomorrow, for that matter. If you want to go home and stay overnight that's fine. If I need you I'll call you. If not I'll see you here tomorrow night."

Jacques smiled and grasped my shoulders, "You're still pretty impressive you know. I remember how good you used to be and you still shoot well, but I thought this physical stuff... well we all get older and I really thought Paolo could take you. I'm sorry."

"What are you sorry for? That I'm not a helpless, decrepit old guy, or that you wanted to show off your son? It's no problem. It was just a bit of fun. I like the boy. I was thinking when things quieten down, I might come and give him a bit of training."

I was glad to be getting rid of Jacques for a day. It avoided me having to make any excuses for going to see Natalya, who I had still not mentioned to him. Jacques is a good and trusted friend, but I prefer to keep things compartmentalised as much as I can. Although I was keen to be with Natalya, I did not relish the idea of trying to get into Monte Carlo in the middle of the Grand Prix, so I decided to wait until after 5pm before heading out. It was a beautiful day. I fetched my drawing pad and some pencils and was just making myself comfortable by the swimming pool when Paolo came out to say goodbye.

"We're off now. Papa's taking me home. He doesn't trust me to get there by myself. Thanks for the money and everything."

He extended his hand for a formal handshake. I grasped his hand and told him to take care of himself. He turned back to me from the doorway into the house,

"You sure you'll be ok operating the computer."

"Don't worry. I'll be fine."

I heard the car starting and moving off down the driveway. For about ten minutes I sat staring at the pool, thinking about the operation and wondering if I had missed anything and whether there was anything else we needed. The water looked very inviting, so I stripped off and dived into the pool. It was as delicious as it had looked. I swam for a while and then got out and lay on a lounger to dry off. I closed my eyes feeling the warmth of the sun on my body, allowing myself to be enveloped by the unceasing tzikatzika tziking of the cicadas, until I fell into a semi meditative state where all that existed was the noise of the cicadas and the scent of the flowers and herbs in the garden, with just the faint sound of a ringing church bell intruding.

The church bell was ringing when I woke up. There were four solemn, evenly spaced dongs, one for each quarter of the hour that had passed since the previous hour, followed by the deep tolling of the hour. I counted twelve before there was silence, still punctuated by the sound of the cicadas, although they seemed also to have succumbed to the torpor of an unusually warm Sunday afternoon, giving no more than a desultory tzikka tzikka or two.

I opened my eyes and wondered whether in a week's time I would be in this same garden, lying in this same chair, but with Natalya lying next to me, her arm carelessly thrown across my thigh maintaining the physical contact with me that she had so seemed to crave in the few days I had known her.

I stood up, feeling a little groggy after having slept directly under the sun. My right knee was hurting. I looked at it and saw that it was swollen. I wondered whether I had injured it as I knelt down low when throwing Paolo to the ground. Was my technique now deteriorating with age? I went through in my mind's eye the sequence of movements and was fairly certain my technique had been perfect. So what had caused the injury? Whatever had happened, perhaps this was payment for intolerable vanity. I had been a little irritated by Jacques' proud boast to me of Paolo being a kick boxing champion. To me, of all people and I had responded with a brief demonstration of my superiority. Or, rather, let us face it, I had been showing off. An arrogant and senseless response to what I thought had been an oblique comment from Jacques on my age and ability. I sat for a minute thinking that I had become increasingly sensitive about my age recently. What the hell. I stood up, my knee a constant reminder either of my age or uncharacteristic pride or both. I limped into the house to find my acupuncture needles and some of the Chinese medications I always carry with me.

After treating my knee with acupuncture I rested it for about twenty minutes then showered, before applying the medication. After I had finished, the knee was feeling much better. I still had three or four hours before I wanted to leave, so I dressed, took out the maps of the target area and some sheets of paper in order to go over all my plans again and try to re-establish my personal sense of detached professionalism.

CHAPTER THIRTY SIX

*"Romance should never begin with senti-
ment. It should begin with science and end
with a settlement." (Oscar Wilde).*

My arrival in Monte Carlo was reasonably well timed. The racing was over and the process of removing all the signs, barriers, advertisements and accoutrements associated with a formula one race were well advanced. I allowed the concierge at the Metropole to valet park my car and entered the hotel lobby, which was crowded with team participants and hangers on. From the celebrations that seemed to be taking place, it appeared that the Mclaren team had beaten Ferrari on this occasion. Someone barged into me trying to push past. I turned to see a young man glaring at me. He was perhaps four or five inches shorter than me and rather slightly built, but the difference in our physiques did not seem to intimidate him in the slightest,

"Get the fuck out of my way."

My grandfather taught me that politeness was a virtue that not only helped in interpersonal relationships but improved one's own spiritual well-being. I therefore had little tolerance for this sort of boorishness and almost dropped the little fucker on the spot.

Self-control and a desire for anonymity prevailed, so I restricted myself to giving him the death look. He seemed to be immune. He probably received ten of those looks every quarter of an hour. He continued in his futile efforts to push me aside and, after a moment's pause, I let him. I was not there to cause a scene, much as I would have liked to. I wondered who he was as I saw people approaching him giving him pieces of paper and books to autograph. Probably one of the drivers who earned in an hour or so what I was unable to accumulate in a lifetime.

I forgot about him as I slipped through the crowd towards the elevators where I spotted Natalya, surrounded by five good looking guys who were probably half my age. I was earlier than I had told her and I stopped, wondering if the waiting around for me was just an act. Perhaps I should just leave and cut my losses, but as I was vacillating she saw me. Her face lit up, she stopped talking, presumably in mid-sentence and left the five young men in her wake as she glided gracefully through the people separating us, put her arms around me and gave me one of the most passionate kisses I can ever remember receiving. As I eventually disentangled myself from her I sighed. She was good this one. She had managed in one brief instant to dispel my doubts. I looked around. The men she had been talking to were looking at me enviously. I straightened up, put my arm around her and started to guide her back towards the elevators.

I stayed with Natalya all night. I was not expecting Jacques to return that night and was due to meet the

Englishman at the Beach Hotel in the morning. I woke early and showered before disturbing Natalya. As I was drying myself off I noticed that the television was also connected to the internet. A keyboard was sitting next to the television. I doubted whether the Englishman had done anything to check for banks, so I googled Monaco Banks and chose three possibilities for him. I obtained the names of different officials from the particular banks' web sites and wrote them down. By then Natalya was stirring. I looked at my watch. Even though I wanted to arrive early for my meeting, to enable me to put the car in the garage away from the hotel, I still had time for a leisurely breakfast a deux in the room.

As I had, up to then, lamentably failed to fulfil my pledge to Natalya not to see her for some ten days, she did not take particularly seriously my parting statement that I would not be able to see her again until the end of the week, Friday. I assured her that this time I meant what I said, but she was clearly unconvinced. Strangely I found this somewhat disconcerting. I was used to people believing me when I said things. I could not help wondering, once again, whether I was perhaps losing my touch. In some ways the rigid structure of my life and my approach to interpersonal relationships was completely falling apart. I felt a certain sense of relief that, after this job was over, it might not be necessary to continue my previous disciplined approach to every aspect of my day to day existence.

After I had parked the car, I used a public telephone to call the banks whose names I had written down, to ascertain whether or not they might be suitable for the

Englishman. I also called my bank in Liechtenstein to ask them if they would be able to make an anonymous, untraceable transfer of around 250,000 sterling pounds to a bank in Monte Carlo. They hummmd and harrrrd a little but eventually agreed that they could manage such a thing.

By the time I arrived at the Beach hotel it was later than I had intended but, fortunately, I was again able to beat the Englishman and do my trick of creeping up on him, even though he was also early.

I wanted the Englishman to make his own choice, without any prompting from me and simply gave him the list of three banks. A Luxembourg Bank, a Monegasque Bank and a Swiss Bank. People are brainwashed to believe that Swiss Banks accounts are totally secret. It used to be true but had not been so for quite a long time. It was not the fault of the bankers. It was all due to Swiss politicians being eager to please their European neighbours, to say nothing of being intimidated by a United States of America, which was very aggressive in pursuing its own economic policies and trying, by fair means and foul, to obtain some degree of transparency from the Swiss. So, as I had rather anticipated, the Englishman immediately chose the Swiss Bank. We took the elevator down to the hotel garage together and got into the British Embassy Audi, which I then drove to the centre of town.

On the rare occasions when I have given it any thought, I have observed that the streets in Monte Carlo all seem to be named either after former members of the Monaco Royal family or after other countries. That might or might not be true, but there is certainly a Quai des Etats Unis (USA), a Boulevard Suisse and Avenue de Grande Bretagne. The latter was where many banks, including the one chosen by the Englishman, are situated. I drove up this street but it was impossible to park, so I continued up to the Place du Casino adjacent to which was a large underground car park. The drawback to this car park was that it was full of surveillance cameras. The Englishman had already noticed this and had covered his face with his hand as we went through the entrance barrier.

As I killed the engine he turned to me and said,

"We'd best walk out of here separately. Have you got a hat or something I could cover my head with?"

As a matter of fact I had. With the proliferation of surveillance cameras everywhere, I made a practice of keeping three or four different hats at all times in cars I was using. I gestured to the rear seat,

"Take your pick." He looked around, turned back to me and nodded approvingly before picking up one of the hats and putting it on, pulling it down low on his face.

"I think the exit comes out in or by the gardens in front of the Casino. I'll meet you in the gardens."

He nodded and slipped out of the car, closing the door behind him. I waited a few moments before picking one of the remaining hats, putting it on above the large pair of sunglasses I was wearing and following the Englishman out of the car park. He started walking towards the Avenue de Grande-Bretagne the minute he saw me. I caught up with him and fell into step beside him.

"I've checked and the guy you need to ask for is Urs Schiele. I suggest you ask for him by name." I was wearing a windbreaker and I unzipped one of the pockets from which I removed an envelope I offered to him.

"Here. 20,000 Euros to open the account. Have you got an ID to give them?"

"I've got everything. Don't worry. This is something around fifteen or sixteen thousand pounds isn't it? When will you be sending the balance of the two fifty?"

"Immediately you give me the name or number of the account it's going to. The maximum it should take will be two days. "

The Englishman's conduct and demeanour were subtly different from the way he had been previously. The most accomplished practitioners of the martial arts are attuned to their environment to an extent that enables them to sense the smallest changes in that environment. Some people describe this ability in metaphysical terms. They say that there are constant vibrations around us, emanations of a primal source of energy, "ki" in Japanese, "Chi" in Chinese. The greatest exponents of martial arts are supposed to be able to harness and use this energy. Although I have witnessed remarkable demonstrations of this supposed energy and indeed, have personally benefited from it, I am not convinced of its existence. I believe something else. An essential element in developing martial skills is the ability to control not only one's opponent or opponents, but also one's environment. This sort of control requires the development of great sensitivity to everyone and everything around. One develops an ability, for example, to sense a hostile feeling from someone across a room. I believe that the most skilful of practitioners develop such sensitivity that they can become aware of infinitesimal sounds or movements that, although they are only noticed on a subconscious level, will yet invoke an appropriate response or defensive movement.

Whatever the source of this ability, I felt strongly a change in the Englishman. There was a new certainty and purpose to him that had not been evident before. It put me on my guard and warned me to be more cautious in my dealings with him. I also knew with certainty, that I would ignore the feeling at my peril. He turned to me as he started to cross the road to the bank,

"Urs Schiele?" I nodded and he continued crossing the road, breaking into a run the last few yards to avoid a car that had appeared, driving towards him without slowing down. I watched him enter the bank, before walking a few yards further on to a cafe with outside tables, which gave me a view of the bank and the street around it.

I was in something of a quandary. It was a problem I had been wondering how to resolve for the past few minutes. I wanted the English officer to feel secure and to know that I could be trusted. To do this would require me to arrange the money transfer as quickly as possible. It only required one telephone call, but I did not want to use a telephone known to the Englishman, that might enable him later to trace what number I had called and thence my principal bank. I had also been wondering whether I could rely completely on the bank to send an anonymous transfer. Ideally I would have opened another account in Monte Carlo. I could use the same name and identity I had been using at the Beach Hotel, then have the money transferred anonymously to that account and thence to the Englishman's new account. This would provide me with an extra layer of security, if things went wrong. But to try and do all that before Thursday would be impossible. I knew very well how banks liked to sit on transfers of client's funds for 24 or 48 hours and, for that period, utilise the funds for their own benefit. Whatever I did, I needed to lose the Englishman before I telephoned. In the meantime I ordered a coffee and sat waiting for him.

CHAPTER THIRTY SEVEN

"Money has no motherland; financiers are without patriotism and without decency; their sole object is gain." – (Napoleon Bonaparte)

Cartwright entered the bank and asked to see Urs Schiele. It turned out that Mr. Schiele was expecting him. He had already been warned that a gentleman had been recommended to his bank. There were several documents to sign and questions to answer. These were put by Mr. Schiele firmly, but in a diffident and respectful way, with constant apologies for having to subject his client to this interrogation, but these days there were strict money laundering laws. Even so, within half an hour everything had been arranged, the account opened and a receipt given for the initial 20,000 Euros deposit.

The Colonel walked out of the bank even more impressed with Traynor. The man certainly knew his way around. He had not known whether or not Frank would agree to his proposition and yet had set this whole thing up within a very short time, so that it had proceeded smoothly and efficiently. He also not only felt pleased with himself but was imbued with a certain excitement at the reality that he was soon going to have a substantial chunk of money sitting in his own private secret bank account. He looked around for the American outside the bank and saw him sitting at a table in a sidewalk cafe across the road. Cartwright crossed the road and sat down beside the American without saying anything other than to order a coffee from the waiter who appeared almost magically the moment he was seated.

After the waiter was out of earshot, Cartwright whispered, "Here's the number" and slid a piece of paper across the table that Traynor immediately palmed and put away.

"I'm going to have to go and arrange the transfer of the two fifty. Can you get a taxi back to the hotel or wherever your ride is meeting you?"

Cartwright had had Ross drive him to Monte Carlo that morning and given the operator instructions to pick him up again at 15.00 at the hotel. He looked at his watch. It was nearly midday.

"Yes. Don't worry about me. I can sort myself out."

"Oh, there's one other thing I needed to talk to you about."

The Englishman sat up, "Yes"

"I mentioned this the other day."

Cartwright looked at him expectantly, "You've got people watching my team." It was said as a statement not a question. Cartwright had thought about how he was going to respond if this issue was raised by Traynor and whether he should simply give an outright denial, but he had eventually decided it would be better to stick to the truth, in so far as it was possible to do so. It would also give the Colonel the opening he needed to ask Traynor about the arab on his team.

"Yes. And, in fact there was something I wanted to ask you that has arisen out of that."

The American looked at the soldier expectantly, nodding his head slightly for the Englishman to continue.

"You've got on your team someone who we have identified as Syrian. He's been having some telephone conversations that seem to indicate that he's involved in planning some sort of operation that looks as if it might take place towards the end of the week. He doesn't seem to be talking about our operation so I wanted to know whether or not you were planning some distraction or other to try and draw my people away?"

Traynor looked mystified for a moment before asking, "What actually has that Syrian been discussing? Whatever it is I can tell you that it's nothing to do with me."

"It's in line with the sort of terrorist chatter we pick up all the time. He's been talking about picking up a package from someone in Marseilles."

"The fucker! I didn't like him from the word go. He's probably using my money to fund his own little gig. He's planning this for the end of the week you say?"

The Colonel nodded.

"That could be ok then, couldn't it? The operation's on Thursday and I assume therefore you'll be taking him and the others out early on Friday morning."

The Englishman did not respond as Traynor continued, "In fact it could be a bit of luck really. Your guys will have a real terrorist plot to disrupt with obviously the terrorists having recruited the others to help them. Unless he's planning something before Friday, it won't affect our operation and will give you some additional cover to throw your team off the track. If he tries anything at all before Friday then I'll get one of my people to waste him on the spot."

"That sounds OK. I can tell you that after the initial surprise, we started to look at the situation in exactly the same way as you. The only problem is going to be if for some reason or other we have to change the timetable of our own operation or he tries to implement his plans before Friday."

"As things are shaping up it doesn't seem to be very likely that our timetable will change. If it does though, then whatever happens, that fucking little arab is going to be gone before he gets a chance to do anything. Anyway, the reason I raised the question of your observation is that I'm going to have to go up to see my men later on today to prep them for Thursday and deliver a few things. I don't want to be spotted or put on camera. Apart from anything else it could make things awkward for you over our arrangement."

Cartwright thought over this request for a minute, "What time do you think you'll be coming up there?"

"Probably not before 19.00."

"Alright then. Try and make it around 8pm if you can. Then call my cell ten minutes before you think you're going to arrive and I'll take my people off watch."

Traynor nodded his agreement, at the same time wondering whether he could trust the Englishman.

"I'll be off then. When should we have our next meet?"

"Tuesday? Midday? Then a final meet on Wednesday evening when I'll give you the latest intel. We can fix a time for Wednesday's meet when we meet on Tuesday"

Traynor signified his agreement, got up and walked away, back towards the Casino. Cartwright watched the way the American moved smoothly and confidently along the street without looking back and was reminded of a sailing boat, gliding effortlessly and swiftly across a calm sea. He put a five euro note onto the table to pay for his coffee and got up to follow Traynor before the latter disappeared from view.

By the time Traynor reached the gardens in the Place du Casino, the Englishman was approximately 300 metres behind the American, watching as the man he was following descended the stairs into the car park where the car had been left. Cartwright stood still for a moment, undecided as to what he should do. If Traynor was going to telephone or speak to his bank why was he going back to the car? He could of course be entering the underground garage as a simple counter surveillance measure. When he had exited the car park earlier Cartwright had noticed that there were at least two other exits in addition to the one he had used and there were probably others, it was quite a large garage. There was little point following Traynor into the garage, if this was counter surveillance he would have disappeared within seconds. Cartwright decided to walk around the gardens to where there were some shops. Either he would or would not see Traynor.

As he walked he was constantly scanning the whole area for someone of Traynor's size and build, because he assumed that, if Traynor was trying to avoid being followed, he would have removed his jacket or even perhaps changed a jacket with some other item of apparel he kept in the car. There was no sign of his quarry. Either he had been given the slip or the man had driven away from the area. He was still looking carefully around as he passed a Cartier jewellery store and nearly walked into a striking looking young woman. She was tall, blonde and slim. As he avoided her at the last minute she directed a delightful smile at him that sent a slight shiver down his spine. She had a confident look about her that told the world she knew all about men and how to manipulate them. Probably a high class hooker, he thought to himself as he watched her walking away from the jewellery shop, confidently swinging her hips. He would not mind betting that that woman would do whatever a man asked. He sighed, thinking about the quick, furtive groping and thrusting under the bed covers that passed for sex with his wife. He stood there, still watching her as the distance between them increased and was surprised suddenly to see her waving and shouting, obviously trying to attract someone's attention, before bending to slip off her shoes prior to running in the direction that she had been waving. He was curious and having nothing better to do, followed. He rounded a corner just in time to see her run into a small shopping arcade. Moving closer he saw that she had dropped her shoes on the ground and was embracing someone. He wondered who the lucky man was. The two broke apart and he could see the man's partial reflection in one of the shop windows. This he had not expected. It looked like Traynor. He ducked into a doorway and tried to get a better view, but the man said something to the woman, before turning and disappearing further into the shadows of the arcade. The girl remained where she was for a few moments before squatting down to pick up and put on her shoes. She then turned, to examine her reflection in the nearest shop window, which she used to adjust her hair before turning back towards where Cartwright stood. She passed right by the Englishman, to whom she gave a quick searching look, before continuing back down the street. At that point he decided to follow the girl. He did not have to do this for long because she entered a nearby hotel surrounded by several parked, expensive and exotic motor cars. The Hotel's name was inscribed next to a logo of a sailing ship, Hotel Metropole. A small brass plaque announced that the hotel was one of the Leading Hotels of the World.

He entered the lobby, looking around for the girl. He just caught a quick glimpse of her entering an elevator. Walking over to the elevators he watched as the numbers lit up sequentially on the floor indicator until they stopped at 9. He pressed the call button hoping that the particular elevator the girl had taken would descend, confirming for him that she had alighted at the 9th floor. An elevator at the furthest end away from him 'dingged' to signify its imminent arrival. It did not matter; the indicator for the car taken by the girl remained at 9.

Partially satisfied he turned to look at the reception desk, wondering if he could get the girl's room number from one of the clerks. After a moment's hesitation he decided to leave it. Perhaps, if it became necessary, he could use Esclimont, or even Hubert, to obtain that information. He walked back to the arcade where he had seen the girl with the person he was sure had been Traynor, trying to retrace the movements of the man after he had pulled away from the girl. By any standard the behaviour of the two had been strange. He stopped by the entrance to some offices and looked carefully at the nameplates. The only name that seemed significant to Cartwright was for the fourth and fifth floors which were occupied by the Deutsche Handelsbank. The fourth floor was listed as being "reception" whilst the fifth floor was indicated as being for "Private Clients". If it was Traynor who had entered, it had been around fifteen minutes since he had gone up. Cartwright decided to find somewhere he could wait and watch the arcade, to verify whether or not it was indeed Traynor he had seen. The only explanation that seemed to make sense to Cartwright for the quick embrace and almost instant departure of the girl was that Traynor was the man the girl had accosted and he had not wanted to be seen with the girl. A small, rather dingy looking café, just by the entrance to the arcade, seemed ideal for observation. There was an empty table in a corner by the window from which he could see into the arcade without being seen. He sat down to wait, ordering a beer and a ham sandwich.

The Colonel had still not decided definitively what to do about Traynor. He could play it straight and take the money on offer or he could just take the first two hundred and fifty thousand pounds and still take out the American. But he could not help thinking that that would be an awful waste of another quarter of a million pounds. He bit into his sandwich, chewing thoughtfully. There was a third alternative. If that had been Traynor and the woman was his girl-friend, he might be able to use that as leverage in some way to extract more money. If he did that then, for safety's sake, he would have to bring in one or more of his men. Did he want to do that though? Ken Collier was a solid loyal man. They had been through a lot together. Could Ken be relied upon to keep his mouth shut? Of course there was always Hubert. He had a bit of a twinkle in his eye and Cartwright had often suspected he was something of a rogue. He might not be too scrupulous about ripping off and killing an international hit man. If they could get their hands on the money Traynor had received they would be able to split probably, say at a minimum, six or seven million euros. He took a deep draught of the beer, still thinking and working out his various options.

Time passed. Cartwright finished his sandwich and was halfway through a second beer. He looked at his watch. He had been sitting there for over an hour. Could he have missed Traynor? Was there another exit to this complex that he had not noticed? Perhaps it had not been Traynor at all and the person he had been waiting for had already long passed him. He decided to wait another ten minutes before calling it a day.

CHAPTER THIRTY EIGHT

In London Featherstonehaugh was lounging on C's sofa. He and C were each drinking a whisky from C's special stock before having lunch with a distinguished guest who was due to arrive at any moment.

"So what's the latest news from our man in the field?"

Featherstonehaugh savoured a mouthful of the old whisky before replying. "His team's set up and has full surveillance of the assassination team. We have no visuals yet of the team, but there are five separate, so far unidentified individuals. Strangely enough one of them has been picked up talking on the phone in Arabic and his voice is being run through the computers for possible voice identification against intercepts from known Tangos. I understand that the point man specifically picked at least one arab for his team in case anything went wrong and the blame had to be fastened on Islamic terrorists. It is sheer chance and a bit of luck for us that he seems to have picked a real live tango. It gives credence to the cover story being sold to Cartwright's people of surveillance and subsequent elimination of a terrorist cell. A couple of the others seem to be Serbs. At least they were talking in Serb. No doubt a couple of mercenaries."

"What about Jean-Michel? Anything from him?"

"His man's been in preliminary contact with our field commander. They have a direct line into the Al Khalifa's security detail and are obtaining real time data on the couple's movements. Jean- Michel's been more than helpful. We're really going to owe him on this one. He's been looking at the data coming in and he thinks Thursday ought to be D day."

"What does Cartwright have to say about that?"

"Apparently, that that was precisely the day chosen by our Operator."

C grunted, "So it looks like we're on target for the end of the week. We'd better tell his nibs when he comes in, so that he can have a suitable public statement prepared for the family." He looked over at Featherstonehaugh's empty glass, "want another while we're waiting?"

"I think I'll wait until he arrives. He's bound to want one before lunch and I don't want to be too far ahead of him."

C snorted, stood up and defiantly poured himself another generous measure of the spirit from the heavy crystal decanter whose facets glittered silver and amber as they briefly caught the light.

"When are you arranging delivery of our other little package to Cartwright?"

"Well, as they're aiming for Thursday I thought I'd courier it out Wednesday night."

At that moment one of the secure telephones rang. C answered immediately, listened for no more than two or three seconds before saying, "Very well sir" and replacing the receiver. He turned to his deputy,

"He's about four or five minutes away. Make sure the underground garage is opened for him and go down and meet him will you."

Featherstonehaugh stood up and left the room without another word. C, alone for a short time, stood up holding his glass and walked over to the window that overlooked the river and a large area of London beyond. It was a grey, totally sunless day and everything looked drab and gloomy, matching his mood. Beneath all his guile and ruthlessness lay a classical scholar who would have liked nothing more than to return to a career of teaching and writing at Oxford. In spite of the fact that he had approved and initiated the action they were taking he did not like it. The Al Khalifa man was of no concern to him one way or the other, although on balance he felt that it would do no harm to teach the arrogant father a lesson that would undoubtedly not be lost on him. The woman though was different. Malicious and, even with a certain amount of cunning, she might be, but he had seen on the television, only the previous evening, a report of her visiting children with AIDS in Africa and had been struck by her apparent tenderness and obvious empathy with the children. If her ex-husband and other members of the royal family were more like her the world might be a whole lot better off. He shuddered as he thought of the resources being squandered on this whole operation.

The door swung open and C turned to greet the visitor who had come for a personal briefing on the up to date situation.

CHAPTER THIRTY NINE

""Oh the night fell black and the rifles' crack
Made perfidious Albion reel". Irish song

W hen I left the Englishman at the cafe I had little doubt that he would try to follow me. I took
off the sunglasses I had been wearing and slipped on
another pair that Jacques had given me. Jacques loved
gadgets of all types. His particular love affair was with
electronic devices and he had furnished me with a special pair of sunglasses that had a concealed micro-video
camera that enabled the wearer to see behind him.
When Jacques first produced them I treated them as
a joke and he had to persuade me to use them. In the
field they actually worked surprisingly well, although
the field of view was somewhat restricted. However the
street I was walking on was not too crowded and I had a
clear view of Frank when he started to follow me. I did
not know how he thought he was going to be able to
track me without a team assisting him. The nearest, easiest place to lose him would be the underground garage
where I had parked the car and for which I now headed directly. The garage had several entrances and exits
and it was impossible for one person to cover them all.
I wondered if Frank was serious about following me or

simply hoping that I might slip up, now that we seemed to have reached a mutually acceptable agreement.

I had been giving considerable thought to the matter of sending money to the Englishman whilst sitting in the cafe waiting for him to finish his business with the bank. After considering all my options it had occurred to me that the easiest course might be to return to the bank where I had delivered the money that was credited to my Liechtenstein account. Perhaps I would be able to open an account there, under the Hassan Ben Kamal name, then use that account as a conduit for the money I was going to send to the Englishman. A problem might be that my previous dealings with the bank had been as Mr. Chau. However, replaying in my mind my previous visit to the bank, I remembered that I had never actually identified myself as Mr. Chau. I had not given the man any name at all, merely referring to the Liechtenstein Bank by name and mentioning they had arranged a certain facility. I had not needed to explain any more. Of course he may have seen the faxed receipt addressed to Mr. Chau, but he did not actually know that was me. All in all I thought it was worth a try. There did not seem to be anything to lose. I had a few thousand Euros on me, enough to use to open an account and if I asked both banks to conceal the source of the transmitted funds it would double my security.

I doubted that Frank would follow me into the car park. His ploy would be to try to situate himself to cover as many exits as he could monitor simultaneously, in order to catch me emerging. The owners of the garage

had very helpfully placed multiple clear signs throughout the inside of the building indicating the various
streets and locations that could be reached from particular exits. I followed signs indicating the Principality's
central post office, which I knew was located in the
same arcade as the bank to which I was heading.
Surfacing cautiously from the subterranean garage, I
looked around for Frank. He was nowhere to be seen.
I walked quickly towards the arcade, anxious to achieve
the cover it afforded before he carried out an inevitable sweep of the area. I had barely entered the arcade
when I heard a female voice calling me. My heart sank.
I should never have ventured anywhere near Natalya's
hotel when I knew I was being followed. I should have
driven around for an hour or so until I was certain I
had lost the Englishman before risking an appearance
in the area of the Metropole hotel. Now it was too late.
I ignored her voice and continued walking into the
arcade but she called again and then a third time and
I half turned to see her running full pelt towards me.
In the few instants when I was deciding whether or not
still to ignore her, she caught up with me and jumped
into my arms. As I held her and received her kisses I
looked over her shoulders at the street beyond.

I caught only the briefest glimpse of a shadow darting into a doorway, but I knew Frank had seen me. I
pulled Natalya further into the arcade, out of sight of
the street, held her by the arms and said to her sternly

"I warned you. I was doing something dangerous.
Now I've been seen by someone I didn't want to see
me. And he'll have seen me with you, which is really

bad. You've got to get out of here at once and try to make sure that no one's following you."

However annoyed I was at this turn of events, I knew it was my fault and that I could not blame the girl. She had no idea what I was doing; she had no training and was simply reacting as any other woman would have done in her place.

"Why? What's happening? Please explain" she was bewildered but I had to give her credit in that her confusion only lasted a couple of seconds. As she disengaged herself from me she said, "The man who was looking at me before. I passed him in the street. It's him isn't it?"

More bad news. So Frank had had a good look at the girl and, at worst, now knew we were connected and at best would suspect it. It seemed the fates had decreed that Frank's future prospects were diminishing in direct ratio to any future I was contemplating with Natalya. As the girl walked away from me and I slipped into the area of the arcade where the elevators and offices were located I wondered whether I should even bother sending Frank the money. Perhaps I should wait for him at the Beach hotel, follow him and take him out as the opportunity presented itself. No. That might jeopardise the whole operation and trigger off all sorts of unpleasantness for me. The schedule of the targets' movements Frank had given me proved I still needed him. If there were going to be any changes he would be informed and would pass on that information. If he was not around, I would be operating blind and would have to implement blanket surveillance on the couple, which would bring its own problems. Then I would not just be able to deal with Frank without having to handle his whole team. I was back to my original quandary over Frank that had led me to make a deal with him. I needed him. That decided, I had to send him the money; otherwise he would know something was wrong. It would be a quarter of a million pounds thrown away, unless I could be sure that Frank was to be trusted to keep to our bargain and I had already decided to take that risk when I first approached him. His being English made it unlikely I could trust him. As a non-commissioned officer in the Foreign Legion I had been encouraged to read French history. One thing I particularly recalled was the label the French frequently attached to the English, "perfidious Albion". I could not remember who had said it, but the warning and the caution it engendered had remained with me. I entered the bank with these thoughts churning in my head.

The man at the bank I had dealt with previously was affable and helpful. But then why should he not have been. I explained to him what I wanted to do. He was quite open about saying that the bank did not as a matter of practice like to be used as a post box for money just to come in and go out again. I thought about this as we were speaking. Assuming the deal with the Englishman went smoothly, I would have to send him an additional quarter of a million pounds. From my point of view one transaction from one source would minimise any possible tracing of the funds. I asked the banker whether it would be acceptable if I opened an account and transferred half a million sterling pounds into it and only sent out 250,000, maintaining a 250,000 balance. This it appeared was more than acceptable. Whilst the man disappeared to obtain the account opening forms I used their telephone to call Liechtenstein to give the necessary instructions. He came back and we completed all the necessary formalities for opening an account and arranging the transfer to Frank. By the time I had finished I had been in there for over an hour. It was now well into their lunchtime and the bank was officially closed until 2pm. I laughed to myself when they apologised for making me leave through the employees' back entrance. If Frank was hiding somewhere, waiting to see me come out, he was going to have an extremely long wait, because the exit I used was on a completely different side of the building from where I had entered.

I made my way back to the car park carefully, without seeing any sign of the Englishman. I continued looking around for him fruitlessly, as I drove out of the garage and headed back towards the Beach hotel. I had decided by the time I returned to my parking place underneath the hotel that I would proceed with Frank as if nothing had happened. Both banks had promised to effect immediate transfers, although these were going to be value dated for the end of the week. What this meant was that Frank would be notified of the imminent receipt of funds into his account, but that the account would not actually be credited with the cash until Thursday at the earliest. I had re-run in my mind several times, the whole incident with Natalya and had concluded that Frank may not have had more than a quick glimpse of me and that it might not have been sufficient for him to make a positive identification. That would be a good outcome, because I was sure that he did not have the resources available to watch Natalya, assuming he would be able to find her, in order to ascertain definitively whether or not we were connected. In fact, if he spent time trying to make a connection between Natalya and me, it would only be an additional distraction for him. The more distracted and confused he became the better it was for me. Chaos and confusion had been my allies for as long as I could remember.

I decided to hang around and see if I could catch Frank when he returned to the Beach Hotel to pick up his ride. It would be an opportunity to try and sow some additional doubt in his mind about the girl and me. I entered the hotel lobby and went directly to the bar area, choosing a seat from where I could see and be seen by anyone entering the hotel. I had been there for around ten minutes, sipping at the beer I had ordered, when a man came into the lobby. He was probably slightly shorter than me, perhaps 5'10 or 5'11, in his mid-thirties, more wiry than broad, but clearly very fit. His hair was streaky blonde having clearly been as exposed to the sun as his face, which had the sort of perma tan that comes from long periods in the desert rather than from the beach. A pink Polo shirt, which seemed completely out of place on him, was presumably intended to disguise him as a vacationer, in spite of his khaki trousers and suede desert boots so beloved by members of the British army. He looked around the lobby carefully, before walking over to where I was sitting and taking a neighbouring stool. He also ordered a beer which he gulped down as if he had been severely deprived of liquid for a long time.

Having almost emptied his glass within seconds, he ordered another beer, before turning his attention to me. I could feel his eyes scanning and assessing me and swivelled to meet his gaze. When he had first entered the lobby he had looked to me like a fairly standard issue British soldier. Close up he did not. He exuded a balance and self-confidence that only comes from having faced life's most difficult trials without flinching. His eyes, constantly surveyed the area around him with a wary vigilance, stemming from a knowledge of how quickly tranquillity can turn into violence.

"Corr, nothing like an ice cold beer in this heat is there?"

He was addressing me,

"Can't disagree." For a moment his eyes remained on me, reflecting a glimmer of interest.

"So, you here on holiday then?"

"No."

"Business then?" He was doing a pretty fair imitation of a cop.

"I came for the Grand Prix." I lied easily, smoothly and naturally,

"Oh yeah."

"Yeah. I'm an engineer with one of the teams."

"Really, which team is that?"

"Toyota."

"How did you do, then?"

"Not very well I'm afraid. I probably shouldn't be saying this but we'd do a lot better if we got some real unified direction. As it is we've got people working in the UK and also in Japan and they never seem to be going in the same direction at the same time." I remembered having read somewhere that a great majority of formula one racing car development was carried out in England and was allowing my imagination to build on that sliver of knowledge.

"Really. That's a pity. Must be a bit of a problem."

I shrugged, "To tell you the truth I was quite excited when they first put me on the formula one project. But after a few years of all the politics, you get fed up. I'm trying to get myself put back on mainstream products. So what do you do?"

He was as good a liar as me, "I'm on a sales team. We work for a division of an oil company that develops plastic products."

"That's interesting. What company?"

"British Petroleum". I assumed that things in Britain were much the same as America and that government and oil company interests often coincided, so that the man in front of me probably had some knowledge of and dealings with the company he had named.

He regarded me with undisguised interest, "You're Japanese are you? I must say you speak fantastic English. You sound American."

"Well I went to school in the States and spent several years there." I decided to change the subject before having to invent my life story,

"You'll have to tell me more about your products. At Toyota and particularly on the F1 side, we're always looking at new lightweight materials and developments in that field."

This seemed to go beyond the scope of his knowledge because he ignored the question and instead thrust his hand towards me saying,

"The name's Harry, Harry Palmer." He apparently thought that foreigners did not read Len Deighton's spy fiction. I hesitated before shaking his hand. My training has left very obvious calluses on my hand that someone like him would notice and, in all probability, identify immediately. I had little choice though; I could hardly leave him dangling his hand in mid-air when I had been so friendly a few moments before. I took the proffered hand and, sure enough, caught him glancing down quickly to verify what he had felt. I sensed an immediate change in attitude in him. He took a sip of his beer and then asked, in what for him presumably passed as being casual,

"So you're Japanese, eh?" I nodded affirmatively, "Something I've always wanted to know. We're all brought up to believe the Japanese are all martial arts experts, you know Judo, Karate that sort of thing. Is that true?"

Without hesitating I responded, "Is it true that all English play football and cricket."

He laughed, "Definitely not mate. I think the favourite sport back home today is sitting in an armchair playing computer games."

I smiled, "Same with us I'm afraid." As I was answering him I noticed him stiffen at something he had seen over my shoulder. I turned back to my original position on my seat in time to see Frank walking into the lobby.

The man next to me stood and raised his hand in greeting towards Frank before turning back to me saying, "My Boss. Head honcho and top salesman."

"Really" I muttered politely. By then Frank had joined us. As he glanced at me 'Harry' said, "We just met, boss." Then turning to me, "Sorry I didn't catch your name"

"Ikeda, Hiroshi" I said with a little bow,

"Yeah, well I was just telling Hiroshi here about the plastics division at BP where we work and how you're the big man and top sales guy there."

"Oh yes." Frank was definitely not interested in any of this. He wanted to try to confirm whether it was me he had seen with Natalya, "Been here long have you?" This was his opening gambit addressed to 'Harry'.

"'Bout twenty minutes,'spose."

I butted in, "Yeh, I've been spending the whole afternoon in the cool and quiet of this bar for a bit of peace, after all the noise and heat of the Grand Prix. Harry here came in about twenty or thirty minutes ago and we started to talk."

A slightly puzzled look passed briefly across Frank's face. "It seems a shame to spend the afternoon in here when it's so beautiful outside. We English don't get to see that much sun."

I thought that was a pretty stupid thing for someone to say when his and Harry's faces so clearly evidenced long periods of exposure to the sun, but I let it pass, after all both Frank and I were play acting.

"I've spent too much time outside this weekend. It's good to be in the cool."

Frank could see that he was not going to obtain any further enlightenment, so he gave up and turned back to Harry saying "We really should be getting going." Then to me, "very nice to meet you Mr... "

"It's OK, it's Hiroshi. Nice to meet you too."

"Yeah Hiroshi, good talking to you. See ya mate."

I let them go without trying to torture Frank any further. I have often had cause to reflect how strangely fate seems to intervene in our lives. I was almost sure that Frank would have told his man to wait for him outside, but Frank had been delayed trying to follow me and the soldier, probably curious to see the hotel and anxious to have a drink, had come in and encountered me, unknowingly giving me the opportunity to plant the seed of doubt in Frank's mind that I had been in the hotel when he thought he had seen me. It was clear to me that this brief encounter had, if not shattered, at least partially destroyed, any certainty Frank might have had that it had been me he had seen. Now he did not know. He was unsure. I was satisfied with this. It was the most satisfactory outcome I could expect to a potentially bad situation. The irony was not lost on me that both of us had been careless and affected by the actions of third parties.

CHAPTER FORTY

Cartwright started the interrogation as soon as they were in the car on their way back to the house from which they were carrying on their surveillance.

"Who was that fellow you were talking to?"

"Said he was an engineer for the Toyota formula one team."

"Did you believe him?"

"No reason not to. Seemed to know what he was talking about. You turning up rather saved me. I got into a little difficulty when I told him we were in BP's plastics division and he started quizzing me about lightweight plastics and how they were always on the lookout for lightweight materials."

Cartwright was silent for a minute. He was thinking that Traynor was quite something. Ballsy. But then that was no more than to be expected from an experienced operative.

"I told you to wait for me outside. How long were you there for?"

"I'm sorry, boss. I waited a long time and when you didn't come, I thought I'd go in, take a look around.

I didn't see you anywhere, but when I saw the bar I thought I'd have a beer."

"And that guy was at the bar when you came in?"

"Yeah. He was sitting there having a drink."

"You didn't see him go into the hotel?"

"No. Definitely not. He was well at it when I came in." Ross was beginning to wonder why he was being subjected to an interrogation about some Jap he had met casually at the hotel bar, "what's this all about boss. Is there something you're not telling us?"

"No. It's nothing. We're on a sensitive mission and I'm just curious about people we come across supposedly casually."

"Well you needn't worry about that boss. He was sitting there minding his own business. Wasn't the slightest bit interested in me. It was me started up the conversation."

Cartwright wondered. It was all a little too pat. But if Traynor had really gone straight back to the hotel after their meeting and after presumably setting up the bank transfer and had just been relaxing in the bar, then it probably could not have been him that he had seen. He wished to hell he had moved in closer and tried to get a better look at the man when he had the opportunity, instead he had held back, not wanting to be spotted and then gone after the girl. He was fairly certain the man with the girl had not seen him. So if it had been Traynor there would have been no reason for the American to pretend he had been in the hotel bar for some time. He would only need to pretend if he had seen Cartwright trailing the girl. Cartwright began to feel very frustrated. What did it matter anyway if he had decided to take Traynor's money?

Cartwright was still worrying away at the problem when they arrived back at the observation post. He walked in, brusquely asking whether there was anything new to report. There was not. Cartwright went into the kitchen to look for a beer. There were several empty bottles but nothing else. He called out to Ross irritably,

"Ross go out will you and get a couple of dozen bottles of beer. Here's some cash."

Andy looked at MacCallister, "what's wrong with the old man?"

MacCallister shrugged and resumed fiddling with the electronic equipment in front of him.

Cartwright remained restless even after he had drunk a couple of the beers Ross returned with. He tried to concentrate on writing up a surveillance report but eventually gave up and called Hubert. He wanted to keep the GIGN people happy and not make them too curious. After satisfying Hubert's questions he spent some time at the monitoring equipment to distract himself. The men they were watching seemed simply to be relaxing. They either spent their time by the pool or were eating in the kitchen. Neither was their conversation very enlightening. It was mostly about the women they had slept with or people they had killed. The arab hardly talked and seemed to be keeping very much to himself.

Cartwright had put his cell phone on vibrate so that no one would hear it ringing. At first he did not notice the vibrations until he suddenly became aware of the insistent buzzing in his trouser pocket.

"I'm going to be there in about fifteen minutes."

Cartwright checked his watch. It was a little after 7.30pm. Whatever he chose to do there was no necessity for the men to know anything about Traynor at this stage. He stretched out his arms, pretending to stifle a yawn,

"Listen lads. If you ask me nothing's going to happen for the next three or four hours. I'd say it's going to be a repeat of last night's sitting around talking crap. Why don't we all go out for a bite this time."

"You sure, boss?" Ken Collier was wondering what had brought about this blatant departure from SOP (standard operating procedure).

"Yes, I'm sure. Of course if anyone is so devoted to this job that he wants to stay behind he's welcome to do so." The chorus of assenting voices indicated that everyone was of the same opinion as their Colonel. They were out of the house and on their way to the local restaurant, within ten minutes.

Perhaps ten minutes after that, a dark grey Audi drew up and parked five hundred metres down the road from the house where Traynor's team had settled in. Traynor got out and looked around, almost seeming to sniff the air like a wild animal testing its environment, before reaching into the car for a large bag and gliding silently on his rubber soled shoes through the darkness towards where his team were housed. He hoped that Cartwright had been able to distract his SAS team, otherwise he was almost certain to be picked up by any thermographic cameras that the English were undoubtedly using.

Surveilled or not, there had been no time to set up a more secure method of making contact with his group. Although it entailed climbing over a fence, Traynor took the precaution of entering the house through the garden on the side furthest away from where he was almost certain the English had set up their surveillance, thus minimising any possibility of his being lit up by the English equipment.

His careful, clandestine arrival, raised immediate concerns with his team, particularly when he insisted on meeting in the kitchen, which was located on the same side of the house from which he had entered.

It was one of the Serbs who first voiced the concerns that it was clear the whole team shared, "Are we being watched?"

"I don't believe so," lied Traynor, "but we're in the middle of an operation and operational security requires me to act as if we are under surveillance."

The team listened in silence. It was obvious to Traynor, from the sceptical looks on their faces, that they were not convinced by what he had said. There was little point in dwelling on the subject or discussing it further and, if Frank had lifted the surveillance Traynor did not know when it would be re-imposed, so he came directly to the point, opening and delving into the bag he had carried to the house,

"I've got some weapons. Side-arms. As well as uniforms you're going to need."

He removed a smaller bag from the holdall, unzipped that in its turn and placed the five handguns which had been in it on the table. There were two 9 mm Glock automatics, a 9mm Beretta, a Smith & Wesson revolver and a 9mm SIG automatic. He handed a Glock to each of the two Serbs, the Beretta to the Russian, the SIG to the Syrian and the revolver to the Croat. Each of them checked the weapons that had been handed to them, noting that they contained full magazines in the case of the automatics. The Croat's gun was fully chambered.

"You're unlikely to need these, but, just in case... "

What he failed to say was that all the weapons had been supplied by Jacques and that he had been very careful to ensure that the SIG had gone to the Syrian. This was because Jacques had carefully filed down the firing pin so that even though the gun was fully loaded, it would not be able to be fired.

Traynor then told the team that the operation was almost certainly on for Thursday night and that he wanted to arrange a rehearsal on Tuesday evening. He gave them a time and marked a spot on the map where they could meet using the car and motorbikes to make their way to the rendezvous point.

Having answered all questions, Traynor prepared to make his way out by the same route through which he had arrived. The Russian was nearest to the door and Traynor touched him lightly on the arm to indicate that the Russian should accompany him. Out in the darkness of the garden and away from the others, Traynor told the big Russian that he did not trust the

Syrian and that the gun given to the arab had been sabotaged so that it would not fire. He asked the Russian to pass on the information to the others so that no one exchanged weapons with the arab. He also told the Russian to ensure that he and the others kept an extra special eye on the Syrian and make sure that under no circumstances did he leave the villa. If he tried to leave the villa he was to be restrained. The Russian nodded his acceptance, a brief smile crossing his face.

Traynor was out of the villa and back at the safe house he was sharing with Jacques before the English SAS team had even finished their meal.

CHAPTER FORTY ONE

As far as the English were concerned the following day was uneventful. It was just more of the same. That was until the early evening. Then suddenly at around 18.30, without any prior warning, the people they were watching seemed to be preparing themselves to leave. MacCallister was on surveillance at the time with Andy. He immediately went into the room where Cartwright was sitting talking to Ken Collier.

"Boss. It looks like they're on the move. Are we going to mount up and follow them?"

Cartwright had, earlier in the day, gone out for his meeting with Traynor. The meeting had been routine, with a final meet arranged for 17.30 the following day, the day before the operation. The Colonel had been forewarned by the American that his team would be going out on the Tuesday evening for a rehearsal. Now, as his men looked at him seeking a decision for a course of action, he pretended to think, as if he was weighing up the different alternatives. He knew Traynor's team would be returning to their villa some time later that night, but wanted to be careful not to let slip to any one of his men the true nature of what they were doing. Eventually he answered,

"Does it look as if they're packing up completely or are they just going out?"

"No. They're definitely not packing up, boss."

"Then I don't think we should follow. We can't afford to let them know they're being watched. Depending on where they're going, we don't have enough people or vehicles to follow them without the danger of giving ourselves away."

"But, boss we could always break off if it looked like they'd made us." MacCallister started to argue.

"Yes. But we've got to assume these people are very well trained. They might not give any indication they know they're being followed and it's not beyond the realm of possibility that they could turn it around, make us think we've lost them and then start following us back."

"Yeh boss, but we could deal with that."

"I don't want to have to deal with that. Our orders are very clear. Watch them. Report on them. Don't do anything to jeopardise the surveillance. It's very simple. We can't afford even the slightest chance of them finding out we're here. What I will do is report to London, then they can do whatever they can from there. In any event everything we're passing back is being collated with the intel they're getting from satellite."

"OK boss," MacCallister's voice and demeanour showed that he was disappointed. Collier took the opportunity to intervene,

"If they're all leaving the house, why don't we take the opportunity to go in and put in video and mikes.

We could improve our intake 100 per cent. As you know boss, at the moment we're missing a lot of what is going on inside the target house."

Cartwright had been wondering when someone was going to come up with that suggestion, "It's a good idea. I'd better speak to London first, though. It's up to them. They might be worried that any stuff we put in the house could be detected. We don't know how or how often they're sweeping the place. But it'd be SOP (standard operating procedure) to carry out a sweep after the house had been left empty."

Collier and MacCallister both nodded their agreement as Cartwright reached for the secure phone he used to speak to Featherstonehaugh.

"Mark? Frank. Got a little problem on which I'd appreciate your input." He went on to explain what was happening and the opportunity they had to plant listening devices and video feedback into the house they were watching. Featherstonehaugh listened in silence before exploding,

"For Christ's sake, Frank, you know we can't do any of that. We don't want your people to hear too much. What are you thinking of?"

"I know all that Mark. This is a fine line and we all understand that you are getting a lot of information that we know nothing about and that it is of the utmost importance that the subjects do not know they are under surveillance. So, I've got that right have I? The absolute priority is that they do not suspect any surveillance, even at the expense of obtaining extra intel."

"Oh I see. Thank God, Frank. I thought for a minute there you'd gone off your head. You're speaking for the benefit of your men are you?"

"That is absolutely correct, Mark. My men are on top of things. We're just a little eager to find out whatever we can. But I'll make sure everyone understands the priorities."

"Thursday's still on is it Frank?"

"As far as I know."

"That means you'll be moving in on what... Friday morning?"

"That's about right. You'll let me know will you if you get any further intel that might require us to move in pre-emptively?"

"Just get on with it Frank. You've said enough to cover yourself. Let's not have any more unnecessary phone calls shall we? Goodbye."

Cartwright switched off the telephone and turned to his men who were clustered around him expectantly.

"Our job is to watch and listen. We are just a part of a much larger operation and we are not allowed to take any action that might jeopardise it. We will probably be given, at very short notice, instructions to take out this cell as quietly and efficiently as we know how to do. There is a possibility that we'll be given the ok for the end of this week."

An almost tangible ripple of excitement went through the room. Action was the reason these men had gone through the agony of selection for the Regiment. All of them recognised how important surveillance was and they were all experts at it. But the truth was, static surveillance, for the most part, was no more than boring routine. If it were not for the prospect of future action the surveillance would, for most of them, have been unsupportable.

CHAPTER FORTY TWO

The following two days were more of the same for Cartwright's team. The cell they were watching had returned to their villa late on Tuesday night, apparently in good humour, from the snatches of conversation that had been picked up. The only anomaly was that one of the terrorist cell had returned a couple of hours after the others. The British soldiers wondered about this but heard nothing to enlighten them.

The five men in Traynor's team had indeed been pleased with the way their rehearsal had proceeded. They had worked well as a team and four of them had returned to the villa confident that they would be able to block the tunnel entrances for at least five minutes, before disappearing in the general confusion that was likely to follow whatever it was that Traynor was going to do in the tunnel. Their employer had been extremely tight lipped about the precise details of the operation and had made it clear to his team that the only concern they needed to have was to make sure that each of them performed his assigned task efficiently.

The fifth, the Croat, had followed Traynor to Cannes after the rehearsal at the tunnel. Traynor wanted him to be thoroughly familiar with the location from which the targets were scheduled to leave Cannes on the Thursday night. The American had already carried out a detailed reconnaissance of the area around the Palais des Festivals, which the couple's schedule had indicated as being where their evening engagement was to take place. It was late when they arrived and traffic was light. Having parked the two cars a few blocks away from the Palais, they walked all around the neighbourhood until the Croat was satisfied he was sufficiently familiar with the area. They noted the various potential exits from the Palais accessible to motor vehicles. The principal entry points were the main entrance and adjacent entry points for celebrities and people with particular accreditation. The artists' entrance was at the side of the building. All these entry points and a further Riviera entrance to an adjoining building, ultimately led out to the Croisette, which is the main road running along the Cannes sea front. They were able to choose a sufficiently close location to enable all the exits to be monitored, which would also allow the Croat quickly to fall in behind the couple's vehicle when he saw them leave. The position they chose was so convenient that it enabled an observer with binoculars to read some of the posters advertising events at the Palais. The Croat tried to pump Traynor for information about the hit,

"I've got to know who I'm looking out for. If I don't know, how will I be able to follow them? I can't just get in the pack with the press and hope everyone's following the right person. Haven't you got any pictures or anything I can look at before, to identify them?"

"Don't worry about identification. It's not going to be a problem. You'll recognise them when you have to. I'll tell you who it is when you need to know, when we all head out. And you'll be the only one I will tell. And I don't want you telling any of the others. Can I rely on you?"

The Croat nodded. He was intrigued. He looked at Traynor thinking carefully before trying again, "So it must be someone famous. Someone I'll know at once. Film Festival. I know, film stars. Must be a film star. Yes?"

"I've said you'll know when I tell you. Stop asking me fucking questions. I'm paying you to do a job not to run a fucking quiz show."

If the Croat had learned one thing in his career, it was when to shut up. He stopped asking questions. Indeed he stopped speaking altogether, meekly following Traynor back to the cars. The American turned to him as he got into the car, "You're sure you can find your way back here and out back to Monte Carlo again?"

"I'm sure, but let's just go out of town and back here again one more time. This time let me go in front. Flash me once if you think I'm going wrong."

He did not go wrong and within half an hour the two cars were driving back to Monte Carlo with the Croat in the lead. As they were approaching the exit to the Principality, Traynor called the car in front on one of the walkie-talkies he had previously distributed to all members of his team,

"The next turn off is the one to MC. I'm going there but you needn't."

"Roger that. Should I continue to base?"

"Affirmative. Unless I contact you we'll be meeting up Thursday at 17.00 at pre-arranged rv"

"Roger. Understood. Over and out."

In the SAS house, although the routine that had been established for the surveillance was being followed, the air was tense with barely suppressed excitement and anticipation of an impending operation. The undercurrent of expectation was fuelled by an intercept made on the Wednesday afternoon. It was another Arabic telephone conversation made from the garden of the villa under observation. The translation reported to Cartwright was to the effect that the operation was going active and that unless a further telephone call was made to cancel, Friday was going to be when the package would be collected, Allah be praised. The choice, checking and preparation of weapons and equipment was quietly commenced by every member of the group.

Amongst the SAS team it was only Cartwright who, after his conversation with Traynor on the subject, was still wondering about the vagaries of fate that had so conveniently placed an apparent real terrorist into the midst of the people recruited by Traynor. He realised, of course, that Traynor had deliberately recruited an arab as one of the team, for potential use as a plant in substitution for himself under the arab identity documents, but he had accepted what he had been told by the American and was sure that it was nothing more than a bizarre and amazing coincidence that had led to that member of the team making telephone calls that, to the experienced SAS group, seemed more than suspicious.

Cartwright himself received a secure call towards the middle of the Wednesday afternoon.

"Frank. Mark."

"Yes"

"I have a courier bringing you a package for delivery to your man. The courier will explain the contents. I would stress that it is of the utmost importance that the package is transmitted on and that the contents become part of the overall operation. The courier will be arriving around 21.30. Jean-Michel's man has been told to be on hand to assist clearance. Would you call to arrange an earlier rv point? The same chap will also have updates for all the information you have so far. Obviously you'll have to make contact with the other group in order to pass on everything."

"Understood. I'll get onto that immediately. Anything else."

"Just good luck and good hunting."

"Thank you."

Cartwright had no sooner finished this conversation than he was calling the number Esclimont had given him. As he spoke and discussed a time for a suitable rendezvous in Nice, he calculated how long he would need for the earlier meeting he had fixed with Traynor. He finally agreed to meet Esclimont at the hotel in Nice an hour and half prior to the courier's expected arrival. This would leave him with a couple of hours to go over details again with Traynor and arrange a further, later, meeting for a final briefing and delivery of Featherstonehaugh's package to the American, whatever it was. Before the end of their conversation, Esclimont told Cartwright to park his vehicle before the meeting, as they would be travelling to the airport in an official car.

Looking at his watch the Colonel decided that there was nothing he could do where he was and that he might as well leave for his first meeting. He might perhaps, for once, get there before the American and be able to have a quiet drink on his own, without his men constantly around him trying to second guess his orders.

He did indeed arrive before Traynor. When the American arrived the meeting was affable, without any of the pre-operation tension that was now permeating the SAS team. Cartwright was surprised and yet not surprised that the man in from of him seemed completely relaxed and, apparently, free from any stress or anxiety about the imminent action. The Colonel had, in the course of his career, been in contact with and, indeed, commanded many highly trained, experienced operatives; men who, almost without exception, had proved their ability to maintain a cool head under fire, probably many times over. Looking at the man sitting facing him, the SAS officer reflected that, on not one occasion during their various meetings, had Traynor seemed anything other than completely calm. No, it went further than that. The American positively exuded a rather contagious sense of serenity that the Colonel could not recall ever having seen in anyone else. Cartwright found the man's calm rather chilling and he gave an involuntary shudder as he wondered, not for the first time, whether he was capable of going up against this man. Perhaps, after all, his wisest course might be the simplest; honour his agreement with the American. His curiosity overcame his usual reticence towards the American. Swallowing the last of the glass of beer he had ordered whilst waiting for Traynor, he leaned slightly forward towards the other man and asked,

"I'm curious. Obviously I've worked with a lot of cool headed operators like you, but here we are, some twenty four hours before a big operation and you don't seem to be the slightest bit nervous or stressed about it. In my experience everyone gets a little tense just before the jump off point. Just between the two of us, professional to professional, do you really feel as calm as you appear?"

Traynor did not in any way change his posture or even move, yet the easy going geniality he had been showing instantly changed to a chill hardness that the Colonel found unnerving. He looked at the SAS officer for perhaps a full minute, with the cold, detached, slits of eyes that the Englishman sometimes found almost reptilian, before replying,

"Just between professionals then" he leaned towards the Colonel, his voice soft, mellifluous and brittle at the same time, "I'm probably not like anyone you've ever known. You're a soldier and you probably compare me to other soldiers you know or have known. It's true I was in the military, one way or another, for probably most of my life, but I've never really been a soldier. I come from a long line of warriors. A line going back hundreds of years, of people whose only interest was in perfecting... " he paused for a moment as he searched for what he considered the appropriate way to convey what he intended,

"... perfecting what is like two sides of the same thing, the art of killing and the art of dying. The art of death. I've never tried to explain this to anyone before, so I may not be making it easy to understand, but I was taught and I believe, that killing and dying are like the two edges of a sword. Both edges are equally sharp. Sometimes you use one edge sometimes the other, whichever is appropriate to the circumstances. What is important is the technique you use, not whether you live or die." He looked searchingly at the Englishman who was now looking a little bewildered.

"I don't think you understand what I am trying to explain. I'll try and put it more simply without any philosophy. When you go into a battle, combat, an operation, you don't want to die. You might even worry about dying. And when it's over and you've survived, you feel relief that you've come through it unharmed." He stopped and gestured to the waiter who was just passing their table, "another beer for my friend and... do you have sake?"

"I think we do. I'll check for you sir. Would you like it warm or cold?"

"Cold is ok."

Turning back to Cartwright, "Sorry Frank, talking about all this Japanese shit made me suddenly really feel like having some sake."

Frank gestured for him to continue, "so, as I was saying, you come through a fight alive and you're relieved. When I go into a fight I don't think about dying at all. Maybe I did, occasionally, a long, long time ago, but I certainly haven't for years. I think only about winning; destroying my opponents. And when a battle, operation, whatever, is over, I don't feel relief at having survived. I go over what I did in my mind, analysing the whole thing and wondering in what ways I might have improved my technique. Of course it's not quite the same with a gun, but there's still technique involved. Even with a long gun, at a distance. There's a lot of technique, as I'm sure you know. So, anyway, I'm not frightened or nervous because I've nothing to be nervous about. Either I win or I'm dead. In a sense we're all dead anyway, we just sometimes don't know when to lie down. That's it. In the end it's as simple as that."

From his position sitting opposite the American Frank contemplated Traynor, sipping from his glass of sake, wondering if he really believed what he had just said or whether it was all bullshit. Watching the American's calm demeanour he decided that perhaps it was not bullshit.

"Well, thanks for that insight. Tell me one thing." Traynor nodded his assent,

"How do you get yourself into this mental state, so that you don't have any fear of death? I mean, it's all very well in theory, but how do you do it in practice?"

Traynor shrugged, he was no longer interested in prolonging this conversation "I don't know. Training perhaps. My training started even before I could walk. I've been lucky enough to have had very special masters."

"Who, when?" The Colonel was interested in pressing, to obtain as much information as he could.

"I think I've said enough, Frank. Enough that you'll know I'm not an ordinary person and not someone you want to have up against you."

Cartwright took what was said as the warning he was sure it was intended to be and duly noted it. He looked at his watch. Time to leave. As he finished his drink, he told Traynor that he was going to collect one more piece of equipment that the American would need. Traynor frowned, "What is it? I've got everything I need."

"Frankly, I don't know. I have no idea. All I know is that my masters in London told me they're sending something important that you'll need. I'm picking it up later on. I can either give it to you tonight or tomorrow morning."

Traynor sat silently for some seconds, wondering what this new piece of equipment could be. "Later tonight would be better. I want to have everything in place by tomorrow." He changed tack, "Have you got any further intel for me? Any changes of plan? Anything like that?"

"I'll know that later as well. I'll tell you when I give you the thing, whatever it is. So can we meet here later? Say, around 22.30, 2300?"

Traynor nodded affirmatively as he got up and offered a handshake to the American, who accepted the proffered hand with his usual iron grip. Within minutes Cartwright was on the road to Nice.

Cartwright had arranged to meet Esclimont at the bar of the hotel in Nice where he had retained the rooms for his group even though they were for the time being quartered in the house from which they were carrying out their surveillance.

The Frenchman was as immaculately dressed as he had been when the Colonel had first met him. His manner, however, was less condescending and considerably friendlier. Cartwright wondered whether the nearly empty wine glass in front of the Frenchman had anything to do with the warmer atmosphere between them.

"Would you like a glass of wine? We have maybe an hour or so. It will take us no more than fifteen minutes to get to the airport."

"Thank you. I'll have the same as you."

Esclimont signalled the barman, who immediately brought over a glass which he half filled with red wine before topping up the Frenchman's glass.

Cartwright left his glass untouched until forced to drink by Esclimont raising his glass to the SAS man in salutation, before drinking. Even to Cartwright's untutored palate the deep red, almost purplish, wine tasted good.

"Chateau Leoville Poyferre '96. A fine St. Julien at a not outlandish price. That is what we have expenses for, non?"

"I suppose. Actually it's very good I must say."

"You are not a wine connoisseur I think? A beer man probably, like all good English." Esclimont looked at him keenly with sharp, bright, bird like eyes.

"I normally prefer beer" Cartwright admitted, "although we do drink wine in the officers' mess. And Port." He added.

"Ah yes, Port. Something of an English speciality I think."

Cartwright frowned, "I believe Port comes from Portugal"

"Yes, I know, but nearly all the important producers are, if not now, then originally, English families, Taylors, Warre, Croft."

"Oh. Yes. I suppose you're right. I've never thought about it. Tell me, do you have any news at all for me? Any changes to the schedules you gave me?" He asked casually.

"As a matter of fact I'm going to meet my informant after we've finished at the airport. You can come with me if you like. We're meeting in the bar of the Metropole Hotel in Monte Carlo. Mohammed Al Khalifa owns it you know. My informant runs security for the family. He was a parachutist in the army, like you, I think, then was recruited by our DST, Direction de la Surveillance du Territoire Exterieur, which was merged into the DCRI, our MI5."

"I know what the Direction Centrale des Renseignements *Généraux* is Monsieur Esclimont." Responded Cartwright a little stiffly, using the full name of the intelligence agency that operates as part of the National Police under the Ministry of the Interior.

"Of course you do. I'm sorry. And please call me Phillipe. Anyway Bernard was with them for about twenty years. Then he retired and became head of security for Mohammed Al Khalifa. He likes to keep in contact with old colleagues and new... like me. It makes him feel he is still... how do people put it in English?... still, ah yes, still in the loop." He shrugged, "Of course for us he is a useful source of information about Al Khalifa, who has many diverse and varied interests, as I am sure you are aware."

"As a matter of fact I am. An interesting man, Al Khalifa. Interesting background, too."

Esclimont looked at the Englishman searchingly but was met with a blank, impassive stare.

"So I take it you would like to come with me when I meet Bernard Picard?"

"Yes. I would."

Esclimont drained the remnants of his glass, looked at his watch and said, "Perhaps time for one more. It would be a shame to leave the bottle."

As they continued drinking, it transpired that Phillipe was a great admirer of the SAS and that when he had first met Frank he had not intended to be stand-offish but had been a little overawed to meet the commanding officer of such an elite corps. Now that the ice had been broken between them, he plied the SAS officer with all sorts of questions, until, finally, he glanced again at his watch and said, "We should be going. In case the plane is early."

Esclimont was driving an unmarked car, but was able to transform it into a fully functioning police car by the simple expedient of taking a blue strobe with a magnetic base from the back seat of the car and placing it on the roof. With the aid of the flashing blue light and the Frenchman's skilful weaving through the traffic, they took ten minutes to reach the airport. Esclimont took a road that led around the terminal buildings to a barrier manned by an armed police guard, who raised the barrier for them immediately. Phillipe brought the car to a halt at the back of the terminal and, without any explanation, got out of the car leaving the engine running, before entering a nearby door. He came out a few moments later, got back into the car and drove between the various tankers, service vehicles, guide vehicles and vehicular tugs that littered the area between the runway and terminal building. He finally stopped to one side of an aircraft parking area.

"Our plane's coming in here," he announced to Cartwright. Sure enough, within approximately ten minutes, a large passenger jet came in to land. It finished braking towards the end of the runway some distance from where they were parked. They watched from inside the car as the aircraft turned and taxied, coming ever closer to where they were, until it was finally guided into its designated slot by an aircraft parking operative.

As the deafening whine of the aircraft engines ceased, Esclimont got out of the car. Cartwright followed suit. Exit and entry at this part of the airport was via passenger steps rather than directly into the terminal through the gate. As soon as the steps had been wheeled into place Esclimont was mounting them and had arrived at the top by the time the aircraft door was being opened. Cartwright watched him enter the aircraft and emerge again a few minutes later followed by another man who was carrying a dark coloured bag about the size of a laptop computer case. As they descended to the tarmac the SAS officer stepped forward a few paces to meet them. The man following Esclimont walked directly up to the Colonel,

"Colonel Cartwright. Major Shawcross, Queen's Messenger. I have a package for you and accompanying letter."

"Thank you Major." Cartwright took the case he was offered and a sealed envelope that the Major produced from the inside pocket of his jacket.

"Is there anything we can do for you? Or anywhere we can take you?"

"Thank you sir, no. I'm overnighting at the airport Novotel and fly back first thing in the morning."

"Well we can drop you at the hotel, can't we Phillipe?"

"Of course we can, Frank." Phillipe was now affability itself.

The hotel was no more than a mile from the airport. The Queen's Messenger was dropped off and Phillipe drove back to where Frank had parked his car. As Frank got out of the Frenchman's car, Phillipe said

"Follow me up to Monte Carlo and we'll go and see what Bernard Picard has for us."

CHAPTER FORTY
THREE

*"The strategy of the beautiful woman can
be a useful tool for espionage and assassination." Chinese military classics*

B ernard Picard was pleased with himself. Bernard
Picard had, in fact, been pleased with himself
for years too numerous to count. As a young man he
had joined the French army and volunteered for the
elite special forces 13th Parachute Dragoon Regiment,
part of the French Army Special Forces brigade. He
had been involved in special operations for the DGSE
and DST before finally being recruited by the latter security service. He had been advised to retire after being involved on the periphery of a scandal involving
the French oil giant, Elf. In return for his refusal to
co-operate with the crusading magistrate who had decided to pursue criminal charges against various Elf executives, Picard was quietly recommended to a job as
head of security for Mohammed Al Khalifa, the owner
of a group of hotels which included three hotels in the
South of France and two of Paris's best known luxury
hotels. Al Khalifa was a man with a large bank balance

and an ego to match. Neither was he above stretching the truth when he wanted. As the length of Bernard Picard's employment with the hotel group started to distance him from the DST, his new employer over time, promoted him from his final employment level at the DST to having been Deputy Director General of that organization. Picard's initial embarrassment at his employer's boastful self aggrandisement, that led to his regularly being introduced as a former senior member of the French intelligence establishment, was partly mitigated by the fact that in 2008 the DST had ceased to exist, having been incorporated into the Interior Ministry's Central Directorate for Intelligence. Over time, the final vestiges of any embarrassment he might have felt evaporated, until he almost came to believe the fiction Al Khalifa propagated about him.

Although Mohammed Al Khalifa was often unsparingly abusive about various members of the British Government and their civil servants, he was, perhaps surprisingly, something of an anglophile and modeled himself and the way he dressed, on his idea of a traditional English gentleman. It was therefore not especially surprising that the well-trained and efficient security force Picard commanded was comprised mainly of English former soldiers; some ex members of the SAS, former paratroopers and retired Military Policemen. Of a force of some forty members spread throughout the two principal centres of Al Khalifa's business empire, London and Paris, only perhaps four or five were French. Whether the stocking of the ranks of the Khalifa security organisation was dictated by Picard or his employer's preference for recruiting English mercenaries rather than French, it enabled Picard to defend and maintain his employer's fiction about his own former status. The practical effect though, was that Al Khalifa had at his disposal a private army of well-trained mercenaries, whose skills ranged from close protection to sabotage and whose loyalty and compliance was guaranteed by very generous salaries.

Fortunately for Al Khalifa's detractors, his team of former soldiers was engaged primarily in security and close protection, rather than any more nefarious activity. Unfortunately for the Al Khalifa family and, ultimately for the woman currently being courted and escorted by his son Walid, professional, skilled advice concerning security and protection measures was frequently overridden by family members' personal convenience and preferences. So it was that, on the day before the Princess's fateful engagement at the Cannes Film Festival, she and Walid Al Khalifa were walking and shopping openly around the Monte Carlo streets, accompanied by two highly trained bodyguards who had, for the afternoon, been designated primary shopping bag carriers. Des Greeley, who had served for twenty years in the British Parachute Regiment and seen combat all over the world, was a favourite of Walid Al Khalifa. Walid enjoyed the former soldier's cockney, crude, bawdy humour and invariably chose Des to accompany him. That afternoon Des's fellow bodyguard was a Frenchman who complained constantly, but quietly, about being relegated to being no more than a porter carrying shopping bags from Louis Vuitton, Ferragamo and other assorted designers.

"Look at it this way, mate" said the philosophically inclined Des, "finally we're getting enough to pay the mortgage, the ex-wife's alimony and have plenty left over. That's a lot better than having people trying to blow your head off while you're worrying how you're going to pay your next electric bill."

The Frenchman merely grunted in response. He was one of those rare individuals who preferred jumping out of planes and shooting people to going on shopping expeditions.

This particular expedition had been arranged on the spur of the moment, when the Princess had found her diary empty of engagements for a few hours. Throughout the previous three weeks or so, when she and Walid had been cruising the Mediterranean, the only time the couple had been free of the attentions of persistent, aggressive paparazzi had been when they had been out at sea, well away from any port. Even then, at around the time the American KH-12 Keyhole Satellite had been passing intimate pictures of the two of them to the MI6 Head Office and the Princess's former father-in-law, one of the more enterprising paparazzi had rented a speed boat and been able to obtain some shots of the couple on a private beach, in poses that some prurient individuals might have found embarrassing.

The Al Khalifa response to the oppressive attentions of the media had been formulated by Bernard Picard in consultation with members of his team. The result had been the hurried installation on the Cleopatra of several extremely powerful water cannon, which were then used very effectively to dampen the spirits of intrusive paparazzi. Fear of the dreaded water cannon had kept the intrepid members of the world press sufficiently far away from the Cleopatra that day to enable the Princess and her faithful knight to slip into Monte Carlo unnoticed, to enjoy a day unusually free of the strain of unremitting media attention.

So, on this occasion, Bernard Picard had yet another reason for positively contemplating his efficiency at shielding his master and his master's, dare he think it, fiancée, from the unwanted attentions of the press.

Throughout the extended late spring courtship of the Princess that Walid was so assiduously carrying on, Picard had set up two command centres for his security operation. What he liked to describe as his naval command centre was, unsurprisingly, aboard the Cleopatra. The other was at the Metropole Hotel which was owned by his supreme commander, Mohammed Al Khalifa. Encouraged perhaps by the feeling of goodwill engendered by the ten year old Corton Charlemagne he had had brought up from the Metropole's wine cellar, Bernard was feeling particularly self-congratulatory. He had always prided himself on his, perhaps somewhat exaggerated, connections within the French security services. Even though his balding, bespectacled appearance and 5 foot 8 inches stature were contrary to cinematic images of the fictional James Bond, Picard, secretly, always thought of himself as a real life version of the eponymous hero of the James Bond novels. His fantasy was bolstered by his military background and his having obtained a pilot's license and participating in several fast driving courses. His fantasy was further fuelled and had, indeed, taken on a completely new dimension since Walid's relationship with the Princess. Within the past month, no less a person than the Head of the DGSE had arranged for his personal assistant to liaise with Picard over the security arrangements for the Princess. The meetings were strictly clandestine. Picard had been warned in no uncertain terms that such meetings were entirely unofficial and not to be notified to anyone, even his boss. Flattered into believing that these "exchanges of information" were initiated solely because of his close connections with the security services, Picard freely gave Esclimont whatever information the latter requested. Some of that information related to the social programme of Walid and the Princess, but neither Esclimont nor his Director were above obtaining whatever other information Picard might be prepared to pass on, about the business and activities of Mohammed Al Khalifa and his son.

The next meeting Bernard had fixed with Esclimont was to take place in the bar of the Metropole late that evening. The Princess had been invited to a private, intimate dinner at the Royal Palace by Prince Albert, the ruler of the Monaco principality. Walid, to his consternation, had been excluded from the invitation and, in revenge for the slight, was hosting his own private dinner for selected dignitaries on the terrace of the Hotel's Presidential Suite. Accordingly Picard was more or less off duty that evening. The following day was a different story. After a number of engagements, the couple were due to attend a film premiere in Cannes, followed by a gala charity dinner hosted and attended by all the icons of the film industry. The dinner would be packed with celebrities and, inevitably, there would be swarms of paparazzi surrounding the venue, frothing at their disgusting mouths in anticipation of being able to snatch a sufficiently candid photograph to sell to the networks for some exorbitant sum.

Picard had come to hate the media and the paparazzi in particular. Prior to Walid's relationship with the Princess his job had not involved very much contact with the media. There had been occasional flurries of interest arising out of litigation involving his boss, but nothing especially intrusive. When the Princess had come on the scene though, it had been a completely different story. The only comparison Picard could think of making to the behavior of the press towards Walid and the Princess was that of a ravenous pack of wolves fighting insanely over a small scrap of meat. They were worse than disgusting. Not like human beings at all. Initially Picard had underestimated the way in which the paparazzi might pursue his charges. The epiphany had come when he was sitting in a car with Walid and the Princess, with forty or fifty members of the press surrounding the vehicle, screaming and banging on its every surface to attract the attention of the occupants, faces and cameras pressed up against every window. Picard shuddered to think of it. He had fought in the Algerian war of independence and the conduct of the paparazzi had reminded him of an occasion when a screaming, berserk mob of murderous, bloodthirsty arabs had literally torn some of his fellow soldiers into pieces. He had been lucky to escape with his life. In his opinion there was little, if any, distinction between the conduct of that North African mob so many years ago and the mob of reporters today. The hatred that the paparazzi had created in him throughout the past month had caused him to do anything he could to taunt and frustrate them.

Whilst Picard was imagining the instruments by which he might inflict indescribable torture on the unsuspecting members of the press, who were either ogling the stars in Cannes or drinking themselves into reasonableness at bars throughout the Cote d'Azur, Cartwright was following Esclimont to Monte Carlo. The Frenchman, with the confident assurance of his nation, had decided that English people only drove at moderate speeds and thus, to enable Cartwright to follow him, he was considerate enough to limit himself to the 130 kilometre per hour legal limit universally applicable on French Highways. The undemanding speed, on a nearly empty road, enabled the Colonel to open the sealed envelope given to him by the Queen's Messenger, hold it against the instrument panel in front of him and read its contents as he drove, whilst still keeping one eye on the road. The letter was short and to the point. It instructed Cartwright to give the contents of the package to Traynor who was, if possible, after the 'accident', to use the hypodermic needle within to inject the driver of the target car. The letter further informed the reader that the syringe contained a potent mix of sleeping pills, neuroleptic and anti-depressant drugs and alcohol intended to enter the driver's blood stream and show up on a post mortem blood toxicology screen. Having read the letter, Cartwright stuffed it into a pocket for later destruction.

They were soon in the centre of Monte Carlo. Esclimont did not waste time searching for a parking space. He drove directly to the Casino where he showed some credentials to a doorman who immediately arranged for the two cars to be parked in the parking area directly in front of the Casino and under the watchful eyes of Casino security. The Frenchman grinned at Cartwright as they walked towards the Metropole.

"Being in the police or security services in France is great. We can get in anywhere or do anything," He boasted and added, laughing. "I just showed him an ID I use showing I'm a Commissaire of Police."

"I thought this was an independent Principality" the Englishman pointed out gently.

Phillipe laughed again, "All the doormen and security people here are French. They know who they have to answer to. Anyway the Monegasque police also know they have to accommodate us. And they do."

The Colonel followed Esclimont through the hotel entrance and into the bar where the Frenchman walked straight up to a man sitting nursing some cloudy liquid in a glass. Turning to the Englishman he confided, "He's drinking Pastis, Frank. It's a popular anise based alcohol down here".

Frank, who had become very familiar with Pastis in the course of his evening with Hubert, said nothing.

The man at the bar turned to look at them as they sat down next to him. Cartwright estimated that he was probably in his late fifties, maybe even early sixties. Stockily built, with large powerful looking hands, he was almost bald apart from a monk-like, semi-circular rim of dark hair flecked with grey. He wore expensive looking gold rimmed glasses, which, if the Englishman had known about such things, he would have recognised immediately as having been manufactured by the designer Cartier.

"Bon soir, Phillipe. Tu vas bien?" He beamed at Cartwright's companion and at the same time looked questioningly at the Englishman.

"Do you mind if we speak English, Bernard? This is an English security liaison officer, Colonel Cartwright. He's been helping with security arrangements for Her Highness."

Picard smiling with pleasure, immediately got off his stool and offered his hand in greeting to the English officer, "Bernard Picard, Colonel, Head of Security for the Al Khalifa organisation and formerly of the Direction de la Surveillance du Territoire." This announcement was made in a rather pompous manner with a slight bow and just a hint of a flourish of Picard's hand.

"How do you do sir?" The Colonel shook Picard's hand.

"What would you like to drink? Have whatever you like. You English like scotch don't you or would you prefer a French cognac? Or, if you like I was drinking before a very fine Corton Charlemagne, before I changed to this," he indicated the glass of Pastis with another wave of his hand.

Cartwright chose a cognac, as did Esclimont. Picard turned to the barman and instructed him, in rapid French, to bring a bottle of the special Louis Treize cognac for his guests. He did not notice the amused conspiratorial wink Esclimont gave Cartwright as Picard barked out his instructions.

Esclimont did not waste any time on niceties, "So Bernard. The Colonel here is concerned about the security for the Princess tomorrow night in Cannes. There will be a lot of famous people and many spectators and paparazzi. He needs to know that security will be tight." Warming to his theme, Phillipe added, "There has been increased chatter from terrorist sources which is causing some concern. That is the reason the Colonel himself has specially flown out here."

"You really need not worry, sir." Picard addressed himself directly to Cartwright, "we have everything very well covered and planned."

"Well what precisely do you have planned?" Cartwright asked.

"The journey to Cannes should be no problem. We were thinking of either sailing the yacht to Cannes or taking a helicopter."

Cartwright's heart sank as he listened. If they did that it would torpedo entirely Traynor's whole plan. He was relieved when Picard continued, not yet having become accustomed to the French security man's tendency to give long winded explanations for simple matters,

"But we decided against that. The yacht idea would not have worked because the harbour at Cannes is even more crowded than the harbour here and, getting the principals from the Cleopatra to the harbour and, from the harbour to the Palais des Festivals, would have been difficult and problematic. The helicopter would have presented similar problems. So, logistically and practically, we decided the simplest approach would be the most effective. To have the principals travel by car."

Cartwright nodded, encouraging Picard to continue, "We will go down in three vehicles. We have two Mercedes S class saloons, one of which is armoured. It is Mohammed's personal car. We had it driven down from Paris a couple of days ago." The Englishman noted the familiarity with which Picard mentioned his boss and mentally contrasted that with the impersonal way the French security officer referred to the princess and her lover as "principals".

Picard continued, "The Principals will be in that Mercedes, which will be in the centre, between the other Mercedes and a Range Rover. The Range Rover is for the bodyguards. All excellent men. Mostly English, from the English Special Air Service." He looked slyly at the Colonel and tapped the right side of his nose with the forefinger of his right hand, "I think you know the Special Air Service, no?"

Cartwright looked at Picard stonily and said, "Go on".

The Frenchman became a little flustered at the Colonel's failure to respond to his attempt to initiate greater intimacy between them, "So, where was I... ah, yes... the Range Rover will have four security personnel. There will be another four in the other Mercedes and one with the Principals." He paused for effect, "I personally will be driving the Principals."

Picard announced his personal involvement not only as if that in itself would be sufficient deterrent for anyone with hostile intent, but also, as if it would be the solution to any security problem.

"And the return trip?" asked Cartwright casually.

"Ah yes" Picard raised the right forefinger he had previously used to tap his nose, "the return trip. Undoubtedly there will be many press outside when we come to leave. They have been a constant problem. They are such... they are more than pests... they are vermin!" the final word was expressed with passionate vehemence, before he resumed in a more normal tone,

"They, the press will be expecting us to leave as we arrived, in a convoy of three vehicles. But we will not do this! Instead we will bring the armoured Mercedes and the Range Rover to the VIP entrance of the Palais, the body guards will get out to clear the area by the cars and everyone will think the Principals will be exiting that way. In the meantime... " he signalled the barman to fill up his glass and those of the two men he was lecturing and stopped talking whilst the barman complied with his unspoken instruction, waiting to continue until the latter had removed himself out of earshot,

"in the meantime, I, one bodyguard and the Principals will be leaving from the back entrance in the other Mercedes. By the time the press realise they are not coming out, we will be well on the road back here.

What do you think?" He asked triumphantly, clearly expecting only praise for his brilliant strategy.

"Yes" Cartwright responded dutifully, "that should work. It seems like you've covered all the angles."

"Yes, I think so." Picard spoke so pompously and with such assurance that the Colonel almost felt sorry for him, knowing as he did that by around this time tomorrow, all that self-assurance was going to destroyed in a crushing accident for which, the way things were shaping up, the man in front of him was probably going to be blamed.

"By the way", Cartwright asked casually, sipping his drink as he posed the question, "Do you have all the car registration numbers? The two Mercedes and Range Rover?"

Picard smiled at the Colonel in a way that managed simultaneously to convey, professionalism, triumph and contempt, "Of course." He delved into his left jacket pocket and removed a folded piece of paper, which he slid across the bar towards the Englishman. Cartwright took the paper, unfolded it and glanced at it. Neatly typed in the centre of the page were the descriptions, colour and registration numbers of the three vehicles.

Cartwright nodded his head approvingly, "Very professional. Very efficient."

Picard beamed, enjoying the praise as Esclimont stood up and drained the last drops of his brandy, "So, I think we've covered everything. Is there anything more?" He addressed his question to Cartwright.

At that very moment though, the Colonel's attention was drawn to a woman sitting at the other end of the bar. She was sitting on her own, but talking to the barman and had laughed sufficiently loudly to cause the Englishman to glance in her direction. It took him no more than a couple of seconds to recognise her as the woman he had seen with the man he had thought was Traynor. It was enough to reignite his curiosity about her. He turned to Picard,

"That's a very attractive woman. Do you by any chance know who she is?"

Both Picard and Esclimont turned to look at the woman.

"Ah ha!" Phillipe exclaimed. He looked at the woman appraisingly "I think she is probably for sale, but perhaps a little out of our pay scale."

"Not in my hotel!" said Picard indignantly. He called out to the barman who responded immediately, breaking off his conversation with the woman to walk over to them.

"Who is that woman?" demanded Picard imperiously, "is she a pute?"

"No sir. Not at all. She's a guest in the hotel. She's been staying here for over a week. She has a suite here. She comes in here most nights for a drink but keeps to herself. As you can see she's very attractive and a lot of men approach her, but I think she has someone. She is certainly no pute."

"OK" Picard seemed satisfied and he instantly became more relaxed. He turned back to the

Englishman, as the barman continued to hover by them "maybe you should try your luck, Colonel."

"Maybe I should," replied Cartwright thoughtfully. He addressed the barman, "do you by any chance know her name?"

"Yes, I think it's Natalya."

"Family name."

"Oh, I don't remember. Something Russian, East European something like that. I can get it for you if you like." He was eager to help in the presence of the hotel owner's security chief.

"Yes please."

"Frank! Are you serious? You English always manage to surprise me." Phillipe Esclimont seemed amused by the Englishman's interest in the woman.

Cartwright had already decided to play along with the idea that he was alone in the South of France and interested in female companionship. He did not want to disclose his real interest in the woman, but he now had every intention of finding out whatever he could about this woman.

The Metropole Hotel had a system universally used in hotels whereby all profit centres such as bars, restaurants and spas were connected to the same central computer that logged arrivals and departures and contained complete details about the hotel guests. As Phillipe was gently taunting Frank, the barman was using the bar computer screen to check the woman's details through the room number given on the bar receipts she had signed.

"Here we are. Her name is, oh, sorry it's not Natalya at all. It's Katarina Kolinsky. She's from the Czech Republic... from Prague."

Picard impatiently took the screen and swivelled it so that he could read the entry. He spoke quickly as he was reading, "Czech passport, number bla bla, place of birth Praha, date of birth, hmm that makes her thirty seven." He looked up towards the woman, "she looks a lot younger than that. Maybe it's the light in here."

As Picard read the woman's details Cartwright became increasingly intrigued. He had seen the woman close up in the daylight and she had not looked a day over twenty six or twenty seven, certainly not ten years older than that.

"Ah here"

The Colonel's attention was drawn back to the information Picard was extracting, "she is here with someone. She checked in with a Japanese national, a Mr. Kenzo Inoue from Osaka."

Cartwright felt his pulse quicken with mounting excitement. This was too much of a coincidence. It must have been Traynor that he saw with this woman. He had to find out more about her. But then as swiftly as the certainty of the connection with Traynor struck him, it occurred to him that perhaps this woman had nothing at all to do with Traynor. Perhaps, because he had caught a glimpse of an oriental man with the woman he had automatically assumed it was Traynor, assumed that an oriental had to have been the man he was following. His head started to ache as he considered the different possibilities. Whatever the position it would not hurt to try and find out some more about this woman and her apparently elusive companion. He looked at the clock on the wall above the bar. He had arranged to meet Traynor around 11.00pm. It was nearly that now, but he was determined to obtain more information about the woman.

Esclimont was yawning and clearly did not want to prolong his social contact with Picard. The security chief on the other hand looked as if he was settled in to continue drinking for some time.

"You know, I'd quite like to try my luck with that woman, if you don't mind Phillipe. Why don't you go off? I can find my way back to the car and out of here."

"Are you sure?" Phillipe spoke very half-heartedly.

"Yes I'm sure. You go off."

"Alright then. We'll be in touch tomorrow, hmm?" Shaking hands with each of them in turn, the DGSE man walked away.

"If you'll forgive me Bernard, I'm going to talk to that young lady." In response, Picard smiled knowingly and waved at him dismissively.

Cartwright walked to the other end of the bar and sat down next to the woman, "Do you speak English?"

She looked at him appraisingly, without in any way revealing that she recognised him as the man Traynor had wanted to avoid the other day, "Yes I speak English."

"Can I buy you a drink?"

She shrugged, "Why not?" Natalya was very far from stupid. She had made one tremendous idiotic, naive mistake in her life that had resulted in her being put on the streets of Italy as a prostitute. She had had a hard time and learned a lot. Traynor had appeared from nowhere, like an angel of mercy and plucked her out of the hell in which she had been living and, in a matter of hours, brought her into the world of luxury hotels and glamorous people she used to dream about. She had never quite believed in Traynor. He was a very strange man. Hard, like granite, yet capable of amazing tenderness. In fact he had shown her nothing but tenderness. She was very grateful to him; very drawn to him. Maybe she loved him. She did not really know. There was something about him that was both reassuring and frightening. The Albanians who had bought her and put her on the streets had been frightening; violent, cruel and ruthless men. Yet there had been something about Traynor when he told her not to worry about the Albanians that made her believe in him. The more time she spent with him, the more certain she had become that the Albanians really would have been no problem for him. She had come to recognise the hard ruthlessness that men like the Albanians and Traynor had in common. She saw it now in the Englishman sitting next to her. He had cold eyes. She could feel that he was attracted to her, but for sure he was married and he was the sort who was unlikely to stray from his wife. Attraction was not the reason he was sitting there. She was sure that this man had recognised her and all this was something to do with Traynor. Why not play along? She asked herself. She was, in any event, herself curious about Traynor. She knew nothing about him other than what she felt and observed. He had said he was involved in something dangerous, perhaps she would find out what.

The man started asking her questions to which she responded readily. She had slipped up with the barman telling him that her name was Natalya, but she was not going to make the same mistake with this one.

"My name's Katarina." She said in answer to his question. The way she said 'Katarina' was charmingly coquettish. In spite of himself, Cartwright could not help feeling attracted to this woman. She was so different from his very correct, rather prudish wife. There was something about the woman that aroused him, however unwilling he was consciously to contemplate such a possibility and a part of him was enjoying just sitting quietly interspersing his questions with trivial, slightly bantering conversation.

"What's your name?" she leaned towards him as she asked and he caught a whiff of her musky perfume.

"Peter. Peter Jameson." The first name that had popped into his head was that of one of his junior officers.

"So what do you do... Peter?" she was leaning forward again, almost touching him. He was very aware of her breasts, which were partly exposed by her low cut blouse, "no don't tell me, let me guess." She leaned back scrutinising him carefully. How could she have missed it before. It was obvious. The suntan; the clothes. The way he walked and sat. Military.

"I think... I think... " she looked at him appraisingly, as she slowly delivered her opinion. "I think you are a military man." The throaty drawl made her conclusion sound more seductive than anything else.

Cartwright frowned, trying not to think how incredibly attractive he found this woman. Was his career so obvious that it was stamped on him for all to see?

"Well you're half right. I used to be. Not any more, though. Now I work for an oil company, British Petroleum. I don't know if you've ever heard of them?"

The game continued for another fifteen minutes with each of them telling the other one lie after another, until they both realised they were getting nowhere. Natalya was the first to capitulate. She stood up abruptly, "Well thank you so much for the drink. It was nice talking to you, but I'm tired. I have to go to bed."

"Well, can I see you again?" He said it dutifully, still uncertain whether or not he was wasting his time trying to investigate this woman.

She smiled at him sweetly, "I don't think so. Actually I'm married. My husband is just away doing some business for a couple of days, but he's coming back tomorrow."

What Natalya did not realise was that this final throw away comment was enough to raise Cartwright's level of interest even higher. This seemed to be stretching coincidence a little too far. He stood up politely and let her leave without further discussion. Picard was still sitting at the other end of the bar. The clock indicated that Cartwright was now more than half an hour late for his meeting with Traynor. He hurried out of the bar, waving politely at Picard as he left.

CHAPTER FORTY FOUR

*" When you take the initiative in battle and attack first,
it is desirable to be prepared with a second and third
strategy up your sleeve." Chinese military classics*

I was wondering what had happened to Frank. It was approaching mid-night, making him already nearly forty five minutes late for the meeting we had fixed earlier. The operation was on for tomorrow and I liked to take my time making sure that everything was properly prepared and would run smoothly. I had a drive of twenty minutes or so back to my safe house and at this rate I was not going to get much sleep tonight and I wanted to be at the top of my game tomorrow.

It was nearly half past midnight when he walked into a lobby where, apart from someone at the reception desk, I was the only sign of life. He was carrying a red container that looked like one of those refrigerated containers that people take on picnics. He did not apologise for being late but simply placed the container on the table in front of me without comment and started giving me the most up to date intel on the targets.

"They'll be travelling down to Cannes in a convoy of three vehicles. A Range Rover with an escort of four. A Mercedes saloon, with another similar escort and their vehicle in the middle, an armoured Mercedes. Here are details of the cars and their registration numbers." He placed a folded piece of paper on the table which he unfolded, smoothing out the folds as he did so.

I was a little annoyed. Frank had previously assured me that the targets would not be travelling in convoy. This was going to call for a different plan altogether that I was going to have to come up with at short notice.

"I thought you said they were going to be in a single vehicle. I don't care whether or not it's armoured, that's not going to make much difference, in fact it could work in our favour because putting armour on a sedan usually fucks up the handling, which ought to make the operation easier. But a convoy... "

"Hold on a minute. I said they were going down in convoy. They're coming back in a single vehicle." He stabbed several times with his index finger at one of the numbers on the piece of paper as he emphasised the vehicle in which the targets would be travelling and went on to explain the strategy devised by the couple's security team to deceive the press. I looked at Frank in disbelief. What an idiotic idea that was. A convoy as a diversion was all very well on some occasions, but this was not one of them. Any decent security man would know that it would be impossible for a subject to leave a known location with only two or three exits leading onto a single road when there were crowds of journalists and other people waiting to catch sight of the subject. The most anyone could hope for would be that they might get three or four minutes start before the press pack set off in pursuit. They would be much better off staying in convoy and using the two guard vehicles to block off anyone following. Still, what was bad for them would be good for me.

"Sounds like their security people are fucking idiots. So much the better for us."

"I agree with you. But I'd say that the guy in charge of their security has no experience with this sort of thing. It's all new to him and he's not about to listen to anyone around him who might know what they're talking about."

Frank finally came round to talking about the container he had put on the table. He pushed it towards me, "There's a hypodermic needle in there. After the crash we want you to inject its contents into the driver." He pulled another crumpled piece of paper from his pocket, placing it on the table and, once again, started smoothing out the creases with his hands.

I glanced briefly at the second piece of paper before drawing the container towards me and opening it. It contained a very large syringe, with a long fine needle. The syringe, which was filled with liquid tinted slightly red, had been packed carefully into the centre of the container, surrounded by wadding and cold packs. I closed the container.

"Hmm. What is it? Drugs? Alcohol? Both?"

In response, Frank pursed his lips, raised his eyebrows and inclined his head towards the second piece of paper he had put in front of me. I picked it up and read it. I do not know very much about pharmacology, but I knew enough to realise that just the anti-depressant and sleeping pill element mixed with alcohol would probably severely inhibit anyone's driving.

"Yeah. OK, I get that. They find a load of shit in the driver's blood and no one's going to look any further for the cause of an accident. The only thing is... " I paused, thinking,

"Yes? What is it?"

"Well the accident's likely to kill the driver. If he's dead, how does this stuff get into his bloodstream once the heart stops pumping."

"Well that's why you're going to have to inject it into at least two, preferably three places. If you look further at the instructions you'll see it's very specific about injecting some into the chest cavity to the side of the heart, some into the femoral artery, as high up as possible and, if any is left, the rest of it into the area behind the eye."

I could not believe what Frank was telling me. I was basically being told to carry out some sort of semi-surgical procedure on the driver's body after the incident, when I should have been spending time ensuring the principal target was dead and getting myself out of the area as soon as possible. I could understand the reasoning, but we were not going to have a lot of time, things were going to be very time critical particularly if there was a pack of journalists on the targets' tail. I picked up the note that contained what were obviously instructions from London and read it through slowly. Yes, it was all there, even down to a little diagram indicating the intended injection points. I looked up at Frank without saying anything. Well, when it came down to it they were paying me a lot of money to do this properly and I liked to pride myself on doing a good job, so I would do my best to comply with their instructions.

Another thought struck me. "Is that stuff in the syringe going to stay liquid and stable? It's not going to become a congealed mass that I won't be able to inject will it?"

Frank laughed humourlessly, "I don't think my people are going to make a mistake like that. I think the stuff is treated with some preservative like carbon monoxide or something."

I nodded. That would make sense.

As we were talking I could have sworn I caught a whiff of the perfume Natalya wore. It was a very distinctive, heavy perfume that had a tendency to cling to my clothes. I looked at Frank curiously, wondering whether I was imagining the smell or whether he had been with someone using the same perfume. Somehow or other I did not think that it was the latter. Lest I be misunderstood, I should make it clear that it was not that I was jealous. I was concerned that Frank might have been able to track down Natalya. If he had taken the trouble to do so, it would mean that he had recognised me after all. As far as I was concerned that was definitely bad news. I like to know what is happening around me and I made up my mind to call Natalya after I had left the Englishman.

After discussing the target's schedule and having given me the refrigerated container, there was only one other matter Frank wanted to discuss.

"One more thing."

"Yes"

"The money. Have you sorted that out?"

I was surprised. He should by now have received the pre-advice notifying him that the money have been sent. "Have you spoken to your bank. They should have received notification that the money's been sent although they don't give value for a couple of days."

"What do you mean, value?"

I explained to him that whenever banks transfer money they like to hold on to it for at least twenty four hours, so that they can lend it out overnight and earn extra interest for themselves. That, as there were a couple of banks involved in this transaction, they would each be taking their cut and holding on to the cash for a time, so that, although his bank would have been notified that the money was coming, he would not actually receive the value of it in his account until probably tomorrow, or rather, as it was past mid-night, later on today. Frank seemed to understand, but I was not sure that he did not think I was trying to play games with him.

"You'd just better make sure that the money is there when I check with them in the morning, otherwise we're going to have a problem."

Right, of course we were. I hate banks. It's always the same with them. They are always fucking things up just to earn a little bit extra while at the same time being prepared to gamble on complicated financial instruments that they have people dreaming up and, on which they end up losing billions. Because they are so greedy, they do not realise that normal, boring day to day banking is the way really to earn money without any risk at all. I did not know whether it was Mr. Smoothie-anything you want we'll do for you, in Monte Carlo or the bank Frank had gone to, or even both of them, but I knew I would have to start working the phones first thing in the morning to get everything sorted out. I did not want to have to start worrying about Frank and his team at this late stage of the game.

While we were talking about the banking Frank had been playing nervously with the two pieces of paper he had brought to the meeting. He now looked up at me. "Have you finished with these?"

I reached for the paper containing the descriptions of the target cars, "Well I need this." He nodded his acquiescence as I put the paper into my shirt pocket and then reached for a box of hotel matches lying on a nearby ashtray. He lit a match and set fire to the other piece of paper. It took no time for the flames to swallow it and Frank then crushed the ashes into dust with the match box before getting up to leave. I followed him outside. This time he was driving himself and he no longer had the Citroen. At least I knew another of the cars he was using. I waited ten minutes for him to get clear. I did not expect him to think of following me, but, just in case, walked in the direction opposite to where I had left my car until I found a payphone. I dialled the Metropole Hotel and asked for Natalya's room. She answered immediately and I hardly had time to say hello before she started to pour out her story of having seen the man I had been trying to avoid when she had seen me in the street. She quite impressed me with her eye for detail. She had seen the man before he had seen her. He had been sitting with two other men, one of whom she had found out from the barman was chief of security for the hotel owner. The barman had further confided in her, with the expansive generosity that barmen sometimes offer regular customers, that the third man, the youngest of the three was also something to do with security, but more official and that he had frequent meetings with the hotel security chief.

It did not take a genius to work out that Frank was obtaining his information about the target from the hotel's security man. It was probably just one of those inexplicable coincidences that I had put Natalya into a hotel connected with the targets. Coincidence or not, Frank was clearly interested in Natalya. It was no great leap of imagination for me to assume that he would have been able to have the hotel security guy access the hotel's client information. When we checked in I had to show the Japanese passport I was using so all the details of that identity would be available to Frank. That would enable him to tie the girl in with a Japanese man. He would be almost certain to assume it was me. So I now had to assume he knew I was connected to Natalya and would have to take the appropriate precautions. Even if he found out the girl was using a stolen passport he would be unlikely to do anything about it. If he was considering reneging on our agreement, he would want to keep the girl in play, to use her as bait for me. My ace was that he probably did not know the girl had recognised him and reported back to me.

I now spoke to the girl," Listen, don't worry. You're going to be leaving there on Friday anyway. I'll have to think about the best way of getting you out of there. In the meantime I want you to go through the hotel carefully. Check every possible exit that you can use without being seen. Check where they come out. I'll call you back tomorrow during the day, probably early afternoon. Stay in your room from mid-day."

"But what is this about? Is it because of the passport?"

"No. It's not about that. Don't worry I'll sort something out."

While speaking to her I wondered why I was bothering with all this. I should just have cut her off completely. The problem was I did not want to. I had even been thinking that she was a bright girl and that I might be able train her to work with me. A few years previously I would not have given the matter any thought. I would have helped her out and gone on my way without bringing her along as unnecessary baggage. Still, it was not simply that I had formed some emotional attachment to her. Doing things alone is not always optimal. Sometimes it is better to have a partner and there was no question that, around the French Riviera, particularly around this time of the year, a man and a woman were less conspicuous than a man alone.

I had been scanning the street carefully while speaking on the telephone. It was as quiet as the grave. I started to retrace my steps, going back to where I had left my car, which I reached uneventfully. When one thinks one is safe, nearly everyone, experienced operative or not, has a tendency to relax. That is usually when problems occur. It is the same in combat. That one moment of relaxation or lack of attention is when you get nailed. So, although the streets were empty and I was sure I was not being followed, I still took my usual evasive action and indirect route back to the safe house where Jacques was waiting.

Jacques was still awake when I got back, cleaning and checking weapons and equipment. I gave him a quick rundown on the latest intel I had been given by Frank. I was wondering whether or not to mention anything about Natalya, but decided not to for the time being. I had plenty of time to tell him, if I needed his help to extract her.

CHAPTER FORTY FIVE

"It is always wise to look ahead, but difficult to look further than you can see." (Sir Winston Churchill)

I woke up early to the welcoming smell of freshly brewed coffee. Jacques had even cut up some grapefruit for me. Over breakfast we joked at each other's expense, dredging up memories of some of our more memorable escapades or fuck ups. This sort of humour was all part of a well-established pre-operational ritual to dispel tension that I have found is common to most combat units. With us it was more habit than that we were really tense or apprehensive.

We carefully went through all aspects of the operation. I booted up Paolo's computer and made sure the battery was fully charged and that I also had a fully charged spare. I then logged into the programme he had set up to infiltrate the traffic cams. It worked perfectly.

Jacques and I had decided to travel together on the powerful BMW 1300 K GT motorbike we were going to use for the operation, with me as the pillion passenger. Jacques had prepared the bike for carrying equipment and had fitted it with side panniers, a rear top case and a tank bag. We agreed that the effect of the extra weight would be negligible. Jacques had already ridden the bike at well over its supposed top speed of 200 kilometres per hour. He estimated that, even with the weight of two of us and the equipment, we would still be able to travel at over 125 miles per hour, enough, he thought, to catch up with most drivers. I was not so sure. When I had driven the 5 series BMW from Liechtenstein I had pushed it along the highway between Cannes and Monte Carlo reaching a maximum speed of between 130 to 140 miles per hour. The targets were going to be in a very fast S class Mercedes. I did not know how good the driver was going to be but, potentially, that car would be able to outdistance us. Our original plan had been to follow the target all the way from Cannes. In view of my reservations about the car outrunning us we decided to pick up the car on a winding stretch of road before the turn off to Monte Carlo. We would rely on our link into the traffic cams and the Croatian, who would be following the target, to tell us when our target was approaching.

We had finished packing up the bike, with the dazzler slipping neatly into the tank bag where it would snuggle against Jacques' chest as we rode, when I brought out the refrigerated package Frank had given me. In response to Jacques' query I explained what it contained. After moving some other equipment, the pack just fitted into the rear top case. I had been contemplating taking the hypodermic out of its refrigerated cocoon and packing it in the black combat vest I was wearing over my shirt. I decided not to risk degrading the contents of the hypodermic, so I decided to keep it in its packing until the time came to use it. We had debated the wisdom or otherwise of carrying weapons. If by some chance we were stopped by the police before, or even after the operation, we both preferred to try to talk our way out of trouble first, if not we should easily be able to handle two or three police without weapons. On the other hand, if we were ambushed at any point by Frank and his SAS team there could be a shootout. Both of us adhered to the policy that you do not bring a knife or your bare hands to a gun fight. I was almost certain that Frank would not ambush us. I was satisfied he did not know anything about Jacques or our safe house. As far as he knew I was staying in the Monte Carlo Beach Hotel. He had found out about Natalya which, he had to think, gave him another lead into keeping tabs on me. I was as sure as I could be, that he was unaware I had found out he knew about the girl. There was no reasonable possibility that Frank would jeopardise our operation by ambushing us anywhere near the site of the accident. In his shoes I would have planned to hit my team at their villa just before dawn on Friday morning and then, if he had decided to do so, go after me.

I told Jacques my thoughts about this. After a brief discussion he agreed with my analysis. Nonetheless we decided not to go completely unarmed. We both strapped on handguns and packed extra magazines. I had the H &K supplied by the Brits in Rome and Jacques had a Sig 250 chambered for .40 S&W ammunition.

Jacques wanted to make lunch before we left. He had a tendency to exaggerate about personal matters and he frequently complained that the French had deliberately starved him throughout his service in the Legion. He claimed that it was a result of this that, after his discharge, he made it a point never to miss a meal. My personal observation was that he just liked to eat, even though somehow or other he managed to remain thin. Anyway I did not object if he wanted to eat before we left. It gave me the opportunity to take a fifteen minute drive to find a payphone in order to check with the bank about Frank's money. I was already feeling a little belligerent about their failure to pre notify the Englishman that a transfer was on its way, but curbed my annoyance and started off being polite. My reward for this exercise in self-control was to be told that the transfer had been made and the money ought already to be in the recipient's bank. I returned to the villa and Jacques' lunch, pleased that everything seemed to be on track.

It was a little after 3pm by the time we had finished lunch. Having cleared the table we carried out final checks on the equipment. I had arranged to meet the team at the end of the road near the Monte Carlo Beach Hotel at 5pm. The road there was quiet and there was a small secluded, untidy and therefore unused, section of beach, where I was sure we would not be disturbed. I had arranged a time well before they were going to go into action, as I wanted them prepped and ready, even if they were going to have a few hours of tedium first. My plan was to have the Croat pick up the targets when they left their yacht on the way to Cannes. He would then follow them, install himself where we had previously arranged and pick them up as they left. The two Serbs would set themselves up in a Highway rest area I had checked out a little distance from the turn off to Monte Carlo. The Russian and the Syrian would locate themselves near the Monte Carlo end of the tunnel so that they could move into position at short notice, when they were informed to do so by radio. If everything went as planned and the Croat did his job, everyone would have at least twenty minutes to half an hour to get into position.

I suggested to Jacques that we bike down to the Children's Hospital to see if we could pick up the woman. We drove down on the Corniche, which is a picturesque winding road, threading along the mountains that drop down to the Mediterranean. I can ride a motor bike but they have never been a preferred form of transport for me. I like four wheels and some coachwork around my body. Jacques, on the other hand, was something of a bike aficionado. He was also an expert rider and it was not unpleasant, on a hot sunny afternoon to feel the wind rushing against me as he pushed the powerful BMW through a series of bends. We rounded a bend and Monte Carlo lay spread out below us, the sun glittering and flashing in the distance from its multiple reflections in the windows of the Principality's tall buildings. I vaguely remember once hearing Monte Carlo described as a jewel set between the blue of the Mediterranean and the rusty white of the coast line and truly, there was no doubting the beauty of the scene spread out before us. There was something incredibly alluring about that small area of land squashed into the wild mountain side and crammed with tall apartment buildings.

I spoke to Jacques through the one piece microphone and earpiece we were both wearing. "Can you stop for a moment?"

I jumped to the ground as he brought the bike to a halt by the side of the road. Even the brief few miles we had travelled had made my muscles stiff and achy. I wondered at Jacques' affection for riding these machines. I took out the telephone the English had given me and put in the Sim card and battery, before switching it on. I called Frank immediately it showed service. It rang four or five times before he answered. Suspicious as I am, I assumed he was setting up a triangulation of my position.

"Yes."

"I checked on the package and had confirmation that it's arrived."

"So I've been informed."

"So we're all set? We can start to get into position?"

"Yes, you're good to go."

"No last minute changes?"

"No, but check back with me at 19.30 for final confirmation, before going silent."

"Copy that."

I slipped off the battery cover, removed the battery and then the Sim card which I put back in a small plastic box I kept for that purpose. In the 1980's I had worked on drug interdiction in Colombia with a specialised intelligence unit called the Activity (Intelligence Support Activity), which like other such units is constantly changing its name. This unit used very high tech electronic equipment that was able to intercept cell phone conversations. Using a control link, they could even programme a telephone that had been switched off to come on at a particular time. Since that time electronics has come a long way and I was taking no chances on any telephone I had operating as a direction finding bug on my conversations and location.

Jacques joked as he watched me dismantling the cell phone, "I'm glad to see you're starting to learn."

I ignored his comment, "The Rupert's got his money. Let's hope he really is now fully on board."

We got back on the bike and were soon outside the Children's Hospital where, according to her schedule, the woman was due to be. We parked about a hundred and fifty metres away, from where we had a clear view of the entrance. It looked good. There were probably around fifty press and television people outside, with a couple of television broadcasting vans in the street, their satellite dishes arcing up into the sky from the roofs of the vans.

We must have been sitting outside for over an hour. It was hot and I was sweating underneath the biking leathers I wore over my combat vest and trousers. Jacques was leaning against the bike patiently smoking his fourth or fifth cigarette when there was a sudden flurry of activity amongst the press corps. Simultaneously a black S Class Mercedes with dark tinted windows drew up to the hospital entrance. The car sat low on its chassis indicating to me that it carried considerable extra weight. I assumed that this was the car that I had been told was armoured. We were not too far away, but all we could see was the crowd of press converging on someone, fluff covered microphones waving wildly in the air and a mass of flash bulbs exploding. I caught a glimpse of a tall bodyguard and what I thought was a woman's blonde head being bustled into the rear of the Mercedes before the car shot off, its tyres squealing in protest, with the paparazzi and television reporters running along the road after it, in an attempt to obtain some final shots.

Jacques had already started the bike and I jumped aboard as we set off after the Mercedes. There were at least seven people on motor bikes already in pursuit of the car and no one took any notice of us as we accelerated through the traffic joining the chase. For the Mercedes it was a losing battle. I had thought the car would be heading for the harbour, but instead it made for the area around the Casino. There was traffic and the streets were not especially wide, so we soon caught the Mercedes. Jacques stayed some distance back but the motorcycle borne photographers rode within inches of the sides of the car, pushing their cameras against the windows, trying to take pictures of the occupant.

Jaqcques' calm voice came over the intercom, "I think we can just sit back and watch. If they behave like that, we're not going to need to do anything. They'll take her out and themselves with her. I've never seen anything like it."

Jacques was right. There was an air of frenzy about the behaviour of the reporters that made an accident seem more likely with every second that passed. The only thing that seemed to me to prevent an accident was the Mercedes pulling up at the Metropole hotel. Apparently the staff at the hotel had already been alerted because, as the Mercedes stopped, it was surrounded by a phalanx of security men who kept the photographers at bay and prevented them from entering the hotel in pursuit of the woman who had rushed in under cover of her protective detail.

As I watched, I thought of entering the hotel as Mr.Inoue, its Japanese guest, but dressed in biker's clothes I was likely to draw unwelcome attention to myself. Neither did I want to run into Natalya.

"Lucky we decided to check the hospital. Otherwise we'd've been warming our asses at the harbour waiting for them. I reckon they'll be leaving from the hotel, not the boat. Drop me off to meet up with the boys."

Jacques dropped me by the Beach Hotel which was a mile or so from the rendezvous point. I walked the distance cursing the fact that I was wearing all those clothes in the heat. I had not wanted to take the time to change in the hotel. When I arrived, the street was empty apart from the team members standing by their respective transports, smoking cigarettes, waiting for me. We moved off the road towards the beach as I gave them their final briefing. French motorcycle police wear a blue smock similar to clothing worn by many civilian motorcyclists in France, so my motor bike team was not going to attract any attention before they went into action with their portable strobe lights. We carried out a thorough check of all communications equipment before I sent the two tunnel teams off to their respective locations. The Croat remained behind for his personal briefing. He gave a low whistle when I told him the names of the targets.

"Now I understand why you're paying so much. None of us could figure out why we were getting so much money for what seemed such a simple job."

"OK. Now you know. You also know how important it is to keep quiet about this, otherwise there can be all sorts of people after us. Don't say anything to any of the others. They'll realise soon enough when it hits the news."

He nodded, "We were thinking of staying a few days at that nice house you provided for us, but now I think we should all clear out first thing tomorrow."

"I agree. I am."

He did not say anything, but probably assumed from the leathers I was wearing and his own experience, that I was going to use a bike to approach the target car in the tunnel before shooting the occupants. There had already been hints from other members of the team that they were familiar with this assassination technique. I saw no reason to tell the Croat anything different. I did tell him that he would now have to wait to pick up the targets outside the Metropole Hotel rather than the harbour. We had not envisaged this possibility and he only knew the routes to and from the harbour. Fortunately the ubiquitous in car GPS system came to our aid. I programmed the hotel in as a destination and then sent him off, telling him that I would check in with him within the hour. As he drove off I tried to reach Jacques on our intercom. I did not feel like walking back to the hotel. Within a few seconds Jacques came roaring up.

"I was watching from a little distance away." One of Jacques' many good qualities was that he did not need to be told when to provide back up.

We stopped at the hotel so that I could finally check out. I had only left a few odd clothes in the bedroom which I threw into a bag I deposited with the concierge, telling him I would collect it in a couple of days, which I had no intention of doing. Jacques then drove me up to the Metropole. I was pleased with the Croat. He had parked in an excellent spot from which to observe the hotel entrance. I left Jacques, walked up to my man's car and got in.

"Anything happening?"

"No. All quiet apart from them" he pointed to the gaggle of paparazzi, standing around, leaning on motorbikes, smoking and generally littering the street around the hotel entrance.

We sat there quietly for another half an hour or so before again being alerted by movement amongst the photographers. They reminded me of wild birds being stirred into flight by a careless walker making their way through a forest or jungle. I reflected that someone had to be feeding them information because, within minutes of them becoming active, the Mercedes I had seen earlier at the hospital drew up, sandwiched between a Black Range Rover and another S Class Mercedes. To my experienced eye, neither the Range Rover nor the second Mercedes were armoured. They both rode noticeably higher than the armoured S Class, although the Range Rover did have tinted windows. As we watched, eight security guards came out of the hotel. They spread out between the entrance and the cars, pushing away, none too gently, those paparazzi who approached too close. The car drivers got out of their vehicles and joined the other security people in their tight formation.

We saw the camera bulbs flashing before the targets appeared. The first to come out was a stocky, balding, late middle aged man with glasses. He walked with a self-confident swagger, stopped in front of the cars, turned to a couple of the nearest paparazzi and said something before giving one of them quite a violent push. At the same instant the woman appeared, diverting the attention of the press away from this minor fracas. Immediately the balding man with glasses moved to the armoured Mercedes and opened the rear door for her. On this occasion, however, the woman did not run into the car. Instead she stopped and waved at the photographers who responded with a blitz of flashbulbs. She was clearly visible to us. Surprisingly tall, she was wearing a long evening dress, with obviously expensive jewellery sparkling from her neck and hands as it was caught by the light of the camera flashes. She seemed in no hurry to enter the car and stood waving and apparently talking to some of the press, until a thickset, slightly shorter man with a dark complexion and close cropped, tightly curled, wiry hair, who had been following her, whispered something in her ear. She nodded and, with a final wave to the press, entered the car followed by that man. That was my cue to leave the Croat to start following them. As I got out of the car I said,

"You're on. Report in if there are any problems, otherwise just confirm when you arrive and when they're ready to leave again. Once they start back you know what to do. Don't forget to keep us all regularly updated.

A growled, "I'm not a fucking amateur" were his final words as the Croat started in pursuit of the three car convoy, which was by now moving off from the hotel. I stood watching as, once again, the press people leapt into a frenzy of activity, jumping into cars and onto motorcycles after the targets' convoy. The paparazzi were so focussed on chasing the woman's car that they appeared to be taking no notice of anyone who was unfortunate enough to be in their path. I saw at least two of them ride their motorcycles on the pavement making several pedestrians jump for their lives.

I turned as I heard the low growl of Jacques' bike behind me. He handed me the helmet I had been wearing earlier. I put it on and we immediately became unidentifiable behind our dark tinted visors. We set off towards Cannes but instead of stopping in the place we had chosen to await the couple's return I changed my mind and told Jacques to go after the convoy. I wanted to see at what sort of speed they drove, as well as wanting to check on the Croat, before coming back and ensuring that everyone else was in position. According to their schedule the couple were going to a film and dinner, so we had plenty of time. The bike leaped forward as Jacques accelerated. When we entered the tunnel I had chosen for the fatal act, the roar of the BMW's engine reverberated off the walls, surrounding us in a cordon of noise that remained unbroken until we shot out of the tunnel. Jacques had to slow to pick up a ticket at the toll booth before coming onto the Autoroute. Within seconds of joining the Autoroute Jacques had accelerated hard. It took another ten minutes before we caught the convoy. I was gratified to note that the paparazzis' bikes were not powerful enough to keep up with the cars and we passed them all a good few minutes before we tucked in behind the three cars. Because of the noise and the wind it was difficult to hear Jacques on the intercom, but I was able to catch his confirmation that they were travelling at around 190 kilometres or 115 miles per hour, a speed well within the BMW's capability. Having caught up with the convoy, Jacques dropped his speed a little, allowing distance to be created between us, whilst still keeping within visual range of the cars.

There was surprisingly little traffic and I could not help wondering whether we should take advantage of this opportunity and do our work there and then. At the speed we were travelling any accident would be massive, almost certainly fatal for the occupants of the cars and a three car pile-up would negate any suspicion of foul play. On the other hand there was the possibility that the armoured Mercedes might protect its occupants more than the standard car. Jacques must have been reading my thoughts because I heard his voice in my earpiece,

"We should stick with the original plan. If they come back in three cars, not one, at this speed, we can rethink. Perhaps do it on the Autoroute."

I thought he was right, "Copy that".

The rest of the trip was uneventful. We watched as they drove up to the Palais des Festivals. Another mass of press, more flash bulbs lighting up the night sky, more glittering jewellery, more waving at the crowd pressing in on the roped off red carpet provided for the celebrities to enter the Palais.

Jacques shook his head, "What a circus!" I laughed in response. It really was, particularly for two guys like us who were used to operating in the shadows.

I left Jacques watching the show and walked over to the place where the Croat was supposed to have installed himself. Of course nothing ever goes as planned. Here was the first problem. The Croat was in position alright but he had had to double park because the street that had been empty of cars when we had reconnoitred the area was now full of cars parked nose to tail. I tapped on the Croat's window. He looked up in surprise as he wound the window down and I leaned in.

"What are you doing here?"

"Just checking. I thought you realised, I'm a very hands on type of guy."

"Well I've driven around three times and there's absolutely nowhere to park from where I can eyeball that place," he indicated the Palais with a movement of his head. I straightened up looking around at the cars on the street.

"We'll just have to move one."

"Yeah, how're we going to do that? We going to ask the owner?" he asked sarcastically.

I did not answer him directly "Just wait here."

I walked back along the street in the shadow of the buildings, to where I had left Jacques.

"Little problem. I need some gear to get into a car."

Jacques delved into one of the side panniers and produced a long thin flat piece of metal, about an inch wide and a foot long.

"Will that do?"

"Perfect. When I come back in the car follow me."

I walked back to where the Croat was still sitting. I saw him look at the metal bar I was holding, but he said nothing.

I had already picked out a suitable car parked three cars down from where we were. It was a Volkswagen Golf, a few years old, without any of the electronics used on modern cars to foil car thieves. In fact it was a bit of a heap and the owner would probably thank me for giving him an opportunity to make an insurance claim.

It took me all of three seconds to get in the car and another twenty or so seconds to hotwire it and start the engine. Within a minute I was out of there and the Croat was parking in the place the VW had vacated. I drew alongside Jacques, who started up the bike and followed me as I drove out of Cannes. I did not care where I put the car, but I did not want to get stopped by any inquisitive policeman. I drove up above the town towards St. Paul de Vence. As I was driving along a section of the road that was quiet, with no traffic, I noticed that I was passing a small, tree lined lane. I made a U turn and drove into the lane. It was perfect. The street was unlit and entirely shaded by large trees. It extended way beyond my field of vision and there were several other cars that I could see parked at various intervals along the lane. I parked the Golf about 500 metres into the lane, underneath a tree. Before leaving it I used my motor cycle gloves to wipe down any parts I might have touched with my hands, although with a car like that there was little chance the police would bother fingerprinting it. I stepped out picking up the metal bar I had used to gain entry and walked over to where Jacques was waiting for me on the bike. I handed the bar back to him. As he replaced it in the Pannier he commented dryly, "It's all excitement working with you isn't it."

I put my helmet back on, climbed aboard the bike and Jacques moved off slowly back to the main road. Before we reached Cannes I asked Jacques to stop and took out a walkie-talkie to try and contact the Croat. He came through loud and clear and confirmed that he was now in position and waiting for our party to leave. After a quick discussion with Jacques, I decided that we should proceed to rendezvous point 1. This was an area nearer to Cannes, where we had originally decided to pick up the target car as it passed. When I had started to have doubts as to whether or not we would be able to match the speed of the Mercedes I had changed the pick-up point to rendezvous 2. Having now experienced the likely travelling speed of our targets, I had decided that we should revert to RV 1. Our communications equipment had a good range, but the nearer we were to the Croat the clearer his transmissions would be.

We reached RV 1 within a few minutes. Jacques parked the bike and we sat down to wait. I estimated that we probably had a good three hours to wait. It was important not to lose focus in that time. Jacques and I talked a little but for the most part we just waited. We walked around from time to time and much to my disgust Jacques got through at least half a packet of cigarettes. I think he took a slightly malicious pleasure in smoking in my presence. He knew I hated smoking. I had always hated smoking, even when we were in the Legion together and I was probably the only Legionnaire in the whole outfit to reject his ration of Gauloise. It was nearly 9pm when I reassembled the English cell phone and called Frank. He sounded irritable,

"I've been waiting for your call."

"Are there any changes?"

"No. I'm told everything will proceed as discussed."

"Be in touch tomorrow then."

After I had returned the phone to its individual parts I checked in with the Croat. I had been doing this every twenty minutes. Our transmissions were in the clear, that is unencrypted and, although I did not want anyone listening to us, I wanted to ensure he remained alert. I also carried out a final check on the dazzler.

Shortly before midnight, the radio emitted three clear distinct squelches, followed after a pause by another three. This was the pre-arranged signal from the Croat that the couple were leaving the Palais des Festivals and that he was following. I turned to Jacques,

"Time to mount up".

CHAPTER FORTY SIX

*"To bother about the best method of accomplish-
ing an accidental result."* Ambrose Bierce.

I t was not just the media circus which was causing
problems at the Palais des Festivals. It was the crowds
of onlookers who had come from far and wide for a
glimpse of some of the biggest names in the film industry. A few of the pushier star gazers had even been
fortunate enough to catch the attention of some of the
more approachable personalities and been rewarded
with personalised autographs. For the glitterati who
were attending the film premier and charity dinner it
was just another pampered evening. For the paparazzi
and the ordinary members of the public it was more
like being immersed in a hot cauldron of noisy pushing, sweating humanity, with occasional flare ups of
temper and even brief violence, that drew an instant,
equally violent, explosive response from the many police who were on duty.

Cartwright's relationship with Esclimont, having
thawed from its initial chill, the Englishman had chosen to turn to the representative of the DGSE in his
quest to ensure that, on the Princess's departure from
Cannes, any pursuing paparazzi would be sufficiently

delayed to enable Traynor to do his job without interference. French efficiency is often greatly underrated.
No one could fault Esclimont's competence. The usual
complement of police for a star studded film showing
at the Cannes Film Festival provided sufficient numbers
to ensure that the stars were able to enter and leave
without excessive harassment. Esclimont had arranged
for a police presence that almost overwhelmed even
the mass of press. The stirring and jostling that accompanied the arrival of the Range Rover and armoured
Mercedes at the Palais at the end of the evening was
met with a forceful, determined and coordinated counter movement by experienced riot trained officers.

Whilst an increasingly ill-tempered melee was
occurring around the newly arrived Range Rover and
Black Mercedes at the main entrance to the Palais, a
small group was leaving through the artists' entrance
and getting into another Mercedes. The group's mood
was sombre. The Princess had started the evening in
very good humour. Her visit to the children's hospital had been satisfying and fulfilling. She was at her
best giving her time freely to the sick. Whether it was
patients with HIV or children stricken with cancer, she
would happily and unhurriedly go from individual to
individual, her obvious empathy creating an immediate bond that was as apparent to her as it was to the
patient she was visiting. She was invariably happy when
she came away from these engagements, feeling useful
and fulfilled. Her good mood had lasted throughout
the screening of the film, until some five minutes into
the formal dinner. It was then that Walid had made the

first of increasingly frequent visits to the men's room that even the most severe prostatic hyperplasia would not have justified. It was common knowledge that the Princess detested recreational drug use. She may have led a privileged life but she was not so naive that she did not recognise at once the reason her escort was constantly disappearing with some of the more dissolute of Hollywood's performers. She had become increasingly irritated with Walid as the evening progressed and, by the time Picard and Des started to usher her through the back rooms and bare corridors that led to the Palais' artists' entrance she was in a foul mood and venting her rage on her escorts, showering them with bitter complaints about the escape plan Picard had concocted. It was no novelty for her to be in the public eye. She had been the object of press attention for years and saw no reason to end her evening through a dingy back entrance just because photographers were waiting to take her picture. To her, Picard's strategy to thwart the press was as incomprehensible as it was unnecessary and she showed her annoyance by snapping both at Al Khalifa's head of security and his son Walid. Des, who privately agreed with the Princess's views, maintained an embarrassed silence. As an Al Khalifa employee he was not encouraged to express his opinions, professional or otherwise. As Picard drove off, his departure, initially unnoticed by the paparazzi who were struggling with the police, a heavy strained silence reigned in the car. It was only when they were on the highway that the silence was broken by the Princess snapping at Picard sharply, with just a hint of hysteria in her voice, that he should slow down, reproving him for driving too fast.

The Croat had been watching the scenes at the Palais through high powered binoculars. He had shaken his head in disbelief as he had focussed on the snarling, frenzied expressions on the faces of paparazzi who were almost completely out of control. He had seen the other Mercedes drive up to the darkened rear entrance and the driver exchange places with a broad shouldered balding man with glasses as a woman was ushered, almost pushed, into the car's back seat by the dark man with close cropped, wiry black hair he had seen earlier.

As the Mercedes pulled away from the Palais des Festivals the Croat put aside the binoculars, manoeuvred his car out of its parking place and followed. He was too far away to see the scenes that took place when Federico Conti, one of the more enterprising photographers, received a call on his cell phone from a colleague he had posted at the back of the Palais, informing him that the people he was interested in had just left in a light coloured Mercedes. Federico had immediately run to his Yamaha motorbike, hurriedly pushed a crash helmet on his head and accelerated the bike at high speed through the cordon of police, the crowd of photographers and any other person unfortunate to be in his way. He was lucky he did not kill anyone but he did not care. He had the scent of his prey in his nostrils and nothing was going to frustrate the hunt.

People who gather news and photographs for the media like to think of themselves as a breed apart, intellectually superior to the common man. They care for nothing and no one. All that is important to them is obtaining a headline story or picture. But far from being the superior lone hunters they imagine, they are, in fact, the ultimate pack animal; the wolf pack of humanity. Others have less charitably described them as hyenas. Conti's dramatic exit was impossible to miss. Within seconds the pack was following, once again to the peril of innocent bystanders.

Even driving at 90 miles per hour the Croat kept a window open in the car. It was a hot night and the car was not equipped with air conditioning. The BMW motorbike had already interposed itself between the Mercedes and his car and he had been intrigued, but not had time to think about, the fact that Traynor was not alone on the bike. He did wonder who the mysterious extra body was and from where he had come. He was certainly not one of the team with whom he had been closeted for the past few days. But these thoughts were filed away as he concentrated on the driving and following the car and motorcycle in front of him.

The cavalcade was probably about twenty kilometres or eight or nine minutes out of Monte Carlo when the Croat was alerted to the imminent arrival of the fast approaching Federico Conti by the tortured scream of a high revving motorcycle engine. He glanced in his rear view mirror, saw the bike coming up fast and then the lights of a large number of other bikes some distance further back. It was time for him to earn his pay.

The traffic was light, but Conti was too impatient too wait for anyone to move over for him. His progress up the Autoroute had been a series of fast weaving manoeuvres as he manhandled his bike past slower moving vehicles. Even at the speed he was travelling his camera was ready, slung diagonally across his neck and waist. It was banging about a bit but Conti was used to that and the camera was built to take a little knocking about. His only concern was to catch up with the light coloured S class Mercedes, which he was sure was heading for the security of the Metropole Hotel in Monte Carlo from where he had tracked its occupants earlier in the evening. He was glad the Princess and her escort had dumped their two flanking cars. Without any other vehicle to block his path he had every chance of getting a close up shot of the Princess and her latest lover. He was wondering how much he would get for his pictures when the Renault Laguna he was passing swung towards him without any warning. Cursing he swerved violently, slowing down substantially as he fought for control of his bike. He risked a quick glance behind him as he started to accelerate to make up the distance he had lost because of the Renault. The rest of the pack was getting closer. By the time he was again level with the Renault the group of twenty or so bikes filling the road behind him was no more than a couple of hundred metres away. Splitting his attention between his side mirrors and the road ahead of him he reacted a little too slowly when the Renault again swung sharply towards him, hitting him a glancing blow. Conti's last thought before losing consciousness as a result of colliding first with the pack of motorcycles coming up behind him and then the embankment at the side of the road, was that the Renault driver had done it deliberately.

The Croat laughed out loud as he looked in his rear view mirror at the chaos he had left in his wake after knocking the motorcyclist off his bike. They had all been travelling at a good 90 miles per hour. Things happen very fast at that sort of speed and from the looks of things there was the most enormous pile up he had ever seen in his life. It had actually been touch and go for him because he had swerved a little too sharply, then hit the motorcycle harder than he had intended and had himself almost lost control of the car. It was only by the skin of his teeth that he had succeeded in pulling the car out of a long weaving skid. But he felt exhilarated. All in all he was enjoying himself. He drove through the toll booth in good humour, wished the toll booth operator a pleasant good night as he paid and mentally prepared himself for his next task.

Once out of sight of the toll booth, on the approach to the tunnel the Croat plugged the magnetic blue strobe light into the point that normally held a cigarette lighter and leaned out of his window to place the light on the side of the car's roof. At the side of the road, just before the tunnel entrance he saw the parked car containing the two Serbs. He swung the car across the left hand carriageway, side on to all traffic, so that it entirely blocked that side of the road. As he was doing this the Serbs pulled across the other carriageway, their own strobe already flashing blue. The Croat got out of his car and removed the raincoat that had previously hidden the police uniform he was wearing and threw it into the car, before standing by the vehicle ready to intercept any traffic seeking to enter the tunnel. In his right hand he held the walkie-talkie that was going to inform him when he could get back in the car and return to the house where he had been based.

As he stood there, the two Serbs, also in uniform, joined him making the three of them look like an official police road block.

At the other end of the tunnel, similarly dressed in uniforms of the French Gendarmerie, with their motorbike parked in the middle of the road, with a similarly flashing strobe to that being used by the Croat, the Russian and Syrian members of the team were also in place to perform the same function as the Croat and his Serb companions.

CHAPTER FORTY
SEVEN

"Patience is not an absence of action; rather it is "timing" it waits on the right time to act" Fulton J. Sheen

The SAS team had that evening been afflicted with the usual combination of nerves and excitement at anticipated action counterbalanced by the boredom of routine. The men they were watching had gone out in the late afternoon. With orders not to follow and not knowing when the cell was going to return, the soldiers had, for the umpteenth time, checked their weapons and equipment for the operation early the next morning. They had all had a break early in the evening when, at Cartwright's suggestion, they had once again gone out to dinner at the restaurant they had come to think of as their local. Returning to their observation post they noted that the cell they were watching was still away from their base. With nothing else to do, they had settled down to packing up all their equipment and cleaning the house in order to erase any evidence of their having been in residence. Cartwright was on tenterhooks, but he successfully concealed the tension he felt as he waited for the news that would tell him his job was almost over and that he would be in action in the morning. He had switched on the television, deducing that the death of the couple in a car accident would instantly become a major news story and the television was probably going to be the first resource for him to find out whether or not Traynor had been successful. Not that he had any doubt that Traynor was going to accomplish his appointed task. There was something chillingly, inhumanly efficient about the assassin that made the Colonel shudder.

He was still sitting at the television at midnight, without any item having come on the news. Most of his men were asleep, with only Andy on the thermographic camera and the RSM to keep him company. Dawn was at 04.45 in a little under five hours. The men had to be in position for their assault well before that time. When the tolling of the bell on the local church clock-tower announced midnight, the Colonel decided to get a couple of hours sleep and instructed the two men sitting with him to do likewise.

CHAPTER FORTY EIGHT

"I don't believe in accidents. There are only encounters in history. There are no accidents". Pablo Picasso

I have seen a lot of horrific spectacles in my life but even I found the crash spectacular and awe inspiring. It was a massively noisy demonstration of how a carefully made, beautiful, luxury motor car can, in seconds, be reduced to nothing more than a smoking, twisted lump of barely recogniseable metal.

When we got the signal from the Croat that the target car was on its way out of Cannes, Jacques and I were able to pick it up on the computer screen through the link with the traffic cams. As Jacques monitored its progress, I removed the dazzler from its box. Jacques watched the screen for eight to ten minutes before shutting the laptop.

"They'll be here in a few minutes" he announced as he slipped the laptop into one of the bike's side panniers.

I climbed onto the BMW behind Jacques, trying to adjust the dazzler into a comfortable position. We were sitting there, the bike's engine throbbing against us, when our earpieces screeched again with the second signal from the Croat that the targets were approaching our position. Jacques eased the bike onto the highway and started slowly accelerating in the direction of Monte Carlo. He had accelerated up to about 80 miles per hour when the Mercedes shot past us travelling a good 20 or 30 miles per hour faster. Jacques accelerated, only throttling back when we were three or four car lengths behind our quarry. At the speed we were travelling, the bike was bouncing around and it was a lot more difficult than I had anticipated to hold on both to the dazzler and Jacques. I had one arm around Jacques' waist and was holding the device with my other arm, simultaneously using the same hand to grip Jacques' jacket, but I still had to clench the sides of the bike hard between my legs to steady myself. I had taken off my right hand glove to enable me to operate the dazzler's trigger mechanism. In my efforts to balance and keep my grip I was pushing the dazzler hard into Jacques' back trying to stabilise it between our two bodies. At one point Jacques was sufficiently discomforted to break radio silence in order to reprimand me for nearly overbalancing the bike.

By the time we slowed for the toll booth my thighs were aching from gripping the sides of the bike and my ungloved hand was feeling numb.

We followed the Mercedes away from the highway towards the tunnel. We must have entered the tunnel at about 100 miles per hour and within seconds were at the chosen critical point. As I said "Now" to Jacques over the intercom, my peripheral vision picked up a white car, stationary on the opposite side of the road. It was too late to do anything about it then, we were already committed and alongside the Mercedes. This was the really dangerous part. I had to hold onto the bike only with my legs, turn my body towards the car and hold the dazzler in both hands as I aimed it at the driver. As we drew level with the front of the car I blanked out of my mind all the potential dangers and physical discomfort, concentrating only on the job to be done. Time seemed to slow as I steadied myself into the sequence of movements, grip, turn, aim, trigger, turn back, grip hard again with both hands to hold on for Jacques' evasive action to avoid a wildly out of control vehicle turned into a dangerous projectile alongside us.

As I aimed the dazzler I was concentrating only on the driver. I did not see any of the other occupants of the car. The driver turned his head towards me. In microseconds my brain registered that he was middle-aged, wearing glasses and balding. I saw a puzzled expression cross his face just before I operated the trigger. The effect was instantaneous. The driver reacted to the sudden loss of vision by slamming his foot on what he thought was the brake and instinctively twisting the steering wheel away from our bike. We were lucky. Instead of nearly hitting us the car was driven hard into the nearside wall of the tunnel. The driver had obviously, in his moment of disorientation, pressed the accelerator instead of the brake. The Mercedes hit the wall at full throttle and actually drove a few feet up the tunnel wall before flipping over. It flipped again in a complete circle, hitting the opposite wall upside down before bouncing back right side up, spinning crazily and again hitting the walls as it spun. With each contact the Mercedes became transformed into something looking less and less like a passenger vehicle. The noise was horrendous, reverberating and echoing through the tunnel; the high pitched revving of an engine, mixed with the screaming of protesting metal being ground inexorably into an unidentifiable mass and, finally, successive bangs as the tyres blew out. When the misshapen mass of twisted metal that had previously been a beautiful luxury limousine, eventually came to a halt the engine was still screaming its protests.

Jacques stopped the bike alongside the wreck. I climbed off and looked at him as I unzipped the tank bag in front of him to remove the refrigerated container. He lifted his visor without saying anything. He did not need to say anything. It was obvious from his expression that he felt the same relief as me that we had not been hit by the careening car as it made its wild progress around the tunnel.

The first thing I did was to reach through what was left of the crushed driver's window to use the electronic stop/start button to cut the engine. The silence was a relief after all that noise. My first priority was the driver. He was not dead. He seemed to be moaning quietly to himself, but it was difficult to make out what he was saying with the exploded airbag partly covering his face and body. I put the container down on the road, opened it and removed the hypodermic before leaning into what was left of the car. I pulled the airbag away from the driver to expose his chest and plunged the hypodermic into the right side of the driver's body, just underneath his rib cage before squeezing the contents into him. With the plunger about half way down I stopped. There was no way I was going to be able to open what was left of the door. If I was going to reach the driver's femoral artery I was going to have to climb half way in through the window space. It was not easy but I managed to jab the hypodermic again into the driver in his groin area. I did not know whether or not I had actually delivered the contents into the femoral artery but I thought it was near enough. By then the driver seemed to be dead and I only had his eye to do. I slid back out of the window awkwardly, ripping my jacket in the process. Glancing at the syringe I could see there was still a small amount of liquid left. I was not quite sure where I was supposed to make the injection so I pushed the needle into the area behind the eyeball and squeezed the plunger until it would not go any further. Having emptied the syringe, I put it back in its box and threw the box to Jacques to catch.

I then directed my attention to the other occupants of the car. The man sitting in the passenger seat next to the driver was lolled over unconscious. He had a number of cuts on his face which were bleeding profusely. He was not my concern. It took a considerable effort to open the rear passenger door which was severely scratched, dented and twisted out of shape. Eventually it came open with a loud squeal of protest.

Car crashes are a blunt instrument of assassination. They do not distinguish between the target and innocents. Their outcome is uncertain. I have seen minor crashes where someone has died without any apparent reason for their demise. I have seen monstrous wreckages which it would be impossible to believe anyone could survive, yet people walk out, unmarked and unharmed. The reason motor accidents have, all too frequently, become a weapon of choice is that pathologists and the police rarely look beyond the wreckage for a cause of death.

The wreck was one of the worst I had ever seen. The front of the car, the chassis, roof and trunk portions had been almost completely obliterated. Yet when I opened the rear door I saw that the area containing the back seat had survived virtually intact. The arab man who I had been told was the principal target of the whole operation was squashed on the floor between the rear seat squab and the back of the front seat. He was not only conscious but seemed unhurt. He looked up at me and seemed about to say something. I was certainly not interested in a conversation with him. I thought of delivering a crushing blow to his sternum either with the palm of my hand or my fist, but decided instantly that it might not be a good idea to leave post mortem marks that might be identified for what they were. Instead I grasped his head with my hands in the approved position and broke his neck. As he slumped back dead I looked at his companion. She was also on the floor between the seats. She was very pale, but conscious and apparently also not badly hurt. A small trickle of blood tinted the ivory skin around her nose, with another small amount of blood around her mouth. The thought crossed my mind that I should have felt relief that she had survived. But I did not. I felt a little sorry for her but remembered wondering, when I had first seen her, what a good looking woman like her was doing with the sleazy looking guy I had just killed. I could not help reflecting that she would not have been in this position if she had stuck with decent people. As I leaned over to feel the pulse at the side of her neck she murmured, "Help me. Please help me." I suppose it should have been heart rending but I felt nothing. Her pulse was faint and uneven. I had more than enough experience to realise that notwithstanding her apparent lack of injury she must have suffered some severe internal damage. I lifted her gently off the floor and lay her along the seat. The least I could do was to try to make her more comfortable. The seat belt was hanging loosely down and I thought to myself that not only was she in the wrong place with the wrong guy but that if she had simply worn the seat belt she would probably have survived, perhaps even unhurt. As it was I did not know whether or not she was going to live. It was time for us to get out of there anyway.

As I extracted myself from the wreck I turned towards Jacques and started giving instructions to the team over the radio,

"Back to base. Break off now. Back to base." Looking up at Jacques I was astonished to see a man standing by his side. I glanced beyond Jacques and the man and saw the white car stationary, further down the tunnel. I now remembered noticing it previously. This guy must have seen everything. The man was gesticulating wildly and babbling away in heavily accented French about what had happened. He was short, stocky and dark and from his accent I took him to be either Spanish or Portugese. He had not yet come to the realisation of what he had witnessed and was functioning on the basis that we were trying to help after the accident.

I asked him if he had called for help. He responded that he had not because he had come over immediately to see if he could assist. I then asked if his car was working or if it had broken down. He said that he had had a problem but the car was now alright.

I looked over towards the bike, saw that Jacques had put away the dazzler and the container for the hypodermic and said to him

"You get out of here. Make sure everyone's left. I'll handle this. See you back there." Jacques nodded, got on the BMW, did a smart U turn before accelerating fast back towards the highway.

The man who had come over was looking puzzled. He was trying to put it all together. I put my arm around his shoulder and started gently to propel him back towards his car. "We've got to go and get help. We've got to call an ambulance urgently."

He had allowed me to guide him to his car before he remembered that he had a cell phone. He was raising it to show me when I hit him with a savage, unrestrained hand blade across his carotid artery. The blow nearly took his head off. I was in position ready to hit him again but it was not necessary. He dropped like a stone. I looked around quickly. The tunnel was still clear. I dragged the unconscious man to the rear of his car, opened the trunk and manhandled him in. In films they make these things look easy, but believe me, it is not the easiest thing in the world to manipulate a limp body. I closed the trunk, removed my motor-cycle helmet which I threw into the rear of the car and got into the driver's seat. The keys were in the ignition and the car started immediately. It was already facing in the direction I wanted to go, towards the Autoroute and within seconds I was driving out of the tunnel. As I cleared the tunnel entrance a car was entering, being overtaken by three or four motorbikes. I looked at my watch. The whole operation, from our entering the tunnel to my leaving it, had taken less than five min-utes. I was now thinking about getting rid of this car and the guy in the trunk. It would be easier to do this with Jacques's help. As I drove slowly towards the villa I heard the sound of several two tone sirens calling to each other urgently in the distance.

The car was running very roughly and was getting oppressively full of exhaust fumes, but at least it was running. I wound my window all the way down and leaned across to the passenger side, also to open that window. The flow of outside air into the car improved things. As I drove I wondered how anyone could drive a car in the condition that this was in. I was also thinking about the disposal of the car and its owner. The house I had acquired above Cannes was in a fairly remote location, well away from any other houses. Its previous incumbent had built a three car garage to one side of the house. I kept a car there permanently for emergen-cies, but it still left more than enough room to hide the heap I was driving. I would need Jacques' help. He knew nothing about the house and I had no intention of enlightening him. He was a good friend, but he did not need to know every little thing about me.

Jacques was waiting for me when I arrived back in La Turbie. He had taken off his motorcycle outfit and was more comfortably attired in Jeans and a shirt.

"Nice car" he joked as I drove into the driveway. I glared at him. After nearly suffocating from exhaust fumes for the half hour it had taken me to get back to the house I had a headache and was in no mood for humour.

"What did you do with that guy?"

By way of answer I jerked my thumb in the direction of the trunk of the car. Jacques walked over to the back of the car, opened the trunk and peered in.

"I'd say he's dead" he announced straightening up.

"You're kidding me" I walked over to look. I had hit the man hard but I did not think I had killed him. In fact I had been intending to put a bullet in his head when I arrived back at the house. The crumpled body still seemed to be lying in the same position where I had pushed it. I felt for a pulse but there was none. I was surprised.

"The guy must have had a heart condition or something. I didn't hit him that hard."

"What are we going to do with him."

"We either bury him or just dump him somewhere."

Jacques turned and went into the house, returning moments later with a powerful flashlight which he shone into the trunk at the body.

"What are you doing?"

"Just checking you didn't shoot the guy and forget to tell me."

I laughed "You've got to be kidding me. You don't think I'd tell you. I wouldn't suggest dumping him anywhere if he had a bullet in him."

"Strange" Jacques mused out loud.

"What?"

"Look at him. He looks alive and as healthy as you or me. Look at those rosy cheeks."

I leaned back into the trunk to look at the body. It was clearly visible in the torchlight and Jacques was right. The face had what I can only describe as a healthy, ruddy glow.

"Fuck me. Would you believe it?"

"What?" Jacques was mystified.

"I'll bet it's carbon monoxide. He died from carbon monoxide leaking into the trunk. That's why he's got the good colour. Carbon monoxide causes oxygen to stay in the blood rather than circulate in the body. It increases the red blood cells or something like that, giving that healthy appearance. I had to open the windows because the exhaust fumes were filling the car. I didn't think about it getting into the trunk. Stupid fucker. That'll teach him not to take care of his car."

Jacques shook his head in wonderment, "Well it saved us doing the job. We can take him to a cliff somewhere and just throw him into the sea. What about the car though?"

"Well I've been thinking about that. I know a guy, ex CIA. He's got a house in the hills near Cannes. Very isolated. He closes the house up for the summer, only goes there in winter. We can stick the car there and come back in a couple of months, drive it up into the hills somewhere, when everything has quietened down and leave it."

"Hmm. You sure there's not going to be anyone at the house for the next couple of months." Jacques sounded doubtful.

"Don't worry. I know the guy well. For sure he's in Washington now. He still does part time work for the agency. In the years I've known him he's never gone to that house before December."

"We'd better do it now then, while it's still dark. Will you drive that thing?" He indicated the white car.

"I suppose so." I looked at it reluctantly, "it'll probably take an hour in that. You'd better just follow close behind in case it breaks down."

Jacques nodded his agreement.

"I'm just going to go in and get this gear off. Is there anything to eat before we go? I'm starving."

While I was changing, Jacques made me a cheese sandwich which I started to eat as I opened all the windows in the white car. I did not want to end up like the man in the trunk. Before we left we planned a route from one of the maps I had of the area. We decided to go along the coast road away from the Autoroute. It would be quieter and we were unlikely to come across any police who would, in all probability, be travelling up and down the Highway en masse following the accident.

It was pleasant driving along an empty road on a warm, balmy night. Even late night revellers seemed to have gone to bed. I had the impression that we were the only people left alive on earth. When we cleared the darkness of the tree lined streets of the villages we passed, the waning moon lit up the landscape giving almost day like brightness. As I looked at the reflection of the moon rippling on the surface of the sea, I thought of Natalya, wishing that it was just the two of us driving along in the moonlight in a decent car.

My romantic fantasy ended abruptly when I realised that I was driving along a cliff that rose up steeply, directly above the sea. I stopped the car at the side of the road and got out. Jacques joined me as I looked over the edge. From what I could see there was a sheer drop straight into the sea.

I turned to Jacques, who nodded. He and I were thinking the same thing. We walked to the trunk of the car I was driving, opened it and between the two of us managed to lift the body out and carry it to the cliff edge where we put it on the ground. We both again looked over the cliff edge.

"Do you think we should roll it or should we try and swing it out a bit."

"I think we should try and swing it out. Try to get it into the sea. You take the legs, I'll take the arms." I leaned down and gripped the arms whilst Jacques grasped the legs. We lifted the body about two feet from the ground and then started swinging it rhythmically.

"On my count."

I counted to three reaching the last number as the body was swung out over the edge. We released our grip at the same time and the body fell into the void.

We looked over the edge again but could not see anything. Even in the moonlight we could not see whether or not the body had gone into the water.

"It doesn't really matter where it went. No-one's likely to find it for a while and if they do... " I shrugged.

We got back in the cars and continued towards the house above Cannes. The white car managed to make the trip without breaking down. When we got to the house I made a bit of a show of not remembering quite where it was and, then, of finding a key to the locked gate, which I kept hidden behind a loose brick in the outer wall.

"How did you know where the key was?" Jacques was curious.

"I've been here a couple of times. Did some work for the guy when he was out. I make a point of remembering things like where people hide their keys." As I spoke I made a mental note to change the hiding place.

We drove in. I never lock the garage. If someone wanted to break into the grounds and steal the car I kept there they were welcome to try. It was the work of a few moments to put the white car into the garage, remove the number plates and cover it with some dust sheets that were lying around. Before we closed the garage doors I waved the number plates at Jacques,

"Better bury these. Just in case."

There were a variety of garden tools in the garage left over from the occupant before me. I picked up a spade, walked a few yards into the garden and dug a hole, deep enough for no animal to scratch at and shallow enough not to be too physically demanding.

I threw the number plates in and covered them with earth. This was not the only hole I had dug in that garden. There was one other, very considerably deeper, that had taken a lot of effort and quite a time to dig. But that was a hole whose contents I wanted to remain undiscovered, at least for my lifetime.

It is essential to maintain an appearance of strength in my line of work. If people you work with even get a hint that you might have a weakness, they start worrying about working with you and worse, how they might double cross you. I have said that Jacques was a good and loyal friend. He had been able successfully to cross the barrier between having a normal family life and operating in the shadow world I inhabited without being perceived as weak. But of course he was vulnerable in a way that I was not. I had seen his vulnerability in his pride in his son. I had been wondering how he would react when he found out about Natalya. He had always seen me as the ultimate example of self-sufficiency and independence. To him I was unassailable, able in times of difficulty instantly to disappear. Immediately I told him about the girl I would shatter this impression. I wondered if I really cared. I was at the end of my career and I needed his help to get her out of the hotel as soon as possible. I could do it without him, but a two man effort would be much more secure. In addition, having to hide the white car and dispose of its owner had taken time out of the night that I had not previously envisaged when thinking about extracting the girl. I had relocked the outside gate to the house and we had got into his car when I decided just to come out with it.

"Jacques there's one more thing I need to do and I need your help with it."

"Sure. What is it?"

"It's something we need to do now."

He turned away from the road briefly to glance at me. I could see he was wondering what we might have forgotten. Before I could say anything more he voiced what he was thinking,

"You mean the English Rupert. You want to hit him now?"

"No. It's not that. I think we're clear of him. That is if your lead blanket is doing its job and blocking any bugs in that dazzler thing."

Jacques sighed, "You're going to hate me for this... I decided it was too risky hanging on to the dazzler. I made a detour on the way back to La Turbie and chucked it and the syringe box over the cliffs and into the sea."

I thought about it. Jacques was right. What was I going to do with that dazzler anyway? I could not carry it around in my baggage. I had not yet decided where I was going next, although I had been thinking of disappearing into my house in Umbria for a few months. If the device had been bugged in some sophisticated way and I had it with me I would have been totally fucked. There was a rather heavy silence in the car as I was having these thoughts and Jacques was wondering how I was going to react to what he had done.

"All right. But you owe me big time. That was a unique bit of kit. I can't see myself ever getting my hands on something like that again."

Jacques let out a breath, clearly relieved at my reaction. I was slightly surprised. Jacques had always been tough and independent, never afraid of anything, yet this small exhalation of breath made me think that perhaps he was a little afraid of me.

"Anyway the favour I want to ask is nothing to do with all this." It was my turn to take a little breath,

"I met this girl I like. I need to get her out of a hotel in Monte Carlo before anyone tries to get on her to get at me."

Jacques slammed on the brakes, stopping the car with a protesting squeal from the tyres. He turned completely towards me with an incredulous expression on his face,

"A girl. You. You're fucking with me." He looked hard at me to see whether or not I was joking,

"No. I'm serious."

"Come on. Where would you find a girl? As far as I know you've only ever been with hookers."

I cannot remember ever before feeling as embarrassed as I did then. I felt too ashamed to tell Jacques that the girl was a street whore I had picked up on the Italian highway. "I sometimes meet girls." I muttered defensively

He was looking at me as if my body had become possessed by the spirit of some bourgeois accountant.

"So when did this happen?"

I could almost see Jacques' mind working, as he ran through in his head where I had been since being with him in Florence.

"It's complicated. I don't want to go into it now, but she's in the Metropole Hotel near the Casino. I need to get her out at once, because the Englishman knows she's there and knows she's connected with me. If I leave her there any longer they could put someone on her and... " I tailed off as Jacques interrupted,

"Whoaaa. Just a minute. So there's a girl. The English know about her and we've now got to extract her from under their noses. Is that it?"

I nodded.

"So would you like to tell me just when and how this all happened between Florence and here. You've been running an operation. When did you have time to get into all this trouble? You... you... of all people." Jacques ended up losing the power of speech.

"Look, Jacques. Never mind about all that. I'll tell you the whole story when we've got more time. Now, will you help or not?"

"Of course I'll fucking help, you prick. I'll just never forgive you for not telling me what you were getting up to. You with a girl. And here I was thinking you only went for hookers."

"Well... I suppose she was a sort of hooker." I muttered, again in embarrassment, wondering at the same time whether I should have told him that.

"Don't tell me she's one of those Eastern European girls they stick on the streets here." He could not hide his disbelief.

I became even more defensive, "She's a decent girl. She's just had a hard time." It was my turn to be surprised at his reaction. He laughed loudly, put the car into gear and began to drive again.

"Well that's ok. That's a bit more like you. I couldn't 've taken it if she'd turned out to be a nice girl from a good family."

"She is a nice girl" I protested.

He laughed again, "I didn't mean that. Truth is I met Carolina, my wife, when she was working in a strip joint and she's been a great wife and a great mother and I just love her to bits."

This was something Jacques had never confided in me before.

He was now driving towards the Autoroute. There was no reason for us to remain on minor roads and we needed to make time to get to Monte Carlo quickly. The car clock read 3.15 am. I estimated that it was probably an hour and a half to two hours before dawn. I had reckoned that Frank would have realised that he only had a small window of opportunity in which to catch my team. That would mean an assault taking place on Friday morning. Whether it was police or Special Forces, standard practice was to initiate assaults just before dawn when people were asleep, sleepy or just at a low level of alertness. Frank ought, therefore, even now be preparing his team for an assault to take place sometime within the next hour and a half. I was hoping that this would mean there would not yet be any surveillance on Natalya.

"Have you got a phone I can use?" I had thrown away the telephone the English had given me as I was driving away from the scene of the accident I had caused and had left the phones Jacques had given me at the house in La Turbie.

Jacques delved in his pocket and handed me a phone. I had to switch it on and wait for it to register a signal. I called the hotel and asked for Natalya's room. The operator was apparently used to people calling each other at three o'clock in the morning and put me through at once. It rang several times before a very sleepy sounding Natalya answered. She soon overcame the sleepiness. The call took no longer than the time I spent giving her terse instructions to dress, pack and check out of the hotel and be ready to be collected by a friend of mine in about twenty minutes. She told me that she still had most of the cash I had given her. I made a quick calculation and told her to use it to pay the bill. It should have been more than enough. I had already paid the bill up to the last time I had seen her on the night of the grand prix so she only needed to cover four days.

Jacques who had been listening to our conversation chuckled to himself, "So is this the one? The one who melts the great iceman. I can see the headlines now – "Cold Blooded Killer broken by a piece of skirt."

"Fuck off". I was already regretting having told Jacques. He was obviously determined to get as much mileage out of this thing as he could.

The area around the tunnel leading into Monte Carlo was alive with police. A temporary barrier manned both by French and Monegasque police had been erected at the entrance to the tunnel. One of the police signalled us to stop, whilst a helicopter with the insignia of the French Gendarmerie slowly rose from the road ahead of us. As the sound of the helicopter faded into the distance, the same policeman who had stopped us waved us on, directing us around the barrier. There was only one open lane in the tunnel. The wreckage of the Mercedes was still there, but was now surrounded by fire trucks and police cars all of which were lit up by large portable lights on stands with the intermittent flickering of blue and red strobes reflecting off the tunnel walls. We drove slowly past looking at our handiwork. The only attention we drew from the police was to be gestured at to move along faster. By contrast, when we arrived in the centre of Monte Carlo it was like the city of the dead. Even the Place de Casino was quiet although there were still one or two late night gamblers filtering through into the street. No one was stirring by the hotel though. Jacques pulled up on a corner about a hundred yards across from the Metropole. He had binoculars in the car and we each in turn used them to scan the whole area. It seemed completely clear. Light from the hotel illuminated the interiors of the luxury cars parked around the hotel entrance. They were all clear. It was not so easy to see whether there was anyone in any of the cars parked in the shadows away from the hotel.

"What do you think?"

"Looks clear. Although they may also have someone inside."

"Yeah"

"We go with the plan?"

"Have to. It's the only way."

As we were driving we had discussed how best to get the girl out without picking up a tail. I had told Natalya to wait in the lobby. I told her just to come in the clothes she was wearing and to leave her bag with the concierge. I did not know what might have been planted in her bag when she was out of the room. Mentally I gave her credit for not even raising a small protest at these instructions. I told her that I was sending a friend to come in to get her. Jacques would simply go in and take a look around. If it looked clear he would get Natalya and leave with her. I was going to watch while he left the hotel and walked with the girl across the square towards the car park by the Place du Casino. If I did not see them being followed I would drive alongside them as they entered a side street leading to the Casino area, they would leap in and I would accelerate out of there fast. Anyone following would have to come after us or risk losing us. If they did we ought to be able to spot them. It was not a very sophisticated plan but it should work. Neither of us discussed what we would do if someone was following, but I suppose Jacques had the same thought about this that I did, namely to trap them and take them out.

Jacques got out of the car and walked across to the hotel. After perhaps five minutes he came out again with his arm around Natalya. They strolled across the road looking like a couple without a care in the world. I saw no indication at all of anyone paying any attention to them. No one followed as they entered the side street. No car started up as they disappeared from view.

Satisfied, I drove in the direction they had taken. The rest of it went as planned. She had not been put under surveillance and we were away free and clear. I felt relief. I was also pleased with the way the girl had performed. She had followed instructions to the letter. There was no drama when she got into the car. She sat there, saying nothing letting us get on with what we were doing.

I drove out towards the minor road that leads to the Corniche, away from the tunnel and the highway. The road was winding and steep and it would have been impossible for anyone to drive along it without lights unless they were wearing night vision goggles. There were no car lights at all behind us and I was as sure as I could be that we were not being followed. Jacques had been constantly looking rearward and eventually it was clear that he, too, was satisfied. He settled back into his seat and spoke to me in French,

"Does she speak French?"

"No. Some Italian and good English."

"She's a good one. I approve. She's not only a looker and too fucking young for you by the way, but she performed well."

I felt the same way as Jacques, but was pleased at his apparent approval.

"Are you two talking about me?" She said it in English. It was the first time she had spoken since getting into the car. Jacques replied before I could,

"Don't worry it was all good. You did well back there."

I looked at her in the rear view mirror. She looked nervous and was biting her lip slightly.

"Don't worry Natalya. We're going to have a few days holiday in a nice little house we've rented."

Jacques interposed, "Do you really want to stay there? Don't you think we should get out of there? You can't rely on that Englishman keeping to your deal. They've not got much checking to do to link up the two houses."

"I thought you said that was a dead end. It was all done in cash with no records."

"It was and it is. But they still might link up the two houses. I think we should clean the place up and get out of there immediately. In fact I already arranged for my boys to come up and get the van. We can take this car and the Audi."

"You're right Jacques. But I need papers for Natalya."

"That's no problem. We can be back to my place in Florence in four or five hours. You'll be safe there. The English don't know anything about me. I'll fix up some papers. It'll take a couple of days. Carolina'll be glad of a bit of feminine company... " he paused turning to look at Natalya, "or maybe she'd prefer to go out with my daughter, they're much closer in age."

I looked away from the road long enough to glare at him viciously which merely caused him to laugh.

CHAPTER FORTY NINE

"The skillful leader subdues the enemy's troops without any fighting; he captures their cities without laying siege to them". Sun Tzu

Friday the early hours of the morning

Cartwright was woken by the ringing of his cell phone. Although he knew it had to be Featherstonehaugh he glanced at the screen out of habit, noting that it was a little before the time for which he had set the alarm, 03.00.

"Go to secure will you?" Featherstonehaugh did not waste time on pleasantries.

Cartwright put on the light and made the connection to MI6's deputy chief through the secure link.

"Have you seen the news?"

"No. I thought I'd snatch a couple of hours sleep before we kicked off this morning and there was nothing about it before that."

"Well, so far so good. Once you've cleaned up today congratulations will be in order."

"So it all went off as envisaged."

"Yes. An excellently executed operation. Very clean. Can you confirm the package I sent was passed over and used."

"I passed it on with the very explicit instructions you included. I have no reason to believe that it was not used."

"The operation... what was the count?" Cartwright asked the question hesitantly.

"Two confirmed that we know of. Her status is uncertain. First reports are that she's injured but alive."

Cartwright did not say it aloud but thought,"thank God." He had not wanted the woman to be hurt. "That's good" he said aloud.

"Yes." Featherstonehaugh did not seem to be very enthusiastic.

"Anyway Frank, I wanted to confirm that we have a Guided Missile Destroyer on station just off your coast, HMS Dauntless. They're under cover of a courtesy visit to Cannes. When you're ready they'll send a Sea King to pick you up". He was referring to the Sea King Mk4 Helicopter in use with the British Navy as an amphibious support helicopter capable of carrying twenty seven troops.

"Is there anywhere near you where it can land?"

Cartwright thought for a minute. In round figures the Sea King was about 60 feet long and had a rotor diameter of a little over 60 feet. It might fit into the garden of the house they were going to assault. If not, it could land on the nearby waste ground.

"We'll find somewhere. We'll activate a beacon and they can home in on that."

"Very good. By the way Frank, I know I don't have to tell you, but you need to take all your waste away with you and dispose of it quietly."

"Don't worry about that. We'll have that handled."

"Well good luck. C and I will be watching on the satlink. Can you confirm lift off at 04.15."

"Confirmed"

By the time the Colonel had finished his conversation his men were up and fully dressed in their black kit of Nomex fire proof assault suits and Kevlar body armour. From long experience Cartwright had snatched his couple of hours sleep only after first dressing in his own assault suit. He called the RSM,

"Ken, do you think we can exfiltrate from the garden of that house by Sea King?"

Collier thought for a few moments before answering, "I think we might. There's that area at the back beyond the pool that's completely clear of trees. I'd say it's more than large enough for a Helo"

"Good. That's what I thought too. Assuming we can do that, we'll call in the chopper when we've finished, load everything up on to it and exfil from there. You'll have to designate two of the lads to stay behind to check that everything's clean and take the hire cars back and pay off the hotel. There's a destroyer offshore of Cannes. When they've finished the clean-up they can come in by Zodiac from Cannes. I'll call GIGN from the boat and ask Hubert to drop the lads at Cannes Harbour."

"Very good, Boss. I'll sort that."

"Any news from Ross and Andy?"

"They reported a few minutes ago. They're in position and ready. All the tangos entered the house around zero fifty and there has not been any movement for over an hour."

The RSM was reporting back on the contact he had had from the two members of the team who had established themselves in sniper positions around the property prior to Traynor's team returning from their operation. The two snipers, Ross and Andy had been reporting back regularly

Before leaving the house they had been using as a base for the past few days, the Colonel and the RSM each walked through the rooms, ensuring that nothing had been left to indicate their presence. The bags with their equipment were already packed away in the trunks of the vehicles they were using. The whole team then squeezed into the cars. It was a tight fit with everyone dressed for an assault that they were hoping could be initiated by stealth but might require forceful entry. Apart from the sniper team, who were using HK417 assault rifles, popular with the SAS for being reliable, effective and with a full silencer option, Cartwright and the rest of the assault team were armed with suppressed Heckler and Koch MP5SD sub machine guns in addition to handguns and knives. Whether or not they were going to succeed in entry by stealth, the house they were assaulting was in a residential neighbourhood. All shooting had to take place with silenced weapons. With the subsonic ammunition they were using, the MP5s would be extremely quiet and no one even passing on the street would be likely to hear anything.

The approach to the house was downhill from where they had started and the final 500 metres was effected with the engines off and the cars coasting towards the target. Approximately 100 metres before the house they braked to a halt. The rest of the approach would be made on foot in the shadows. Although the house they were assaulting was surrounded by a two metre wall, the assault team scaled it in seconds and crouched below the wall scanning the garden and house beyond with their night vision goggles.

"Sniper 1 are we clear for white?" When assaulting a building the assault force would designate each of the four sides a different colour. In an ideal situation each colour would be under observation by a separate sniper. Lacking the manpower to provide complete cover for the building Andy and Ross had positioned themselves so that they were able to cover the front (white), the back (black) and as much of the two other sides (red and green) as they could.

"White is clear" was the whispered transmission followed by Ross's, "Black is clear".

The days of surveillance and the two snipers' earlier reports had confirmed the location of the xrays or tangos on the first floor of the building.

Cartwright looked at his watch and then, briefly, up at the sky. The sun would start to rise in approximately ten minutes. Using hand signals, the team approached the house quickly, slipping between trees and shrubs for cover. Once at the house, the team divided into two, one group moving to the French windows at the rear of the house and the other group remaining at the front door. Although both groups had to cope with locked doors they were in the house in a matter of seconds. The group who had entered from the rear swept quietly through the downstairs rooms ensuring that the rooms were clear, while the second group stealthily climbed the stairs. At the top of the stairs the three members of the second group moved down the corridor towards the bedrooms before stopping to wait for the first group to join them.

The principal assault was over in seconds. Doors crashed open, targets were located and shot. The Russian was the only one of the five men in the house not to die immediately. He had always been a poor sleeper and had had particular difficulty in falling asleep that night. Unknown to the assault team he had been in the kitchen getting himself some water as they had gone over the wall. Perhaps it was some battle honed instinct or he had heard the faint creak of a floorboard. For whatever reason it was, he had sat up in bed and reached for the 9mm Beretta he had been keeping close ever since Traynor had given him the weapon. He very carefully and quietly pulled back the slide an instant before the door burst open. He dived to one side and fired the instant he saw the black clad figure and felt rather than heard two rounds hitting the bed where he had just been lying. He was a good shot and the bullets he fired hit their target, knocking the person who was firing at him backwards into the path of another black clad figure who had started to enter the room directly behind the first attacker but had not had time to deploy separately. Although this caused a delay in the assault of no more than fractions of a second, it was long enough to enable the Russian to smash through the bedroom window in a desperate leap. Radio silence was now broken and almost simultaneous transmissions were heard in the assault team's earpieces,

"One down"

"One xray loose"

"Engaging target on black moving fast. Xray down."

"All xrays down."

The brief action over, Cartwright and the others removed the respirators and hoods they wore on their heads, taking deep breaths as they did so.

"Let's take a look at what we've got." Cartwright spoke as he moved into the rooms to look at the faces of the dead members of Traynor's team. When he reached the room where the body of the only arab looking xray lay, he examined the body quickly. Holes in the forehead and chest, which were still seeping blood testified to the accuracy of the assault team's shooting. He glanced around surreptitiously to ensure no one else was anywhere near him before manhandling the body onto its front. He then withdrew from his pocket an envelope Traynor had given him at their final meeting, which he slipped underneath the body before stepping back and drawing his silenced pistol. Looking around again, to ensure he was still unobserved, he fired once into the back of the arab's head. Satisfied that the hollow point round had, on exiting, almost completely destroyed the arab's face, he left the room and went to check on the other bodies.

In the meantime the snipers had left their positions and entered the house, dragging the body of the Russian with them through the French windows.

Someone had switched on the lights in the house and Cartwright went to check on MacCallister who had been hit by the Russian's bullets.

"I'm fine boss. Got me in the Kev. Just a bit of bruising. Might perhaps've cracked a rib."

"Bloody lucky you are." The voice was Collier's, "you two fucked up your entry my lads. When we get back to Hereford you're in for a spell at the killing house to brush up."

The SAS team split up and went through the house methodically. They took the bodies of what they believed were dead terrorists and put them in large black plastic bags which they lined up next to a BMW motorbike which had been parked in the front driveway.

The sun was just starting to rise on another beautiful day as the SAS group gathered in the sitting room to examine the results of their search of the premises. On a table in front of them was a large pile of Euro bank notes, an assortment of handguns and various passports, one of which had been found in a bloodstained envelope along with a set of credit cards and driving license. The envelope had been found beneath the body of the terrorist whose face had been shattered in the assault by a shot through the back of the head that no one could remember having fired, but everyone promptly forgot about in the after action euphoria.

"Throw the guns in a bag with one of the bodies" Cartwright ordered as he picked up the various passports and started flicking through them.

"But Boss there's some decent weapons there. We could use them. They'll be untraceable too."

Cartwright looked up, glancing at the assorted handguns on the table, "very well. Pack them up then, with the rest of the gear."

"What about the money, Boss?" Andy was the first to put into words what everyone was thinking.

"How much is there?"

"Give or take, around a quarter of million Euros". Collier had counted the money twice.

Cartwright was silent. He looked around at the expectant looks on the faces of the men clustered around him. He did not know how many of the officers under him had ever been faced with a similar situation, but this was a first for him. As commanding officer of the Regiment he not only had to maintain the respect of his men he also needed their trust. Neither did he fail to consider that men who had walked away with a generous cash bonus would be unlikely to indulge in post operation discussions that might raise awkward questions. He made a rapid calculation, seven men, two hundred and fifty thousand Euros,

"Well, we could turn it into the Treasury" he paused looking at the disappointment that instantly appeared on the faces of the men surrounding him, "but what the hell will they do with it other than tart up some bureaucrat's office. Ken, you and the men take 30,000 a piece and donate what's left to the Sergeants' Mess."

"Yes Boss." Although Cartwright had addressed Collier, the whole team had spontaneously chorused his answer, followed immediately by a slightly embarrassed silence. Again it was Andy who broke the silence,

"Err, what about you, Boss. It doesn't quite seem fair... " his voice tailed off.

"I'm your CO. Whatever my wife might want me to do, I'm afraid I can't participate." The reference to his wife caused the men to laugh and broke any incipient tension.

As the men gathered up the weapons and the money, Ross winked at Collier, "Well sarge, not a bad night's work, even if I say so meself." Collier just grinned back. He had a reputation as being something of a stickler for regulations but was as pleased as the others at the unexpected windfall.

"Would it be too much to expect you lot to make yourselves useful, set up a beacon, mark out a landing area and call in the Chopper" Cartwright's jovial tone matched the prevalent mood in the room,

"Right away, Boss" the chorus of voices once again echoed around the room.

By the time the Sea King landed, the team's vehicles had been driven down to the house and all their equipment and everything else for loading had been placed alongside the area set up for the helicopter. It was the Colonel who had had the idea, as he looked at the black plastic bags lined up next to the BMW motorbike and two Renault Laguna motor cars. The Sea King Helicopter had an external cargo hook capable of carrying a Land Rover underneath it. Cartwright ordered the bodies to be placed in one of the Renaults which was to be securely tied to the motor bike. The Helicopter was going to be flying with considerably less of a load than its maximum and his idea was for the Sea King to carry the car and its cargo of dead bodies, together with the motorbike out to sea and then dump the whole lot into the Mediterranean before they reached the Destroyer. He explained what he wanted to the Helicopter crew when they arrived. They listened without turning a hair. They were primarily used by Special Forces and, in that context, the Colonel's request was not so outlandish as to cause them much surprise.

"What are we going to do with the extra car, sir?" It was Collier who voiced the question that the whole team had been considering.

"Check to see whether the keys are amongst the other keys we found. If they are then it's going to be one less on the helo and a three car convoy back to Nice. Maybe you can use the car after you return the hire cars, or I don't know, dump it or give it to the GIGN with our compliments. In fact, yes. Give it to Hubert. I'm sure they can use a car that's entirely off the books. The three of you remaining behind I want to go over the house again carefully. Make sure it's all clean and there's no blood or mess left. Ken, " Cartwright addressed himself to the RSM, "make sure any bloody sheets are in the car with the bodies before we take off."

The RSM nodded his consent and disappeared into the house for a further check as to whether or not any sheets and bed covers with blood on them had been removed.

In very little time the Helicopter was flying low over the Mediterranean. It was flying a little further out to sea than had originally been envisaged by the officer commanding its floating base. The pilot, mirroring Cartwright's caution, wanted to choose a point at sea to drop part of his cargo in sufficiently deep water and well away from the prying eyes of other shipping.

Collier, Peters and Ross the three left behind to effect a final clean up, had watched the Helicopter as it took off into the dawn. They walked back into the house they had raided and carried out a final check to ensure that no trace of their presence had been left. It was Collier who found two shell cases from the Beretta in the room previously occupied by the Russian. He picked them up and put them into his shirt pocket. The three members of the SAS team were now dressed in jeans and shirts, their black kit in the Helicopter on its way to the Destroyer. Collier looked at the broken window frame, nothing to be done about that. Walking carefully one last time through the house he was finally satisfied it was clean and joined Peters and Ross outside. Each of them got into a car and followed Collier in convoy as they took the road towards Nice. Collier had in his pockets the credit cards that had previously been used at their hotel and the Car rental agency. He was in an exceptionally good mood as he drove, almost feeling the 30,000 Euros he had added to the money belt around his waist.

By the time Collier, Peters and Ross had arrived in Nice, the Helicopter had dropped the dispensible part of its load and continued on to its mother ship to land the other members of the SAS team. As they settled on the deck and the pilot cut the engines, Cartwright noticed that the ship's ensign was flying at half-mast.

He was met by the ship's commanding officer who walked with him to the wardroom for breakfast.

"I notice you're flying your flag at halfmast. Has someone died?"

"Oh. No you probably wouldn't know. Very sad news I'm afraid. Our Princess died in a car crash last night. Although we haven't had specific instructions to fly the flag for her, I'm sure that they'll be standing instructions everywhere to do so."

"Good God" Cartwright feigned shock. "When and how did that happen?"

"Very close actually. Somewhere over there in fact." The Lieutenant Commander pointed with his finger in the approximate direction of Monte Carlo. "I haven't heard all the details but apparently some newspaper people were chasing her car and forced it off the road or something. Anyway, we just heard an hour or so ago that she died in hospital. They say that that arab chappie she was seeing died instantly, as did the driver. The only survivor seems to have been a bodyguard."

"Grief. I can't believe it," responded Cartwright dutifully shaking his head and composing his face into an expression of sadness and shock.

CHAPTER FIFTY

Monday London SIS
Headquarters Vauxhall Cross

The conference table in C's office was strewn with newspapers whilst the large flat screen television, on a wall next to a picture of the Queen, was flashing its images, although the sound was turned down low. Television or newspapers there was only one headline item. The premature, accidental death of the Princess and the enormous, spontaneous, national outpouring of grief.

C and Featherstonehaugh were alone, each occupying an easy chair and each sipping from a crystal whisky tumbler.

"Who'd've believed it Mark? We knew she was popular, but this... " He made an expansive gesture with his free arm taking in everything from the newspapers to the television screen

"I know C. It's absolutely incredible. It's like the whole nation, perhaps even the whole world, has gone into mourning. I have to say I never envisaged this...

look at that... " he pointed to the television screen, which was showing an apparently infinite vista of flowers that members of the British public had been placing outside the Princess's two residences ever since the news first broke on the previous Friday morning.

C got up and poured himself another generous measure of whisky. "I don't think we'd've seen anything like this if it had been the Queen who had died. I'll tell you Mark, not only is this unprecedented, but I can't imagine that we're ever going to see its like again in our lifetime. It's incredible."

"I'm sure you're right C."

"And did you see our Prime Minister on television on Saturday giving that maudlin, platitudinous eulogy. God I dislike that man. He's not like a real man. He's more like some advertising agency's... what do they call those things... those computer generated images of people they use in games and things... "

"You mean avatars?"

"Do I? Is that what they're called? I always thought an avatar was an incarnation of a hindu deity. Avatars eh? Well anyway. He's like one of those."

"I'll say one thing if I may C."

"Yes"

"This incredible demonstration of the affection the public had for her, well, can you imagine what would have happened if she hadn't died and gone on to marry that man. Everyone would not only have accepted it, they'd probably have rejoiced with her. It shows that we were right after all to have sanctioned the operation."

"We're not speaking about that anymore Mark. It never happened." C's admonition was sharp,

"It never happened." He repeated softly, "Though I must say" he mused, "our soldier... Cartwright... performed very well indeed. Which reminds me... ".

He put his glass down, stood up and walked over to his desk. Opening a drawer he removed a bundle of five or six passports held together with a large elastic band and brought them over to his deputy, "Put those in a burn box will you. The Colonel arrived back yesterday and dropped them in to me last night. He thought I might want to look at what's left of his cleanup, in case we had any of them on our radar."

Featherstonehaugh took the bundle, removed the elastic band and looked through the passports, examining all the photographs carefully before holding up two of the documents, "We ought to tell counter terrorism they needn't waste resources looking for these two."

"Who are they?"

"A couple of Serbs wanted for war crimes in the Balkans. Been after them for years. It's an ill wind isn't it?"

C grunted, "What about the chap who got all our money?"

Featherstonehaugh flicked through the passports before holding up a bloodstained European Union Passport issued by France, "that's him. Do you want to see?"

"No. What I would like is to get our money back? Any leads on that?"

"I'm very much afraid that's gone, C. I don't know how or where, but he managed to make it disappear almost immediately it was handed over. No trace whatsoever."

"So they didn't recover a penny."

"No. Not a penny. They found no trace of anything. No cash, no bank books, no deposit slips. Nothing at all to indicate where or how the money went."

"Ten million Euros. Gone just like that. I told you we should have used funny money. Now he's gone and so's the money. I am disappointed. I was counting on you, Mark, to get it back you know."

Featherstonehaugh shrugged. As far as he was concerned this was a pointless discussion. The money had gone and that was it. The operation had gone off spectacularly well and as far as he was concerned it was money well spent. He voiced this opinion to C who responded with a grudging "I suppose you're right. Did you see the unofficial results of the autopsy the French carried out by the way?"

"No I didn't. When did that come through?"

"Jean-Michel sent me a note this morning. It's on my desk if you want to see. Over there." He pointed towards a small bundle of papers sitting neatly on his desk top.

"The Monegasques thought the thing was a bit too touchy and allowed a French government pathologist to deal with it." He paused to sip his drink, "you can look at it later. In short they found that the driver of the car was drunk and probably also under the influence of various medications that didn't mix very well with alcohol. Apparently a standard tox screen revealed substantial quantities of alcohol in his blood as well as some drug, I've forgotten the name, that people take to try and overcome alcoholism, as well as some anti-depressant."

"Really. Can you imagine that? A man driving in that condition. Almost beggars belief doesn't it?"

C's eyes twinkled, "And just between these four walls, a very nice touch of yours." He continued after finishing his whisky," I also spoke to Jean Michel this morning. The French magistrate in charge of the enquiry is intending to charge some journalists with a whole slew of offences, including culpable homicide, for having started a chain of events that ended with the accident. About five or six journalists were arrested when the police arrived on the scene. It seems they were too busy taking photographs of the wreck, the dead and injured, to call the police or an ambulance."

"It's appalling the way these journalists behave. They deserve everything they get." His indignation was genuine although he failed to see the irony of the feelings he was expressing.

"True. But from our point of view it's another neat little distraction."

Although the Palace was informed about the accident shortly after it was known that the Princess had died in the early hours of the morning, a senior official decided it would be inappropriate to awaken the Queen. It was her equerry who finally brought the news to the Queen's quarters at Buckingham Palace. The Queen had finished breakfast by the time the equerry passed through a huge oak door opening onto the red carpet that covered the Queen's corridor. He passed the Pages' vestibule, where pages wait to serve the Queen and, when he was signaled that he could enter, he came solemnly into the private sitting room where the monarch sat at her desk in a bay window, reading state papers. Several of the 9 or 10 corgi dogs she had with her in her room raised their heads and growled briefly, before forgetting the visitor's presence and going back to sleep. The Queen's reaction to the news was muted. She had, from time to time, intervened half-heartedly into her son's life, trying to impress upon him the obligations that he had been born into, attempting as best she could to patch up the relationship between her son and his former wife. She had faced a losing battle. Her son accepted advice only from his grandmother, the late Queen Mother. The Queen Mother had always displayed particular affection for the heir to the throne. In public she was a dignified elder statesperson. In private she was a doting, indulgent grandmother to her first grandson, sanctioning whatever he wanted to do with the seal of her approval. The Queen had watched and read about the incessant guerilla warfare that her son and his spouse seemed intent on conducting and simply gave up. When she was informed that the Princess's liaison with Walid Al Khalifa appeared to be a serious long term relationship, rather than a brief fling, she had sighed, realised there would be serious implications for her grandsons, the Princess's children and heirs to her throne and felt weighed down by yet another of the many burdens she bore. She was genuinely shocked to hear of the Princess's sudden death and indeed saddened, because in her world, people of the Princess's age simply did not die like that. Even her wild sister, a heavy smoker all her life, had lived well into comfortable twilight years. However, to be honest, the shock and sadness was tinged with feelings of relief that this unexpected tragedy had brought a sudden and welcome end to a most unpleasant and unseemly chapter in her family's life. She reflected, not for the first time, that God, in his own mysterious way, had once again shown her the mercy she sought in her regular devotions to him.

The Princess's former husband was similarly, but more overtly conflicted in his reaction. His immediate reaction was shock, followed swiftly by feelings of relief at the sudden and complete removal of the burden of the woman who had been causing him so much difficulty and been responsible for such considerable public odium and ridicule being directed towards him. However strongly feelings of guilt made him try to suppress the relief he felt, he was unable to. He felt at once happier and lighter. He had gone to sleep gloomy and depressed as usual. Each day he awoke with an uneasy feeling of dread, wondering what further private revelations about him might have been leaked in time for the morning editions of the nation's news networks. This morning everything was different. He had woken up and before he had even dressed, miraculously the enormous cloud that had darkened his life for so long was abruptly dissipated. Behind the sombre, sad expression with which he received the condolences of his staff, he felt like smiling. The joy was however, strongly mitigated by overwhelming feelings of guilt at his reaction. He was not supposed to feel pleasure at such a terrible occurrence. Neither was he supposed to be thinking of all the things his older mistress might do to him when he told her that this news meant that the way would now be open for him to bring her openly into his life, perhaps even to marry her. From time to time, as he had frolicked wickedly with his mistress, he had wondered if he would suffer divine retribution. It seemed though, that God in his infinite wisdom had decided to alleviate his suffering. The whole time that he was wracked by these conflicting emotions he was mentally composing himself, to show to the public how grief stricken he was, notwithstanding his differences with his former wife. After all, the woman who had died was the mother of his sons and they would be devastated. So, when he faced his sons and finally appeared in public, he was the very essence of melancholic dignity, making a special, poignant journey to accompany his ex-wife's remains as she was flown back to England for burial.

The public's reaction to the death of the Princess, their "fair lady" as she became dubbed by the English newspapers, reached a crescendo with her state funeral. Following that, although her tomb became something of a place of pilgrimage, public interest waned rapidly, only being revived from time to time by Mohammed Al Khalifa's public attempts to characterise what had happened as a murderous conspiracy to prevent his son marrying the Princess.

A few newspapers, seeking to boost their circulation figures, pursued the conspiracy theory from time to time, in so far as they had no better story that particular day. One or two articles referred to a mysterious white car that had been seen in the vicinity of the accident but had then disappeared. No one took much notice of the white car and even the conspiracy theorists were unable to explain how it fitted into their hypotheses. The French and Monegasque police, who carried out a joint investigation into the accident, made no attempt to trace the white car, doubting its existence and, in any event, dismissing it as irrelevant.

No one, least of all the conspiracy theorists, made any connection between the accident and a body that washed up on the beaches of the Italian Riviera some months later. The body was severely degraded from its time in the water but showed no signs of violent death. The Italian police, who had considerably more important matters to deal with than an unknown body that could have come from anywhere along the Mediterranean, or the many boats that plied its waters, designated the death as natural causes and promptly forgot about it. Neither were they any more interested in the burnt out wreck of an old Fiat that lay rusting, unexplored and uninvestigated, in a deserted quarry off the Ligurian coast.

Equally unnoticed, except amongst a small circle of fellow army officers and of course the men he led, was the investiture at Buckingham Palace a few months later, of Colonel Franklin Cartwright OBE DSO MC, as a Knight Commander of the Most Honourable Order of the Bath. Present at the ceremony was Colonel Cartwright's proud wife, who had been given a dress allowance for the occasion by her husband, which was as unexpected as it was generous. Co-incidentally, on the very day Cartwright had received the gold embossed card requiring his attendance at the Palace for his investiture, he had gone to a public phone and called his offshore bankers to ascertain whether or not they had received a further credit of 250,000 pounds. It was a call he had made several times previously, to which the response had always been negative. He had already resigned himself to managing on the first payment Traynor had sent to him and wondered how he could have allowed himself so easily to be deceived. To his surprise and gratification, on this occasion he had been informed that, yes, a credit of slightly less than 250,000 pounds had entered his account, the small shortfall being bank charges that had been deducted. It was in the flush of pleasure at this good news, he had announced to his wife that he wished her to spend on clothing what, previously, they might both have regarded as an excessive amount.

Lady Cartwright, as she became on the day of her husband's investiture, chose neither to question the source of the funds for her dress nor for the magnificent party hosted later by Colonel Sir Franklin Cartwright, to which all the members of his regiment who were not at the time posted abroad were invited. Seven members of the Regiment, who felt they had particularly close ties to their Colonel, clubbed together to buy him an expensive silver salver, suitably engraved, to commemorate the occasion. As the newly knighted Colonel warmly thanked his men for their gift, he thought briefly of a Japanese American assassin and wondered where he was that day.

Made in the USA
Lexington, KY
21 August 2014